THE TASTE OF TEMPTATION

It was a gentle kiss at first. It might have even been a cousinly kiss. Then Alex kissed her again, harder.

Mary felt as though hoofbeats were still pounding in her ears, but it was her pulse. She felt boneless, but at the same time sensed that she was holding him so tightly he couldn't have escaped if he'd tried. How strong and hard his muscles were, how smooth that place on his neck where her hand lingered.

"Dear God, you are beautiful," he murmured. "And you're so small!" he added in wonder.

"Oh, Alex, I do love you. I always have," she said softly.

It was as if God had snapped His fingers and flung a thunderbolt. Alex stiffened and stepped back. "I must be *mad*," he said.

Mary knew he was right . . . this was madness . . . sheer madness . . . this madness of love. . . .

CINNAMON WHARF

Janice Young Brooks

A SIGNET BOOK

NEW AMERICAN LIBRARY

PUBLISHED BY
PENGUIN BOOKS CANADA LIMITED

PUBLISHER'S NOTE

This book is a work of fiction. Names, characters, places, and incidents either are the product of the author's imagination or are used fictitiously, and any resemblance to actual persons, living or dead, events, or locales is entirely coincidental.

NAL BOOKS ARE AVAILABLE AT QUANTITY DISCOUNTS
WHEN USED TO PROMOTE PRODUCTS OR SERVICES.
FOR INFORMATION PLEASE WRITE TO PREMIUM MARKETING DIVISION,
NEW AMERICAN LIBRARY, 1633 BROADWAY,
NEW YORK, NEW YORK 10019.

Copyright © 1988 by Janice Young Brooks

FIRST PRINTING, JANUARY, 1989

2 3 4 5 6 7 8 9

SIGNET TRADEMARK REG. U.S. PAT OFF AND FOREIGN COUNTRIES
REGISTERED TRADEMARK — MARCA REGISTRADA
HECHO EN WINNIPEG, CANADA

SIGNET, SIGNET CLASSIC, MENTOR, ONYX, PLUME, MERIDIAN and NAL BOOKS are published in Canada by Penguin Books Canada Limited, 2801 John Street, Markham, Ontario, Canada L3R 1B4
PRINTED IN CANADA
COVER PRINTED IN U.S.A.

Prologue

June 1927

Castlemere still smelled of rosemary.

Had it always been that way? Was the scent from the bushes outside, or something inherent and in the great house itself? Had generations of Beechams identified that scent with home? Natalie wondered about it as she stood in the dim hall waiting for her eyes to adjust to the near-darkness. She was aware that all her senses were more finely tuned than usual. The slight rosemary scent was so evocative, so characteristic of Mary Beecham and all she touched.

Before the front door closed completely Natalie heard an English robin burbling its liquid song, the Daimler's engine providing a faint bass undertone as the chauffeur pulled around to the garages. She heard, or imagined she could hear, the faint, hypnotic shushing of the waves beyond the cliffs. Someplace in the depths of the house there was the soft, melodious clink of fine glassware and the rhythmic thump of a rolling pin being expertly wielded. Though the day was warm for June, it was cool in the great entry hall—cool and dry and very still, just like always. But today there was the special aura of "significance" that Natalie had often experienced in museums and at the opera as the lights dimmed.

"May I take your wrap, Miss Natalie?" the butler asked in a hushed, mournful tone.

She'd forgotten his presence and thought irreverently that he must have had his early training in a burial firm. Nobody but a mortician had any business sounding so grieved about the commonplace. "Thank you, Bartlet," she said, handing him her pink linen coat and matching cloche.

"I've put you in the Prince William suite, Miss Natalie."

"How considerate of you to remember it's my favorite. How is she, Bartlet?"

"Fading, if I might say so, miss," he confided funereally. "Though the doctor is hopeful that she may rally. She'll be glad to see you, Miss Natalie. She was most concerned that you come to see her. I'm afraid she worded the telegram quite strongly. Shall I show you upstairs?"

She could practically hear his aged joints creaking at the thought. "Of course not. I know the way. My driver will be in with my bags momentarily. Send them up with him. Don't trouble to carry them yourself." Since the Great War, domestic help had been hard to come by, even for great country houses like Castlemere. It wouldn't do to overwork anyone as loyal as Bartlet—or as old. He must be even older than Grandma.

"Very grateful, Miss Natalie."

She went up the huge curved staircase, running her hand lightly along the smooth walnut banister. Family history had it that the young Queen-to-be Victoria had once stuck her head between the third and fourth posts and gotten stuck. As a youngster, Natalie had examined the spot closely for some proof of the story—a hair, a thread of ribbon, anything. Naturally, generations of housemaids had long since cleared away any evidence that might have existed.

Natalie paused at the landing, gathering her strength of will. Should she wipe off her pale lip rouge? Mary Beecham didn't approve of women who painted. Papa claimed she'd once made a guest wash her face before she could come to dinner. Was that true or merely apocryphal? Either way, she took a lacy handkerchief from her handbag, wiped her lips, and wished she'd worn a longer dress instead of the flimsy drop-waist flowered chemise that had seemed so lovely in the London shop and seemed so vulgar here.

Smoothing down her stylishly shingled hair, she tapped lightly on the linenfold paneled door to the sickroom. A plump, florid woman in a white uniform and unflattering headgear opened it a crack. Was she a nurse or a nun? Probably a nurse, unless Grandmama had turned Catholic in the last two years. "Hello, Sister," Natalie said, feeling that covered either possibility. "I've come to visit my grandmother. Is she able to receive a guest?"

The woman opened the door wider and gestured for her to enter. "Yes, dear. We're ever so much stronger today. It would do wonders for us to have a visitor. In fact, I was just about to nip down for a spot of tea. Why don't I have some sent up to the two of you."

This room was dark. The heavy green damask draperies were pulled shut, creating an eerie underwater look. Natalie almost stumbled over a small table. "So, you've come at last," a voice said.

"Yes, Grandmama. I was in Scotland visiting friends when your telegram caught up with me. I hurried here as soon as I could. I hear you're getting well now."

"I'm dying and you'd be a fool to believe anything else. Open the draperies, Natalie, and let me see you. My attendant seems to believe that fresh air and sunlight are deadly."

Natalie did as she was told, and light flooded the room. It was an elegant room, a perfect setting for Mary Beecham. Tall ceilings made her seem even more petite than she was. Small herself, Natalie had only recently come to appreciate why Grandmama had always preferred a large stage: her dainty stature made her seem delicate and harmless to anyone idiot enough to gauge her by physical size.

Natalie studied the room she'd so often visited. For many decades the pier glass and ornamental mirrors had reflected the image of a woman said to be the greatest beauty of her age. The bed, of course, was the centerpiece of the room. It was a vast piece of furniture, crafted of golden oak with bas-relief carvings of fruit and flowers, and canopied with swags of white watered silk. There Grandmama had spent two wedding nights and sat sentinel as one husband died. Natalie's cousins had dropped hints that yet another man had died raving in this bed, but would never enlighten Natalie as to details. Here Grandmama had borne her children, and soon, here she would spend her final night. And then what? Could everyone really continue without her?

Natalie had known the few facts about Mary Beecham's life since childhood. Today, for the first time, she realized how skimpy they were, how very nearly meaningless. How had Grandmama felt about any of it? About her husbands, her children? About the deaths and births? Had she ever cried herself to sleep in this bed? Had she whispered endearments to her husbands, or had she merely "done her duty," as Victorian ladies were supposed to? What had happened to the first child—the one nobody ever talked about—and who was the man who died here, the man her cousins had alluded to, or had they made the story up to tease her?

The outburst about the fresh air must have tired Mary,

for she lay perfectly still, her eyes closed, only the faintest sound of her breathing reassuring Natalie. She was still beautiful. Wrinkles hadn't ruined the perfect complexion, only given the face more character. ("If she had any more character, they'd have to put a sign on her and erect her in a public square!" Natalie's father had once said after a harrowing visit.) The old woman's hair, braided and wrapped around her proud head like a crown, was still thick, but white now and showing no hint of the auburn depicted in the portrait in the morning room. Natalie had always wondered if there had actually been those dark plum-purple highlights in her hair or whether it was a whim of the artist.

"Does the light bother you?" Mary asked softly. Natalie had assumed she was asleep, but Mary had been studying her, assessing her, wondering how she would react, it she would readily assume responsibility.

"No, I prefer it," Natalie answered. "Your telegram said you had something important to ask of me. What is it, Grandmama? You know I'll do anything I can."

Mary was silent for long moments and then merely said, "That bureau by the window. Open the top drawer."

She caught her breath painfully. Was this the right thing to do? Could she trust this sweet-natured, untested girl to understand and do what must be done? If not her, then who could assume the responsibility? It had to be Natalie.

Natalie rose and did as she was asked. The drawer was shallow, full of handkerchiefs. She started to take one out, but Mary said, "Turn the drawer knob clockwise and pull harder."

There was a faint click and the drawer slid open farther, to reveal a row of small books, perhaps twenty of them, stacked horizontally, spines upward. Those to the left appeared quite old, their covers faded and battered. They were all leather-bound, but of different colors and slightly different sizes. None had a label. "What are these?" Natalie asked quietly.

"Diaries," Mary answered. "Take out the one at the far left and bring it here." There was still time to change her mind. She need not lay this duty on the girl's shoulders. Was her heart big enough to understand?

Natalie removed the book carefully and closed the drawer. Approaching the bed, she held it out, but her grandmother said, "Sit down. Read. What are you thinking?"

Natalie had almost grown accustomed to the sudden disconcerting questions that were almost a hallmark of the old woman in the huge bed. "That even this book smells of rosemary."

Mary opened those blue, undimmed eyes that had pierced so many souls and secrets. "Yes. Shakespeare said that. *Hamlet*, I believe: Rosemary for remembrance. Child, you must heed me and remember . . . remember . . . someone must remember." At the sight of the small book, a virtual storm of memories had gathered and begun to swirl around her like the typhoon winds that sometimes lashed Singapore.

She suddenly felt dizzy and helpless, but she must not cry in front of Natalie. She must not seem the senile old lady. It was bad enough she was hardly more than the empty shell of herself now. Inside those books was Mary Beecham, the real Mary Beecham, girl and woman, who had poured out her heart onto the pages.

"Remember what, Granmama?"

But Mary had closed her eyes again, and the only answer was the soft sound of her breathing.

Singapore. Alex. The heady scent of cloves.

Natalie opened the book cautiously. The paper was old and brittle, the writing small, round and childish and faded with age:

> 10 July, 1859. I'm Mary. Mr. Beecham gave me this buk to write in. He said I shud write every week. So I wil rememmer everythin. I can come in his libery. We wil both write in our very own buks. He is a very nice man. I cam here to live las month. I was sick. . . .

1

June 1859

George Beecham was in the library at Castlemere studying a new map of the Caribbean and enjoying the rare sensation of having the entire house to himself. Well, almost to himself. Most of the servants were there, quietly doing whatever they did. But Portia and the girls had accompanied his parents to York to visit some distant relatives, and his Aunt Nellanor had gone to stay with an ailing friend in Brighton for a few days. Still, when he heard a faint shriek from the kitchen regions his first thought was that whatever the problem was, Portia would deal with it. Even without her, he amended, it would probably sort itself out. Household matters usually did.

This comforting thought was short-lived, however. Hurried footsteps approached the library and he sighed resignedly as there was a frantic tapping at the library door. "Come in, Mrs. Mackey," he said.

The housekeeper, her usual condescending dignity left behind, entered and said, "Mr. Beecham, much as I dislike disturbing your work . . ." She paused, got her breath, and brought her voice down to a lower register. Folding her hands in the gesture that was so irritatingly characteristic, she went on, "I'm afraid a problem has arisen which is beyond my authority to rectify. With the mistresses both gone, I must appeal to your judgment."

"Very well," he said. Why did she always make him feel like a slightly unwelcome guest in his own home? His father's home, he corrected himself mentally. "What is the difficulty?"

"It's a child, sir. She's been left at the back door and she's ill. I don't know what should be done with her."

"Who left her?"

"I don't know, sir. Cook said she caught a glimpse of a person through the window a quarter of an hour back, but didn't open the back door until she was set to dump some dishwater, and there was this child."

"What sort of person?"

"I don't know, sir."

"Very well, I'll come see what I can do."

Mrs. Mackey stood aside to let him lead the way, but followed so closely he felt as though he were being pushed. The cook and scullery maid had laid the child on a blanket in the pantry. George studied her for a moment, murmured, "Oh, my God!" then knelt on the stone floor and studied her more closely.

She was quite small and might have looked wiry if she'd been conscious. As it was, she merely looked fragile, her orange-red hair emphasizing the extreme pallor of her skin. She hardly seemed to be breathing. He put his hand to her throat and felt a faint, fast pulse fluttering under his fingers. "Send a boy by horseback for Dr. Engle and put her to bed in the dressing room adjoining my room. Hot water bottles would not be amiss, I think."

"But, sir, that's hardly proper. I can make a pallet for her on the servants' floor."

"Mrs. Mackey, I decide the proprieties at Castlemere," he said sharply. "Now, do as you're told." His hands were shaking and he'd become nearly as pale as the child.

She gasped and nodded obediently, her neck nearly cracking with the effort.

An hour later, Dr. Jonathan Engle was sitting across the desk from George. Engle was a young man, barely twenty-six. He and George had been boys together; they'd learned riding and shooting and drinking and been bosom companions until they were adults and the differences in their social status became obvious, even to them. They were still friends, but they'd passed the stage of sharing secrets.

"I hardly know what to tell you, George. A proper little mystery. She's very ill. Of course, you could see that. Without anyone to tell me about the initial stages of her ailment, I can hardly make a diagnosis. There's been a fever; you can tell from the dryness of her lips, but it seems to have receded. Frankly, I can't guess whether this is a deep, healing sleep or the final stages of debilitation. All there is to do is keep her from becoming chilled, and introduce liquids. Time will tell. Who is she? What's she doing here?"

"I don't know," George said rather sharply, as if responding to an accusation rather than a question. "Passing transients must have left her, thinking she'd get better care from us than they could provide. I've heard of many such cases."

Dr. Engle shook his head. "It happens, but it's usually a dirty Gypsy sort of child. This child was very clean, did you notice? Her hair and nails and clothing were immaculate. Poor clothing, but of fairly good quality even if much patched and darned. And . . . Oh, I nearly forgot! How stupid of me!" He reached into his waistcoat pocket and pulled out a locket. "She had this on a chain around her neck. The chain had broken and fallen down in her clothing. Perhaps there's a clue in it."

George reached across the desk quickly and took the ornament before Engle could open it. "Yes, perhaps," he said.

Engle waited for George to open the locket, but George just slipped it into his own pocket without another word. He stood, and the physician, recognizing his dismissal, rose also. "I'll come back this afternoon and see how she's getting along."

"How old would you say she is?" George asked.

"Odd that you should ask that. I put her age at about four years, maybe almost five, when I first saw her. She's such a tiny thing. But when I looked at her throat, I realized that she's older. Probably seven. She's already lost and replaced several of her front milk teeth."

At that, George half smiled. Engle wondered why the assessment should please him. "I see. Thank you, Jonathan. We'll take the best care of her we're able."

"Are you going to make an effort to trace her people?"

"I've sent my man to town to make inquiries."

"I wouldn't expect much to come of it. But still, if she lives, she might make good enough extra help in the kitchens. You might as well get something from your investment, what?"

George waited until the doctor had been shown out, then opened the locket. He gazed at the small, faded face that stared back at him. Nodding, he snapped it shut. Tucking it away again, he went up to see the child. Agnes, a plump upstairs maid who was as eager and good-hearted as she was clumsy, had been assigned to sit with her and was nodding in a chair by the window when George came in. "You may go to eat, Agnes. Bring me a tray of sandwiches when you come back. The cold veal from last night, if any is left."

"Yessir, should I send someone in to stay with the poor little one?"

"No, I'll stay until you're back."

Agnes went off, clearly perplexed by why the master should interest himself in the matter, but relieved to get an opportunity to eat. She'd been afraid they'd just put her in here and forget about both of them until they starved to death. Agnes wasn't a girl to miss meals if she could help it.

George sat down next to the cot and studied the little girl. They'd put her in a cast-off nightgown that had belonged to one of his daughters. Though they were both younger than this child, the garment was still too big, making her look lost in the flannel folds. She stirred a little and made a squeaky whimper. George poured a cup of water from the carafe and tried to lift her gently to a semisitting position. "Here, girl. Drink some of this."

For a moment her eyes opened slightly and she took a few painful swallows before going limp. George laid her back against the pillow and tucked the blankets around her. Leaning back in his chair, he took the locket out and studied it again, then looked for a very long time at the little girl.

She wasn't well enough to speak until the next morning, and then she woke up disoriented and terrified. Agnes came to George. "She's scared half out of her wits, poor little mite."

George went to her immediately. "Now, now, child," he soothed, "you mustn't be frightened of us. This is Agnes and she's been taking very good care of you."

The little girl was huddled against the wall, her legs drawn up to her chest, her eyes big and wild. But she looked every bit as defiant as scared. "Who are you?" she demanded in a voice still weak and raspy from her illness.

"I'm George Beecham. More important, who are you?"

"I'm Mary Grey," she said.

"And where are you from, Mary Grey?"

"London . . . sir. Where's this place? What am I here for?"

Her speech was quite good, George thought, the pronunciation curiously uninflected. "That's a good question. You were left here. You were very ill."

"Where's my mother? Have you done something to my mother?"

"That's what we'd like to know too. What is your mother's name?"

"Mrs. Grey," the girl said, as if explaining something obvious.

"I mean her first name. What do her friends call her?"

The girl hesitated. "Mrs. Grey . . ."

Well, perhaps she didn't know. The child herself wouldn't call her mother by her Christian name, and if they lived among friends who weren't intimates . . . "What does your father call your mother?"

"I don't have a father. He died when I was a little baby. Where is my mother, sir?"

"Now, you must not worry about it. Your mother wanted you to stay here with us until you're entirely well."

"Where *is* she?"

"Very near, I'm sure. I'll find her for you. But you must help me. Whereabouts in London did you live?"

If Mary caught the verb tense, she didn't say anything. "We live in a house near the market."

"Near the market? Which market?"

"The one where they sell food and clothes."

Hopeless. The child had no idea the size of the city she was talking about. "When did you come here? Was it before you were ill?"

"Where is here?" the girl asked in response. She was beginning to relax, but it was exhaustion, not ease, and her paleness was becoming alarming, as was her labored breathing.

"You go back to sleep for a bit and we'll talk more later," George said, nodding to Agnes, who'd been hovering. Agnes plumped herself down on the edge of the bed and carefully tucked the child back under the covers.

George called several members of the staff together. Arms crossed in mute disapproval of all these goings-on, Mrs. Mackey, the housekeeper, had been questioned first. "So you say you have no idea who this child is?" George asked.

"I told you, sir, no. Cook said—"

"Let's let her speak for herself," George said. "Cook?" he asked, wishing he could remember her proper name. Portia and his mother would know, but he never had occasion to speak to her.

She was a young countrywoman from the neighborhood who had trained under the previous cook and taken over the position when that formidable lady had elected to retire some ten years earlier. She looked as though she'd be of a hearty, open disposition, but she was surprisingly taciturn. "I dunno nothing about her, sir. Just found her there on the back steps, didn't I?"

"I'm told you saw a stranger out the window a few moments earlier?" George prodded.

"Not to say 'saw,' sir. Just an eye-corner look, you might say. I was dicing up a nice turnip and paid no mind."

"Was it a man or a woman?"

"I couldn't say, could I, sir? Not thinking it was important and all. People go by that window all day. To the stables and kennels and what-not."

"You don't even know if it wore skirts or trousers?" George asked with obvious disbelief.

The cook folded her arms in unconscious imitation of Mrs. Mackey. "No, sir."

"Very well. What were you able to find out, Tutin?"

The clerkish little man George employed as a secretary and errand runner was seated at the edge of a hard chair and popped up when addressed. "I asked about the village, sir, about anybody seen traveling with a girl child. The hotel and two of the boardinghouses had entertained guests lately who had such an individual with them. One was a single woman, two were couples. One of them had several children. Not having seen the child, sir, I couldn't describe her to them. But I asked what they looked like, the little girls."

"And what were you told?"

Tutin pulled a well-worn notebook out of his vest pocket and consulted it myopically. "At the hotel, a couple stayed on Monday and Tuesday of last week. Believed to be on their way to Canterbury from Southampton, from things they said. The child with them had dark curling hair and a cast to one eye, but pretty just the same, they said."

George shook his head. "What about the others?"

"At the one boardinghouse it was a couple with three little ones, a boy of about twelve and twin girls. Nothing known about them. Very secretive like . . ."

Tutin obviously favored these suspicious characters as the culprits who had unloaded a child on his master, but George dismissed them. "And the third?"

"At Mrs. Renault's—you know, that run-down old farm

out along the cliffs to the west. She takes in boarders sometimes."

"What did she say about her guests?"

"Not nothing, rightly. I mean, folks in town said as how she had a woman and girl abiding there for a bit, but Mrs. Renault herself wouldn't tell me aught. Said it was . . . was none of my damned business. I quote her, sir."

George had run into Mrs. Renault before. A small section of her land adjoined Castlemere land for a stretch and there had been a slight misunderstanding over fifty feet of boundary when her husband died a year back. It had been resolved in her favor without any hard feelings on either side, or at least not on the Beecham side, but George had cause to remember what a very harsh-tongued old lady she was.

"Very well, Tutin. I'll go speak to her myself."

"I wouldn't advise it, sir."

George's patience with Tutin's timidity suddenly ran out. "What would you advise, then? Should I just find another back step and dump the child on someone else?" He immediately regretted this outburst. "Never mind, Tutin. I'll take care of it."

"Mrs. Renault? I'm George Beecham from—"

"I know right well where you're from," she answered, stepping outside her door rather than inviting him in. "What is it you want? That rabbity young man of yours was here this last eve and I sent him off."

"Yes, I know. I'd sent him to ask you a question or two."

"Didn't get an earful of answer, did he, now?" Mrs. Renault smiled as if she expected him to enjoy the joke.

George grinned back at her and watched her smile falter. "I hope I'll learn more than Tutin. Mrs. Renault, we had a child left on our back steps yesterday and have no idea whose child she is. The staff claims she's not from the village or they'd recognize her. I sent Tutin around to inquire about anyone who might have passed through lately, and he was told you'd had a guest—"

"That I did."

"Was it by chance a Mrs. Grey with a daughter Mary?"

"That was their names, yes."

"Then where is Mrs. Grey now?"

Mrs. Renault shrugged. "They went off yesterday morning."

"Come, Mrs. Renault! The child was so ill she was nearly

unconscious. Certainly the woman wouldn't have set out with the child in that condition."

"She weren't so sick when they left. Just a little poorly."

George wanted to shake her, but restrained himself. "Very well. If that's what you say. How did they set out? In a hired carriage?"

"No, sir, on foot they was."

George gritted his teeth. "What did you learn about them? Where were they from? Where was the mother going?"

"I'm not a magistrate, Mr. Beecham," she said haughtily. "When I have a person or persons visiting my home, I don't feel it's my job to go prying and prodding into their personal affairs. 'Twas none of my business and I don't see that it's yours neither."

"Of course it's my business, woman! I've got the daughter in my house and have no idea how to find her mother!"

Instead of rising to this bait, Mrs. Renault began to carefully clean her fingernails with a long spinter she broke from the door frame. When the silence had stretched far enough, she sniffed and said, "So how's the little mite doing?"

"Better. It appears that she'll survive. Mrs. Renault, I must find her mother. Can't you help me?"

"Would if I could, sir," she said.

She stood leaning against the door frame as George mounted his horse and rode off, a frustrated stiffness in his bearing. Then she entered the house, and after closing the door, spoke to the redheaded woman who was leaning against the wall. The young woman had tears on her cheeks and was trying to repress another bout of coughing. She held a blood-flecked handkerchief to her lips.

"There, dearie," Mrs. Renault said. "He's gone. Now, you stop taking on. You heard him say little Mary's going to be fine."

2

Beechams, though they excelled in many areas, had never been very good at marriage.

The first of the line had set a pattern that had recurred throughout the centuries. A Crusader, John Beecham had dallied in the mysterious East long enough to marry an infidel and father two children before returning to England. He brought this exotic family home and had hardly time to settle in before his darkly beautiful wife and children died of the climate and homesickness. Fortunately, he'd also brought back several small crates of spices, which he sold to finance his return to the sunny land. He went back, half-hoping to find another wife he could love as much as his first, and while he was there he bought more of the aromatic stuff his English neighbors had found so valuable.

"Where does it come from?" he asked the traders in Calicut as he rolled a quill of cinnamon between his fingers. The Arab traders smiled behind their plump brown hands and told him what they told other gullible Westerners: "From a mysterious place deep in the origins of the Nile River—a fearful forest called Paradise that's guarded by dragons and serpents that fly and blood-drinking bats. Every year the monsters go into a frenzy and rip the bark off the Paradise trees. The bark, it floats down the Nile to where the Egyptians catch it in nets in secret places no Westerner may go."

John Beecham shuddered and bought more.

Finding no woman who could compare with his first wife, he eventually packed the cinnamon and saffron and cloves (had he really bought so much? what would he do with all of it?) and started a long journey back to England. He was nearly sixty, an extraordinary age in that day, before grief subsided and he realized his need for an heir to inherit the family fortune he had almost inadvertently founded. He formed an alliance with the village tanner's daughter, which might or might not have had the blessing of the church, but which did produce a fine brace of sons to carry on.

The elder son and his descendants lacked the first Beecham's impulse to travel, but they loved spices and eventually set themselves up in a modest home on Mincing Lane in London, near the docks, where they could conveniently act as brokers, buying and reselling the products from the East that came on the Venetian galleys. For many generations they got along, extending their contacts, gaining customers, and learning the trade without attracting notice and leaving no trace in the history of the era except a few ledgers attesting to their slowly growing prosperity.

Finally, in the 1300's, some of them started learning their letters as well as numbers, and a spotty record began to appear in the history of the family. According to a letter preserved at Castlemere, Gervaise Beecham, whose lifespan paralleled Edward III's, had as his patroness Queen Philippa, to whom he presented a golden casket of precious cloves. A highly respected leader of the Pepperers' Guild and the first Beecham to enter public life, he must have been both attractive and witty, and spent many years as the darling of the court before finally falling in love and marrying at the advanced age of forty-two.

One of his descendants, a boy of gentle disposition, Alain Beecham, fell passionately in love at fourteen with a cousin who proved to be quite barren. But she, like Alain, loved spices, and during their marriage, the business prospered as never before. It wasn't until after her death in their middle age that he was persuaded to remarry and keep the line going. This wasn't a happy marriage, though it did provide him with a son. To provide himself a bolt-hole from his shrill, prolific second wife, Alain Beecham bought land in Essex and attempted to plant crocuses with the intention of producing home-grown saffron. The weather conspired against him the first three years, and he gave up the attempt, but kept the land.

Later, his son Edmund Beecham who was a portly, ruddy, and unwise in love as his monarch, Henry VIII, married a woman with six sisters. Though he was a canny businessman, Edmund became a figure of fun within the family. His younger brother, who hoped to inherit, celebrated gleefully as Edmund's wife produced daughter after daughter after

daughter. Eventually she produced a son, by which time
Edmund had lost interest in both the bed and the nursery
and had instead turned his eyes to the land his father had
purchased and the saffron possibilities. Crocuses grew well
for him, which was timely. All around him, spice merchants
were going broke because the Venetians had lost their hold
on the trade and England hadn't yet come to terms with the
new masters of spice—the Dutch and Portuguese. Edmund
and his son and grandsons, however, their fingertips stained
the brilliant golden yellow of saffron, stayed afloat and started
looking around for more property.

The Beechams bought many parcels of land over the
generations; sold a few, but never abandoned their home
near the increasingly smelly docks in London. Finally, Philippe
Beecham, a man with intensely attuned olfactory senses, a
man who preferred spice to sewage, found a large stretch of
land in East Sussex that suited his fancy. It was on the south
coast near Beachy Head. At the site of what he was told was
a former Roman hill fort, he laid out the plans for the
family estate, positioning the house itself close enough to
the lip of the sheer chalk cliffs to smell and hear the sea
and—on very fine days from the uppermost windows—even
catch a glimpse of France across the Channel. Or so some
exceedingly long-sighted Beechams claimed. Philippe called
the house what the locals had always called the place:
Castlemere. Having finally completed the great Palladian
home in 1702, at the age of fifty, Philippe spent another five
years looking for a wife before going giddy over a penniless
wallflower with a slight squint. But to Philippe, she was
beautiful and he loved her to distraction—a love that was
fully and generously reciprocated.

This domestic delay was characteristic, if not downright
genetic. Again and again, Beecham men tended to leave
marriage until their autumn years, raising hopes in junior
branches of the family, only to dash them as they married
late in life. These junior branches, however, had their uses.
Younger sons and cousins were sent all over the world to act
as company factors in such far-flung places as India, Jamaica, and the Spice Islands.

If they'd had a gift for making better marriages—better in
the political sense—the Beechams would certainly have become one of the great titled families of England. Instead,
they became one of the richest families. For although their
hearts ruled their heads in love, emotion never overshad-

owed business, and every third or fourth generation tended to throw up a Beecham who, if not a genius, at least had a firm grasp on the importance of money and a burning desire to acquire even more of it.

George Beecham's grandfather Henry had both family traits in large measure. Born in 1740, he'd expanded from spices into the tea trade, made a hefty profit, then prudently got out again just before the trouble with the American colonies broke out. Seeking adventure and further profits in the pepper trade, at which the new country was excelling, he'd gone off to observe the conflict firsthand and incidentally buy a bit of property in Virginia. He stayed on until 1789, at which time he finally wed an American girl of a mere seventeen years, who died giving birth to a daughter named Nellanor a year later.

This event stunned Henry into thinking of the future of the Beechams. He didn't like the idea of leaving the company to a daughter. Not that women hadn't run it in the past—several strong-minded young widows over the years had taken the helm during their sons' childhood. But Henry wanted a son. Now obsessed with procreation and feeling that America had betrayed him, Henry returned to England and Castlemere and tried again. This time his bride, a redhead from Cornwall named Charlotte, gave him a son named William before giving up the ghost. Henry himself followed her into the graveyard barely five years later. Nellanor and William had been put into the care of a cousin and the family money had been nursed along by a firm of bankers until William came of age.

William, who ran to gout and pomposity at an early age, was one of the few Beechams to make a good marriage, at least by external standards. Evelyn Robsart was a beauty of nineteen when William, an extremely wealthy bachelor of thirty-six, came on the horizon. Though untitled themselves, the Robsarts felt it would take little more than the joining of the two old names and fortunes to create at least an earldom. In this they were mistaken.

The only impediment, the Robsarts felt, was the presence in the household of William's half-sister, Nellanor. Her American heritage was, of course, a drawback, but that could be overlooked. The real problem was Nellanor herself. Tall and plain, she was a decided eccentric—contemptuous of society's rules and altogether too intelligent for a decent woman. Worse, there were her "marriage" and son to take into consideration. No one with any common sense believed she'd ever actually been married, but no one with social sense openly challenged her. If only she and that boy Claudius ("Where did she get *that* name?") didn't live right there at Castlemere with William! If only she'd stayed in India, where she'd lived during her "marriage." But when the Robsarts had delicately hinted to William that perhaps his half-sister would be happier living elsewhere when he was married, he'd gotten quite snippy and defensive about it, so they dropped the subject.

In the end, the Robsarts weighed the pros and cons, the money and Castlemere against Nellanor, and shoved Evelyn down the aisle to plight her troth to William Beecham. Evelyn had done her duty promptly, giving birth to George in 1830, then had two miscarriages in rapid succession before retiring from the matrimonial bed. She settled in to the serious business of putting on weight and enhancing the Beechams' social status, often accomplishing both at the sumptuous dinners to which only the best people were invited.

Knowing the family history, Evelyn looked forward to long years in which to select a proper wife for her son, George, but he was an atypical specimen of the family in many ways. For one thing, he was extraordinarily good-looking. In a family of men who were generally barrel-shaped, spindle-shanked, sandy-haired, and inclined to alcoholic flushes whether they drank or not, George Beecham was slim, broad-shouldered, and fair, like the men in Evelyn's family. He was also a dreamy, scholarly boy, a trait Evelyn blamed on Nellanor's disturbing influence. After her own son, Claudius, was shipped off to manage the family's Singapore office, Nellanor devoted all her attention to George, who appeared to adore his eccentric half-aunt.

Most distressing, George had shown a decidedly non-Beecham interest in girls at an early age. Or perhaps it would be more accurate to say they'd shown an interest in him which he had no inclination to resist. At sixteen he'd been caught in the barn exchanging kisses with the estate manager's bosomy daughter, and then there was An Incident involving a Welsh governess when he was twenty-one.

Evelyn and William put their heads together and decided George couldn't be trusted as a bachelor. By no means a young man of strong character, he was occasionally impulsive and might make A Serious Mistake if left to his own devices. They started casting about for a suitable wife and found one in the daughter of one of William's business associates. Portia Ridley's family imported vanilla from Mexico, and she appeared to be malleable.

George had been curiously reluctant to marry.

"Pretty filly, can't follow your thinking!" William huffed.

"I just don't want to marry her," George said, giving his father a hand up as the older man mounted his long-suffering bay stallion in preparation for a hunt.

"Don't matter, boy. Family obligation, don't y'see?"

In the end, it was Evelyn who convinced George. With a combination of threats, expertly staged tears, and bribery, she persuaded him to give pretty Portia Ridley a diamond-and-ruby engagement ring that Beecham brides had worn for six generations.

A chapel had to be built adjacent to Castlemere, an oversight by previous Beechams which Evelyn had long intended to correct; it was completed just in time for George and Portia to say their vows. This was in the spring of 1853. A bare ten months later, their first child, Charlotte (named for George's grandmother), was born, and thirteen months after that, Hester (named for a character in a book Portia was reading the week before the birth). Since that time, four years had passed, and except for one false alarm, there had been no further sign of additional children.

They'd settled into a contented existence by the time Mary came into their lives. At least Portia was contented. Her father-in-law, William, was still in control of the household and the family spice business, though George was becoming involved and was often in London at the offices and warehouses. Her mother-in-law, Evelyn, had added another wing and was fruitlessly engaged in attempting to get George's Aunt Nellanor to inhabit it. Aunt Nellanor, now in her sixties, but as vigorous and outspoken as ever, had no intention of being shunted aside, but the battle kept both her and Evelyn out of Portia's way.

George, whom Portia genuinely loved, although she'd never understood him, occupied himself with his work and his studies, spending much of his free time at home in the combination library and map room that served as an office away from the office. He read, he studied his maps, he invited scholars and explorers and geographers to visit Castlemere, and corresponded with them when they were absent. He was always willing, if never eager, to appear for the social situations she created. He danced beautifully and made small talk with a preoccupied air she found both exasperating and charming.

That George didn't reciprocate the love she'd been prepared to lavish on him had become apparent to Portia early in the marriage. Not that he was cruel or even rude; he was the very soul of kindness. It was a remote kindness, however, with no true heart in it. But Portia didn't brood. Her daughters soon became the center of her life and absorbed the affection that was wasted on George. Pretty, dainty girls with the Robsart coloring and the Beecham charm, they filled her days and her thoughts. Before much longer, Portia was certain, they would have a little brother. After all, she was only twenty-four and had years of potential childbearing ahead of her. George would enjoy a son, she felt. He'd never been quite at ease with the girls; men weren't with daughters, she supposed. He loved them, she was certain, but seemed to be vaguely afraid of them.

Portia was a contented woman until her return from the trip to York. From that day on, nothing was ever quite the same for any of the Beechams. "Left on the doorstep?" she asked incredulously of her husband after she had gotten a report from her maid and hunted down George in the map room. "And you took her in the house?"

"I could do nothing else," George answered. "I made a search for her mother, but the woman had gone—back to London, I assume. I'm continuing the search, of course, but until she's located, the girl is our responsibility. And we must face the fact that the mother may never be found."

"Hmmm. Well, I suppose there's always room for more help in the kitchens—"

"No, this is a well-bred child. Nicely spoken. Very clean. She's not a scullery maid."

"Then a housemaid. Perhaps trained as a personal maid for the girls as they get older."

"No, Portia. You don't understand me. The child isn't of the servant class and we won't make her into one."

"What on earth do you intend for her, then?"

"To raise her with the girls, as our own."

Portia was too shocked to speak—at first. After a few incoherent sputters, she said, "George! You can't mean that! A foundling, of God knows what unsavory background, raised with our own dear daughters. Absurd! I won't have it!"

"You *will* have it. I expect obedience in this, Portia."

She was more stunned by this than his previous announcement. In the years of their marriage, he'd never spoken to her in such a way. It made her unutterably angry, and at the same time, it was rather exciting. Still, she wasn't going to give up quite so easily. "Do your mother and father know of this?" she asked, not realizing how very sly she sounded.

"Not yet, although I imagine Mother has heard about the child by now."

"They won't like it."

"They don't have to."

This was a new George, a man Portia had never seen before. She left the interview with a strange fluttering in her heart. Like the controlling crown wheel in a clock, a domestic crown wheel was turning, and like the subsidiary wheels of a clock, all of them were forced to move, to engage teeth in new patterns. Portia was the first to notice and the last to understand it.

Not everyone was pleased with the change. The subject broke after dinner that evening, a tactful silence having been preserved all day while the combatants marshaled their troops. Evelyn, very plump now but seeming angular and edgy, picked at her food, making a silent, martyred point of how upset she was. William kept up a running commentary on the hunts and shoots of his long life that his recent trip had brought to mind. He seemed unaware of the tension.

His half-sister, Nellanor, who had been on one of her rare trips away from Castlemere to visit friends in Brighton during the absence of the rest, had returned shortly before the evening meal. George assumed from the sparkle in her dark eyes that she was fully cognizant of Evelyn's anger and was thoroughly enjoying it. In contrast to Evelyn's dainty eating, Nellanor shoveled in her food as if she hadn't eaten for weeks and even allowed herself a small belch, which made both Evelyn and Portia shudder. Nellanor would come to George's defense even if she thought he was dead wrong, just to take an opposite view to Evelyn and Portia. But he didn't need her support this time.

When the final course was cleared, William leaned back in his chair and said, "Well, what's it all about, then, son? This brat you've brought in the house is causing an uproar. Got your mother's digestion all in a dither. Explain yourself."

"There's little to explain. She was left on the back step, very ill. I had her brought in and nursed. The doctor says she'll recover, probably without any ill effects. I've attempted to locate her mother, but the woman has vanished without a trace."

"Yes, yes. I see that, but what's all this nonsense about treating her like one of us? Why isn't the kitchen good enough for the brat?"

So Portia had reported their conversation to his parents. He shouldn't have been surprised. He cast a cold glance at her and she wouldn't meet his eyes. "Because she isn't of the servant class, Father. She seems to have been gently reared."

"Nonsense!" Evelyn said.

"Have you spoken with her, Mother?" George asked.

"Of course not!" This was true enough, but Evelyn had wasted no time looking the child over as soon as she'd heard about her presence in the house and the mysterious circumstances of her arrival. The child had been sleeping soundly when she went in, however, so she could truthfully say she hadn't spoken to her. Not that strict adherence to the truth normally mattered a great deal to her. There were more important virtues, in Evelyn's view.

William flapped his hand impatiently at his wife. "If she's not a servant, what the hell is she, then? Who is she? What do you propose to do with her?"

"Let her grow up," George said simply. "With whatever advantages we can give her."

"We?" William asked. He was thoroughly enjoying himself. Hadn't had a good spitting-and-hissing family row for years. It was about time. "Do you forget this is my house, boy?"

"No, nor do I forget that it's entailed to the eldest male heir. You can't throw me out or take it away from me," George said.

Nellanor belched again and grinned.

"I can damned well take the business away!" William blustered. Good for the boy. He'd never shown this kind of spirit before and William had feared it would never happen. "That's got no entailment."

"You could do that," George answered, remaining very calm. "But then my wife and daughters would be paupers. Of course, I could teach in the village school. I know a great deal about geography. Portia could probably take in sewing. She does fine handwork. And if we let all the staff go—"

"George!" Portia wailed. How had this gotten so far out of hand? She'd anticipated that William and Evelyn would simply straighten it out, but here was George threatening to take her to the poorhouse. Take in sewing!

William glared at his son, bursting with pride inside. He himself didn't give a damn about the little wench George had taken in, but the courage she'd made George show was worth taking in a whole damned orphanage.

Suddenly Nellanor burst into a loud, cackling laugh. "Good show, Georgie! You keep the little one. I'll look after her for you."

At this announcement, both Evelyn and Portia looked up sharply, their thoughts running along parallel lines. Evelyn saw a possibility of getting Nellanor moved into the new wing and keeping both her and the child out of sight. Every hour Nellanor spent with the child was an hour Evelyn wouldn't have Nellanor in her hair. Portia's hopes were that George's half-aunt, interested in the foundling child, would take less interest in her own darling daughters. She'd feared from their birth that the vulgar old woman might influence them the way she'd influenced George, and win their affection. Let her have the other child, and good riddance to both of them.

Though they wrangled and harangued a bit longer about it, the battle was done, each side feeling it had won.

The crown wheel silently turned another notch.

3

———◆———

Mary Grey's physical recovery was rapid. The next morning when Dr. Engle called at Castlemere he reported to George that he was quite certain now that she would be entirely well in time. "Amazingly recuperative, children are. If you or I became as ill as she was, we'd be in bed for a sixmonth."

"When will I be able to take her to London to search for her people?" George asked.

"Well, that's a wearing sort of trip. I wouldn't say for a few weeks at least. But, George, you don't mean to take all this trouble yourself, do you? Why not let Tutin do it?"

"She was left at my home. That makes her my responsibility."

"I think that's damned fine of you, but I do believe it's unnecessary. Of course, it's up to you. I'll come back tomorrow."

When George went to look in on the child later in the morning, he met his Aunt Nellanor just coming out of the room. "Pretty little redhead," she said.

George responded to the knowing look in her eyes. "You know who she is, don't you?"

Nellanor looked away. "I only know what my eyes tell me. And I know you fairly well. Or I thought I did."

Nellanor's disapproval was something he couldn't bear. In many ways she'd been more truly a mother to him than Evelyn. He took her arm and said quietly, "It was a long time ago and I was very young, Aunt Nell." The saddest thing about it was, he'd forgotten the young woman's face—until he saw Mary Grey. All he remembered of her, when he thought of her at all, was her soft, yielding body. She'd been all milk-white skin and delicious curves. Big, shapely breasts that filled his hands, candy-pink nipples that fasci-

28

nated him, and thick soft hair that smelled faintly of cinnamon. He'd been a hungry, randy boy, wanting nothing more than his own satisfaction.

Nellanor was waiting for him to go on.

"Mother told me that Gwenith had come to her asking for money to go to a midwife—to 'fix' things. To get rid of the child. A week later, she told me Gwenith had died in the process. I had no way of knowing it wasn't true."

"None at all?" Nellanor asked. It was a rhetorical question and clearly critical. "Were you ever *that* young?"

"She lied to me, Aunt Nell."

"Women have been known to. To protect their territory. Never mind, George. You can't be faulted for believing your own mother, I suppose. Men are so gullible. Fools, nine out of ten of them. I thought you were the tenth."

George clasped his hands behind his back. "I wasn't altogether gullible. I'm equal parts fool and scoundrel. I suppose I wanted to believe it or I would have tried to stop her at the first. It was spineless of me, and now I'm reaping the consequences. I must make it right—or at least as right as I can. As soon as the girl is well, I'll take her to London and try to find Gwenith."

"That would be an error, George."

"What else can I do?"

"Just take care of the child as she wanted you to."

"She could only have left her because the child was so ill and she hadn't the means to provide her with medical care. Gwenith was a very sweet, loving girl. I'm sure she'll want her back."

"Oh, George, don't do this to little Mary."

"Do it *to* Mary? I'm proposing to do it *for* Mary."

"What? Fling her back and forth like a shuttlecock?"

"Aunt Nell, you don't understand!"

"Somebody doesn't, that's a certainty. Do as you think you must, George. But tell me this: what will you do if you can't find her mother?"

"I've decided to adopt her."

"Fine. That's what I hoped you'd say. But how long will you give yourself to look for your Gwenith?"

"As long as it takes."

"No, George. It won't do. Would you leave the child a motherless, fatherless orphan forever? You've all of England, Scotland, and Wales to search. She might have even gone to the Continent. The woman might die, or remarry and not wish to have anything to do with you or the girl."

"Oh, she wouldn't marry."

"Say you! Your understanding of her probable behavior has already shown to be faulty to the extreme."

"Still, she wouldn't—"

"Regardless, you might search for years. And what of Mary all that time? Should she be here on sufferance, neither fish nor fowl? If you sincerely wish to do right by her, you must decide now how long you will allow for the search."

George looked away, remaining silent as a servant passed along the hallway. When they were alone again he said, "I'll go on looking for her until I find her. But I see your point. I'll proceed with adoption in six months."

"And what of Portia?"

"I suppose I'll have to tell her the truth," he said, again dropping his gaze.

He's keeping something from me, Nellanor thought. She recognized the signs. He might be a man grown to the rest of the world, but she knew him better than the world did. "She'll know without being told. If nothing else, your mother will inform her."

"You think Mother knows?"

"Oh, Georgie! Haven't you realized yet that your mother knows more about this than you do? That she always has?"

"I doubt that," George said firmly. It was the first time during their conversation that he seemed to be in control, as he had been at dinner the evening before.

Nellanor studied him, wondering what he was thinking, but sensing it was better not to ask. "Do as you think best. I'll support you in whatever way I can."

"I know that, Aunt Nell," he said, kissing her cheek.

"The doctor tells me you're doing well," George said. "You'll be healthy in no time at all."

Mary was sitting on the edge of the bed wearing a clean but shabby dress George had never seen before and shoes and stockings that he thought might have been some that Charlotte had outgrown. She was no longer as ghost-white as before, but she still had a pallor he associated with city dwellers. Her hands were folded primly in her lap and she was sitting very straight. "Please, sir. Tell me where my mother is."

He pulled up a chair and sat down. "Mary, I don't know where she is, but I promise you I'm going to help you find her."

"What am I doing here?" she asked, seemingly unmoved by his promise. "Why did you make my mother go away?"

"To tell you the truth"—why did he feel this was a child who would accept nothing less than the truth?—"I don't know why your mother left you here, but—"

"My mother left me here?" she asked.

"Yes." Why did she seem surprised? They'd talked about this before. But that had been the first time she had awakened. Perhaps she didn't remember. "You were very sick and she wanted us to take care of you."

"Did she say that?"

"Well, no. I didn't—"

"And you didn't make her go away?" She raised her hand to her mouth as if to nibble on a fingernail, then, catching herself, very deliberately clutched her hands together.

"We wouldn't have done that, my dear girl."

Mary got up and walked across the room, turning her back on him. "My mother left me," she said. It sounded like a vow. She could have been a young princess making a troth-plight, recognizing its importance without quite understanding the implications.

George was strangely frightened and felt as if he'd inadvertently set something dangerous loose. "Only for your own good, my dear," he said overheartily. "Now, let's get you out for a bit of a walk. Look the place over if you feel up to it." Dear God, he sounded just like his father.

She straightened her shoulders and tossed her head in a curiously adult way, then turned to face him. "Yes, sir. If you wish, sir." And while the words were subservient, the stance and the set of her small jaw were haughty and angry.

"Shall we go to the barn first, then? There are some horses there, and dogs, and probably even kittens. Do you like kittens?"

"No."

"Oh. I see. Well."

She stared back at him defiantly and he met her gaze with guilt and consternation. Then, not quite knowing what else to do, he put his hand out toward her. She looked at it for what seemed minutes, and then, with seeming reluctance, put her hand in his. George was fully aware of the reluctance, but was gratified at the firmness of the grip.

Mary wasn't sure what she thought of the country. She'd never been outside London and it was all so different, so open, so green. Grass seemed to spread for miles and she wondered what it was *for*. Later in life, Mary came to the firm conclusion that she didn't like cities, but on this, the first day of her new life, she hadn't balanced those scales. Anyway, she had more important matters churning her thoughts than comparing the urban existence to the rural.

Her mother had *left* her. It was a stunning and horrible realization. She and her mother had no one and nothing in life but each other. No other friends, no other family. And yet she'd done something to make her mother simply abandon her, throw her away to strangers. Still fuddled by her illness, she raked through her memory for some explanation. Was it because she got sick? She'd been sick before, and so had her mother. Mother was sick a lot of the time. But they had stayed together.

She tried to recall what she could have done. Was there some breach of etiquette—Mama was very serious about good manners and proper speech—that she'd committed? Had she said something ugly or done something naughty? She couldn't remember. In fact, she couldn't remember very much of anything since she came down with that cough and Mama put her to bed with a dose of honey and expensive lemon juice. Then there were hazy impressions of a journey: the jolting of a carriage, Mama holding her on her lap, some lady putting damp cloths on her head and talking about her red hair. Was that here, or someplace else?

They had reached the stables. "The horses here pull our carriages, and two of them sometimes run in races," the nice man was saying. Had he told her his name? She should have tried to remember it. She made herself pay attention. "Would you like to ride? No? Maybe later, when you're feeling better. I think it would be too tiring for you now. Ah, here are the kittens. I knew there would be some."

Mary's concept of cats was based wholly on her city experiences. Cats meant either the scrappy, mean vagrants that lived in alleys and unused drains, or the fat, repulsive lap creatures that belonged to some of the ladies Mama did sewing for. Sometimes Mary went with her to take mended dresses back and she'd seen the useless creatures being fed tidbits that made Mary's mouth water.

But these might have been a different breed of animal entirely. The mother cat was a sleek, lithe tortoiseshell who walked up and butted her head against Mary's leg. Her fur was smooth and shiny. As soon as the cat approached the visitor, four kittens came tumbling and romping out of hiding and joined her. One of them, an orange ball of fluff with a white face, looked up at Mary and meowed demandingly. The nice man leaned down and scooped the baby up. Cupping it in his palms, he held it out to Mary. "Would you like to hold it?"

"Yes, please, sir." She was astonished at how light and yet strong the little cat was. It grabbed at the front of her dress with minute needle-sharp claws and clung to her, making a funny rattling purr. Mary bent her head and felt the kitten's soft fur against her face. She could feel its whole tiny body trembling in tune with the remarkable noise it was making.

The nice man was watching and saying, "Would you like to have this kitten as your pet? You could let it sleep in your room at night, if you like."

Mary couldn't bring herself to answer; she just cuddled the kitten closer.

"You'd have to give it a name, you know." He leaned forward, lifted the kitten's tail for a moment, and said, "It's a male—I think. It's hard to tell when they're so little. Do you have a name you'd like to give it?"

Mary stared at him wordlessly.

"Well, then. How about Ginger? It's a good cat name, especially for an orange cat. It's also a good Beecham name. Do you know what ginger is? It's a spice. Someday we'll go to the warehouse in the city and I'll show you some ginger and tell you all about it. There are boxes and boxes of it there."

George realized he'd never made such an offer to Charlotte or Hester, or even thought about voluntarily doing things with them. They were, he recognized for the first time and with sadness, Portia's children. Only his by genetic accident. But this child—this child needed him. Charlotte and Hester, adorable as they were, didn't.

Looking up at him, Mary said, "Ginger is a good name. Thank you, sir."

After that, Mary never asked about her mother again.

4

Nellanor's approach to Mary was unlike George's. "Do you plan to lie about all day long?" she asked, marching into the small room adjoining George's one morning. The child was still staying there. "Awful little hideyhole this is. We'll get you up to a nice room where there's a bit of light and air. There's one next to mine that would do nicely for you. Agnes!"

"Yes'm?" The maid had appeared behind her with a breakfast tray.

Nellanor looked at the tray with an expression of outrage. "What in the name of heaven is this in honor of?"

"Well, the poor little mite—"

"Poor little mite, my eye! She's a perfectly ordinary child who's quite capable of getting her arse down to breakfast like the rest of us."

Agnes giggled. She adored being shocked by the old lady. Nellanor went out of her way to oblige her. "Yes'm. What should I do with these things?"

"Run back downstairs and wrap them up for us to take along."

"You're going on a journey, ma'am?"

"Only round the place. That is, if this spindly creature will get out of bed and stop lolling about like visiting royalty. What about it, girl?"

"I'll get up when I like," Mary replied, terrified into a rudeness her mother would never have allowed.

Nellanor laughed. "Got a mind of your own, have you? And a temper to match. Should have known you didn't have that carroty hair for nothing. Well, my lass, I'm going off on a bit of an adventure today, and you may come along if you choose. Here's some clothes for you. Old trews and boots and a shirt of George's. Saved them up, I did. Figured there'd be another boy about the place someday."

"I'm not a boy!"

"Doesn't matter a fig. Climbing clothes are what you need, and climbing clothes you'll get. Now, put them on or not. It doesn't matter a fig to me. I'll wait for ten minutes, not a second more. And keep that mangy cat here. It's too little to go hauling around, and I'd end up having to carry the damned thing."

She flung the neat bundle of clothing on the bed and stomped off.

"She's a right terror, is Miss Nellanor," Agnes said admiringly.

Mary had scrambled out of bed and was using the chamber pot behind the screen in the corner. "Aren't you scared of her?" she called.

"Aye, near to wet myself half the times she talks to me, I do. But when my little brother Francis came to see me one time—bringing some things from me mother, he was—and fell and broke his arm, it was herself who nursed him. Splinted him up without so much as a blush or a by-your-leave. 'Struth. So I figure she ain't as mean and all as she talks. Hurry up with that pissin'. She means what she says. She won't wait."

Wearing George's old clothing and sporting hasty braids that had bits fraying out like fine copper wires, Mary appeared in the allotted time. Nellanor looked her over critically. "Turn around, child. Bit baggy in the bottom, but all the better for getting around, I suppose. Where's the food?"

"Right here, ma'am," Agnes said. She was only a few steps behind Mary and waddling along with a picnic basket.

"Not that great fool thing, Agnes. It would take a draft horse to drag it along!"

She dumped the contents out on the floor of the entry hall and started rummaging around. "Here, girl, put as much as you can in your pockets." She started handing Mary the oiled-paper-wrapped lumps of bread, bacon, and cheese, and stuffed some tiny jars of jam down the front of her own dress. "Where's a knife?"

Agnes handed her a butter knife. "That's a sad excuse for a knife, but never mind," she said, jamming the knife into the twisted knot of hair at the back of her head just as if it were a perfectly normal thing to do. Mary was awestruck. The old woman looked like an elderly female pirate.

"Now, my girl, we'll look at the cliffs first," she said, setting off at a brisk pace. Mary had to run to catch up. In spite of her still somewhat weakened condition, running felt good. Mama had never let her run anywhere. She said it was unladylike. And Mama would have never allowed her to wear trousers like a boy.

But Mama wasn't around anymore.

Nellanor was an amateur naturalist and this child provided her with a student upon whom to vent her copious knowledge. George and Portia's daughters had a distinctly sugary turn of mind where natural science was concerned. Everything to them was either "pretty" and elicited little squeals, or "ugly" and reduced them to making nasty faces. Nellanor tried to make allowances for their being so young yet, but now she didn't need to. She had a new audience.

She sent Mary climbing up a tree to fetch an abandoned bird nest, and then sat on the ground and dissected it, explaining to the little girl what sort of bird had built it and what the different twigs and grasses of its construction were. With the butter knife she opened up part of a mole's burrow and told Mary about the creature who dug it. She identified trees and flowers and birdcalls and then tested Mary's recall. "Well, at least you're not stupid," she said, meaning she thought Mary was very bright indeed.

When they reached the edge of the cliffs, which they had approached by a circuitous route through the woods, Nellanor said, "This is the English Channel. Across there is France. Beechams like to say you can see France on clear days, but that's nonsense and evidence of an overactive imagination. Do you want to rest a bit, or shall we go down to the beach?"

It was the first concession she'd made to Mary's health, and the girl promptly answered, "I've never seen a beach."

"Then we'll take a close look. Over here is a sort of path. It's very steep and rough, so go slowly and carefully or you'll fall down and I'll have to carry you back. I'm too old for that. This isn't a sandy beach. Someday you'll probably see that kind too. This is a chalk-and-flint-rock beach . . ."

She went on explaining as they picked their way down, her voice rising as the sound of the waves grew louder. Several times she hoisted her heavy skirts past her knees to facilitate her progress. Mary could see her voluminous linen drawers and nubby stockings and was fascinated. Her mother had never undressed in front of her, so she had no idea what grown ladies wore under their outer garb.

Once at the bottom, Nellanor allowed herself a few deep, refreshing breaths. "Here's a nice flat rock. I've been having picnics on it for many a year. When I was younger than you, my nanny brought me here and sometimes made a fire and cooked eggs for us. The odor of salt breeze always makes me think of eggs. Put the food out and let's see what we have."

Mary emptied her pockets. The bread had gotten mashed flat, but Nellanor claimed it was best that way. After wiping the multipurpose bread knife on her skirts, she cut up some cheese and slapped it and some bacon between the doughy slabs of bread. "Now, girl, ask me a question," she said through a mouthful of food. Her manners were abominable, but Mary didn't mind, even though she felt sure she should. "Any question you want. I'll allow you three today, then one a day for as long as you want to keep asking. And I'll give you an honest answer if I can and if I think you deserve it."

Mary took a bite of her sandwich, trying to be dainty. But she was hungry and bit off more than she usually would have. Around Nellanor that seemed acceptable, if not actually required. "How old are you?" she asked after she swallowed.

"Sixty-nine," Nellanor shot back. "That's a silly question. Ask me a better one."

"Why does that house smell funny?"

Nellanor grinned. "Still silly, but you caught me out. The smell is rosemary, but I don't know why it's there. I usually don't even notice it after so long—only when I've been away for a while and come back. Don't you like the smell?"

"Yes, I do, ma'am."

Nellanor shook her head emphatically. A hairpin flew loose and landed on the bread. "No, no, no! I'm not 'ma'am' to you. I'm 'Aunt Nell.' "

"But you're not *my* aunt," Mary countered.

Nellanor glared at her. "What in hell difference does that make?"

Mary hadn't an answer to this.

"You've got one more question," Nellanor said, stuffing the last of her sandwich in her mouth.

Mary looked away, afraid to meet the old woman's eyes. "Do you like me?" she asked.

"What do you think?"

"You said you'd answer my question, and I asked first."

."I suppose I like you well enough, girl," Nellanor said. "Do you like me?"

Mary met her gaze directly. "Perhaps."

Nellanor's booming laugh drowned the sounds of the waves.

The reactions of the rest of the family to Mary varied widely. George's father, William, simply took no notice of her. Little girls weren't a significant part of his life except in the vague realization that several of the women in his family had, he supposed, been such creatures at some time. If he'd been forced to take a side for or against her, he probably would have supported her, albeit halfheartedly.

On the day Mary and Nellanor had their picnic, William was looking over some repairs to the gutters and saw them return. Nellanor was striding briskly, the girl occasionally giving a skip to catch up. Nellanor shooed Mary into the kitchen door and came over to stand with William looking up at the workers. "She's a good 'un," she said.

He nodded. Nellanor liked the fiery-haired little wench and he had a high regard for her opinion in most matters. It was all that was said between them on the matter. It was all that needed to be said.

Also in Mary's favor, in William's view, there was the change the orphan's arrival had brought about in George. He'd stood up for his decision (bird-witted as it was) and acted as if he had a real spine for a change. William couldn't understand it—the girl was a by-blow, he supposed. The child of one of those village girls who'd been throwing themselves at his son a few years back. Or maybe that ladies' maid or governess or whatever she was that Evelyn had run off. But what was so remarkable about that? Every man of consequence, and a good many of no account at all, had a bastard or two someplace. William himself had a daughter someplace, or so he'd been told by a woman he'd had in a hedgerow, who then tried to get money out of him. He'd sent her packing fast enough.

Now, if this newcomer had been a boy-child . . . Ahh, that might have been a different thing entirely. William would have interested himself in the matter. Since the Crusades, there had never been a complete failure to produce a male heir—a few close shaves, a posthumous infant or two, and some whose sires were open to question—but the line had never passed sideways that he knew of. Always from father to son or grandson. They needed a young male Beecham to carry on the line, and Portia didn't seem to be getting the job done. Two girls in a row, that was acceptable, but no sign of breeding for several years now.

"They still having at it, George and Portia?" he had asked Evelyn one evening when he'd been brooding over the question.

"I beg your pardon?" Evelyn said. She knew perfectly well what he meant, but persisted after years of marriage in pretending she didn't quite understand his vulgarities.

He made his query more specific, in language that brought a genuine blush to his wife's cheek. "Dear! How would I know?"

"You damned well do know. You know everything that goes on here."

Evelyn couldn't decide whether to be flattered or insulted, but she answered, "I believe they are still fulfilling their marital duties."

"Then why isn't she getting on with giving us a boy?"

"In good time, William," she'd replied, but she was as worried as William.

Evelyn, too, ignored Mary, but in her case it was deliberate and fueled by anger. Years before, a cousin of Evelyn's had come for an extended visit after her husband died. She brought along her children and their Welsh governess. Concerned with her cousin's distress, Evelyn had been slow to notice the interest George and the young woman took in each other. But when she did realize, some months into the visit, that "meaningful looks" were being exchanged between the scion of the Beechams and a young woman who was only half a step above a common servant, she was quick to take action. "George, I fear you are forming an attachment to this unsuitable young woman," she said. "It must stop. It's quite undignified and will make you a laughingstock among the household staff."

"Damn the household staff, Mother. I love Gwenith," he'd said.

"I *cannot* have heard you right!"

"I want to marry her."

She stared at him, aghast. He was only twenty-one years old, and (owing to Nellanor's malignant influence, she considered) a strangely immature twenty-one. Now, as he stood before her, he had a stupid, starry-eyed look, like a Crusader in quest of a holy relic—all obsession and no brain. "I see," she said quietly, resolving to take care of the matter herself. Nothing would be served by further discussion with him.

She summoned the governess to a private interview and said, "Your name is Gwenith, I believe? Well, Gwenith, it pains me to have to open such a personal subject, but I believe it's necessary to point out to you some facts of life. My son is the heir to a long tradition as well as the family estate. This is a heavy responsibility, perhaps heavier than he now realizes. He must make a good marriage. By that I mean, of course, a marriage to a woman of his own class and status. Now, perhaps you don't quite realize why that is. I shall explain to you—and I do so with the belief that you do entertain a serious affection for my son and will understand that such affection is best proved by doing what is right."

"Yes, ma'am," the young woman said, looking at the carpet in Evelyn's elegantly appointed sitting room, where the interview was being held. Evelyn was seated sideways at her writing desk, her plump, heavily beringed hands folded in an attitude of composure.

"Very good," she said with a hint of a cool, polite smile. "Let us suppose for a moment that George, in his youthful enthusiasm, made an unsuitable alliance—it might seem, at first, quite democratic, not to mention romantic. I'm not insensitive to such concepts. However, others would not regard it as such. His eventual position as head of this household would suffer enormously. The servants would have no respect for him as their master if he had been so foolish as to marry into their own class. Nor would such a woman ever be accepted as mistress of the house.

"In addition, the social stigma would be insurmountable. His friends would turn away from him, laughing behind their hands. Guests might continue to visit, but only to . . ." She paused as if stricken by the distaste she felt at even putting such a concept into words. "They would come to gawk. The Beechams, as you may have failed to realize, are respected in the very highest circles. Our own dear queen has even been a guest at the Beecham table. Do you suppose Queen Victoria would actually deign to sit down with a former governess who had so far forgotten her place as to engineer a marriage with her betters?"

The young woman had wilted. "No, ma'am," she whispered.

But Evelyn wasn't through. Her chin jiggled as she spoke

more forcefully. "There is also the business to consider. Beecham's Fine Spices is a far-flung empire, the head of which—as you know George will someday be—must command respect. If George were to make an inappropriate alliance, he would also make himself a laughingstock among his hundreds of employees and business associates. And it wouldn't just be George. His children would suffer as well."

At this the young woman looked up sharply, but said nothing in the face of Evelyn's lecture, which was going on relentlessly. "I suspect that George, in his youth and idealism, would say none of this mattered. And in fact, it might *not* matter to him—for a while. But, my dear young woman, you and I must consider the long view. In time, it is inevitable that the flush of romance would fade. George would get weary of being the object of fun and derision. Not truly being master in his own house would irritate him. So would having his friends look at his wife and children askance. The business would inevitably suffer, making him feel like a failure.

"I shall tell you something about men that you are probably too young and inexperienced to have realized: even the best of them cannot admit their own failures and mistakes. They are casters-of-blame. They like to see themselves as martyrs to the errors of others—especially what they perceive as the errors caused by women. I presume you grasp what I'm telling you."

Gwenith nodded. There were tears trickling down her face.

Undeterred by this evidence of weakness, Evelyn went on briskly. "It would be only a matter of time until George became seriously discontented with the situation, and he would blame you. Whatever softer feelings he thinks he feels now would change. An unsuitable wife would become a millstone to him, a detriment to his home life, his social life, and his business life. It is, you should know, quite possible that George may be elevated to the peerage, provided the wife he eventually chooses is the right sort."

To Evelyn's credit, she firmly believed every word she was saying, and had anyone been present to chide her for the terrible pain she was inflicting, she'd have countered that her son's happiness and welfare were more important to her than anything else in the world. It was not only her right, but her sacred duty to protect him. She would be morally remiss to allow such a situation to continue unchecked.

"You do understand what I'm telling you, don't you? Any

thought of an alliance between you and my son is utterl unthinkable. Even if it is what he thinks he wants, it woul be a terrible thing for him, and ultimately a terrible thin for you."

"I . . . Yes, ma'am."

"Very good. I knew you were a girl of enough intelligenc to see reason." No point in withholding a harmless compli ment now.

"But, ma'am. There's something else—"

"Yes, your employment. I can understand how it woul be most difficult for you to continue to serve my cousi here, but I've spoken with her and she says she intends t go back home later in the week, and has agreed to send yo and the children ahead today."

"But, ma'am, I'm with child and—"

"Oh, my God!" Evelyn exclaimed, coming quickly to he feet. A diamond-ornamented watch pinned to her ampl bosom fell off and bounced on the carpet and she didn't even look down. "You're lying to me. Confess it!"

Gwenith was weeping openly now. "It's true, it's true!"

"Stop! I don't want to hear any more. Sit down." She gestured at the chair she hadn't offered earlier and went to the window. Gazing out, she tried to think this through and compose herself. There was the ragged sound of crying from Gwenith, but she ignored it. Finally she came back and looked down at the young woman. "You must pull yourself together! This is not the time for Welsh emotionalism."

She resumed her place at the writing desk. "This doesn't alter a single thing I said. It simply means that something in your character or upbringing was faulty and has created an additional problem for you. If you think you are going to use this story—if it's true—to bring some leverage against us, you're quite mistaken. I am not, however, entirely with- out human sympathy."

She opened her desk drawer and took out a piece of writing paper. "I'm addressing this to my banker. I will direct him to give you a sum of money that should provide adequately for you—and the child, if there really is to be one—for several years. I shall, in fact, be quite generous, but you must understand, there will never be any more. If you use this gift sensibly and invent a believable story to account for the baby, there's no reason you shouldn't find some man of your own class to marry you. You're really quite attractive, you know. You may regard it as a dowry of sorts."

At this, Gwenith burst into fresh tears.

Evelyn ignored her and wrote out the letter.

She sanded and sealed it and held it out to Gwenith. "Take it, young woman. You may depart as soon as your bags are packed. I shall explain to my sister without prejudice, and if ever you need an employment reference, direct your inquiry to me and I shall see that you have it. But understand this." She paused until Gwenith, red-eyed and despairing, looked up at her, then went on in a venomous tone, "If you ever come back here, or attempt to communicate with my son, I shall spare no effort in destroying you. I can do it, never doubt. And I will—without any mercy. You do believe me, don't you?"

Gwenith didn't answer.

"Don't you?"

"Yes, ma'am," Gwenith sobbed.

Every time Evelyn saw the child Mary, with Gwenith's red hair and delicate stature, she heard the whole conversation over again. The young woman had betrayed her, and what maddened Evelyn was that she had "played by the rules" that Evelyn herself had drawn up, and the stupid Welsh girl appeared to have won the game. She hadn't contacted George—not that Evelyn knew of. She felt sure, had there been a meeting between them, he would have told her so instead of carrying on with the pretense that he had no idea who the child's mother was. Nor had the ex-governess asked for more money.

No, far worse. Cuckoolike, she had just left her egg in their nest. And there was nothing Evelyn could do about it! The nasty woman must be gloating like a pig in truffles over the way she had worked it out. She herself might not have acquired the comfortable life she'd hoped for in the bosom of the Beechams, but she'd made sure her bastard did.

The most awful part of it all was wondering what George was really thinking. He was no longer that naive young man. He'd drawn into himself and excluded her from his confidence after that day when he came home from hunting and found Gwenith gone. She'd had a good story ready, of course. She told him that the young woman had come to her in tears and hysteria, confessed her condition, and asked for money to go away to a midwife in London and get rid of the baby. It all reminded her of times when George was a little boy and would beg to do something and, upon hearing her refusal, stomp about in front of his friends, but secretly smile at her. He hadn't smiled about Gwenith, of course, but Evelyn sensed his relief.

There had been a few bad moments later—when she told him the story of Gwenith dying. Perhaps that was a flourish she should have˜ resisted, but she feared he'd change his mind. He'd taken it hard—not so much grieved at her death, but guilty at his role in it. Evelyn had suffered a twinge of remorse at this, but he would survive and be strengthened by it, she'd told herself.

"Of course now, with the living, breathing evidence of her lie living right in the house, wearing her granddaughters' hand-me-downs, skipping through the grounds with Nellanor, she'd expected a terrible confrontation, and when it didn't come, she became more and more perplexed and nervous. At first she'd dreaded it. But as the days went by, she found herself hoping the explosion would come, just to have the horror of it over with.

But while she lost sleep, and gritted her teeth when she saw Mary, and grew nervous and worried, she knew she would never bring it up herself to him—or to William, who had never known the full truth of the matter. No, to open the subject would be to admit some degree of culpability. Her only hope was that Nellanor, who appeared to like the child (she *would*, just out of spite), would take her over and keep her out of sight and hearing as much as possible.

And soon enough, she told herself, with any luck Portia would give them all a boy and that would effectively eclipse George's morbid interest in the little redheaded bastard.

5

Fifteen-year-old Alex Beecham stood by his trunk, surveying the docks and attempting to look relaxed. Leaning back, hands in pockets, he struck a casual pose. He was typical of his age in some ways: coltish, gangling, with feet and hands just a little too large to manage as well as he wished, limbs suddenly too long, a voice that often betrayed him by shifting between octaves without warning. But in spite of the drawbacks of youth, he was, by anyone's standards, an arresting-looking boy—straight blue-black hair with a crisp part and eyes so pale they seemed very nearly without any color at all. He had a wide intelligent brow, ears perhaps a little too large, and finely chiseled features. His nose was narrow with a slight arch which contributed to the impression that he'd already begun to develop the unintentional but characteristic look of faintly bored haughtiness that was considered the mark of well-bred Englishmen.

There were signs, however, that this wasn't the average English schoolboy. His complexion was tanned, not from a summer beach holiday in the south of France, but from a lifetime spent in the tropics. The faint squint lines around his shockingly pale eyes looked as if he were more accustomed to the glare of equatorial sun than misty English days. And the air of comfortable ennui was only a thin glaze barely concealing excitement and anticipation as well as desperate homesickness and fear.

Could she have forgotten him? he wondered, gnawing for a moment on a hangnail, then stuffing his hands back into his pockets as if an invisible mother or ayah had reprimanded him. How long should he wait? If she didn't come to fetch him, what would he do? Could he have come halfway around the world only to be forgotten? And in a strange country. No, his country, he mentally corrected himself. He was English and this was England. He was home for the first time ever. He'd never quite expected England to be so very unlike Singapore, however. Rather, he'd expected it to be much the same in appearance, merely cooler in temperature and without the monsoons. His parents had told him the climate was different, of course. His mother had talked about snow and tried to make him comprehend what it was, and he'd tried very hard to imagine it. Think about snow, he told himself firmly. Think about anything but the fact that your grandmother isn't at the docks to meet you—

"Alexander! Is that you?"

A tall, homely old woman was striding toward him. She wasn't at all as he'd pictured her. Grandmothers were supposed to be plump and twinkly-eyed. At least his other grandmother had been. This woman was big and horsey, with a mannish walk and loud voice.

"How long have you waited?" Nellanor demanded, then went on without waiting for an answer. "Glad to see you had the sense to hold your ground until I turned up. The carriage wheel came loose and held me up. My, you're tall, aren't you, and so very good-looking. I wouldn't have recognized you as a Beecham. Nothing like your father. You must favor your mother's people. Come along," she said, snapping her fingers at a servant who'd finally caught up with her, puffing with the effort. "Take the baggage, Hector. Now, Alex, we must decide what you're to call me. What did you call your mother's mother?"

"Just 'Grandmother,' " Alex said, swamped by this flood of words spoken at a fast pace. He was fascinated by the little collection of stiff gray hairs sprouting from a mole on her chin, and could hardly tear his eyes away.

"Then I shan't be 'Grandmother' also. 'Gram' sounds terribly intimate and childish, considering your age and the fact that we've never met before. I understand some grandmothers are called 'Granny,' but I despise the sound of that. You could call me 'Aunt Nell' like George's girls do, but then, I'm not your aunt. Why don't you just call me 'Nell' until you decide on what you like? Everyone else does, all the adults in the family, and it would make us seem friends. We're going to be, you know. Friends, I mean."

Nellanor knew she was drowning the boy in all her ridiculous talk, but couldn't seem to stop. Normally she kept her wits under control even when her tongue was busy, but she'd been so moved by the sight of him standing there, so terribly forlorn, near tears—impossible for a boy that age, of course, to cry—and looking so awfully exotic and foreign and out of place. She'd have to make George take him to a tailor and fit him out in clothes that didn't look like they'd been made fifty years ago and stored away until now. The boy must not start an English school looking like such a colonial. He'd be at enough of a disadvantage without wearing that horrible outdated tweed his father had put him in. Claudius should have had more sense, but then, when had he ever shown decent judgment? What kind of father had he been to this lanky, beautiful boy with the classical nose and big ears, who looked so pitifully lost and frightened? He'd grow into those ears when he caught up with his feet, she hoped.

"We've a long ride ahead, Alex," she said. "But I've had a dinner packed for us, things boys like. Sweets and hearty sandwiches, and lots of sugared tea. Up you go, into the carriage."

Alex took his place and the carriage lurched into motion. As they bowled through the town, his grandmother kept up a running commentary that even to him was beginning to sound a little shrill and nervous. Could she possibly be as wary of him as he was of her? Wondering this, he began to think he might just come to like her in spite of the funny hairs on her chin. He'd been predisposed not to. His father didn't like her, and she was his own mother. Not that his father had ever said so in exactly those terms. It was just that he hardly spoke of her at all, and his silence was more eloquent than any spoken criticism.

As they left the town behind, Nellanor took a deep breath and said, "Too bad about your mother's death." Expressions of sympathy didn't come easily to her, especially those she didn't mean.

Alex didn't say anything; he couldn't. His feelings about his mother were so complicated and contradictory that he hadn't sorted out yet how he felt about her dying. In a way, he was sad—at least he knew he should be. It *had* been horrible, the emptiness in the house when she was suddenly gone. And the way his father seemed to just shrink into himself without her was frightening. His father was a colorless man at best; when his wife had died, he'd become nearly invisible.

But it was also a relief to be without her. Alex would never have to hear again about his older brother, the one who died as a child. With his mother gone, there wouldn't be any more visits to the cemetery to put flowers on the grave of that boy whom he'd never known and had come to hate. No more reminiscences about how good a baby he'd been, what a wonderful future he would have had, no more implications of how much better than Alex he would have been.

"You'd love me, too, if I died!" he'd shouted at her once. She'd started crying hysterically, and his father had taken the strap to him for upsetting her, so he'd never expressed himself again.

". . . actually, I'm glad," his grandmother was going on. "Not about your mother dying, exactly. I didn't even know the woman myself. She might have been a good enough sort, though I've often wondered about anyone who married Claudius. Beside the point, really. I just mean that it meant you could come to England. I was beginning to think your father would never let go of you and send you here to me. I've been asking him to for years, you know."

"You have?" Alex asked, turning to face her for the first time since they'd started the journey. Had she really been asking for him, wanting him there?

"Of course!" Nellanor saw the boy's pale eyes light up at last, and it made her heart contract. He really was in need of affection; that was obvious. But she realized that he'd find overt evidence of love hard to accept at his age. If only she'd known him when he was little—she could have cuddled and kissed him before he outgrew it—but he'd probably turn to stone if she so much as touched him now. He'd given a fair imitation of a granite statue when she embraced him at the docks.

Damned pity Claudius hadn't sent him earlier—even earlier in the summer. He and little Mary could have taken their places in the family at one time. Now fall term would start in a few days and there wouldn't be much of an opportunity to make him feel loved and welcome. Barbaric, sending boys off to school that way. Boys were delightful creatures one at a time; in school groups they were hateful little beasts. Thank goodness there wasn't any danger of having Mary snatched away from her that way.

"I've brought along a map, so you may follow the road we're taking. I've never known a Beecham who didn't like

maps. It's in our blood. I've also brought along some books
that your Uncle George enjoyed at your age. I kept them,
in case he had sons while I was still around. I thought you
might like to have something to read along the way. Naturally, you may sleep, if you feel like it. You've had a long,
tiring journey."

She was going out of her way to be polite to him, sensing
instinctively that the blunt treatment Mary had needed wasn't
right for this child. He was a good deal older, and male
besides. And he might well have already learned at his
father's knee to hate her—she didn't want to start out by
confirming the worst of whatever opinion he might have
formed of her.

"I don't need to sleep," Alex said, exhausted, but vaguely
embarrassed at the suggestion of a nap. Naps were for
children and old people. But he was grateful to have the
books. He didn't so much want to read as he wanted an
excuse not to talk to her for a while. So many new impressions to sort out, especially his impression of her. She
wasn't physically what he'd supposed, nor in any other way.
He'd never met a woman so mannish and outspoken, and
while he was fascinated by it, he wasn't sure whether he
liked or disliked her for it. Nell. Could he really call his
own grandmother by her Christian name that way? He
opened one of the books, occasionally turning a page so
she'd think he was actually reading, but he was only looking
at the words while his mind drifted.

By the time they'd gone ten miles, he'd nodded off.
Nellanor eased sideways and let him topple gently so that
his head was in her lap. She smoothed his dark hair back
from his forehead, kissed her finger and touched it to his
temple, then felt like a fool for making such a silly gesture.
That was the sort of thing Portia would do when she was
sure she had an audience to appreciate the touching femi-
ninity of it. Still—this was her son's son.

She'd never really gotten to be a mother to Claudius.
He'd been such a stolid, loutish child, seeming to resent her
even when he was far too young to realize he might have
reason to. And he'd gotten away from her as soon as he
could. First, to school, then to the East, where he took up
his duties as company representative in Singapore. His letters had been few, boring, and dutiful. He hadn't even
invited her to his wedding.

She'd been compensated for her failure (for she did realize it was at least partly her own failure) with her son. She'd enjoyed the years with George, her half-nephew. By the time George was born, Claudius was already ten years old and she knew she'd lost him, so she turned her affection on Evelyn's boy. Nellanor had adored George, still did, in fact. However, he was a grown man with a wife and daughters of his own now. No longer so much in need of her. But she had this boy now—at least for a few short years—and she had Mary.

They were well along the road to Castlemere when Alex began to stir. Nellanor leaned back, pretending to be asleep too. She maintained the fiction as he woke, realized he was sleeping on his grandmother's lap and sat up, startled and embarrassed. After giving him plenty of time to compose himself, she opened her eyes and said, "Oh, dear. I seem to have dropped off. How rude of me! Riding always does that to me, I'm afraid. Old ladies make dull company on a trip." Was that really her own voice saying all those insipid things? She sounded as dithery as Portia or Evelyn. How disgusting! "Ask the driver to stop and let us get out and have something to eat."

Alex leaned out the window and called to the driver, hoping that no one noticed that his voice cracked as he did so. At the next wide place in the road, they stopped. The driver and the servant Hector, who'd carried the trunk and suitcase, climbed down and headed off into the woods to take care of natural functions. Nellanor, seeing the boy squirm uncomfortably, said, "Go along with the other men, Alex. I'll put out the picnic things."

Go along with the *other* men, Alex thought, and a flare of genuine affection for the old woman took fire.

Nellanor, who prided herself on a superlative bladder, that rarest of organs in a woman her age, settled in to setting up their repast. When Alex and the men returned from relieving themselves in the woods, the coach driver and Hector took the sandwiches Nellanor had unwrapped in their absence and went back to their perch to eat, leaving the woman and boy to sit together on a tartan rug in the grass. Alex tried not to eat greedily, but he was nearly starved and had gulped down two thick sandwiches before he realized he was probably taking more than his share. "Sorry," he mumbled, offering his grandmother the third one, which he'd been about to bite into.

"Please, you have it," she said. "I can't bear to eat when

traveling. It makes me queasy." She hoped he wouldn't hear her stomach rumble at this lie. She could have plucked a nearby fern and swallowed it whole. "I expect you're wondering what Castlemere is like," she said, so he wouldn't feel he had to talk while wolfing down the rest of the food. "I believe your father had a picture of it."

Alex nodded. It was a faded watercolor which he'd rescued when his mother tried to throw it away years earlier. He'd hung it in his own room and hardly a day passed when he didn't study it and wonder about the big house where the other Beechams lived in apparent grandeur. The picture had always inspired an odd mixture of feelings in him, mainly a deep longing to see the house for himself. Now he was only hours from that dream.

"It's quite a big house. When I was a little girl—hard to imagine, but I was, once—I got lost several times and had to cry until the housekeeper came and found me. But you won't have any trouble."

"Is it a real castle?" Alex asked around a mouthful of cheese.

"No, not really. It hasn't got a moat or crenellations or any of that. It's called Castlemere because there used to be a castle there. Or at least that's what people in the village claim, but I believe it was a fort, a Roman fort. The 'mere' part of the name probably comes from the French *mer*, for 'sea.' The site overlooks the English Channel. Someday when you have time away from school, I'll take you to see some real castles, though. Dover isn't far, and Battle Abbey is quite near. We'll go to London too."

Seeing that he was finished eating, Nellanor started to gather things up and put the dishes and cups back into the picnic hamper. The coachman hopped down and came to pack it away as Nellanor and Alex strolled back to the carriage. "Do you know very much about your family you're going to meet? I don't expect your father talked very much about any of us."

"My father doesn't talk much about anything," Alex said, immediately feeling disloyal.

Nellanor laughed, a noisy sort of bark. There were jungle creatures that made raucous noises like that. It was a comfortable, welcoming sound, even if it was odd to be coming from an old lady. In spite of his heritage (he'd never heard his father laugh) and circumstances, he had an irrepressible sense of humor. Squelched by the long, lonely journey, it was now beginning to reassert itself.

"He was never one for conversation, your father. Even when he was a little boy I could hardly get five words out of him a day. Well, then, I'll have to make up for it. First, there's your Great-Uncle William, my half-brother. He's horribly fierce, but you mustn't pay any mind to his manners. Under it, he's a good person. William and I grew up without parents, rich little orphans with nobody to raise us but hired servants who didn't really care how we turned out. I suppose our manners suffered for it. William's wife Evelyn, your great-aunt, is as fat as I'm skinny. I'll let you make up your own mind about her."

There was a distinctly naughty look in her eye that made Alex smile, and she grinned back. "Their son, George, is your father's half-cousin, so I suppose he's your half-second cousin, but that's getting terribly complicated and I suggest you set right out just calling him George or Cousin George. He'll like that; there's nothing stuffy about him. His wife is named Portia, like in the Shakespeare play. They have two—now three—little girls. Charlotte is five and Hester is four. Then there's Mary. She's their new daughter."

"A baby?"

"No, older than the other two. She's a foundling who was left with them, and George is adopting her. Mary's quite a delightful child. All red hair and temper and talk, now that she's settled in and gotten used to us all. She's as bright as a new penny. I'm sorry there's no one your age in the household. It might be boring to be around older people and all those little girls. If you find boys at school you want to go visit during the holidays, you must not feel obligated to spend your free time at Castlemere."

He unfolded his map again. "Are we far?"

"About another hour. I believe we're just about here," she said, pointing a long finger with a ridged nail to a spot along the coastline. "Alex, your father didn't like me. I suppose you know that."

Alex knew he ought, for courtesy's sake, to deny this, but before he could formulate a reply, she went on, "Do you know why?"

"No, ma'am."

"That's as well as might be, then. You can make up your own mind about me and the rest of the family."

6

Between two arms of Castlemere there was a secluded terrace that opened out from the map room. Flagged with great sheets of slate that were tufted at the cracks with velvety moss, it was a cool, private retreat. Alex met his cousins there en masse. They were having tea. Dressed in pale colors and seen in the delicate European summer sun that filtered gently through the ornamental maples, the women seemed like a flock of large, fragile birds. His first impression was surprise that they were all complete strangers to him. He'd anticipated having an instant sense of recognition, of kinship, in spite of never having met any of them. They were, after all, Beechams, like him.

But unlike him too: they were the "superior" Beechams, the part of the line that happened to be born first and born male. Alex knew his father harbored a resentment of them for it. He felt he should share the feeling, but being a far better-natured individual than his father, he did not.

"This must be Alexander, then!" George said, rising and shaking the boy's hand vigorously. "What a pleasure it is to welcome you."

Alex was pleasantly surprised at George. He'd pictured him much older. Handsome, dashing-looking, and friendly, George could almost have been an elder brother to him in spite of the difference in their coloring. In fact, Alex had expected both George and his father, William, to be plump and ineffectual-looking, if not downright effeminate. So many of the Englishmen who came out to Singapore were—second sons looking for a place in the world. He'd also formed this impression of the elder English Beechams from what his father *hadn't* said about them. Alex always had the

dim sense, without actually being told so, that his father felt
his labor in Singapore and surroundings was something of a
waste because of a lack of business sense or intelligence at
the English end of the process.

Alex's father, Claudius Beecham, was the family spice
company's head factor in the East. His job was to select and
purchase the spices the company exported to England for
packaging and sale. To do this work he had to spend much
of his time traveling from island to island, watching crops,
judging potential yield quality, guessing about the weather,
and deciding whether to bid in advance on an entire plantation's output or wait and buy when it reached the central
clearing place—the teeming harbor of Singapore. If he predicted a good crop, put in a preemptive bid and was wrong,
the company paid too much for inferior goods. On the other
hand, if he failed to commit a grower and the crop was
exceptional, he'd either miss buying it or have to pay too
much because of the competition.

It was a job that carried a heavy responsibility and for
which he seemed to receive little praise. Or at least little
that Alex had ever heard about. In fact, Alex had the
impression there was an absolute minimum of communica-
tion of any sort between the England Beechams and the
Singapore branch. Alex was beginning to wonder if his
impressions might have been wrong all these years. These
people seemed far too nice to have mistreated his father.

Claudius never commented on just what became of the
product of his labors once it reached London. When Alex
had gotten old enough to be interested in the business,
Claudius would merely wave his hand as if brushing away a
mosquito and say, "They do what they do. I've nothing to
say about it." As Alex scuffed his toe lightly on a small
mound of moss, it crossed his mind for the first time that his
father's implicit criticism might have been nothing more
than a disguise for sheer ignorance.

This suspicion that he might have been encouraged to
form an entirely erroneous impression of his relatives deep-
ened a moment later when Uncle William, ruddy and boisterous and clearly a force to be reckoned with in his own
home, came onto the terrace bellowing about his riding
crop. "Those girls have run off with it again. How many
times do they have to be told it's not a damned plaything?
Oh, you must be Claudius' boy. Good to have you here," he

said, pumping Alex's hand briefly before turning to his wife. "Evelyn, where is my riding crop?"

"You left it in the lumber room with your filthy boots," she said, frowning at his lack of manners. "If you wouldn't mind, dear, we haven't all been introduced to Alexander yet."

"Sorry, Mother," George said, and got on with the social business at hand.

Alex decided immediately that while the Beechams as a whole were a pleasant surprise, he didn't much like Evelyn. "How nice for you to get to *finally* meet your grandmother," she said. It was clear she meant it as a criticism of somebody, whether Nellanor, Claudius, or himself, Alex couldn't guess, but he instinctively bristled. "You find us in an informal moment, I'm afraid," Evelyn went on, "but I suppose you won't mind. I presume the social niceties are rather frequently neglected in your part of the world."

"Why should you presume that?" he asked. He knew it was bold and rude, but it just came out.

Evelyn was taken aback. "Why, the heat and all," she said.

Nellanor yelped with laughter. "Got you there, he did, Evelyn. What do you suppose they do, turn native and skip around wearing fig leaves?" It was nice to know that the boy recognized when he was being condescended to and could fight back so effectively. That it amounted to an undeclared state of war with Evelyn didn't worry her.

"Nellanor, really!"

Portia left practically no impression on Alex. She was sitting on a bench with a feverish-looking little girl on her lap and a very shy one with masses of dusty brown curls sitting by her skirts playing with a doll. Portia greeted him politely enough, but was preoccupied with the child whose forehead she kept stroking absently. "George, I do wish you'd send someone for Dr. Engle to look in on Charlotte. I don't think she's well," she said as soon as the introductions were decently completed.

The family fell into a discussion of the possible sources and importance of Charlotte's fever and Alex was left to observe them. Out of the corner of his eye he caught a hint of motion and turned to discover yet another person on the terrace, a person no one had introduced.

This person, a third little girl, was sitting on a rock ledge that was part of a wall that a spray of wisteria cascaded down. Half-concealed in the greenery, she would have been invisible if it weren't for her brilliant red hair and sparkling, curious eyes. She sat very still, as wary and cynical as a forest creature. She was staring at him and he wondered how long she'd been doing so.

Charlotte was very ill indeed. By midnight her fever had soared and she'd come out in a blistering rash. Portia was frantic and Dr. Engle could do little to relieve her anxiety. "Measles, I believe, but an extremely violent case."

"It's that horrible little girl you brought here," Portia shrieked at George. After the day she discovered Mary's presence at Castlemere, she'd never brought the subject up again and now all the bitterness she'd been hoarding for a month spewed forth. "That filthy child. Diseased. She was diseased, and now look what's happened! She's given her sickness to our own daughter!"

"Now, Portia, you don't mean that—" George said.

"Mrs. Beecham, you're upset," Dr. Engle put in. "You don't know what you're saying. I'm sure Mary Grey isn't responsible for Charlotte's illness. It's been too long. And I don't believe she had measles anyway. There was no evidence of a rash—"

"Don't you dare stand there telling me your diagnosis of that brat's illness when my own is so ill. I wish she'd never come here! Oh, George, why did you do this to me?"

Dr. Engle gave Portia a sleeping draft and instructed Agnes to put her to bed. Evelyn sat with Charlotte while the two men went outside the door to talk. "What is the true situation, Jonathan?" George asked.

"We've never lied to each other, George, and I can't start now. I'm afraid it's very likely she might not survive. There's nothing I can do but pray with you for the best. The thing you must consider now is the rest of the family. This sort of thing is hardest on the young and the old, and it's highly contagious. You must keep all the other children as far from her as you can. Your mother is already exposed, but your father and aunt must be protected as well."

George set about making arrangements for the endangered members of the family to all move into the wing of the house Evelyn had been trying to push Nellanor into for months. Then he went to visit Portia. She was still too overwrought to sleep, but the medication had calmed her considerably. "Portia, do you want to talk?" George asked, sitting at the side of the bed. There was only a single dim candle burning and it cast her face in profile.

"Not to you, George."

"Then you must listen to me instead. About Mary—"

She turned away and her disordered hair picked up the light and made a fuzzy halo. "No!"

"Portia, there is no reason for you to be so angry about her."

"There's every reason. She's your bastard. Don't think I'm too stupid to realize it."

She still wouldn't look at him. He put a hand to her face and turned her head gently. "She *is* my child. I never thought you were stupid. I had no idea of concealing the truth, I just thought you felt it best not to say anything. But that was wrong. I should have talked to you before. Whatever sin or indiscretion of mine brought about her existence, I cannot double that sin by casting her out into the world. You must see that, don't you? She's my child, my responsibility, and because you married me, she has become your burden as well. I know that's not fair, and I don't expect you to love her or even like her. All I ask is that you don't hate her—or me. She has as much right to a pleasant life as any of us."

"She has no rights! Not in my house, with my daughters!"

"Now, Portia—"

"And what of her mother? Who was she, George? What did she mean to you?"

"It doesn't matter in the least who she was, and as for what she meant to me—well, I don't suppose very much, actually. I was very silly and young for my age. I fancied myself head over heels in love."

Portia flinched away from his hand, which was still resting on her cheek.

But George, once set on telling her the truth, was relentless in his need to unburden himself. "But I must have been quite wrong in that fancy. My mother told me she'd asked for money to have an abortion and even though I should have known how very out of character that was, I didn't question Mother. I made no attempt to find the girl. A week or so later Mother told me she'd died. Looking back now, all I can remember is an overwhelming sense of relief, to tell the truth. I'd gotten myself in far more deeply than I meant to, and it seemed a solution had been handed to me on a silver salver. I accepted it gratefully.

"I know that makes me sound very selfish and callous, but that's what I'm trying to make you see. I was selfish and callous then. But I've changed a great deal in the few years since then, and the situation has changed. Our own children have made me realize how important a single human life is, how deserving of its proper place and dignity. . . ."

She'd closed her eyes and her breathing was slow and even.

George smiled to himself. What a thing! To make such a damning self-analysis and have the audience fall asleep in the midst of it. He tucked the blankets around her shoulders, touched her hair briefly, and went back to sit with his mother at Charlotte's side.

"Who are you?" Mary demanded of Alex. In the hubbub of Charlotte's illness and the move to the new wing, they'd both been temporarily forgotten and had crossed paths in the hallway.

Alex looked down at her. "I'm Alexander Beecham. Who are you?" he demanded.

"I'm Mary Grey. What are you doing here?" Since Mary had recovered from her illness and the shock of finding herself in new surroundings, her natural curiosity had come to the fore and been given new life and energy by Nellanor's unconventional encouragement.

"I'm on my way to attend school, and am visiting for a few days. Nellanor is my grandmother." Why did he even bother answering her blunt questions? Still, she was a cute little thing and it wasn't as though there was anybody else to talk to.

"I call her Aunt Nell, but she's not really my aunt. Why don't you like people here?"

"Whom don't I like?"

" 'You find us in an informal moment,' " Mary said, in perfect imitation of Evelyn's tone.

Alex laughed and said, "You shouldn't mock your elders. You're a rude little girl."

"Not as rude as you," Mary said, ignoring the laugh and taking his words literally. "I have lovely manners when I want to use them. My mother taught me. Aunt Nellanor says that's useful—you should have good manners available to wear when you need them. Like an umbrella for when it rains."

"You talk too much!" he said, unable to resist the impulse to tease her.

"I have a cat. His name is Ginger," she said, not in the least put off by his assessment. "I'll let you pet him if you want."

"I don't like cats."

"Why not? Where do you come from and why do you look so different?"

"What do you mean?" Perhaps she wasn't so amusing.

"Your skin is dark and your hair is black and your eyes aren't any color at all. It's very pretty."

"Men aren't pretty!" That was really too much!

"You're not a man."

He found her maddening. "Go away, little girl. I want to find my room."

"I can show you. And my name is Mary, not 'little girl.' "

If she'd been a boy, he'd have cuffed her for her impertinence. As it was, he was tempted. "If you know so much, where *is* my room?"

"Down there. On the right-hand side by the stair. I'll bring my cat for you to see."

"Don't bother!" he said, walking off.

Nellanor came along a moment later and found Mary standing unusually still and staring down the empty hallway. "I've been looking everywhere for you. And Alex. Have you seen him?"

Mary turned to face her. "Oh, isn't he pretty, Aunt Nellanor?" she asked rapturously.

Nellanor was puzzled. "I suppose so, child. But I don't think he'd like to hear it."

"No, he didn't."

Alex wanted to explore the house he'd wondered about for so many years, but Charlotte's illness made that impossible. He was banned, along with most of the family, from the main section. Staying inside all day was unthinkable. The long, stifling ocean voyage, plus all the dread and anticipation, had built up an enormous amount of undischarged energy that needed outlet. In addition, the littlest girl, Hester, was distraught at being separated from her mother and sister and, being half-afraid of her Aunt Nellanor, cried almost continually, a pitiful sound that frayed the nerves like sandpaper. To escape the sound of her whimpering and get some necessary exercise, Alex decided he'd spend the next day exploring the grounds.

He hadn't counted on Mary.

"Where are you going?" she asked as he set out to see what sort of trees grew in the woods. He'd seen the distinct shape of oaks in the distance, but he didn't recognize any others.

"I'm going for a walk," he said.

"I'll come with you," she said, stroking the orange cat in her arms. Her flaming red hair and the brilliant orange creature formed an island of color in the misty morning light.

"No need."

"You'll get lost without someone to tell you where you are and how to get back. But I know my way around now. Aunt Nellanor showed me where everything is and now I get to go wherever I want. Except the cliffs. I'm not allowed to go to the cliffs by myself. It's dangerous for children. I'll take my cat inside. He's too little to go along."

He made his escape while she was returning Ginger to her room.

She caught up with him an hour later.

"Do you think Charlotte will die?" she asked, popping out from behind some bushes like a forest spirit.

"How would I know?"

She shrugged and fell into step beside him. "Aunt Nellanor says she might. I don't like Charlotte, do you?"

"I don't even know her."

"I like Hester even if she is only a baby. She's only four years old. I'm seven."

"No, you're not."

"Am so! I'm just small for my age. Aunt Nellanor says I'll always be small. She knows about these things—because she's so tall. She says she was tall even when she was a baby, but that's silly because babies don't stand up so you can measure them. Aunt Nellanor measured me against the door in her room. She says she'll make marks there so I can see how much I grow. Did you ever do that?"

This was the talkingest child he'd ever come across. Unaccustomed to being around younger children and their questions, he found himself alternately amused and bewildered by her. "No. What *are* you doing here, anyway?"

"I've come here to live. And I'm going to stay here forever," she said, skipping around in front of him and looking into his face as if in challenge as she spoke.

"What about your own family?"

She fell back into step with him, making long strides to match his. "I don't have a family. Only the Beechams. Mr. Beecham is going to adopt me if he can't find my mother. Aunt Nellanor told me that, but it's a secret, so you can't tell anybody. Promise?"

"You're making that up, little girl."

"I'm not 'little girl' and I'm not making it up. I don't tell lies. Well, not real lies, just stories sometimes. Aunt Nellanor says it's wicked to tell lies. My mother said so too."

"Where is this mother of yours?"

"Gone. She's never coming back."

"Then Cousin George will find her "

"No, he won't. Nobody will find her. Ever."

Charlotte died that evening.

Alex, who didn't know her, still grieved. The death of a child, even an unknown one, was a frightening reminder of mortality, especially to one who was still struggling free of his own childhood. Moreover, Alex kept finding himself perilously near tears for reasons that were wholly selfish. He knew they were selfish and unworthy, but couldn't help himself. For as long as he could remember, he'd looked forward to coming to Castlemere; it was to have been a homecoming of sorts, and he'd imagined it a hundred different ways, every one more wonderful than the others. All those times his mother draped him in the sticky robes of his dead brother's potential, all the words he'd hoped for from his father and never received—all of that was going to be made up for at Castlemere. They would welcome him, open the familial arms to him, accept him as one of them, make him feel he was somebody very special. And instead, he'd become merely an outsider, a nuisance guest in a house of sudden death.

He didn't blame them, but his disappointment was severe, nevertheless. Even Nellanor, the one Beecham who seemed to genuinely care for him, was cast down by the child's death, and her brash personality was suddenly muted. By the end of the day after Charlotte died, Alex would even have welcomed—or at least tolerated—the nosy little girl who'd dogged his footsteps the day before. But she had disappeared and he certainly wasn't going to seek her out.

Mary had gone to earth in the room she'd been given in the new wing. Though she was too young to have put the concept into words, her instinct told her that, like Alex, she was an unwelcome outsider, far more unwelcome than he. And those who were most deeply grieved were also those whose resentment of her was the deepest. It was time for her to fade quietly into the background, otherwise she would merely stoke the fires of their dislike.

She was also frightened. If Charlotte could die, so could she. She knew old people died, she had once sat dutifully beside the coffin of one of her mother's elderly friends. She'd seen death in the streets of London as well—poor beggars, ageless in their despair, curled into ragged balls in alleys and stinking only slightly more in death than in life. But it was a shock to realize that anyone young and clean and surrounded by the magic of Castlemere could actually cease to exist.

When it came time for the funeral, Mary allowed herself to be buttoned into the little black dress Agnes had hastily stitched together for her. She didn't want to go, but knew better than to argue about it. As the family was about to file into the chapel, she crept close behind George and heard him speak in a low, fierce tone to Portia: "You must get a grip on yourself and stop making these wild accusations."

"It's only the truth. Your Mary brought that disease here. She killed Charlotte. I wish she'd died instead of my own dear baby."

Mary stopped short, paralyzed by what she'd heard.

Alex, just behind her, had heard as well, and was furious at the meanness and injustice of Portia's words. It *was* an injustice, he knew all too well. He grabbed Mary's elbow and pulled her around the corner, out of sight of the rest. Alex had been so busy looking after his own emotional defenses that he'd never thought of coming to anyone else's aid, but this little girl needed his help. "It isn't your fault. She didn't mean that."

"Yes, she did," Mary answered, her lip trembling.

"No, mothers say beastly things if their children die. Mine did too, because my brother died. Now, we must go to the service," he said.

"I don't want to go," she said defiantly, prepared to do battle, even with him if necessary.

To her surprise, he smiled—the first time he'd smiled at her—and said, "I don't either."

Then he did an extraordinary thing she was never to forget. He held his hand out to her and said, "Will you please show me the cliffs?"

Nobody noticed the two of them set off across the grounds—the lanky, lost boy who'd come so far to bury his cousin and some dreams, and the little redheaded girl in her sloppily made mourning dress.

7

The first trip to London to search for Mary's mother was a disaster even before it began. Portia, still crushed by her elder daughter's death two months earlier, insisted on believing in the face of all evidence to the contrary that George was going to leave the child there, no matter whom he found or didn't find. "A nice respectable orphan asylum, perhaps," she said to her mother-in-law over morning tea the day George, Mary, and Nellanor were to depart.

Nellanor, standing at the dining-room sideboard in her stiff traveling clothes and balancing a plate of toast and marmalade, answered for Evelyn. "There is no such thing as a *nice* orphan asylum, Portia."

"I'm sure there must be. Or perhaps put her into service somewhere."

"She's a bit young for heavy work, Portia." This time it was Evelyn who spoke. As much as she sympathized with Portia's desire to get the child permanently out of sight and out of mind, she couldn't convince herself it would happen. George was being insanely determined about the whole matter.

"Well, then, he could just place her with some family, couldn't he?" Portia went on, becoming shrill. "Pay somebody a few pounds a year for her clothes and food. Somebody would be glad for the money, I'm sure."

Nellanor just shook her head and took another bite of toast, creating a cascade of crumbs down the front of her bodice. Brushing them off casually, she left the other women and went to the front entry. George was there, waiting. "I just sent Agnes up for you, Aunt Nell. Where were you?"

"Having another bite to eat. Are we ready?"

She glanced around and saw Mary sitting on a valise just

64

beyond the door. Her face in profile was drawn down into a shockingly sad expression. Instead of the vivacious seven-year-old Nellanor had grown so fond of, she looked like a miniature old woman who had seen the worst of life. "Ought you to be bringing her along, George?" Nellanor asked.

"Of course! She's the only one who might recognize the neighborhood where she lived. I can't possibly search all of London on my own and hope to find her mother. Her help is essential."

"And if she doesn't want to help?" Nellanor asked wryly.

George was genuinely perplexed. "What on earth can you mean? Why wouldn't she want to find her own mother?"

"Oh, George, George," Nellanor said.

Mary could smell London before she saw it. She recoiled from the mixed scent of people, sewage, coal smoke, and breweries. It had once been so familiar she wasn't even aware of it; now it sickened her. She wanted to go back to the rosemary-scented house where the smells were of earth and grass and salty fogs. As the carriage rolled on, relentless mile by mile, she became aware of the sound of the city too. People again, so many people. And machines. Castlemere always had the underlying repetitive sound of waves breaking on the beach and the trills of birds.

If only this could be over with soon so she could go back home, her real home now, Castlemere.

George had questioned her about her previous home and she had tried to give him answers that were satisfactory. She'd been torn by the process. She had come to love the soft-spoken man who had taken her in and seemed to like her so much, and because of that, she genuinely wanted to give him the information he wanted. It was the only way she had to express her affection and gratitude. At the same time, she didn't want to help him with this attempt to return her to the life she'd had before. In the end, her love for him had won out over her own best interests, but even when she tried to cooperate, she hadn't been a source of many useful facts.

She lived near a church when she and her mother lived in London, she told him. Oh, yes. A big church. They went there for Sunday services and she could hear the bells all day. The name? No, she didn't know the name. They just went to "church." They never called it anything else.

Did they live near the river? No, far away. How far? A

long, long way. They walked there once and it took a long time. Half an hour? Two hours? She didn't know.

Were there any public buildings near? Or businesses? Yes, there was a brick building where men carrying important-looking papers went in and out. What sort of business was it? She didn't know.

What about parks? Were there parks near? Yes, a small park with grass and many trees she replied. As far as she knew, it had no name.

In spite of the lack of concrete evidence, George had studied the London maps and picked ten or twelve areas he thought might be likely, and was determined to drive her through all of them. Certainly she would recognize *something*.

They arrived late in the day, and instead of beginning their search immediately, they went directly to the Beechams' old London house on Mincing Lane. "Who lives here?" Mary asked Nellanor.

"Mostly nobody. But all of us stay here when we have to come to London on business or shopping or visiting friends. Now, get out of those clothes and put on your nightdress. I'll have a tray of dinner sent up and we'll eat here."

"What about Mr. Beecham?"

"He has some business people to see tonight."

"If nobody lives here, who will fix our dinner? Do you know how to cook things, Aunt Nellanor?"

"There's a staff here. A housekeeper and odd-job man. Turn around, let me do those buttons for you. We'll sneak away from George and get you some new frocks before we go back."

Mary sighed happily. Aunt Nellanor, at least, believed she would go back to Castlemere, and Mary trusted her to make it happen. "Does your grandson live here in this house?" she asked, relaxing for the first time that day.

"Alex? No, he goes to school. You know that. You've asked me a dozen times."

"When is he going to visit you again?"

"I'm getting a bit weary of that question too, child. I told you before, I don't know. He doesn't get to leave school until the Christmas holidays and he may choose to spend them with someone else. Now, you've had all the answers you'll get from me today. Take those braids out and brush your hair while I see what's keeping our food."

They began their quest in the morning. Riding back and

forth through the crowded streets, Mary began to get the conflicting impression that everything was familiar and that none of it was. A house here, a church there, a market stall in another spot—all looked as if she might have seen them before, but nothing around them ever seemed entirely right. Surely that was the man who sold brooms on the corner, but it wasn't a corner she recognized, and the man, when approached by George, claimed to have never laid eyes on Mary before, even when George gave him a pound note to jog his memory. And wasn't that the church she and her mother had gone to? No, the door was in a different place. Only once was she sure of a sight. She'd seen that market cross before, but it had been when she and her mother walked a very long way to pick up some sewing.

"Where was the house you visited? Nearby?" George asked.

No, she only remembered because she'd gotten a stitch in her side and they'd sat down here until she felt better.

"Never mind, Mary," George would say at the end of every day. "You mustn't worry that we won't find her. London is a big place and we've only started to look."

And every night she'd cry herself to sleep.

Finally, after a dreadful week, Nellanor put her substantial foot down. "You're wearing the child to a nub and I feel like a chewed string, George. Enough!"

"Just another day or two, Aunt Nell. We're sure to have success soon."

"No! I'm an old lady and you've rattled my bones around enough stinking streets and alleys. You may keep looking if you want, but I'm taking Mary shopping tomorrow. I'll buy her some pretty things, maybe go see the Tower. No, better yet, take us to the warehouse tomorrow. That would be most entertaining."

"The warehouse? A little girl wouldn't like that."

"You liked it when you were little, didn't you? And so did I. I've never forgotten the first time, and that was sixty years ago. Mary's a very curious child, George. She'd enjoy it."

The next morning, wearing old clothes ("It's very dusty," Nellanor warned) and carrying thick handkerchiefs ("You might need to breathe through it. The smell can be very strong"), they went to Beecham's Fine Spices' main warehouse. The odor, powerful and pungent, coiled out through the surrounding streets and drew them in toward the vast

brick-and-timber building. The cobbled yard inside the
wooden front gates was a bedlam of activity. Carts and
horses moved among barrels and crates with mysterious
markings. Burly men staggered under the weight of small
casks and tossed large ones as if they were no more substantial than pillows.

Mary's senses were overwhelmed. For once, she, who was
never short of questions, didn't know what to say. George
looked down, noted her astonished gaze, and smiled. "These
spices come from all over the world, and many of the most
valuable of them come from the hundreds of islands near
Singapore," he began, as his father had once introduced
him to the warehouse. "They are brought here and stored
until they go out to the shops where they are processed to
sell."

Mary looked up at him in speechless wonder and sneezed
violently.

George laughed. "It does that to you, doesn't it just! You
know, I had a friend when I was a boy, who worked here
with me one summer, and he liked what he learned so much
that he became an explorer and geographer. His name is
Winston Foxworth-Wilding and he's very famous for writing
books about the places he goes."

"What are those things?" Mary asked, pointing to where
a man had accidentally dropped a cask, causing a gush of
green liquid full of lumps to spurt out the side.

"Come and see," George said. He approached the worker,
who had turned the cask to stop the flow, and gestured for
him to give it a twist so another spurt came out. George
cupped his hands, catching some of the liquid and what
Mary thought were tiny dark green peas. "Taste," he told
her.

Mary gingerly took one and popped it in her mouth, then
made a face. "Sour! And salty!" she exclaimed, her lips still
pursed.

"They're capers," Nellanor said, helping herself to a
handful.

"What's that?" Mary asked.

George nodded to the workman to get back to his job.
Wiping his hands on his handkerchief, he said, "They're the
flower buds of a bush that grows in southern Europe. It's a
weed, really. Grows in gutters and cracks in old walls. The
Colosseum is covered with it. Do you know about the
Colosseum?"

Mary shook her head.

"Then I'll get some maps out when we get home and show you where it is . . ."

When we get home, Mary echoed happily in her mind.

". . . Of course, these are cultivated—that is, grown on special farms, not just picked wherever they happen to grow," George was going on. "The flowers open in the sunlight, so the buds have to be picked very early in the morning. The workers put the flower buds into wooden barrels of salted vinegar, and when the barrel is full, they're sorted through copper sieves for size. It's the copper that makes them such a rich, dark green color. In fact, some of the growers just leave a few copper scraps in the bottom of the collection barrels to make sure they all get dark green. The smallest and most perfect are the most valuable."

"Do they taste better if they're greener?" Mary asked.

Nellanor gave George a quick, victorious look, as if to say: I told you so.

"That *is* a good question," George said. "But no, the color doesn't make any difference in the taste, but customers seem to think it does, so we buy the darkest ones we can. And if we find very good ones that aren't dark enough, we sometimes dye them."

"I think we ought to have lamb with caper sauce very soon, so Mary can see how they taste cooked," Nellanor said. "I'll ask the housekeeper to arrange it for supper tonight."

Pleased at the suggestion, George snagged a passing messenger and jotted a note for him to take to the London house.

"Ah, here's Clyde!" he said when the messenger had gone.

The warehouse manager was approaching with a plump hand outstretched in greeting. He was only a year or two older than George, but had risen to his present position after many years with the company. He'd started as a husky lad of nine, carrying and fetching, and had shown such intelligence and loyalty that George's father had recently put him in charge. Now that his manual labor had decreased, and his hearty appetite hadn't, he'd grown quite roly-poly. "Didn't know you was coming 'long here today, sir."

"You remember my aunt, don't you, Clyde?"

"Yes, sir. Good to see you again, Miz Beecham, ma'am."

"Nice to be here, Mr. Gordon," Nellanor replied politely and with sincere warmth. She liked Clyde Gordon and it was partly her advice that had caused William to put his faith in the young man.

"And this is Mary Grey. She's—" George suddenly stopped, stymied by how to explain who Mary was. Instead he said, "She's wanting to see the place."

"Right exciting place for the young'uns, ain't it? Well, you come right along, young lady, and we'll show you around."

Mary remembered few of the actual facts she'd been exposed to that day, though in years to come she learned a great deal about spices. That day, only isolated bits of information took her fancy: the tiny mild capsicums from Hungary ("People call them peppers, but in the trade we're exact, Miss Mary," Clyde said) were to be ground into paprika, the best quality called rose paprika, the second best called king's paprika, but the similar-looking capsicums from Mexico called devil peppers were so hot they made her nose run and her eyes water just to be near them. They would be made into hot sauce. "Don't touch them, miss," Clyde Gordon said. "You get just a speck of the dust on your fingers and touch your eyes and you'll think you've gone blind from the burning."

Mustard seeds were much in demand, not for eating, but for grinding up and making a footbath, so Beecham's sold them in small containers as a spice and ground up and sold in big canisters for medicinal purposes.

Mary liked the nutmeg smell better than anything else in the warehouse, and George gave her a handful of nutmegs— smooth, hard nuts with a whitish coating. "Anytime you want to enjoy the scent, you can scrape the seed a bit against a rock," George said, demonstrating against a brick wall, then pocketing a handful himself. Mary liked the fresh, slightly soapy smell.

But her very favorite part of the day was when George gave her a little tin of candied ginger. "This is the root, or rather the rhizome, which is a kind of root, of a plant that has been known to man almost forever. Here, take a bite. Even before William the Conqueror came to England, it was brought here from Asia," George explained. Again, it was much as his father had first explained it to him, and he passed the information to Mary as if it were a treasured family secret. "The early Greeks and Romans used it, and it's been common in Chinese life for as long as anyone can remember."

"Is there any growing at Castlemere?" Mary asked, chewing happily on the sweet. It had a pungent bite to it, like mint.

"No, it won't grow this far north. It lives in the tropical parts of the world, where it can get brilliant hot sunshine and huge amounts of rain. The best comes from Jamaica. It is used fresh, just as it comes out of the ground—after the skin is scraped off—or dried and ground up or cooked down in syrup to be candied. It's also used in medicines. In the barrels along that wall are the raw product."

Mary and Nellanor followed him, and he took out a dried, branched rhizome. "It looks like a witch's hand!" Mary exclaimed.

George laughed. "That's why they're called 'hands' or sometimes 'races.' "

The day went all too quickly. They paused in their explorations of the warehouse for luncheon with Clyde Gordon, but Mary's stomach, stimulated by the rich odors of the spices, was complaining by midafternoon. "I'm hungry, Aunt Nellanor," she whispered.

"So am I. There's a tearoom I like to visit. Cavett's. Let's see if we can get George to take us there."

"Cavett's?" Mary said too softly for Nellanor to hear. In spite of the warmth of the day, she felt a chill. She'd heard that before. Her mother had mentioned it. "No, I don't want to leave here. I'll eat some more of my candied ginger, Aunt Nellanor."

"Nonsense. You'll make yourself sick as a dog filling up on sweets all day. George . . ."

That was how, when they had finally stopped looking, they found Mary's London home. On the way to Cavett's Tearoom they passed the house where she and her mother had lived in the small rooms at the back and up one flight. Mary instinctively clutched at Nellanor's arm. "What is it, child? Your hand is as cold as ice."

"Mary, what *is* wrong?" George asked, alarmed at her sudden paleness. "Stop the carriage, Hector. Mary . . . ?"

She blinked back the tears and fought for control of her voice. She struggled for a convincing lie to account for her behavior, but no story presented itself. Besides, she couldn't lie, not about this. They'd been good to her; she couldn't betray the trust, no matter what it might cost her.

"That's . . . that's my old house," she said, nearly choking on the words.

She pointed to the building they'd passed, afraid to look. Was her mother in the window, watching? She didn't want to know. She clung to Nellanor's arm, unaware that her small fingers were biting into the older woman's flesh. Nellanor acted like she didn't feel it.

George wanted them all to go to the door, but Nellanor shook her head. "We'll wait here, George. You go ask after Mary's mother." She disengaged Mary's fingers and put her arm around the child, who was staring straight ahead and shivering.

George, his own feelings in turmoil, walked back to the house. It was a tall, narrow home with a miniature front yard planted in roses. A tiny paperboard sign in the lower left corner of the window said, "Rooms to Let" in small, discreet printed lettering.

George knocked. Waited. Knocked again. The door opened. A woman with an obese frame and a dainty manner smiled sweetly. "May I help you, sir?"

"Yes, I'm trying to locate a Mrs. Grey. Gwenith Grey. Is she here?"

The woman didn't answer for a moment, merely studied him curiously. "No, I'm very sorry, she's not."

"Then could you tell me when she might return?"

"That I could not, sir. She's moved house."

George glanced back at the carriage. Nellanor and Mary were sitting quite still, not speaking. Mary half-turned. The woman at the door followed his gaze. "Is that . . . could that be her little Mary? Why, you must be Mrs. Grey's cousin, then."

"Her cousin?"

"Why, yes. When Mary came down with that awful cough, she said she was going to take the child to live with some cousins in the country. She could have used some nursing herself, even though she claimed she was feeling fine. I heard her with her own coughing at night. But I didn't think it was wise of her to travel with the dear little mite sickly, but she said the country air would do her good. Looks like it has."

"Did she say who these cousins were, or where in the country she was going?" George asked.

The woman drew back suspiciously. "Just who are *you*, if you don't mind my asking, sir?"

"Please, don't be alarmed, Mrs. . . . ?"

"Norton. Miss Mabel Norton."

"Miss Norton, my name is George Beecham, of Beecham's Fine Spices. You may have heard of—"

"I certainly have. But what are you doing with Mary? That *is* Mary Grey in the carriage?"

"Yes, it is, and I'm not sure precisely what I'm doing with her. That is, her mother, who knew my family, left the child with us several months ago. Mary was very ill. Her mother left no message, no word of where she'd gone. That's why I'm trying to locate her."

"Mrs. Grey *abandoned* her child? Forgive me, but I find that difficult to believe."

"So do I, Miss Norton. Can you tell me where you think she might have gone?"

Mabel Norton thought hard. "I just haven't any idea. She was a very quiet young woman. Very self-contained. Never said anything about her people. That's why it particularly stayed in my mind about her cousins. It was the only time she ever mentioned having family. She said they lived on the coast. Near Brighton, I got the idea. She never mentioned old friends and didn't seem to have any in London. She wasn't close to anyone here, either. Not exactly stand-offish, just private and very shy."

George took one of his cards out of a gold case and started writing on the back. "Miss Norton, I'd be very grateful if you'd sift through your memory for anything that might help me find her. This is my business address; this is my London home; the last is my country address. You may reach me through any of the three if you think of anything."

She took the card. "What about the little girl? What's to happen to her?"

"Don't worry. I'll see that she's taken care of very well. My aunt—that's the older lady in the carriage—is very fond of her, as am I."

Miss Norton nodded, satisfied. George returned to the carriage and sat down heavily. "Well?" Nellanor asked. Mary continued to stare at the back of Hector's head.

"She's gone. Moved out when she brought Mary to us."

Mary suddenly made a horrible noise, a rasping intake of breath, as if she hadn't breathed for a long time. For a second George thought she'd taken another bite of the candied ginger and was choking on it, until she flung herself, sobbing, onto Nellanor's lap.

"Mary, Mary, don't worry, we'll find her," George said, patting her back gently. "I promise you, I'll find your mother for you."

Nellanor slapped his hand away. "George, you *are* a fool!" she said. "Take us back to Castlemere. Now!"

8

George returned to London two weeks later to talk to Mabel Norton in the hope that she had remembered something—anything—that would help him in his search for Gwenith. But all she had recalled was that Gwenith had once talked about visiting her grandmother in one of those Welsh towns that start with "Ll" and are pronounced like someone clearing his throat. This triggered a faint memory in George's mind as well. He remembered her mentioning such a town and thought at the time how oddly pretty the name sounded when she said it. Once again he felt the sick surge of guilt at how very little he did know about this woman who had borne his child. If he hadn't been such a lusty, self-absorbed lout, he might at least remember where she was from—if, in fact, he'd ever bothered to ask her, which he doubted. Their conversations were entirely concerned with his opinions and his feelings. He was coming to hate that overgrown boy he had been only a few years ago.

But upon consulting with his maps, he realized there were at least a dozen such towns. Even if he knew the right one, the grandmother might not still be living, and she might be on the maternal side of the family and have an unfamiliar family name. Still, he put Tutin to work making inquiries.

While he had the maps out, he summoned Agnes to find Mary and send her to the library so he could show her where Italy was, as he'd promised when they were visiting the London spice warehouse. She came to the library with Ginger in her arms a few minutes later. There was a piece of straw in her hair and a faint air of the stables about her. Normally George wouldn't have allowed a child into his sanctum, much less a cat, but it was so easy to indulge Mary.

The library held the maps accumulated by many generations of Beechams. Some of the oldest, the crackling parch-
ment maps with fiery-eyed sea serpents showing where the
earth ended, had been given to museums now, but many
remained. Philippe Beecham, the builder of Castlemere and
first master of the library, had built in huge, shallow drawers where the maps could be stored flat. George consulted
the small tags labeling the drawers and took out a recent
map of Europe. He put it on the large central map table. He
was pleased at the degree of Mary's interest, which seemed
genuine. "But you said Italy was hot," she said, leaning
over the map. "It sticks out into the water. Why isn't it cool
and nice from the sea breeze like it is here? Aunt Nellanor
says the sea breeze is what makes it so pleasant here."

That led to a discussion of climate and the role that
latitude played in temperature. "Does Alex live near Italy,
then?" she asked. "Aunt Nellanor said it was very, very hot
where he comes from."

"No, Alex comes from the other side of the world." He
put away the map he'd been showing her and dusted off the
big globe that had stood, neglected and forgotten for years,
in a window embrasure. He could remember how his father
had pointed out places on this globe to him and how he'd
liked spinning it. He gave it a half-turn. It squeaked. He'd
have to get it fixed now that there was someone interested
in using it.

"Here is China and here is India," he told her. "Between
China and India are a lot of small countries: Burma, Siam,
Tibet. And here, coming down like a long, fat tail from
Siam, is the Malay Peninsula. At the very point of it is an
island. That's Singapore, where Alex lives. The large islands
to the east and west of there are Sumatra and Borneo. You
see, the equator goes right through them and just beneath
Singapore. The long, thin island to the south is Java. Now,
somewhat to the east of this area is a group of islands called
the Moluccas, better known as the Spice Islands. That's where
it all started, though there are hundreds, possibly thousands
of islands in this part of the ocean where spices grow. They're
all very hot because of their location, and that's why the
spices that grow there won't grow here. They come from trees
and plants that must have a hot climate all the time."

"All the time? Even in the winter?"

"Even in the winter. In fact, I don't think they have
anything that Englishmen would recognize as winter."

"Have you been to this hot place?" Mary asked. She'd taken a chair close to the globe and was sitting on the edge, absently stroking Ginger. She kept inching forward and Ginger nearly rolled off her knees several times as she talked and wiggled.

"Yes, when I was a very little boy my father took me there. I was even younger than you are, and I don't remember very much about it."

"Did you like it? Did you get a heat rash? I got a heat rash when I was littler, in the summertime."

"I think I probably did. Mostly what I remember is the long sea voyage. It took most of a year to get there and stay awhile and come back. I had my birthday *and* Christmas on the ship."

"I'd like to have my birthday on a ship! I've never been on a ship, only in the little boat with Aunt Nellanor along the beach. Are you going to take another trip there?" Mary asked.

George looked down at her and felt his heart contract with affection for this fey child. Her wild red hair framed a face that was alight with questions. How strange it was that Gwenith's child should have such eager curiosity. Gwenith's primary trait (and her appeal, he realized now) had been a quiet passivity. She had been—and still was, as far as he knew—a docile, quiet young woman, not given to questioning very much of anything. She had been willing to accept tranquilly anything George said, anything George wanted, anything George believed. That was why he had thought he loved her for one luscious spring season. There was nothing like unquestioning adoration to touch the heart of a self-centered young man. But now, not terribly much older but considerably wiser, he found himself more deeply touched, in a wholly different way, by the quick mind of a bright child who never seemed to run out of questions.

"Maybe I'll take another trip there someday," he said. "The whole family could go."

"Or maybe just me and you and Aunt Nellanor . . . and Hester," she added as an afterthought. "We could all have birthday parties on the ship, couldn't we? How do you bake a cake on a boat? Cook won't even let me open the oven door when she makes a cake, because it would shake it and make it fall. But on a boat . . . ?"

George laughed. "I don't know how to make one on dry land! Ask Aunt Nellanor, she knows everything."

Mary leaned forward again, dumping Ginger on the floor, and said very seriously, "She does! She really does! Do you know, she can tell the names of all the birds we see, and she knows all about fishes and can tell what it's going to be like tomorrow by looking at the clouds!"

"Mary, that cat is doing something suspicious in the fireplace—"

"Ginger, *no*!" she said, dashing to gather up the cat, sooty-pawed and smug. She hurried to the door, but turned and asked, "How do you have Christmas someplace that's always hot?"

"You'll have to ask Alex that, next time he comes to visit."

She grinned. "I will. I'll ask him."

But Alex didn't come back, not that year. Events at Castlemere conspired against a visit.

On October 3, William Beecham woke up complaining of a pain in the stomach. Midmorning, he leaned over the paddock rail while examining a new colt and vomited blood. He took to his bed and the pain in his stomach grew rapidly worse. The doctor diagnosed a tumor, and although he tried different medicines, William grew steadily and rapidly worse. By the end of the month he was in constant agony and couldn't keep any food down. Once robust, he became a pale, skeletal creature almost overnight. On November 10 he sighed, suffered some brief and quite horrible spasms, and died.

Evelyn, who'd been sitting by the side of the vast carved bed for five weeks, collapsed. She was unconscious for fully twenty minutes, and when she woke, she was lethargic and confused and kept asking for someone named "Doddie."

She never recovered.

As William was laid to rest in the Beecham section of the church graveyard, Evelyn stared blankly at the horizon and hummed to herself. "I don't think she knows where we are or what's happening," Portia whispered to George.

"It's just as well."

By the end of the week it was apparent that this wasn't simply shock over her husband's death, but the symptom of something having gone badly awry in her mind. She suffered laughing and crying spells; when thwarted, she threw things; and she took to wandering about the house in the night. Once the housemaid Agnes found her, clad only in her nightdress, sitting outside in the rain. She was soaked to the skin and developed a bad cold. From then on Agnes slept in the big bedroom with Evelyn, with the door locked. She seemed to have lost track of who the family members were.

She kept calling Nellanor "Doddie," from which they surmised the mystery person must have been a grandmother or nanny or some other older woman she was remembering from her childhood. She believed George to be the family solicitor and persisted in asking him confused questions about the arrangements for her marriage settlement. She seemed to have no idea whatsoever who Portia was and continually asked her to identify herself. This reduced Portia to tears nearly every time it happened, and she would rail at George as if it were somehow his fault.

The oddest sign of Evelyn's affliction, however, was her interest in Mary and Hester. They had become, in her crippled mind, her little sisters, though she'd never had siblings. Strangely enough, she allowed them their own names and insisted that they call her "Evie." She was happiest when they were in her room with her playing with dolls.

This was a hideous trial for Mary. She'd disliked Evelyn since her first day at Castlemere, and rather than being comforted by her apparently harmless childishness, Mary was terrified by the anomaly of a grown woman acting like a child. Evelyn was old—by Mary's standards—and quite alarmingly fat, and played too roughly. She seemed to remember, in some dimly lighted recess of her mind, that she didn't like Mary, though the reason has escaped with all her other recent memories. Consequently, if unsupervised, she would pinch and slap the child whenever the urge took her. Mary would have been reluctant enough to tattle on another child; she couldn't bring herself to tattle on this bizarre adult.

Then, the week before Christmas, she was spared. Agnes interrupted the family at breakfast to announce tearfully that she couldn't waken the mistress.

Evelyn had slipped away silently during the night, and once again the family assembled in the churchyard. It was the third time in six months that a Beecham had come to a final rest here. It was a gray, rainy day, and as Mary stood half-hidden behind Aunt Nellanor under a big black umbrella, she kept studying George's face. He looked awful, and Mary pondered it. How could anyone really care that the crazy, fat old woman had died? She had been mean before she got sick, and meaner afterward. Mary was enormously relieved that she was gone, though she knew better than to let anyone suspect she felt that way. Still, this fine, kind man who had taken her in, who had taught her about maps and given her the little leather-bound book to write in, was obviously saddened by her departure.

Suddenly it came to her: he was an orphan now, just like she was. No wonder he was sad! She sidled away from Nellanor.

George was staring into the wet black hole in the ground, thinking how many more dead Beechams than live ones currently surrounded him, when he felt the little rough warm hand slip into his. He gave it a squeeze and was surprised at how much comfort there was in that small, openhearted gesture. That was when he decided that the adoption of this child must be the next order of business. He would continue to search for Gwenith, he had to. But Mary had to be recognized as his child.

Christmas that year was a bleak, black-clad holiday. There were still delicious meals, but no generous presents. There had been too many sorrows to be put aside so soon; too many deaths, too many empty chairs at the table. There was no tree, no holly wreaths hung on mantels and doors, no waxy mistletoe, no excited talk of St. Nicholas. Mary's previous Christmases had been penniless affairs celebrated with handmade gifts and a hand-knitted stocking where a tuppence and an orange appeared on Christmas morning. Once there had even been a small doll with a china face. Because of her background, she didn't mind that the holiday was subdued. She had no idea of how it was usually celebrated in a household like this.

But she was terribly disappointed for another reason. She'd expected that Alex would share it with them. "When is he coming?" she asked Nellanor on Christmas Eve morning. She'd bounded, bright-eyed, into the old woman's bedroom as soon as she heard her stirring.

"My Lord above, child. Where do you get the energy? Sit down. You make my old head spin. When is who coming?"

"Cousin Alex. Your grandson. When is Alex coming? You said he got a vacation from his school at Christmastime. That's today. Where is he? Will he come in a carriage or will we go meet him someplace like you did when he came on the boat from Singapore?"

"Oh, dear. I had no idea you thought he was coming,

child. He's gone home with a boy from his school instead of coming here."

All the exuberance suddenly drained from Mary and she seemed to wilt. "But why would he do that?" she asked.

"I wrote and told him about William dying, and then Evelyn became so strange, and I thought he'd enjoy himself more someplace else without all the death and sickness shadowing the holiday. He seemed to welcome the opportunity to go elsewhere."

"He's not going to come to Castlemere *at all*?"

"Not this Christmas. I'm sorry you misunderstood."

"But he *has* to come! I made him a present and everything."

"You did?"

"Yes, I knitted him a new belt. It's red."

Nellanor suppressed a smile. Agnes had been teaching Mary to knit, and for the last few days Nellanor had seen Mary several times bent over a long, mangled red strip of knots. *That* was to be Alex's gift? There was no boy on earth who could have accepted such a thing with good grace.

"You can send it to him, Mary. We'll wrap it up in pretty paper."

Mary stood up and tossed her head. "No. I'll keep it for myself. I don't want to give it to him!"

The first week of 1860, George Beecham gathered a leather satchel of papers together and went to London to see his lawyer. He returned two days later, shaken but pleased with what he'd done. He found Portia in the master suite, packing up William and Evelyn's belongings in preparation for moving herself and George in. Dismissing the servants, she sat down on the edge of the ornately carved bed. "I've arranged to adopt Mary," George said.

"I see." She had a tight smile.

"You see? Is that all you have to say about it?" George had expected a battle royal and had all his ammunition ready.

"What else could I say? This is something you are set on doing, regardless of my opinion. Why should I bother to express it?"

"Portia, I'd like to feel that you understand why it's necessary. If I'd been a widower when we married, you wouldn't have harbored this sort of resentment of a child of mine, would you?"

"But that's not so, is it?"

He wasn't certain what she meant by that: that he wasn't a widower, or that this wasn't his child. Surely she realized that Mary was his daughter. She couldn't have forgotten all of the conversation they had the night before Charlotte died. Or had she? His nerves were already strained to the point of snapping; he no longer wanted to thrash it all out.

Portia watched as he sat down on the flimsy chair Evelyn had used at her dressing table. She knew she had it within her power to make this easier for him; she suspected that she should do so. But she couldn't. It was her price. Privately she'd come to realize that this adoption was as relentlessly inevitable as the seasons. She didn't like it, but as the weeks had passed, she'd come to hate it slightly less. But George had to pay for her acquiescence.

She'd looked at it from a hundred different vantage points and had found a few that made it slightly easier to reconcile herself to Mary's presence in the family. One of them was the child herself. She wasn't nearly as rough and common as her background and violent-colored hair had first made her seem. In fact, her manners were really rather good. The way she ate was nearly prissy-proper, and she treated Portia with a respectable deference. She had the good sense, or natural inclination, to keep herself scarce, spending most of her time with Nellanor or outdoors. Also in her favor was the fact that she provided little Hester, who might have been quite bereft without her older sister, with companionship.

Most important, the child and Portia's token acceptance of her gave Portia a certain hold over George. Until now, their relationship had been heavily weighted in his favor. It was Portia who wanted his concern and his affection. And for reasons she'd never analyzed, she felt she had to earn his love. Now, however, it was George seeking her approbation. There had been a subtle shift in their relationship. While George's character had strengthened and gained determination, it was he who felt the guilt and responsibility for the child, and in spite of his words to the contrary, his attitude was faintly apologetic. Mary's presence, abhorrent as it was in some ways, had given George an extra chip in the marital game of power, but it had given Portia two.

She found it easier, also, to acquiesce now that Evelyn was gone. Evelyn had known more about the situation than Portia and had been forever trying to share her knowledge. Portia didn't want any illuminating revelations. Her ignorance and innocence were her best weapons in the silent battle she was waging with George. With her mother-in-law hovering, it had been necessary to keep up a constant air of disapproval of Mary; it had been wearing to seem perpetually irritated when, in fact, she had been largely apathetic to the child herself.

"Portia, please say you understand," George was saying.

Portia glanced around the room. It was truly grand, enormous, luxurious. The windows overlooked the best view Castlemere had to offer; the furniture and *objets d'art* were the most elegant of the Beecham holdings; the fabrics were the highest quality that money could buy. It was a room deserving of the appellation "master suite." And George was now the master of Castlemere and Beecham's Fine Spices. More important, Portia was the mistress. In this huge bed with the ornate carvings and heavy velvet swags, she would certainly conceive the son she hadn't yet provided. That would further consolidate her position in the house and in his heart. Then he'd forget about this little girl.

"I'm trying to understand, George, really I am," she said, touching the corner of her eye with a lace-edged handkerchief.

"That's the way, Portia. I know this isn't something you had any way to be prepared for, but I do appreciate your being such a fine sport about it," George said, delighted that he was to be spared the terrible scene he'd feared she might stage. "I suppose I'd better tell Mary now."

Portia was gazing down at the floor. She looked so wistful and hurt that he felt a flash of mixed remorse and fondness.

Actually, she was considering whether she should replace the carpet.

George invited Mary and Nellanor to take a walk with him that evening. The sun had set and it had grown quite cold, but George needed to be outside.

"In weather like this?" Nellanor snorted. "I'd catch my death."

"I'll go!" Mary exclaimed, already searching for the cable-knit hat Agnes had made for her from the red yarn Mary had given up attempting to knit with.

George glared at Nellanor. He'd wanted his aunt along to have this conversation. She understood the child so much more clearly than he did. She often served as translator for them. Mary was ready in a few minutes and tugging on his coat sleeve. "I can see a fire from my window. Out near the cliffs. May we go see? What do you think is burning? There's no house there. Maybe a tree?''

"Probably just a bonfire to get rid of some trash. Mrs. Renault has one every year," Nellanor answered. "I've often wondered where she gets all the things to burn. I suppose the neighbors must help her collect it because they enjoy the fire so much. It does make a nice little holiday at a dreary time of year."

George looked at his aunt with surprise. "This happens every year? I've never known."

"That's because you're always looking the other way. Toward London," Nellanor said. "I look out to sea."

George pondered this as he and Mary walked across the frosty ground toward the orange glow of Mrs. Renault's bonfire. Mary was bounding along in front of him, prattling on about the fire, speculating on its contents, scheduling, ownership, dangers, benefits, and meaning. It seemed like she never ran out of comments and questions. Funny, he thought, her talk was saved from being as boring as most children's by the fact that it was almost never about herself. That was, when he considered it, very odd indeed.

Finally he interrupted her. "Mary, there's something I must speak to you about. In a few months you are going to become our daughter. You'll be Mary Beecham. You would like that, wouldn't you?"

She stopped so suddenly that he nearly fell over her. She seemed to freeze. It was an effort to make her mouth work, she was so afraid she might say the wrong thing and jeopardize this offer. "Oh, yes. I would like that," she finally managed to whisper. Her breath made a cloud on the air.

He patted her thin shoulder awkwardly and started to walk on toward the bonfire. She hurried to catch up. "I spoke to two lawyers," he said. "They agreed that in a case like this, it was best to wait a full year and let your mother have that opportunity to come back. After that length of time, and with proof of diligent search, they consider that I am justified in thinking she won't, and we may legally make you our daughter. Now, in some cases—"

He was talking just to fill the void with a sound, afraid of Mary's silence in the crackling cold. This was when he could have used Nellanor. She'd have said something that was neither inane nor over the child's head. It had grown quite dark now, the sliver of moon and the orange glow of the bonfire the only beacons.

For her part, Mary was so full of astonished questions that she didn't know where to begin. Her greatest hope had been that she would be allowed to stay here at Castlemere for a long, long time. She hadn't even dared consider that she might remain permanently. That George Beecham would adopt her (Did she actually understand the word correctly? She would have to ask Nellanor. Pray God she had it right. Suppose it meant something else?) was beyond even her fertile imagination.

They'd reached the fire. Several families of villagers had congregated to watch it burn and the children were standing as near as they safely dared, holding their hands out to the warmth. Among the adults, there was laughter and drinking and even a bit of singing, all of which became muted when George and Mary appeared within the circle of light. George sensed that they were intruders, dampeners of enjoyment. He was the lord of the manor; he had a role to play and so did they, and he was an uninvited guest. He greeted a few of the men, nodded to the women, and smiled at the children, then took Mary's hand and firmly led her away.

She would normally have wanted to stay to observe something so strange and interesting as a midwinter bonfire, but tonight her mind was fully occupied with the news he'd imparted. They were nearly back to the big house when George started speaking again. "You must not think this means I won't still try to find your mother for you, Mary. This is merely a legal move to ensure your position."

She wasn't sure she understood, but she didn't like it. "My mother's not ever coming back," she said firmly.

"She might, Mary."

"*No!*" She stopped walking.

He turned and looked at her. The moonlight made her look like a small, defiant ghost. Her red hair looked black. "Mary, you can't know that."

"I do. My mother doesn't love me anymore and she won't ever come back."

Her words hung, brittle and sharp-edged, on the cold night air. "Oh, Mary. You can't believe that," George said, his heart aching with her pain. "Come inside. I have a fire in the library and there are things we must talk about."

She obeyed reluctantly, wishing she hadn't said anything. She'd lost her mother's love; she didn't dare risk losing his.

Once inside, he stirred up the hearthfire and put on another log. Prodding it into life, he realized he'd been a fool. Just as Aunt Nellanor said. She understood; why had it taken him so long? "Take off your hat and coat, Mary," he said, noticing that she was still standing at the doorway, as if ready to bolt. "Come sit here on my lap. I want to be sure you hear me."

She discarded her outdoor clothing and snuggled up to him. She liked to be close to him, but he'd never invited her to actually sit on his lap before. She liked the smell of his jacket—it was like tobacco and something spicy that reminded her of the pervasive rosemary scent of the house itself.

He smoothed back her hair, partly from affection, partly to keep the fuzzy strands from tickling his chin. "Mary, I knew your mother. I didn't tell you that before, but I did know her and she was a very nice person. The nicest kind of person there is."

She looked up at him, surprised at this revelation. It had never crossed her mind that her mother had been acquainted with anyone here. She'd assumed Castlemere had been a random selection of a place to leave her and she'd counted herself lucky that such a good choice had been made by accident. "How did you know Mama?"

George paused, debating how much truth to tell her. "She stayed here once," he said, hoping that Mary would assume he meant as a guest. He didn't want her to know her mother had been a servant in this house. "But that's beside the point. The thing I want you to know is this: your mother loved you very, very much. And that's the reason she left you here. I know that's hard to grasp, but I promise you it's the truth."

"No, I did something bad," Mary said softly into his shirt-front. "I don't know what, but it must have been very naughty."

"I know it must seem that way to you, but you must believe me, you're wrong, wrong, wrong. Your mother wanted to do the very best she could for you, *because she loved you*. But for some reason she knew she couldn't take the best care of you. I don't know what that reason was. Maybe we'll never know. But this I can assure you: she knew she'd be so lonesome for you that she'd almost die of it, but she decided to leave you here for your own good. She knew that I'd take care of you no matter what."

Mary stuck her finger in one of his buttonholes and twisted it. "Did my mama tell you this?" she said, frankly disbelieving.

"No, she didn't have to. That's just how parents are. I know she felt that way because I'm a father and I would. I would do anything at all for you and Hester, no matter how much it might hurt me. To be a good person, each of us must follow that precept."

She looked up at him finally, unconvinced, uncomprehending, but eager to listen. But the fire was warm, she was tired and comfortable, and it was getting difficult to concentrate.

"You see, we must do what is right. Do you know why?"

"Because God wants us to?" That was something she'd learned at church in London.

"That's one reason, but there's another reason. It has to do with conscience. Do you know what that means? Conscience?"

She shook her head.

"Your conscience is . . . it's what you think of yourself down so deep nobody else knows about it. Whether or not we are good, happy people depends on the condition of our conscience. If we do what's right—no matter how painful it is or how much we hate doing it—then we will like ourselves. If your conscience is troubled by things you've done or even by things you haven't done but think you should, then it doesn't matter a jot what you have or what other people think of you. You can't be happy if you don't like yourself. Mary, are you listening to me?"

She was resting her head against his chest, her finger caught in his buttonhole. She'd gotten quite limp.

He got her finger loose and stood up, scooping her along as if she were no more substantial than a rag doll. "Poor child, what am I doing? Pouring my own pitiful philosophy into you when all you need is your rest." Then he chuckled to himself. Why was it when he poured out his soul and philosophy to the women in his family, they tended to fall asleep?

He took her upstairs and handed her over, sleepy and mumbling, to Agnes. Then, taking a little-used staircase, he climbed up and up and onto a flat section of roof that faced south. The bonfire had died down to a mere crimson spot. He stood, heedless of the cold, for a long time, looking out to sea.

9

June 1864

Mary was looking over Hester's doll collection and wondering how on earth the younger girl could find the little china-and-cloth people so interesting. At twelve and nine, the difference in the girls' ages should have started to matter less and they might have grown quite close except that Portia discouraged it. George often wondered how in blazes he could have fathered two daughters who had so little in common.

Hester was thoroughly an indoor child. She didn't like bugs or rain, and even a good sharp wind took her breath away and left her pale and trembling. Her ideal day was a quiet one of sewing or playing house in front of a cozy fire with the curtains pulled against any hint of the elements. Timid and of vaguely frail health, though the doctors never found anything specifically wrong with her, Hester was content to be her mother's daughter.

Mary, devoted protégée of Nellanor, would probably have been content to live in the woods if she could have had Nellanor, George, Ginger, and her maps and books with her. She liked to be out on drizzly days, loved rainy ones, and went half-mad with joy when a violent storm swept along the coast. Some of her happiest moments were spent standing on the roofs of the big house watching the lightning split the skies around her and cringing happily at the deafening thunder. She was a tree-climber, a kite-flier, and was getting to be a good fisherman. The only outdoor activity in which she did not excel was horseback riding. "You've got a seat like a demented pigeon!" Nellanor told her. "All flapping and squawking and head-bobbing."

"I don't care. I don't like dumb old horses anyway!" Mary replied haughtily to these criticisms. Somewhere in the dimmest, most inaccessible reaches of her mind there was a tattered vision of a great horse rearing over her, pawing at the air, and making horrible noises. Once in a while she dreamed about it, and when she did, it always took place in London and she was very, very small. All in all, it was a memory she didn't want to know anything more about, and in time, the dreams ceased.

Today, however, horses weren't on her mind. Birds were. She had several nests she'd been watching and she was eager to go check to see if the fledglings were learning to fly yet. Unfortunately, Nellanor had gone on one of her rare trips away from Castlemere to visit some old friends, and the rules were that Mary couldn't venture out on her own. She was tempted to go anyway, knowing she could perfectly well stay out of danger, but the thought of Nellanor's wrath if such a breach were discovered kept her inside. She'd tried to get George to go with her that afternoon, but he was in the map room having a very serious discussion with Tutin and sent her along to play with Hester. Her indoor confinement and the subsequent boredom was why she had been reduced to the prebedtime business of helping her half-sister get her dolls ready for sleep.

"Mama says she's going to make me a fine wedding dress for this one," Hester was saying, holding up a doll that was clad now in a frilly nightdress that matched the one Hester had on.

"What would a doll get married for?" Mary asked. "It can't have babies or anything."

"I'll pretend she does."

"But—"

Mary's objection to this foolishness, which was going to include some references to nature that would have surprised the younger girl, was interrupted by Agnes coming in the door. "Your papa says you're to get yourself to bed early and in the morning we're to throw your things together for a short trip," she told Mary.

Mary leapt up. "Oh, good! I bet we're going to go get Aunt Nell back."

"I wouldn't know about that," Agnes said. "He said I'm to come along, since Miss Nellanor is gone."

"I don't have to go too, do I?" Hester asked.

Mary looked at her with wonder and despair. How could someone pass up the chance to do something to get out and about? She had the fleeting thought that if she put her mind to it, she might reform Hester someday.

The next day, Mary was so delighted with the mystery and adventure of it all that she didn't notice until the journey was well under way that George wasn't his usual cheerful self. Mary gazed out the window of the railway carriage as Agnes quietly snored in her corner, and wondered what was wrong. But she was half-afraid to ask. She sensed that something important was going on. She didn't like "important" things without sufficient warning.

"Where does this train go?" she asked, instead of inquiring outright: Where are we going?

"I'll show you," George said, taking a folded map from his pocket and spreading it on his knees. Odd, how many things we Beechams talk about over maps, he thought. "We're about here and we're going to a village right there."

Mary looked at the long Welsh word. "How do you say it?"

"I'm not sure."

They fell into silence again and George cleared his throat and noisily folded the map.

"Why are we going there, Papa?" Mary finally asked.

"To see a grave," he said, then went on with obvious discomfort, "Tutin brought me very sad news yesterday, Mary. He found out something I must tell you and you must be very brave about."

Mary's heart seemed to leap up into her throat. Something's happened to Aunt Nell! she thought frantically.

". . . it's about your mother, Mary. She's dead."

Good. Mary was so relieved that she almost spoke the word before she caught herself. Thank God it wasn't Aunt Nell!

"I'm very sorry, Mary. I know it's a sad thing for you and I wish there were a less-painful way of breaking the news. I'd always hoped we'd find her someday and she could see what a fine, pretty, smart girl you were growing up to be, but it wasn't God's plan, I suppose. According to Tutin, she died several years ago. Not long after she left you with me."

Good God, the child looked like a statue, staring at him as if stunned. This was a mistake. He should have waited until Nellanor got back and had her help him with this awful moment. But Aunt Nell always acted so odd about the subject of Gwenith. He'd thought he could handle it himself. He knew he should. It was his responsibility. "Mary, dear, won't you say something?"

"I—I don't know what I should say, Papa."

That was the understatement of her life. She knew she must not say what she was thinking; she couldn't tell him how happy she was to hear that her mother was dead and there was no longer any threat of having to go back to her. Not that her mother would ever have taken her back. People only give things away because they don't want them. She was so relieved she felt like weeping.

"We'll go visit her grave and then we'll talk with her people. Your people too. Tutin says you have a grandmother in this town, and probably cousins. You should know them."

"Do we have to, Papa?" She wanted no connection with these people. What if *they* wanted to take her away from Castlemere?

George had no idea of what her true concern was. "It will be sad, seeing her grave," he replied, "but good also. It's hard, sometimes, to really understand and accept life's endings without the physical proof. I know you're young, but someday you'll see what I mean."

"Yes, I guess so, Papa," Mary said, looking out the window again.

Mary never forgot, try as she might, her first sight of the Welsh mining village. Despite a recent shower, the very air of the grim little place was gritty with coal dust. The shops and houses were gray with it. The people in the streets were stooped and mean-looking to her frightened eyes. Several stopped and stared with open hostility at the rich man and his daughter who walked through their dismal town. They left Agnes, who wasn't one for walking under any circumstances and was suffering from a bunion today, at a bakery where she could drink tea and rest her feet.

Outside the village, on a hillside that overlooked another hill that looked as if it had been gnawned on by giants, there was a tiny, dreary cemetery. George found the headstone reading:

GWENITH GREY
1835–1860
Gone to Rest

He stood for a long moment, staring with a horror he

hadn't expected to feel at the thin slab, already covered with dingy lichen and beginning to settle unevenly. It might have been there for decades rather than a few short years. It was impossible to imagine that strawberry-and-cream flesh gone to dust, the round cheeks, lush lips, and sparkling eyes no more than a skeleton now. This visit to the grave wasn't the comfort he'd sought for himself and Mary; it was a desecration of her life. He put his hand on the cold stone and felt all the guilt and remorse he'd fought back for years settling on him like a physical weight. Poor, innocent Gwenith—cut down in her prime, moldering for eternity here.

Mary edged away, crushed by the look of pain on her father's face. Papa was truly unhappy, more unhappy than she'd ever seen him look. She must not—*must not*, let him know how she was feeling. If she'd been alone—but she'd have never come here of her own volition—she'd have kicked at that ugly gray headstone. She might have raged and cried out: I loved you, Mama, and I thought you loved me, but you gave me away! Gave me away like an unwanted puppy.

But of course she wouldn't say such a thing around George. He'd tried several times over the years to talk to her about her mother. He'd explained patiently that her mother had been a sweet, loving person who would never have parted with her except under the most dire circumstances. Even today, as the train pulled into the station, he'd reminded Mary that Gwenith must have been very ill, must have known she was dying when she left Mary at Castlemere. The grave was proof of that.

At twelve, Mary was bright enough to understand and accept all of that. Nor did she ever lose sight of the fact that she had been singularly blessed by living at Castlemere with George and Nellanor. She shuddered at the very thought that she might have had to live in this terrible, bleak village. But that was all purely mental recognition. It meant nothing to a wounded young heart. In the most vulnerable, delicate core of her spirit, Mary couldn't forgive her mother for abandoning her. It was the ultimate disloyalty, a colossal betrayal she could never forget.

She knew George had brought her here to clear that slate, but as much as she adored him, she couldn't do so. Not even for him.

"I think we should pray," George said.

"Yes, Papa," Mary said, folding her hands and bowing her head. She could think of nothing to say to God.

* * *

The worst, she discovered a half-hour later, was yet to come. George insisted that they go meet her grandmother. "I won't have to stay there, will I, Papa?"

"No, of course not," George said, surprised at the question.

"Do you promise? Swear-to-God promise?"

"I promise."

Following the directions Tutin had given him, George went up a steep street and stopped at the second cottage from the top. A woman who couldn't have been more than forty-five, but looked old, opened the door, looked George over, and adjusted her features to reflect a mixture of respect and wariness. "Yes?"

"Are you Mrs. Grey? Gwenith Grey's mother?"

"That I am, or was," she answered with a thick Welsh inflection.

"I'm George Beecham. I knew your daughter."

"Oh? She's dead now. What would you be wanting?"

"I thought you might like to meet her daughter."

"Sorry, sir, but Gwenith never married. She was in service."

"I know that, but she had a daughter."

"Begging your pardon, sir, but you've got it wrong."

George was beginning to realize what an error this visit was, but didn't know how to get out of it. He'd also noticed that Mary had slipped around behind him. He reached back and pulled her forward. "This is Mary, Gwenith's daughter."

The old woman looked at Mary, registered recognition for a second, then drew herself up. "No sir, this is no child we know."

"But look at her, woman! She's the image of her mother." This was turning into a nightmare. He must have been mad to make this journey at all.

"No, sir, there's no likeness."

"But, Mrs. Grey . . . Oh, never mind!"

Before they'd even turned away, the door had closed.

"Can we go home now, Papa?" Mary asked in a very small voice.

"Yes, as soon as we can," he said, taking her hand and hurrying down the street as if pursued. "She's an old lady, Mary. Her wits are addled," he added firmly.

"Yes, Papa," Mary replied. She'd have agreed to anything rather than risk delaying their escape from this hideous place. But she knew the truth: her mother had never

even told her people about her daughter. The denial made
the betrayal complete.

"We'll never talk about her again, if that's what you
want," George said.

"Thank you, Papa. That is what I want."

Mary didn't think about that day again consciously. She
buried the memory of it, and it wasn't until many years later
that she had good reason to remember and reevaluate it all.

They didn't speak of it. When they got back to Castlemere,
George confessed to Nellanor, who swore that he deserved
a good thrashing. He agreed entirely. Later, Nellanor said
to Mary, "I hear you and your papa took a trip."

"Yes, we did," Mary answered.

Nellanor waited for her to go on, but she didn't wait long.
If the child wanted to talk about it, she would. Otherwise
Nellanor wasn't of a mind to poke her own stick in. "I had a
letter waiting when I got back," she said. "From Alex."

"Alex!"

"Yes, we're going to London next week. He's finished
with school now and is going to stay with us for a month
before he goes back to Singapore."

"A month? A whole month?" she said blissfully, her
mother entirely forgotten.

10

Mary had come to like the Beechams' London house very well during later years. It was a house any imaginative child would love. It was on the site of the original Beecham property, owned by the family since the Middle Ages. None of the first structure remained, having burned in the Great Fire of 1665, but parts of the house dated back to the rebuilding the next year. It was a modest home then, a few small rooms and a narrow staircase leading to loft-type rooms above. Over the intervening centuries, however, as Beecham fortunes had grown, several houses on either side and behind it had been purchased and either leveled to build new rooms or added to the original by means of enclosed walkways. There was even a small garden where roses fought to survive in the dirty London air.

The result of the piecemeal building was a mazelike floorplan and a veritable museum of architectural and decorating styles. The unwary guest, innocent of the structural vagaries of the house, was more likely to *fall* than walk into some of the rooms. The oldest section was Tudor-style half-timbering with sagging and bulging walls, uneven floors, and doors that tended to either stick or come open of their own accord at unexpected hours of the day or night. Mary adored this, certain it was the ghosts of previous Beechams wandering the house. "A poor lady whose husband died very young and left her with a dozen beautiful, unhappy children," Mary would explain dreamily.

"Too bad she didn't marry a carpenter," Nellanor would answer, closing the offending door with a firm slam.

The newest wing, added in William's youth, was mock Tudor, just as picturesque as, but far cleaner, airier, and more convenient than, the old part. Mary and Nellanor had taken over rooms in the old section; George and Portia, who had far less tolerance for ghosts and drafts, had their suite in the newest; and the rooms in which the Beechams entertained were scattered throughout the rest of the house.

Mary loved her bedroom, a funny L-shaped room that was two steps down from the hallway. It smelled ancient and ghostly—in a friendly way. The thing Mary liked best about the house was its proximity to the spice warehouse. When the wind was right, the delightful, if overpowering smell of Beecham's Fine Spices blanketed the neighborhood. Mary would often drag a chair over to her high, narrow bedroom window and hang out, sniffing the air with her eyes closed, attempting to separate and identify the odors. At her request (and delighted beyond measure at her interest), George had made her a little box with circular holes fitted with small glass bottles of various spices which she frequently consulted with her nose when a scent eluded her.

But on this summer's visit to London, Mary was less concerned with spices than with guests. Alex Beecham was going to stay with them! She still couldn't quite believe it. He'd been to visit Castlemere only once since that first time he'd come, and Mary had been confined to her room with chickenpox and had seen him only when his activities took him onto the section of the Castlemere grounds visible from her room. It was one of the gravest sorrows of her childhood. "It's just as well he can't see me. I wouldn't want him to remember me all spotty. I shall die of this dread disease!" she told Nellanor tearfully. "He'll have to come back to my funeral and he'll grieve all his life, never marrying and always wearing a black armband."

"I think not," Nellanor had answered astringently. "Don't scratch, or you'll end up looking like something the cat gnawed on."

Though Alex didn't come back, Nellanor had visited him several times, short grandmotherly visits that meant she traveled several days just to have luncheon and a walk with him around the school grounds before returning to Castlemere. George, too, had been in touch with Alex, most often at the London house, where he'd invited his nephew to make himself at home during school holidays. Mostly, however, Alex had spent his vacations with the families of friends from school.

Nellanor lamented this, but George approved. "Of course

it would be nice to have the boy with us, but he's making the social and business contacts he'll need the rest of his life."

But now Alex was through with his formal education and would be returning to Singapore to take up his official apprenticeship in the overseas management of Beecham's Fine Spices under his father's expert guidance. Nellanor was determined that he delay his departure until autumn and spend the summer with the Beechams. She'd approached George about it the Christmas before the last term. "You must insist, George. It's important that he get to know us. Make sure that he understands that he's welcome for as long as he wants to stay."

"He's a nice young man besides being family. Naturally he's welcome, but he's undoubtedly anxious to go back to Singapore and begin his adult life. He came here as a boy and is going back as a man."

Nellanor suddenly looked and sounded her age. In a far more subdued voice than she normally used, she said, "George, it's the last time I'll ever see him and he's my only grandchild."

"Nonsense! He'll be back, or you can visit him."

"I'm too old to travel that far and I don't think he'll ever return."

In the end, they both wrote and Alex accepted the invitation.

Mary was disappointed when the move to the city was made. She'd imagined it would be only her and Aunt Nellanor and they'd have Alex to themselves. But everyone went: George, Portia, Hester, the servants—even Ginger, the cat. "We look like a traveling band of Gypsies," Nellanor complained as they set out, and Mary suspected the old woman was as unhappy as she.

Alex was to arrive the day after the rest of them, and Mary was up at dawn. She'd been saving up her best dress to wear that day. It was a summery white frock with a pattern in a dark purplish red that went well with her hair—or so Aunt Nellanor said in the face of Portia's insistence that redheads must never, never wear red. It had a lacy white collar. Mary thought it looked very grown-up even if it did make her neck itch. It had a very full skirt that swirled nicely when she turned, but she'd wanted it floor-length with crinolines. "You're not a grown woman yet," Nellanor had said. "When you have a bosom, you can have long skirts." Mary felt like she'd been waiting for the elusive bosom forever, but there was no sign of it yet.

Early that morning, she put on the dress and climbed the staircase to the servants' floor to rouse Agnes from her bed. "Will you fix my hair?" she asked the sleepy maid.

Agnes rolled over and pulled the covers over her head. "You know how to braid your own hair, you daft thing! Leave me alone."

Mary sat down on the edge of the bed and bounced up and down a few times. "Please, Agnes, I don't want plain old braids. I want it fancy and I don't know how."

"I'm too tired."

"I'll tell about that soup tureen you broke."

Agnes sat up. "You wouldn't!"

She wouldn't, but she just smiled.

Agnes did her hair in braids that wound around her head, and even put a strand of silky white ribbon through.

Finally ready to make her grand appearance, Mary perched in the narrow window well in the front stairway so she'd be the first to see Alex arrive. After the first hour, she overheard a perplexing conversation from the hall below. "I hope you don't mind that I told Alex he could bring his friends along to visit during the summer," Nellanor was saying.

"Mind? Why should I mind?" George answered. "He could have a dozen young men with him. This and Castlemere are the Beecham houses—his as much as ours. I'm looking forward to seeing him again. He's a charming young man. Just turned twenty, hasn't he?" George mused. "When I think of the stupid things I was saying and doing at twenty . . . The mistakes—"

"Not all your mistakes have turned out so badly," Nellanor said, lowering her voice and making it hard for Mary to make out the words.

George laughed, a warm chuckle that made Mary smile even though she had no idea what they were talking about.

Alex didn't arrive until midafternoon and Mary was stiff from her long, cramped vigil, which had been interrupted only by a midday meal that Nellanor made her take. Her dress was wrinkled, her neck itched so badly she wanted to scream, and she suspected it was probably red and blotchy. Her hair had come loose in spite of her efforts to keep the fuzzy strands all tucked in. The carriage, piled to a tottering height with trunks, stopped immediately beneath her and all she could see of Alex was the top of his head. She dashed down the steps to be the first to greet him.

Flinging the door open, she stared for a minute. He'd grown up! Tall, broad-shouldered, and powerful-looking, he was a wonderful vision to her. With his glossy dark hair and startlingly light blue eyes, he was even more handsome than she remembered. But he was a man now, a real man, and she was just a skinny girl who didn't even have a bosom. He had a friend with him, too. She hadn't expected that. A slight young man with wren-brown hair that kept falling in his eyes was helping Alex sort out luggage and get the driver properly paid.

She was suddenly struck so shy it hurt. Just as she was about to quietly close the door again and slink away so a servant would be the one to greet them, Alex turned from supervising the unloading of the trunks and noticed her. "Hello there, child, are the Beechams in?"

"I'm a Beecham," she said.

"Are you? Oh, yes. One of George's girls. I should have remembered. No, not that trunk, Hector. It goes on to Castlemere along with the one with the broken strap and the large one at the bottom."

Mary fled.

Back in the safety of her room, she succumbed to a flood of tears. She wrapped a pillow around her head to close out the increasingly loud sound of greetings from the ground floor. After a while, Nellanor came to her room. Mary knew how difficult it was for Nellanor to climb the stairs unnecessarily and felt both guilty and gratified that she'd made the effort.

"Mary, what's come over you?" Nellanor demanded, "Alex is here. Come down and see him."

"I don't want to see him ever again. He can just go back to his stupid Singapore. I don't care," Mary mumbled through the pillow.

"Don't be a fool, girl. You've been watching for him all day. You're making a wreck of your hair."

"I won't come down!"

Nellanor dragged the pillow away. "Sit up and speak to me properly! Mary, this is no time to have one of your tempers. Alex has come to visit us and it's important that we all be courteous."

"He has no manners! Why should I?" Mary said, scooting back to get out of Nellanor's reach.

But the old woman grabbed her thin arm and shook her. "You may be as rude as you want when you're an old lady like me, but right now you're a little girl in my care and I won't have this! You will wash off your face and comb your hair and get downstairs in five minutes. Do you understand?"

Mary sniffed.

"I mean this, Mary Beecham. You had better pay heed."

"Yes'm," Mary muttered, and gave Aunt Nellanor the most thoroughly scathing look she could manage.

The old woman was impervious. "Don't think making ugly faces changes things. I've had more people make faces at me than you've had baths. What *is* the matter with you?"

Mary tossed her head defiantly and was sorry to see a length of the white ribbon flash by her eyes. She really had wrecked her hair. "He didn't remember me, Aunt Nell. He thought I was just some guest he didn't know. I went to the door and he asked me if any of the Beechams were here, and when I said I was, he just said, 'Oh, yes, one of George's girls.' He didn't even know who I was."

Nellanor looked at the ceiling and shook her head. "If I didn't know better, I'd think God hadn't given you the brains he gave a chicken. Mary, you're not such a ninny, are you? Of course he didn't recognize you, and you should be glad he didn't."

This was the last thing Mary had expected to hear. "Why should I be glad?" she asked, wondering if Aunt Nellanor had suddenly gone strange in the head like Evelyn did so many years ago.

"Think it out, child. The last time Alex saw you—the *only* time he saw you—was the first summer you came to Castlemere. How old were you then?"

"Seven. You know that." Mary had given up on fashion and was thoughtfully sucking on the end of one of her braids. She was starting to sense where Nellanor was going.

"And you're twelve now, aren't you? Almost twice as old. The only reason Alex didn't recognize you is that you've grown up so much. If he'd bounded out of that carriage and said, 'Why, look here, it's little Mary,' it would have meant you hadn't changed."

"Do you really think so?"

"I certainly do, and if you keep chewing on your hair, you'll get hair balls like Ginger does. It's bad enough having that cat puking all over the place without you doing the same. Now, fix yourself up. You look like something that got left out in the rain overnight."

Nellanor could hardly take her eyes off the boy. To think that the son of her son should have turned out so well. He must have gotten that lovely blue-black hair from his mother's people; Beechams were mainly fair or redheaded. The smile, of course, was from a different source, a source no one else at the table had ever seen. Claudius' father had possessed that same fine sensuality of the lower lip and the tendency of the very corners of his mouth to turn up before the full bedazzlement of the smile was evident.

Dear God, it had been so long now. She was surprised and a little angry at herself for remembering him so vividly. It was a good thing Claudius hadn't resembled his father; she'd have been tortured by the memory of him all her life. As it was, she hadn't thought about him for years; only now, seated across from Alex at the dinner table, did she recall her lost and misspent youth. No, not entirely misspent. For those few months while they lived in isolated bliss in the summer house in India, she had been the happiest a woman could be. And then, when she found out her marriage was a mockery . . .

She shoved the thought aside. She'd put in her full quota of suffering years ago. The present was what counted. And the future for those young enough to have a future. She was desperate to question Alex, but remembered her manners well enough to address a few remarks to his friend. The poor young man looked rather overwhelmed, as anyone was when thrown into the midst of a large, unfamiliar family. "Mr. Turner, are you going abroad as well, now that you have completed your schooling?"

"I wish I were, ma'am. And I wish you would call me Henry. No, I'm going home to catalog the family library. My father recently inherited a large estate near Carlisle with an enormous but utterly chaotic book collection." His eyes sparkled at the prospect. "I wish I could do some traveling, but the book chore certainly won't be onerous."

Feeling she had done her duty to the guest, Nellanor turned at last to her beloved grandson. "Alex, will you be going into your father's office as soon as you return?" she asked.

"Not immediately," he said. "According to his letters, Father plans to send me on a tour of as many of the spice-producing islands as possible first. To see what's being grown, to meet the plantation owners, and so forth. Then he wants me to spend a season on his plantation on Penang."

"He's bought land?" George asked.

"Yes, a clove plantation. Penang is about four hundred miles northwest of Singapore—"

"I know where it is," George said. "At least on the maps. I think I was there once, when I was a child. Oh, here's Mary . . ." He broke off, holding his hand out to the child. "Mary, tell your cousin Alex where the island of Penang is."

She took George's outstretched hand, looked at her feet for inspiration, and said softly, "Penang is an island just off the Malay Peninsula in the Strait of Malacca. It was given to Francis Light, an English trader, in 1786 by the Sultan of Kedah. Penang and Province Wellesley, facing it on the mainland, and Singapore, are called the Straits Settlements."

Alex was genuinely impressed, in addition to feeling guilty about slighting her earlier. He hadn't meant to hurt her feelings. It was just that she'd grown so much and he was preoccupied with getting the luggage sorted out. "That's very good, Mary! I can't think of a single one of my class-mates who could do so well. Except maybe Henry here, who seems to know everything. Englishmen as a rule are astonishingly uninformed about the empire. There were boys at school who didn't even know where India is."

Portia muttered something sour about children who didn't know their places and nodded to the servants to clear the soup course.

"Would you like to see Penang and Singapore, Mary?" Alex asked.

She nodded wordlessly. Was he offering to take her back when he left?

"You really ought to bring the family out, George," Alex went on.

"I've thought about it. There never seems to be a time I can leave England, though. Since Father died, I've been busy all the time. But yes, it would be good to see it all again firsthand. Would you like that, Mary?"

Portia interrupted. "George, shouldn't Mary be excused now to take her dinner in the nursery with Hester?"

"Is that where Hester is? I wondered. Please send for her. I want the girls to get to know their cousin Alex. They're old enough to sit at table with the adults."

"I hardly think—"

"It would please me, Portia," he said firmly.

"Very well."

Portia was angry, but soon gave up sulking when she realized no one was paying the least attention. She gave orders that two more places be set, and went back to her meal.

"Think about it, George," Alex was urging. "I'd like showing you around."

"I will. I truly will. It would be an enlightening trip and I'd like to see if it's all really as I remember. Even as a boy, I was impressed by the heat. I can't imagine how you stand it year round."

"I never noticed it as a boy. I'd never known anything else," Alex said. "I suppose I will now. But I can't say I'll ever miss your English winters. That first year I was here . . ." He shuddered. "George, you really must come. All of you."

His enthusiasm was contagious. "Yes, we'll do it," George said. "Not right away, but when the girls get a little older and you've had time to settle in. Portia, you'd enjoy the trip," he added, blissfully unconscious of the fact that Portia hated the sea, wilted in the heat, and had an unremitting contempt for the society of colonials.

Two places had been squeezed in next to Nellanor. Summoned from the nursery, Hester had taken her place and was looking perplexed at her own presence with the adults. Mary was on the other side of her, eyes glued to Alex. She'd leaned forward to catch his every word and was dragging her lace collar in her gravy. Portia had noticed it too, and looked horrified.

Nellanor just smiled.

That evening, after hours of brandy and cigars with George, Alex ascended the stairs. The house was quiet, at least as quiet as a house in the middle of London ever got. At the landing, he was startled that a ghostly little nightdress-clad figure appeared before him.

"The stairs are uneven. You could trip without someone to show you the bad ones," Mary said.

"You shouldn't be up so late, child."

"My name is Mary. Mary Beecham. You can remember it because of the Virgin Mary. Of course, we're Protestants and we don't say very much about her. Not like Catholics do. I knew some Catholics when I was little and living with my mother . . ." She rattled on as she accompanied him up the stairs. "Watch that one. It makes a horrible squeak if you step on that end. We used to be Catholic. Beechams, I mean. Did you know that? Everyone was. And then there was this king who wanted a divorce and the pope wouldn't let him, so he started his own church."

"You don't say?" Alex said with a smile.

"Oh, but I do. It's really true. Papa—your cousin George is my papa now that I'm adopted—said so. He gives me books to read about history and then he asks me questions. Just like going to school, but I'm the only pupil. Aunt Nellanor—that's your grandmother, Mary—says—"

"I know who Nellanor is, Mary." This was the strangest girl! he thought with amusement.

"Aunt Nell sometimes calls Castlemere the Beecham Academy for Girls. Sometimes Hester studies too, but she doesn't like history. She likes sewing and painting and things like that. What did you study at your school? Did you take maths? I'm very good at addition and subtraction and multiplication, but I don't like division at all. Do you?"

"I hate it, except for the nines tables."

"Oh, me too! You should like nines, because your birthday is the ninth day of the ninth month."

He stopped outside his door. "How in the world did you know that?"

"I asked Aunt Nellanor. Don't you remember we sent you cards and a lawn-tennis racket last year on your birthday? You wrote a nice letter back to Aunt Nell about it, but I guess you didn't know I helped pick it out."

"You did? I'm so sorry I didn't know. It's a wonderful racket. You'd better get back to bed. I hear someone else on the stairs."

"All right. Good night." She scampered down the hall a few feet, then ran back and whispered, "Cousin Alex, I love you." Then she was gone.

He went into his room, smiling and shaking his head in wonder. He was, to his surprise, genuinely touched by her confession. It was so sincere, so wholehearted. Were all little girls like this? He knew very few, but suspected this one was unique. What sort of woman would she someday become? Impossible to imagine.

They stayed in London for a week, then adjourned to

Castlemere for the rest of the month of Alex's visit. Henry Turner went off to Carlisle to catalog his books with great reluctance. A well-mannered, but quiet, even dreamy young man, he'd fitted into the family very well. His departure seemed to signal the beginning of a hectic month. Portia and George normally had frequent company, but in going all-out to entertain Alex, they filled the London house, then Castlemere, with guests in an unbroken stream. Several of Alex's friends from school, along with their parents, were invited. A host of distant cousins—most of whom were connected with Beecham's Fine Spices in some way—was brought in for visits. Portia used the presence of her husband's handsome nephew to pay back a few social debts by inviting a number of her friends and their marriageable daughters to stay for a few days.

Mary despised all these guests. She'd wanted to have Alex to herself, and hardly got him alone at all. When his friends from school were around, he was hunting and sailing and staying up late playing cards with them. The rest of his time was taken up with long, cigar-smoky discussions in the map room with George and the relatives. Occasionally she'd slip in to listen, but the talk would be of the weather in Mexico and what it would mean to the vanilla pods, or the possibility of rubber importation into Malaysia increasing land values, or which growers were adulterating their ground ginger with ground mustard, or what the chances were of anyone ever inventing a machine to crack nutmeg hulls. They never seemed to stop talking about these things so Alex could be left alone for her to talk to. Nor did he ever take much notice of her except to nod or smile when she came in. Once, however, he grinned and winked at her at breakfast and she was giggly all day.

The worst guests were the husband-hungry daughters of Portia's friends. They were a simpering, sissy lot with eager eyes, flirting laughs, elaborate curls, and oversize crinolines. Mary was disgusted that poor Alex had to sit by them at dinners, pay them compliments, and take them for walks. Oh, he acted as if he enjoyed it well enough, especially with the pretty ones, but Mary alone was certain he was miserable and his apparent pleasure was mere courtesy.

Mary was exhausted by her vigilance. She woke early every day and stayed up as long as she could on the chance of snagging Alex, but it seldom paid off. The result was that she grew hollow-eyed and started falling asleep every time she sat down quietly for a few minutes. Nellanor noticed and thought she was sickening. "You've been indoors too much lately, girl," she said. "I want you outside today getting some fresh air. Let's go look at the construction in the west wing."

Mary went along reluctantly. Normally this sort of snooping around was her cup of tea, but Alex had gone to Brighton overnight with a friend and was due back this morning. She didn't want to miss him. But Nellanor's orders, however kindly phrased, were not to be disputed. "I'm only free for an hour," she said.

"I beg your pardon?" Nellanor said, grabbing her by a loose braid.

"Nothing, Aunt Nell. I didn't say anything."

There had been a small fire in one of the guest rooms in the west wing the previous week. George had been ready to simply patch up the damage, but Portia insisted that both it and the adjoining room were too small to be useful and ought to be knocked together as long as work was going to be done anyway.

They found George standing in the middle of the rubble that had been hauled outside for carrying away. "Aunt Nell! Mary! The most extraordinary thing. I've solved a mystery. Look at this." He handed each of them a slab of the plaster that had been taken out with the wall.

Nellanor studied it and said, "Look at the layers of wallpaper and paint! I had no idea these rooms had been redone so often."

"No, Aunt Nell. Not the front, the back. Look at the back. Smell it."

Nellanor fished around in her bosom for her spectacles, donned them, and studied the plaster. A smile spread across her face. "So that's the reason. Mary, look. See what's mixed in? Dried rosemary needles."

"I got curious because the scent was so much stronger than usual when they started tearing the wall out. I thought maybe there were rosemary switches in with the lathing, but it's the needles—used to bind the plaster. Do you imagine old Philippe Beecham had it done this way on purpose for the smell, or the builder just used it because so many of the bushes were handy?"

"Does this mean that Castlemere will smell the same forever and ever and ever?" Mary asked.

"Forever and ever and ever," George answered.

Nellanor started laughing, a delighted cackle that was probably heard in the next shire. "Won't Portia be sorry! She hates the smell. Always has."

"She does?" George replied.

"Oh, George, haven't you ever noticed how she's got the windows open airing the place out every time it isn't actually snowing? I can't wait to tell her it's hopeless."

"Aunt Nell—"

"Oh, very well. I won't tell her, but I want to be around when you do."

"Let's don't tell anybody," Mary said. "That way it can stay a secret for just us to know. Us and Philippe. And Alex. Can we tell Alex?"

"Tell Alex what?" He had come around the corner just in time to hear Mary's last words.

George nodded to Mary with suitable gravity, careful not to smile and betray his amusement. Alex followed suit and listened very carefully as she explained about the rosemary leaves in the plaster. "And what is your belief?" he asked seriously. "Did Philippe Beecham instruct the builder to do it this way?"

"I'm certain he did," Mary said. "You see, he might have been desperately in love with a beautiful woman who liked the scent, but she was married to someone else. Or died young"—this was one of her favorite romantic themes—"and he wanted the house to smell like her favorite perfume throughout eternity so that no one would ever forget their undying love."

"God in heaven!" Nellanor exclaimed. "Where do you find those trashy books to read?"

"I didn't read it. I made it up myself," Mary said indignantly.

Alex turned away, his shoulders shaking.

Mary ran to him. "Don't cry, Cousin Alex. I didn't mean to make you sad."

His face was contorted with repressed emotion. "I think I can manage to hold back my tears," he said.

Halfway through Alex's visit, Mary started suggesting to Nellanor that they take him fishing. She'd decided the only way she could get Alex away from everybody else—everybody but Nellanor—was to get him out on the Channel in a boat.

"I don't know that he cares for fishing," Nellanor said.

"I bet he does, Aunt Nell. Ask him, please. Or maybe I can ask?"

A few days later, she reminded the old woman again, and the day after that, when she started nagging, Nellanor said, "I did talk to him about it and he said he'd like to go with us."

"Tomorrow? Could we go tomorrow?"

"I suppose. It looks like rain, though."

"It doesn't matter. We aren't sissies, Aunt Nell. You said only sissies come in from fishing just 'cause it rains."

Nellanor replied, "I must have been feeling younger when I said that. But very well, I'll tell Alex we'll go tomorrow."

The next morning was miserable. Cloudy, drizzly, and much too cold for the season. Nellanor tried to dissuade Mary, but the child was so clearly crushed at the idea of giving up the promised trip that Nellanor relented.

"I'm sorry, Alex," she said to him out of Mary's hearing, "but Mary's set on doing this, rain or not. I think we might as well get it over with. She'll get cold quickly enough and be ready to come back."

"I don't mind in the least, Aunt Nell. It's probably the last time for a good long while that I'll be cold. But I don't think you ought to go out."

"You mean you'd take her yourself?"

"Why not?"

"Because she's awfully intense company without anybody to dilute her enthusiasm. She's a lot like using a whole spoonful of pepper when a sprinkle would do."

He leaned down and kissed her cheek. "You're just the same way. It's what makes you both so charming. Tuck yourself up in front of a fire. I'll take Mary out for a while."

Nellanor's predictions of Mary objecting to the cold were utterly wrong. She was afire with enthusiasm from the second she found out that she and Alex alone were going. "All by myself with Cousin Alex! Oh, I'm in raptures, Aunt Nell! Raptures!"

"When in the world did you pick *that* word up?"

"What shall I wear?"

"Your fishing clothes, of course. Or had you thought about having Agnes alter one of Portia's ball gowns?"

"Would she?" Mary said.

"My God, child! I think your raptures have melted your brain."

Midmorning, they set out. Mary insisted on Alex using

her best pole. "But if it's your best, you should use it," he said.

"Oh, I can do fine with another one. I'm a good fisher with any pole. Aunt Nell taught me. Can you clean a fish? I can."

"I can't say I'm an expert," he replied, smiling.

He put his hand on her shoulder and tapped out the rhythm of a tune he hummed as they walked along. Mary was so thrilled at this evidence of friendship that she kept missing her footing and tripping over tussocks of grass.

"Hadn't you better watch where you're going? Instead of staring at me. What's wrong, have I got my breakfast on my chin?" he asked.

Though it was still drizzling, there was little wind and the sea was calm. "Aunt Nell said we couldn't go out in the boat if it was rough," Mary reported.

"That's not too rough," Alex said.

"Not for us! We're not sissies."

They set out in the old boat she and Nell often used. It didn't look seaworthy, but in spite of the faded paint and battered exterior, it was a sturdy craft and cut through the water surprisingly well. Mary sat in the bow watching Alex row. "You're a very good rower," she said.

"I would guess that's high praise, coming from you," he said.

They didn't go far, just out enough that the waves wouldn't bring them back in immediately. Mary insisted on baiting both their hooks. "Aunt Nellanor and I catch these little fish in a tide pool down the beach," she explained. "Then we put them in a bucket she made by punching a lot of little holes in it. She figured it out by herself so the holes are big enough for water to go around without the fish getting out."

"You really love Nellanor a lot, don't you?" he said, watching as she impaled a fish on the hook. Was there another well-bred little girl in the world who would do that? Probably not.

"Oh, I do. I love her the most. Except for my father. I love him the most too. Do you love Nellanor or do you just like her because she's your grandmother?"

"I love her, just like you do."

"Why?"

"Hmmm, I never thought about why. Does there have to be a reason?"

"I don't know. Here's your pole, all ready."

He took the pole she held out and dropped the hook over the edge of the boat.

"No, it'll snag on the bottom of the boat that way. You have to stand up and throw it out. Like this . . ." She stood up to demonstrate.

"Be careful! You'll fall over," Alex said, reaching out to grab her arm.

She eluded his hand. "No, I do this lots. Aunt Nell showed me how you keep your body in the same place, but you let your knees bend with the boat. Aunt Nell says I have superb balance—"

It was quite true. When she was paying attention to the motion of the water, the movement of the boat, and what her own knees were doing, she could stay upright easily. But she wasn't paying attention to these things, she was concentrating on Alex. And as she spoke the last word, a wave tilted the boat and Mary went flying, head over heels, into the water.

She bobbed to the surface a surprising distance from the boat and opened her mouth to assure Alex she was all right, but as she did so, she got a mouthful of water and started choking. Thrashing and flailing, she saw Alex dive in and swim toward her with long, powerful strokes. In a matter of seconds, though it seemed like hours to her, he'd grabbed her by her braids, dragged her back to the boat, lifted her up to dump her over the edge, and climbed in after her.

He made her lean over, and pounded her back until the coughing and retching had stopped. Then he started rowing back to shore. Mary sat huddled in the bow, her wet clothes heavy and frigid in the breeze. She started shivering, and by the time Alex dragged the boat up onto the shingle, her teeth were chattering so violently it made her whole body shake.

Without a word, he scooped her into his arms and carried her up the path. The cold and shock were making her faint and woozy. She knew how hard it must be for him to climb, carrying her. But she couldn't find the strength to object. As they neared the house, she became aware that she wasn't the only one shaking. Of course, he was wet and cold too. Knowing she ought to insist on being put down to walk, she merely tightened her grasp around his neck.

"I've m-m-made a f-f-fool of m-m-myself!" she cried as Alex banged on the kitchen door with his foot.

"Nonsense!" he replied briskly, and to the scullery maid

went on, "Send for some warm clothes for her and some-thing hot to drink. We'll keep her by the fire until she's all dried out."

He put her down on a stool and started peeling her still-dripping jacket off. She suddenly flung her arms around his neck and started weeping into his soggy shirtfront, and he hadn't managed to extricate himself yet when Nellanor stormed into the kitchen. "Dear God! What happened to the two of you? No, don't tell me. I can imagine. Mary, you were showing off, weren't you! And poor Alex got drenched hauling you out of trouble. I should have known—"

"No, Nell. I was the one who fell overboard," Alex said.

Mary pulled away and looked at him with astonishment. He winked at her and went on. "Mary only got wet trying to help me back into the boat. I'm afraid I pulled her in. But we're both fine. We're *not* sissies, you know."

Nellanor glared at both of them for a long moment, then left to find out what was taking Agnes so long getting dry clothes.

"Why did you tell her that?" Mary whispered.

He started taking her shoes off. "Oh, I just don't think everybody always has to know the whole truth about every-thing, do you?"

Alex was to leave on Wednesday morning. On the Mon-day evening before, he came to Nellanor. "I know George and Portia mean well, but I've hardly had any chance to talk to you. If I have to spend my last full day at Castlemere being polite to strangers, I'll go mad."

"So you seek me out for rudeness?"

He laughed. "Let's run away, Nell. All day tomorrow, just you and me."

"Portia has a big going-away party planned for the eve-ning. Everybody who's anybody for a hundred miles around is invited."

"Then just for the day. We'll put on false whiskers and nobody will know it's us creeping off across the lawn."

Nellanor yelped with pleasure. "I can't wait. Oh, say, would you mind very much if Mary came along? She adores you and would never recover if we both abandoned her."

"That's fine. So long as there's no water involved."

"Why did you lie for her?" Nellanor asked.

He didn't bother to deny it. He'd never expected his grandmother to believe him anyway. "Just because she was so miserable. And it had happened just like you said. She was so busy showing off her skills for me that she flung herself right into the water. She's an odd child, isn't she? I don't know much about little girls, but I doubt that many of them are so proud of their fishing skills."

Nellanor said, "She's been the joy of my autumn years. She and you, my dear boy."

Alex kissed her withered cheek. "Now, now, that sounds nice and I was counting on you for good, astringent discourtesy."

Mary was up at dawn and waiting in the carriage a full hour before Nellanor and Alex joined her. Their plan was a trip along the coast to Hastings and then to Battle Abbey, but none of them really cared whether they made it to their destination or not. In spite of her best intentions, she was so tired she fell asleep after the first gently rocking mile of travel and didn't wake until they stopped for luncheon. She was mortified, first at having fallen asleep and then at the realization that they'd apparently managed to enjoy conversing without her help.

Alex liked the abbey. They stood together at the crest of the hill where Harold's troops had stood on that fateful day so many hundreds of years earlier and looked down to where William's invading forces had taken their stand.

"To think, if Harold's men hadn't fallen for the false retreat and followed down this very slope, we might not be standing here today," Alex said.

"Why not?" Mary asked. She'd been ready to show off how much she knew about the battle itself, having studied up to impress him, but this speculation was outside her understanding.

"Everybody's history would have been changed. If Harold had won, Richard the Lion Heart wouldn't have been king and gone Crusading and our ancestor wouldn't have gone along and gotten interested in spices," Alex explained. He'd completely forgotten that Mary was adopted and wasn't, so far as he knew, a Beecham by birth.

"Do you mean her majesty wouldn't *be*?"

"She'd be somebody, but not queen," Nellanor answered. "Probably a cook in somebody's household. She looks like a cook."

Mary's eyes widened with shock; then she dissolved into laughter. She laughed so hard she got the hiccups and Alex had to bend her over his arm and hold her almost upside down and shake her to stop them. By that time Nellanor was giddy too, at the sight. She'd been lucky to have Mary in her life, and she shouldn't be ungrateful, but why, oh why, couldn't she have had both of them for longer? Alex was everything a woman could ask a grandson to be, and now that she'd finally gotten to know him, he was going away.

Mary, however, hadn't a scarcity of years before her like Nellanor, and while she was unhappy at his going, she looked on it as a temporary condition. "You'll come back to England, won't you, Cousin Alex," she said when the carriage was rolling back toward Castlemere. It was a statement, not an inquiry.

"Someday, but it's a very long trip so I won't make it anytime soon."

"That means I'll be grown up when you come again."

"You? Don't ever grow up, Mary. You're just right like you are."

"Oh, but I have to grow up and get tall and have—" She was about to say "a bosom," but a glance at Nellanor's warning look made her suspect that this degree of forthrightness might not be appropriate. "—and have crinolines and bloomers with lace at the knees and such."

"I doubt that Alex is much concerned with your underwear, child."

"I wasn't being personal, Aunt Nell. I was speaking in general terms." This was a statement she'd heard Nellanor make when Portia took offense at remarks Nellanor made. "Does Aunt Nell let you ask a question every day like I do?" she asked Alex.

"A question every day?"

"Yes, ever since I came to Castlemere I've gotten to ask questions. Sometimes I forget and sometimes it's a silly question—"

"Most times it's silly," Nellanor put in, trying to fix the end of one of Mary's braids that had come loose.

"And sometimes Aunt Nellanor won't answer me."

"*Will* you stop bouncing around until I've got this tied?" Nellanor asked, swatting at the fine red hair that kept blowing in her face.

"What kind of questions?"

"Sometimes about things I'm studying. Aunt Nell knows all sorts of history and numbers. And sometimes I ask about you," Mary confessed. "Like when you are going to visit us again and how old are you and when is your birthday. Sometimes I ask accidentally. Like yesterday, I said to Aunt Nell at breakfast, 'What time is it?' and she said it was nine and that was my question for the day."

Alex leaned forward conspiratorially. "She's a tricky one, isn't she?"

Mary giggled.

Late in the afternoon, they returned. Many of the guests for the dinner had already arrived and the house was a beehive, with Portia an extremely irritable queen bee. Before she could complete her full tirade about how late they were, Alex dashed upstairs to get bathed and dressed. He was at his door before he discovered that Mary had galloped along behind him. "What is it, Mary?"

"Cousin Alex? If you'd like me to, I could come back to Singapore with you tomorrow. I wouldn't mind."

He bent down and put his hands on her arms. "Mary, that's very kind of you and it would make me happy, but think how sad Aunt Nell and your papa would be without you. They'd never forgive me if I took you away."

"But someday I can come to Singapore, can't I?"

"I hope so. Now, run along, I have to change for dinner."

Mary went to her room and scooped up Ginger, who was curled on her bed sleeping off the rabbit he'd caught and eaten earlier. "Oh, Ginger, I'm the happiest girl in England. I'm going to go visit Cousin Alex when I'm grown up and he's going to fall hopelessly in love with me and we'll get married and have dozens of pretty babies and live happily forever. I'll take you along and you can marry a lady cat and be happy forever too."

11

June 1927

Natalie passed along the dining-room sideboard. To look at it, you'd think this was Castlemere in its heyday. There was enough food here to feed a dozen guests: kippers, sweetbreads, eggs cooked three different ways, bacon, sausage, scones, toast, and six kinds of jam. She took a tiny portion of each, knowing these choices had been prepared and put out primarily so that she, the only guest, could have anything she wanted.

She'd read throughout the afternoon before, and by the time the light began to fail, Grandmama was soundly asleep and Natalie couldn't ask any questions. But her own sleep that night had been disturbed by the queries that jostled through her mind, tumbling over each other. Natalie had never even known that Grandmama was adopted. Nor had she heard of Aunt Nellanor, George Beecham, Portia, Evelyn, or William except as names in the family records. And she'd certainly never heard of Gwenith Grey. But as she read the diaries, they were beginning to come alive as real people who were important to her grandmother.

Her musings were interrupted by a hearty, "Good morning, dearie. Hoped I might find you here."

"Good morning, Sister. How is Grandmama today?"

"Perking along like a sweet little kettle on the boil."

Natalie finished her breakfast hurriedly and went up to Mary's room. "How far have you read?" Mary asked her as she came in.

"Up to the discovery when the wall was torn out. Rosemary mixed in the plaster. How extraordinary. I've always wondered, but never asked. I just assumed it was a mystery to everyone."

Mary was having her breakfast on a wicker bed tray. Her

color was better and she seemed to have regained strength and vigor. "When I was sixteen, Papa had some perfume made for me that had oil of rosemary as an ingredient. It was so typically thoughtful and understanding of him."

"Do we make oil of rosemary? I've never seen it for sale with a Beecham label. In fact, I don't remember ever seeing it at the chemist's at all."

"Yes, Beecham's still makes it, but we sell it only to perfumers and soap makers. And I have a few bottles of the oil that's been distilled in an alcohol base sent here every year. A teaspoonful is put in the rinse water of all linens. I started that when I became mistress of the house. It resulted in a terrible tragedy, but I kept on."

"A tragedy?"

Mary's expression had become grave as she gestured toward the drawer beneath the bookshelves where the diaries were hidden. "It's all in there," she said.

Sensing that her grandmother didn't want to talk about the rosemary oil, Natalie said, "What an interesting child you must have been."

"Interesting? Looking back, I can't see why I didn't drive the household mad. I was, thanks to native intelligence and Papa's teaching, a very bright child, but extremely immature at the same time. Imagine my thinking all that romantic nonsense about Alex. But I believed it completely at the time. Natalie, would you take this tray away?"

"Not unless you promise to eat your bread and butter," the younger woman said, removing the tray, but handing back the plate in question. "There's little mention of Great-Aunt Hester in your diaries."

"Isn't there? How strange. No, I don't suppose it's strange. I have very slight memory of her in those early years. She made very little impression on me until we were older. Portia—Mama, as I finally learned to call her—kept Hester close to her. She was a nice child, but bland and boring to me at that age. And I must have terrified her. I was such a wild little hoyden. And so immature. So extraordinarily immature. I think I started actually growing up about the time of the nutmeg blight. Do you know anything about that?"

"Some. Daddy's talked about it. All the trees died, didn't they?"

"Most of them in the Straits Settlements. It was caused by a tiny, almost microscopic beetle that attacked the trees exposed to direct sunlight. But no one knew that then. It must have looked like God had just struck the European planters down. Because of the way the English and Dutch cleared the land, their crops were the most vulnerable. The Chinese and Malays planted their crops between other trees without clearing the forest, as nature intended the trees to grow. Theirs suffered, but not as much. Thousands of acres of nutmeg and cloves died."

"There must have been dozens of planters bankrupted."

"Hundreds. And the list might have included Alex's father, Claudius, if he'd been on hand full-time to keep the groves cleared. Fortunately for him, he had to live in Singapore most of the year, serving the company's interests. He died of malaria the same year the trees died. Later we found out he'd suffered it periodically for some time, but we didn't know then. His contact with the rest of us was purely business. How he must have hated all of us!"

"So Cousin Alex inherited a worthless plantation of dead trees?"

"Not entirely worthless. A fair number of the trees survived. Most of the planters abandoned the land. A few, like Alex, who had another source of income, burned off the diseased trees and waited a few years in hopes the blight wouldn't recur. At that time, you see, rubber seedlings had already been smuggled to England from Brazil and there was great hope it would be a more valuable crop than spices. Which, of course, is what happened. Alex spent far more years than he should have out there trying to get the crop to recover. At least, that was why he said he stayed in the Straits and I suppose he believed it himself at the time. Natalie, you must take this awful bread away."

Resigned, Natalie did as she was told.

"Are you wearing lip rouge?" Mary asked as Natalie moved away.

"Yes, Grandmama, a little. I'll take it off if you want."

"No, it brings out the color in your cheeks. I wondered if I might try just a tiny dab."

"Grandmama! I thought you disapproved."

"Will you put it on me and bring me that hand mirror? The large one with the silver handle."

A few moments later, Mary was studying herself in the mirror. "That's quite nice, isn't it? Does it come in different shades of red?"

"Yes, I think you'd look even better if it were a little bit lighter with a touch of orange. I'll go to town tomorrow and get you some."

"That would be very nice, dear. Now, where was I?"

Natalie started to remove the hand mirror, but the old woman's fingers closed around the handle. "You were saying you grew up so much during those years. Certainly it wasn't because of the nutmeg blight."

"No, I only mentioned that because I don't think it's in the diaries. Actually, I think the first time I came out of that hazy pink world I'd created was two or three years after the blight. I must have been . . . oh, seventeen or so. A letter came from Alex to all of us. Normally he just wrote business letters to Papa and personal notes to Aunt Nell, and he was very good for remembering cards for my birthday and Hester's, but this letter was all formal, with all our names on it. In the letter he announced his recent marriage."

"Oh, no—"

"Yes. A Dutch woman named Anjanette. I was destroyed, absolutely destroyed by the news. I'd never questioned that my ridiculous dreams might not accord with Alex's own. I fully expected that he was just patiently waiting for me to grow up so we could marry. Oh, dear, it makes me feel silly even now, to think what a self-centered little fool I was. Well, that letter brought me down to earth with a terrible thump, but it didn't last long. I was young and resilient and determined to believe only what I wanted to believe. I invented some ridiculous story to console myself with, about how she was probably an orphan he'd only married out of pity and she was sickly and would be carried away by malaria just in time for me to marry Alex as I'd planned."

Her voice was becoming weaker and slower. Natalie shifted the pillows and helped ease her into a more comfortable position. "Go on, Grandmama." Why was she being told all this? Natalie wondered. It certainly wasn't just an egotistical urge to say her piece. If that were the case, Grandmama wouldn't be so fatally honest about her own feelings. She wasn't making an attempt to make herself appear noble either in the diaries or in conversation.

Mary's voice was faint and the words dragged out. "Then, when I was nineteen . . . another letter . . . came. . . ."

When Natalie was certain her grandmother was sleeping, she got up and took another diary from the drawer. Then she closed it back up and rang the little bell for the attendant.

"I'm going outside for a while now," she told the woman.

"Grandmama is sleeping peacefully. I think she's better today, don't you?"

"Oh, we'll pull her through this, don't you worry, dearie."

The remark was so aggressively positive that Natalie was alarmed rather than comforted. Telling herself she was letting her imagination run away with her, she went outdoors and settled herself in a shady nook. She opened the diary she'd brought from her grandmother's room.

> 13 April 1872. Life is no longer worth living! The most *devastating* news ever! Cousin Alex is a father. His wife has given birth to a horrid daughter. This is the death knell of all my hopes and dreams. . . .

12

October 1872

"Mary Beecham! You stop carrying on that way," Nellanor warned.

"I'm not 'carrying on,' Aunt Nell. I merely said that making a baby-size dress for a Dutch child's first birthday is a waste of time. This Katie is probably the size of an English four-year-old. The Dutch are big lumpy people and—"

"That's a ridiculous remark from someone who doesn't know a single Dutch person, and it's a vain remark besides. Just because you're small. Well, in my opinion you're a Welsh midget. And you don't know anything about Alex's wife or the little girl. Except that they *are* Alex's wife and child," she said shrewdly.

"It couldn't matter less to me," Mary answered airily. "And I am *not* a midget!"

"Don't you flounce around me that way, acting as if I can't see through you."

"I can't think what you mean."

"Mary, this silly imagination of yours is going to get you in trouble. I thought it was harmless when you developed that devotion to Alex when you were a child; I can see now that I was wrong not to nip it in the bud. But it's surly and ugly of you to begrudge him his happiness now just because he isn't as dreamy as you."

Mary relented. Nellanor had just celebrated her eighty-second birthday the month before and suddenly seemed old and fragile to her, her remarks delivered in a voice that had an unaccustomed tremor. It frightened Mary. "I'm sorry, Aunt Nell. But you must let me help you finish the baby dress. It's already October and the birthday is in February. As long as it takes to make the trip—"

"I know that, child. What's a chit like you who's never

been anywhere but London and back in all her twenty years doing telling me about travel around the world? Why, I came from America when I was an infant and was on my way to India with nothing but a lady's maid for company when I was your age. Now, get that cashmere wrap of mine and help steady me to dinner."

"Wouldn't you rather have a tray in your room?"

"And miss watching Portia trying to fling you at those young men she's invited? Pimple-faced boys, I'll bet. Don't ever marry a man with pimples, child. They aren't to be trusted. Now, boils are a different matter. A good man can have an occasional boil and have his character strengthened by it, so long as it's only occasional. More often and it sours him."

"I'll make inquiries about boils and pimples before I accept a proposal, Aunt Nell. Pardon me, your lordship, I love you madly and I know you're rich as Midas, but have you ever had a boil? I can't marry you otherwise."

"Don't be fresh with me, child. Get that cat out of my way, unless you want me to break my leg or his."

The guests were already prepared to be seated when Mary and Nellanor finally arrived. Among them were Dr. Engle and his wife, a local matron and her daughter, a sandy-haired young man named Jamison something, and two very pimpled youths. Mary and Nellanor exchanged smiles.

Whom are those two laughing at now? Portia wondered as Mary and Nellanor took their places. They always seemed to be secretly poking fun at somebody—most of the time, she suspected it was herself. What an irritating combination they were—the coarse old woman and the outspoken girl who was turning into such a beautiful woman. Portia studied Mary as she sat talking with Dr. Engle.

The freckles had all but disappeared and the carroty hair that had been so wild and brazen in her youth had turned darker. It was almost purplish red, echoing the maroon highlights in the taffeta gown she was wearing. Though very small, barely five feet tall, she had a superb figure with a tiny waist. While she wasn't as generous of hip and bosom as was fashionable, she was beautifully proportioned, Portia admitted bitterly.

She and Mary had effectively ignored each other all these years. In a sprawling household, with the child under Nellanor's wing, it had been relatively easy. Portia had left

Mary's education (silly thing to think a girl needed all that book learning) to George and the tutors he'd hired, and whatever domestic instruction was necessary to Nellanor and a governess. All the child's other needs were taken care of by servants. All in all, she had not been nearly the burden Portia had anticipated.

Now, however, this happy arrangement was undergoing changes, and Portia didn't like it one bit. There was the matter of Hester to consider. Until a few years ago, Portia had dominated her. What with governesses and her own lessons in the wifely arts, and the fact that the child was terrified by Nellanor, Portia had been the ruling, indeed the only, force in her daughter's life. But then Hester had "received evidence of her womanhood"—Portia's vocabulary did not include "menstruation," and even "monthly courses" was far too vulgar to utter. One endured such things; one did not mention them.

It had been the beginning of a horrible change in Hester. She had apparently discussed it, actually *talked* about it, with Mary in a rare moment when Portia didn't have a thumb right on the girl. And from this feeble and unsuitable common ground, a bond had begun to form between the girls. They started taking walks together, visiting each other's rooms to talk about clothes, chatting across the table at dinner and altogether behaving like friends.

It was appalling! Portia wasn't a stupid woman and had the sense to realize that forbidding Hester Mary's company would invest the older girl with even more appeal. But Portia didn't know what to do to stop it. If Evelyn had been living, she'd have known how to strangle the friendship before it was born, but Evelyn was gone and Portia had no other support in the household. George positively glowed when he saw the girls together. There was no help there. And Nellanor encouraged their growing closeness at every turn simply because she knew Portia was opposed to it.

Portia convinced herself that two such different personalities as Mary and Hester could not long remain compatible. She gave them a while to get tired of each other, then started putting out a few feelers:

"I'm so glad you got your father's fair coloring, Hester. Violent coloring, red or black hair for example, is so unattractive."

"Oh, but Mama, if only I had beautiful auburn hair like Mary. I would be the happiest girl."

"Try on this ring, dear. You have such lovely long fingers for jewelry."

"I wish I had tiny, dainty hands like Mary."

She decided then that the only way to break it up would be to get rid of Mary. And the only acceptable way of doing that was to marry her off. George objected. "She's far too young to even think about it, Portia. She's just a child."

"A child! George, she's twenty years old. Most girls are married at that age and have children of their own."

"Well, perhaps we could arrange a coming-out season for her," he said. "It would mean staying in London for months."

But when he broached the subject to Mary, she nearly went berserk. "I despise London, Papa. Except for our house and the warehouse on Mincing Lane. You know that. And I positively will not be tarted up in frills and scent and be trotted out for examination like a prize hog carcass on market Tuesday."

George laughed. "You're letting your tongue run away with you again, my dear. Since when does anybody put frills on a hog carcass?"

Mary was undeterred. "The point is that a 'season' is one of the most mortifying, barbaric customs the Western world has ever come up with, second only to slavery. No, Mother will have to find some other way to get me out of her hair."

"Now, Mary, Portia isn't the least eager—"

"Oh, Papa, you dear lovely man," she said, kissing his forehead where the hair was beginning to recede.

So Portia was thwarted again.

Well, if she couldn't haul the girl to London, she'd bring London to Castlemere. Calling in a few of her social credits, she created a steady stream of suitable young men. Not the cream of the crop, naturally; those she was holding in abeyance for Hester in a few months, but there were a good many acceptable second sons bound for nice country vicarages or pleasantly remote army postings. Any one of them would do nicely.

As soon as she got Mary off her hands, she could concentrate on getting Hester ready for the marriage market. And it was going to take some doing, she had to admit. While she complimented her daughter on her fair coloring, she secretly despaired of her generally washed-out look. Hester's hair was an indefinable shade between brown and blond, and no amount of pinching her cheeks could bring up a pink glow, only the occasional disfiguring bruise. Her eyes, though pale, were her best feature. Extremely myopic, she had a dreamy, unfocused look that had a certain appeal. Unfortunately, she insisted on ruining it by wearing ghastly spectacles that magnified her eyes to bugginess and left a dent on the bridge of a nose that threatened to become rather too prominent.

Yes, Mary would be a serious threat to Hester's chances if she weren't gotten out of the way before it was time to start luring in potential husbands for her own daughter. Glancing from one to the other, she could imagine a young man's reaction. Mary was as brilliant and sparkling as a jewel, Hester as lumpy and boring as rock chalk.

Portia hardly took her eyes off Mary during dinner. She really was outrageous—all the animation of voice and expression was downright tiring. And her talk! She never even seemed to pause for breath, unless it was to turn a devastatingly brilliant smile on some unsuspecting soul. The Welbourne twins—the vicarage and the army in one family—were nearly drooling in their custard. That wouldn't do. She didn't claim to understand the girl, but she knew her well enough to grasp that gaping adoration didn't appeal to her.

But Jamison Hewitt—now, that was a different matter entirely. A devilishly handsome specimen with a strong jaw, thick sandy-blond hair, and eyebrows always arched in amusement, he was leaning back negligently, watching Mary with an amused detachment. He apparently found her attractive, but wasn't overwhelmed by her. A nice balance. And he was a little older than the others, old enough to rein in a headstrong girl like this one.

"I do believe you're making that up," he was saying to her now with a grin. She'd been telling some asinine story about collecting hen's eggs and being attacked by a peahen who thought they were her eggs. Mary's dramatic exaggerations had everyone at the table laughing uproariously. Everyone but Portia.

"Why, Mr. Hewitt, are you calling me a liar at my father's board?" Mary said. It was downright sparkling. Portia flushed with anger. Why wasn't Hester saying anything? And how could she discreetly signal to the girl that she had a dab of custard on her chin?

"I wouldn't dream of calling you anything but the beautiful Miss Beecham—at your father's table, or anywhere else."

Yes, he might do quite well, Portia thought. She reviewed what she knew about him. He was the nephew of the sister of a friend of hers in London. An only child? No, she thought there had been an older brother, or was it sister? Mother dead for years, her friend told her. The father, said to be in very poor health, was a solicitor in London with a decently wealthy practice and some minor bits of property around Canterbury, if she remembered correctly.

The young man himself had taken up the law in a desultory way, and she heard he was considered a bit of a rogue in the city, but to a respectable degree. Parties, cards, racing, a few stories about women (not nice women, of course: that would have been worrisome), but nothing out of the ordinary for a young man of his age and circumstance. Yes, he might be ideal. He was polished enough to cope with Mary's youthful high spirits, poor enough to want to marry into what he might assume was a good portion of Beecham money (time enough later for him to find out how wrong *that* was), and well-bred enough to suit George's exalted ideas of a husband for his adopted daughter.

When the men rejoined the ladies after their port and cigars, Jamison headed straight for Mary, who was sitting by Nellanor talking about birds. Before he could reach her, however, Nellanor made one of her imperious demands and Mary crossed the room to fetch her a fan. As Mary was obediently rummaging in a drawer in the cherrywood occasional table Nellanor favored for depositing her possessions, Portia noticed the older woman rise.

"I think I'll go to my room, I'm not feel—"

And with that, Nellanor collapsed, joint by cracking joint, into a brittle heap.

After all the guests had tactfully departed, Jonathan Engle told the family that Nellanor was almost certainly dead before she got to the floor. He meant it as a comforting thought, that she had not suffered for more than a fraction of a second.

But Mary found no comfort in his remarks; there was no comfort to be had. She'd known, given Nellanor's great age, that she wouldn't have her forever, but she'd always imagined that there would be time for last words and loving reassurances. Death should have escorted Nellanor from this life with measured steps, with dignity, and in privacy.

As Ginger sat in the windowsill, eerily howling his own

feline grief, Mary and Agnes bathed the bony, wrinkled body and dressed it for burial in her favorite blue dress. It was a sturdy, shabby garment and Portia objected. "It's not fitting to meet her Maker in such a dress. She had lovely things she hardly ever wore."

Fixing her with a direct gaze that Portia found bold and disconcerting, Mary stood her ground. "This is Aunt Nell's climbing dress, the one she wore when we went birding or down the cliffs to the beach. God knows her in this dress."

Portia shrugged. Under six feet of earth for eternity, what did it matter? She was finding it difficult to conceal the sense of victory she was feeling. She had finally beaten the old woman, with years as her only weapon. Though Portia did all the dreary everyday duties of running a household, the firing and hiring of staff, planning menus, supervising cleaning, and sorting out of domestic squabbles, the family and staff had always regarded Nellanor as the mistress of the house. Now, at last, Portia could take her rightful role, if only by default.

George disappeared into the map room and was hardly seen until the funeral. He was shocked at the sense of loss he felt. It was even worse than when he lost his own parents. He'd known how much he loved Nellanor, but he'd never imagined how gigantic an empty space her passing would make in his days.

But his sorrow was nothing to Mary's. She loved George and depended on him for the big important things in life, the sweeping philosophy, the sense of love and security. But Nellanor was her everyday mainstay, the one who fixed her braids, told her the facts of life, bandaged her cuts, berated her lapses in manners, laughed at her jokes, and clipped burrs out of her cat's fur. When she was sick or scared or bored, she went to Nellanor, who comforted, explained, or bullied her, according to her needs.

Never again to hear her imitate a bird call or sing a slightly bawdy song just to see Portia sputter? Never see those brown-spotted spidery hands baiting a fishhook or threading a needle?

Mary was dry-eyed and bossy at the funeral. Her color was high and her disdain awesome when the vicar, who was new to the neighborhood and might have been forgiven his ignorance, compared Nellanor to a lamb going home to her Lord. The evening of the funeral, however, Mary disappeared.

George found her much later, dressed in the ratty hand-

me-down trousers and shirt of his that she wore fishing with
Nellanor. Stroking the orange cat on her lap, she was sitting
by a driftwood fire she'd built on the beach. He sat down
next to her without a word, and held her while she cried.

George started talking about Singapore a week later. Nellanor
had left some money and the deed to a piece of property in
America to her grandson, Alex. Her father had bought it to
grow pepper on before she was born. When pepper wouldn't
grow there, he converted it to tobacco. When he died,
Nellanor's advisers had put it in the hands of a series of
overseers and she had continued the practice all her life.
She'd never seen the land she left Alex. All the rest of her
belongings—money, books, jewelry—she left to Mary.

"I think we ought to consider that trip to Singapore we've
always talked about," George said at breakfast one day
shortly after the reading of her will. "I hate for Alex to
receive nothing but a letter and paperwork regarding her
death. After all, she was his grandmother and we're his
family and it seems very cold and unfeeling."

A week later, he brought up an article he'd read about
the Suez Canal. "They say it's a miracle of engineering and
takes months off the trip to the East. We could be gone the
length of time it used to take and have much more of it in
visiting instead of getting there and back."

Then, a few days later: "The girls will be married and
gone in no time. If we're ever to take them, it ought to be
soon."

Hester loved the idea. Having only recently discovered
that life had horizons beyond her mother's rigid sphere, she
was eager to go anywhere. "Sampling life," she called it. A
favorite phrase of Mary's from a book they'd read together.

Mary said nothing. She wanted to go for several reasons.
Her curiosity was the primary one; she had studied that part
of the world for nearly all her life. In George's map room
she'd learned the names, configurations, and facts about all
the islands where spices were grown or transported, and
naturally she longed to see them with her own eyes. A long,
interesting journey would also help take her mind off how
much she missed Nellanor, and best of all, it might effectively divert Portia from her maddening attempts to marry
her off.

On the other hand, she dreaded seeing Cousin Alex. It

was heartbreaking enough to know he was married and a
father without having to witness the proof.

George received unexpected support, however, from Portia on his third attempt to interest the family in his scheme.
When she had married George, she had brought her own
family's smaller spice concern under the Beecham standard.
Wouldn't it be lovely if Hester were to bring in another?
And what better place to make the social contacts that
would lay the groundwork than in Singapore? Most young
men preparing to go into the business served their apprenticeship there.

In January George wrote to Alex of their intentions and
started making plans in earnest. In April they went to Southampton, where they would stay with a cousin of Portia's for
a week before sailing. As they stepped through the front
door of the cousin's house, Portia caught her heel in a throw
rug, tumbled over a table, and broke her leg.

Portia had hysterics; the cousin fainted twice while the
doctor was splinting the leg; Hester couldn't stop crying.
Even George, despairing at their behavior and the wreck of
his plans, so far forgot himself as to shout at the physician.
Only Mary was calm. She took it as a sign from God, the
exact interpretation of which wasn't quite clear yet, but
would be in good time. Perhaps it was merely that she'd be
spared seeing Alex and having to confront, once and for all,
the truth of how her silly hopes had been crushed.

By the next morning, however, Portia had it all figured
out. She sat up in bed thinking about the situation, and the
pieces of her reasoning fell together in a lovely pattern.
She'd never wanted to go to Singapore anyway. Having
been there once as a girl of twelve with an aunt who wanted
a young companion for the journey, she had a vivid recollection of the aimless, petty existence of women in colonial
society, the hideous heat, the endless sickening ocean voyage, and most of all, the wealth of disgusting creatures that
lived in the tropics. The whole point in agreeing to the trip
had been to have Hester make a debut, and Hester could do
that under her father's supervision.

Portia adjusted her frilly new bed jacket, took a sip of her
tea, and considered. He wouldn't do it as well as she, of
course, but she had to weigh against that the fact that
sending them out would spare her the trip (with an excellent
excuse) and would keep George happy. If he didn't get to
go, he wouldn't be fit to live with. In addition, she'd have

that irritating Mary out of her life for the duration and could go back to Castlemere and get the domestic staff whipped into shape to suit her without any interference.

George was unable to put up anything more than a token resistance to the idea of leaving her behind. He'd suspected all along that she wasn't going to be a good traveling companion, and without her, he wouldn't have to become involved in half the entertainments she would have expected.

Informed of the second reversal of their plans, Mary was bewildered. If God was going to give her signs, she wished He'd make up His mind.

By the time the big steamer pulled into the Channel, she had it sorted out. Alex had probably become portly and potbellied and thoroughly colonial in outlook—this prejudice she'd unwittingly absorbed from Portia. He would certainly be graying at the temples by now, and have taken up drinking, which would blotch that fine skin. Yes, this was probably The Reason for the trip. She would surely come home completely cured of her infatuation.

13

George hated the voyage.

As a boy he'd made the trip to Singapore on a China tea clipper. Clippers had been lofty, elegant sailing vessels. It was said that a perfectly rigged clipper could catch and propel itself on a breeze so slight it wouldn't put out a candle on deck. A trip aboard one meant months at sea, with plenty for a boy to watch in the daytime as uniformed sailors scampered like monkeys in the flapping, snapping sails, and silences at night so profound you could hear your own heart beat. To travel on a clipper was to live for a timeless space in a sea world unlike anything on land. A China clipper was a work of art as much as a mode of transportation.

But with the opening of the Suez Canal, the clippers had all but disappeared. Tall, deep-draft sailing vessels couldn't negotiate the canal, and as carriers of goods from the Far East, the clippers became, almost overnight, financial dinosaurs, their effective range having shrunk to only a part of the globe.

Their place was taken by squatty, shallow-draft steamers—immense broad-shouldered bullies of the ocean that could shove their way through calm or turbulent seas with equal ease. It took only weeks instead of months to reach Singapore, and George hated every hour of it. The steamer was a vast, noisy machine; its terrible mechanical heartbeat thumped and pounded ceaselessly. It was felt in the ears, the brain, the soles of the feet. The crystal drops on chandeliers vibrated hectically; the sound made ripples on drink surfaces; it made the high C on the piano in the first-class lounge whine in sympathy. It frayed George's nerves; he found himself involuntarily tapping his foot or nodding slightly to the inescapable, penetrating rhythm.

Worse, it stank. The faintly salty, fishy odor of sea was gone, replaced by an oily, sooty stench whenever the wind was to their backs. The fresh green scent that told them land was near, even if it wasn't visible, was no longer discernible. And there wasn't anything interesting to watch. Those who worked the ship now sweated and strained in the ship's bowels, feeding its ravenous furnaces. No lithe sailors swarmed the complicated maze of ropes and canvas; the delicious, brisk sense of urgency when an order was given and the deck burst into life was gone.

It all made George feel old and cranky. It was as if a memory had been blighted, a childhood treasure stolen and vandalized. This wasn't "sailing"—this was just getting from one place to another in a machine. It was as different as riding an aristocratic stallion in a race was from riding a clunky donkey to market. He had let his attention wander for a few years, and when he looked back, an era had ended without giving him a chance to bid it a proper farewell. And to think he'd taken such enthusiastic interest in the completion of the Suez a few years ago.

Of course, as a spice merchant (and George never forgot that role), he was still delighted. The only event in the last eight hundred years that could compare in benefits to the English spice trade was the French theft of clove seedlings from the Dutch in 1770. The shorter, faster route through the Suez meant spices got to England weeks fresher, the cost of transportation dropped significantly; mildew and salt-water damage were now merely an occasional nuisance, not a devastatingly frequent fear. But why did there have to be such an awful loss of beauty and elegance for those benefits?

The rest of the family party was miserable enough in other ways, and so failed to notice his discontent. George's valet turned greenish before the engines ever started up and became so ill he had to be under the ship doctor's care. Hester was ill, though not alarmingly so, nearly the whole journey. Her governess was afflicted too. The lady's maid who was to attend both Hester and Mary was called into service nursing the two of them. George's clerk was busy most of the time in his cabin preparing the list of planters and plantations George wished to visit, and his secretary spent his time going over a tottering stack of ledgers George had brought along to have rechecked and summarized.

George was not only unhappy but also downright lonesome. It wasn't his habit to strike up friendships with strangers. He wasn't shy by any means, he just hadn't the patience it took to get through all the preliminaries of getting to know people. So often it was such a waste when one discovered the effort had been spent on a bore.

The only one who should have been free to share George's company was Mary. But he had seen little of her during the journey. She wasn't seasick; in fact she seemed to be thriving, her color good, her step as brisk and confident as on dry land. But she was withdrawn, always reading a book, or leaning on a rail staring out to sea, or pacing the deck as if she had a destination. At first he thought it might be because the maid who looked after her at home, Agnes, had refused to come along, claiming she'd rather die than face the sea. But when he asked her about missing Agnes, she looked at him as if he'd lost his mind. In fact, the few times George approached her and tried to talk about the journey, she was snappish, and once even told him to stop whining.

"Oh, Papa, I'm sorry," she said, seeing the hurt look in his eyes. "That was horrid of me to say. I didn't mean to speak so rudely. It's just that I can't help it that you're not liking the ship, and I have things on my mind as well."

"What kind of things, Mary?"

She opened her mouth, then shut it again, thinking better of how a confession of her own might sound. "Very silly things, Papa," she replied, putting her arm through his and leaning her head against his shoulder. "Partly I'm missing Aunt Nell. Aren't you?"

"A great deal."

"She'd have liked this. She'd have been striding around the deck knocking over the slow walkers, disrupting the sissy shuffleboard games, telling the seasick passengers there isn't any such thing as *mal de mer*, demanding that God send her some weather that was a real challenge."

"That she would!" George laughed. "And what about you?"

She looked up at him, her eyes sparkling. "I'd give my best pair of stays and second-best pantaloons for a good storm! I'd lash down the luggage, tie Hester into her bunk, secure myself to a sturdy rope, and stand out here daring the waves to wash over the deck. Wouldn't it be thrilling! Just try to get me, storm! I defy you!"

She'd spoken loudly, and two perambulating ladies stopped and stared at her with disapproval. "I'm so sorry," Mary said to them. "I was just recounting to my father what happened once when the ship I was on was attacked by pirates in the midst of a typhoon. Just a day or so from here, it was. Yes, it was awful, but my sister and I managed to get a gun away from the pirate captain, and we tied him up. Of course, she was terribly disfigured later when she got in front of a cannon as it fired, but . . . well, we survived, and that's all that counts."

The ladies gasped with horror.

When they had scurried away, no doubt to lock themselves in their cabin for the duration, with letter openers at the ready to defend themselves, George did what he could to reprimand Mary, but it was ruined because he kept laughing. "The poor things will probably be terrified the rest of the way out and back."

"Nonsense, Papa. They loved it. Besides, they were eavesdropping on a conversation that was none of their business. They deserved to get their ears full."

"Now, you know your mother wouldn't approve of that kind of reasoning," George said, still trying to do his best by the absent Portia.

"No, but Aunt Nell would have. Why are you smiling?"

George laced his fingers together with Mary's and looked out to sea, grinning. "I was just remembering: once, when I was just old enough to be allowed to eat with the adults, I sneaked my dog into the dining room and hid him under the table, planning to feed him everything I didn't want. He got away from me, however, and started wandering around underneath, bumping into people and alarming them. Aunt Nell came to my rescue. She told everybody that her digestion was absolutely ruined if her feet became overheated while she was eating. That, she said, was why she had a blackamoor under the table fanning her feet. I was taking a drink of water as she said it and I laughed it up my nose and was sent from the table in disgrace, but less disgrace than I would have been in if the dog had been revealed. I'll never forget the look on my mother's face when Nellanor launched into the story. She couldn't have looked more surprised if she'd been told there was a crocodile under the table."

"Oh, Papa, I do miss her so terribly! Don't you?"

"Well, I've got you instead."

Mary said, "Whatever do you mean by that?"

They first sighted Singapore harbor at ten in the morning. They'd been passing miles and miles of the Malay Peninsula —so lush and green it was impossible to believe that humans could penetrate it and live without constantly fighting the growth. But for the last hour or more, the water had become nearly as dense as the land. Ships and more ships passed or sailed alongside with progressively closer spacing. When they finally heaved into sight of the city, George, again standing at the rail with Mary, was astonished. "I wouldn't know it was the same place! It was a busy harbor when I was here last, but this . . . this is simply unbelievable!"

The captain had heard his exclamation and joined them. "It's an astonishing sight, isn't it, Mr. Beecham? It'll take us a while to ease through. We probably won't dock for a good two hours or more. Miss Beecham, have you ever seen the like?"

"I certainly have not, Captain Woodson. How do they keep from running over all the little boats?"

"It's the job of the little boats to keep out of the way."

"To whom do they belong? What are they called?"

"They belong to all sorts of Asian people mostly, Miss Beecham. The steamers are almost entirely European. There are sampans and junks. Sampans often carry passengers and luggage. That flat barge is called a *tongkang* and conveys heavier loads. Those belong to South Indians called Klings. See the ladder-masted boats? Those are characteristic of the Bugis—a Malayan people. Also that one—a *prahu*—it'll be watched very carefully by the authorities. They are often pirate vessels."

"Pirates? You mean there really are pirates? I thought they were only in books."

"Indeed there are. There are whole islands and tribes hereabouts who have been pirates for years, for centuries in fact. It's their economy. These are rich and therefore very dangerous waters."

Mary stared at George with surprise and mouthed, "Pirates?"

The captain, pleased to have an audience, was going on: "Over there are many of the clippers that are still making the Hong Kong–Singapore–Australia run. That huge spiderweb of masts and spars and rigging is something to remember, Miss Beecham. By the time you have grandchildren, there won't be any such things as tea clippers. There's hardly a kind or nationality of floating vessel that hasn't been here. In fact, not long ago a Confederate cruiser called here after sinking three American ships nearby."

George and the captain fell into a technical discussion of tonnage entering and leaving port and freight comparisons of various lines. Mary simply gawked. How did so many vessels manage to get around such a place without scraping each other's sides? As they edged ever closer to their berth, it became virtually impossible to see water at all except by leaning over the rail and looking straight down. There must be a system to it, or a referee who was visible to all but her, or there would be constant catastrophe. But the captain himself seemed unconcerned.

Mary became uneasy. It was a touch of claustrophobia, reminiscent of her first trip to London with George and Nellanor. The heat was also a factor. Throughout the trip, it had grown steadily hotter. But at sea there had always been a breath of wind. Now, rocking gently in the crowded harbor, the smell of land and people and cooking drifted out to them, mingled with the humid air, and lay like a stinking blanket. Someone was cooking on a small boat that was lolling beside them, and the smell of cooked pork and hot peanut oil was overwhelming. Mary was uncomfortably aware of her stays, her camisole, her petticoats, hose, and heavy dress—and the gentle, sickening rocking of the ship. Maybe there was such a thing as seasickness after all. Feeling smothered and wishing to take her mind off herself, she said to her father and the captain, "I must see that the others are getting ready. Will you excuse me?"

"Come back in time to meet your cousin when we dock, Mary," George reminded her.

That was the last thing she wanted to hear. "I will if I can, Papa, but I must take care of Hester."

It turned out to be far more of a job than she'd anticipated, and she was spared having to make any decision about joining her father. Hester had lost an earring, a gift from Portia the previous Christmas. She, the governess, and the maid were all searching frantically. Everything that had been packed was being unpacked to look for the jewelry. "I was sure I saw you put it in the blue case," the governess said.

"Such a thing would never be packed in the blue case, madam," the lady's maid said haughtily. "Unless, of course, you wish to question my system?"

"I am merely questioning your memory!" the governess snapped.

Hester started crying. "I'll never get an exact match made! Mama will be furious at my breaking the set! Oh, dear, how will I ever explain?"

The tiny cabin was the temperature, and approximate size, of an oven. Mary watched in consternation as the servants rummaged, complained, cast aspersions on each other's upbringing, and bumped bustles against each other and the furniture. Mary listened to the whimpering and the bickering and even attempted halfheartedly to help them for a while. It grew hotter and hotter and the crying and criticisms grew nastier and her stomach got touchier.

"Mama will never forgive me for ruining the set by losing one," Hester sobbed.

Finally Mary could stand it no longer. She clapped her hands loudly, palms cupped, and virtually screamed, "Stop it! All of you! Absolute silence."

"Really, Miss Mary, I hardly think—" the governess began.

"That's the problem. All of you are 'hardly thinking.' I can solve this. Hester, give me the other earring."

Hester, wondering what sort of mysterious means Mary meant to employ, unfastened it and handed it to her sister, expecting magic.

Before anyone could say another word, Mary flung the earring out the porthole and said with satisfaction, "Now they're both gone, so the set isn't broken."

"Mary!" Hester wailed.

"Be sensible, Hester. Mama won't ever notice. We'll have new ones made here. This is where pearls come from. Now, pack as quickly as you can."

The three of them were stunned into complete silence and obedience by her sudden air of command and her absurd logic. They fell to packing as if she were holding a pistol on them.

The steamship had been docked for a quarter-hour when Mary finally ventured on deck. Approaching the rail with care, she looked about, trying to spot George. She'd misjudged how long it took to secure the vessel. All the passengers were still on board. George joined her. "Do you see Alex? Oh, there he is—see him?"

Mary looked where he was pointing. Alex was waving at George.

She had really wanted him to be fat and sloppy and middle-aged, with his fine bronze skin blotched and pasty. She was sure that that was why God had caused this trip to happen in spite of all the obstacles. She'd come to regard it as almost a promise. But Alex was broader-shouldered, slimmer-hipped, and more tanned than ever. His black hair glistened in the brutal tropical sun.

Mary turned away, looked up, and muttered furiously, "Well, You've dragged me halfway around the world, God. Just what have You got in mind?"

"Come along, Mary."

"No, you go on. I've got to make sure Hester is ready."

"No need. I'll send my clerk for her."

There was no escape. Mary felt a rising sense of panic. What if she simply refused to disembark? She could run back to her cabin and lock herself in—no, of course she couldn't. She had to see this out.

It took some time to make their way to where Alex stood waiting. Seeming not even to notice Mary, he shook George's hand enthusiastically and said, *"Selamat datang, tuan abang!"* That means Welcome, honored elder brother."

George was flattered that Alex thought of him more as a brother than an uncle. "How do I reply?"

"You could say, *'Saya tidak menggerti bahasa malay.'* which means, 'I don't understand Malay,' or you could say, *'Sama-sama, 'adik,'* which means, 'Thank you, younger brother.'"

"Then *Sama sama, adik.* You're looking well, Alex. The tropics agree with you."

George had completely forgotten Mary, understandably enough, as she'd slunk around behind him. The two men exclaimed and clapped each other on the shoulders and shook hands again. Finally George grabbed Mary's hand and dragged her forward. "You remember Mary, of course."

Alex stared at her for a long moment in obvious surprise and appreciation.

"This . . . *this* beautiful young woman is Mary? Why, you were just a child the last time I saw you. Anjanette will think I've lost my mind. I've told her all about all of you, but I had no way of describing Mary adequately, I see now."

"Is Anjanette with you?" George asked.

Mary was glad to be spared the necessity of making conversation. Part of her was giddy to the point of speechlessness by his flattery, another part huffy that he was so very surprised. He must have entirely forgotten her to carry on so much about the change. She hadn't changed that much, had she? Most of all, she was practically feverish from his having taken her hand. She knew she was being a fool and couldn't seem to help herself.

"No, Anjanette is home. I didn't want to expose her to all the noise and jostling. She's with child again."

"Alex, how wonderful. Congratulations! You're building a family so quickly I'll soon lose track," George said.

With child again, Mary thought bitterly. This was too horrid to endure. "I'm going to see what's keeping Hester," she said, turning on her heel.

She didn't see Alex again for an hour. When the baggage was all identified and piled onto a cart to be taken to Alex's house and the servants had been dispatched in a hired carriage, the family was escorted to Alex's own carriage.

As they were ready to get in, George spotted someone he knew. "Had no idea he was here. I'll just have a quick word with him. Hester, come along. You know his daughter, he'll want to meet you."

Mary and Alex were left alone—or as much alone as was possible in the crowd. "I see you made it safely," he said, smiling. "You didn't fall off the boat this time."

It took her a moment to remember. "Oh, yes. The fishing trip. I never thanked you for saving my reputation with Aunt Nell. What a silly child I was. I don't know how you endured me."

"Not silly. You were very interesting. And now you're not only interesting but also quite beautiful besides. I can't quite believe yet that this is really you. George must be fighting off your suitors with a stick!"

Mary didn't know what to say. She was pleased, of course, but sorry in a way. It would be a lot easier to get over him—as she was determined to do—if he weren't nice to her. And so flattering. She couldn't claim to know the workings of his mind, but she was quite certain he hadn't meant what he said as an idle compliment.

"Fine pair of bays, Alex," George said, rejoining them.

"Thanks, George. I keep ten horses, six in Penang, four

here. But I rotate them. City use is hard on them. Here, Hester, sit by me so I can sit facing your father."

Hester, still weak from the journey, all but collapsed against him. She could just as well have sat by George, Mary thought—and realized how very cranky she was being. As the carriage began to roll slowly through the crowd, she chided herself. This attitude was impossible. They were going to be here for a long time, probably four or five months altogether. She just couldn't make herself miserable for such an extended time.

She took a deep breath and launched into being polite. "I heard you speaking Malay to my father, Cousin Alex. Do you really know the language, or just a few phrases?"

"About halfway between. I know enough to converse for a short time or instruct the servants. This is the most cosmopolitan city in the world; it's necessary to speak several languages if you're going to do business. I speak Dutch because my wife and her people are Dutch, though we use English at home to each other, and Malay to the staff. I also speak a little Mandarin and Hokkien. You can hardly do business in Singapore without them, unless you have a full-time interpreter as a permanent shadow."

"What are Mandarin and Hokkien?" Hester asked.

"They're Chinese languages. The two most common of many. You see, this is primarily a Chinese city, but a very odd one. There's an enormous lower class of Chinese, coolie labor brought in over the decades, and there is a very elite upper class of Chinese, the traders with whom we deal, but not much of anybody in between. There's also a large Indian community—Tamils, Sikhs, Bengalis, Pashtuns, Parsees—who have the same strange imbalance, though many of the relatively upper classes of Indians are in civil positions like the police and government administration. If you look around, you'll notice that the Chinese and Indians are almost all males. They consider Singapore and all of the Peninsula a place to go to make money or pay off a debt. Then they go home. They don't bring their families. It causes many problems."

He was addressing his remarks to Mary, and for a moment she had the feeling they might as well have been alone in the carriage together.

"Like the *kongsis*," George put in.

"Who are *kongsis*?" Mary asked. In spite of everything,

she was fascinated. She'd thought herself remarkably well-informed about Singapore before coming here. Too smug by half, Nellanor would have said. But her books and maps hadn't taught her any of this.

"A *kongsi* isn't a who, it's a what," Alex explained. "They're Chinese secret societies, based on language, primarily. But it's more than just a club; it's also a subgovernment, a religious affiliation, a militia, and a huge extended family. A *kongsi* takes the place of virtually everything the Chinese have left behind in China, and they're fiercely loyal, fanatic really, to them. Unfortunately, in the name of loyalty, they've become very warlike. They're constantly battling among themselves, and there are terrible riots from time to time."

Hester was looking pale and cringing away from the sight of the many Oriental faces on the streets they were traversing. "They aren't much danger to Europeans," George reassured her. "Except I understand they occasionally make threats against the European Catholics because they think Catholicism is a rival *kongsi.*"

"I don't think I feel well . . ." Hester said.

"You're tired from the journey. I'm taking you all straight home to rest. We'll have plenty of time to see the city," Alex said. He glanced from Hester to Mary, including her in this assessment of their namby-pambiness—as Mary saw it.

"I'm not the least tired," Mary said. "I adore travel."

George and Alex both smiled. She was pale and wobbly and her voice wasn't nearly as firm as she'd hoped.

They didn't know that her stomach was being distinctly troublesome as well. She was sure she just needed a little food and perhaps the tiniest nap and she'd be ready to see Singapore. She looked at Alex and found that his gaze was already on her. He smiled as their eyes met. Had he been watching her for long? And if so, why? He didn't seem to be staring at Hester or George.

They were leaving the city, rolling now at a good pace along a road that ran through the section where the English and Dutch lived. Mary made herself turn and look at the area they were passing, but she could still imagine that she felt Alex's eyes on her. Stop it! she told herself. You're just thinking he's interested in you because you want to think so. That's what Nellanor would have told her if she'd been there to see her acting so stupid. Mary looked back for a

second. He *was* looking at her! Pay attention to the
scenery, she ordered herself.

The houses they were passing were painfully European,
and were all set on generous lots and surrounded by lush
gardens. There were hedges of rhododendrons, thick lawns,
graceful coconut palms. "A monkey!" Hester exclaimed.

"They're as common as cats here," Alex said. "Some of
them are kept as workers, as well. They're trained to climb
up and get the fruits out of tall trees."

Mary laughed. "Imagine trying to train Ginger to do
anything!"

"I'd start with training him not to do a few nasty things,"
George said.

"Oh, Papa, could I have a monkey for a pet?" Hester
asked, brightening for the first time in weeks.

"Well, I don't know . . ."

Mary hoped he'd refuse. She didn't like monkeys. They
seemed too much like odd little almost-people. She found
them unnerving. Besides, she was missing her own pet. She
had wanted to bring Ginger along, but George had convinced her the journey would be too hard on him. He
was too old, and used to a pampered life with nothing
more strenuous than occasionally interrupting a nap to
get petted or brushed or to make a mess in a fireplace.

Mary leaned back, fighting off sleep. The gentle rock of
the carriage was so soothing . . . she kept letting her eyes
close for slightly longer intervals when she blinked. George
and Alex were talking steadily, something about harbor
boundaries land reclamation, and the words washed over
her. She wanted to be bright and alert when she met the
hateful woman who'd tricked Alex into marriage—for there
was no doubt in her mind that it was a vicious trick—but she
couldn't seem to keep her head upright.

She was jolted awake by Hester reaching over and shaking her arm. "We're here, Mary. Wake up."

"I *wasn't* asleep," she snapped. "Just resting my eyes
from the sun."

They were going up a long gravel drive with circular
patterns raked in the surface. She glanced back and noticed
that a small dark man in white trousers and shirt was already out on the drive fixing the damage their passage had
done.

The house was large, brick, and surrounded with wide,
shaded porches. As the carriage stopped and Alex started

helping them out, a tall, stately blond woman came down the steps. She had her hair in a thick rope around her head and wore a dove-gray dress with a high collar. A majestic, if not particularly pretty woman, Mary thought fleetingly as she struggled to step down without tripping on her skirts. A housekeeper, perhaps.

"Welcome to Singapore," the woman said in a voice that was soft and husky and very slightly accented. "I'm glad you weren't delayed. So often the sailing schedule is merely wishful thinking."

Alex was no longer looking at Mary. His whole attention was on the woman who'd just spoken. "George, allow me to introduce my wife, Anjanette," he said, taking the woman's hand and gently pulling her forward.

14

"Shame on you, Alex, for not telling me what beautiful young ladies your cousins are," Anjanette Beecham said. She spoke quietly and with deliberation, as if she weren't absolutely certain of the language. In spite of this, there was enormous warmth and sincerity in her voice.

She stepped forward and took Mary's and Hester's arms and led them up the steps. "I knew I'd like them, but I had no idea what an ornamentation to our home they would be. You must be Hester. Welcome, dear. Such lovely hands you have. Perfect for jewelry. And, Mary—your hair. Alex said it was red, but I've never seen a more arresting color. You make me very envious. Come along, girls. Your servants are already here. They've unpacked your things and been shown to their quarters . . ."

On a wave of friendly greetings, she swept Mary and Hester into the house, leaving George and Alex behind. Inside, the walls were white and cool. The rooms were enormous, and most were divided with hinged silk screens instead of walls. Mary immediately noticed one painting, a faded old watercolor of Castlemere, hung in a place of prominence. "It's a little confusing at first—sometimes a wall is in a different position from week to week," Anjanette was continuing in her soft, soothing voice. "Using movable walls is something of an Eastern mode, I assume. Most of our European visitors find it a bit disconcerting for a while, but quickly adjust. In a day or two I hope you'll feel like this is your home. I promise I won't move anything until you're settled in."

Hester paused, putting a hand to the only solid doorframe near her. "I'm so warm . . ."

"I know you are, darling. I've a lovely cool room ready

for you and the adjoining one for Mary. Come along and get those hot clothes off. Normally we'd be having tea now, but I'll have it sent to your rooms instead, so you may rest until dinner. We eat quite late, when the worst of the heat is over." As she was speaking, a young Indian woman clad in a sari came in carrying a bouncy, sturdy little girl nearly eighteen months old. She had white-blond hair. "Oh, this is our Katie. She is most anxious to see you—aren't you, love?"

Both girls spoke briefly to Katie, who regarded them with owlish curiosity and jabbered an incomprehensible greeting. Then Anjanette smilingly dismissed the ayah and child and they went upstairs and entered a lovely long room with tall windows across the whole length. They were shaded now with more screens. These were gauzy and painted with serene landscape designs. They were arranged to slide across the windows. Halfway along the room a partition divided it into two areas so that each had privacy, but the airy, open impression remained. Low beds were canopied in fine white netting to protect against mosquitoes. The floor was covered with deep blue carpet with a green pattern. It was a very restful room.

Summoning a native maid in liltingly spoken Malay, Anjanette saw to their every comfort with a minimum of fuss. Her soft voice, her gliding movements, her very presence was enormously soothing. "I'll leave you now to see that your father is settled. Please rest. The heat is so difficult at first for Europeans. When dinner is ready, you may join us downstairs or have it on a tray here, whichever you prefer. Just send a note by the maid. We call her Susu."

The tiny, sprightly woman, her dark hair skinned into a tiny bun at the very top of her head, nodded and pointed to herself. *"Nama saya Susu."*

Anjanette leaned forward and whispered. "It means 'milk,' and we've never known if it's really her name or just what she was asking for when she came to the door."

Mary smiled at Susu and pointed to herself. *"Nama . . . saya . . .* Mary Beecham."

"Very good," Anjanette said. "By the way, the fruit is here more for decoration than nourishment." She gestured to a large crystal bowl filled with a variety of remarkable fruits. "I would advise against trying it until you are most accustomed to the food here. I hated to remove it. The colors are so lovely."

"Don't worry," Mary said. "I have an iron digestion."

"You'll need it, my dear. Hester?"

"I'm not hungry anyway," she said as Susu helped her step out of her dress.

"Very well. I'll send tea up."

Hester was in bed and asleep before Mary could get undressed. Once she was down to her pantaloons and chemise, she dismissed the maid with, *"Sama-sama."*

The tiny woman grinned. *"Selamat tidur*, Marree Beeshum," she said, putting her folded hands beside her cheek to indicate going to sleep.

"Sama-sama, Susu," Mary repeated. She'd have to learn more. It would be extremely difficult to instruct a servant in her needs with a single phrase that meant "thank you."

She picked over the fruit and chose a waxy yellow one with indentations along the length. It was nice of Anjanette to warn them, but she was starving and had always been able to eat anything without ill effects. Mmmm, very sweet, she thought, nibbling it as she went to explore the bathroom. It had white tile flooring, a water closet with wood and brass fittings, and instead of a tub, a huge, flat porcelain basin with a shelf above where a large jar of water stood. Mary supposed a bath meant standing there naked while the maid climbed up and poured from the jar. Not an ideal way of bathing, but better than washing little patches from a washbowl.

She suddenly felt very tired indeed. The slight sense of nausea she'd felt earlier was returning. She climbed into the bed, noting the fresh, spicy scent of the soft white sheets. The laundress must put cinnamon oil in the washwater. What a nice touch for a spice merchant's house, she thought drowsily. Dragging the mosquito netting into place, she put her head down, meaning to think over everything she'd seen. But sleep caught her immediately.

It was dusk when she woke. Hester was shaking her arm. "Mary, what's wrong? Are you having a bad dream? You're whimpering in your sleep."

Mary was rolled into a tight, sweaty ball. She tried to stretch out and couldn't. "My stomach, Hester. It hurts so much—"

"I'll get Anjanette."

"No, Hester, don't," Mary said, too late to stop her

sister. She didn't want Anjanette of all people to see her at her worst. Not only did her stomach hurt, it was making alarming gurgling noises.

In a moment Anjanette was there, pulling aside the netting and helping Mary to sit up. "There, dear. I was afraid of this. I'll bet you weren't sick on the ship. For some reason, the seasick ones seem to have less trouble when they get here. Now, let me help you to the bathroom. I'm afraid you're in for a difficult bout."

They were barely in time. Mary felt as though she were full of boiling acid. Diarrhea and vomiting overcame her in feverish waves. Her skin was scalding and freezing and all her joints hurt so badly she could hardly move. Her throat hurt, her whole torso ached. Her legs were so wobbly she couldn't stand without help.

"There, there, dear, the worst of it is over now," Anjanette finally said. "We'll just clean you up a bit."

Anjanette and the Malay maid Susu took off her sweaty, sticky underwear. Nobody but Aunt Nell and her maid Agnes had ever seen her without her clothes before, and normally she would have been mortified. But she was too sick to care. Anjanette helped hold her upright while the maid poured cool water over her. "You're getting wet too," Mary apologized. Anjanette's sleeves and skirt were sopping.

"Yes, it's quite refreshing—is that right, 'refreshing'?—and I'll dry in no time. There, now, you're as fresh as a bunny. Now, wrap up in this sheet and let's put you back into your bed."

Anjanette stayed with her all night. Every time Mary moaned, the older woman was there, not saying much of anything, but helping her to the bathroom or bathing her forehead and shoulders with cool water. Mary kept having a dream of her own mother doing this for her when she was very small. Once she even mumbled, "Mama?" Anjanette patted her hand and laughed in a soft, throaty way.

It was barely dawn when Mary came wide-awake at the sound of a loud *boom*! She sat up suddenly. Anjanette reached under the netting and pressed her back down. "I should have warned you. They fire that cannon from the fort every morning at five. You may get used to it in time. I never have. It startles me every morning."

"I smell awful," Mary said. "I'm disgusting."

"You're just sick. But you'll be fine in a few days."

"What's the matter with me? Am I dying?"

"Heavens, no! But I know you feel like you might be. It's the climate and the water, and I'll bet you ate some of that fruit."

"Just one."

"It takes people that way sometimes. I shouldn't have left it in here."

"How *do* you stand this heat?" Mary asked. She could feel trickles of sweat between her breasts and where her arm had been touching her side. She ought to wash, but she felt faint even reclining. She felt sure she couldn't stand long enough, and the thought of water—or anything else—touching her skin made her shiver.

Anjanette lowered the netting and leaned back in the rocker she'd pulled up to the bed. Seen through the net, she looked pale and fuzzy and rather saintlike. She had a beautiful strong profile. "Everybody who comes here asks me that, and it seems odd. You see, I have nothing else to compare it with, except a few trips upland. I was born in Java—do you know where that is?"

"A big Dutch island to the southwest of here."

"Yes, you're very knowledgeable about geography. All the Beechams seem to be. Alex says you use maps for swaddling clothes. I grew up in Java, as did my father and his father and grandfather before him. The Van Rijns have been there for over a hundred years."

"You've never been back to Europe?"

"Only in a way. My parents took a wedding trip to Amsterdam and I was born on the return trip."

"Don't you ever want to go?" Mary asked. She was already nearly exhausted from the effort of talking for a few minutes.

"Oh, I'll go someday when . . . Never mind. You just rest, dear."

The doctor came at eight and pronounced her to be suffering the consequences of travel and climate. She was to eat nothing for three days but tea and tiny amounts of unseasoned rice. "Perhaps a few ounces of barley water, as well," he said, and smiled at her expression of distaste.

Hester fluttered around her, trying to be helpful, until Mary was driven to faking sleep to escape her ministrations. George called on her, as did Alex, but Anjanette ran them off with news that the patient was feeling better, but wasn't to have her rest disturbed by visitors, however well-meaning.

At midmorning Mary said, "I *am* feeling better. You must rest yourself. I've kept you up all night, and that can't be good for you—and the baby."

"I'm quite accustomed to this sort of thing, my dear child. But I will take your advice. I'll leave the maid with you and I'll come back this afternoon and start teaching you how to talk with her. She understands some English, but pretends not to."

The maid, standing by the door, ducked her head and giggled into her hand.

Mary searched through her memory for what the maid had said yesterday that apparently meant "sleep well." "*Selamat tidur*, Anjanette," she said hesitantly, not at all sure she had it right.

"*Sama-sama*, Mary," Anjanette said. She lifted the netting once more and kissed her lightly on the forehead.

Alex was getting ready to take George into the city to meet some of their growers who were in town when Anjanette came to their room. "You should have told me she was so beautiful, Alex. We'll have to put fences up to keep the young men away!"

"I'm as surprised as you are. I remembered her as a skinny little tomboy with scabs on her elbows and straw in her hair. She was a funny little thing, and that's whom I expected to see. When George introduced her at the wharf, I was dumbfounded. She's stunning, isn't she?"

"Not at the moment," Anjanette said, smiling. "Poor thing. She's such an interesting girl, your Mary."

"My Mary?" he said with a laugh that had an edge to it. "You know, she did have quite a crush on me when I was in England. It was charming, but uncomfortable. I've been rather dreading that aspect of their visit, thinking of her still as that devoted child . . ."

He stopped, apparently deep in thought—a thought that made him frown.

Anjanette sat down at her dressing table and Alex came over and stood behind her as she let down her hair. Leaning forward, he put his hands on her shoulders and nuzzled her neck.

"She is still a child, you know," Anjanette said. "In some ways. And I'd wonder if she were quite sane if she *didn't* still adore you."

"Flattery, flattery," Alex said, smiling at her in the mirror. There was something distinctly uncomfortable about the tone of his voice. "I don't want anybody in love with me but you. You shouldn't have stayed up all night with her. Susu could have watched over her."

"I know, but Susu's a stranger to her and she was so very miserable, poor dear."

Alex started unbuttoning the back of her dress. "You're a stranger to her too."

"I suppose I am. But I don't think she felt that I was."

"No one feels like a stranger with you, Janette. You take a cloud of comfort with you."

She stood up, letting her dress fall past her taut abdomen to the floor, then stepped into his open arms. "Such a poet you are."

He kissed her lingeringly and then said, "George wouldn't mind if I were delayed—"

She stepped back. "Alex, he is our guest! But," she added softly, "perhaps he wouldn't mind if you came home early."

Mary spent several days feeling extremely fragile and hating it. She'd virtually never been ill before except for the unavoidable childhood diseases, and she had no idea how to be a good or sensible patient. Every time she felt better, she was convinced she was well and would leave the bed, only to be nearly brought to her knees with fatigue. She took this as a sign of some moral failing and fought it. She knew she ought to rest, but everybody else was getting to share Alex's company and she couldn't bear being left out.

Her first trip downstairs, four days after their arrival, ended with her almost fainting—a silly thing she'd never done before. "I know she wasn't ready yet," Anjanette said, forcing her to lean over. "It's the lack of real food as well as the sickness. Alex, would you take her back to her room?"

Mary was both embarrassed and thrilled when Alex scooped her up like a child and carried her upstairs. She closed her eyes, trying to memorize the feeling of being in his arms, but felt guilty for even thinking that way. How ugly and disloyal of her. She must learn to see Alex in a different light; he was Anjanette's husband and she'd come to love Anjanette every bit as much as she'd always loved Alex, though in a different way. And if she thought he was holding her more tightly than strictly necessary, well, that was just her imagination working far too hard.

Eventually she did recover, and became aware of the rhythm of the household. They started stirring at the sound of the cannon from Fort Canning. Servants padded softly through the house, bringing hot water to the men for shaving and freshly ironed clothing to everyone. Alex and George went out riding for an hour or two early every morning. The women took an early tea in a latticed bower behind the house. The first morning Mary joined this ritual, she was made aware of an important aspect of life in Singapore that she would never have learned from her books and maps. "I think I'll just stay out here and rest a little longer," she said when Anjanette and Hester got up to go back indoors.

Anjanette glanced around the garden and grounds, which were empty. "No, dear, I think you had better not," she said hesitantly.

"Why not?"

"Well, I don't mean to alarm you both, but you should know. Never stay out here, especially in the early morning or late evening, unless there are servants about. It's the tigers, you see."

"Tigers!" Hester shrieked, and gathered her skirts to bolt indoors.

"We don't see them very often. They don't like people any more than we like them, and they never go into the city, but out here . . . well, there is the occasional incident. If you're sitting quietly by yourself, one of them could wander onto the grounds without being aware of you until it's . . . too late."

"But Papa and Cousin Alex are out there somewhere every morning!" Hester exclaimed. "Won't they get eaten up? How horrid!"

"They're on horseback and they carry guns. They're quite safe, Hester. But nearly every day or so there is a death. Usually workmen on the new roads being built into the jungle."

That was when Mary started to become really aware of the animal and insect life in Singapore. Having grown up under the influence of Nellanor's interest in the natural world, Mary found the variety and density of living things fascinating. The most ubiquitous creature was the little *chichak*, a tiny lizard that was everywhere. One could look up at almost any time and see at least one walking upside down on the ceiling. Occasionally they fell off, and this occurrence reduced Hester to hysteria several times. The servants routinely knocked them down with brooms and killed them, but it was a hopeless task.

"I know they're really harmless and they eat a lot of insects, but they do distress the guests," Anjanette said, picking one up by its tail and casually handing it to Susu to dispose of. Mary suspected that the *chichaks* were ignored when there wasn't company. Except for their disconcerting habit of diving into the soup at dinner, Mary didn't mind them much. She caught one and examined it, but couldn't figure out how its feet could hold on upside down on a smooth surface.

The grounds, too, were alive with creatures: flying lizards and tree lizards and tiny skinks that raced through the grass. Small monkeys shared the trees and shrubs with swifts, swallows, sparrows, and doves, along with the occasional exotically plumed bird Mary didn't recognize. Oh, how Nellanor would have loved this place! she kept thinking.

One morning, while Mary was still lying in bed, listening to the garden sounds of bird calls, crickets, grasshoppers, and the croaking of big bullfrogs that always came out after a rain, she heard human voices raised in alarm. "What's happening out there?" she asked Hester, who was sitting by the window as Susu brushed out her night braids.

"I don't know. The gardeners are all in a bunch, talking and pointing. Oh, here come Papa and Cousin Alex."

Mary joined her at the window. More servants had gathered to watch, and Anjanette was standing just under the window holding the baby, Katie. Alex, carrying a huge, wicked-looking knife with a long blade, approached a clump of bushes. The gardener and one of his assistants followed close behind with hoes raised. Another carried a heavy, flat shovel. Edging around the bushes carefully, Alex peered into the greenery and suddenly lunged with a fierce sideways sweep of the knife.

A chorus of excited voices from the gardeners went up as Alex reached back in and started pulling out a snake so enormous it defied belief. He walked toward the house, still dragging the snake. The gardeners followed, holding up loops of the creature. "This one's twenty-five feet if it's an inch!" he said to Anjanette.

"What in the world is that thing!" Mary called down.

"A python! It's the third one this year, and the biggest yet!" Anjanette replied happily. Alex and Anjanette's daughter had staggered over on sturdy little legs and was chattering with happy animation as she slapped a section of snake.

Hester was leaning back in her chair, the color of farmer's cheese. "I'm never setting foot outside again," she said. The last word was accompanied by a retch as she leapt up and ran for the bathroom.

Mary's eyes were bright, however. If only she'd gotten up earlier, she could have been down there watching from a better vantage point. She threw on her clothes, eager to examine the snake up close before the gardeners disposed of it.

Mary had just started to understand life in Singapore when she learned they were to leave. "We'll be going to Pulau Penang next week," Anjanette told the girls over a light luncheon of prawns and curried rice. They always ate together after a long leisurely morning of letter writing, which seemed to be the primary activity of European women in the East. Mary found letters tedious in the extreme, and had no one she wanted to write to. Everybody she cared to communicate with was here. She spent the time filling page after page of her current diary.

"It's almost time for the clove harvest and Alex likes to be there for as much of the time as he can," Anjanette was going on. "I'm sorry you haven't been here long enough to really meet anyone, but when we return, perhaps you can attend some concerts and entertainments. Your mother will never forgive me if I don't introduce you both to some nice young men."

"Oh!" Mary exclaimed. "That's why—" She stopped.

"That's why what?" Hester asked.

"Nothing. Just a thought," Mary said with a smile. She'd just had an inkling of a possible reason why Portia had been so insistent on her going to Singapore. Portia had thought a suitable husband would turn up and keep Mary in the East forever. She had sent along a letter to Anjanette, and instructions to get Mary married off must have been in it.

"Where's Pulau Penang?" Hester asked Anjanette, disappointed that Mary wouldn't explain what she'd started to say.

"About four hundred miles northwest of Singapore. You passed it on the way here."

"You mean we have to go by boat?"

"Yes, *'pulau'* means 'island.' Singapore's an island too. Didn't you realize? We go everywhere by boat. But just a small boat that hugs the coast. You won't be seasick again," Anjanette assured her.

"Isn't there a road?"

"Oh, I suppose there is. Some tracks through the rain forest up the length of the peninsula. But it would take ages and you wouldn't like it. It's mainly *kampongs*, native villages. All the Europeans there are engaged in tin mining and logging. The main roads all run from inland to the strait, and they're clogged with business traffic."

"No cities at all?"

"Well, there's Malacca and Kuala Lumpur. We could stop at Malacca on the way, or you may go back and visit them for longer if you want to. I think they both have long histories. I'm afraid I'm not too interested in that sort of thing, but Alex is, and he'd take you. Mary, you like history, don't you?"

"Oh, yes," she said. An image of traveling with Alex sprang to her mind and she squelched it. "Will we be seeing more of Papa and Cousin Alex when we go to Penang?" she asked.

Next to her illness, the segregation of the family had been her biggest disappointment. Mary wasn't overly bothered by Singapore's roaches and lizards and snakes; Aunt Nellanor's nature studies had cured her of being finicky. But she hated being excluded. The two men had both been all but invisible except at dinner. They spent the early morning riding, the late morning and midday at Alex's offices, and the late afternoon at some men's club. After dinner the two of them usually retired to port and cigars and card games with business associates Alex invited over.

"Oh, yes. We are all very cozy at Penang. Much less formal."

Late that night Hester crept into Mary's bed, whimpering. "Oh, Mary, can't we just go home? Please ask Papa. He'd do it for you if you asked."

"Hester, why would we want to go home? We've been here only a few weeks."

"I hate it here. I hate the nasty bugs—there was a hairy spider the size of a shilling in the washbasin this morning—

and all those other awful creatures. And I'm always so hot and I've had a headache ever since Suez. I *even* miss Mama!"

Mary put her arm around the younger girl. "But, Hester, you'll never get a trip like this again."

"Thank God!"

Mary laughed. "I mean it. This is all so fascinating. We'll go back and spend the rest of our lives in England. It would be awful to miss learning all we can about this part of the world while we have the chance. Think how interesting it's going to be to see the plantations where the spices are grown! Every time you have custard with a sprinkle of nutmeg on the top, you'll think of how and where it's grown."

"All I'll ever think of is hotness and greenness and crawly things. Oh, Mary, you like all that kind of thing. I don't. You should have been born a boy, the way you love books and maps and birds and things. I don't want to know anything about spices—or birds—except how to use them in cooking when I have a household."

"Is that all you want? To have a household?"

Hester drew back so she could see Mary's face in the soft moonlight filtered through the mosquito netting. "Of course. What else is there to want of life? Don't you want to marry a handsome man and have babies and your own house?"

"My own house? I never thought about living anywhere but Castlemere."

"Oh, Mary, you're the older one and you're being silly. We won't live at Castlemere when we get married. We'll live at our husbands' houses."

"But who *will* live at Castlemere?"

"Mama and Papa, of course."

"But when—?" She cut the words and the thought short. She couldn't contemplate life without George.

"Mary, how many babies do you want to have? I want at least six. Three boys and three girls."

"Leave Castlemere . . . ?"

Hester went back to her bed and was soon sleeping. But Mary was awake for a very long time. She'd never thought about her future in a very real sense. She'd imagined a fairy-tale future many times—what girl didn't? But that misty pink vision had included Alex for as long as she could remember. Now she knew, in her mind if not yet her heart, that wasn't going to be how her future was.

This was the real world, and in this hot green world Alex

had a wife—a fine wife—and a child. Soon there would be two children. This was his world and she was merely a visitor. Before the end of the year she'd be going back to England, back to reality. And she was going to have to face up to the rest of her life and decide what to try to make of it.

That brought her back to Hester's question. What did she want?

Against her will, she started crying. All she wanted was to have Aunt Nell back, to have her happy childhood back, to reclaim her wonderful, stupid belief that Cousin Alex was going to love her when she grew up.

15

Life in Penang was, as Anjanette suggested, very different. Theirs was a working plantation with all the hustle and work that implied. Moreover, instead of undergoing a constant round of social visits, as in Singapore, the Beechams formed a tiny European community of their own most of the time. The family members were the only non-Asians they normally saw. The household staff were Malay, the army of plantation workers Chinese, the overseer and clerks Indian.

Claudius Beecham had purchased the plantation from a Chinese owner with the intention—an intention never revealed to the senior branch of the family—of retiring from Beecham's Fine Spices at the earliest opportunity and becoming an independent grower. Unfortunately for him, the clove blight made this impossible on the very eve of his planned departure from the family's financial bosom.

"I suppose I shouldn't be telling you this, George," Alex said as they wound their way upward from Georgetown along a road bordered by thick tropical growth, "but I don't share my father's aims nor do I love the place as he did. It was to be a bolt hole for him; it's merely a responsibility to me. In fact, had I inherited it in its prime, I believe I would have sold it. As it is, I feel obligated to restore it to its previous value. After all, he invested his life savings—and my inheritance," he added, trying to keep the bitterness out of the voice, "in this venture."

"Will you be able to do so?" George asked, slapping at a fat mosquito on his neck.

"I'm not sure," Alex replied, his face clouding. "We're better off than some of the other English and Dutch planters. Fewer of our trees were destroyed by the blight, but still, bringing the groves back is a long process. We put

156

nearly as much effort into nurturing along the saplings as we do in cultivating and harvesting the mature trees. There's also the problem of my own time. I can't be here very much of the time—don't get me wrong, George, I don't want to be here full-time . . . I like my work for the family business— and leaving the year-in-and-year-out duties to an overseer isn't satisfactory. I've got a good man, but nobody has the incentive I do to make it prosper."

In the carriage following them, Anjanette was explaining some of the same information to Mary and Hester in more domestic terms. "Alex's father always meant to make this a real English plantation, with a European house and grounds. Sadly, it was not to be. You will find the house very strange, I'm afraid. But perhaps you will like it, as I do."

They rounded the last curve as she spoke and Mary was enthralled with the sight that met them. The main house was a huge low structure of whitewashed wood with a palm-leaf roof. Beautifully proportioned, the entire house was built on short stilts and was surrounded by an enormously wide covered porch. In fact, it was more porch than house. There was a serene Oriental air about it. "It's wonderful!" Mary exclaimed.

"Well, it's more practical in many ways than the homes most Europeans have," Anjanette replied. "It is cooler, certainly, but quite primitive. If we were here more often, we would have the jungle cleared back farther and nice gardens planted, but there is never time for that. We work very hard when we are here, then we go away. Almost the only alteration we have made is to have latticework put around the base so Katie can't crawl underneath the house." She was on the verge of mentioning how many snakes and other creatures liked living under the house until she remembered Hester's feelings.

"Work? You as well?" Mary asked. This was more like it. She had quickly come to dislike the lethargic, pointless life the women and girls led in Singapore.

"Yes, everyone. You will help me, perhaps?"

"Gladly. Doing what?"

Anjanette laughed. "You should ask *before* you agree. Hester, are you not well?"

"Just hot," Hester replied weakly.

"You have been taking your quinine and using your mosquito netting, have you not?" Anjanette asked with concern. "It is so important here. Once you have malaria, it can be a lifetime affliction. I cannot send you back to England ill. Your mother has trusted you to my care."

"It's only the motion of the carriage," Hester said, glancing up at the heavy growth around them. Mary felt a flash of sympathy at the way Hester seemed to cringe from the wildness of the place. Though she herself was fascinated by the same quality, she recognized dimly that it frightened Hester, though she couldn't understand why. Too bad she hadn't spent more time with Aunt Nell when they were little. But then, Mary wouldn't have liked sharing the old lady.

"I can smell the cloves!" Mary said.

"Can you really? What a good nose you must have. By midday, everyone can smell them even though all the work areas and godowns are a distance from the house."

"Godowns?" Hester asked.

"Storage sheds," Mary explained automatically before Anjanette could speak. The older woman glanced at her and smiled.

Alex and George's carriage had pulled up and the men were already walking away, looking things over and receiving the overseer's report. Mary was the first out of the ladies' carriage, but was too late to attach herself to her father and cousin. She was forced to spend the rest of the morning unpacking with Anjanette, Hester, and Susu. "When will we be able to go out and see everything?" Mary asked, chafing at this domesticity.

"Not until quite late this afternoon," Anjanette said firmly. "The midday heat is too much to endure." She handed sleeping Katie over to Susu, who'd been with the servants in the wagon behind them. "Make sure she's bathed and powdered, Susu. She's getting a heat rash. The ayah has all her things in a blue valise."

"But Alex and Papa are outside," Mary said.

"They are men," Anjanette replied placidly. "Now, I'm going to bathe and change my clothes. I hope you won't be disappointed, but we are quite informal here. We must, naturally, maintain a certain standard in front of the workers, but none of our European friends will call without sending a message first, so we may relax a few standards. Don't worry. We will go back into town for parties as soon as we are settled and the peak harvest is done."

Mary didn't quite follow her meaning about informality until Anjanette returned an hour later, freshly bathed and attired in a lightweight, loosely fitted dress of pink cotton with white eyelet trim around the neck and three-quarter-length sleeves.

"You're not wearing stays!" Hester exclaimed, lifting her mosquito netting and peering out from the bed where she had been resting.

"You need not follow my example if you would feel uncomfortable," Anjanette assured her.

Mary was fascinated. She'd never seen a lady who actually looked pregnant. Women of the lower orders, yes, but not a lady. Yet there stood Anjanette with her abdomen obviously distended and she didn't even seem embarrassed. Mary suddenly felt very naive; she'd assumed, when she thought of it at all, that ladies didn't swell up like common people when they were with child. But what must Alex think of her this way? How could she risk repulsing him with her ungainly shape? Didn't she care what he thought?

"Oh, you *are* offended," Anjanette said, seeing the perplexed look on Mary's face.

"No, no. I'm not," Mary assured her. "I'm just wondering if I may also wear what I like."

"Of course you may," Anjanette assured her, unaware of what Mary had in mind. "Now, I must see to tea. Susu will serve it on the porch in a few minutes."

When she was gone, Mary threw herself into unpacking the single trunk that had remained untouched throughout the journey. "Mary, you didn't bring those trousers, did you?" Hester exclaimed when the objectionable garments were unearthed. "Mama said you must not."

"Mama isn't here," Mary pointed out, slipping the friendly old trousers on and shaking out the baggy man's shirt she'd secreted in her baggage.

It was with some trepidation, however, that she stepped onto the porch a few minutes later. "Anjanette?" she queried quietly.

The older woman was sitting in a deeply cushioned bamboo chair. A soft white blanket had been spread on the wooden floor and Katie was playing with some colored blocks, talking happily to herself in a mixture of English and assorted other languages. She was wearing only a nappie and a loose white blouse. Her ayah, an Indian girl of about fifteen, was squatting watchfully a few feet away. Anjanette turned and gazed at Mary with obvious surprise, then, astonishingly, began to laugh softly. "This is the Mary Beecham I expected!"

"What do you mean?"

"When Alex told me about you before you came here, he always said what a strange little girl you were, climbing cliffs and trees in your boy's clothes."

"Is it all right if I wear these?" Mary had been prepared to be defiant, but found, to her surprise, that she really wanted Anjanette's approval.

Anjanette considered for a moment. "It is strange garb for an Englishwoman, but if Alex and your father think it is acceptable, so shall I."

When asked that evening, George agreed to Mary's garb, subject to Alex's opinion. "After all, this is your world," he said. "We wouldn't do anything to embarrass you."

"I think it's charming," Alex said. "It makes me feel Nellanor might come striding around the corner of the house any moment." Then, dismissing Mary's wardrobe from his thoughts, he spoke to Anjanette, who had come onto the porch. "Have you rested, Janette?" He gave her a light peck of a kiss in greeting, but Mary noticed that he laid his hand lightly on her abdomen for a fraction of a second and they exchanged very private smiles that made Mary's heart feel like someone had driven a stake through it. He not only wasn't disgusted by his wife's appearance, he seemed to actually like it. It was incomprehensible and it made her feel very young and intrusive and hideously jealous.

The daily schedule was dependent on the climate. Before the sun was even up, the household stirred to life. Early morning was the best time of the day for any physical work that had to be done. They took a light meal, merely tea and fruit. Usually this was repeated in midmorning. Shortly after the noon hour, they all gathered and had a large meal, then retired to their netted beds for a few hours because it was too hot and oppressive to function. The plantation grew very quiet, man's endeavors stilled.

After this rest and another light tea, work was resumed until nearly sunset. Again, retreat was ordered by the climate. Sunset was the worst time for mosquitoes. Instead of napping, quiet indoor activities took place: sewing, letter writing, or menu planning for the women, bookkeeping or reading for the men. Finally, when it was dark, dinner was served and the family spent a few hours together. They talked, read aloud, played cards, and occasionally indulged in silly, old-fashioned parlor games. On rare occasions there were guests, most often neighboring plantation owners who came to smoke cigars and talk business with the men.

On the second day, Mary started accompanying Anjanette on her daily rounds. Though Anjanette was at the Penang plantation only infrequently, she took her role as "Mem" Beecham seriously. "On Tuesdays and Thursdays I visit the neighboring *kampongs*, and on Monday, Wednesday, and Friday I'm available to the plantation people as well as any villagers who wish to come for medical help," she told Mary as they set out for the first round of visits.

Mary had seen herself as being trained for a gracious benevolent role, but it didn't work out quite as she expected. As they neared the closest village, a bevy of small children ran out to greet them. "Mem Beeshum! Mem Beeshum!" they cried, crowding around Anjanette.

A girl of about nine cautiously approached Mary and said something in Malay. "What a pretty child you are," Mary said, patting her on the head. The girl cried out, backing off and holding both hands up in alarm. She ran to a woman who was apparently her mother and who was shaking her head unhappily.

"What's wrong with her?" Mary whispered to Anjanette.

"You will learn their ways in time, but you should never touch anyone on the head. It's natural to reach down and touch the children, but resist the impulse."

"Why? Is there something wrong with their heads?" Mary asked, looking at her hand, imagining nits or scalp diseases.

"No, that is where their spirits hover. You could harm their souls if you brush the spirits away."

Mary noticed that Anjanette hadn't said: They think that . . . In fact, Anjanette had explained it as if she believed it. Perhaps she did.

Resolving not to give any more offense, Mary followed along with her hostess, pretending to show an avid, slightly maternal interest in all that was being said. This was rendered difficult by the fact that she didn't understand anything that was being said. While the people were attractive and friendly and Mary was convinced that Anjanette's efforts to keep in touch with their concerns was worthwhile, all the talking was Malay. Anjanette was quite fluent in the native tongue.

Anjanette began by translating everything that was said to

Mary. Halfway through the first village, however, she was merely giving her the gist of the conversation at intervals, and before long had become so involved in what she was doing that she all but forgot that Mary didn't understand a word. For her part, Mary smiled and nodded—and nodded, and nodded. She used the few words she'd learned when she thought they might be appropriate, but they elicited hysterical laughter several times and she gave up. "Those . . . are . . . nice . . . shoes!" she said to one gentleman who was wearing elaborately woven leather footwear.

Anjanette smiled. "He doesn't understand you, Mary dear, even if you shout."

"I didn't know I was shouting," Mary said, blushing to the roots of her hair.

Anjanette hugged her. "I know. Just smile and be beautiful. They'll love you."

"Anjanette, I'm not any good at this."

"Not now. It's your first time."

She didn't blame Anjanette, but she quickly became bored. She followed her hostess into hut after hut to admire babies, consult about rashes, and chat with a few ill or injured individuals who were not working.

"Everyone seems young," Mary commented on the way home, trying to dwell on something besides her own failure. "There are a few old people, but so many children."

"The lifespan here is short," Anjanette said sadly. "So many diseases and a climate in which they all thrive. In your part of the world, you have winter. That makes a difference. The insects that carry disease die out and have to start over in the spring. But in the tropics, there is no respite. Everything thrives. Everything except people. It's most strange, isn't it? Europeans think of paradise as a place where it is warm and where green things grow all the time. But even paradise has another side."

Maybe that was the difference. Mary had been trying to play a role. Anjanette hadn't. She felt very deeply for the welfare of the people they had visited. "Are you happy here?" Mary asked.

"I know no other way of life except in books and from hearing people talk. I speak of snow so knowingly, but I cannot imagine it. Still, how could I not be happy? I have a fine husband and child. Two homes and another child soon. Yes, Mary, I'm happy for myself. It's only for others I'm sometimes sad."

That evening, as they all sat on the wide porch before retiring, Alex echoed his wife's reflections on the transience of human life in the tropics. Mary, sensing that boredom loomed large in her immediate future, inquired about sites of historical interest in the hopes of provoking him into suggesting a short trip or two. Anjanette had mentioned several cities they might see on the way, but Alex and George had been anxious to get to Penang to supervise the height of the clove harvest and so they had made no stops.

Alex said, "There is, one assumes, a long history of the Malay people here, but very little physical evidence of it. The land, you see, is voracious. It literally eats up man's pitiful attempts to make his mark. An area is cleared for a home or building, and within a few years the forest has recaptured it unless constantly held back. If you leave a godown alone, for instance, a year later it will be so thickly covered with vines that you can't find it without knowing where to look. In another year the termites and wood rot will have reduced it to a lacy shell the vines pull down. In three, it's as though it never existed."

"But surely the people left monuments, artifacts?"

"Have you felt the urge to drag a great stone around in the heat and laboriously carve a message? Would you enjoy firing up a kiln to make a plate and cup when it's so easy to use a big leaf and half a coconut? Of course not. There's no need here to build a stone house to keep the warmth in during the winter. Stone is hard to work with; wood is easy, free, and perpetually available, and there is no winter cold to protect yourself from. The arts of these people are transient: dancing, singing, the weaving of beautiful fabrics."

"But—"

"But you are English. You want stone cathedrals and eternal castles and Domesday books. You're a Beecham and you crave ancient maps and histories."

She wondered if this was somehow derogatory. "No, I don't. And you're a Beecham too. You're as mad for maps as Papa. I'm merely interested in this place and the people, and find myself wishing I knew more of the history."

He smiled, the moonlight shining on his teeth eerily, and she knew he'd not meant to criticize her. "You could make it up, Mary. You're good at making up stories. Remember the one about why Castlemere smells of rosemary? Anjanette, you should have known Mary as a girl—she had a wonderful imagination."

"She still does. That's part of her charm," Anjanette answered softly.

"Are you not well?" Alex asked his wife suddenly, alarmed by the weariness in her voice. "Janette, don't leave the house tomorrow. Promise me?"

As a topic of conversation, Mary's character was forgotten as Alex took Anjanette off to bed. George and Hester followed them a minute later, and Mary was left to sit by herself for a moment. Alex's solicitude for his wife made something deep inside of her ache. It was the thing she wanted most for herself—his love and the open evidence of it. At the same time, she couldn't bring herself to begrudge Anjanette. She herself had felt instant concern when she heard the tired little quaver in her tone.

Mary didn't improve much in her efforts to help Anjanette. "You're too bossy, and you can't boss people who don't understand what you're saying. That's your problem," Hester summed it up as they sat in their cotton chemises and pantalets, combing out their freshly washed hair. Mary's had turned fuzzy in the humidity and she despaired of ever getting a comb clear through it again.

"At least I'm doing something when I'm bossy," Mary countered, losing patience and taking a pair of embroidery scissors to a snarl. "You don't do anything but write endless letters, though what you have to write about eludes me! You never leave the house."

"The mosquitoes outside like me better than you. I'm sweeter."

Mary smiled. "That you are. Oh, Hester, I'm bored, bored, bored. I want to do something!"

"For instance?"

Mary threw her hairbrush at a lizard on the opposite wall. It shot away. "I don't know. Ride a horse, climb a tree, wade in a river, run a race, play a huge trick on somebody I dislike, build a bonfire, cut all my hair off—something!"

"Oh, don't cut your beautiful hair. Remember, Mama says a woman's hair is her crowning glory." She picked up a long lock of her own mousy brown glory and held it out to look over. "I don't know . . ."

Mary perched on the end of Hester's bed. She wrapped her arms around her knees and let her damp hair tent out around her. "Hester, don't you ever wonder what would happen if you did something altogether strange. Suppose

. . . suppose we cut our hair and wore men's clothes and went out and hunted wild animals. We could go anywhere we wanted and nobody would know we weren't men. We could even go fight in a war."

"It wouldn't work. You have too much bosom."

"Oh, Hester! Just try to imagine doing something exciting."

"Mary, exciting things are usually scary too. I just want life to be pleasant and happy."

One morning, about two weeks after their arrival Anjanette became ill. "It's malaria," Alex told the rest of them at breakfast. His face was grim. "She hasn't had a bout for nearly a year, and we hoped she was over it."

"What can I do for her?" Mary asked, rising from the table.

"Please, sit down. There's nothing. Susu will take care of her. With enough quinine and bed rest, she ought to be well in a few weeks. She usually is. It's the three-day variety. A three-day cycle, that is. Susu has no trouble keeping her down on the bad days, but on the two days between, she invariably thinks she's well and wants to get up and do too much. That's when you and Hester will be needed."

Mary rattled around in the house all day. She tried darning some stockings, but Hester took them away from her. "You'll have them ruined with all the bleeding you're doing on them. This end of the needle is sharp, have you noticed?"

In the afternoon, she found a map of Penang and spent several hours poring over it, examining every detail and trying to picture the actual land it represented. Here was a precipitous drop-off, probably with a rock outcropping. But what sort of rocks were they? And there a stream went straight, meandered for a mile, then went straight again. What topography could account for that? The next morning, when Anjanette was feeling better, as Alex had predicted, Mary took the map into the older woman's bedroom and questioned her. But she knew nothing of the island except who lived where. Apparently sensing Mary's frustration with her lack of information, she said, "You are very like your Aunt Nellanor, aren't you? Alex has told me many times about her—her love of nature and her interest in plants and animals."

"Alex talks about Aunt Nell?" Mary asked, smiling.

"All the time. He adored her, and I think you did too."

"She was wonderful, Anjanette. Most people were terrified of her, but I loved her more than I can say. She was always on my side, even when everybody else in the family was against me. Except Papa. He was never against me."

"Nor Alex. He loves you," Anjanette said, patting her hand.

Mary couldn't speak for the lump in her throat. If only he could love her the way she loved him—but it was impossible and would hurt Anjanette.

"Ask Alex about the map, dear Mary. He knows every inch of the island."

"He's too busy. He and Papa are out all day and too tired to even talk in the evening."

"Then don't wait until evening. Go along with them."

"Do you mean it? I've asked and they keep saying it would be too hard on me. That's stupid, of course. I'm as hardy as a cart horse."

Anjanette laughed. "Not quite, I hope. But I agree that you should at least try it. If the heat is too much, you can come back and rest. I'll talk to Alex about it tonight."

Thanks to Anjanette's intervention, Mary was ready at dawn to accompany the men. Clad in her trousers and shirt and a wide coolie hat, she was sitting astride a large horse waving away the flies when George and Alex came out of the house. "You really are coming along?" George asked.

"Where are we going first?" Mary asked.

"To one of the main groves that's being harvested today. Why don't you tell me what you know so I don't waste my breath," Alex said, swinging into his saddle.

"That cloves are the dried unopened buds of a fragrant, bushy, cone-shaped tree; that you should average about five pounds of cloves per season per tree, and there are about a hundred trees to the acre. So, about five hundred pounds per acre. How many acres do you have?'"

"Five hundred, but you're overlooking the fact that only about two-thirds of the trees are in full bearing condition at any one time, so your numbers are high." He was amused by her eagerness to show off the information she had garnered, but was very careful not to show how he felt. Besides, it was damned refreshing to have an intelligent woman around. Most of the guests they'd had over the years were woefully ignorant of the business at hand. And the women were far worse than the men. Most of them were actually proud of how little they knew and seemed to feel it was a charming attribute. Trust Mary Beecham to run against the tide.

"How much do you harvest, then?" she asked, turning her horse to follow Alex. George rode behind her, grinning with besotted fondness at his beautiful, bright daughter.

"Only about two hundred fifty, as so many of our trees are young," Alex replied.

"Tell us about cloves, Papa," Mary said over her shoulder. "Like you did when I was a little girl."

"Both of you know the story," George said, touched.

"I know, but I like to hear you tell it."

"Oh, very well," he said, thinking back to those days. Hester had wanted bedtime stories about castles and fairies. But Mary had wanted stories about real adventures, like the Great Clove Theft. "In the faraway old days, the Portuguese ruled the Spice Islands of the East. They were cruel masters and the people hated them. Then the Dutch learned to be fine sailors and they came and took the islands away from the Portuguese. The people were glad at first—"

"—but the Dutch were as cruel as the Portuguese," Mary put in, as she always did at that point.

"Cruel and selfish too. Cloves and nutmeg were as valuable as gold, and they didn't want anybody else to grow them," George continued. "The Dutch made raids on other islands where the seeds were carried by birds, and burned any trees they found—"

"But they couldn't find all of them, and there were so many islands—"

"They also dried the nutmegs with charcoal heat instead of sunlight—"

"So nobody could buy the seeds in Europe and plant them—"

"The Dutch held their monopoly for a long time—"

Alex rode ahead, half-listening to the counterpoint of their voices, but thinking more about the speakers them selves. How fine it was for a father and child to be so close. He hoped that his little Katie and the baby on the way would be as fond of him as Mary was of her father. Her father? For the first time in many years he remembered that George wasn't really Mary's father. That first time he had visited Castlemere, Nellanor told him George had adopted her as a foundling. Then there was some awful remark Portia had made the day the other little girl was buried. What was her name?

"—and they even burned huge piles of cloves in the streets of Amsterdam to keep the supply scarce and the price high," George was saying. "They killed any of the natives they caught selling to anyone else, and they even burned their own trees on the islands if pirates came near. Then a Frenchman—"

"Pierre Poivre—"

"Which name in English is—"

"Peter Pepper!" Mary said with the happy yelp she'd used at this point since childhood.

"Poivre learned that about fifty islands were growing plants and the Dutch couldn't guard all of them."

Isn't it odd, Alex thought, how alike they are in spite of not being related by blood at all? And yet they had the same interests, the same quick minds. Even a similar timbre of voice, though Mary's was so young and high. He glanced over his shoulder. Mary was half-turned in the saddle, listening to George and smiling. When George turned for a second to glance at something, Alex suddenly saw both of them in profile. Identical profiles. She *is* his daughter! he thought. Of course! Did she know? Probably not. If she did, she'd talk about it, just as she relished talking about everything she knew.

"So he raided them, didn't he, Papa?"

"He got together an expedition, and in a few months in 1770 he and his men kidnapped four hundred nutmeg seedlings and—"

"—and seventy clove seedlings. Good for Peter Pepper!"

"He planted them in French possessions all over the tropics—"

"—and the Dutch monopoly was ended! Aren't you glad, Alex? What are you smiling about?" she asked.

"Just enjoying you—and your father," he said. "We turn to the right up here. Do you smell them?"

As they passed through a small clearing between the densely overgrown path and the clove grove, the hot, sweet smell enveloped them like a cloud. Mary closed her eyes, took a long, deep breath, and let it out with a long sigh. "This is what heaven must smell like!" she said.

16

Mary spent the morning in the fields with them. But by afternoon, when the sun was blazing fully and everyone retired for a few hours, she'd changed her mind about heaven smelling like cloves. As it became hotter and hotter, the odor became overwhelming. The inside of her nose hurt, her eyes felt gritty, and her head throbbed from the smell. Hell, not heaven, might be what smelled of cloves.

"Have you a headache?" Alex inquired, the heel of his hand to his temple. "It takes people that way. Especially Europeans."

"Why, no," Mary answered, when in truth she could have banged her head on the nearest tree trunk in desperation. But she wasn't about to admit any weakness on the first day, for fear she wouldn't be allowed to accompany them again. The alternative was sitting indoors being bored senseless and wishing she were near Alex.

Aside from the pain, she'd enjoyed herself. The grove had been busy, scores of small neat Chinese coolies working purposefully. This, not the leisurely life of the ladies, was what she'd wanted to be part of. Something was getting *done* here. The coolies spread large canvas cloths under the trees to catch any buds that might fall off; then they began pulling down branches and picking the fat pinkish green flower buds. She watched with fascination as they selected which to pick. Too early, and the cloves would be small and rock-hard when processed, Alex told her. Too large, and they'd crumble and flake. Each tree would be gone over two or three times during this, the peak month for harvest. As their hand-held baskets filled, other workers collected the buds and took them away for processing.

Not one to merely observe, Mary got a basket, a stick to

pull the brittle branches down, and worked for an hour or so. The coolie who was working the tree with her looked over her results, shaking his head and bobbing little apologetic bows as he threw out more than half of what she'd picked. The next basket passed his approval, however.

When they finally went home for luncheon and a rest, Mary was full of questions. "Why are the workers all Chinese instead of natives?"

"Because the locals aren't very ambitious."

"Lazy?"

"No, there's a difference. The natives don't need to be ambitious, by our standards. The land provides them with a good life without having to knock themselves out in the heat so the European sahibs can make money. It just shows good common sense," Alex said. "But the Chinese are fiercely ambitious people. Most of these men came from parts of China where life is hard and improving their lot is difficult. They leave their wives and children and indenture themselves for a term of five to ten years. Then they go back rich men. They work hard, but they're well paid for their work and they're extraordinarily thrifty."

Late in the afternoon, when the men prepared to return to the groves, Mary had bathed and rested and was ready to go back with them. George was concerned. "You look tired. Hadn't you better stay here and rest some more?"

"Papa! That's not very flattering. Next thing, you'll be saying I look like a worn-out hag," Mary said, hooking her arm through his. "Let me come along with you, please. I'm fine, and this morning was the most fun I've had since we left England."

He was inordinately pleased at her interest and her stamina, as though both reflected on him, which was only partially true. He was also glad to have her along because her very presence seemed to enliven everything around her. The coolies, normally so solemn, liked having her in the grove and watched her smilingly, vying with each other to help her. Even Alex had been different this morning. Previously he'd been very intense, like an overage schoolboy trying to impress an older brother with the true and earnest value of his work. But this morning he'd loosened up and shown his genuine enthusiasm for the business. And it was because Mary's eager curiosity had brought it out. She was a good influence on Alex, just as George knew she was a good influence on himself.

Too bad Alex and Mary couldn't . . . Oh, well, it was too late to be speculating about that. Still, it was a pity.

As the next weeks passed, with Mary always at his elbow, asking questions and throwing herself into each stage of the clove processing, Alex, too, became aware of a lifting of his spirits. But he attributed it to the fact that Anjanette was getting better. She was still feeling low every third day, but it was nothing like the feverish, death's-door illness she'd suffered in the past. However, even he, if pressed, would have admitted that Mary did make those days pass more easily.

He'd simply never known anyone, man or woman, with her energy. She never seemed to wear down or run out of questions. Nor did she confine her interest to words. There was virtually nothing she wouldn't try—or could be kept from trying. She climbed the trees to help pick from upper branches; she carted baskets; she helped with whitewashing the godowns. One day he'd gone back to the house for something, and when he returned, she was helping two coolies bury a dead pariah dog near the base of one of the trees. "What an interesting way of fertilizing the trees," she said, cheerfully dumping a shovelful of soil. She had blisters on her hands and didn't seem to even notice.

And if there was something a little hectic in her determination, there was only one member of the family who sensed it and had a partial understanding of it.

"She's a wonder," Alex told Anjanette late that night as they lay in the darkness listening to the distant thunder that hinted of the coming monsoon season. Already there were more rainy days than clear. Soon they would be deluged. "Imagine a well-bred girl doing something like that without so much as flinching at the work or the sheer nastiness of it!"

Anjanette turned on her side and rested her hand on his chest. "But she's not a girl, Alex. That's where you're very mistaken."

"Oh, not in years, I suppose. But in spirit—"

"That spirit is her character, not her age. She's simply a rare young woman." She was quiet for a long moment, then added, "She's in love with you, you know."

"Janette! What a ridiculous thing to say! I think the fever *has* gone to your brain."

"Don't puff up so indignantly, my darling. I'm not accusing you of anything and I'm not being the jealous wife. But she adores you. She can't take her eyes off you. She lights up like a lamp with the wick turned high every time you come in a room."

"If you're right—which I don't think for a minute that you are—what the hell shall I do about it?"

"Do?" She chuckled. "You must do nothing at all. Let her enjoy her romantic dreams and she'll go back to England in a few months and find someone else to love and marry. She is of an age to be smitten. If you try to discourage her, you'll embarrass her and she'll remember that always." She paused, then laughingly confessed, "I had a crush on a dancing master once when I was a girl, and he told me he knew and I must get over it. I blush even now to recall my chagrin. No, let this trip be a good memory to her."

"A dancing master?" he asked, taking her in his arms and nibbling her shoulder.

"A brittle, effeminate little creature. I can't imagine what I thought was so grand about him," she said. "That tickles."

"So, someday Mary Beecham will tell someone about her pathetic Cousin Alex whom she was stupid enough to adore—?"

"No, Mary made a better choice the first time than I did. Oh, Alex, don't do that—everybody will hear us!"

The family sat on the porch, watching the rain sheet down. "Good thing you got the harvest in," George said, lighting a cigar with some difficulty. The moisture permeated everything.

"Oh, there will be a few more dry days," Alex said. "How would everybody like to go over to the mainland and go upcountry to see the rain forest before the full force of the monsoon is on us?"

Hester, normally too ladylike and shy to express discontent, spoke up. "No, thank you. I've seen enough jungle."

"But a rain forest isn't a jungle," Alex explained. "A jungle is low, impenetrable growth. A rain forest . . . well, it's a magical place. Unlike anything else in the world. You'd like it, but of course, you don't have to go unless you want."

"I want to," Mary said. "Can we, Papa?"

"I don't know . . ." George answered, giving up on his cigar and tossing it over the porch rail. A sodden monkey dashed out from the trees, grabbed it, and ran off.

"Won't his friends think he's important when he leans back in the crotch of a tree and smokes *that*!" Mary said.

This struck Anjanette as very funny and she laughed so hard she got tears in her eyes.

"Really, Papa. I want to see a rain forest. Please, let's go."

"Very well," George said, feeling very tired at the thought, but pleased to make her happy.

"I think I'll stay here," Anjanette said.

"You're not getting sick again, are you?" Alex asked.

"Not in the least, you worrier. But it's such an effort, and I'd rather stay back with Hester. We'll go as far as Georgetown with you and do some shopping and visiting and meet you back here."

They set out a few days later. Winding down the hill toward the coast of the island, Mary got a view she'd been unaware of on the way up. The town nestled below them, with a narrow ribbon of water between Penang and Province Wellesley on the mainland. "What are those square greenish blue areas? Oh, let me guess. Rice fields. Am I right?"

"Rice paddies, yes," Alex said. "But look across at the dense green area higher up. That's where we're going. If we went clear up into the really high country, it would be cool and pleasant. Not as cool as England, of course, but a different climate from the one you've been in here."

They left Anjanette, Katie, and Hester with friends named Trask in Georgetown. The family had been invited to a dinner and dance at the Residency the next week and the two women were aflutter with plans for new dresses. "What will you wear, Mary?" Anjanette asked.

"Oh, Mother had a dress made for me before we left. It's packed away someplace," she said.

Mary and the men took a boat across to the mainland, rented horses and equipment at Butterworth, and started the climb to the rain forest. At first, it was disappointing, but as they went deeper in, Mary began to appreciate the eerie beauty. Unlike the land on Alex's plantation, which had been cleared and worked and then regrown, there was virtually no low growth here. The ground was nearly bare except for tiny lichenlike plants, ferns, and plush moss. The trees grew as straight and tall and unbranched as randomly placed pillars, and the light grew dimmer and dimmer until it seemed they were in a strange foggy underwater world of faint greenish light.

"But there's no color but green. No flowers," she said with surprise as they dismounted at the end of the day and the attendant coolies began to unpack gear to fix dinner.

"You're wrong, Mary, there are millions of flowers. You're just not looking for them in the right place," Alex said. He stepped over to the nearest tree and grabbed hold of a ropy vine that was hanging from the invisible upper reaches. He gave it a great jerk and they were showered with bright flower petals and a clump of orchids. They were also soaked with raindrops.

Mary exclaimed over the flowers, tucking one behind each ear. "So there's a beautiful garden over our heads! It would be perfect if only the rain would stop," she said.

"It won't. Ever. It probably isn't even raining above the canopy. This constant drizzle is why it's called a rain forest. Under here, it rains all the time. The tops of these trees are so high that they're literally in the clouds much of the time. They drip this way even when there isn't a cloud in the sky for miles."

They spent three days in the forest and Mary became absolutely enchanted. It was beyond anything that even her fertile imagination could have conjured up. Occasionally they would come to a place where one of the enormous trees had fallen and let in a long shaft of sunlight. Beneath, there was always a tangled profusion of colorful growth—figs, dozens of orchids, great exotic plants and flowers even Alex couldn't name. And often where the tree had stood, the vines that originally used it for support still stood even though the tree was gone. Alex broke off sections of one such vine for Mary and George and they found its woody exterior concealed a juicy center full of pure, sweet water.

"Papa, let's take home tons and tons of this soil and grow our own rain forest at Castlemere," Mary said on the last night before their return to Penang. "We could build a big conservatory with lots of windows . . ."

George was tired. The travel and heat hadn't seemed so enervating when he'd been here as a boy. Now he was feeling his years. He suspected he had a mild touch of malaria, though he wouldn't have said so and had a fuss made, and he was getting sick of the constant green vista and rain. He wouldn't have wanted to take this home with him even if it were possible. At home, in a few months it would be time to hang the mistletoe. Here, it was growing all around them. "It wouldn't grow a thing," he told her, sitting down on one of the folding camp chairs set up in front of her tent. "It's very poor soil."

"No, Papa, look at the millions of plants that grow in it."

"That's why it's poor. The plants suck every nutrient from it. When a leaf falls, it's barely started to rot before its value is used by the roots. All these plants have roots that grow very near the surface. Some of them, like the orchids, are above the ground. In fact, some of the vines we see aren't really stems, but the roots of plants that grow high in the canopy and send their roots down a hundred feet to the soil."

Mary suddenly felt sad, partly because—being so well-attuned to George's moods—she had sensed the shortness in his tone and his growing desire to go home. In addition, her own mention of Castlemere had brought a realization she hadn't wanted to face. They were going to return before long. No matter how she threw herself into the enjoyment of every moment, this magical place, as Alex had called it, was merely an interlude in her life. Then she would be like the plants he'd talked about—sending long emotional roots halfway around the world.

Thinking Mary had grown quiet because of his having corrected her, George went on explaining, "When I was here as a boy, I watched as a forest like this was being felled for planting. It's nearly impossible. The trees are dense and hard and very wet inside. They're difficult to cut and almost impossible to burn. And once the trees and plants are gone, nothing else wants to grow because there is no leaf mold to fertilize the ground."

Mary forced herself to pay attention. "That's why Alex's clove groves require so much extra fertilizer, isn't it? The dead dogs and prawn dust and all."

They sat together watching as the coolies, under Alex's supervision, prepared their camp for the last night. A ring of fires was started around the site to keep wild animals away. Alex and George each had a small tent on either side of Mary's. In the center of the site a folding table and chairs were set up where they would eat, and on the opposite side of the ring, the coolies would sleep, out of reach of snakes, on the spindly folding cots they brought along. Mary watched these preparations and felt her eyes filling with tears. Why couldn't time just be stopped right now? She could spend eternity in this strange green place with George and Alex, the two people she loved most in the world.

She wanted to say: Let's forget the rest of the world exists and stay here forever.

George wanted to say: Let's go home now to the cool, scholastic quiet of Castlemere. My strength for adventure has ebbed.

Neither of them said anything.

She was uncharacteristically quiet that evening. "Are you feeling ill?" George asked over dinner. She assured him she was the picture of health in such forceful terms that he abandoned the subject with a puzzled smile. Afterward George talked to Alex about his trip when he was a boy. "There was a plantation we visited—a man named Parker, I think. He had pierced ears. Only man I ever saw with such a thing. Dennis Parker or Packer I think his name was. Ever heard of him?"

"Oh, yes, he's a sort of legend," Alex said. "Went a bit mad. Married not one but two Malay wives and set out to rid the earth of tigers. Or so it seemed. My father visited his house once and said it was virtually carpeted in tiger rugs." He started laughing. "My father never went back. He'd gone to see about leasing some land Parker owned, but first there was a big dinner party at which unidentifiable things were served. My father thought the dishes were just vegetables he didn't recognize stewed with some sort of fish. He ate it all very politely, until he started to sip his drink and realized it was watered-down blood. If you had known my father . . . oh, but of course, you did. When you were a boy he lived at Castlemere with Nellanor."

"I hardly remember him. He'd come out here by the time I was eight or nine. Then, of course, we corresponded when I came into the business. Hard to believe you're his son. He was so . . ."

"Boring?" Alex said with a laugh. "You don't have to be careful what you say about him."

"No, I was going to say 'unhappy.' "

"He was that. I never knew why. Maybe because he wasn't you."

"Me? Why would anybody want to be me? Whatever do you mean?"

"He had good cause to envy you, George. You're heir to the business and that wonderful house. You have a very stylish wife and a daughter who loves you—two daughters, I should say," he caught himself, having momentarily forgotten Hester entirely. "Although I have to admit it was probably the business he wanted most. Speaking of your daughters, where did Mary go?"

Neither of them had noticed that she'd slipped away to her tent while they were talking.

"We squinted for hours when we came back out in the open," Mary was telling Hester. "I hadn't realized how really dark it was in the forest until I was dazzled by the sunlight."

"It sounds grim and horrible. I suppose there were creatures . . . ?" There were always creatures in this part of the world. That was what she hated most about it. That and the heat.

"Of course. Bats and snakes mainly. It seems like everything in the rain forest either flies or climbs. Even the squirrels can fly. They have to, to get to sunlight. I don't believe things like deer could live there. They couldn't find enough to eat on the ground."

"Well, I'm glad I didn't go. We had a good time in Georgetown. Wait until you meet the Trasks. That's who we stayed with. They have the two most divinely handsome sons. They'll be at the party."

"Pooh, party! What a waste of time to come out here, then get all rigged up like it was London."

"Don't talk like that, Mary. You know Mama wanted us to meet some young men."

"What's the use, Hester? You'd kill yourself before you'd marry some oaf who'd keep you here, and I don't intend to marry at all."

Hester would normally have fallen on the last bit, objecting to the concept of spinsterhood, but the first part of the sentence had rendered her speechless. Dear Lord above! Mary was right. Imagine having to actually live all of one's life with lizards on the ceiling and bats forever threatening to entangle themselves in one's hair. That was very well for someone like Anjanette, who'd never known any other sort of life, but for herself? She suddenly hated the very thought of the frothy fuchsia gown with the silver spangles she'd bought in Georgetown. It might make her pretty enough to get a proposal and she might lose her head and accept.

Once more the Beechams loaded up their carriages with

servants, clothes, boxes, and themselves and came down the hill to Georgetown. "Next time we do this, we'll be on our way home," Hester said. Mary gave her such A Look that she was silent the rest of the way.

The monsoon was now on them in full force. It poured down rain almost every day. At least the winds that accompanied it were slightly cooler, which would have been refreshing had they not all felt soaked to the skin.

The Trasks welcomed them to their big stucco-trimmed, impressively pillared villa that overlooked the harbor. Their handsome sons, whom Hester now regarded as threats rather than attractions, were out doing whatever business they did, and Mary was spared being introduced to them. Colonel Trask was a leathery little man with a gigantic walrus mustache and an apparent terror of the opposite gender. He spirited Alex and George away almost at the moment of their arrival.

Mrs. Trask, Yorkshire born and bred, was a handsome, strapping woman half a head taller than he. "Dismal weather for travel," she said cheerfully, snatching little Katie out of the ayah's arms and bouncing her around with violent affection. "Shouldn't be having another so soon, Anjanette. Still, it's the way of things, isn't it? Nice to see you back again, Hester. Smile, girl! Now, let me look you over, Mary Beecham." She thrust the screaming Katie back to her keeper. "My, my! You are a bonny thing, aren't you just? And so little. I've got just the thing for that hair of yours. Mine's the same, goes all to fuzz when it rains. My gardener grows a great ugly plant that I smash up and then put a bit of its juice in the rinse water. You use it this afternoon."

Mary smiled. She'd expected to dislike these people who were in league with Anjanette to make her be English and proper, but Mrs. Trask's well-meaning tactlessness was refreshing.

"I'm sure one of the boys will fall in love with you," she said later as she supervised the washing of Mary's hair. "I hope so. I am so tired of them hanging around here dropping cigar ashes on my rugs, when they could be off getting me grandbabies. Great oafs of boys, actually, but good-natured and hard workers. You could do worse. Of course, you probably could do better, too."

"I don't intend to marry, Mrs. Trask," Mary said, wincing as the maid worked on a tangle.

"No, nor did I. But then one day I got to be twenty-five

and looked around and everybody else was married and having babies and I wanted some of my own. There I was, a big lump of a girl who hadn't had an offer since I was twenty, and not like to get another. I got my father to send me out to an old auntie in India and I found myself a husband. I was no beauty, but I had a nice dowry and that helped. Of course, you won't have any trouble. That bosom of yours is enough if you didn't have a shilling. Men are fools for bosoms. If I'd had a decent one, I wouldn't have had to go clear to India."

The mysterious hair potion worked wonders and the ball gown that had been packed away in layers of tissue since before they left Castlemere was beautiful even if it was too heavy and hot for the climate. Studying herself in the glass, Mary was pleased with the result. Hester looked very pretty too, although fuchsia wasn't the perfect choice of color for her. But she was happy to be getting back to a familiar kind of life and her myopic eyes sparkled.

"Janette, don't be a fool," Alex said. "Take those damned corsets off and lie down."

"But I can't go out without lacing. My dress won't fit. I don't understand it. I wore this same dress when I was six months gone with Katie and I had no trouble."

"And you can't truss yourself up that way without feeling miserable. I find it hard to believe that even you are subject to female vanity. You've got too much sense."

"Alex, it isn't a question of sense or vanity. I don't mind looking all bulgy, but I can't go with the back of my dress gaping wide open and I didn't bring anything else that would be suitable for a ball."

"Then borrow something from Mrs. Trask."

"Oh, Alex, that is the kind of thing a man would say. You're all so blind. Emma Trask's shoulders are twice as wide as mine and she's long-waisted too. Nothing of hers would fit me. It would take days for the alterations."

"Then we won't go. That would suit me fine. I'd rather just sit here with you anyway."

"We must go! I promised Portia I would see that the girls were introduced to the right people, and so far the only people they've met are us and about a hundred coolies. They're probably ready anyway and would be crushed if they couldn't go show off their dresses."

"Then let Mrs. Trask take them."

"Alex, that would be disgracefully improper. We are their family and sponsors. It's our duty—"

"Then I'll go with them. But you get those horrible torture instruments off and rest. No, not another word. I'll watch over them like a jealous father hawk. It'll be good practice for me. For when Katie gets to be this age."

Satisfied that Anjanette was comfortably settled, Alex went out on the veranda to talk with George and wait for Mary and Hester. The Trask "boys," Robbie and John, were in the drive, laughing uproariously at bawdy jokes. George was alarmed at the news that Anjanette would not accompany them. "It's not illness, it's common vanity that's keeping her away," Alex explained. "So it's up to us to squire the girls."

"Then I'll take charge of Hester. She's easier to keep an eye on," George said. "Craven of me, I suppose, but I'm feeling a bit doddery."

"Doddery? You're hardly forty."

"I feel eighty. It's just the heat, I expect."

Alex pulled his watch out of the pocket of his waistcoat. "What's keeping them?"

At that, the sound of Mrs. Trask's voice ordering the servants to bring the carriages around floated out to them. Alex went inside. Mrs. Trask was decked out in a vivid green dress encrusted with lace and pearls. There were already sweat circles under her arms, but she didn't seem to notice or care. Hester was darting around the hall like a trapped bird, looking for her evening bag. "You look lovely, Hester," Alex said, meaning it. Her cheeks were flushed, giving her the color she needed, and the dress was designed to enhance her rather angular figure. "Are we ready? Where's Mary?"

"Right here," a voice answered from the top of the stairs.

Alex looked up and was struck dumb. *That* was Mary? It couldn't be. Mary was a child—a girl with a fuzzy mass of dark red hair dragged back from her face and straggling in the heat. She was a freckled sprite in boy's clothes. Of course, he'd seen her in dresses and knew she'd make an effort to look like a proper English miss for the party, but not like this! Why, she was ravishingly beautiful. Her hair was pulled into a high chignon atop her head, and long glossy ringlets fell down the back. All sunburn and freckles had disappeared under a dusting of rice powder and her skin looked like Dorset cream. The maroon dress belled out, nipping in at an incredibly tiny waist. Draped ivory lace at the low neckline framed a generous bosom—more generous than he would ever have guessed, even if he'd considered the matter, which he certainly hadn't.

She floated down the stairs, her eyes as bright as the tiny diamond earrings she wore. Her skirts swayed provocatively. "Mary, I can hardly believe this is you," Alex said.

"Is that a compliment?" she asked, smiling up at him.

Dear God, this wasn't little Mary, the tomboy cousin.

"Of course it is!" he said. "We'll be late if we don't hurry," he added, turning on his heel.

She watched him go and wondered what had made him speak so sharply. She shrugged it off, telling herself she was imagining things. Having been forced to go to the party, she was determined to enjoy it as fully as anything she threw herself into.

George and Alex had their work cut out for them, keeping track of Hester and Mary. As eligible young Englishwomen, they were swamped with attention from all the bachelors who were the bulk of the European population in the East. The Trask boys alone were a challenge. The Beecham men had nearly been forced to throw them out of the carriage before they could even depart for the Residency. John, in particular, didn't seem to be able to keep his eyes off Mary. He followed her every move with all the feral intensity of a cat approaching an unwary bird. And unwary she was, Alex felt. She seemed utterly ignorant of her own appearance. If she knew the power of that shapely shoulder, she wouldn't shrug it so coquettishly, he told himself. Dear Lord, she needed a woman along to guide and protect her, somebody with a better appreciation of the subtle dangers of being a beautiful young woman than Mrs. Trask had.

Alex hardly noticed what he ate at dinner except to note in passing that it was typically English food. Heavy, overcooked, and altogether unsuitable for the tropics. Any other time he might have reflected on the mystery of why the British always insisted on taking their cooking with them. But not this evening. He was too busy trying to conduct a polite conversation with the matron sitting beside him while actually eavesdropping shamelessly on the talk across the table from him. Were those boys treating his cousin properly? From the moment of their arrival, Mary

had been surrounded by a flock of young men begging to sit
by her. The two who won out, the Scarecrow and the
Butterball, as Alex mentally dubbed them, were vying frantically for her attention, bragging of their exploits in the
office and jungle respectively.

She handled it well, turning first this way, then that,
appearing to take a sincere but impersonal interest in each
in equal portion. When the Scarecrow finished a highly
colored version of a tiger hunt in which he played a heroic
role, Mary looked across, catching Alex's eye.

Without thinking, he smiled and winked. Her politely
schooled features broke into a wide grin and she laughed
out loud. The table fell silent for a second, all eyes on her.
She put her hand over her mouth and glanced back at Alex,
her eyes sparkling with heartfelt amusement.

He suddenly felt a bond between them that utterly elimi-
nated everyone else at the table. It was a bit like that time
at the other little girl's funeral when he took her hand and
they both escaped. But this wasn't, he reminded himself, a
sad little seven-year-old in a shabby black dress. Nor was he
a fancy-free adolescent anymore. For a heady moment he'd
forgotten.

After dinner there was an entertainment—a sweating harp-
ist labored away at an instrument that seemed to be going
out of tune even as it was played. Some of the older people,
stuffed to the gills with roast, stewed vegetables, and heavy
pastries, nodded off, only to be stirred awake by the sharp
elbows of their spouses. Even Alex felt his eyes growing
heavy, and could see Mary, in a chair at the opposite side of
the room, deliberately lifting her chin at intervals, as though
she was about to doze. Poor Hester did actually fall asleep,
and would have toppled right off her chair had George not
saved her. Finally this dreary interval was over, the dais was
set up for other musicians, and the chairs were whisked to
the edges of the room by uniformed servants. A band culled
from the lower ranks of the local regiment struck up a lively
tune and dancing commenced.

Seeing Mary safely in the short arms of the Butterball,
Alex proceeded to do his duty. He presented his compliments and Anjanette's apologies to the Resident's wife and
then asked Hester to dance. He whirled her around, making
sure she was noticed, then spun her to a stop in the midst of
a clump of shy young men. Once he saw her off on the arm
of one of them, he asked Mrs. Trask to dance. Not surpris-

ingly, she turned out to be an enthusiastic and hearty dancer, all but dragging him around the floor, inadvertently brushing aside any number of other couples. He genuinely enjoyed her boisterous conversation, so much so that his responsibility to watch over Mary slipped his mind for a while.

When Mrs. Trask finally released him, he looked around for his charge. She wasn't to be seen. That wasn't alarming. The ballroom was crowded and she was so petite he might not see her if she were only a dozen feet away. He took a watching post and reviewed the couples dancing past. When he spotted Mary, she was dancing with John Trask. He was holding her quite close, and the stiffness of her right arm indicated that she was trying to increase the distance without outright rudeness. As Alex watched, Trask bent his head and whispered something. As he whirled her around, Alex caught the look of distaste on her face.

He strode through the dancers and tapped Trask on the shoulder. "Sorry, old boy, but I haven't danced once with my cousin."

Trask looked angry. "I have this dance with Miss Beecham, sir."

Alex laid his hand firmly on the younger man's shoulder and said in a low voice, "Go away. Now."

Mary threw herself into his embrace and they moved away, leaving John Trask alone in the middle of the floor. "Thank you for getting rid of him. I was afraid I was going to have to hurt him."

Alex laughed. "I meant to be your rescuer. I should have known you didn't actually need help. What did he say?"

She looked up at him. "Never mind what he said. What pretty music this is. It makes me wish I knew how to sing."

"I'll bet you sing like a nightingale," he said chivalrously.

"Aunt Nell always said I had a singing voice like a kestrel. An uncontrolled screech signaling imminent death of some harmless creature."

They danced without speaking, then applauded politely when the musicians paused before starting a slow number. Alex held his hand out to take hers. "Another?"

"My pleasure," she replied. Her grip was firm, quite unlike the limp-fish feeling most young ladies offered their partners.

How very small she was, he thought as he put his arm around her. Strange that she could be so fragile and yet so strong. Her hand in his was almost as little and delicate as a child's, and yet he knew, under the long ivory gloves, there were calluses on those fingers from her work at the plantation. Her light floral scent enveloped him and her glossy garnet-colored hair tickled his chin.

Suddenly the room seemed hotter, more crowded. He could feel sweat trickling down his side under the layers of clothing he wore. Damn! Why did they have to dress up as if this were Edinburgh instead of Penang? He could see a light sheen of perspiration on Mary's shoulders as well. It made her flesh glow.

She tilted her head up, and when he met that clear blue gaze he knew, without any doubt, that Anjanette had been right. That wasn't cousinly affection in her eyes. But Anjanette had also been wrong. This wasn't a childish crush on a dancing master. The woman in his arms was a woman, not a silly girl. He realized he'd pulled her quite close and could feel those deliciously generous breasts against his chest.

Something dangerous and painful was unfurling in his heart.

He stepped back quickly. "It's getting late. It's time we got you and Hester home."

"Alex, what's wrong? What did I do?"

"Nothing," he said firmly. Then, more pleasantly: "You did nothing wrong."

But *I* very nearly did, he thought.

17

Anjanette Beecham was a perceptive woman, and her assessments of people were usually to be trusted. But when she had told Alex that Mary was a woman, not a child, she was only partially right. Mary was still teetering on the fine invisible line between girlhood and adulthood, wobbling one way, then the other, sometimes in the same minute. In the areas of life that required logic and learning, she was preternaturally mature—especially for a female. George and Nellanor had both expected her brain to absorb anything a boy's brain could, and had filled it to the brim with facts.

But they had, out of their love for her, encouraged a flamboyant imagination, and it was in this area that she was surprisingly immature. Other girls at a far younger age had their sights firmly—if not downright cold-bloodedly—set on acquiring husbands of the correct financial status, personal habits, and lineage. Oh, some of them mooned about over unattainable men—it was one of the greatest feminine prerogatives. But few of them threw themselves into it with Mary's energy and intensity. Nor did many of these other girls—who entertained passions for their friends' older brothers, black-sheep uncles, and father's stewards—have the underlying structure of genuine respect and admiration that Mary had for Alex.

Still, Mary was belatedly reaching an age of change. Bit by bit she was coming to see herself and her desires objectively. And in the last days of her visit to the East, she was destined to learn a great deal more about life, love, and herself.

Three days before we have to leave, Mary thought bleakly as she stared through the film of netting at the moon's long bar of blue light across the floor. This night and two others to sleep under the same roof as Alex, then the trip back to Singapore and then to England. It could be years before she saw him again. It could be never. Sometimes the thought made her heart constrict into a lump of pain, but lately she'd been trying to force herself to give up her romantic image of him.

Yet tonight that was very difficult, and as these last days passed, she succumbed more and more often to a sort of suffocating panic. There would be no sleep for her yet. She got up and donned a light cotton wrap. Careful not to disturb Hester, she opened the bedroom door onto the porch. She paced nervously for a few moments, then leaned on the railing, watching as the shadows of night creatures darted through the yard into the surrounding jungle. A light breeze carried the scent of cloves from the godowns where they were stored, ready for shipment. How would she bear that scent again? Wouldn't she be carried back here, where her young heart had been broken?

Naturally she would never marry and have children or grandchildren of her own, but she could see her great-nieces and great-nephews gathering around her when she was an old lady (but an attractive, interesting old lady—not fat or warty), wondering why her eyes grew so misty when a cup of clove-spiced wine was handed her at Christmas. They would whisper to one another, wondering what terrible heartbreak the noble old lady had suffered in her youth. She would speak to them softly of the jungles of Penang and—

She caught herself embroidering this little melodrama and shook her head. No, she must not think that way, she told herself, lifting her braids off her neck so that the breeze might cool her neck. As Nellanor had so astringently and frequently noted, her love of Alex was a childhood fancy allowed to run amok. Nothing more. Alex was her cousin and her friend. She must content herself with loving him in those roles.

"Oh, Aunt Nell, why aren't you here to help me?" she whispered into the darkness.

She would walk three times around the house, three counterclockwise circuits—that would make her tired enough to sleep. It had worked before. Going very slowly, so the boards wouldn't creak and disturb the sleepers whose bedrooms she was passing, she tiptoed along the porch, whispering her private incantation: "One to sleep, two to sleep, three to sleep . . ."

She passed the room where Katie and her ayah slept and heard the baby make a sweet cooing sound in her sleep. Katie was such a good baby, a gabby, busy little creature who clung to Alex as if by magnetic attraction every time he was near. She was a lucky child, to have Alex as a father. He always took time to play with her every day, and gave her little gifts and treats.

Passing her father's room around the corner, Mary could hear him snoring lightly. Papa would be glad to start home. She was beginning to worry about him: he'd dropped some weight and seemed tired. Sometimes he was even irritable, a trait she'd never seen him exhibit. It was a pity he wasn't thoroughly enjoying this trip. He'd looked forward to it so eagerly. For his sake, though not her own, she was glad they were leaving soon.

Hester was talking in her sleep when Mary came past the open window. Mary smiled. Hester talked more at night than during the day, but it might as well have been a foreign language for all the sense it made. Her conversations—for they were, by tone and cadence, clearly conversations—were conducted in an incomprehensible mumble.

As she approached Alex and Anjanette's room, Mary stopped. Anjanette was talking. No, crying. No, not that either. Mary, thinking at first that Anjanette's soft moans were a signal that her labor had begun early, moved closer to the window. Worried, she listened for a moment.

"Oh, Alex . . . yes, yes. Oh . . . yes. Now . . . now . . ."

Mary stepped back, hands clapped to flaming cheeks. Nearly tripping over her wrap, she turned and fled.

She fought her way through her netting and flung herself into her bed, pulling the pillow over her head. She was embarrassed to her very core. Anjanette wasn't having a baby, she was . . . she was *having intercourse.* Mary couldn't even think the forbidden phrase (which Nellanor had once used, then explained in blunt but general terms) without blushing all over. She actually felt like she had a fever.

Alex and Anjanette did that with each other! Alex!

I am a great silly fool! she thought. Of course they do. They're married. They're in love. They're supposed to.

And yet it didn't make sense. Being a proper Victorian girl in spite of her unconventional upbringing, Mary knew virtually nothing about sex except what she had observed in the stables. But horses and cats and dogs were different. She had never had occasion to consider that act in relation

to people. From snatches of whispered talk she had overheard between Portia and her friends, Mary had formed the
opinion that it (whatever "it" entailed) was something that a
lady endured with good grace. Like tooth extractions or
monthly cramps. She and Hester had giggled over the subject from time to time without having much idea what they
were giggling about.

But Anjanette hadn't been a woman performing a distasteful duty. She'd sounded happy. No, "happy" wasn't the
word at all. Her voice had been . . . Mary didn't know a
phrase to define how Anjanette had sounded. It was like
when she was talking baby talk to Katie, only more so.
Much more so.

She lifted the pillow, took a great gulp of fresh air, and
flopped over onto her back. But there was something wrong
here. Anjanette was with child. Mary had done enough
eavesdropping to know that married ladies usually regarded
pregnancy as a respite from their husbands' hungers. Was
Alex being "a beast" like Portia's friends sometimes mentioned in hushed, scandalized tones? Not from the sound of
what she'd heard.

It was as if a whole new universe had opened beneath her
feet. A thrilling universe of roiling red and orange and gold.
And it did strange things to her. She suddenly felt aware of
her own body in a new way. She had tingles and aches in
places she'd never noticed before. She was shocked and
embarrassed by what she'd overheard, but excited too.

As if opening her eyes on a new landscape, she was
beginning to see Alex in a different way. Her romantic
fantasies had included handholding, chaste kissing, and gentle embraces, but had stopped short of anything more physical.

No, that wasn't quite true. There had been that day when
she'd seen him come in from the fields, removing his
sweat-soaked shirt as he headed for his room. She'd had
very peculiar feelings about the sight of his gleaming naked
torso and muscular arms and she'd thought about it far
more than a nice girl should. And she'd been touched in a
very strange way by how he looked at her when she came
down the stairs the night of the ball at the Residency.

But now her imagination ran riot.

She felt sweat trickling along the curve under her breast
and she put her hand up to cup its fullness. What if it were a
man's hand? Alex's hand.

Involuntarily a little groan like a kitten mew escaped her.

Hester stirred, turned over, and said, "Whissen formin ga?"

Mary slapped her hand back down on the mattress and turned her burning face away.

"I hate for you girls to leave tomorrow," Anjanette said, holding one hand to the small of her back. "You've been wonderful company and I don't know how I'll stand staying up here next year without you."

"Perhaps we can come back," Hester said, swatting at a fly and shuddering.

Anjanette smiled. "I doubt that. By next year you'll probably both be married ladies with homes of your own."

"Oh, do you really think so?" Hester said with a happy sigh.

Mary sniffed. A delicate little noise, but fraught with unspoken opinion.

"What shall you do today, Mary?" Hester asked quickly. "Anjanette and I are going to two of the *kampongs* to dispense medicine."

"I don't know."

"Would you like to come along?" Hester prodded.

Mary just looked at her.

"Why don't you have Alex take you along to supervise while they load the cloves on the wagons?" Anjanette asked.

"I'd just be in the way," Mary said self-pityingly.

"Nonsense. I'll arrange it," Anjanette said.

So it was that Mary found herself riding beside Alex as he made his way to the godowns. "Anjanette and Katie will miss you. So will I. It's been wonderful getting to know George better," he added, making clear that "you" was plural.

In spite of her determination to be stricken with sorrow, Mary found her spirits lifting once she was out in the open. The rain had let up and the burlap bags of cloves were being quickly taken from the godowns, loaded onto wagons, and covered with protective rubberized canvas. Cloves, as most spices, were extremely susceptible to mildew and mold, and it was imperative to keep them as dry as possible.

The long banks of low fires over which they had been gently dried were cold now, their ashes soupy gray mud; the sorting trays were empty and stacked; the big needles with which the burlap bags were sewn were stabbed into their cork boards and put away; the empty godowns were being swept out and made ready for the next crop.

"What will they all do now?" Mary asked.

"The workers? They'll have plenty to do. The seedlings and saplings need tending. The bearing trees will be pruned and fertilized. The ones that didn't produce will be cut down to make room for young stock. And of course the harvest goes on year-round to some extent. This was just the peak." He glanced around contentedly. "It all seems to be under control. Would you like to go for a ride?"

"Where?"

"Well, there's a spot I don't think you've seen that's the closest thing to a meadow I can provide. Not a well-tended English meadow, but I think you'll like it."

They wound down through some unfamiliar paths and came into a large flat clearing. Apparently it had been cleaned up for another grove that hadn't been planted. New growth had begun, but hadn't gotten weedy and rank yet. "The ground is too low. It turned out to be too wet for cloves," Alex explained. "A lot of work wasted, but it's a pretty place while it lasts. Does it make you homesick?"

As he spoke, a tiger walked out of the jungle at the far end, looked at them, and then with an indignant swishing of its tail turned and bounded back into the heavy growth. Mary laughed. "Not exactly. But I would love to see Portia's face if such a thing stalked out of Castlemere's woods while she was having a garden fete."

She eased her horse down the last few feet of the path ahead of Alex. Her mount, skittish at best and unnerved by the tiger, pranced around and managed to slip on a muddy patch. Having frightened itself, it suddenly bolted and streaked away across the clearing.

Mary, taken by surprise, lost the reins and nearly toppled off, but quickly bent and got a tight, two-fisted grip on the stupid creature's mane. What a wild ride! She'd never really liked horses and this convinced her she'd been right. She flattened down so it couldn't pass under a tree and scrape her off, and screamed at the horse to stop. It paid no attention, but continued to gallop, jagging back and forth to avoid obstacles.

Unaware of anything but the desperate need to hang on, Mary didn't see Alex's frightened expression as he spurred his horse after her. "Hang on, Mary!" he shouted. It was not only unnecessary but also unheard.

They passed through some high growth. Thorns tore at the horse, maddening it further. They slashed through Mary's trousers, but she was so intent on keeping her seat—and her life—that she hardly felt the pain. A vine seemed to fly out of nowhere and slapped her in the face. She closed her eyes, afraid a repetition might blind her.

At first the wild ride had been exhilarating, but as the horse galloped on, dodging bushes and imaginary tigers and flinging her from side to side, it became painful and frightening. Mary's horse had nearly completed a huge erratic circle by the time Alex and his big sensible mount caught up with them. Mary heard the thundering of hooves and watched with horror as he leaned over to snatch the loose reins. He defied gravity and she was terrified that he would fall under the feet of the animals.

"Alex, no!" she screamed, trying to reach forward with one hand to grasp the reins herself as they whipped in the wind. She felt herself slipping sideways and abandoned the effort.

Somehow Alex straightened up, his own and her reins in his hands. He didn't dare yank as sharply as he would have liked, for fear the horse would throw her, but he kept a firm constant grip and finally both horses slowed. Before they had even stopped, he'd flung himself to the ground and come to her side.

There were bloody rips in her trouser leg. A long red welt snaked across her cheek and the bridge of her nose. Her hair had come loose and stray leaves and twigs had caught in it. Her face was stark white and her lower lip was trembling.

"I'll kill this horse with my bare hands. Are you hurt badly? Come on. I'll help you down. Careful. I've got you," he urged.

She lifted her right leg over the horn of the saddle and started slipping helplessly. It was as if her joints had turned to gelatin. Alex put his hands to her waist and she fell forward.

He meant to set her down gently, but before her feet could touch the ground, he found her face-to-face with him. Only scant inches away. She was breathing heavily, and with each breath he could feel her generous breasts against him. Both wore light cotton shirts, and hers clung to her admirable figure damply. He held her for a long moment, looking into those huge, terrified eyes. Then, in spite of her scare, she smiled shakily.

"Thank you for saving me," she said, wrapping her arms around his neck. Her breath smelled like sweet grass and nutmeg. Or was it her hair? He couldn't tell and didn't care. She slipped farther, her body shaping itself to his, and without volition his arms went around her. Then he bent and kissed her.

It was a gentle kiss at first. Had it not been that they held each other so close, it might have been a cousinly kiss. But then, as he tried to draw back, he found he couldn't. He kissed her again, harder. He was aware with some awe that his hand nearly spanned her back.

Mary felt as though the hoofbeats were still pounding in her ears, but it was her pulse. She felt boneless, but at the same time sensed that she was holding him so tightly he couldn't have escaped if he'd tried. How strong and hard his muscles were, how smooth that place on his neck where her hand lingered.

He drew back slightly, his lips brushing hers as he spoke. "Dear God, you are beautiful. And you're so small!" he added in wonder.

"Oh, Alex, I do love you. I always have," she said softly.

She never knew if it was her words or the unexpectedly close whinnying of the horse at the same instant, but it was as if God had snapped His fingers and flung a thunderbolt.

Alex stiffened and stepped back so suddenly that she nearly fell forward. "I must be *mad!*" he said. His voice was as cold as an Edinburgh winter. "Get on my horse. I'll take this one back. *Now!*"

There was no question of not obeying the order. Shaky, but propelled by surges of conflicting emotions, she mounted his horse and had hardly settled herself when he started out ahead of her. She wheeled his horse and followed.

"Alex, wait. I'm sorry. I shouldn't have said that," she cried.

But he either didn't hear her or didn't choose to hear her. He rode ahead, picking up speed. His glossy black hair and strong back were all she could see. His face was a mystery to her. But there was fury in his rigid posture. He only glanced back once to see if she was following.

He didn't slacken his pace until they were within sight of the house. He suddenly stopped and dismounted. His face a composed mask hiding whatever he felt, he tied the reins to a tree and came back to where Mary waited. "Do you need help?" he asked. It was an absolutely emotionless query, bearing neither anger nor affection.

"No, I can manage, thank you," she replied, matching his

tone. She was swimming in guilt and remorse. She'd acted like a fallen woman! She deserved to be treated like one. Would she never learn when to keep quiet?

And yet there was a mass of indignation that was rising to the surface. She hadn't been entirely responsible. It wasn't as if she'd clung to his legs, being dragged along and kicked loose. He'd kissed her first. Yes, she had said the forbidden words—she hadn't meant to and was mortified—but he'd said she was beautiful and he'd held her.

She dismounted, willing her quavering knees to hold her up, and started to walk toward the house just as he had— with dignified, rigid posture and without looking back. But her body failed her and she stumbled over a tussock of grass. As she fell, she caught a glimpse of her father coming down from the porch toward them. Alex was instantly at her side, helping her up, slipping an arm around her waist to support her.

"Mary, I'm sorry," he said. "I—"

"Alex, I'm glad you're back early . . . Mary! What happened?" George said, rushing to her other side.

"That damned horse bolted with her. She didn't fall. Nothing's broken, but she's cut up. I shouldn't have let her ride him. Anjanette will have to—"

"—but that's why I was getting ready to come find you. It's Anjanette—"

"Janette? What's wrong?" His hand fell away from Mary as he clutched George's sleeve.

"It's the baby, I think. The women won't be more specific."

"Oh, God! It's too soon. And there isn't a doctor for miles. We were supposed to be back in Singapore before—"

"I've sent your overseer into Penang for a doctor."

Mary was forgotten. She might not have existed, for all Alex cared now. He didn't even wait for George to finish talking before he went striding to the house. He vaulted the porch railing and disappeared into the room he and his wife shared.

"Mary, those are nasty cuts. Let me get something for them," George said.

"Oh, Papa!" she cried, flinging herself on him. "I want to go home. Please take me home!"

18

Anjanette's labor was not prolonged, but was agonizing nonetheless. Fearing for the welfare of a baby born too early, she fought all the way, apparently believing that she ought to be able to stop the process by sheer willpower.

"Janette, relax," Alex said, sitting at the side of the bed holding her hand while the doctor was out of the room for a minute. "You're not helping yourself or the baby."

"It's too early, Alex," she cried, nearly crushing his fingers as another contraction gripped her.

"Now, now," he attempted to soothe her. "You heard the doctor. He said you must have miscalculated and the baby isn't nearly as early as we think. It'll be fine if you just relax."

"Oh, Alex, Alex. This baby has to live. I won't have another."

Alex was shocked at this pessimism, but tried not to show it. Was there something about her health she was hiding from him? "Of course you will have other babies. As many as you want. And this one will be fine too."

Mary and Hester sat on their beds through the long afternoon and evening, listening to Anjanette's cries. Hester wept out of natural sympathy and out of her own fear. "It's too awful! Someday that will be us," she said fearfully. "I'm not sure I ever want to have babies, Mary. It must be unbearably horrible if even Anjanette can't hide her suffering. Oh, Mary, what can we do to help her?"

"Nothing, you ninny!" Mary snapped. "What with Susu and the doctor and Alex, that room is as crowded as a country market on fair day."

"Mary, don't you care about Anjanette and the poor little baby?" Hester asked, scandalized.

"Don't talk to me in that prissy, superior way! Of course I care, but what earthly good does it do for us to whimper and wring our hands and worry?"

For all her harsh words, Mary felt every bit as bad as Hester did, but for different reasons. She regarded Anjanette's plight as a form of divine retribution that had struck the wrong victim. Already distressed and confused by the passions she'd recently been introduced to, Mary kept thinking wildly that this ought to be her punishment, not Anjanette's. It was, if nothing else, God telling Mary Beecham to behave herself or look out for what He could do.

"Well, I would think you could at least clean up and get those bloody clothes off," Hester said, worried sick and unwilling to leave Mary alone to her own misery.

"In good time."

"You look a perfect wreck, and those cuts will get infected. I think that's what you want." Hester had passed beyond caution. "You want to get sick yourself and steal the stage from poor Anjanette."

"Hester Beecham! That's the meanest thing you've ever said!"

Hester burst into tears.

Mary stomped out to take a bath and clean her wounds. The welt on her cheek had gone down, leaving only a long bruise. But the thorn slashes were all surrounded by puffy, itchy flesh, and for the first time all day, Mary wondered if by her neglect she might have actually courted illness. After dabbing herself generously with iodine, she pulled on fresh underwear and a clean cotton dress and pulled her hair into a severe knot on top of her head. If I do get sick, she told herself, nobody will ever know. I'd drop over dead before I'd complain. That would show Hester how wrong she was.

The baby was born shortly after nine o'clock. Mary had gone to the central room to try to divert her mind by studying some maps. It didn't help. She was crossing the room when she heard the little ragged squawl of the baby's first cry. She sat down suddenly and put her face in her hands. The baby was alive! God hadn't done His worst!

Susu came to the door a few minutes later and jabbered a rapid stream of information. Though she'd picked up a good deal of Malay in the weeks they'd been in Penang, Mary was too rattled to understand a word. She grabbed the small woman by the shoulders and pleaded, "Susu, please, *please* speak English!"

Susu looked over her shoulder, then whispered, "Him baby boy. Do good, that little little baby."

"And Anjanette? How is Anjanette?"

"Smiling lady, mistress is. Do fine, that lady."

Mary ran to tell Hester and then realized she'd seen and heard nothing from her father for hours. She found him around the opposite side of the house from Anjanette's room. He was sitting on the porch, his feet on the rail, a cigar in his hand and a pile of ashes next to him. "Is it over?" he asked guiltily.

Mary smiled. "Papa, you've been hiding, haven't you?"

"Even a husband is in the way at a time like this. I don't suppose any woman will ever know how useless and unwelcome a man feels when a birth is going on."

"I've felt pretty useless and unwelcome myself, Papa." She pulled a chair over and sat down upwind of the cigar. "When may we go home?" She didn't refer to her earlier outburst on the same subject. George had assumed her distress then had to do with her horse bolting, and she was content to let him go on believing that.

"I don't know. This complicates things. We'll have to take our direction from Alex. I don't know if it's ruder of us to stay or to leave. We'll see how things are tomorrow. You had better get to bed, Ginger," he said, calling her by the affectionate nickname he had sometimes used when she was little. It made Mary feel warm and safe for the first time in months.

"Ginger . . . How do you suppose my cat is? Portia never mentions him in her letters, even though I always ask."

George had noticed that Mary had stopped referring to her as Mama or Mother and now always used his wife's first name. It signaled a change he doubted she was even aware of. How would Portia take it? "Your Ginger has probably messed in every fireplace in the house by now. Castlemere will smell more of cats than rosemary some day."

She put her arm through his and leaned her head on his shoulder. "Fireplaces . . . Ginger . . . rosemary. Papa, it all makes me so homesick. Please, let's go as soon as we can. I want it to be cold enough for a fire in the fireplace and to walk out in a freezing English drizzle. I want to cuddle Ginger and admire his mouse carcasses. I want to breathe rosemary until I'm dizzy with it."

He lifted his hand and stroked her cheek with his knuckles. "So do I. Except for the dead mice."

Alex joined them at breakfast and reported on his family. "Anjanette is quite well. Tired, of course, but the doctor says she's in excellent health. The baby—we're calling him Richard—is a different matter. He's very small, and although there is nothing else wrong, the doctor warns us we must not hold out too much hope."

He was addressing his remarks to George without meeting Mary's gaze.

"Alex, I hope you'll be forthright with me," George replied. "We want to be useful—or at least not nuisances—in whatever way you wish. I know you haven't had time to consider what to do with us yet, but—"

"On the contrary, George. Janette and I have talked it over. To be honest, we'd like to be selfish and make you stay with us until she's ready to travel back to Singapore and we know about the baby's future—"

"Then we'll stay, happily," George said with a brave show of sincerity. Even Mary, who knew better, almost believed him.

Alex held up a hand to stop him. He smiled. "That's what we *want*, but we've agreed it's not best. You and the girls have your plans to think of. There are your steamer reservations and your servants left in Singapore to be fetched. And besides, I need a favor of you—"

"Anything, Alex."

"Well, I'd like to ask you to step down a peg and do my job for me, actually."

"Take the cloves to market?"

"Exactly. And meet with our suppliers. My crop is usually among the earliest, and you probably won't have to do much haggling, but if necessary—"

"I'd enjoy it enormously. That's the heart of the whole business and I'd be a poor businessman if I couldn't handle it."

Mary noticed how much healthier and happier her father suddenly looked with the prospect of something worthwhile to do. It crossed her mind to wonder if George knew she'd be right at his side every minute of any haggling that went on.

But Hester had other concerns. This conversation was

merely an obstacle to what they ought to be discussing. "Cousin Alex, can we please see the little baby?"

"Yes, Anjanette would love to show him off. In fact, she sent me to fetch an audience. If you're through eating . . . ?"

Mary trailed along, keeping a distance from Alex, who didn't seem to even be aware of her existence anyway. She held back until Hester's exclamations of admiration had died down, then came forward. Anjanette was sitting up in bed, looking radiant. Her long blond hair was loose around her shoulders and her face glowed. She held out a tiny bundle and said, "Would you like to hold him? Hester? Mary?"

"Oh, I couldn't! I'd be so afraid I'd hurt him," Hester said.

Anjanette looked at Mary. Such dithering was expected and understandable from Hester, but if Mary tried it, Anjanette would be curious if not insulted. Mary Beecham wasn't afraid of anything. She leaned forward, cradling her arms so Anjanette could place the bundle in them. She found herself looking down into the tiniest, prettiest face she'd ever seen. The baby's eyes were open and its little lips were pursed and working in kissing movements, as if still nursing.

Mary felt a sudden surge of vicarious happiness. This was surely the most perfect creature in the universe. "Oh, Anjanette, he's wonderful!" she said.

Somebody sighed with relief. Mary wondered later if it had been Alex or Hester.

"He's nearly five pounds. The doctor said he would have been enormous if he'd gone full-term," Anjanette said proudly. "He says he's seen a lot of five-pound babies thrive after the first week or so."

"He's so . . . so *real*," Mary said in wonder.

Alex stepped toward her, his arms out to take the child back. As she transferred the baby, their fingers brushing, she looked up at him. His gaze caught hers for a long, intense moment, as if to say: Yes, *this* is real. Yesterday's kiss wasn't. It didn't happen.

Mary nodded.

They were only two days late in departing for Singapore. The wagons were loaded with their precious cargo of cloves and waiting in a line. The luggage of the departing Beechams was piled onto a cart and the carriage was waiting for George and the girls. Hester had wept all morning and was red-eyed and hiccuping. "I don't want to stay here, but I wish they could come back with us all the way to England. I'll miss them all so much—even Susu and the ayah."

Mary was packed, her climbing trousers—now torn and bloody—once again packed away in the very bottom of a trunk. She knew she would never wear them again, and Hester had urged her to pitch them in a dustbin, but they were a sort of talisman to Mary, a remembrance of the day she was rudely jerked out of a romantic haze and into the cold light of adult feelings and consequences.

George had been pacing since dawn, eager to be gone. He had a book of figures Alex had prepared for him to study on the way to Singapore. In it were notes on the men he might have to deal with, past history of Beecham's dealings with them, bits of advice on their strengths and weaknesses in bargaining, records of previous and potential future crops. George was like a starving horse in sight of a trough of oats.

Anjanette had dressed and come onto the porch to bid them farewell. She was holding the new baby and Alex was holding Katie. The sight of the four of them, a happy world of their own, made Mary feel that her heart was being turned inside out. In one way she rejoiced in their happiness, their completeness. In another, she was devastated by an acid jealousy that she despised herself for feeling.

It seemed the actual departure might never get under way. Hester wept all over everyone, including her sister and father. "We're coming with you, you ninny!" Mary pointed out.

George and Alex talked a mile a minute, trying to cover all the odds and ends of business they hadn't touched on in the previous weeks. When it looked like it might soon be over, Mary hugged and kissed Anjanette, and instead of addressing Alex directly, spoke to Katie in his arms. "You hurry and grow up so you can come visit us in England, Katie. Make your daddy bring you. Good-bye, Cousin Alex." She blurted it all out in a hurry, then turned and went to the carriage before he could reply.

George joined her, half-dragging Hester, who was still trying to extract promises from Anjanette that she'd come to England and bring the children. Anjanette was sweet and sympathetic, but didn't promise anything.

At the last moment, Alex handed Katie to the ayah and

came to the carriage. He shook George's hand once more. "We'll miss you. All of you."

The carriage lurched forward.

"Good-bye! Good-bye! Oh, thank you for a wonderful, wonderful time!" Hester cried, waving.

Mary, seated with her back to the house, turned briefly, forced a smile, and waved once.

They stayed in Alex and Anjanette's home in Singapore. Without the proper mistress of the house present, both George and the staff expected Mary to fulfill her role. "You like bossing people," Hester said without rancor. "It ought to suit you."

"I don't want to bother with planning menus and sorting out squabbles in the laundry room and all that foolery," Mary grumbled.

"Too bad. You're always lording it over me for being the eldest. Now you have to pay the price. Just don't get the idea you can tell me what to do. Now, Papa has given me money for shopping, and I'm taking our governess along. Good-bye." She paused at the door and added, "I'll want a substantial luncheon. See to it, would you?" She breezed out the door with a smirk. Mary threw a sofa cushion after her and heard a shrill giggle before the front door closed.

George came in the parlor a moment later, carrying the cushion and looking perplexed. "What's this doing on the floor?"

"I threw it at Hester."

"Mary, you're in charge here. You can't act like a child."

I'm not a child anymore, am I? Mary thought. I'm twenty-one years old. Practically an old lady. "Papa, I don't want to be in charge." Catching his skeptical look, she amended, "Well, I do, actually. But I don't want to do only that. Take me along with you, please. I've never seen the warehouses here or the ships we hire or anything."

George sat down on the arm of a sofa. "Mary, be honest with me—do you really want to do all that, or do you just want to do something other than staying in the house."

She didn't hesitate. "Both."

"Fair enough."

She tied up the few household chores that demanded her attention and was sitting beside him in the carriage a half-hour later. He was impressed with the way she'd gotten herself up. Wearing an attractive but plain dress, she'd smoothed her hair back into a tidy figure eight at the back of her neck and dusted her bright complexion with a fine layer of rice powder. She was still pretty, but in a more mature, less flamboyant way than usual. It was a very suitable appearance for a daughter coming along to be in the background of business.

"What's first?" she asked.

"First we deliver Alex's cloves to his agent."

"Why? Alex is a factor. Why does he need an agent? Can't he just buy his own cloves for Beecham's?"

"He can't act as both buyer for Beecham's and seller for himself in the same transaction. He turns his crops over to an independent agent who sells them for a commission. He's free to sell them for whatever he can get, to anyone he chooses. That way, if Alex had an enemy in the company, he couldn't be accused of giving himself preferential treatment."

"I see. But has Alex enemies?"

"Not that I've ever heard of. But his importance to Beecham's is second only to mine. Power and position always create jealousy and enemies eventually."

Mary thought this over, nodding, and asked, "Then what?"

"I—that is, we—have meetings with representatives of three steamship lines to get comparison prices for transporting what we buy. I'm almost certain of the outcome. We've been dealing with the same line for the last five years, but there's always a chance somebody else may come in with a better offer."

"A lower cost, you mean?"

"That's the important factor, but not the only one. I've been reading those journals Alex prepared for me and it appears that Enoch Bowsman will probably give us a lower figure, but his ships are badly cared for. They lose a lot of travel time to repairs. That increases the percent of spoilage—"

"But if the percent of spoilage might rise by, say, ten percent, but the cost of transport is twenty percent less, it would be worth it, wouldn't it?"

George looked at her sharply. "That's right. But tell me, would it be true no matter what the quality of the crop?"

Mary thought for a moment. "Do we buy only what we need for ourselves? Haven't I heard you talk about selling surplus to other spice merchants?"

"That's right. We sometimes buy excess and resell it to

small operations that can't afford to have their own factors all over the world."

Mary considered for a long time, then said, "Then you'd have to take into consideration more than cost and spoilage. Time would matter too."

"Explain yourself," George ordered.

"Well, if we were sure we were shipping unusually good quality, and if we'd only bought what we needed for Beecham's—which would be true, since the best would be expensive—we could afford to get it back to Europe later than our competitors. If it were mediocre and we could afford to buy a surplus, we'd need to pay the extra to hurry home and sell what we didn't need at the best price possible before all the other big merchants came along with their shipments. Is that right, Papa?"

George whistled through his teeth. "That's a garbled way to put it, but you've got the idea. Have you heard me talk about this before?"

"I don't know. Maybe so." Mary didn't understand why he was asking. There wasn't anything particularly extraordinary about it all. It was simple logic, given the various factors she had to weigh and consider. It was like doing a mathematics problem. She was eager now to see it in action. It was all she could do to keep from rubbing her hands together in anticipation.

For the first time since the day the horse bolted, her mind was occupied with something other than Alex and her secret heartbreak.

Mary learned that the longer and busier the day was, the more quickly she fell asleep. To cut short those dark, private minutes between waking and dreaming was a blessing, for it was then, without distraction, when logic and intellect stepped aside for emotion, that she found it hard to avoid thinking of Alex and of her own hopeless passion for him. She knew now that it was not only hopeless but also wicked, and she was determined to cure herself of it. But it was still too soon. All she could do now was avoid the pain as much as possible.

She rose early to see to domestic matters and was always ready to accompany George. On a few occasions she was disappointed; business was a male activity, sometimes conducted in the forbidden (to her) sphere of men's clubs. But

George cooperated in scheduling most of his meetings in such a way that she could attend with him.

As for the evenings, one of her first acts was to raid Anjanette's household records. Like any good housewife and company wife, Anjanette kept a combination diary and account ledger. Looking through it, Mary could determine who had been invited to dinners and parties the year before at the same time; what they had been fed; their special preferences in the way of drink.

She made a list of people who were customarily entertained and gave it to George the middle of their first (and presumably last) week back in Singapore. "Papa, I'd like to have some of these people over to dinner. I think we should do that for Alex and Anjanette—"

"—if not for ourselves," he added. "I'd do better dealing with some of these men if I could talk to them here at leisure."

"That's what I thought."

"Not to denigrate your talents, my dear, but do you have any idea how to have a dinner party?"

"You tell the servants to fix food and you invite people," she replied. "That can't be very difficult, can it?"

George smiled at the thought of how Portia would react to a remark like that. Over the years, Portia had nearly convinced him that a dinner for eight was of a level of complexity very close to that of arranging an international treaty. Still, if she botched it, everyone would undoubtedly be very tolerant. Alex's acquaintances all knew of his situation and the fact that a green girl was trying to fill in for Anjanette.

"Very well. Let's try it. After all, we're leaving next week and they can hardly hunt us down to get revenge if it goes badly."

It went well enough.

There were mistakes, of course. She'd arranged to chill the brandy instead of the table wine. She had plenty of cigars out for the men, but no ashtrays. There wasn't really enough duck (Mary didn't like duck and was astonished that people could actually wish to eat so much of it), but an embarrassing excess of saffron rice (which she loved) more or less made up for it. She inadvertently seated the newspaper editor's wife next to the man who'd jilted her fifteen years earlier, and she'd written the wrong time on one of the invitations, causing one couple to arrive while she was still dressing.

But in spite of the ostensible formality of the occasion, a sort of happy picnic atmosphere prevailed. The ladies were sympathetic to an English girl who had the misguided courage to take on such a project without Anjanette's experienced guidance; the men were charmed by her vivacity and beauty.

George thought he might actually explode from his pride in her. He'd never been happier in his life.

When it was all over and Mary had trilled her last cheerful good nights, she kicked one of her silver slippers across the parlor and did a little sailor's chanty dance. "I did it, Papa! I really did it. Nobody got mad enough to throw food or hit me. It must have been a success."

He congratulated her and participated in a blow-by-blow rehash of the whole evening, successes and failures alike. When Mary had finally wound down, he said, "I've been thinking about our plans . . . ."

"So have I."

"Do you think—?"

"Do you—?"

"You go first."

"I think we should stay awhile longer. But only if you want to, Papa."

She'd been toying with this idea all evening. When they got back to England, she would revert to being the elder child in the household, under Portia's rule. After this single heady success as an adult, that would be hard to take. But as Alex and Anjanette wouldn't be able to travel to Singapore for at least a month or six weeks yet, it had become the ideal sphere for Mary.

"I think we should do our duty to Alex and Anjanette," George said.

He, too, had enjoyed himself tremendously since their return. In spite of not feeling top notch physically, he'd been fascinated by actual participation in this end of the business and hadn't done badly at it. The dinner party had put a sweet frosting on his content. It would be a pity to deliberately walk away from it all too soon.

"If we stayed another month, we could still be home well before Christmas," Mary said.

Hester was sent ahead on schedule with a respectable family they'd met several times. She took the maid and governess with her. Mary and George settled in to the most enjoyable month imaginable. Mary studied the journal Alex had prepared and tagged along with George as much as she could manage. He even offered to let her negotiate with one planter who was too young and powerless to openly object, but she demurred. "He'd be too insulted at having to talk to me, Papa. You talk. I'll listen." This was a triumph of realism over ego that impressed him far more than she suspected.

She planned two more large dinner parties and a half-dozen smaller get-togethers. There were no disasters.

George had always loved her; he had enjoyed her quick mind. Now he came to respect it as well. There had been times over the years when he deeply regretted having no sons. He was resigned to the fact that Portia would probably never give him one. But in that month in Singapore, he realized he did have a perfect son—an intelligent, eager, strong-minded son capable of understanding the subtleties of business.

But this "son" happened to be a beautiful girl.

It gave him a great deal to think about.

19

—————◆—————

June 1927

"I always thought we'd go back to Singapore, but we never did," Mary said.

She didn't look any more rested, but her voice was firm and sure. She sounded more like her old self than at any time previously during Natalie's visit.

"Why didn't you go back again?" Natalie asked.

"No one reason. It was never the right time. Except once. I wanted to take your father, as my father had taken me. We were ready to sail and he got measles and they wouldn't let us take him on the ship even though we promised to keep him chained in a stateroom. I can't blame them."

"He never told me."

"He probably doesn't remember. He was only four. It was too soon to take him anyway. He wouldn't have enjoyed it."

"Why didn't you try again?"

"I don't know, exactly. After that one attempt, we just never quite got around to going. Business interfered, family problems made it seem best to put it off just a bit longer." Mary took a sip of the tea Natalie had brought to her.

"You regret not seeing Singapore again?"

"In a way I do, but I suppose it's changed, and that would have made me sad. A violation of my rose-tinted memories. It seems strange to me to realize how long ago it was when I was there with Papa and Hester. I can close my eyes even now and picture it as vividly as if I were there."

She shut her eyes and smiled. Natalie asked, "What do you see, Grandmama?"

"Not Singapore. I never think of Singapore. I always see

the plantation on Penang. The big house on stilts. The lizards running underneath when you come around a corner and surprise them. The banana trees that we weren't to get near because of the spiders that liked to live in the bunches of fruit."

"I'll bet you broke that rule."

Mary smiled without opening her eyes. "Occasionally. I liked bananas. I liked everything about Penang. Even the heat and the lizards. I especially liked the parrots. You know where you are with a parrot."

Natalie giggled. "What does that mean?"

"They don't mince their words—not the silly words people teach them when they're caged, their own words. When you go into their jungle, they tell you in no uncertain terms that it's their home and you're trespassing. Aunt Nell would have loved them with their violently colored plumage and rude manners. That was my one constant sadness about that trip—that Aunt Nell couldn't be there to enjoy it with me. She'd have sorted me out, too."

Mary's voice drifted off, but into memories, not sleep. Natalie sat in silence with her for a long time, then finally said, "Why are you letting me read the diaries?"

Mary's eyes opened immediately and she gave Natalie the direct look that used to sometimes frighten her when she was a child and had done something wrong.

"Don't you want to read them?" Mary asked.

"Of course. I'm fascinated. But I keep wondering why you want me to."

"Because there's something you must know. Something you must see to for me."

"Why can't you just tell me?"

"Because something happened and you must know why and how it came to be. It's very important that you understand thoroughly. I shall be gone soon and you're my heir in more ways than you know."

"Papa's your heir, not me."

"And then you after him. You are the only child of my only . . . son." There was a pause before the last word. "Beecham's will someday be yours, but being my grand-daughter comes with a responsibility."

The finality in her tone was unmistakable. Natalie was more confused than ever and wanted to question her further, but knew it was no use. She poured her grandmother a

fresh cup of hot tea and said, "I'm pleased to read the
diaries, Grandmama, and I'll do anything you ask of me."

She picked up the little book from the table beside her
and opened it to the flat silver bookmark.

> 28 September 1873. We go home in two days. I
> can't bear to go, but I couldn't bear to stay
> either. . . ."

20

September 1873

They got word from Alex that Anjanette and the baby were both well and they were going to attempt to make the trip back to Singapore with an arrival date that was to be three days after George and Mary's planned departure. "Do you think we ought to change our plans again?" George asked Mary. "Won't it seem rude to miss them by such a short time?"

"No, Papa," Mary said firmly. She'd taken on Portia's role of social arbiter for the time being. "They expected us to be gone long before this. We'd be putting them under the obligation to entertain us if we stayed, and I'm sure that wouldn't be good for Anjanette. She'll need to rest from the journey."

George, who was secretly wrestling with a digestive distress, gladly accepted this at face value.

Mary's last two days were taken up with frenzied shopping. Hester had been purchasing and stashing away presents during the whole trip and had had no such errands when she left, but Mary had utterly overlooked the tradition that returning travelers were expected to bear gifts. Unfortunately, many of the best shops in Singapore carried European goods. Mary snorted about how utterly stupid it all was, then got the Chinese cook and a translator and ventured into the Chinese section of town. George handed her wads of banknotes, grateful to be spared the necessity of shopping for himself. Mary came back frazzled and sweating, but pink-cheeked with victory. She'd gotten a lovely long strand of fat pearls for Portia and a pair of cloisonné vases. She had an ivory-backed comb, brush, and mirror set for Agnes and pretty little carved ivory boxes for the rest of the servants.

She also got a half-dozen small ornamental bowls for

everybody she hadn't thought of but who would expect a gift. For herself she bought two batik shawls and a huge, fragile bird cage, *sans* birds. She didn't believe in caging birds and she knew the bamboo structure would probably crumble before she got it home, but it was too beautiful to resist. She purchased a small porcelain bowl with a vivid crimson glaze for Ginger.

There was a nice crowd of friends they'd made in the last month to see them off. But as soon as the waving was done, George retired to his stateroom. They had hardly cleared the Strait of Malacca when he fell ill. He'd been building up to it for months, although he had been more perky and energetic during the six weeks in Singapore than during the time in Penang. Mary wasn't entirely surprised when she knocked on his stateroom door and his valet informed her that her father wasn't at all well. What surprised her was the extent of his illness. For several days, she feared for his very life. He was so violently nauseated he couldn't even keep water down, and quickly became nearly comatose.

"It isn't malaria, is it?" she asked the ship's doctor.

"No, it's not. But I'm afraid it's every bit as serious. It's an intestinal parasite," he told her, sensing immediately that this wasn't the sort of weepy, fainting young woman you had to mince words with. "It could be any one of a half-dozen sorts. If it's one of the worst, I don't hold out much hope. If not, he may recover quite nicely, though slowly. Has he lost weight recently?"

"Yes, over several months now."

"That's a good sign, on the whole. It means he's probably had it for some time. It's not one of the fast, deadly ones. I don't have the equipment aboard to do any testing. We'll just have to wait and see."

Mary wanted to take him ashore at the next stop to recuperate, but the doctor argued with her. "He's miserable and will stay miserable wherever he is. He might as well be coming closer to home while he's too sick to know the difference. Perhaps as we near the south coast of France . . ."

Mary sat by his bed all day and evening, and only the doctor and George's valet joining forces got her to go to her own cabin at night to get some sleep. On the third day, George was well enough to be cranky and ask for food— although he wasn't able to keep it down—which encouraged the doctor greatly. "He's going to make it, Miss Beecham.

Now, why don't you just get some rest yourself. Or get out on deck and have a good time with some of the other young people."

There was no question of that. She stayed with him as if afraid he might get away from her if she let him out of sight. They didn't talk much—George was too exhausted from his ordeal—but Mary had a great deal of time to think. That, of course, was the one thing she didn't want. At first, all she could think about was George himself and the possibility that he might die. It was something she had never contemplated and it shook her to the core.

George was the one person in the world who was wholeheartedly on her side, and she'd never realized until she faced the very real possibility of losing him just how much that meant. It would leave her with only Portia and Hester as family. Portia didn't like her, and Hester, though beloved, was determined to marry and start her own family at the first opportunity.

All those scenes in which Mary had imagined herself as an interesting spinster suddenly rose to haunt her. She didn't *want* to be an interesting spinster.

What is there to do, then? she asked herself fiercely. Marry, of course, she replied. Marry whom? Not the only person she'd ever considered: Alex.

As she sat by her father's bedside, preparing him cooling drinks and wringing out cold compresses for his head, she circled the thought, coming at it from odd angles, justifying, imagining, twisting the facts, and speculating. But in the end, she couldn't fool herself. Alex was happily married to a wonderful woman and was the father of her children. Mary shouldn't, couldn't, and wouldn't ever attempt to interfere in that relationship again. It was a silly and dangerous dream that had to be retired and forgotten.

George was well enough to come out on deck and be settled into a chair with blankets tucked around him by the time they passed Gibraltar. "You love Hester, don't you?" he asked Mary.

"Hester who?" she replied with a laugh. Then: "Did you really mean that? Of course I love Hester, Papa."

"And you'd take care of her if she needed you?"

"Why should Hester need me to take care of her? I would, but I don't underst—"

"And Portia? I know she acts as if she's capable of handling anything, but she was raised by a father who believed in keeping girls ignorant. If I were gone, would you—?"

"Papa, that's enough! You're not going to be gone anytime in the next few decades. You've been very sick, I know, but the doctor says you're recovering at a marvelous rate."

He sat staring as the vast rock seemed to slide past them silently. "Still, if I were to die, you'd take care of Portia?"

Mary was still determined to jolly him out of his morbid mood. "Yes. I'd probably have to tie her up with stout twine and gag her before she'd let me, but I'd certainly try."

"Good," he said solemnly.

George was well enough to disembark at Southampton without any signs of his devastating illness. Mary could see the new lines of age and strain in his face and thought his pallor was obvious, but no one else seemed to notice. "Portia, my dear, you didn't need to come to meet us," he said.

"I wouldn't have missed your return," she said, slightly offended. "Mary, how very freckled you've become in the sun. You must have buttermilk facials when you get home."

"Thank you, I am glad to be home," Mary said. At George's sharp look, she put aside the urge to continue in this sarcastic vein and kissed Portia's soft cheek. "I'm happy to see you again, Portia."

If Portia noticed they were on a first-name basis, she either approved or decided to ignore it. "Hester is about someplace. I declare, that girl is never where she's supposed to be."

As if summoned up by this remark, Hester appeared through the crowd. She was being steered by a very handsome man. "Oh, Papa, Mary!" she cried, flinging herself at them in turn. "I thought you were never going to come back. I'm so thrilled to see you!"

Mary noticed Hester's hair was done with fashionably crimped bangs and her eyes sparkled as they never had in the East.

"Aren't you going to introduce your escort?" Mary asked after a bone-crushing hug. The tall sandy-haired man was standing back from the family reunion. He looked slightly amused; whether it was fond amusement at Hester's antics or a patronizing attitude, Mary couldn't tell.

"Oh, Papa, you remember Mr. Jamison Hewitt. Mary, Mr. Hewitt. He brought Mama and me down to meet you in his carriage. Wasn't that kind of him?"

"Very kind, sir," George said, already looking around for their baggage.

"I'm glad to meet you, Mr. Hewitt," Mary said.

He put a hand to his chest. "I'm wounded to the heart, Miss Beecham. We have met before."

"We have? I'm so sorry . . ."

"Mr. Hewitt was a guest at Castlemere. I think it was the night Aunt Nell died, wasn't it?" Hester said.

Hester was unaware of her *faux pas*. He wasn't. "Sadly enough, that is true. A very tragic occasion. I should not have mentioned our previous acquaintance and recalled such an unhappy time."

Mary excused herself and went to help George and his valet locate and identify their belongings. Just for a moment there, her heart had constricted as if Nellanor had died only the day before. It had been eleven and a half months—Mary didn't even need to count up; some internal calendar kept track for her. There had been very few days in those eleven months that she hadn't thought of Aunt Nell. She was perpetually thinking: "What would Aunt Nell have said?" "How would Aunt Nell have handled this?" "How Aunt Nell would love this view."

She didn't like Mr. Hewitt for being a part of that tragedy. No, that wasn't fair! she told herself firmly. It had nothing to do with him and it certainly wasn't his fault it happened the night he came to dinner. Nor was it his fault that Hester had so tactlessly pointed out the connection. Still, she must be nice to him. Hester was obviously smitten and Mary didn't want her beau scared off the family by a cranky sister.

They set out for Portia's cousin's house, where they would stay the night before an early-morning departure for Castlemere. Mary was perplexed when Portia took charge of the transportation and forced Mary into sitting next to Mr. Hewitt. Oh, well, she probably just wanted him seated across from Hester so he could see her better. "So nice of you to bring the rest of my family along, Mr. Hewitt," George said.

"I thought you and Mrs. Beecham might like to take my carriage back tomorrow and I'll hire a rig to take your daughters, and another for your servants and luggage. That is, if you'd trust the Misses Beecham to my care?"

"Oh, Papa, what a good idea!" Hester all but screamed. "Please, Papa!"

George was willing to acquiesce, but Portia looked distinctly unhappy. Mary, full of good resolutions to get along with her, said, "Why don't I ride with you and Papa, and Hester can go with Mr. Hewitt."

"No!" Portia exclaimed; then, in calmer tones, "that would be quite improper. I think if Mr. Hewitt took both the girls directly ahead of us . . . ? George?"

"Yes, yes. Very good. Where is that brown valise with my paperwork?"

It was a cool, sunny day and Mary felt she wanted to embrace it with her eyes. "Aren't you chilled, Miss Beecham?" Jamison Hewitt asked. "I have another carriage robe here." Hester was bundled up to the ears and her nose was an unbecoming red.

"I *am* chilled, but I want to be," Mary replied. "I had almost forgotten what it is to be cold, and it's wonderful! And I think you should stop 'Miss Beechaming' us both. It's too confusing altogether. Please call me Mary."

"And I'm H-H-Hester," Hester said through chattering teeth.

"I'm Jamison, but my good friends call me Jemmy."

"Then I'll address you as Jamison until I feel we've became true friends," Mary said.

"Mary, that's r-r-rude!" Hester exclaimed.

"Not at all, Hester," Jamison said. "Your sister is just going to make me win her over, which is only right. But our acquaintance is more mature. Do you consider me your true friend yet?"

"Certainly, *Jemmy*," she said emphatically, glaring at Mary.

Mary smiled at her sister. "Well, Jamison, tell me all about yourself. Where are you from?"

Hester, pleased that Mary was making an effort, took up the subject and put Jamison through a rather intensive hour of questioning. He was, they found out, thirty years old, the only child of a Canterbury barrister who was himself the youngest son of a highly respected baronet. Jamison had studied for the bar, but did not practice law very much of the time. He lived in London and his interests were in property and horses.

A good family name and not much money or ambition, Mary thought to herself. But then, why shouldn't Hester marry such a man if that's what she wanted? Hester wouldn't be a good helpmeet to a man of enormous business energy, but she would bring a tremendous dowry to marriage. She didn't have to marry a rich man, and Portia would be pleased at the family connection. Still, Mary found herself wishing that Hester would set her sights on someone more—more admirable. It would make it easier to be happy for her.

"Of course, I do find the spice trade interesting," Jamison was saying. "I always have."

Hester glowed. Mary frowned. That was a bit blatant of him.

"Tell us all about London, Jamison," Mary said. "We have little knowledge of the city, living in the country as we do." She had quite honestly forgotten that it was the city of her own origin. Anyway, she'd spent her formative years in a different London—a shabby, hungry London he probably didn't know existed.

He regaled them with stories that were so funny that Mary had all but discounted her reservations about him by the time they neared Castlemere. He was, for all his apparent negligence where business was concerned, a very bright, witty man-about-town. He knew everybody who was anybody, and told delightful stories on the great and near-great without ever giving the impression of dropping names.

Mary lost interest in his stories, however, when Castlemere came into view. She had to fight down the urge to leap out of the carriage and run the rest of the way. "I'm home, house!" she said under her breath. She'd never noticed how long the drive was before.

When the carriage stopped, she hopped out before anyone could make a move to open the door for her. The servants, forewarned of their arrival, were lined up by the open door to greet the returning master. Mary ran up the steps and threw her arms around Agnes. "Oh, I'm so happy to be back! Agnes, you've put on weight while I was gone. Half a stone at the least. I'm going to work it off you."

"Get off me, you big silly," Agnes said, smiling and crying. "You look as brown as a Gypsy."

Portia had come along behind. She'd never approved of this sort of familiarity with the servants. "Mary, really . . ."

"Where's Ginger?" Mary whispered to Agnes.

Agnes crooked a finger and they slipped away upstairs.

George, all his baggage finally accounted for, watched her go. He hoped Portia didn't notice how Mary hitched up her skirts and took the stairs two at a time. She had grown up so much on this trip, and yet was still a delightful child in some ways. Would that she could stay just as she was forever.

He repressed a sigh. How he longed to spend a quiet, solitary hour in his library getting his bearings, and then go to bed for a day or two. But Portia would be insulted about the first part and fuss horribly over him about the second. He just couldn't face a fuss. And there was this Hewitt person to take into consideration. He didn't much like him; a bit brash and pushy, it seemed. Still, he had been helpful, and it would be surly not to invite him to stay. "Mr. Hewitt—"

"Please, sir, if you'd call me Jamison . . . ?"

"Jamison, then. Will you be able to stay with us for a day or two and let us express our appreciation?"

"Oh, please do," Hester put in soulfully.

"Thank you, but that would be a pleasure that I must deny myself. An outsider has no place in a family reunion after such an extended trip," he said. "May I take you up on the invitation at a later date?"

He'd saved himself in George's eyes. Suddenly he seemed quite a good sort of fellow.

"If my husband is agreeable, I'm hoping to have a house party shortly after New Year's Day," Portia said. "Perhaps you would join us then?"

"Papa, look how fine he is!" Mary said, coming back down the stairs with an orange armload of fur. "Oh, are you leaving, Mr. Hewitt? Thank you for escorting us."

Hester went to the door with the guest and saw him off. She came back and gripped Mary's arm and pulled her aside. "Isn't he the most divine man in the entire world, Mary? I think he likes me. I truly think he does!"

For all her happiness at being back at Castlemere, Mary felt a strange jolt at these words. Hester had always talked about marrying, but it had all been subjective. Now there was a real man who appeared to be courting her. It could happen! If she didn't marry Jamison Hewitt, she would marry someone else before long.

Mary had a sudden presentiment that all their lives were about to change; just like coming around a bend in the road and knowing you can't look back anymore and see where you came from. "I'm sure he does, Hester," she said, burying her face in Ginger's fur to hide her expression.

21

Dr. Jonathan Engle put his instruments away and sat down to light a pipe. As George rebuttoned his shirt and tucked it in, Engle studied the great bed in the master suite. All that elaborate carving really was extraordinary, and the size of it! He and George had once sneaked in here when they were small boys and played on that bed as if it were a ship and they were pirates. There'd been hell to pay when George's mother found out, but that was just part of the adventure. "George, do you remember . . . ?"

George grinned and grabbed a corner post of the huge bed. "These were the masts and we draped the sheets around as sails. Were we ever that young?"

"We're not exactly in our dotage now!" Jonathan said. He was slightly vain of his youthful appearance.

George pulled up a chair and sat down. "Well, Jonathan, how am I? Am I going to make old bones?"

Engle was all professional now. "George, I just don't know. I don't see a lot of tropical diseases in my practice, you know. Now, if it were a touch of gout . . . You're in need of rest, that much is obvious even to a backward country doctor. But I think you'd also better see someone in London. I'll write some letters, ask some questions, and find a good man for you."

"So you think it may be serious?"

"It may be. Asking me that is like pointing at a distant rise and asking me to identify the types of trees. Living around here, I can make a guess of what's likely to grow, but haven't the vision to be sure. Somebody might have planted an olive grove that I can't see."

George laughed. "Even your metaphors have gotten bucolic, Jon!"

Engle shrugged. "I'm a bumpkin, but even bumpkins have their uses."

"Let's go down and have a drink and a good cigar together before I send you along to the rest of your patients," George said, leading the way. "Do you remember Winston Foxworth-Wilding from school?"

"The Fox? Of course! Even if I didn't remember him, I'd know who you mean. Turned himself into quite a famous man, our old Fox."

"We've corresponded over the years, and I had a letter from him when I got back."

"Posted from some Himalayan peak or a Mexican temple, no doubt. Is there anywhere the man hasn't been?"

"Probably not, but the letter came from London."

"And you want to go running up there?"

"I do need to for business reasons," George said, justifying himself to his physician, even though he'd already made up his mind.

"I can't stop you. Never could. Well, get what rest you can and give my greeting to the Fox. I'll make some inquiries about a doctor to see there. Didn't Foxworth-Wilding marry that pretty girl we were both smitten with for a week or so? Dotty? Dorothy?"

"Dorothea. She died over the summer. That's one of the things he said in his letter."

"It's no wonder, the way he dragged the poor woman all over the face of the earth. She must have been a rare one to survive that sort of life as long as she did. About that drink you offered . . . ?"

"You actually *know* Winston Foxworth-Wilding!" Mary exclaimed over dinner that night.

"Mary, would you please modulate your voice," Portia ordered.

"I've mentioned him before," George said.

"You never!"

"I most certainly have. I've known him since we were in short trousers. In fact, it's my doing in a way that he became so famous. He and I got sent down from school one term—"

"What for?" Hester asked.

George grinned. "I don't think you need to know."

"George, you're giving the girls the wrong impression," Portia said.

"No, I'm afraid I'm giving them the right one. In any case, we got sent down and my father put me to work doing dogsbody work at the London warehouse. Foxworth-Wilding's father thought it was a good punishment and put him to work with me. Sadly for them, we thought it was grand. It was there, in the midst of the spices, that the Fox started getting curious about the places it all came from and started studying geography. In fact, over the years, he's maintained his interest and given me some valuable information. Impending revolts in the countries we buy from, droughts, and such."

"Oh, Papa, imagine knowing him! Are you going to see him when you go to London? May I come along? Please!" Mary begged.

"I suppose so, but understand, I'm going to conduct business and visit with an old school friend. You can't—"

"Interfere in your conversations. I know. I just want to listen to him. I won't talk at all."

George gave this promise the skeptical look it deserved.

"Papa, he's been everywhere, just everywhere. And he's brilliant. I'm reading one of his books now. The one about the White Nile. I think it's mean of you to keep him a secret from me all these years. I really do."

"If you'd stop chattering and listen once in a while . . ."

"I have so many things I want to ask him. If I could be excused, please, there are some notes I want to make right away so I don't forget anything."

Hester had been listening to this discussion and toying with her potatoes. "Mary, you must be mad! Why would you go trailing all the way to London to talk to some dusty old geographer?"

Portia nodded her agreement, but George and Mary both stared at her as if she'd grown an extra head.

"Mary, quit pacing," George ordered.

They were in the library of the London house. It was three minutes until seven and their guest was due at seven. Mary was ready with a stack of books and a notebook full of questions she'd jotted down from her reading.

The young footman, Bartlet, opened the door of the library. "Mr. Foxworth-Wilding," he said ominously.

George and his old friend fell on each other with handshakes, back slaps, and greetings. Mary was agog. Even though she knew this man was a contemporary of her father's, she'd been imagining him older and more professorial. He should have been tall and storkish. But Fox-

worth-Wilding was half a head shorter than George, with a
sturdy, compact frame that might well run to fat someday.
He had a broad, intelligent brow and carrot-colored hair
only lightly interwoven with gray. He had a wide smile with
a slight gap between his front teeth. Bubbling with energy,
he didn't appear young so much as youthful. He simply
didn't suit the picture Mary had invented and she was having a very hard time believing this was Mr. Foxworth-Wilding.

"I want you to meet my daughter, Fox," George said.
"This is Mary."

"Who would have thought?" his guest replied, taking
Mary's hand and bending over it to bestow a gallant kiss. "I
always told people I knew you were good for something,
George. I wasn't widely believed, but I guess your secret
skill was in fathering beautiful daughters. Where is Hester?"

"Hester is in the country with her mother. I hope you'll
come down and let us entertain you there."

"I'd be honored. I'm pleased to meet you, Miss Beecham."

"Mr. Foxworth-Wilding, I'd like to ask you a few—"

"Mary, I told you—"

"Yes, Papa, I'm sorry."

Winston Foxworth-Wilding looked from father to daughter. "Is there something wrong?"

"Not at all," George replied. "I told Mary she could have
dinner with us on the condition that she kept very quiet and
left us alone afterward to rehash our boyhood sins. Mary
has promised, but I warn you, it's a promise I don't expect
her to keep unless constantly reminded."

"Well, you must act the father, but you can't expect me
to help you. I'd very much like to hear what your daughter
has to say," Foxworth-Wilding said with a grin. He did look
a little foxish, Mary thought. Not in a pointy, feral sense,
but like a well-furred, well-fed fox who knows the stupid,
yappy dogs have no idea where his earth is.

"I would just like to ask you some questions," Mary said,
"but I'll wait." Her tone was so martyred that both men
laughed.

"Dinner is served, if that is convenient," Bartlet said
sorrowfully.

"He's training to become butler," George explained quietly as they went into the dining room. "I don't know if
we'll withstand the process. I keep expecting him to burst
into tears. Now, Mary, will you be hostess?"

Mary hardly got to speak a word, and after a very short

time she ceased to want to. Winston Foxworth-Wilding was every bit as fascinating a man as she'd hoped. His last trip had been to the Outback of Australia and he spoke with knowledge and wit about the landscape, the weather, the people, and the history. Dinner was finished much too soon for Mary. But she'd promised George she'd leave him alone with his old friend, and so she excused herself as soon as they had finished the meal.

"She's a perfectly lovely child, George," Foxworth-Wilding said. "She must be a great joy to you. A bright girl."

"She is really extraordinarily intelligent, if I may be forgiven such a distinctly fatherly assessment. We just returned from a trip to Singapore." He explained to his friend about the circumstances that had caused him to temporarily take up Alex's reins, and the amazing grasp Mary immediately had had of the business principles involved in the spice trade. "My Aunt Nell and I had seen to it that she had a good education, probably too good an education for a girl. Most men are intimidated by a pretty girl who's as smart as they are. But I didn't realize until recently how quick she was to apply book knowledge to real life. It was most gratifying."

"If I have a single regret in life, it's that Dorothea and I didn't have children. I envy you the opportunity to take such pride in the accomplishments of a child."

"About Dorothea . . . I was very sorry to hear of her death."

"Thank you, George. But I think I regret the life I put her through more than her death."

"Surely not!"

"She despised travel. If she'd had her way, she'd have snuggled into a pleasant little house in the country and joined the ladies' sewing circle and had church fetes on the lawn. I knew that and I always rather meant to give her that someday. But there was always one more trip, one more unknown to chart and map, one more challenge to take up before settling down. I never really thought about how very devoted she was. She could have stayed in her cottage in the country while I wandered all over the world, but she never even hinted at the possibility. Every time I went, she packed and was on the boat a step ahead of me. A rare woman."

"Then she must have loved your work as well as you."

"Not in the least. I don't fool myself, George. I miss her and feel a terrible guilt, but that doesn't change the facts.

Dorothea was the dearest soul ever, but not very smart. She had absolutely no curiosity and wasn't faintly interested in what I was doing. She was one of those intrepid English-women who can go anywhere and take England with them without even noticing where they are."

"We saw a lot of those people in Singapore."

"The day she died, we'd gone to Ayers Rock and she'd worn wool stockings and a high-necked day dress. She had a heat stroke and went wild when the aborigine guide tried to undo the buttons so she could cool off. She literally pre-ferred death to impropriety. I was out in the field. They told me about it later."

"That must have been terrible for you."

"Horrible. I don't believe I've ever been quite so angry with anyone in my life as I was with her for dying so stupidly. But it's been a long time now. I'm not good at keeping up grief or guilt. Tell me about yourself and Portia. I remember your wedding. She was the prettiest bride I ever saw."

"I'll tell her you said that. Portia is very well. Very contented with our life, I think. You will come down and see us before you go off again, won't you?"

"George, I don't think I'll leave England again. I've al-ways told myself the reason I go around learning about other peoples is to share the things I learn. But I've not lived up to that as well as I should. I've done the five books, but one of them is badly outdated since I wrote it and I intend to revise it for reissue. I've got my Australian notes to compile and publish, and trunks of other material I've always intended to get in order."

"I can't imagine you staying put."

"I couldn't until recently. But it was strange—when En-gland heaved into view this time, I felt an extraordinary sense of relief. It was almost as if some voice spoke to me and said, 'There! Now you're home safely. You never have to leave again.' A foolish notion, I know. But there it is."

They talked until well after midnight, catching up on the missing years and frankly gossiping about old friends and acquaintances they had in common. By the time Foxworth-Wilding's carriage rattled off into the chill night, George felt happier than he had for a long time. He was beginning to see possible solutions to a number of things that had been troubling him. There would be some additional ground-work, but yes, it might all work out very well.

*   *   *

George's primary aim in visiting London was to see to it that the spices he'd purchased in Singapore had arrived in good order. Neither he nor Mary questioned whether she would accompany him. She'd had nearly as much to do with the purchase as he. She was perplexed, however, when they left the London house the next morning and headed the wrong way. "We're picking up the Fox at his hotel," George explained. "He was anxious to see the old place, and I thought you'd like to have him along."

"He's so interesting, Papa. You're lucky to have a friend like that," she said. "I wish I had interesting friends. I wish I had friends, come to think of it." She said it lightly, but George could hear the genuine pain in the remark.

"Your Aunt Nell and I have done you a disservice, Mary. We've nearly cut you off from the opportunity of having women friends. Most women aren't trained to fill and use their minds, and they will resent you for it. So will many men."

"You mean I'm never going to have friends, Papa?"

"No, I mean you'll have to be selective. You're a wealthy young woman; you have a good family name; you're very attractive. People will like you, or pretend to like you, for those things instead of what you really are inside. You'll have to learn to distinguish between the climbers and the real friends. There are a fair number of young men in this world who can act the lover for a generous dowry."

She cast him a sidelong look. "You sound like you're thinking of someone in particular."

"Whom do you suppose I mean?" George asked, unwilling to commit himself.

"I think you're talking about Mr. Hewitt."

"Yes, I did have Mr. Hewitt in mind. But I may be misjudging him. He may be as devoted to Hester as she seems to wish. Still, Hester has neither beauty nor outstanding intellect. Perhaps—"

"I'm worried about Hester too, Papa."

She said it in such a fussy, motherly way that George laughed affectionately. "Don't be concerned, Ginger. It's my job to worry about my girls. Ah, there he is, waiting for us."

They scooped up Foxworth-Wilding and went to the warehouse. "I can't wait to get back to the old place, George," he said. "Such memories!"

"You liked the warehouse, Mr. Foxworth-Wilding?" Mary asked.

"I loved it. I told myself I wouldn't settle down until I'd seen every place the spices came from. I think I just about accomplished that goal."

When they rolled into the open center yard of the warehouse, he closed his eyes and breathed deeply. "That's the living perfume of adventure and history!" Opening his eyes, he addressed Mary. "Do you realize that gold and spice are the two most important elements in human history? It was the search for both that made all the great voyages of discovery happen. At times, certain spices have been worth far more their equal weight in gold. Saffron still is."

Mary stared at him with awe. Here was someone who felt as she and Papa and Aunt Nell did about spices. Not even Alex had shown the mystical appreciation Mr. Foxworth-Wilding expressed.

Clyde Gordon, grown plumper and happier than ever, came out of the offices to greet them. "Thought you'd caught me a bit unawares, didn't you, Mr. Beecham? Thought I'd be napping!" he said cheerfully. It was a pretense of his that George dropped in unexpectedly to try to catch him not doing his work, whereas both of them knew full well that Clyde not only did his job well, he did it almost perpetually. He was the first person in every morning and the last out in the evenings.

George introduced Foxworth-Wilding and Clyde replied, "I got a slivery-bit of a memory of you, sir. Wasn't you with Mr. Beecham one school term when we was all youngsters? Seem to recall you knocking over a whole case of cardamom."

Foxworth-Wilding clapped him on the shoulder. "You've an exceptional memory, my man. I could use you when I start feeling my head swell. Was that ever a mess! I thought Mr. Beecham's father was going to thrash me."

"Here, let's get out of the way," Clyde warned as the double front gates were dragged open and an enormous workhorse pulling a heavily laden cart came toward them. "That's them vanilla pods we been getting such good reports on. I got word from the docks they was in this morning. Would you gentlemen and Miss Beecham like to see?"

"We certainly would," George replied.

They stood aside while two burly workers dragged a heavy wooden case off the cart and opened it. Inside were three large tin boxes of nearly a hundred pounds each. Clyde pulled out a steel tool and got into one. Lifting the lid and then a couple layers of paraffin paper, he exclaimed, "Right nice, Mr. Beecham. Smell."

The four of them leaned over the box, taking deep breaths. "Take out a bundle, Clyde, and let's see how they look."

"Mexican primera, aren't they?" Foxworth-Wilding asked.

"Yes, we buy mainly first grade. Although we usually bring in some chica prima for the soap and perfume trade. But anything below that is useless. Have you seen vanilla grown?" George asked. "What a question. I know you have. You wrote to me about Potier's Process."

"Who or what is that?" Mary asked.

Foxworth-Wilding explained, "Normally the pods are put through a number of elaborate, time-consuming processes before they're ready to ship. In Guiana they're put in ashes until they start to shrivel; then they're cleaned off and rubbed with olive oil and left to finish drying in the open air."

"But don't they keep the flavor of the ashes?" Mary asked.

"That's one of the problems and the reason most countries don't use the process. In Peru they dip them in boiling water, sometimes three or four times, then hang them out to dry. The best results are from Mexico, but it's the most tedious, too. They're 'sweated'—spread out on wool blankets every morning, then wrapped up in the blankets and put in airtight boxes to sweat all night. That goes on for about two months. The Potier Process is much easier. The pods are picked, put into barrels of rum, and left alone for a month, then aired for three or four days before being put back into the rum and shipped. Very little labor, and it makes for perfectly wonderful rum as a by-product, so to speak."

Mary had been listening with interest. She'd never learned as much about vanilla as some of the other spices. "Still, it must be a very expensive process. All that rum, and the cost of transporting liquid instead of dried pods. So much heavier to pay by the pound. And the pods still have to be dried again at this end before they can be sold. They might mildew before they dry in this climate."

George grinned at Foxworth-Wilding's expression.

"Quite right you are, young lady," the geographer replied. "I believe I may have just made a fool of myself. Mr. Gordon, would you like to tell everyone again about what a clumsy boy I was, just to puncture my pretensions?" It was apparent that he wasn't offended, merely amused at his own expense.

"I'm sorry. Did I say something wrong?" Mary asked.

Foxworth-Wilding smiled. "No, you just got to the end of my stuffy little lecture before I did. Mr. Gordon, let's see those pods."

Clyde was smirking happily over the way little Miss Beecham had put the famous man in his place. ("Without never knowing she done it," as he told his wife that evening. "You ought t'see her, Millie. Perky and bright as a new penny, she is.")

"Here you are," he said, laying a sheet of paraffin paper on the ground and setting a bundle tied with raffia twine on the paper. The pods were all of a length, about ten inches long, and tightly packed together. The outside of the bundle consisted of sixteen perfectly matched pods stacked side by side, all a deep, leathery brown and glossy with their own aromatic oil.

"Handsome specimens, eh?" Clyde said as proudly as if he'd grown them himself.

"What else do you know about vanilla, Miss Beecham?" Foxworth-Wilding asked, having learned his lesson.

"Almost nothing. They're a sort of orchid and grow on vines, don't they?"

Foxworth-Wilding told them about the year he had spent in Mexico and the process of planting, fertilizing, and harvesting he'd observed. Much of what he described was new even to George. Both he and Mary were still asking questions when they dropped him off at his hotel late that afternoon.

"No wonder he's so famous, Papa. He must be absolutely the smartest man in the world. Don't you think so?"

"Oh?"

"Well, next to you. And maybe Mr. Gordon. He talks in a funny sort of way, but he knows a lot, doesn't he?"

"Yes, I think the two of them may just represent the ends of the spectrum. Clyde is all 'do,' Foxworth-Wilding is all 'know.' "

"But Mr. Foxworth-Wilding does a lot, Papa. He travels everywhere and writes books and gives lectures."

"But he writes books and gives lectures about what other people do, not any accomplishments of his own. Now, our Clyde couldn't be less interested in the little Mexican children who climb around fertilizing the vanilla pods because the bees won't. Didn't you see him itching to get back to real work while Foxworth-Wilding was telling us that? But Clyde could cart all those crates around himself, fix the wagon, pay the weekly wages of every man in the place, and tell you in the dark exactly what grade a pod is and what it will sell for."

"I think I see what you mean. Papa, I think you really are smarter than both of them—for knowing the difference."

"They're a good combination," George mused. "Just as I hoped."

"What do you mean?"

"What . . . ? Oh, nothing. Just something I've been thinking over."

Mary tried to get him to explain further, but George changed the subject and wouldn't elaborate.

22

"Is my hem straight? Nothing's straggling loose at the back of my hair, is it?" Hester asked twirling in front of Mary.

"You look like a sherbet. You're beautiful enough to eat," Mary stated.

It was almost true. Portia's Christmas gift to Hester had been a cream-and-mint-striped velvet ball gown. Judicious padding and wiring in the dress made her figure look quite good, and the colors were flattering to her fair complexion. Agnes had been washing her hair every other day for the last month, and rinsing it with vinegar to bring out the auburn highlights Hester imagined were there. Hester had even gone without her spectacles for the duration so that the awful little dents on the sides of her nose would go away. It had worked, though Hester had earned a good crop of bruises by running into things. Fortunately, none of them showed, except a faintly greenish one on her elbow. If she remembered to keep her gloves pulled up, nobody would notice. "Anyway, it matches your dress," Mary said encouragingly.

In order to avoid a charge of favoring Hester, Portia had also arranged for a dress for Mary to wear to the formal ball during the house party that she intended as Hester's launch into the marriage market. The little gray square of taffeta had looked suitably dreary—she didn't want Mary to outshine Hester—but made up, it didn't look as she had imagined. Yards and yards of the fabric together looked like rich antique silver. On Mary, with her fair skin and Aunt Nellanor's eight-strand garnet choke collar to echo the garnet of her hair, the result was stunning.

Hester looked pretty; Mary was breathtaking. They'd have happily changed places.

"Certainly Jemmy will propose tonight. Don't you think so?" Hester asked, taking one more look at herself in the glass.

"Stop squinting. Do you really want him to, Hester?"

"Who wouldn't? Mary, I think you're becoming quite peculiar. Jamison Hewitt is the handsomest man alive. He's terribly smart and stylish and says divinely funny things. His manners are wonderful. Now, what girl in her right mind wouldn't want him to propose to her? Tell me that, if you can."

Mary avoided the obvious answer by replying, "But Hester, you're only eighteen years old—"

"Nineteen next month."

"But wouldn't you rather meet some more men and make sure there isn't one you like even better? Hester, there are thousands of men in England!"

"That's some advice, coming from you. You'll be twenty-two in March, and how many of those thousands do you know? Mary, you had better start looking for a husband or you won't get one at all. You're getting to be of a great age, as far as marriage is concerned. You're very beautiful and all, but you have such a terribly strong character, and that puts gentlemen off."

"Stop nagging at me, Hester. I'll marry someday. But not until I'm sure it's the best person." *Or the second best* she added mentally. "Stop trying to shove me into somebody's bed."

Hester's pale cheeks reddened. "Mary, what a vulgar thing to say."

"Well, it's part of getting married, you know."

"Not a part nice people talk about."

"You know I'm not a nice person. Put on a little more of that scent, Hester, and let's go downstairs."

At the landing, Hester grabbed her elbow. "Mary, do you think it's really awful?" she whispered.

Mary instantly thought of that night on the porch in Penang. Anjanette's voice throbbing with passion. Heat flooded her face. "Probably not," she mumbled, ducking her head so Hester wouldn't see her blush.

The ball was a grand success. Whatever else one might say about Portia, no one could deny that she was a superb hostess. She drew people together as if they were parts of a cake recipe; the bulk was the flour—the pleasant, substantial bland element. Some were exceptionally nice—the sweetness. A judicious few strong personalities were selected as spice, and even fewer for their purely decorative value. If Mary had not been a member of the family, Portia would probably have invited her anyway for her sheer beauty.

But Mary's usually outspoken personality was—mercifully, in Portia's view—subdued during the week of the house party.

Mary had a great deal on her mind, and having Castlemere filled to the rafters with guests was making it difficult for her to sort out her thoughts. There were people everyplace! Every time she settled in for a quiet hour of petting Ginger and brooding, somebody had hysterics in the hallway outside her room, or mistook her door for theirs and spent hours apologizing. She tried escaping the house entirely, but the surrounding meadows were crawling with other strollers or hunters. Even the chalk and flint beach attracted a hardy few.

And most of them, she was forced to notice, were in pairs. Apparently attempting to set a highly romantic atmosphere to inspire Mr. Hewitt—though Mary couldn't quite comprehend why she'd want to—Portia had selected a disproportionate number of dewy-eyed young couples who showed a tendency to hold hands and sneak kisses when they thought no one was looking. Whether or not it would influence Mr. Hewitt remained to be seen, but Mary was finding it a most disconcerting climate.

These lovebirds were particularly noticeable the night of the ball. Why did getting dressed up inspire them to greater excesses? Mary wondered, noting with irritation the meaningful looks and longing smiles being exchanged over the roast beef and parslied potatoes.

Part of her found this tedious and silly. She was almost embarrassed for the couples who gazed at each other with such gooey expressions. One lovely girl had trailed her pearls in her brandied peaches while batting her eyelashes at her new husband. A perfectly agile, able-bodied young man who could ride point to point with the best of them had taken a spectacular fall in the marble foyer because he attempted to walk and gaze up adoringly at his beloved on the stairway above at the same time.

"Perfect asses, all of them!" she snorted to herself while he was being sorted out and petted by the object of his love.

In spite of her intellectual contempt for this evidence of stupidity, she was sometimes almost giddy with jealousy. Nobody fell down and made a fool of himself over her and she half-wished somebody would. Oh, men looked at her too, but it was with cool appraisal, not adoration. She'd been troubled for several weeks by her father's remarks about men who wanted women for their names and looks instead of their character, and it seemed to her that all the interest shown in her was of this sort.

Hoping in some obscure way to disprove her father's warning, or perhaps prove it and get to wallow in self-pity, she turned rather fiercely on the young man who had insisted on accompanying her through the buffet line. "Mr. Jones-Pryce—"

"Pryce-Jones, Miss Beecham."

"Whatever difference does it make? Names are so pointless, aren't they? If I'm clearly addressing you, for instance, what difference can it make what I call you?"

"None, I suppose," he said with condescending amusement.

"As for what you call me, why, it's subject to change, isn't it?"

"How do you mean?"

"This year you call me Miss Beecham. Next year you might be calling me Mrs. Somebody-or-other. But I'd be the same person. That's why I believe I'll keep my own name when I marry."

"You wouldn't really, would you?" He was becoming uncomfortable.

"No reason to change it and confuse everybody, trying to remember a new one."

"But that's hardly the way—"

"Or perhaps I'd make my husband use my name," Mary rolled on. "Better yet, we might both select a wholly new one. For example, if you and I were to marry, we could be Mr. and Mrs. Spicedaughter-Barristerson."

Pryce-Jones was looking distinctly alarmed. "That would be rather unusual," he said with an attempt at a hearty laugh that came out as an anxious titter.

"Have you an aversion to the unusual? I don't. I adore unusual things. Like dragons," she added, and without further explanation plunged on, "Do you think women are inferior to men, Mr. Pryce-Jones?"

"Well . . ."

"I do hope not. It's my opinion that women ought to have all the rights men do. Oh, voting in elections and driving milk wagons and fighting wars and things like that—"

"I don't know that I—"

"Surely you don't think we're too frail, do you? Why, women are far more resilient than men. Take childbirth, for example—"

Pryce-Jones surged to his feet and snatched her plate. "Allow me to get you some more cake, Miss Beecham," he all but screamed.

He made a quick escape, carrying both their plates. Mary heard a low chuckle and turned to discover that Mr. Foxworth-Wilding was sitting beside and a little behind her.

"That was wicked, Miss Beecham. I thought the boy was going to wet himself with terror."

Mary burst into laughter. "It was rather awful of me, wasn't it? You won't tell Portia?"

"I'm not a snitch," he said, seeming to savor the nursery word.

"No, I don't think you are. What do you think of women, Mr. Foxworth-Wilding?" she asked with a naughty grin.

But he was no callow boy to be thrown into confusion by the likes of her. "As individuals or as a race?" he asked coolly.

It took her down a peg. "I'm sorry I was pert with you, sir," she answered sincerely.

"I'd be sorry if you weren't. And please don't be so awfully respectful. It makes me feel very old. Would you like another plate? I don't believe poor Pryce-Jones will ever come back. In fact, he's probably hiding in a closet someplace, fearing you'll find him."

"Thank you, no. I can't really eat in this rig, anyway. Not without bursting some seams."

As she spoke, George passed her line of vision. Portia was on his arm, smiling and nodding to people. "Mr. Foxworth-Wilding, may I ask you a frank question?"

"I hardly think I could stop you," he said.

She ignored the implication. "It's my father. I don't think he's well. You've known him forever; don't you think he looks ill?"

Foxworth-Wilding took the question seriously. "I was surprised at how he'd aged when I first saw him this autumn.

But of course, I'd not actually seen him for years. I thought perhaps it had been a slow process."

"No, it's only since our trip. He was very tired nearly the whole time. And then he was terribly ill on the journey back. I thought he would recover at home, but it's been two months and I think he looks worse. No, it's not exactly his looks. If it were that, everybody would notice. It's the way he acts. Sort of sad and preoccupied."

"Exactly what I felt. But, Miss Beecham, you must realize that an illness like he had may take months and months to fully recover from. It's especially hard to get over anything in the midst of an English winter on the seacoast. Has he seen a doctor?"

"Only the local, his friend. I think he told Papa somebody to see, but he didn't do it."

Foxworth-Wilding studied her for a moment. She was terribly concerned and it broke his heart to see a fine spirit like hers brought down by a worry she could do nothing about. "Miss Beecham, I'm supposed to have some sort of meeting with your father in London next week—"

"He's going to London? He didn't tell me."

"Will you smile again if I promise to make him have a medical consultation while he's there? I know a physician who served in Delhi and knows a great deal about unusual diseases."

"Oh, would you really do that? I'd be so grateful. But please don't tell Papa I talked to you about it. He'd worry about me worrying."

Encouraged by Mr. Foxworth-Wilding's promise, Mary cheered up and vowed to behave herself. She even sought out Mr. Pryce-Jones (who shied like a frightened filly at the sight of her) and made a very pretty apology for her earlier behavior.

She then went looking for Hester, to see if Mr. Hewitt had declared his intentions yet. But her sister was being galloped around the ballroom by a sparsely bearded youth. Portia was looking on with obvious approval. "Everybody's enjoying the party," Mary told her. "I've heard lovely compliments."

Portia acknowledged this effort at amiability with a surprised smile, but without taking her eyes off Hester. "How nice of you to tell me, Mary. I do wish she wouldn't duck her head that way when she's dancing."

"I think he's treading on her toes horribly."

"He's a third cousin of the Duke of Marlborough," Portia replied, as if this explained everything. "Are you enjoying yourself, Mary?"

Mary was perplexed by this query. Portia had never shown the slightest interest in Mary's feelings about anything. "I suppose so."

"Oh, here is Mr. Hewitt," Portia exclaimed loudly enough to draw his attention.

"Have you seen Mr. Beecham, Mrs. Beecham? I wanted to ask him about the shoot tomorrow."

"I believe he's in the billiard room," Portia replied. "Mary, will you show Mr. Hewitt where it is?"

"But Jamison knows perfectly well—"

"Mary!"

"Yes, Portia," she replied.

Jamison took her elbow protectively and led her off through the crowd. Mary glanced back at Portia and saw her smiling at them.

It was as if lightning had struck at her feet. In a blinding flash of insight, Mary suddenly understood something. Portia was trying to shove her—not Hester—into Jamison's arms. And bed. Of course Portia wouldn't approve of him as a husband to her darling. It had puzzled Mary all along that Portia would settle for a mere Hewitt when there were bigger fish to fry. All those times Portia had made Mary accompany Hester and Jamison on their little strolls and rides and picnics, it wasn't for the sake of propriety, but for the purpose of engaging his interest elsewhere.

Of course!

Mary started laughing.

"Was it what I *didn't* say?" Jamison asked.

"No, no. I'm sorry. Did you really want to find Papa or were you merely trying to avoid Portia's snares?"

"The latter, since you ask. You look very beautiful tonight, Mary. You always do, but especially so tonight."

"Thank you, Jamison. So does Hester. Did you notice?"

"Yes. But she can't hold a candle to you."

Suddenly her smile faded. This wasn't amusing at all. Hester fancied herself madly in love with Jamison. It was bad enough that Jamison didn't fully reciprocate those feelings, but this sort of compliment coupled with the discovery that Portia opposed the match boded ill for everyone. Even if Mary had been attracted to Jamison, she would have denied such feelings for Hester's sake.

"I'm afraid it doesn't please me to hear you say that, sir," Mary responded coldly.

"Don't play that part with me. All beautiful women like to be called beauties."

The very arrogance of it made her blush with a combination of embarrassment and anger. "My sister is very fond of you," she said.

"And I of her. And you, Mary."

"You must not bother nurturing an affection for me."

"Oh, but I do. I can't help myself. And I suspect you can't either."

"I hope I mistake your meaning," Mary said.

She tried to disengage her arm from his grasp, suddenly disliking his touch. But his fingers tightened marginally and she couldn't have drawn away without making too much of the action. They had strolled out of the ballroom and down the length of the picture gallery. It was dimly lit and Mary suddenly realized there wasn't anyone near. All week she'd hardly been able to run to the loo without tripping over guests, and now the silly geese had all disappeared when she needed them.

"I don't think you do mistake me," Jamison went on, bending slightly as he spoke, so she could feel his breath on her ear. "In fact, I'm inclined to think we understand each other quite well. You're obviously a passionate woman—"

"I beg your pardon!" Mary said at her huffiest.

The Pryce-Joneses of the world might be frightened by her, but Jamison Hewitt wasn't. He just laughed, and the sound echoed in the deserted picture gallery. "I think we're destined for each other, Mary. Why struggle against the inevitable?"

". . . and then she said her mother came from Scotland. Scotland! Now, I ask you!" Someone else was entering the picture gallery. Thank God!

"Oh, Colonel and Mrs. Blackwood! I was hoping you'd take an opportunity to see our pictures," Mary said. She tried to get out of Jamison's grasp, but he held tight.

"Is that little Mary Beecham?" Mrs. Blackwood asked, peering into the gloom.

"Yes, it's me, Mrs. Blackwood. And this is Mr. Jamison Hewitt. Oh, Mr. Hewitt," she added with heavy sweetness, "your hand seems to be caught in my sleeve. Perhaps Colonel Blackwood can help you get free, unless you think we ought to call my father?"

He let go of her with an admiring grin and she made her escape.

"Agnes, I'm not here if anyone comes looking for me," she said. "Help me get out of this harness, would you?"

"That's a fine way to act when Mrs. Beecham's laid out such a fancy party," Agnes said sleepily. She'd been taking a little lie-down on the daybed in Mary's room.

"I'd rather face an execution squad than go back down there."

"What did you do to get in trouble?" Agnes asked knowingly.

"Me? I didn't do anything. Oh, Agnes, Agnes. Why is life so complicated?"

Agnes wisely chose not to delve into the philosophical. "Suck yourself in so I can get this hook undone," was all she said.

"Brrrr!" Mary exclaimed, stamping her feet as soon as she was inside the door of the London house.

The long ride to the city had been miserable in spite of the little brazier in the carriage and the heavy wool blankets they had over their legs and feet. There had been talk of a railway spur to the village near Castlemere for years, but it hadn't materialized yet and it meant long freezing carriage journeys for the Beechams in winter. It had seemed even cooler because of the emotional atmosphere of the passengers. George hadn't wanted Mary to come along and he wouldn't explain why. This both hurt her feelings and made her all the more determined to go with him and pick apart the mystery of it.

"I can't imagine why you need or want to come to London in the dead of winter anyway," George said by way of discouragement. "You know you hate the smell and the cold in that drafty old museum of a house."

"The same can be said of you, Papa. And it's not the destination, it's the departure point that matters. I have to get out of Hester's way."

"Are you and Hester squabbling again?"

"No, but we will if I'm around Castlemere just now. You see, Papa, Mr. Hewitt didn't propose as she expected."

"That's a blessing."

"Not as far as Hester's concerned. She's crushed with disappointment." "Crushed" was hardly the word; she'd worked herself up to thinking of her engagement to Jamison as a *fait accompli* and had even confided in other guests that it was to be expected momentarily. She was hurt and mortified.

"What has that to do with you, Mary?"

She hesitated and decided she wouldn't burden him with the whole truth of Jamison Hewitt's perfidy. No point in upsetting him. "It shouldn't have anything to do with me, but she expects me to sympathize—which I do—but, Papa, if she weeps on my shoulder one more time, I'm afraid I'll come to bits and tell her what I think of Mr. Hewitt, and then she'll hate me."

"I suppose being able to predict your own bad behavior and trying to avoid it is a sign of something. Very well, you may come along. But you're not dogging my steps and nagging me about what I eat and when I sleep."

"I only nag you for your own good, Papa," Mary had said prissily. But she was fighting back tears. Dogging his steps, indeed. She'd thought he liked having her come along on business. It had always been at his invitation. What had she done wrong to make his attitude change?

All the way to London, she was under attack; old emotions she'd all but forgotten resurfaced and darted at her like fanged creatures out of the dark. She was a little girl again, sick and confused because her mother had abandoned her. Now it seemed like her father was wishing to cast her off as well. She hadn't understood when it was her mother, and she understood even less now. What really alarmed her was the fear that she *did* understand. Mama had left her, then died. Could that be what Papa had in mind? Had he lied about seeing the doctor that Dr. Engle had recommended? Was it possible that he had gone, and got terrible news? That might mean he was trying to make Mary turn loose of her ties to him now before death took him away permanently. Why else would he be so unkind to her? He was usually the most thoughtful man in the world.

So they went off to London, both deep in their own thoughts—Mary shivering from more than just the cold.

"May I take your wrap, Miss Beecham," Bartlet said. The old butler was due to retire in a month and Bartlet had already taken over most of his duties.

"Thank you, Bartlet. And, Bartlet . . . ?"

"Yes, miss?" he asked miserably.

"Could you try to smile occasionally?"

He made a hideous grimace that was the closest he could come. "If that's your wish, miss."

He went off with her fur-lined cloak and George's great-coat, and George and Mary went into the library to stand before the fire and warm up from their long, frigid journey.

Ginger, who had been popped into a basket (much against his own better judgment) and brought up earlier with Agnes and George's valet in another carriage, was curled in a leather armchair with the remains of a mouse on the floor.

"Mary, how could you saddle me with that cat?" George asked.

"I thought as long as you were saddled with me, Ginger wouldn't make it much worse," Mary said. She hadn't meant to say anything so self-pitying, nor had she meant for her voice to quiver the way it did. It had just happened. Worse yet, tears sprang to her eyes and spilled over.

George looked at her for a long moment with surprise, then wrapped her in a hug. "I have been rude to you, haven't I? Poor little Mary. I'm sorry."

"Papa, it doesn't matter," she sobbed. "But I want to know what's wrong. You're not . . . not . . . dying, are you, Papa?"

"Oh, Mary! Where in the world did you get an idea like that? Of course not. In fact, I'm feeling better every day."

"Then what *is* wrong?" she asked, somewhat indignant now that he had so firmly allayed her worst fear. How dare he scare her like that!

"Nothing at all. Here, sit down in front of the fire and I'll explain." He dislodged Ginger and pulled the chair closer for Mary, then dragged over another for himself. He sat down, the fire flickering on his fair hair. "I *was* worried about dying—I might as well be honest with you—when we first got back to England. And it made me see things in a new light."

"What things, Papa?" she said, drying her eyes with her sleeve.

He smiled at her action; it was, in a sense, a denial of what he was preparing to say. "It made me see that you and Hester are grown up. Not my little girls anymore. I've been thinking a lot about making arrangements for your futures and marriages—"

"Marriages? You don't mean you're arranging marriages for us, Papa!"

"No, nothing like that. Just boring legal arrangements for dowries and such for when you do marry. I guess I've been so preoccupied with it that I let myself become very selfish. But it was never anything you should have worried about."

"Worried? Worried! Oh, Papa!" she exclaimed angrily.

He shook his head. "Now what's wrong? Mary, I'll never understand you."

If Nellanor had been there, she'd have agreed.

Mary stayed in bed late the next morning.

"I knew it!" Agnes scolded. "I told you it was addle-headed to come out in the awful cold for no good reason. It'll be a wonder for sure if we don't all die."

"I'b nod sick. Leab be alone."

"I can't understand a word you're saying." She laid a plump hand against Mary's forehead. "A raging fever! I told you so. And I won't shed a tear at your funeral, my girl! Such foolishness. Pigheaded foolishness. I'll bring up a hot-water bottle," she added, making it sound about as easy as moving France across the Channel.

"Agdes, if you run to by fadder, I'll neber forgib you. I bean that!"

Mary had never been able to abide the inactivity of illness. By midday, after a long morning's sleep, her head had cleared a little and she decided to venture downstairs for a change of scenery. There was no question of calling Agnes for help dressing, because Agnes would stop her in her tracks if she learned of the plan. Agnes was getting too bossy by half. It came from having trained under Aunt Nell, probably.

She dressed in a dark wool dress and put on two pairs of stockings. Papa was right about the draftiness of the place. She hadn't ever spent much time here in the winter and hadn't realized what it was like. She only got as far as the first landing before deciding this might not have been such a good idea. So woozy she had to sit down on the steps, she huddled miserably, hoping that Agnes wouldn't catch her.

The door beneath the stairway opened and Mary considered moving toward the wall so nobody would see her. Papa would think she was sitting there to snoop—not that she was above snooping, but it would be an unjust accusation in this instance. Deciding the tread might squeak and give her away if she moved, she stayed put. She heard several male voices. Oh, dear, this must have been the secret business of setting up the future for her and Hester. Probably lawyers and bankers and clerks and such.

She peered cautiously between the uprights. Below, she could see George's London lawyer, just as she had suspected. But who was that next to him? Mr. Foxworth-

Wilding. That was strange. Even more peculiar, the next man to enter her line of vision was Clyde Gordon from the warehouse.

A hand fell on her shoulder and she nearly shrieked with fright. Choking back a cry, she looked up at Agnes, who gestured fiercely—but silently—for her to get back to her room.

"How does someone as heavy as you manage to sneak up so quietly on people?" Mary demanded when the door to her room was safely closed behind them.

"Sneak up? I was just going about my business and damn near fell arse over topknot down those steps, with you hiding there in the dark spying on your da."

"I was *not* spying!"

But she was wishing she had been able to. Whatever did that odd company of men have to talk about together? Certainly not her and Hester. But that was what Papa had said he was coming to London to do.

Mary's illness was a recurring one. Fortunately no one but Agnes noticed the pattern of its recurrence. "What if she marries Mr. Hewitt? Will you just get sick forever?" she asked.

"No, if she marries him and he comes here to live, I'll move away," Mary answered.

On two of his visits, she managed to be away—once with George to London again and another time on a longer trip with him to the crocus farm near the Wash. This trip was fascinating to her; the landscape was so utterly foreign that it might have been another country entirely. Low, flat land that sometimes squished alarmingly if one stepped off the safety of a path.

They passed through Newark and poked around in the ruins of the big yellow castle where King John had died. "He'd spent the night before at a monastery, where he had a big meal of cider and peaches. He got very sick, but insisted on continuing. He got this far and died of dysentery. It's too bad we started the journey where his life ended," George said. "We should have come the other way, from the Wash. That's where his heart broke, I think."

"What was King John doing there?" Mary asked. The early Plantagenets formed a sort of void in her learning. She vaguely remembered Aunt Nell making her memorize dates, but little else had stuck in her mind.

"He was fleeing his own barons. They'd made him sign the Magna Carta and were trying to take all his powers from him. After he signed, he repudiated the document because he'd been forced to accept it. The barons had started fighting among themselves, and so King John started traveling around the country, making friends with those who might come over to his side. He had virtually everything he owned with him. Jewels, plate, money, even his grandmother Matilda's crown."

"King John was a bad king, wasn't he?" Mary asked.

"The history books say so," George replied. It was an area of special interest to him and he'd even written a paper in defense of King John's character when he was in school. "I'm not so sure. He wasn't a good man, but he probably wasn't any worse that other kings of the time. What always amazes me is that his brother Richard was revered as such a hero."

"Richard the Lion Heart? The Crusader? But he was a great man! Everybody says so."

"He was a . . . ." George would have said "sodomite" if he'd been talking with a man. Instead he skipped that criticism and said, "He was King of England for ten years. He visited England only twice in all that time. He left his greedy friends at home to cheat and tax the people into poverty while he went off slaughtering people. Anyway, John followed him on the throne and stayed home to be hated in person."

"What happened to all the things he had with him when he died? The jewels and everything?" That part interested her more than the political assessments.

"I'll show you when we get to the farm," he said mysteriously.

Mary liked the farm far more than she had expected. A couple named Haycraft lived in a small cottage behind the larger house, which was itself just a big cottage. With its freshly thatched roof and brightly colored gardens, it looked like it was a family home in constant use, though Mary knew George visited only once or twice a year for a few days. But the Haycrafts kept it always ready for him.

The couple were quiet and reserved, which was fortunate in a way, as they spoke with accents so heavily East Anglian that Mary could barely understand them. Mr. Haycraft was the "croker" or grower of the crocuses, and Mrs. Haycraft looked after the houses and gardens and did the cooking when George was there.

Mary was sorry to miss the harvest, which she assumed was in the spring. "No, it's the autumn crocus that we grow. We'll come back then, if you like. It's a sight to take your breath away, all those flowers in bloom. It takes about seventy-five-thousand flowers in bloom to make a single finished pound of saffron."

She sat in while George spent their first full day at the cottage discussing business with Mr. Haycraft. The next day, they took the pony cart out for a ride. "Where are we going?" Mary asked eagerly.

"Treasure hunting," George answered, clucking to the pony as it plodded along a narrow raised path across the center of the farm. "You must never get off the paths here, remember. This is dangerous land, half-soil, half-water in places. You can take a few steps from solid land and get sucked down."

At the far side of the farm they came to a small river. It was wide, but obviously shallow and sluggish. "This is the Nene. It empties into the Wash and it's tidal. Somewhere along here, King John and his army crossed in a heavy fog. John went first, I imagine, and may have been some little way ahead when he and his courtiers realized the army had gotten left behind. They'd become disoriented in the fog and meandered around in confusion. Then the tide came in. It comes in very quickly and the surrounding land turns to quicksand. By the time John got back, the army was knee-deep in it."

George fell silent for a moment, imagining the scene. "He must have heard the shouts, the screams of fear, and the terrified whinnying of the horses as they sank deeper and thrashed to get free of the quicksand. The fog was too thick to even see where they were. It all went down, Mary. Everything was lost. Men, horses, jewels, his fortune, his grandmother's crown."

Mary stared at her father in disbelief. "Do you mean to tell me there's a fortune right there in front of us? Why haven't we dug it up?"

George smiled. "People have been trying to find it for more than six hundred and fifty years, but nobody knows just where on the Nene they crossed. Nor does the Nene stay put. This is flat country; the river meanders and moves. The treasure might be right under our feet; it could be several miles that way . . . or that way . . . or that way," he said, pointing.

"The gold might be on our land," Mary sighed.

"We have our own gold on this land. The saffron. But who can say? Perhaps the roots of our gold grow down and twine in King John's gold."

Mary felt tears well in her eyes and didn't know why. George put his arm around her shoulders and she leaned against him. They stood that way for a long time, looking out at the placid, innocent little river that held such tragic secrets.

They returned by way of London, making a leisurely visit before returning once more to Castlemere. By the time they got there, Jamison Hewitt had once again departed and Hester was distraught. "Mary, I can't understand it. He must like me, otherwise why would he stop and visit so often? But if he does intend to make an offer, why doesn't he just do it? It's not as though he's shy."

Indeed, he is not, Mary thought, supressing a shudder of distaste at the memory of his boldness with her.

"What does Portia think?" she asked instead.

"Oh, Mama is beastly about it all. I don't think she really cares anything about me. She won't even discuss it. All she can talk about is having a season for me next year and all the rich men I'll meet. Rich men? Mary, why should she care about that? We have all the money we need; what difference can it make that Jemmy doesn't have enormous wealth?"

"Still, what would be wrong with meeting these other men Portia has in mind?"

"It would be a waste of time."

"Still, Hester, you have to face facts. If he hasn't proposed yet, you must consider that he might not intend to, ever."

"Mary, that's mean of you. He will. I know he will. There's some good reason we'll find out later that's causing him to delay."

"And if there's no good reason?"

"Then I just won't marry at all. If I can't have Jemmy as my husband, I don't want anybody."

"That's about the stupidest thing I've ever heard you say!" Mary exclaimed, and then realized to her great chagrin that it was the very thing she'd said to herself about

Alex. But it took hearing Hester say the words to fully
recognize what an idiotic thought it was. But it's different
with me, she argued with herself. Alex is a wonderful man,
worth the sacrifice; Jamison Hewitt is a disgraceful roué.
No, that was merely justification of her own folly. What
mattered was what Hester felt for him—the same obsessive
adoration Mary felt for Alex, even though Mary found it
incomprehensible that anyone could so admire Jamison.

"Hester, let's both find husbands in London. Or maybe
Bath, or Southampton, or . . . or Paris! That's it. Let's make
Portia take us to Paris to find divine dispossessed royalty.
Poor but devilishly handsome Bourbon princes would suit
us. With fairy-tale castles with madwomen in the attics who
make eerie noises in the full moon. We could start now
brushing up on our French and getting new dresses made
with wonderful bustles and ribbons and hats to match—"

"Mary, stop that foolishness! You're just making fun of
me."

"No. I think I'm making fun of myself."

"You're absolutely no help at all. I want to know what to
do about Jemmy."

"I've tried to tell you what to do. Put him out of your
mind. Find somebody else to marry. That's my advice, if
you want it."

"Then I don't want it. You're being ugly about him because you're jealous of me. You don't know what it's like to
be in love and you probably never will because you're so
bossy and mean that no man will ever want you. So there!"

"Hester, let me tell you—" Mary started, then caught
herself.

"Tell me what?" Hester asked, hands on hips and face
flushed with fury.

"Never mind."

"Just exactly what is *that* supposed to mean?"

"Nothing, nothing, nothing! I'm going for a walk.
Good-bye!"

It was a warm Sunday in April when George disappeared.

At first nobody was alarmed. He often missed the midday
meal, but Portia was somewhat surprised when she inquired
in the kitchens and discovered that he hadn't asked for any
sandwiches to take along. But all that meant was that he
didn't plan to be out in the fields for long. Perhaps he'd
gone to town to see someone and was planning to eat there.

But on a Sunday? Not business, then. Portia mentioned this curiosity to Mary in the late afternoon when she came into the map room to look for a piece of needlework she'd misplaced.

"Did he take a horse or carriage?" Mary asked, looking up from the map of Australia she was studying. Winston Foxworth-Wilding had sent it down along with a handwritten copy of the first chapter of the book he was working on.

"I didn't ask. A carriage, I would suppose. We'll ask him at dinner where he went. Let me know if you find my petit point."

But Mary's curiosity was piqued. She put on boots and went to the stables to inquire. No, the grooms said, Mr. Beecham hadn't been there at all today. All the horses and carriages and even the farm cart were accounted for.

She sought out Tutin, the estate manager, in the tidy little house up the hill, where he lived with his mother. "Was my father visiting tenants today?"

"On a Sunday, miss? Not that he mentioned to me. I don't think he would on the sabbath. He says people don't like having the lord of the manor around on their day of rest."

It was most peculiar.

By dinner, Mary was becoming fearful. "Where could he have gone?" she asked.

Portia wasn't concerned. "I expect he's given a message to somebody who just didn't tell us. It's almost dark. He'll be here shortly."

But Mary insisted on having the servants called in one by one. George's valet knew only that the master had worn old clothes that morning, the sort he put on when he intended to potter around the house and grounds. The butler had been engaged in seeing that all the silver was polished and knew nothing about Mr. Beecham's whereabouts. The tweeny, unused to such attention, and thrilled, averred that she'd seen a mysterious man in a black cape hanging around since the last full moon and he was probably a ghost who was responsible. The head housemaid pinched her and told her to stop showing off with that nonsense.

Finally even Agnes was summoned to the dining room to be questioned. She'd been in the village visiting her married sister for the afternoon. "Why are you asking me?" she asked Mary in an overfamiliar tone Portia would have set her down for under other circumstances. "You know where he went. He came looking for you this morning to see if you wanted to go fishing with him."

"He didn't ask me to go fishing," Mary said, glancing out the window. It was pitch dark now. If he'd been fishing on the beach or in the stream, he'd have been back long before now. Unless something happened. . . .

"Guess he couldn't find you."

"Why didn't you give anyone this message?" Portia demanded.

" 'Tweren't no message, ma'am. He just asked where Miss Mary was and mentioned why he wanted to know. He didn't tell me to talk to anybody about it."

"Fishing where?" Mary asked.

"He didn't say."

"Agnes, run to the stables and tell them to get Peter and Harry from the stables and some torches so we can go down to the beach and see if the boat is gone. Send for Tutin and Dr. Engle, also." Mary was already on her feet.

"I'll come with you," Hester said, suddenly realizing the full implications of Mary's orders.

"No, you won't. You'd just fall down the cliff and make a fuss of yourself."

Portia looked like an alabaster statue. "You don't think...?" Mary didn't reply.

They reached the lip of the cliff ten minutes later. Mary had run ahead of the men and her heart was beating so strongly she could hardly hear the sound of the waves on the flint shingle. "Stay back with those torches," she ordered the men coming behind her. She cupped her hands at the sides of her face to cut out the glare and squinted down to the dark beach. "Look, Tutin! Isn't that the boat?"

Tutin, his fear of heights momentarily overcome by his concern for George, nearly stepped over the edge in his efforts to see what was below. "Yes, yes, miss, I think it is."

"What is this all about?" Dr. Engle shouted from some feet away. He'd run most of the way.

Mary didn't take time to explain. "Peter? Harry? One of you give me a torch, and the other come with me," she said. A gust of wind jerked her words away and nearly extinguished the torches.

"You can't climb down there in the dark, miss," Tutin whimpered. "It's dangerous."

"Somebody has to go down and I know every rock," she said, but she'd already taken the stableboy Harry's torch and was disappearing over the edge as she spoke. Peter scrambled along behind her, and just behind him came Dr. Engle, the handle of his medical bag in his teeth to free his hands.

Mary missed her step just where George had.

She fell, cracking her heel and the back of her head against a rock and skinning her elbows. The torch flew into the void. Mary put out a hand in the darkness and felt fabric.

"Dr. Engle, I've found him!"

But she knew when she felt his cold hand that they were too late.

24

"Ashes to ashes, dust to dust . . ."

The words echoed in the small village church, filled to overflowing this April afternoon with the family, friends, business associates, servants, and neighbors of George Beecham. An intimate family service had been held earlier in the chapel at Castlemere. Here, as there, incense was being burned, not as a religious tradition, but as a Beecham tradition. It was rosemary, and Mary had arranged for it.

Winston Foxworth-Wilding sat slightly sideways at the outside end of a front pew. Trying to avoid the unexpectedly sharp pangs of his own sorrow, he studied the faces of those around him. Poor Clyde Gordon looked stunned. Naturally enough, he and George had known each other from the vantage points of their very different classes nearly all their lives, and had, in the ways available to them, been friends. Clyde no doubt had seen himself and George growing old together just as Clyde's father and George's father had.

Next to him, Tutin, the estate manager, was sitting bolt upright, his eyes red. Occasionally blowing his nose noisily, he looked as bereft as Clyde. There was true grief there, but probably fear for his position as well. His job was dependent on George's goodwill. Now, without George . . . ? Next to Tutin, the family's London lawyer, Porter Wambolt, looked as inscrutable as lawyers were supposed to look. Did they teach them that in school? Foxworth-Wilding wondered. Or did a lifetime among wills and writs do that to a man?

His gaze wandered to the family.

Portia looked as if she were held together with cobwebs that might disintegrate at a strong gust. He'd seldom seen a woman quite so devastated by the loss of a husband. Who would have thought she cared so much? Her grief had been almost savage when he arrived at Castlemere the morning before—face ravaged with tears, clothing in disarray, voice shrill and manner hysterical. The normally cool, proper Portia Beecham had thrown herself at him—a man she hardly knew—like a crazed animal desperate to be set free from a snare. As if he could help her!

This afternoon she seemed very fragile. Apparently the funeral service itself had finally convinced her of the truth of George's death. The fight had gone out of her and her blurred features were slack and empty. Even her black dress looked ill-fitting, as if borrowed at the last moment from a far larger, more robust woman. She leaned a little toward Hester, as if she might actually topple any moment.

Hester herself was holding up well—better than anyone might have anticipated. Tears were running down her pale cheeks, but she seemed composed and unaware of them. He supposed it was the necessity of supporting her mother that kept her upright.

Foxworth-Wilding's gaze came to rest inevitably on Mary Beecham. She sat on the other side of Portia, but a little apart. Her head was held high, as if in pride. No tears marred her features. The black dress, hat, and gloves accentuated her extraordinary paleness, but there were spots of hectic color on her cheeks, as if she were containing anger rather than grief.

Suddenly people were stirring. So deeply in his own thoughts that he was almost caught unawares, he rose with the other pallbearers and took his place at the side of the coffin. Tutin was in front of him, Clyde Gordon behind, Porter Wambolt across, the family banker, a man named Stanford, and Dr. Engle made up the rest of the group. Together they lifted their burden and walked with measured steps down the center aisle and around the corner to the village graveyard. There, in a corner delineated by a wrought-iron fence, were the family graves, going clear back to Philippe Beecham.

When the last of the prayers had been said and the coffin lowered into the grave, there was a long uncomfortable silence. Finally Mary reached behind a headstone marked "Nellanor Beecham," then stepped forward and bent slightly to toss a branch of rosemary into the hole. There was a swish and a light thud as it came to rest on the mahogany lid of the coffin. Mary then stooped for a handful of earth, which she placed in Portia's hand as one would give something to a child. She spoke quietly, and Portia held her hand out, allowing the soil to dribble between her black-gloved fingers.

At that, Hester put her face in her hands and began to sob. Mary turned and gave a sharp look to a handsome sandy-haired young man. Somebody Hewitt, Foxworth-Wilding remembered. It was the first time he'd seen Mary show any emotion at all, and the flash of temper was gone as quickly as it had come. As silently commanded, Hewitt stepped forward and took Hester and her mother by their arms, leading them away. Mary stayed where she was, head bowed as the rest of the mourners filed past. Foxworth-Wilding paused a long moment in his turn, hoping she would look up so that he could express his sympathy or admiration in some way, but she remained still and he passed on.

Most of the mourners came to Castlemere afterward; many of them stayed only long enough to give their condolences, drink a glass of sherry, and leave. But those Foxworth-Wilding knew stayed, including Clyde Gordon, who looked most uncomfortable among his "betters." Some of the others, not knowing what the tubby little man with the funny lower-class London accent was doing there, gave him daunting looks. But Gordon, knowing his duty, nodded to them, smiled uneasily, and held his ground.

Portia had disappeared, presumably taken to her bed. Mary and Hester were serving in her stead and Mary was fulfilling her role as mistress of the household with terrible dignity. When he saw her alone for a moment, Foxworth-Wilding went to her and took her hand. "Mary, I hardly know how to tell you how very sorry I am."

"I know you are, Mr. Foxworth-Wilding. One of my greatest regrets is that you and Papa didn't have longer to renew your old friendship. His last months were made happier by his opportunity to be with you."

Foxworth-Wilding didn't know quite what to say. In spite of her composure, he'd expected something more girlish. But her words, though obviously sincere, were so . . . so *adult* that it rather surprised him. "I will be all the help to you that I may," he said.

"I'm certain you shall be," she said, but looked a little perplexed that he'd expressed a promise rather than an offer. He knew she was waiting for him to explain, but that would come soon enough.

Eventually the servants started bringing in platters of sandwiches and scones, a sign to those who were not invited to supper that it was time to go. One of those who remained was Clyde Gordon. Mary, who was fond of him, nevertheless gave him a questioning look. Foxworth-Wilding caught the expression and came to her to say softly, "He's been asked to stay for the reading of your father's will."

"I see. I hadn't thought that we still had that to do."

Jamison Hewitt, as if summoned by the mention of George's will, appeared at Mary's other side. "May I get you a plate, Mary?"

She gave him a long level look. "No, thank you. Mr. Foxworth-Wilding has offered to take supper with Hester and me."

"That I have," Foxworth-Wilding replied, though no such discussion had taken place.

"Thank you for coming, Mr. Hewitt," Mary said dismissively.

"I'm free to stay on for a day or two, if you can put me to use," Jamison Hewitt offered, undeterred by her tone.

"That's very kind of you, but quite unnecessary."

Jamison glanced at Foxworth-Wilding, apparently hoping he would take the unspoken hint and leave him and Mary to speak privately. Foxworth-Wilding, understanding the look perfectly well, but sensing Mary's determination to get rid of Jamison, stayed rooted to the spot. Jamison gave up waiting for him to step aside and said, "Look here, Mary. You need to be looked after. You have no uncles, no brothers—"

"My mother and sister and I will be looked after. I'm certain my father had the foresight to make adequate arrangements."

"Then you're not familiar with the disposition of his property?" Jamison asked.

Foxworth-Wilding was stunned by the brashness of this remark, but apparently Mary wasn't surprised, only irritated. "I can't imagine how that can possibly concern you, Mr. Hewitt."

He spread his hands and smiled. "Only as a friend, Mary. Only as a friend. I *have* studied the law and would be happy to be of any help—"

"Mr. Wambolt has studied law too. Good night, Mr. Hewitt."

Still smiling insolently, he bent over her hand and made his departure. Watching him go, Mary said with a touch of humor, "He's not easy to offend."

Foxworth-Wilding didn't know if she was talking to herself or to him. "What is his interest? Certainly he doesn't suppose there's anything in the will for him?"

"No, Papa didn't even like him and made little attempt to disguise his feelings. No, Mr. Jamison Hewitt wants to know which branch to pick from."

"I beg your pardon?"

"Which of us—Hester or me—stands to be the best investment," she replied coolly, still looking away. "He has the impression the choice of wife is open to him. If I had my way, both avenues would be closed off. Unfortunately, Hester is taken with him."

"Of course. I should have seen that," Foxworth-Wilding replied. Those matters which occupied the minds of young men searching for a bride had been out of his mind for too long. Nor had the financial aspects of romance much concerned him when he fell in love with Dorothea's pretty face and charmingly vacant mind so many, many years ago.

"I suppose it's hopeless now," Mary went on, finally turning to speak to him directly. "Hester will be by far the greater heiress of us and Mr. Hewitt will spring into a proposal. You see, Mr. Foxworth-Wilding, what Mrs. Hewitt doesn't know is that I'm only an adopted daughter. Hester is Papa's real daughter. I suppose my father told you that."

That and much more, Foxworth-Wilding thought. "Yes, he mentioned it. As a matter of fact, he wrote to me when . . . when you came here."

Her face brightened for the first time since George's body had been found. "Did he really? What did he say?"

He was spared having to reply by Porter Wambolt. "I beg your pardon, I'm sure, but as the hour grows late and some of us have a long journey ahead, I wonder if we might proceed, Miss Beecham?"

"Proceed? Oh, the will. Yes, of course. What . . . what do we do?"

"Perhaps you should get Portia?" Foxworth-Wilding suggested.

"Yes, that's good. A formality, of course, but best if she's there with the rest," Wambolt replied.

"I'll fetch her," Mary said.

Foxworth-Wilding watched as she mounted the stairs. She

seemed to float up them, her posture rigid, her pace deco-
rous. And it saddened him. He thought of her as a girl who
always galloped up steps. But the small black-clad figure
disappearing at the landing was a woman, and a very sad
woman at that. Something had gone out of her—her childish
sense of joy. And in its place was a mature reserve that was
most attractive but still a poor substitute for that rare verve
that made her so remarkable.

Would she regain the qualities he'd found so charming?
Her wit, energy, curiosity—temper, even? Or had George,
in death and good intentions, weighted her with a burden
she couldn't hope to carry? Well, he would be ready to help
her in whatever way he could.

For the first time, that responsibility seemed a privilege
rather than a duty.

The first of many surprises—and the one that shouldn't
have been a surprise—came when Mary went to Portia.
Hester was in the room, wringing her hands and crying.
Portia was flinging around clothing and ornaments. "What's
happening here?" Mary asked.

"She's been given something to help her rest, but it's just
made her strange and confused," Hester whispered.

"Portia, what are you doing?" Mary asked, taking away
the nightdress the older woman was trying to fold.

"I'm packing my things."

"But you're not going anywhere."

"Of course we are. We have to move away," Portia said,
swaying as she took back the nightdress.

"Now, Portia, we don't have to go anyplace," Mary said
firmly but pleasantly, as if speaking to a child who'd had a
nightmare.

"Yes, we do. This is Alex's house now. You know
Castlemere's entailed."

Mary stepped back as if slapped. "Entailed?" she whispered.

"Mary, make her stop this," Hester pleaded. "Get Dr.
Engle or somebody."

"Entailed? Hester, *is* the house entailed?"

"Mary, you're acting as strange as Mother. Of course it
is. Even I know that."

Mary sat down suddenly at the dressing table. Dear God!
It was true. Raking through her memories, she found a
wealth of evidence. All those stories George had told her
about past Beechams—old Philippe's roué son who should
have been disinherited but couldn't be because of the entail-

ment! But she'd never thought about it in the present tense.
It was just part of the history of the house.

That meant she'd not only lost her father, she'd lost her
home. Castlemere meant more to her than anything but
George, and both were gone now! It was unbearable!

She glanced up at the mirror at the sound of glass breaking. Portia had thrown a perfume bottle across the room,
then flung herself across the enormous bed. Well, at least
nobody was going to catch Mary acting like that, no matter
what shock or grief she might sustain. She rose, knees still
shaking, and jerked sharply on the bell-pull. In a moment,
Agnes appeared. "Will you stay with Portia while Hester
and I join the lawyer?" she asked. Portia had finally fallen
into a deep, exhausted sleep and was unlikely to cause any
more trouble to anyone. Mary helped Agnes get Portia into
the bed properly and led Hester downstairs.

"Will Alex make us move away?" Hester asked.

"I have no idea. I shouldn't think so. There's that old
dower house we could live in. Portia is the dowager mother
now, even if she isn't Alex's mother. It just needs fixing
up." Her voice trembled as she spoke, and she talked louder
to overcome the quaver.

"When will he be here?" Hester persisted.

"I have no idea. Mr. Wambolt wrote to him. A few
months, I should think."

Winston Foxworth-Wilding was waiting for them at the
foot of the stairs. Mary explained that Portia was asleep and
in no condition to be roused. He led them to the map room,
where Dr. Engle, Clyde Gordon, Porter Wambolt, and
George's banker, Mr. Stanford, were already assembled.
Mary faltered for a moment; many were the times she'd met
all these men, except Gordon, here in the room with George.
Now they were all gathered together without George. Getting a grip on herself, she made Portia's excuses and took a
seat next to Hester on the small Empire sofa that sat in
front of the north window.

After much throat-clearing and paper-shuffling, Mr.
Wambolt began a long and tedious reading. There were
several minor bequests to longtime servants and the village
church, to be used in repairing the roof, with the balance to
go toward cleaning and resoldering the small rose window.

Tutin was granted lifetime rights to inhabit the cottage he
lived in, but could not keep it to rent if he took employment
elsewhere.

Dr. Engle received a set of pictures he'd always admired and a thousand pounds to administer, in whatever way he chose, to benefit the villagers' health needs.

Clyde Gordon was to receive a hundred pounds a year in addition to his salary from Beecham's Fine Spices and "another remuneration to be detailed later." Mary glanced at Wambolt questioningly at this, but he didn't pause to explain.

One hundred pounds was also given the village mayor for the purpose of replacing or restoring the market cross, which had recently been damaged by lightning.

Mary felt very tired and she noticed that Hester's gaze was clouding with weariness also, but there was no rushing Porter Wambolt in the performance of his duty.

He went on to explain that the estate was entailed and now belonged to Mr. Alex Beecham of Singapore (Mary was glad that she'd been made aware of this earlier; the shock of hearing it in front of all these witnesses would have caused her terrible embarrassment) and that said Alex Beecham had been informed by letter of the broad outline of the bequest. Details would be given him upon his return to England.

"The lifetime rights to certain properties to Portia Beecham for her personal use or income, but not to be sold or mortgaged," Wambolt intoned, and went on to list them. They included, besides the dower house, several places Mary had never known about, such as the hunting lodge and fifty acres near Carlisle, and the cottage, farm, and fishing rights of a seaside property in Kent. These were for Portia's use, Wambolt explained, but in the event of either her death or her remarriage, they would revert to Hester. "Except for the dower house, of course," he went on. "Miss Hester Beecham in her turn will own them entirely and may use or dispose of them as she sees fit."

"I beg your pardon," Hester said sleepily. Only the mention of her name had kept her from dropping off entirely.

"I'll explain it later," Mary said in an undertone.

"Look here," Dr. Engle said to the lawyer, "Hester is about to fall over with exhaustion. If there is no more that concerns me directly, may I take her away? I want to check her pulse and temperature and see that she's tucked in with a hot-water bottle."

Neither Hester nor Wambolt made any objection. As soon as she was gone, clinging unsteadily to the physician's arm, Wambolt went back to the property distribution.

Mary was to have, free and clear, the London house and the saffron farm. She smiled at this. Neither was of enormous value. The London property, being in the heart of the city, was probably worth a fair amount, but the house itself was a monstrosity and in a neighborhood that had declined sadly in the last few years. Still, George had left her two places to which she had strong and happy emotional ties. The income from the farm would be enough for her to live comfortably, if not extravagantly. It was nothing like Hester's portion, but Mary felt no resentment. Hester, being the true child of George and Portia, should have a far greater share.

She stood up. "Thank you, Mr. Wambolt, for—"

"I'm afraid we aren't quite finished," he said. "There is the matter of Beecham's Fine Spices."

She was so tired she actually felt faint, but sat back down with a pretense of gracious willingness. The lawyer would, in good time, have to talk to Alex about handing the family business over to him, but in the meantime she *was* the only family member available to listen to the rest.

Once again Wambolt shifted the papers and drew breath to resume his reading, but Foxworth-Wilding, seeing the strain in Mary's face, forestalled him. "Sir, since the rest of us here are familiar with the details of this section of the will and Miss Beecham is obviously weary, I wonder if it would not be adequate at this time to merely summarize the remainder of the document?"

Wambolt looked resistant, almost shocked at this breach of legal propriety, but the banker and even Clyde Gordon expressed their agreement so firmly and promptly that he acquiesced. "Very well, Miss Beecham, in the past, the spice company has always been inseparable from the estate —morally, if not legally, entailed to the eldest male heir. A very wise and farsighted tradition, if I do say so—"

The banker nodded, but Winston Foxworth-Wilding cleared his throat as if urging Wambolt to leave his opinions out of the matter and get on with his account.

"In this instance, however, Mr. Beecham has seen fit to break up the interests. Miss Beecham, you and your mother and sister and your cousin Alex Beecham are to have shares of the business, in a sense."

Mary wasn't following this except to realize the lawyer strongly disapproved of whatever he was trying to explain. "What do you mean, 'in a sense'?"

"To begin with Portia Beecham: she is to receive a one-sixth share of the profits during her lifetime, this portion to be divided among you, your sister, and your cousin, or whichever of you survive her, at her death. Miss Hester Beecham's one-sixth share is also to revert to the remainder of the four co-heirs. They are to have no participatory rights concerning the company interests. Miss Mary Beecham and Mr. Alex Beecham each hold one-third interest."

"I'm sorry . . . ?" Mary said, feeling fuddled. She was getting a sharp headache behind her eyes.

"Miss Hester and her mother have no decision-making power, they may not assign or sell their share. Whereas you and Mr. Alex Beecham will jointly hold all the powers of a single heir—if you so desire."

Foxworth-Wilding came to sit beside her. "Mary, what it amounts to is that you and your cousin Alex own the business and share the profits with Hester and Portia."

"Alex *and* I? Not just Alex?"

She felt her eyes filling with tears and was afraid if she let a single one fall, she'd go to pieces. She lifted her chin in a gesture that would have looked defiant to anyone who didn't know how touched she was by her father's faith in her. "I see."

Wambolt, trying to dampen the contempt he felt for this arrangement, said, "Miss Beecham, you should know at the outset, that you are under no obligation to bother yourself with business matters. You will not violate any principle of the will if you step aside and let your cousin take full control. It's entirely possible that your father intended this as a gesture only—a way of making a legal recognition of your . . . ah, intelligence." He said the last word as if it were faintly distasteful when applied to a young female.

Receiving no response, he went on, "If, in the unlikely event you choose to take some limited role, your father made provisions for a board of advisers. Mr. Foxworth-Wilding, Mr. Gordon, and Mr. Stanford are to receive a generous sum per annum to be available to consult with you until you attain the age of twenty-five. At that time, you may ask them to continue in this role or not, as you choose."

"Does my cousin know anything of this?"

"Yes, your father corresponded with him some months ago."

"And he made no objection?"

"Not that your father mentioned to me. Now, Miss Beecham, I must be going. I will leave a copy of the entire will with you for your perusal. If at any time you need further clarification, feel free to write or call upon me."

He rose and took a sealed envelope from an inside pocket of his waistcoat. "There is only one more matter—something Mr. Beecham left with our office to be given you upon his death."

"What is it?" Mary asked, taking the large brown envelope.

"I'm afraid I have no idea. Good night, Miss Beecham."

Tired as she was, she saw that the banker, Mr. Wambolt, and Clyde Gordon were all turned over to the butler, who had their overcoats ready and a carriage waiting at the door. Winston Foxworth-Wilding was staying at Castlemere, and stayed with her until she should excuse him.

"Do you know what this is?" she asked him when the door had closed behind the other men.

"I think so."

"Please . . . stay with me a moment, then."

"As you wish." He was pleased that she'd asked. He took a silver letter opener from the top of George's desk and held it out to her. All the color had gone from her face but the faint blue circles under her eyes.

She reached out, but her hands were shaking. "No, my fingers are hopeless right now. Please open it for me."

He did so. There were a letter and a stiff paper document with an oxblood-red seal at the bottom left. Without looking at the writing, he handed the document to her.

Mary walked around the desk and laid the yellowing paper in the circle of light cast by the desk lamp. Head bent, she studied it for a long moment. When she finally looked up, her eyes were wide with surprise.

"This is a marriage certificate, Mr. Foxworth Wilding."

"Yes. I thought it might be."

"But the names on it are George Beecham and Gwenith Grey."

25

"Gwenith Grey was my mother," Mary said. "What does this mean?"

"There's a letter. I'm sure it explains," Foxworth-Wilding said, handing her the folded sheets.

Mary spread the letter flat and started to read:

> My dearest daughter,
>
> As you can see from the enclosure, your mother and I were married. It was a secret marriage and I've never told anyone, not even Aunt Nell. But you are entitled to know, even though you may come to despise me for the knowledge. Before I could tell my parents of the marriage, my mother convinced Gwenith to go away and subsequently told me she had died. I didn't find out until years later that she had actually gone to London to give birth to you—my daughter.

Mary looked up at Foxworth-Wilding. "I'm really Papa's daughter. His real daughter."

"I know," her father's friend answered.

"I'd always hoped and dreamed I was, and sometimes I even convinced myself of it for a while, but I couldn't be sure whether it was true or I just wanted it to be true. I'm really Papa's daughter!" she repeated. "But why didn't he ever tell me?"

"Read on," Foxworth-Wilding said, pulling up a chair and half-turning to face the fireplace.

> In the meantime, I had married Portia in the belief that I was legally and morally free to marry.

Hester and Charlotte (do you remember Charlotte?) had both been born by the time Gwenith left you with me and I realized the truth.

I can't excuse what I did to your mother, letting her go away, but I've tried to make it up to you, even though I couldn't make it right. You must see what this means by now. You are my daughter—my legitimate daughter—my *only* legitimate daughter. While you have borne the stigma of illegitimacy all your life, it is Hester who is illegitimate and Portia was never my legal wife.

Now I shall ask more of you because I know you have the strength of character to give more. Having borne this stigma, I ask you to continue to carry it. That's not fair; I have no right to ask it. But out of your love for me, I *do* ask. What's more, I beg you not to tell Portia or Hester the truth. Portia believes so sincerely in the proprieties, it would break her heart to know she was never a true wife. I don't know how Hester would feel—I've never understood Hester as I understand you. But I do know this about her: she cannot keep a secret from her mother.

My beloved Mary, you have been the light and joy of my life. If we hadn't shared a drop of blood, I'd have loved you just as much. I'm sorry I could never tell you this in life, but I was afraid I might see contempt in your eyes and I could never face it. To have lost even a morsel of the love and admiration you had for me would have destroyed me.

As for the division of the business between you and Alex, I'm sure you see why I've done this. Both my lawyer and my banker feel it is a terrible mistake and I suspect, from a practical business viewpoint, it is an error. Beecham's Fine Spices has thrived partly because it has never been divided between branches of the family. But you are as fit to inherit it as a son and I owe you something besides a few bits of property for the injustice I have done you—an injustice that I ask you to continue to perpetrate against yourself.

I can hardly bring myself to a conclusion. But I will do so before I become disgracefully maudlin. I ask one more thing of you: marry. Choose carefully and without haste, but do marry. I want you to have children in the hope that one of them will give you the happiness and the purpose that you have bestowed on me. I do love you, my dear daughter.

Your true father,
George Beecham

Mary folded her arms and laid her head on them. Winston FoxworthWilding went on smoking his pipe and waited until her sobs had subsided. Then he came around behind her, and putting his hands firmly on her arms, urged her to get up. "Come sit by the fire, child. You're shivering."

Mary did as she was told. Handing him the letter with an unspoken request that he read it, she went to the sofa before the fireplace. He sat down beside her and read in the flickering light. When he finished, he folded the letter and handed it back to her. "Is it too much of a burden, knowing?" he asked.

"Not as long as you know. It would have been too much to bear alone. I'm glad you were Papa's friend. And mine. How could my mother have left him? They were married! She was the rightful mistress of Castlemere."

"Now, Mary, you may have forgotten Evelyn, your grandmother, but I haven't. She was the most forceful woman I've ever known. She could have moved continents for the sake of your father's welfare."

"But why wasn't my mother good enough for my father?"

"She was governess for the children of one of your mother's relatives."

Mary was quiet a long moment. "I see. Papa told me she was somebody who visited here. I didn't know she was an employee. A governess. Yes, she would have been a good one."

"Do you care?"

"In the face of all the rest of it? No, of course not. Did you ever meet her?"

"No, but your father wrote to me about her. He said she was very sweet and very beautiful. As you are."

At this she laughed, a shaky little sound that made something in his heart twist. "I'm anything but sweet, Mr. Foxworth-Wilding. But Papa . . . Papa loved me anyway."

On the last word, the tears came back again, as if sweeping over her. She put her face in her hands and shook with sobs. Foxworth-Wilding put his arm around her, pulled her against his chest, and held her tightly until the storm subsided. He was astonished at how small and vibrant her body felt against his. I could fall in love with this girl, old fool that I am, he thought.

"I'm sorry," she said, finally sorting herself out and sitting upright. "I didn't mean to break down like that. I promised myself I wouldn't behave like Portia." She took the handkerchief he offered and mopped her eyes. Once she had a grip on herself, she said, "I would like to ask you a favor, if you would grant it for my father's sake."

"For his sake or yours. Anything."

"Would you stay here at Castlemere?"

"I was planning to, unless you have a carriage at the door," he said with a smile.

"No, I don't mean just overnight. Would you stay until my cousin Alex can get here and take over the house? I don't know if I can cope with everything right now on my own—Portia, Hester, the business, the house—it's more than I ever anticipated having to deal with at once. You can use Papa's room here for your writing. I'll make sure you aren't disturbed and I'll send for your books and clothes and things first thing tomorrow. I need a friend, Mr. Foxworth-Wilding."

"I'd be pleased to be your friend and stay as long as you want. But there is one thing I want in return."

"Anything."

"Don't keep calling me Mr. Foxworth-Wilding. It's such a mouthful. I always wished I were a Smith. My friends call me Winston."

"I don't know . . . I'd feel very fresh. Uncle Winston—how would that be?"

"Hideous!" he replied, unaccountably hurt and feeling quite foolish for it. "I've never been an uncle and it makes me feel a thousand years old. Winston or nothing."

"Very well—Winston," she said, and giggled at the sound of it.

Foxworth-Wilding had to clench his hands behind his back to keep from sweeping her into his arms and kissing her. Dear Lord, was he going mad?

It had been a blistering hot day in Singapore. A heavy

morning rain had steamed in the afternoon sun and wilted everybody. Alex had spent the afternoon at the docks and felt wretched. He dismissed his secretary an hour early and went home. The house was quiet when he came in. "Gin and tonic," he told the hovering servant. "Where is the mistress?"

He was directed to he shaded gazebo at the back of the house. Not expecting him, Anjanette was there, doing some darning. Baby Richard was lying on a pile of quilts on the floor of the gazebo. Kicking his still-thin legs, he was cooing to the ceiling. They had stopped worrying over him hourly. Though small for his age, he was now growing steadily and filling out. Katie and her ayah were sitting nearby, playing some game with colored sticks.

Anjanette looked up with a happy exclamation when he came across the lawn. She put down her sewing and came to greet him. "You look very tired," she said, kissing him lightly. "Take the children inside, please," she added to the ayah.

Alex sat down on a rattan chair and accepted the drink that had been brought out to him while the young woman gathered up the children, Katie protesting the interruption of her game. He was a little surprised at Anjanette sending them away so quickly, but she must have something to talk to him about that she didn't want the servants overhearing. Some domestic crisis or other, he supposed.

When they were alone, she took an envelope from the pocket of her dress. "This came for you today. From England. It looks important."

"What is it?"

"I didn't open it. It's addressed to you."

"Anjanette, I have no secrets from you. If you were worried about the contents, you should have opened it." He took the envelope and turned it over. It was heavy paper, very official. The return address was that of Porter Wambolt, a name he recognized. He was the lawyer George had mentioned in his letters the last few months. Alex felt a frisson of alarm. Taking a penknife from his pocket, he slit the envelope and took out the single sheet.

The writing was tiny, dense, written margin to margin, and it was long moments before he looked up at his wife. "George has died," he said. There was a catch in his voice. He cleared his throat and went on, "He fell on the path down the cliff face at Castlemere. Mary found him—"

"Oh, no!" Anjanette's hand went to her mouth. "Poor, poor Mary!"

"This is from George's lawyer, asking me to come to England immediately."

"You must go, of course."

"I? *We* must go."

"George, you know we can't just run off like Gypsies. There are the houses, the servants, clothing to purchase for a different climate—and you must go immediately, not wait for all that to be tended to."

"Yes, I suppose you're right. It wouldn't be worth the upheaval for such a short visit."

"What do you mean, visit? You will not stay?" she asked.

He shook his head. "Not this time," he said, then was silent for a long moment. "George gone. I can hardly believe it. I had a letter from him just last week talking about plans for the summer."

"Poor Mary, my heart breaks for her. She must feel all alone," Anjanette said.

"Yes," Alex answered shortly. He didn't like discussing Mary. He felt like some people did when near an open window high above the ground—an insane fear that something might snap inside, and against all instincts, they would fling themselves out. Alex was afraid he might someday blurt out that he'd kissed Mary and that the searing memory of that single kiss haunted him still.

"What do you mean about visiting? Are we not to go to England to stay? As George's heir . . ."

Alex could hear the reluctance in her voice, though she was trying to disguise it. "You've never wanted to go live in England, Anjanette."

"No, but it is your destiny. I've always known that. I just didn't expect it to happen so soon."

"Nor did I. I'll go back as soon as I can, Janette, to pay my respects to the family and make myself known to this lawyer, but there is no need for us to move there right away."

"But the business . . . ?"

"It will function quite well without me. I've not inherited it whole—unless George had a change of heart since he wrote to me last, and I doubt that."

"You don't inherit the business?"

"Yes, I do, but jointly with Mary, as George had planned. Portia and Hester are to share a third portion of profits during their lives, and Mary and I are to receive a third portion each. And unless George changed his mind, Mary is to share the operation of it with me and she has a group of advisers. Sound men: the banker George had dealt with all his life—a conservative but good man; Clyde Gordon, the main warehouse manager, who knows everything there is to know about spices; and Winston Foxworth-Wilding."

"The man who writes those books about his travels?"

"The same. He's an old friend of George's. Apparently got his start from an interest in spices and has kept up the interest. The three of them will advise Mary—should she choose to take a role. If not, then I suppose we will have to go there permanently."

"Alex, you talk as if you don't want to go. I do not understand this. You have told me always about how much you loved England and most especially how you loved Castlemere. Now it is yours and you hang back and talk of 'visits.' I do not understand."

Alex took a sip of his drink and leaned back, thinking. Until a few moments ago he'd never had reason to seriously consider what would happen to all of them when George died. It was a hazy situation, too far in the future to think about. When he dreamed about that time, in his mind's eye his children were grown and ready to go to school, Anjanette was in perfect health, and Mary was a married matron.

Suddenly the future was upon them and it wasn't anything like that. "Janette, I'm important to the company here. If there isn't a good man at the Singapore end, the company will be in serious trouble. I don't even have a good potential replacement in mind. It was something I assumed I had years, if not decades, to figure out," he replied with absolute, if not complete, truth. There was also Mary to consider, but he wasn't ready to talk about her.

"More important," he went on, "I worry about your health if you were to go to England now."

"Alex, you know I'm well now. You must not hold back on my account."

"Yes, you're well enough now, but, Janette, you can't imagine the cool, damp climate. After a lifetime here, I'm afraid it would be hard on you to stay for any length of time."

"This you must not consider, Alex. As long as I am with you, my darling, I will thrive anywhere." She came to sit on the arm of his chair and he put his arm around her.

"And I am the same," he said, "so why should we need to go anywhere?"

Anjanette glanced around to see if any of the servants were watching, then slid onto his lap. "Do you mind that it's not all yours? You *are* the heir. It should all have come to you."

He reached up and twisted a loose strand of her hair around his fingers. "I did mind at first, when George wrote to me," he admitted. "But then I considered the amount of money involved and changed my mind. At least, I lost my resentment. A family could live in luxury on a tenth of the profits of this company. A third will be almost an embarrassment of riches. What concerns me is the future. Mary's advisers and I will have no difficulty. But what will happen several generations hence when Mary's descendants and ours are yoked together? Will they be able to agree on decisions?"

Anjanette got up and said, "Oh, but, my darling, that is no difficulty at all."

"No?"

"No. Our sweet Mary will certainly wed, and if she has a daughter, we have to arrange a marriage with her daughter and our Richard. That way her grandson and ours will be one and the same."

He smiled, though his heart had given a funny lurch at the thought of Mary wed and giving birth. "As easy to arrange as that? What if they don't like each other—this imaginary daughter and our boy?"

"Ah, but they will. Like you, they will be curious about everything and they will love maps better than books and believe the whole history of the world stems from spices. Mary's daughter and our son will live at your wonderful Castlemere and think it is the pivot of the universe. Beechams are all alike and they all like Beechams better than anyone else. You are a strange family that way. Will you go tomorrow?"

"Tomorrow? No. I can't leave until that shipment of cinnamon comes through. I will write to the lawyer and to Mary immediately, but I don't see how I can get away in less than a month. It might be two. Come with me, Janette. Leave the children with someone. It will only take six weeks or so."

"If it were only Katie, I would do so, but not Richard. He

requires such care yet. I would worry about him, and so would you."

"I suppose I would. Still, I'll miss you."

Alex couldn't get to sleep that night. Finally, he got up and wrote to Mary:

> My dear Cousin,
>   I have received a letter from Mr. Wambolt giving me the sad news of your father's death. I hardly know how to say how very sorry I am, for all of us. You and George meant the world to each other—that much was obvious to the most insensitive observer. Your only comfort, I suppose, is the knowledge that you shared a rare relationship that few of us are granted. If it was cut tragically short, at least it existed during your youth and you must remember that blessing.
>   For myself, I think I must feel the loss almost as much as you do. Never having had a cordial association with my own father and not having had a living brother, I cast George in both those roles and he fulfilled my highest hopes in each. He was a respected mentor, admirable head of the family, and beloved friend. It's my dearest wish that I may repay that debt by serving as father and brother to you, as he was to me.
>   As for the rest, the official problems attendant on his death, I had previously corresponded with George regarding his disposition of the business. I wholeheartedly agree with his intent, if perhaps doubting the long-range wisdom of it. For the present, I will confidently trust your advisers and your own quick intelligence to take care of the London end of the company. As Clyde will no doubt explain to you in detail, I cannot leave the Singapore branch without a specially trained substitute for some time. Perhaps weeks, perhaps several months.
>   In the interval, and beyond (if it is your desire, as I hope it must be), I sincerely wish you, Hester, and Portia to remain at Castlemere without making any changes except those you desire. It has always been your home; you must all

continue to regard it as such. I can't bear the
thought of Castlemere dust-sheeted, with the life
and love gone elsewhere. Until you and Hester
marry, Anjanette and I most sincerely wish you
to stay there, whether we are in residence or
not.

I will write as soon as I know a tentative date
for my return. In the meantime, let me assure
you of our great love and sympathy. Anjanette
and I regard you as sister, friend, and cousin and
wish there were some way to alleviate the sorrow you must feel. If there is anything whatsoever that we may do, say, or send you that will
give the slightest comfort, do not hesitate to call
upon us for it.

Your cousin,
Alex

He reread the letter once. It sounded stiff, paternal,
uncomfortably proper, almost priggish. But that was just as
well. It was the sort of letter he must write.

And yet—he leaned back, his face in shadow, his pale
eyes clouded with sorrow and confusion—how he wished he
could offer the comfort he longed to give. She must be
devastated, lonely, frightened. If only he could be there to
put his arms around her, to say, "Yes, I loved him too," to
wipe away her tears, to give her some assurance that her
grief would pass and she would be happy again.

But he knew, even as the thought crossed his mind, where
such a moment of comfort could lead. And with a wave of
guilt so real it hurt, he sensed where he would want it to
lead. He sat forward suddenly and put the letter into an
envelope and sealed it before he could write—or think—
anything more.

26

Mary folded the letter and set it down on her breakfast tray. Ginger, sleeping beside her in a nest of pillows, uncurled himself, stretched, and butted his head against her arm. She broke up her last piece of sausage and fed him bits. "He and Anjanette regard me as a sister, friend, and cousin," she told the cat. "Alex wants to be my father and brother. That's nearly every family combination there is." She picked the cat up and tried to snuggle him, but he'd dropped a bite of sausage on the counterpane and wriggled to get free to recover it.

"You're a greedy thing—and so am I, Ginger. So am I," she said with a deep sigh. She set the tray aside and got up. The maid had opened the windows when she brought the tray up, and the balmy June air was billowing the curtains. It was the sort of day that always made Mary feel happy and energetic. In the old days, she and Nellanor would have put on their climbing clothes and gone out for the day with sandwiches in their pockets. More recently, she and her father would have slipped away together to fish or ride or call on neighboring tenants.

But those times were past. What would she do now? Put on one of the wardrobe of heavy black dresses—dear God, how she hated black!—and keep busy all day in the house. Portia, more emotionally adrift without her husband than anyone would have expected, had begun to abdicate duties, and her responsibilities had fallen to Mary. "It's not my home anymore," Portia sniffled. "I'm but a poor guest in a strange woman's house."

"Yes, but your hostess happens to be halfway around the earth," Mary replied astringently. "Hardly able to order meals and pay the servants' wages."

This had thrown Portia into full-fledged hysterics and Mary hadn't chided her further. In a way, it was a good thing that Portia had given up interest in Castlemere. The proper running of the big house gave Mary a great deal to do, even if it was not what she would have wished. The trusty housekeeper who had served Portia for so many years had turned in her notice of retirement the week before George's death and Mary was involved in trying to find a replacement. Since she'd never particularly noticed what a housekeeper did, she had a lot to learn before she could begin interviewing applicants.

"Why don't you be housekeeper, Agnes?" she asked when she first realized the duty had come to her.

"Lord, no, miss! I like fine what I do, even if I do have to put up with the likes of you. I don't want no job that takes my whole day and night."

The problem had served to occupy her mind while waiting to hear from Alex, but now the letter had come and it was clear that he wasn't dashing to England to move in and take over Castlemere and the spice company. It was time to face some hard truths. The rosy vision of Alex as protector, man-of-the-family, and romantic figure had to be erased. "Well, what did I expect?" she asked herself out loud. "That he would say he was leaving his wife and family to dash into my arms?"

Ginger hopped off the bed and joined her at the window, balancing daintily on the sill and arching his back for a petting. "I'd have despised him for that, even if it had been his intent," Mary told him. "Oh, Ginger, you're so lucky to be a cat. You don't even care about things like I worry myself sick over."

"What was that?" Agnes asked from the doorway.

Mary rubbed her eyes as if the sun had caused them to water. "I was just talking to Ginger. What do you want?"

"No cause to take that huffy tone with me. I'm just reminding you that you have a guest."

"Oh, Mr. Wambolt. I'd forgotten about him!" Mary said. The lawyer had come down from London the evening before to sort out some legal details with her this morning.

Agnes was carrying a freshly pressed black dress. "It's going to be a warm day and this is the lightest weight I could find. It's Hester's, but she's wearing another today."

"Do I have to—?"

"You know you can't go into half-mourning for another four months. Then we'll get you some nice mauves and purples and grays. But I think you could put a bit of white on this so long as you're at home, not going out in public."

"I don't think Papa would have liked us all looking like ravens," Mary said, slipping out of her nightdress.

"You're not doing it to please him. It's everybody else expects it. Folks'd think you didn't care if you went dashing around in bright colors."

"Folks? What folks, Agnes? We're as isolated as if we had the plague!"

"Not so, miss. You got that nice Mr. Foxworth-Wilding here still, and now Mr. Wambolt and tomorrow Mr. Hewitt is coming for luncheon. Why don't we pin this nice white collar on here? And that gray brooch?"

"Miss Beecham, I don't believe your mother and sister quite understand the provisions of your father's will yet," Mr. Wambolt said. The portly little lawyer had come to Castlemere four or five times since George's death, usually with business papers for Mary, as the only resident owner of the company empowered to sign legal documents. But he tried to engage Portia's interest in her own situation every time he came.

"My sister has other matters on her mind and Portia believes it's unseemly for a woman to comprehend such things," Mary replied.

"But when I spoke to Mrs. Beecham last night, she seemed to think that you, she, Miss Hester, and your cousin Alex each got a third of the company profits. I tried to explain that there cannot be four thirds of a whole, but . . ."

Mary smiled at him. "I would advise you to cease your explanations, Mr. Wambolt. Portia will not ever grasp the fact that my portion is larger than hers for the simple reason that she doesn't wish to. And there's no real need for her to understand that, is there?"

"No, I suppose not," he admitted. As frustrated as he was with his own explanations falling on such sterile ground, on the whole he approved of women leaving such things to men. It was the natural order of things. "So long as your cousin is willing to look after her interests, as I'm sure he is."

"My cousin and I," Mary reminded him.

"Harumph—yes, quite."

Just as Portia refused to face facts, Mr. Wambolt had his blind side. While he knew better than anyone else the legal ramifications of George's will, he couldn't conceive of the idea of a woman being involved in business. And so far, Mary had not shown any interest in becoming involved. But since reading Alex's letter this morning, Mary was undergoing a slow change in attitude, and even Wambolt, not a man noted for his sensitivity, was vaguely aware of it.

"Mr. Wambolt, I received a letter from my cousin this morning. It seems he's not returning to England immediately."

"Yes, Mr. Gordon has explained your cousin's role in the foreign market to me and he felt it was unlikely that he could leave without a substantial delay."

"It would appear that means there is nobody at the helm, so to speak."

"I'm not sure I understand your analogy," Mr. Wambolt said uneasily.

"I believe you do," Mary answered firmly. "If my cousin is halfway around the world and I'm here at Castlemere, there is actually no one presently acting as head of the company."

"There are your advisers—"

"Yes, but Mr. Foxworth-Wilding is here as well. That means that Mr. Gordon and Mr. Stanford are running Beecham's Fine Spices. Two excellent men, but neither of them actual owners."

"You distrust their judgment?"

"Not in the least, but Beecham's has been run by Beechams for centuries. I feel it's letting down generations of my family to let the company rest in the control of others. Don't you think my father would have felt the same?"

That put Wambolt on the spot, because he was certain that was precisely what George would have felt. As good a businessman as he was, George was positively woolly-minded about family ties. His father had been the same way. "You're suggesting, then, that your cousin be requested to return immediately, no matter the wisdom of leaving the Singapore branch unattended?"

"Quite the contrary. I'm proposing that I take the role my father allowed for."

Wambolt's face went red. "I really don't . . . that is, I wonder if—"

"I think it's an excellent idea," Winston Foxworth-Wilding said from the doorway. "Excuse me for eavesdropping. It wasn't intentional. I was looking for my pipe."

"Please come in, Winston. I was going to ask you to join us. This matter is very much your concern, as my participation in the business will naturally take up a good deal of your time. You agree, then?"

"Conditionally. I think you should go to London and learn all you can about the job you want to take on before you make a decision. You might find it a dead bore."

"I doubt that."

Mary moved to one end of the love seat and gestured for him to sit beside her. Then she turned her attention back to the lawyer, who was glaring at Foxworth-Wilding. "Mr. Wambolt, I cannot help but notice that you disapprove, and I'm sorry about that, but I hope you will, nevertheless, give me your honest opinion—"

"My personal judgments need not concern you," he said, not meaning a word of it.

Mary, understanding perfectly, smiled and said, "These documents you have along today, for instance—tell me what they are."

Mr. Wambolt took out his case and extracted several papers. Spreading them on the desk, he said, "Of course. I need your signature here, and again here—"

"But what for?"

"They're contracts," he explained courteously, but as if on the brink of impatience.

"I know they are. But what are they contracts for?" Mary's impatience was undisguised.

Winston Foxworth-Wilding, still seated, grinned at her. She was like a perky little black terrier with a rat. Any moment, he expected her to pounce on Wambolt and give him a good shake with her teeth.

Wambolt knew when he was cornered. "This is an agreement to lease a warehouse near the docks for a period of one year with the option to renew for three years."

"Why do we need an extra warehouse?"

"We . . . ah, *you* are purchasing a smaller spice company and need a place to store the extra products."

"Are they of good quality, up to Beecham's standards?"

"Mr. Gordon says they are, Miss Beecham."

"Why is this other company for sale?"

Wambolt looked surprised at the question. "It is a family firm, like Beecham's, though on a much smaller scale and of shorter duration. The heir has died and the elderly couple who own it do not wish to continue."

"If we don't buy it, what will they do?"

"Probably sell off their stock and allow it to disappear. Unless they can sell it to someone else."

"What is our advantage to buying it? They can't be serious competition. Is their stock that exceptional?"

"No, in fact they purchase most of their stock from Beecham's in the first place. But they have a number of stores in Wales that purchase exclusively from them. You would be buying entry into a geographical market that has been traditionally difficult to penetrate."

Mary cast a quick look at Foxworth-Wilding, who nodded. "Very well, Mr. Wambolt," she said, briskly signing the contracts.

Wambolt sighed, clearly relieved that this silly inquisition was over and done. Waste of time, if you asked him. Still, if it made the girl feel better . . . She'd lose interest soon enough when she realized how well her advisers were looking after things. He gathered up his paperwork and Mary walked him to the front door, where his carriage was waiting.

"Mr. Wambolt, this is a very long trip for you to make every time there's something that requires a signature."

"I am adequately reimbursed," he replied.

"You mean from the estate? Well, in future, I don't think it will be necessary for you to take so much of your time. I'm planning to come to London on a regular basis in the next few months."

"You are? How peculiar that your mother didn't mention such plans. I've never known her to visit the city much in the heat of the year."

"I don't believe she will be joining me. I was speaking for myself, not the family."

"You're planning to stay in the city by yourself?" he asked.

"Not exactly by myself. I'll have my maid and the staff of the Mincing Lane house. You need not fear for my safety or my reputation, Mr. Wambolt."

He went off grumbling under his breath, unable to formulate a convincing reason why she should not do what she wished, but disliking the idea very much. It was one thing to explain selected bits of business to her at his convenience, quite another to have her underfoot asking questions all the time. He hadn't anything to hide, but he found it distasteful to talk business with a young woman.

Mary went back to Foxworth-Wilding, who had found his missing pipe and was lighting it. "Poor Mr. Wambolt," she said with mock seriousness, and they both laughed. "Did I ask the right questions?"

"Some of them," Winston replied.

"Oh, I thought I'd done very well," Mary admitted. "What did I neglect?"

"The warehouse. Where is it? What is the rental cost? Is the location convenient? What does this little company cost? Would it have been cheaper if a month or two had passed, or would it have gone to someone else?"

He paused and Mary stared at him openmouthed for a moment. Then she went on: "What is the cost of transporting to the market in Wales? What are the special buying habits in that area? What were the profits in the small company for the last few years?"

"Exactly," he said, impressed at how quickly she had taken his point.

"Oh, dear! Have I done a stupid thing?"

"No, you haven't. Mr. Gordon and Mr. Stanford have already looked into all of that and showed me the figures for my approval. It's quite a good arrangement. Don't worry."

"I think perhaps I'm being as foolish as Mr. Wambolt believes. What use is there in my interfering when such knowledgeable men are already looking after Beecham's interests so well?"

"You know the answer to that. You said it yourself. You are a Beecham. We are not. That gives you an extra responsibility that none of us has."

"Then you wouldn't mind if I went to London and started learning more about the business?"

"I wouldn't mind in the least. I'd be delighted to help you however I might."

"And Clyde? How do you think Clyde would feel?"

"Mr. Gordon thinks you're 'as bright as a new penny'—to quote him—and would love nothing better than to teach you everything he can. He had an enormous respect for your father is perfectly willing to transfer it to you. You may not know this, but Clyde's wife is raising nine children and successfully running a boardinghouse at the same time. He knows what a woman can do if she sets her mind to it. Now, your banker is a different story."

"Yes, Mr. Stanford is very like Mr. Wambolt, isn't he?

"Very like. Doesn't that worry you?"

"No, it merely annoys me. Do you play cards, Winston?"

"On occasion. Why?"

"Well, Aunt Nell taught me a lot of card games and I always rather disliked getting a terribly good hand because it wasn't any fun winning if it was too easy. It seems in this case I've been dealt two very good cards and one bad one."

He laughed. "And which am I? A knave?"

"Indeed no, a king of hearts, I should say."

Foxworth-Wilding had to turn away and pretend to tend to his pipe so she couldn't see the look on his face. He was certain he had an embarrassingly besotted expression.

Jamison Hewitt came to visit the next day. To her own surprise, Mary was actually glad to see him. She supposed it was because they had become so isolated in the last month or so. The only callers they had were old friends of Portia's who stopped in solemnly to offer condolences. Hewitt, at least, brought good cheer. Hester brightened at his visit, and even Portia, who had been unalterably opposed to Hester's interest in him before George's death, apparently forgot her misgivings when he kissed her hand and told her with a radiant smile how lovely she looked. More than any of them, Portia dearly loved and missed the social round.

Jamison smelled of brandy and leather and expensive tobacco. He was, even Mary had to admit, astonishingly handsome, especially to eyes starved of the sight of dashing young men. His breezy insouciance seemed to make the air lighter and clearer. He had the gift, too, of telling people what they wanted to hear. "But, ladies, there is no reason for undergoing all the restrictions of deep mourning in your own home. Not even the queen would expect that. And as long as there is no one else present but your closest friends . . ."

"Do you really believe so?" Portia asked. She looked so very pasty in black and was beginning to look in mirrors again.

"My respect for you is too great, Mrs. Beecham, to mislead you. I assure you, in London such rules are often lightened without any social stigma." He turned and winked conspiratorially at Mary.

She began to think she might have misjudged him. And yet, as the thought crossed her mind, it collided with the memory of the night of the ball, when he had taken her arm in the dark picture gallery and frightened her with his strange talk. Still, it must have just been a momentary aberration that he was no doubt as anxious to forget as she was.

"Are you taken with Mr. Hewitt?" Winston Foxworth-Wilding asked her after dinner as they took a stroll in the balmy night air.

"Me? No, he's Hester's beau."

"You hardly took your eyes off him at dinner," Winston persisted, hating the nagging, jealous tone he thought he heard in his own words.

Mary didn't detect it or take offense. "I guess I didn't. I was just wondering about him. I used to dislike him very much. I think I may have been wrong about him, however."

"I'm not so certain," he said.

"Why, Winston, do you know something to his disadvantage? If so, you must tell me. Hester has no father to protect her interests now. I suppose my cousin Alex is really the head of the family now, but he's so far away . . ."

He noticed the wistful sound in her voice, but attributed it to loneliness for her father. "I know nothing to his disadvantage, only my instinct. I don't favor him, but I couldn't tell you why."

He had opportunity to define his judgment more sharply later that evening. When the ladies had retired, Jamison asked Winston if he could have a word with him. Taking brandy and cigars into the map room, which Winston now used as his own office, they settled themselves and Winston waited.

Jamison had his speech ready. "As the closest friend of the late Mr. Beecham, I would like to appeal to you, Mr. Foxworth-Wilding, for advice and some information. You see, I'm very fond of Miss Beecham and would like to make an offer for her hand. With her father gone, and her cousin so far away, however, I don't know to whom I should speak." It was very deferential.

"There is no question of an engagement so close upon George's death."

"Of course not. But eventually there are matters that

need to be discussed. Financial settlements, for instance. I have no knowledge of Miss Beecham's situation . . ."

Winston twirled his brandy glass thoughtfully. "Which Miss Beecham are we discussing?"

"Why, either one."

"I beg your pardon!" Winston nearly shot out of his chair.

"Please, don't misunderstand me. I am exceedingly fond of both ladies. I could imagine a long and happy life with either. But I know myself. My tastes are expensive. I have debts. If I were to marry any woman who didn't have substantial resources, I would make a poor husband in several senses."

"I have never heard anything so cold-blooded in my life," Winston said, disgusted at even being a part of this conversation.

"I find that hard to believe," Jamison said, a slight edge to his voice. All deference was gone. The talk now was bluntly man-to-man. "It is the way of the world, and you are a man of the world. I differ from others only in that I'm not cloaking my thoughts in euphemisms and pretty speeches. Do you think your friend George's marriage was one jot less 'cold-blooded' in intent? Or that Portia Beecham's parents would have allowed the marriage if there hadn't been enormous money and social prestige attached to it? Well, I have no important parents to sell me off to the highest bidder. I must make my own way."

Winston didn't reply. As much as he'd suddenly come to despise Jamison Hewitt, there was hard truth in every word he spoke, and Winston wasn't the kind of fool to pretend otherwise.

"I will make a good husband," Jamison was going on. "I am considered good-looking, an asset women appreciate, I'm well-liked in society, and I'm neither brutish nor stupid. If Miss Beecham—either Miss Beecham—marries me, she will have made a good bargain, as the only asset I lack is money and they have plenty. The only question is, which of them has the most?"

Staring at him in astonishment and a grudging sliver of admiration for the sheer gall of it all, Winston didn't reply at first. Then he carefully picked his way through. "I suppose you know that this house is entailed upon Alex Beecham, a cousin."

"Hester has told me that, yes. But there is some question as to whether he intends to take up residence."

"I wouldn't say 'whether' so much as 'when.' "

"Perhaps. In any case, Hester and Mary have both inherited other property of their own and they are entitled to equal shares in the profits from Beecham's Fine Spices."

He paused briefly, waiting for confirmation.

Winston remained silent, even though his first impulse was to correct this error. In the first place, he had absolutely no right to reveal any confidential information to Hewitt or anybody else. In addition, if he informed Jamison that Mary owned the greater share, the young man would undoubtedly shift his suit wholly to her. From the favorable way Mary had spoken of him earlier in the evening, Winston was afraid she might succumb to the very charms Jamison had just enumerated. On the other hand, if he let the error stand, Jamison would probably choose Hester because she had inherited so much more land.

Was it fair to throw Hester to the wind that way? he wondered. Or was it throwing her to the wind? Was it, rather, throwing her into the arms of the only man she wanted? Hester made no secret of her fondness for Jamison, and everything he'd said about his personal assets was quite true. If she never knew of his desire for her money, she would probably be entirely happy with him. And what difference could it really make to her that he was poor? Her inheritance was more than adequate, it was enormous.

"Go on," Winston said, allowing Jamison's misunderstanding to take the illusion of fact.

Jamison nodded. "There is little more to say. I would, however, hope for your support. You are greatly respected by the family." His manner now was conciliatory.

"I will not support you, Hewitt. But I haven't decided whether or not I will actively attempt to thwart your plans. I will consider all you've said and let you know in a few days' time."

"I'll look forward to continuing our discussion, then," Jamison said.

But Jamison knew better than to let anyone have time to analyze his motives. He'd found out—he thought—what he needed from Foxworth-Wilding. The next day, at luncheon, with everyone present, he gave Hester a silver-paper-wrapped box. Inside was a large topaz ring. "It was my mother's betrothal ring and her mother's before her. I hope you will accept it with my love and admiration."

Hester burst into tears of joy.

Portia said, "Well, I hardly . . . this is so . . . I just don't . . ." then began to cry too.

Jamison shook Foxworth-Wilding's hand and said insolently, "Thanks so much, old man, for your advice. I'll never forget you."

Winston was silent, filled with self-contempt. He, a man who had convinced cannibals that he'd be better as a friend than as a meal, had been taken by this young man. "Continuing our discussion" indeed. Hewitt had the ring along and was determined to give it to one or the other of them on this visit.

27

Mary had felt a very odd sensation the Friday afternoon she walked into the London house. None of them had come to London since George's death and she'd hardly thought about the place, but suddenly she saw the strange old house in a new light. This is mine. It belongs to me alone, she thought. Except for clothing and personal items, nothing had ever belonged wholly to her. Now all these odd rooms that were set up or down from the hall and led into each other in unexpected ways were Mary Beecham's. And the staff, including the mournful Bartlet, now the full-time butler, were in her charge. It was a little daunting and very exciting.

Feeling charged with home-owner energy, she addressed him with brisk, if false, confidence as he stood staring sadly at the pile of baggage being brought in. "Bartlet, I shall be taking the suite of rooms my Aunt Nellanor used to use, but I think I shall have them redecorated and spruced up a bit first, so you may put my things in my usual room for now. And Agnes in the room next to it. No point in her running up and down all those steps to the top floor. Come to think of it, I've never seen the servants' quarters here. I'll look them over later and see if there's anything we should be doing with them."

Bartlet came as close as he could to a smile at this evidence of the new mistress's concern for the comfort and welfare of the staff. "Welcome, Miss Mary, Mr. Foxworth-Wilding. May I express once again, Miss Mary, the gratitude of the staff for your thoughtfulness in sending the rector over to conduct a memorial service for your late father. It was much appreciated."

"Thank you, Bartlet. I was only sorry I could not come to town to attend the service myself. If you'll send the housekeeper to me in twenty minutes, I would be grateful. In the meantime, Mr. Foxworth-Wilding and I will take tea in the drawing room."

"You did that very well, Mary," Winston said when they were settled over their steaming cups of Darjeeling.

"Did I really? I was so frightened that Bartlet would look down his nose at me and know I was terrified of saying something wrong."

"Are you going to keep that young man on? Don't you find his grimness depressing?"

"Bartlet? Yes, I rather think I'll keep him. He's a constant reminder that life is real and earnest and that I must take things very seriously indeed," she said with a giggle.

He smiled at her, amused and strangely touched at the switch from the confident mistress of the house she'd been moments before to the bubbling young woman she was now. He was saved saying something foolish by a knock on the door. Mrs. Coomb, the housekeeper, had arrived. She was a ramrod-backed lady with a fierce set of eyebrows. "Mary, you're going to be busy," he said, rising. "I'm going to go home."

"Your man found you a house, then?"

Foxworth-Wilding had been staying in rented rooms before George's death. He gave them up and put his belongings in storage when Mary asked him to stay on at Castlemere. Now he was taking up residence in London again and had asked his publisher to find him a small house as near as possible to Mary's house. "Yes, I'm to see it and sign the papers this afternoon. Then I've got to see the movers and get some staff lined up." He'd never have admitted how uneasy he was about these simple tasks. Dorothea had always taken care of such things. He had only to say where they were going next, and somehow lodgings and servants were in place when they arrived.

Mary, her mind spinning with the duties of her new role, didn't notice his unease as she saw him off with expressions of gratitude for his support. She returned eagerly to Mrs. Coomb, a very dignified widow in her forties. Mary found her stiff posture and imposing expression a litte intimidating, but was determined to get things off on the right foot. "Mrs. Coomb, I think we should be quite frank with each other today so that we may know if it's going to be comfortable for both of us in this house."

"Certainly, miss."

"To begin with, although I am a single woman, I am mistress of this house and prefer to be addressed as 'ma'am.' Now, the family has visited here very little in the three years you've been housekeeper. You've had relatively few responsibilities—"

"That was not as I would wish, ma'am. If you desire my frankness, then I must tell you I feel this position has been a waste of my talents."

That won Mary over entirely. Nothing the woman could have said would have impressed her more. "I'm delighted to hear that. I shall now commence to use your talents to the fullest. First, I have engaged a housekeeper for Castlemere and I made a botch of it. She's slovenly and has offended the rest of the staff. I would like for you to interview as many women as necessary for the post. If you would prefer to take the position yourself and find a replacement for this establishment, you may do so, but I prefer that you remain here and will give you a raise in salary if you do."

"I have friends and relatives in London, ma'am. And the country life doesn't appeal to me. I shall remain."

"Very good. Now, as to the running of this house, I wish you to engage a new cook. Give good references to the one we have, but get somebody who knows the proper use of spices. As spice merchants, Beechams are expected to serve guests well-seasoned meals. The food here has been too bland of late. I've prepared a list of foods I like and dislike, but when there are guests, my own preferences may be ignored."

"Very well, ma'am. If I may say so, I'm entirely in agreement with you. I know of a cook who would be very good, but she might require higher wages than you currently pay."

"I'm not a spendthrift, nor am I parsimonious, Mrs. Coomb," she said, thinking how ridiculous that really was. Truth be told, she knew next to nothing about money, never having handled much of it. George had paid all her bills without her even seeing them. She knew to the shilling what a ton of cloves ought to cost, but no idea what a scullery maid should be paid. "If you would prepare a list of the staff members, we should talk about their wages and whether adjustments are in order."

Mrs. Coomb pulled the very list from her pocket.

They spent the next three hours together, going over accounts, furnishings, linens, schedules, sources of household friction and solutions. At the end of that time, Mrs.

Coomb was nodding her satisfaction with the new young mistress (who had always seemed a helter-skelter sort of girl, and for whom she had held out very little hope) and Mary was sighing with gratitude that fate had handed her such a wonder of a housekeeper.

Mary had a simple dinner, then tackled Bartlet. "I wish to see the servants' rooms and the stables. I would also like your entirely honest opinion of those members of the staff under your control. Any opinions you express will remain confidential between us. But before we get to that, Bartlet, are you familiar with Mr. Clyde Gordon?"

"An employee of your late father's company, ma'am? I believe he has visited here once or twice before." His tone was overly fastidious on the word "employee," as though it was a condemnation.

"Bartlet, Mr. Gordon will, I hope, be a frequent guest here from now on. I shall welcome him as a friend and equal; I wish the staff to reflect that attitude. I will not have my servants looking down on my friends. Is that clear?"

Bartlet gulped down his disapproval. "As you wish, ma'am."

They went over the house from top to bottom. Mary inspected the top floor—"How hideous! It's like an oven. How do these girls stand it? I want larger windows cut in, fresh paint, and a decent lavatory installed. Arrange it, Bartlet."

The stables—"This is more like it, though the straw could be fresher. Why are horses treated so much better than most people?"

The garden—"I suppose the London atmosphere makes it difficult to grow anything, and there isn't much space to spare, but I'd like a new undergardener who can do something with those roses."

And the cellars—"I bow to your superior knowledge, Bartlet. Handle the restocking to your satisfaction."

By the time she went to bed, she was happily exhausted. She had learned to see this beloved and familiar home in a new light. Strangely enough, the things that had charmed her as a child were the very things that bothered her the most. Long winding hallways were fun for playing hide-and-seek, but a dreary nuisance for servants who had to walk miles out of their way in the course of a week's work. The cozy little kitchen she'd enjoyed visiting when she was young was inconvenient and badly arranged and much too far from the dining room. No wonder the food was always tepid by the time it reached the table. The creaking stair she and Hester used to like to make squeal was a possible sign of structural insecurity and had to be repaired before the whole staircase tumbled down and hurt somebody.

There were a good many changes to make, and at first Mary had avoided considering them, wishing to keep the house as it had always been, the way she had always loved it. But by bedtime she had realized that generations of Beechams had been making additions and alterations to suit themselves, and there was no reason she should not do the same.

"After all, it's *my* house," she said to herself, sliding a little sideways in her narrow bed so that the shaft of moonlight from the open window wouldn't shine in her eyes. This room faced the street and she could hear the muted rumble that was London at night. Muted voices, the muffled clatter of carriage wheels on cobbles, the soft moan of ships' horns on the river. She could also smell the river, the poor old Thames that was such a sewer and reeked so horribly in the summer. The odor was awful, but her ally in a funny way. If old Philippe Beecham hadn't hated the stench so much, he'd have never built Castlemere and this would have remained the main house and would have belonged to Alex.

Philippe's nose had made it hers. She chuckled to herself at the thought. She must remember it, to tell Winston tomorrow when she told him about all the ideas she had for fixing up the house. But no, Winston would not be around tomorrow, nor probably Saturday or Sunday either. He had his own responsibilities to keep him busy.

She rolled over and balled up her pillow under her head, suddenly feeling unutterably sad. What a disappointment it was to have so much on her mind to talk about and no one to share it with. George, who loved her, would have liked to talk about alterations with her; Nellanor, who loved her, would have had fiery opinions of her own to contribute. But there was no one who loved her now. Oh, Hester loved her in her way; many were fond of her, some had some measure of respect for her, but there was no one who truly loved her as George and Nellanor had.

She buried her face and sobbed for the sheer loneliness of her life. Would it always be this way? If only Alex could love her . . .

*   *   *

The following Monday began her apprenticeship at the spice company. At the house she had felt it imperative to take charge immediately, whether she was prepared or qualified to or not. Here, it was a different matter entirely. Cheerful, rotund Clyde Gordon was to be her mentor and she the student. Dressed in dark gray, knowing none of the society tattletales were likely to see her there, and carrying a sheaf of paper on which she could jot down notes, she trailed him silently for the first few days. Though he was more than willing to tell her all he knew—which was considerable—he was a very busy man with little time to step away from his work and explain it.

"Please, proceed with your duties, Mr. Gordon," Mary said the third time he paused in the midst of something, remembering her presence and attempting to explain why he had given the order he had. "I will makes notes of anything I don't understand and we can talk after-hours. In fact, I would like to suggest that you join me for dinner on Tuesdays and Fridays for the next month or two—unless that infringes on your home life? Feel free to bring Mrs. Gordon along if you like."

Thus, a pattern was established. Clyde and Winston dined with her twice a week and Winston was prevailed upon (with almost no urging) to accompany her to church and Sunday supper each week as well. She quickly learned that the long summer evenings were long indeed without anyone to talk to. Even though her busy days at the warehouse were tiring, she tried to have other guests once or twice a week. Mostly older people: the banker and his wife, the lawyer and his, some other old business associates of George's.

Hester and Portia came up for a week and Jamison joined them and Portia's friends at several dinner parties—"We're still in mourning, no more than eight," Portia reminded her, though she was as anxious as Mary to break the rules. But the heat and smell soon drove them back to Castlemere. Mary, with Winston at her side, watched them drive off with a surge of homesickness. Much as she loved this house for its memories and the fact that it was hers, Castlemere was her spiritual home. How she missed the taste of salt in the air on windy days and the pervasive scent of rosemary.

When they were gone, she called Mrs. Coomb. "I'm going to have a bottle of rosemary oil sent over," she told the older woman. "I'd like a few drops to be added to the rinse water of all the linens, and mixed with the candle wax."

"Is that what makes Castlemere smell of rosemary?" Winston asked when the housekeeper had gone. "I'd often wondered."

"No, but if I ever live there again, I'll do the same. Didn't I ever tell you about the rosemary?" She recounted the story of the time the wall had been torn out and the dried needlelike leaves found mixed in the plaster. "I made up some perfectly silly romantic story to go with it, I'm afraid. My cousin Alex was there that day and I'm sure he thought I was quite mad."

"Your cousin Alex lived in England?"

"Only while he was in school, and then we saw him too rarely. I was insanely in love with him when I was little. You see, he's very handsome and very, very nice. A little girl's passion must have been very trying for him. Let's sit in the garden, shall we?"

When they were seated, Winston said, "You've hardly mentioned Alex. Tell me more about him." He'd had the impression that she simply had no interest in her cousin, an impression that had just been proved wrong. But how wrong?

Mary smiled. "I hardly know where to start. Of course, you know his business abilities and his relationship to the family. His father was Aunt Nellanor's son and Nell and my father's father were half-brother and sister. I'm not sure what relation that makes Alex to Hester and me, but we've always called him cousin. I think his father was a very sad, sour person, but Alex isn't like him at all. He's very smart and well-read and makes the same sort of wry jokes that Papa used to make. And, as I said, he's extraordinarily handsome. Slim and strong and tanned from the tropical sun, with very dark hair and startlingly blue eyes. Nothing like the rest of us. He must get his looks from his mother. None of us ever saw her."

How odd it was to sum him up this way. The description, while accurate, conveyed nothing of his magical, magnetic appeal. There simply weren't words for that, she supposed.

"And you were in love with him," Foxworth-Wilding said.

"Quite madly! I trailed him about like a puppy when he visited. I would count the days for months ahead when he was to come to Castlemere."

"And now?"

"Now what?"

"Are you still in love with him?"

"Good heavens, no! He's a happily married man with two children. His wife, Anjanette, is a wonderful woman. Now I love him only as a cousin and head of the family, and for those reasons I am looking forward to his return."

It was a measure of her newly found ability to sound convincing and confident that she could say this so lightly and with such apparent sincerity. It was a measure of Winston's growing love of her that he could believe it in the face of the evidence to the contrary.

Mary was, in fact, slowly learning to be able to think about Alex without the awful lurch of her heart that had tortured her for so long after the trip to Singapore. Her work at the warehouse brought her into contact with his name frequently. All their shipments from the Singapore/ Java/Penang area came under his name, and as she walked through the warehouse she often noticed the bags of cloves with the name of his plantation stamped on them. At first she was almost carried away on a flood of memories, wondering if perhaps she herself had picked some of the tiny dried flower buds in those bags. But after several weeks she ceased to notice them very often and never allowed herself the luxury of remembering those hot tropical days when she was so close to him.

Alex kept in constant touch with Clyde through letters. With Clyde's help, Mary instigated a policy of writing him a long account of each week's work. Whereas Clyde had been sending copies of ledger sheets, Mary added comments. "I think we made an exceptionally good bargain with this turmeric shipment," she would write. Or: "Clyde and I decided against making a bid on the Harlinger plantation ginger this year. The ginger was of excellent taste and texture, but the hands were so oddly shaped that they couldn't be sold whole. As we have a sufficient backlog of powdered ginger, we shall try to find another source for the whole hands."

And Alex replied frequently and lengthily in kind. "I have found another source of ginger out here. Samples to follow." Or: "I'm sending a shipment of black pepper from Siam. As you know, we normally buy the bulk of it from Borneo, but this year's crop was heavily adulterated with dirt. P.S. Remind me to tell you about the old BEIC's orders on white pepper when I get there."

She asked Foxworth-Wilding about this comment that evening. "Didn't your father ever tell you that story? I'll bet Clyde knows it too."

"Yessir, it's a right funny thing. You see, Miss Mary, the British East India Company sent men out to Sumatra and the like to grow pepper. Actually, the natives grew it, but the BEIC men was to make sure they grew enough and shipped it back here. But the company men in England, they didn't have no idea how it was done, don't you see. Once, they sent an order out that the factors weren't to let the natives plant any more black pepper. All they wanted grown was white pepper."

"But they're the same plant. The same berry. The outside is the black and the inside is the white."

"Just so, Miss Mary. Took them near on a year to make anybody back here understand that. Then the English end decided it wasn't a good idea to ship pepper and sugar in the same boats. They said fill the boat with pepper because it's worth more."

Winston laughed, but Mary gave him a questioning look. "That makes sense," she said.

"In a money way, yes. But think about pepper, Miss Mary. It's right light. You could toss a big bag of it around yourself if you didn't mind the smell."

"Oh, I see. The sugar was heavy. It was used for ballast."

"Right. They sent out a ship or two—back in them days they went clear around the Cape of Good Hope, the Suez not being dug yet—and the ships near tipped right over, they was riding so high in the water. It must have been tricky for your ancestors, miss, having to put up with the old BEIC men sitting back here running things without no idea of what was what."

Later that evening, when Clyde had gone and Mary had taken Winston out to the small garden to show him the work being done on the roses, she said, "It never fails to amaze me how much I have to learn from Clyde and you. I find myself looking forward to these dinners with a sort of greed. Not for the food, but for information, for insights. I wish I could stop the clocks and make the evenings last forever. See the small yellow roses, how nicely they're coming along . . ."

But Winston's mind wasn't on the roses, it was on Mary

and what she had said. When, much later, he knocked the cold ashes from his pipe and started gathering up the paperwork he'd brought along, she said, "Oh, I hate for you to leave," and he said, impulsively, "There is a way, Mary, that I could stay. Would you marry me?"

"M-m-marry . . . ?"

"I'm sorry. I shouldn't have flung a question like that at you without warning. Let me try again, and don't feel you must say anything right away. I've come to love you more than I can say, Mary. You've become a part of the fabric of my life, all my thoughts and opinions and perceptions. I know I'm old enough to be your father, but if you'll allow me, I'll be the best husband I can. No, don't speak unless you're so offended at my nerve that you wish me to go."

"Offended? Winston, I'm flattered. But surprised—"

"Of course. I haven't exactly courted you—"

"Courted me? Do you think I would prefer some silly boy bringing me flowers and writing foolish poems more than I enjoy and appreciate all you've given me?"

"I hope not. Please . . . please don't say anything more now. Take as long as you want to give me your answer. I'll see myself out. Good night."

He came as close as dignity allowed to running from the room.

28

———————◆———————

The afternoon was frigid, even for late November, with a nasty, wet wind. Alex stood at the ship's rail, the cold salt air blowing straight into his face. He shivered and grinned broadly. He'd nearly forgotten what is was to shiver. It had been eleven years since he'd been cold—that last English Christmas before he returned to Singapore—and he was enjoying it immensely. A real English winter was one of the best things in life. How fortunate he was to have such fond memories of winter; glossy holly speckled with frost, warm fires, fur-collared coats, hot chocolate late at night with a cousin who was a friend, and visits with his beloved eccentric grandmother. And how unfortunate that he couldn't recapture all of it. England would seem very different indeed without George and Nellanor. Standing at the rail now, he found himself wishing there had been more time with them when he was younger, instead of those few short visits to Castlemere and the busy times when they met in London or at his school.

Still, it wouldn't all be different. There would still be holly and Yule logs and the evocative rosemary scent of Castlemere. And he would see Mary; he would probably see a great deal of Mary, in fact, as his purpose in coming here was primarily to catch up on the business, and she was taking such an interest in it.

Mary . . .

He turned away from the wind, which was beginning to carry wicked bits of sleet. Had he remembered her betrothal gift? Yes, he was sure he'd seen Anjanette pack it for him. Just to be certain, he went to his cabin and looked in the bottom of the brown portmanteau. Yes, it was there, just as he'd thought. He opened the velvet-wrapped box. It contained a long rope of fat satiny pearls with a matching pearl-encrusted tiara. This last had a series of tiny concealed holes around the base to which a wedding veil could be sewn and later detached. That had been Anjanette's idea.

What an extraordinarily beautiful bride Mary would make, he thought, picturing the milky pearls nestling in her red hair and draped about her fine, fair throat. Unless she'd begun to lose her looks, he added mentally. Surely she'd never lose that beauty, and yet he half-hoped she would. It would make it so much easier to be around her without feeling her allure.

But then, it wouldn't be for long. As he had told her in his last letter, this was just to be a short visit. A duty visit—although he hadn't said that. Beecham's Fine Spices didn't need him; the business was thriving under Mary's and her advisers' stewardship. If there had been so much as a hint of a problem, he would have felt obligated to pack up Anjanette and the children and move back to England.

He rewrapped the gift and replaced it at the bottom of the portmanteau and tried to put away his thoughts at the same time. But they were not so easily dispensed with. He sat down and tented his fingers thoughtfully. Mary was engaged to be married as soon as her mourning period was over. That news was the single thing that had made him feel comfortable booking passage. Mary was no fool to marry impulsively. If she was to marry this Foxworth-Wilding person, it must be because she was truly in love with him; she never went into anything half-heartedly. And from all he'd read by Foxworth-Wilding and heard about him, he was an excellent choice of husband, albeit a bit long in the tooth. Still, he was probably quite fit and youthful from all his adventures.

Alex's valet stepped into the cabin. "The steward says an hour until docking, sir. Will you wish me to arrange transportation?"

"Yes, Morgan, if you would. I haven't informed my family of my precise arrival date. They won't be there to meet me."

"Indeed?"

"Don't you arch your eyebrows at me like that, my man," Alex said with a smile. Morgan was an Australian descendant of convicts and his overcompensation for his background gave him a terribly superior air. Alex rather enjoyed puncturing his dignity from time to time.

"What address should I give the transport?"

"Hmmm, I've never had to stay at a hotel in London. Ask about, Morgan, and make the choice yourself."

"Very good, sir," the valet answered smugly. Having such decisions left up to him was the right way of things.

Alex was still chuckling to himself over Morgan's pretensions when London came into view. He'd never approached England this way, up the Thames, having taken transport that docked at Southamption before. Too bad it had been such a bleak day; he might have been able to spot Castlemere from the Channel if it had been clear. He'd never seen the house from the sea. He might have, that day he and Mary went fishing, if only she hadn't fallen in before they got out from shore very far. He smiled at the recollection of that day when she'd accidentally flung herself right out of the boat. He hadn't thought of it for years. What a strange, fey child she had been.

He probably should have told Morgan to have his things sent straight to the Beechams' London house, he thought. Mary's London house now. But he'd had an almost superstitious feeling that he should greet the old country by himself. Get his land legs, so to speak, on his own. That was the reason he'd not written about his exact travel plans.

Going back on deck, he searched the banks for the spice warehouse, but it was hopeless. Not only were the buildings cheek by jowl in a confusing jumble, but the light was nearly gone even though it was only late afternoon. He'd forgotten that part of English winters; how early it got dark. He remembered how disconcerting long and short seasonal days were when he'd come here as a boy. In Singapore, so close to the equator, the longest day was only nine minutes longer than the shortest. Here, there were hours and hours of difference; summer evenings that seemed to never end and winter days that were over before they began. Of all the things he'd told Anjanette about England, he couldn't remember ever mentioning that fact. He'd tell her about it in his next letter.

He felt a sudden stab of longing for her. If only Richard had been a sturdier infant, she could have come with him. But his progress had been set back by a fever the month after news of George's death reached them, thereby making it impossible for her to leave. He was well enough now, but at more than one year old, he still looked and acted like a six-month baby, barely able to get into a sitting position and keep it. He wasn't anywhere near walking yet. The doctor assured them he would catch up by the time he was five or six years old, provided there were no more fevers.

"Would he be better off in England?" Alex had asked. "Would my wife be healthier there?"

"There's no way to guess," the man had replied cautiously. "I've seen people leave here weak as sick kittens and go home and thrive. On my last trip back, as a matter of fact, I called on a former patient whom I hadn't even expected to survive the journey. He's the most robust specimen you'd ever hope to see now. On the other hand, it can work the opposite way. The child might be better off, though not if you plan to send him to one of those dreadful boarding schools where they half-freeze the little mites. Your wife . . . I don't know. She's never known a cold climate at all, has she?"

Someday they'd have to take the chance, Alex knew. He had a home and a business in England that not only belonged to him as a profitable privilege, but also was his moral responsibility to look after. Not to mention that he'd always dreamed of living here, taking his rightful place at Castlemere. It couldn't be put off forever. It certainly wasn't fair to expect the paid advisers to keep on forever, and Mary was soon to be a bride and probably a mother soon enough after. She would naturally lose interest in running Beecham's in his stead. Yes, Anjanette would have to come to England, but not until Richard was more mature.

"Shall I send the portmanteau, sir," Morgan asked, holding out his hand to take it.

"No, I'll keep it with me," Alex replied.

Morgan, in his efforts to keep the cabin tidy, had been trying to separate his master from the battered bag from the time they left Singapore. Now he gave up with a shrug.

"Morgan, have you ever been back before? Have you family here?"

"No and yes, sir. My sisters came over some years back as ladies' maids and married."

"Then why don't you take two or three weeks on your own? I won't need your attentions while I'm here. Have yourself a nice English Christmas with your family."

Morgan was delighted to be free. Alex explained where he would be and Morgan, in turn, gave his sisters' addresses. Alex felt relieved to be temporarily free of him.

Thus, when he entered the room of the hotel Morgan had selected, he was entirely on his own. It was an eerie feeling to be alone, responsible to no one, not even a superior valet. He had a fire built in his room, ordered supper sent up, and had a hot bath while waiting. He intended to review some of the documents he was bringing and then turn in early, but by nine o'clock he was wide-awake and restless.

He could see if his old friend from school, Henry Turner, was in town and free for brandy and a cigar; he'd promised to visit him on this trip. But it was a bit late to be dropping in on someone unexpectedly. No, he'd get in touch with Henry a little later.

On an impulse, he decided to go for a walk. Putting on the heavy coat and hat he'd purchased in Singapore, and feeling, once again, decidedly "costumed" in such heavy garb, he left the hotel.

A winter's-night walk turned out to be a better idea in theory than in practice. Unused to the climate, he found himself genuinely chilled in a few blocks. Hailing a hansom cab, he started to give the name of the hotel, but instead gave directions to Mary's house. This hanging about like a schoolboy who was skipping classes was downright silly, he decided. He'd just drive by the house, and if it looked as if she were still up and about and didn't have guests, he'd stop in and tell her he'd arrived. How he'd know any of that from the shuttered street facade wasn't something he considered.

As it was, he didn't have to make any determination. As his cab stopped across the street, another pulled up by her front door. "Wait a moment," he directed, and silently watched.

A man stepped to the cobbles and held out a hand. Mary stepped down a moment later. It was too dark to discern details, but there was no mistaking her. How very tiny she was, he thought. How could he have forgotten that in little over a year? he wondered. The man accompanied her to the door, and as it opened, Alex could see them in silhouette. The man, presumably Foxworth-Wilding, put his hands on her shoulders, leaned forward and kissed her lightly on the forehead, then turned and departed. A curiously paternal parting, Alex thought. But then what else were they to do on the street? It brought his mind back with a jolt, however, to a memory he could usually keep at bay—the memory of the time he had kissed her in the meadow in Penang. Dear God, wouldn't he ever be allowed to forget that single dreadful mistake of judgment?

She was still standing in the doorway. For a moment Alex thought she was looking at him, seeing him spying on her—which wasn't at all what he had intended to do. But then she stepped back and closed the door. Alex told the driver the name of his hotel. "Drive me back there," he said. "I don't believe I'll call on my cousin tonight after all."

Mary was in such a bustle the next morning that Bartlet couldn't catch up with her to tell her she had a caller. While he was chasing around the big house trying to find her, she ran across Alex quite by accident as he stood in the entry, gazing around at the changes she'd made. The whole place looked fresher and brighter, and hadn't that doorway been cut in since he last saw the house?

"Alex! Good Lord! What a fine surprise," she said as she came flying through the entry and saw him. She rushed up and gave him a quick peck of greeting on the cheek. "How fit and brown you are! I'll bet you're freezing in this horrid weather. I'm so glad you arrived. We're just getting ready to move to Castlemere for the holidays. You'd have missed us if you'd come later today."

"I think I could have found you," he said wryly.

"Yes, but you would have had a long cold ride all by yourself. Did you dock in London? I assumed you'd arrive at Southampton like always. Why in the world didn't you give us any specific information? Oh, I'm so glad you're here. Bartlet! Bartlet, where are you?"

The sorrowful butler appeared. "I was endeavoring to find you, ma'am."

"You've found me. Now, you'll need to send somebody for Mr. Beecham's things and arrange to have them loaded up with ours. Are your trunks and cases at the docks, Alex?"

"No, at a hotel," he said, giving Bartlet the name of the establishment.

"A hotel? You didn't come straight here? Playing the truant, were you?" she asked impudently.

How well she understood him, he thought. Perhaps better than he understood himself.

"I've often wished to do that," she said. "Spirit myself away someplace where nobody will ask me about colors of paint or menu selections or ships of cinnamon that haven't arrived. But I guess I couldn't get away with it. I'd have to drag Agnes along. It's so different for a woman—"

"Mary, stop gabbling for a minute," he said with a laugh. "Let me just look at you."

"Am I gabbling?"

"Charmingly. You look radiant."

I feel radiant now that you're here, she thought, then shoved aside the notion. "Thank you," she answered briskly. "Now, you'd better stand aside or you'll find yourself trussed up and bundled onto the cart with the Christmas parcels. Come along and we'll have a nice hot tea out of the way of the servants. How is Anjanette? And Katie and dear little Richard?"

She swept him along on a tide of friendly chatter and he decided he'd been a fool to worry about seeing her. She seemed to have completely gotten over her schoolgirl crush on him. It was exactly what he had hoped, but it was odd how much sadness there was mixed with his relief.

"I was remembering the time we went fishing," he said when she'd ordered tea.

"Oh, such a thing to remember about me! I did make rather a fool of myself that day. I was so determined to show you my skills, and I made a mess of it. You were kind to me that day. I don't suppose I ever told you how grateful I was?"

"There was no need," he replied, touched. "Tell me about your Mr. Foxworth-Wilding."

"Not until you've told me every detail about Anjanette and the children. You write exceedingly non-informative letters, you know. All business. Of course, Anjanette writes too, but I think she only tells me the happy things. Is the baby really and truly well? You ought to have brought him here, to get him away from the jungles and the mosquitoes. When are Anjanette and the children coming? Have you sold your Penang plantation or are you going to let it to someone when you move back to England—?"

He held up his hands. "Slow down! Only eight or ten questions at a time!"

"Ah, here's tea. Very well, I'm going to drink a half-dozen cups in becoming silence, but you must tell me everything," she said, snatching a cookie from the silver tray Bartlet so majestically set on the table.

So Alex talked. Comfortable now, he told her all about

Richard's bouts of fever and his progress, about Katie's shyness that worried Anjanette, about his wife's activities. Even listening, Mary gave an impression of vivid energy that seemed to literally brighten the room itself. "Now, you have to tell me about yourself and the family," he said finally. "How is Portia?"

"Portia? She's very strange. All the starch has gone out of her since Papa died. It's rather sad, really. I knew how much he meant to me, but I had no idea what a mainstay he was to her life. Portia is like a soufflé that's slowly collapsing before our eyes. But Hester is well and violently happy with her Jamison."

"Do I detect a hint of displeasure?"

"No . . . well, a bit. I don't very much like Jamison and neither does Winston, though he won't ever admit it or say why. I'm certain Jamison is marrying Hester for her money, but he's ever so nice and attentive to her, so I shouldn't worry. Still, I wonder what he'll be like when the courtship is over."

"You sound like you're her mother instead of her sister."

"Do I? I suppose I feel that way. Papa asked me once if I would take care of her and I said I would. I don't feel I'm doing a terribly good job, but there was no dissuading her from her passion for Mr. Hewitt. I suppose it should have fallen to you, as head of the family now, to sort it out, but you weren't here."

From anyone else, he might have taken that as an implied criticism, but it was clear Mary simply stated it as a fact.

"You haven't told me anything about your own intended," he said.

"Oh, you'll meet Winston yourself. He's coming down to Castlemere for the holidays. Not with us. He has to see his publisher about progress on his Australian book tomorrow; then he'll be along. Alex, do you hear somebody shouting? It sounds like a row in the kitchens. Will you just make yourself at home while I sort things out? We should be ready to leave in an hour."

She hurried off and Alex was left with his own thoughts. Why wouldn't she talk to him about her fiancé? She'd been quite frank about Portia and Hester, but changed the subject when he brought up Foxworth-Wilding. But then, what right had he to question her? he chided himself. As she'd pointed out nicely, he should have been here sooner if he were going to come over all fatherly.

Mary went to the kitchens, where two of the housemaids had gotten into a noisy, weepy dispute over a man they both admired. Solving the problem by forbidding either of them to see the man, she took the back stairs to her room. Closing the door, she leaned against it and let out a long breath.

"Alex . . ." she whispered shakily, then closed her eyes very tightly to keep the tears from coming.

29

At Mary's urging, the Beechams of Castlemere had decided to defy convention and truly celebrate Christmas as if they'd never heard of mourning. Winston had wholeheartedly agreed with her decision. It was healthier for everyone. Poor dreary Portia had lolled around in her grief long enough. It had already affected her mind, in his opinion. And both Hester and Mary were happy young women who ought to be able to thoroughly enjoy their (unofficially) engaged states with a bit of celebration.

"I stayed once with a tribe in Africa that had lost its chief," he had told Mary some weeks earlier. "They buried him with solemnity and ritual. They tore their hair and wept and flung themselves on the ground and rolled around in the smoldering ashes of a fire, screaming. When they'd exhausted themselves they formed a big circle. They slept, and when they were awakened, they silently looked at the grave for twenty-four hours. Then they all rose, took out their musical instruments, roasted a pig, got drunk, danced until they dropped, and when they'd recovered, it was over. Over! Life went on exactly as before, as if the chief had been gone for years instead of two days. It was a far more civilized way to mourn the dead than this morbidity the English are afflicted with."

"Then we shall be civilized too. We'll hang mistletoe and wear spangles in our hair and red dresses and remember how much Papa loved happy Christmases," Mary said.

"I'll go along with the mistletoe, but I refuse to wear a red dress," he said.

She'd laughed and kissed him on the nose and hurried off to do one of the hundred things she seemed to do every day.

Now, as his carriage approached Castlemere, he smiled at

the memory of the conversation. He wished he'd been free to ride down with her, but she'd sent him a hastily jotted note saying her cousin Alex had arrived and would be accompanying her, so at least she hadn't been forced to go alone. Not that the introduction of Alex into the household made him comfortable. Far from it. But after all, he reminded himself, Castlemere was Alex's house and he had every right in the world to be there.

As his carriage rolled to a stop in front of the big entrance doors, Mary came down the steps with more enthusiasm than lady-like grace. Winston much preferred the enthusiasm. "I've been watching for you for an hour," she said, taking his arm. "Come inside and get toasty warm. There's a nice fire in the map room for you. Unless you'd rather go upstairs and rest from your journey?"

"I'd much rather be with you, and why should I rest? I'm not such an invalid as all that. You look very pretty today."

She was wearing a burgundy-colored wool dress with cream piping. She twirled around. "It's new, do you like it? It's not exactly red, but it's not black either. I've planned a party for the twenty-eighth and invited everyone on earth. Do you suppose they'll all be too scandalized to accept?"

"The more scandalized they are, the more of them will come."

"Let me send a servant to find Alex. I'm so eager for you to meet him," she said.

When Alex entered the room a short time later, Winston's heart froze. Alex in theory was a worry; Alex in the flesh was a downright terrifying threat. Though normally unaware and totally unappreciative of other men's attractions, Winston could hardly imagine a woman not being positively mad for this man's looks, never mind what his character might be. Straight, glossy black hair that, while neat, looked faintly windswept, a noble patrician nose, penetrating sea-blue eyes set off by suntanned skin—how could he have thought he could compete with a demigod like this? Winston suddenly felt squatty and old and beat-up in comparison.

While Winston was making this assessment, Alex was forming opinions of his own. The world-famous Mr. Winston Foxworth-Wilding looked like a good, sturdy, sensible man. The carrot-colored hair had as much white as red in it now, but that wasn't a bad thing. The gap in his front teeth when he smiled gave him a youthful, endearing quality. And

if there were a few lines and scars in that face, they were
honestly come by. "It's a pleasure to finally make your
acquaintance, sir," Alex said, smiling and extending his
hand.

There was such genuine warmth in his voice that Winston
decided not to despise him after all. "The pleasure is all
mine. Mary and her family have been anxious for your
return and have talked about nothing else."

Alex grinned at Mary and said, "Surely not. Mary is fully
capable of covering a dozen topics in ten minutes if she's
allowed to."

"I see you really do know her," Winston replied.

Mary smiled at them. "Neither of you knows me if you
think I'm such a chatter-bird. I'm the most restrained individual I know. Hardly a word from one week to the next. I
think I could take a vow of silence and nobody would even
notice."

"Notice! We'd rush you to a doctor!" Alex said.

Mary settled happily in front of the fireplace and listened
as they fell into conversation with each other. Singapore
being one of the few places in the world Winston hadn't
been, he was eager to question Alex about the people,
climate, plants, and animals of the area. Alex was all too
pleased to oblige. Mary left them alone, taking a "temporary vow of silence" so that they could get to know each
other. She turned sideways, tucked up her feet, and rested
her head on the back of the sofa. She nearly dozed.

They'd been talking for almost an hour and a half when
Jamison Hewitt's arrival was announced. Mary was disappointed that he'd come along to interrupt the others, but
full to the brim of Christmas spirit, she was determined to
make him welcome. "Send him in here, please," she told
the butler. "And inform my sister of his arrival."

"Hello, Mary," he said. "Oh, Mr. Foxworth-Wilding. I
see you've arrived ahead of me," he said in the faintly
sarcastic drawl he'd come to use when addressing Winston.

"I have, indeed," Winston replied, either failing to notice
his tone or deliberately ignoring it.

Mary introduced Jamison to Alex. They smiled, shook
hands, and said all the right things in the right way, but
Mary sensed an immediate and intense dislike spring up
between them. Impossible as it was to define or explain, it
was nevertheless obvious. She suddenly noticed that Winston was watching her watch them. He gave her a quick

smile and a wink. Yes, he sensed it too. It wasn't her imagination. The only one of them who seemed unaware—or at least unaware that the antagonism was reciprocal—was Jamison himself. "I suppose we ought to be having a talk now that you're here."

"Oh, what about?"

"About Hester and financial settlements and such," Jamison said airily. "You are her legal guardian, are you not?"

"I suppose I am," Alex said. "Although I would think Mary . . . No, you're quite right. I have been remiss in my responsibilities. Why don't we go to my room right now. We can have a glass of Scotch and get the formalities over with. Would you excuse us? Mary? Mr. Foxworth-Wilding?" Anybody who knew Alex's usual friendliness would have been frozen by the coolness with which he spoke, but Jamison was undaunted.

"I think our Jamison may be in for a surprise," Winston said when they had gone.

"What do you mean?"

Winston came to stand in front of the fire, warming the back of his legs. "Just that he tried once before to have this little chat with me, and because I would not oblige him with information I felt was none of his concern, he leapt to some erroneous conclusions. I suspect he is about to have them corrected."

"What erroneous conclusions? Winston, what have you done?"

"Nothing. Exactly that. Nothing."

"Oh, dear. Are we going to break Hester's heart?"

"Bruise it a bit, but save it, I would think."

In spite of her questions, he would say no more. In a remarkably short time, Jamison was back. His face was red, his motions jerky and his voice venomously low. "You bastard!" he said to Winston.

"Jamison!" Mary exclaimed.

But Winston touched her arm and gestured for her to sit back down. He himself lazily refilled his pipe. "Didn't go so well?"

"You lied to me!"

"On the contrary. I told you nothing."

Mary looked at them—Jamison furious, Winston calm and smug. "Will someone please tell me what this is about?"

"Gladly!" Jamison said. "Foxworth-Wilding tricked me into proposing to Hester by deliberately misleading me."

"Tricked you—?"

"Yes, he led me to believe that you and Hester got equal shares of the spice company and of course I already knew that Hester had inherited more property than you and—"

"What in the world has my inheritance to do with it?" Mary asked. She'd shaken off Winston's restraining hand and was advancing on Jamison menacingly.

"I would have proposed to you if I'd known the truth. You're the one I really wanted. Of course, that's why he didn't tell me the truth. He wanted to have you himself."

Mary stopped, gasped in amazement, and finally got out, "You arrogant cad! Are you suggesting that you believed I was yours for the choosing? That you would simply point to me, say, 'You're the lucky one,' and I'd fall swooning into your arms?"

He stepped forward, put a finger under her chin. "You can't fool me with all that indignation, Mary. That's exactly what would have happened, and we both know it. So does Foxworth-Wilding. You'd have never accepted an old warhorse like him if you could have had me."

Mary stepped back, nearly tripping over an occasional table. She ignored the clatter of a breaking vase. "You are the most unspeakably self-centered, self-absorbed . . ." She knew she was sputtering and stopped to draw a deep breath. "No, you're mad. That's what it is. You ought to be in Bedlam with the other lunatics. Well, if you think you're going to marry anybody within a hundred miles of here, you're mistaken, Mr. Hewitt. I'll have you thrown in jail or an asylum before you ever speak to my sister again. I'm going to her right now and telling her everything you've said."

"You go right ahead," he said. "I'll deny every word of it."

Winston had come to stand between them, half-fearing that Mary might strike him and precipitate more damage to the furniture. Not that it wouldn't be worth replacing a few vases for the pleasure of seeing it happen. "I'll back her up, Mr. Hewitt. You really can't get away with this game anymore. Give it up like a good sportsman and take yourself back to London to find another heiress."

"Good sportsman? You stupid old fogy! If you think I'm a good sportsman, you're really senile. This is no game. This is my life at stake. You can both talk to Hester until you're blue in the face and she'll still believe me."

Mary suspected this was true, but could hardly admit it to herself, and certainly not to him. "Hester may have her head in the clouds, but she's not quite the fool you take her for. I'm going to talk to her right this minute, and I'd advise you to be out of the house by the time I come back downstairs."

Suddenly, as if a trump had slipped out of his sleeve, Jamison laughed. "I think I *will* go stay at the inn in the village. You can reach me there when you're ready to invite me back. Your grandpa here"—he gestured at Winston— "can send me word."

Winston lunged at him, but Mary flung herself back between them before he could make contact. "Get out!" she said. "You pollute the very air of this house."

Jamison shot his cuffs, picked an imaginary speck of lint off his sleeve, and started for the door at a leisurely stroll. As he reached it, he turned and said, "Oh, by the way, when you're talking to your sister, you might want to ask what she has planned for next June."

"Not marrying you!"

"No, not quite that," he said, and with a final smirk, he opened the door and ambled out.

"A baby? A baby! You can't have a baby, Hester. You're not even married."

"D-d-don't be such a goose, M-M-Mary," Hester sobbed. "Of course I c-c-can. And I'm going to be married b-b-before it's born."

"I'd like to slap the stuffing out of you, you bird-witted ninny. How . . . ? Where . . . ? Never mind, I don't want to know. How could you be such an idiot?"

"I'm not an idiot. It just happened b-b-because we're so much in love."

"No, *you're* in love. He's just greedy. He wanted to marry you because he thought you had more money than I do. He actually said he would have preferred me. He said that, Hester!"

"You're making that up!"

"I am not. Why would I make up something like that?"

"Because you wanted him yourself, but he preferred me. Don't act so superior. Jemmy told me about that night in the picture gallery. The night you threw yourself at him and nearly made such a scene."

"He said *what*!" She nearly choked on her fury. "Hester,

if there weren't laws against murder, I'd throw you straight out the window for believing such a thing. It happened, all right, but it was Jamison who made the overtures."

Hester gave her a pitying smile. "That's what Jemmy said you'd say if I mentioned it."

"Oh, he did, did he? That . . . that . . . oh, God, Hester, please find your brain and put it to work. Jamison Hewitt is a slimy—"

"I won't have my future husband spoken of that way."

"You are not going to marry that man!"

Hester had flung herself on her bed early in the discussion. Now she rose from the disarray of petticoats and bedclothes, her self-pity replaced with anger as hot as Mary's. "I'm going to have his child and I'm going to marry him. It's none of your business, Mary Beecham. You're not my mother or father; you're not even my real sister! You're just some poor London foundling Papa took pity on. You might have forgotten that, but I haven't. You can quit acting like you own us all."

Mary felt a huge, agonizing lump rise in her chest. Knees shaking, she walked to the door, praying that her legs wouldn't give out before she reached it.

"Mary! Mary, I'm sorry. I didn't mean that!" Hester cried hysterically.

Stepping into the hallway, Mary took a deep breath and started toward her room. She had to get out. Get away before anything more terrible was said or done.

Hester caught up with her. Grabbing her arm, she said, "Please, Mary. Forgive me. I only said that because you made me so angry . . ."

She found herself staring into such lifeless eyes that it frightened her. It was as though Mary were dead. She clamped her hands to her mouth to stifle a scream that was welling up, and stood there frozen as Mary turned and walked away stiffly.

Alex found Mary; he was the only one of them who knew, without even searching, where she must have gone.

He picked his way carefully down the cliff path, glancing now and then at the small figure sitting by the driftwood fire. She was perched on the flat rock where his grandmother had said she'd had picnics as a girl.

"May I sit with you?" he asked when he reached her.

She didn't answer or look up, but made a sketchy acquiescence with her hand. She was wearing some sort of trousers and boots and he could see the ribbing of a fisherman's sweater at her neck sticking out of the heavy coat she was wrapped in.

"Everybody's worried about where you went," he said.

"No, Winston was probably worried. You might have been worried. Nobody else." It wasn't at all self-pitying, but rather as though she were a professor correcting a bright but sadly mistaken student.

"Hester is frantic with worry," he corrected in turn. "We've had to call the doctor for her, she got so hysterical. Some talk about throwing herself out the window because that would make you happy."

"It's her condition. I'd feel the same way if I were going to have Jamison Hewitt's child." She still hadn't looked at him, but looked out at the dark sea, speaking in a flat tone.

"No, it's not that. She's thrilled about that, as hard as it is to imagine. She told me everything that passed between you two. She's devastated by what she said to you. She swears she never thought it in her whole life until she heard the ugly words coming out of her mouth. She's afraid you'll never forgive her."

Mary said nothing for a very long time. Leaning over, she picked up a piece of driftwood and laid it carefully on the small fire. The wood was wet; it smoked and hissed in the flames. She finally spoke wearily. "I suppose we'll have to arrange for her to go to France or someplace to have the child secretly and then give it up. I don't know how one arranges such things. Will you help me?"

"I'd help you with anything in the world that I could, Mary dear, but that won't work. Hester wouldn't go along with it, and the one thing such a plan absolutely requires is the mother's agreement."

She faced him. "Then what am I to do?"

She sounded as if she had the very weight of the world on her small shoulders. Alex felt a terrible wrenching in his heart. He wished he could take her away and spend his life making sure nothing ever hurt her again. If it weren't for his love of Anjanette . . .

"You are to do nothing but put on a pretty dress and smile at her wedding," he said firmly. "You can do nothing. You *should* do nothing. It isn't your responsibility to force her to live her life intelligently."

"But it is. I promised Papa I'd take care of her, and I've done a terrible job."

"Mary, if George were alive now, there would be nothing he could do either."

"Did Winston tell you the horrible things Jamison said to me? And to him?"

"He told me everything. I'm sorry I wasn't there. I believe I would have beaten the man to a pulp and enjoyed every second of it."

She smiled a little at that. "Alex . . . I have a secret that hurts to keep. Papa told Winston, but I've never told anyone."

"Then why must you keep it?"

"Because Papa asked me to."

"I see. Is it that you're his real child?"

"Did he tell you that when we were in Singapore?"

"No, I guessed. I never spoke to him about it."

"That's part of it."

Again they fell silent. It was an electric but strangely comforting silence. Picking up a handful of small flat bits of flint rock, Alex put them in a tiny pile. "You have your beacon, but not your cairn," he explained, smiling. "Do you want to tell me? Would it help you to carry the weight of your secret?"

"More than anything. But Papa didn't want me to tell anyone."

"Why?"

"Because it would hurt . . . some people if they knew."

"Would it hurt me?"

"No."

"Then I'm sure he wouldn't mind my knowing too. He would trust me as he trusted you, wouldn't he?"

"I think he would. I'm a little surprised that he *didn't* tell you, in fact." Mary put one more rock on top of the little pile and the whole structure collapsed. Taking a deep breath, she plunged in. "I'm Papa's real daughter, as you guessed. But I'm his legitimate daughter as well. He married my mother, you see. I have the marriage paper. But he thought she was dead when he married Portia, so he never got a divorce or an annulment."

Alex stared at her for a long moment, then leaned back on his elbows and chuckled. Chuckles turned to laughter, which turned to positive hoots.

She got very stiff. "It's not funny!"

He sat up abruptly and gave her a bracing hug. "Of course it's funny. It's the funniest thing I've heard in years! Mary, it means that Portia—the dignified, cream-of-the-crop, looking-down-her-nose Portia was his mistress. His . . . his *kept woman*." He laughed so hard his eyes started watering and he had to wipe away the tears. "If I'd had an inkling when I was a gawky colonial boy and she scared the pudding out of me with her haughty looks . . ."

Mary looked at him with astonishment and then his laughter caught her like a contagious disease. "What *would* our dear queen think?" she said, quoting one of Portia's favorite sayings. Then she fell into a fit of giggles that took away her breath.

"Do you think Nellanor knew?" he finally asked.

"I'm sure he couldn't trust her with knowing. She'd have hired a band and had it announced by a chorus," Mary said, howling at the image of a group of villagers marching about, singing at the top of their lungs about Portia's marital status.

"Oh, Alex, you won't tell anyone, will you?"

He wiped his eyes again, took a long breath to regain control, and said shakily, "No, I promised and I'll keep my promise. But it will probably kill me to keep something this wonderful to myself. I'll wake up laughing in the night and people will think I've gone mad. If I waste away before I'm forty in some genteel home for the insane, it'll be your fault."

She leaned against his arm. "Oh, Alex, I *do* love you so."

When she'd said it before, it had scared him. This time, he merely draped his arm around her and said, "And I love you, Mary." And at that moment, it felt good and right to say it.

They sat that way for a long time before Mary said, "It's not right, is it? The way things work. Portia loved Papa and he loved my mother and Winston loves me and I love you and you love Anjanette and Hester loves Jamison and he only loves money. I think it's damned shabby of God to have arranged it all so badly. When I go to heaven, I'm going to talk to Him about it."

"I'm sure you will," Alex replied with a smile. He leaned his head against hers for a moment. "We'd better go back soon or Winston will have half the county out looking for you."

Above them, at the lip of the cliff, Winston saw the two

figures silhouctted by the small fire with their heads together. The faint glow had drawn him here and he'd been prepared to risk his neck on the treacherous path to go down and comfort her. But there was obviously no need. He couldn't hear them over the sound of the waves and the wind, but there was no need to. He turned away sadly and walked back to Castlemere.

30

The next month was a nightmare none of them ever forgot. All plans for a happy old-fashioned Christmas were forgotten. Hester blanketed Mary with apologies for her remarks about their sisterhood—apologies that drove Mary nearly mad. She wanted to wipe out the memory of what had been said; Hester kept it constantly fresh by her frequent and tearfully expressed regrets. But Hester was utterly and proudly unrepentant about her "condition" as they came to call her pregnancy. Like a religious convert, she wanted to talk about sex and pregnancy, and that was a subject *nobody* wanted to discuss with her.

"Remember when we used to wonder what it was like?" she asked Mary with a gooey girlishness that made Mary want to slap her.

"I expect I'll find out for myself in good time," Mary said repressively.

To Alex: "I probably should write to Anjanette for advice about marriage."

Alex looked horrified.

Even Winston came in for his share of her confidences. "I would imagine other cultures have entirely different attitudes toward it."

"It?" he asked innocently.

"You know. Men and women. Love. Consummation."

"They certainly do, but they aren't upper-class women living in England in the reign of the most prudish monarch in history," he said.

She laughed sweetly, unconscious of having been rebuked.

Tutin was dispatched to the village to ask Jamison to come to Castlemere the next evening to work out what was to be done. He was pointedly not invited to bring his bags and move in—for the present. Believing that he now had the upper hand, he turned up strutting with arrogance.

After dinner they gathered in the map room, where Alex sat at the desk. Portia took her place in front of the fireplace and glared at Mary. She'd been trying to find some way to pin blame for the whole thing on her, but so far had been unable to accomplish this goal. That Hester was an innocent victim was clear to her; surely the problem could be laid at Mary's feet.

Winston was an unwilling member of the audience. "I'm not part of the family," he objected when Alex asked him to be present.

"But you will be soon enough," Alex insisted. "I'd like your support."

Aware now of the range of responsibilities that being head of the family entailed, Alex took charge of the meeting from the first. "We don't like you and you don't like us, Mr. Hewitt," he said at the onset of the family meeting. "Having put that out in the open, I see no reason any of us should continue to make the point." His voice was as stony and unforgiving as the flint beach below the cliffs.

"Cousin Alex, I don't think that's a nice thing to—"

"Hester, you are the problem being discussed. Not a participant in the discussion. We already have ample proof of the quality of your judgment. If you can't keep absolutely quiet, you'll have to leave the room," he said as if he were talking to a spice supplier trying to sell him shoddy goods.

Jamison, still stunned by Alex's initial remarks, made no attempt to come to her defense.

"Yes, Cousin Alex," she sniffled.

"We need to think out how we can preserve Hester's reputation, if that's possible. There will have to be an immediate marriage. Nobody will be fooled as to the reason for the haste, but I think we can keep the proof out of their hands. This party that Mary has planned—"

"The party! Oh, no! I'd forgotten," Mary exclaimed. "I'll cancel it, of course—"

"No, I think the best thing is to go ahead with it. We'll cart them off to some distant rector and get them married right away and then act as though the party had been planned deliberately to announce the 'happy news.' That way, it will look like the family scheduled the wedding at least a month or so before it actually took place. In fact, we might exaggerate slightly how long before the party the ceremony was performed. As for marrying during the year after her father's death, we'll tell people it was because she wanted to marry while I was here to act in lieu of her father."

"Alex, that's brilliant," Mary said.

"Not brilliant. Desperate. And all those old biddies with the calendars in their heads will see through it when the baby is born. That's why it might help if the baby were born elsewhere—some remote part of Brazil would be my country of choice," he said wryly. "One doesn't run into very many English there. However, I think it would be best if they went to America. Winston, have you any suggestions?"

Winston had been watching with some amusement and considerable admiration as Alex stepped in to sort things out. "Let me think. New York probably has more upper-class English people at any given time than London does. She'd run into everybody she's ever known. That wouldn't do. Chicago would be worse—she'd be lionized. In Boston they'd make a great show of ignoring her, but would secretly know every move she made and the precise moment of the child's birth. I think California would be good. Civilized enough to have good doctors and midwives, but more Spanish than English. The problem is getting there. When I went, we walked across Panama. I don't think that's quite Hester's style. I think there are adequate trains, however."

"California . . ." Jamison mused, apparently thinking he had some choice in the matter. "Yes, that might be amusing. I know a chap who went to San Francisco and quite liked it."

They all looked at him as if he were some variety of plant life that had suddenly spoken. All except Hester, who was quietly weeping into a handkerchief. Mary had a sudden sense that Hester might be starting to regret her circumstances, and she felt pity. But, she reminded herself, Hester got herself into this predicament; she would have to face the consequences.

Alex took responsibility for arranging for the marriage itself. A school friend of his who'd gone into the church and had a parish about twenty miles distant was hastily summoned and the situation was explained. To their relief, he showed no shock or distaste whatsoever. "Happens all the time, old man," he told Alex. "More of the time than not, it seems to me. Send them around to me day after tomorrow and I'll take care of everything."

When the pitiful little ceremony was done and the rest of them returned to Castlemere, Winston made a quick visit to London to make travel arrangements. He returned with a leather wallet full of tickets, letters of credit, and copies of a rental agreement for a staffed, furnished house near San Francisco that belonged to a very discreet friend of his.

Orchestrating the party itself was Mary's job. Barely resisting the temptation to make faces while she wrote, she penned sweet little letters to those who had accepted the invitation. "So glad you're going to be here with us. We have a delightful announcement to make, but I'd hate to spoil the happy surprise by telling you now. With anticipation . . ."

Portia took upon herself the duty of seeing that Hester had an adequate wardrobe for a year-long wedding trip. A great deal of fabric, time, and money were spent on clothes Hester wouldn't be able to fit into in a few months. "But I can't tell the dressmakers she's *enceinte*. They'd tell everyone else they work for and the word would be all over the country," she pronounced when Mary questioned her about the impracticality of the wardrobe.

"You could at least ask them to construct dresses that could be let out in case they decide to start a family right away."

"Oh, no. It would put the idea of a child in their minds."

"Does she think a bride whose engagement is only a week long and is going halfway around the world on a wedding trip *won't* suggest anything suspicious?" Mary said in wonder to Winston.

"She's doing the only thing in her sphere of knowledge to help," he said. If he sounded a little short-tempered, it was because he was feeling irritated. Having spent many of his adult years around peoples who accepted pregnancy as a perfectly natural part of life, he found the strictures of Victorian England basically nasty-minded. He knew that if one expected to reap the benefits of society, one must play by the rules; that was one of the reasons he himself went to so much trouble to help with the deception. But he felt the rules were basically hateful.

That was why he was pleased the morning Mary leaned over her eggs and toast and said, out of the blue, "I don't really think we should be trying to conceal the fact that Hester had sexual relations. The great secret should be that she was stupid enough to have them with Jamison Hewitt."

Christmas Day itself would have been largely ignored by
the family had it not been for Mary. She was determined
that decorations go up and the servants get to celebrate. She
also got up early, dragged everybody to church services, and
made a round of visits to the tenants with Alex. For once,
she didn't think to invite Winston and he was unreasonably
cast down about it. It wasn't anything he wanted to do and
it certainly wasn't his place. He would have gracefully refused an invitation, but he wished he'd received one.

He was, he had to admit, as jealous of Alex as he'd been
before they met. More so, in fact, but in a different way.
After that night he'd seen the cousins head-to-head on the
flint beach, he'd been aware of the odd insular strength of
their relationship. It was a comfortable sort of "completeness" he'd once observed in twins and had sometimes sensed
in old married couples. It was nothing more than an occasional quick glance of understanding between them or half-
smile of private amusement over a family story. It was as
intangible but as impossible to ignore as the scent of a peat
fire on the first cool day of autumn.

It wasn't as if they sought each other out; there were no
dewy looks or furtive touches. Nothing sexual or romantic
that he could discern and be alarmed about. So why was he
so uneasy? Because they seemed to understand each other's
thoughts before the words were done? Or was it simply
because they shared some mysterious Beecham bond of
blood? He had the eerie primeval sense that if, during a
very proper tea, an enemy attacked, they would link arms
and charge a foe like practiced warriors.

Indeed! He scoffed at himself for such flights of fancy. He
must truly be getting old and dotty. Still, even if a literal
image was fanciful, there was a metaphorical truth in the
thought, he believed. There *was* something between them
that nobody, not even he, could be a part of. And that
made him sick with regret.

The day of the party was cold and the air was clear and
sparkling with frost. There were to be ten couples including
Alex's old school friend Henry Turner and his spinster sister. In spite of the upheaval, Alex was eager to see Henry.
A big afternoon tea and light supper were planned, with
music and cards afterward. The next morning, the men were
to go on a hunt while the women spent the day gossiping
and preparing for a formal dinner. On the third morning,

after a big breakfast, the carriages would be called around and it would be mercifully done with. "Forty-five hours at the most," Mary had said at breakfast. "Surely we can all endure anything for forty-five hours."

"I heard of a poor woman who was in labor for forty hours," Hester said brightly.

"Hester, please!" Alex and Mary said in unison, and then laughed at each other.

The first carriage rolled up the long drive about three in the afternoon. "We look like a stable of horses rigged out for a show," Mary said of them as they paced around the great hall waiting to greet the guests.

It was true. They were all in their best. Alex and Jamison were so fresh, young, and handsome that it made Winston feel quite woolly and rumpled in comparison. Alex stood slightly apart with a rather impressive dignity in one as young as he was. One seldom saw the patriarch played with such ease by a man less than fifty years old.

Portia, with the prospect of company, had spruced herself up physically and mentally. She was nearly her old self, throwing orders at servants, complaining over details, sweeping regally down stairs and up as if it wouldn't come off properly without her constant diligence. It was nice, really, to see the old bitch in good form, however temporary it might be, Winston thought to himself.

At her side, Hester glowed with happiness. Her normally sallow complexion was pink with anticipation. Mary's maid, Agnes, had done something very nice to Hester's hair, making swoops and swirls that gave the impression that it was quite thick and curly. She wore a periwinkle-blue gown with a big bow on the bustle and a mandarin sort of neckline (at least he thought that's what Mary had called it) that flattered her. All that dressmaking upheaval hadn't been for naught.

Of course Mary outshone Hester without meaning to. Mary's coloring and natural vivacity always made her seem like a single candle in a dark room—certainly in Winston's eyes. In amber shot silk with an ivory silk shawl with long shimmering fringe, she seemed to absorb the warmth of the room and reflect it back.

"I believe Mr. and Mrs. Wilbur Ridley are approaching," the butler announced.

"Shall we all greet them?" Portia commanded, verbally

herding them along to their stations. "Dear old Wilbur. How nice that he could make it. He must be having a good week."

"Who is this Wilbur?" Winston whispered to Mary.

"Portia's uncle. Up until about five years ago he was a sprightly little man; then he took a young wife. Alta, I believe her name is. He went into a decline and there were a lot of cruel jokes. Poor Alta loves invitations to go anywhere—it's a bit like that story they tell about Juana la Loca. Do you know what I mean?"

"The daughter of Ferdinand and Isabella. Her husband died and she went mad and carted his embalmed body all over Europe with her like part of the luggage," Winston said.

"Yes, Wilbur isn't quite ready for embalming and Alta isn't the least mad, but . . ."

He saw what she meant when the carriage drew to a stop. Alta Ridley was a handsome woman in her late twenties. She came up the steps briskly, greeted everyone with enthusiasm, and said, "Wilbur will be along in a moment."

They all stared as two menservants hauled the pitiful little man out of the carriage and half-carried him up the steps. His hair was wispy, his eyes dull, and he had birdlike limbs. Even outside, it was apparent that he had soiled himself on the journey.

"Dear Wilbur does love a ride, don't you, my dear?" Alta said. "But it's so tiring. If he could go straight to his room for a little bath and a rest, it would be ever so kind of you."

Portia, upwind, rushed forward to embrace him, but reeled back at the last moment.

The rest of the guests arrived with less impact.

Mary found an unexpected treat among the guests: Henry Turner and his sister, Elaine. "I don't expect you remember me, Miss Beecham," he said.

"I'm afraid I—"

"Of course not. You were only a child. A very precocious child, I might add. I came to the London house with Alex for a few days when we finished school."

"Oh, of course. How could I forget?" Mary said, but the truth was, she still didn't remember him. During that time, as at many other times in her life, she'd had eyes only for Alex.

Henry still looked very boyish. He was one of those men who would probably continue to until old age. His thick brown hair kept falling in his eyes and Mary noticed a spot of ink on his finger, as if he'd just come from the schoolroom.

His sister, Elaine, was an exceedingly plain woman with protruding teeth and a faintly mannish manner. "Good to meet you, Miss Beecham. Glad Henry trotted me out for this. I'm no beauty, but I know how to behave myself, I assure you."

"I never doubted it for a moment," Mary said, smiling. "I'm the one who can't be counted on to behave. You may have to keep me in line."

"Good show!" Elaine turned and brayed. "Damned good show! She's a fine one, Henry. I think we're going to get along."

Elaine promised to be the bright spot of the weekend.

For Hester, it was her hour of glory. Everyone congratulated her with apparent warmth. They were, after all, guests in the Beecham home. The whispers behind hands and counting on fingers would take place later. For the time being they all put a good face on it. "How naughty of you to keep it a secret. We'd have brought along a lovely wedding present, if only we'd known," they gushed.

Jamison was happy too. Although Alex had retained as much control as he was able of Hester's assets, she being a minor, he had paid off all Jamison's debts and settled a generous allowance on them. Jamison was now a man among men; a Beecham among Beechams. Or so he thought. Without actually saying so, he attempted to give the impression that Castlemere was his home as much as it was Alex's. His primary advantage was his familiarity with Castlemere; he knew where the guns were kept, all the servants' names, the best hunting areas, what was in the cellars.

Alex was fully aware of what was going on, and when Mary complained, he merely said, "Anyone who is fool enough to be impressed with him will get exactly what he deserves. Cultivating a friendship with Jamison is a self-defeating effort."

"I know it is, but it makes me angry to see him swanning about like he's the lord of the manor."

Mary kept to herself as much as she could during the invasion, seething with a number of resentments she was unable to accept gracefully. She had forgiven Hester's cruel outburst and could almost make herself accept, if not understand, her sister's indiscretions, but to see her made over as though she were a veritable princess of a bride galled Mary. To see Hester get all that apparent admiration for being so stupid infuriated her.

Portia was being especially hard to bear as well. Though Mary had done all the planning and preparation for the weekend party, Portia took all the credit. "I had to simply insist on observing the holidays as I'm sure dear George would have wanted," she said. "It was so painful, making the servants put up all the decorations, but I felt I positively owed it to George. He would have insisted on Hester being married in a festive atmosphere."

And: "Thank you so much, dear. I feel like menu planning is the essence of entertaining, don't you? I did so adore thumbing through all the old recipe books with Cook."

That nearly pushed Mary over the brink of her patience. "Then you can answer something I've been wondering," she said with poisonous sweetness. "What *is* the mysterious spice in this cake?"

"I don't remember at the moment, Mary," Portia replied in kind.

As for Winston, he found himself fascinated by Alta Ridley in the same way one is fascinated by a burning building: it's appalling, but impossible to look away from. Alta was a handsome young woman who put an extraordinarily brave face on her situation. While she should have been dancing with energetic young men, she sat quietly by her pitiful old husband, occasionally blotting a bit of drool off his chin or gently reinterpreting his remarks when he became especially confused.

Driven by morbid curiosity into more frankness than was proper, Winston said, "He wasn't like this when you married, was he?"

Sensing his genuine concern, Alta didn't take offense. In fact, she welcomed someone to whom she could speak honestly. "No. My dear Willy Ridley was a dashing, charming man. He quite swept me off my feet. For the first year of our marriage I was the happiest woman in the world. He was so romantic; once he hired a whole orchestra, a little one, of course, just so the two of us could have an evening of dancing at our London house. No guests, just the two of us. It was lovely."

"What happened to him?"

"I've never been certain. He took a fall down the steps and he was never the same again. His doctor said the fall might have either caused or resulted in a stroke. My Willy just went away," she said, gazing sadly at the old man, who had nodded off at her side. He was twitching and mumbling in his sleep, and Winston, astonishingly, felt tears gathering behind his eyelids.

"Let me get you a plate of cake, Mrs. Ridley," he said, making his escape before he could disgrace himself.

They closed the house up a week after the party. Hester and Jamison had to go to London to begin their long trip. Portia had received a number of invitations to visit from the recent guests and she was planning to take them up on it, one after the other. Alex was anxious to finish up necessary business and get back to Singapore. Winston had left earlier to complete the index for his Australian book.

Mary took a long, solitary walk through the house. Sheets already covered the furniture in some of the rooms. Fireplaces were cold and clean in spite of old Ginger's efforts to leave his signature. There was a damp, dead feeling that even the familiar rosemary scent couldn't overcome.

Alex found Mary in the map room. She'd pulled aside a closed curtain and was looking out toward the sea. "Are you ready?" he asked softly.

She didn't turn around. "I've sometimes wondered why old Philippe didn't build the house closer to the cliffs so you could see the Channel from the ground-floor windows."

"I know you want a poetic answer to that," Alex said with an affectionate smile, "but it was probably because he was afraid the weight of the structure would make the cliffs crumble and dump the whole place onto the beach."

She turned and let the curtain swing back. The room got very dark, but he could see her answering smile. "Alex, when will you come back with Anjanette and the children?"

"Who can say? When the time is right, I'll know, and I'll be here. Mary, I hate Castlemere this way. Will you come here often and keep it alive?"

"I think not. It's not my home anymore. It's yours, and your family must keep it alive."

"You don't mean that."

"No, but it's the truth, just the same."

"Still, I wish you and Winston would come live here when you're married."

322 *Janice Young Brooks*

"Winston," she said, and he knew from her tone that, for a moment only, she had completely forgotten him. "Yes, well, perhaps . . ."

"Are you ready to go?" he repeated.

She looked down at a fold of curtain she'd been absently creasing. "I . . . I'm afraid to leave. It's the end of something, Alex. My childhood, I think."

There was a loud howl and furious scratching noises from outside the door, where Ginger was boxed up ready to travel.

"You can't hold it, Mary. We can't hold on to anything."

"Or anybody," she said softly.

He came to where she stood and put his arms around her. "Or anybody," he affirmed sadly, resting his chin the top of her head lightly. "Now, we must go or that cat will chew his way out of his box."

She looked up at him for a long moment. Slowly, with tender caution, he leaned down and kissed her and could taste the salt of tears on her soft lips. It was a long, gentle kiss that was meant to be the last one ever and must be perfect. Finally it was Mary who drew back reluctantly. She put her hand on his arm, patted it lightly, and forced a brave smile.

"Now I'm ready to leave Castlemere, Alex," she said before turning and walking away quickly.

"I didn't really think you'd be here," Winston said to Mary when Bartlet showed him into the morning room of the London house.

"Why?"

"Isn't Alex leaving this morning?"

"Yes, but there was no need for me to see him off. Henry Turner took him to the docks," Mary answered crisply. She put aside the paperwork she had been looking over and gave him her full attention.

"You look tired."

"Thank you," she said. "Sorry, Winston. That was rude of me. Thank you for your concern. It's just being in town that's getting me down, I think."

"What do you hear from Hester?" he asked.

"Nothing yet," she replied. "Why do you ask?"

"Just wondered. And Portia? Is Portia having a good time with her old friends?"

"I suppose so. Winston, will you please sit down and quit that pacing. What's wrong?"

He sat down across the small table from her. As he did so, the clouds parted and a shaft of sunshine struck her hair, making it look as if it were afire. "Mary, I've come to tell you something."

"Yes?"

He paused, hating to go on. Even though he'd rehearsed this mentally a hundred times, the words were gone for the moment. He took her hand and came out with it. "I've decided we shouldn't marry."

"You have?" She half-smiled, as though she suspected it was a joke of some sort.

"I'm serious, Mary. I've given it a great deal of thought. In fact, I've hardly thought about anything else for three weeks. Ever since I met Alta Ridley."

"What on earth has Alta Ridley to do with us?" She gently pulled her hand out of his grasp.

"Alta Ridley was a lovely young woman like you a few short years ago, who married an older man. Now she's doomed to being a doddering old vegetable's nurse."

"Great-Uncle Willy is thirty years older that Alta," Mary pointed out. "She might have expected it."

"Mary, I'm twenty-three years older than you. There's little difference."

"Of course there is! You are fit and healthy and don't seem nearly your age."

"So was your great-uncle Willy when they married."

"Winston, you're being quite foolish. Just because such a thing *can* happen certainly doesn't mean it *will* happen."

He'd known she'd get angry and argue with him about this, but he'd hoped against all hope that she would simply refuse to talk about it at all and beg him tearfully to change his mind. But that wasn't Mary's way.

"But it will happen, Mary. Eventually. Even if I hold up terrifically well until I'm sixty or so, you'll still be in your thirties—in your prime. I don't want to make you into an Alta Ridley."

"Winston, you're being ridiculous."

"No, just farsighted. Mary, your youth and vitality are the main reasons I came to love you. I can't bear the thought of being the one who saps and drains you of them before your time. I'm going to be an old man before you're even middle-aged. That's how calendars work. You can't hold them back."

She stood up suddenly and turned her back on him.

Taking a few steps to distance herself, she said, "You speak of loving me, and yet you reject me?"

"I'm not rejecting you. I'm freeing you. I'm opening the cage door and shooing you out into your proper element. I know I've taken you by surprise and you're angry, but don't ever doubt that I love you. If I loved you a little less, I wouldn't be saying any of this. I'd think of myself and the happiness I feel with you and not worry about your future happiness for a moment. It's only because I do love you so much that I'm telling you this is how it must be."

She whirled and faced him, her face paler than ever. "Have I nothing to say about it?"

"Nothing."

Her shoulders sagged a little, her only sign of weakness. "Has it crossed your mind that I might like the cage I'm in?"

"I'm flattered to think so. But you won't in ten or fifteen years' time and then the door will be stuck shut forever. What a foolish metaphor that is! Mary, I know what I'm doing is right. I also know you're angry and insulted, but someday you'll realize it's for the best."

She raised her hands in a helpless aborted gesture. "Because you *might* grow old and ill many years from now, are we really to forgo the intervening years of friendship and companionship that could enrich our lives? Why should we both be lonely and alone all that time?"

He noticed she didn't mention love. Come to think of it, she never had used the word. "You won't be lonely and alone. You're young and beautiful and fascinating. You'll have a dozen proposals in the next few years. You'll be able to take your pick of young men."

"I don't want a young man."

"You only want Alex."

He hadn't meant to say it. He hadn't even been certain he believed it until he heard the words come from his mouth. But it was suddenly as obvious as pebbles on the bottom of a clear stream. The silence crackled.

"What do you mean?" Mary said in her very haughtiest tone.

He sighed wearily. "I mean no offense. Simply that you're in love with him and probably he with you."

"Alex is a happily married man. The father of two children!"

"I'm not saying there's anything immoral between you."

"I should hope not!"

"Mary, please don't use that tone on me. I'm not a frightened boy who's going to run away in terror. I'm a man who genuinely loves you. Aside from anything else, I was your father's friend and I hope I'm your friend. I've never known you to be afraid of speaking the truth."

"What you're suggesting—"

"I'm not suggesting anything. I suppose I'm just surprised that I didn't realize it all sooner. I kept attributing it to some familial bond—some special Beecham relationship—when it was simply love."

She didn't deny it. Coming back to him, she said in a flat, exhausted voice, "I'd be a good wife to you."

"Oh, my poor, poor dear Mary! I know you would have."

She sat down without meeting his eyes. After a long silence she said, "Would you please leave me now?"

"I'm sorry to have—"

Holding up her hand, she shook her head. "No more. Not now, please, Winston."

"Tell me you forgive me."

"Forgive you? For what? For knowing what I won't even admit to myself? For being honest when I'm living a lie? For being a dear friend? There's nothing for me to forgive, Winston. You're the one who must try to absolve me of my sins."

"Surely how we feel in the secrecy of our hearts isn't sin?"

"I'll leave the theological subtleties to the clerics," she said, looking away. "Please . . . go now."

"Mary . . ."

She was right, however. There wasn't anything more to be said. He squeezed her shoulder briefly and left her.

31

June 1927

"How is she, Robbie?" Natalie asked the young physician sitting across from her on the shaded terrace. The wisteria vine where Mary had once hidden and observed Alex now covered the entire wall and completely concealed the herringbone brickwork.

Robbie—Dr. Robert Engle, grandson of Jonathan—was scuffing the toe of his shoe gently at a tuft of moss between the paving stones. "Oh, Natalie, I honestly don't know. If I hadn't grown up knowing you, I'd give you a terribly professional, technical answer, but it would mean the same thing. If she were anyone else, I wouldn't hold out much hope. Her heart is weak; her blood pressure is a bit high one day and rockets up and down the next. She ought to have days or weeks at the most. But she's Mary Beecham. She may live on for another decade by sheer strength of will. Lord knows she's got enough of it."

"Robbie, let that moss alone. You know how she hates having it torn up."

"You sound just like her."

Natalie looked both embarrassed and pleased. "I suppose I will turn into the same sort of old tartar some day. But she wasn't always so terrifying. She was once a scared little girl in this house. She hid in that vine right there and studied her handsome cousin Alex. Later, she was a desperately lonely young woman. . . ."

Robert Engle looked at Natalie questioningly. "How would you know that? You haven't gotten into this séance claptrap all the bright young things in London are doing, have you?"

Natalie laughed. "No, it's much simpler than that. Grandmama is letting me read her diaries."

"Hmmm."

"What does that mean?"

"Just that I don't like it. It sounds like an end-of-the-road sort of thing."

"Pardon me, Doctor," Bartlet said sadly from the doorway, "but there is an urgent telephone call for you."

"Natalie, I believe this is about the twins I've been expecting to deliver any day. No, don't see me out. I know my way. I'll call you later."

When he'd gone, Natalie went to her grandmother's room. "I'm sorry, but she's sleeping, miss," the nurse said.

"I won't wake her, then." She wanted to get another diary, but was afraid to rummage about for fear of making noise and disturbing the patient, so she left the room and went for a long walk.

Her stroll took her to the cliffs and she saw the scene with a new perspective. Before, it was a place she liked well enough, but seldom went because her mother was so afraid of her getting hurt going down the steep path. "People, they have died there," her mother claimed with a Gallic air of doom. Funny, all she could remember of her mother were her gloomy remarks. Certainly she had been cheerful some of the time, but Natalie couldn't recall when.

"Who died there, Maman?" she'd asked when she was little.

"Never mind who."

Now she knew. George had died here. George Beecham, her great-grandfather, who had never been anything more to her than a name in the family tree until this week, and was now as real to her as her own father.

And there was the big flat stone where Nellanor had picnicked as a child and taken Mary when she in turn was a little girl. The flat stone where Mary and Alex, young and beautiful and miserable with regrets, had briefly, simply, confessed love and gone back to pretending it didn't exist. Was that why Grandmama wanted her to read the diaries? So that the importance of these places would live on in somebody's memory?

Natalie contemplated climbing down the path, now that there was no one around to tell her she shouldn't, but she'd surely ladder her stockings and ruin her shoes. Unlike her grandmother, she hadn't been brought up on climbing. She had brought along some stout shoes and slacks. Perhaps tomorrow, if it were fine, she'd come back. In the meantime, she took a long walk eastward along the lip of the cliff until she came to a low spot and took one footpath that led to the village. There she bought some pale coral-pink lip rouge for her grandmother and a tin of candied ginger.

Sitting on a bench outside the chemist's and nibbling the sweet, she wondered: Had her own father been taken to the warehouse and given the same lectures about spices as Mary and George and Nellanor had? Why hadn't he taken her in turn? She was his only child, the presumed heir to Beecham's. Probably because she'd never shown any interest. The company was just something that shared her name and provided the family's wealth. But she was begining to feel the stirrings of curiosity. It had meant so much to all of those Beechams through the centuries; it was in her blood and marrow and she was starting to sense the magnetism.

She was saved the long walk back to Castlemere by the fact that Bartlet had come to the chemist for a prescription for his mistress. "Oh, Bartlet, I could have saved you the journey if I'd known."

"It's quite all right, Miss Natalie," he mourned. "I've quite enjoyed the trip. The car is outside; would you care to accompany me on my return?"

"I would love to."

On the way back, she asked, "That portrait of Grandmama—when was it done?"

"The large one in the morning room, miss? It was done a few months after her marriage to your grandfather."

"She's very beautiful in the portrait. Was she really so lovely?"

"She was even more beautiful. Very proud of the mistress, we were. Still are, come to that."

It was probably the longest single speech she'd ever heard him make and she was delighted to find that the more cheerful his words were, the more sorrowful his manner became. He probably giggled when he was truly sad. "You've known her most of her life, haven't you, Bartlet?"

"I'm pleased to say so, miss." His face looked like that of someone who'd just heard about a mine disaster.

But there was reason for his apparent grief, Natalie realized on reflection. He had been, in his way, a part of the family nearly forever. He had been Mary's butler for half a century, longer than most marriages last. It was he, she recalled, who had carried Grandmama all the way back to the house the time she fell and broke her ankle some years earlier. Though he'd had little firsthand part in her sorrows and her happinesses, he had been a constant audience to them. He must know—and love—her as much as anyone living, Natalie thought with a pang of guilt at her flippant attitude toward him.

As she got out of the car, she said, "Bartlet, whatever happens, you'll be looked after. I promise you that."

For a second it looked almost as if he might smile; then he bowed slightly and said, "You mustn't trouble yourself about that. Miss Mary says she has provided for me. Whatever she sees fit will suit me."

When Natalie went to deliver the medicine, she was met with a very nice surprise. Grandmama had taken a long nap, then the nurse had helped her take a hot bath. Her hair was washed and freshly braided into a shiny white chignon. Wearing the frilly pink bed jacket Natalie had brought along as a gift, Mary looked as fluffy and sweet as a baby lamb.

Her manner immediately dispelled this pretty notion.

"Useless potions," she said of the medicine. "That Robbie boy is just a worrier. Worrying should be left to old people like me. I'll take it, but it's a waste. I'm feeling fine and will be up and about in a day or two. What's in the other parcel?"

Natalie gave her the lip rouge and Mary softened. "How lovely of you, my dear. If I had dared to wear this at your age, I'd have been snubbed from here to Land's End. How times change."

"I've been reading about Mr. Foxworth-Wilding. I read all his books when I was in school. They were required reading, but one of the assignments I genuinely liked. He made me feel as though I'd actually been to the places he described."

"To think—children today still get to know my dear Winston. How pleased and embarrassed he would have been. I don't think he ever knew how truly brilliant he was. That was part of his charm. Dear old Winston. Why, more than twenty years after he set me down, he went to the Yukon on that gold rush. He wrote a book about it and dedicated it to me. He didn't pass on until the beginning of the Great War. Eighty-some years old, Winston was when he died. And active until the last week. We did stay friends, very good friends. I finished his last book for him. The one on Celtic history. Did you know that? It was all written. I just organized the chapters, checked the footnotes, and saw it through production."

"So he was wrong."

"About us marrying? No, he was right, but for the wrong reasons."

"I've been wondering about Great-Aunt Hester's baby too, Grandmama. I didn't know my father had any older cousins."

"He didn't. She miscarried on the way to California," Mary replied. "At least, that's what she and Jamison said."

"Do you mean there never was a pregnancy? They pretended in order to force the marriage?"

Mary shrugged. "I've never known. It's a possibility. They were both very determined."

"Imagine. . . . I never knew Jamison, did I?"

"No, he died long before you were born. Before your father was born, for that matter. He died in this bed."

"What!"

Mary was obviously enjoying the shock she'd caused. "Yes, he died cursing me, and Hester claimed I'd killed him. In a way, she was right. You see . . . No, it's in the diaries later. You'll find out all about it. I hadn't meant to come back here, but I did. Very shortly after Alex went back to Singapore, in fact."

"Why was that?"

"Because Portia died. She had a bad fall while staying with some people in Corbridge and broke some ribs. She got pneumonia. We all came back for the funeral. Hester and Jamison decided to stay on, so I came back here to live most of the time too. Out of spite, I suppose, as much as anything. I just didn't think they had any right to be here. Hester had other property that was truly hers, but none of it as grand as Castlemere, and Jamison felt he needed a grand house. The very idea of Jamison Hewitt playing master of Castlemere infuriated me, so I came back and got underfoot and squabbled with them. The battles we had! I started the first one the very day I returned. Before anyone could say 'Boo,' I moved into this room so they couldn't. Oh, *how* Jamison carried on!"

Natalie sat quietly for a few moments, longing to ask questions, but knowing her grandmother would only refer her to the small row of books. She'd never really believed her cousins' gossip about someone else dying in Grandmama's bed. So it was Jamison Hewitt. But when? And why?

It was Mary who broke the silence. "Well?" she asked sharply.

"Well what, Grandmama?"

"Aren't you going to read? Or do I have to keep you occupied? You young people these days don't seem to have any self-sufficiency. I'm too tired to entertain you forever."

Natalie went to the drawer. She glanced back and noticed that her grandmother was tactfully pretending to take a little nap.

18 June 1875. Mr. Henry Turner and his interesting sister, Elaine, are coming for a visit. What a refreshing change from Hester and Jamison that will be.

32

June 1875

"Awfully nice of you to have us down," Elaine Turner said to Mary, throwing open the window of the room she'd been given at Castlemere and taking a deep breath. She was an angular, hearty young woman who looked like she might start doing knee-bends to illustrate her appreciation of the atmosphere. By no means pretty, she had an attractive and unusual appearance—a wide, generous mouth, deep-set eyes, a jawline far too strong to qualify as beautiful, and hair so curly it fell into little crinkled rows when pulled back tightly. She was the sort of woman people tend to stare at and wonder just what the collective appeal of those features was.

"Such nice air by the sea," she said. "I do loathe the stink of London, don't you?"

"Most of it smells abominable, but our house there is near the spice warehouse and I rather like that when the wind is from the right direction," Mary answered. "Miss Turner, I'm so glad you and your brother accepted my invitation. You can't imagine how pleased I am to have such amiable company."

"Don't get along with the brother-in-law, eh?" Elaine commented, coming right to the point.

"Oh, no, it's not that at—" Mary caught her knowing look and laughed. "Why should I start our friendship by lying? No, I don't much get along with him. We mix about as well as two strange cats tied in a sack together."

"I shouldn't wonder. He's got a hungry look. Women like me see it in men like him because they're not looking at us. Do you fish, Miss Beecham?"

"I adore it. But you mustn't be so proper. I hope we're going to be great friends. Please call me Mary."

"And I'm Elaine. Do you really fish? Bait your own hook and everything?"

"I certainly do. My Aunt Nell taught me. She abhorred sissies. She was wonderful . . ." Mary gave her guest a character sketch of Nell.

Elaine listened with great interest. "How I wish I'd known her. And you say she lived in India. I'm going to India in the winter. Not my destination, of course. On my way to China."

"China! Why are you going there?"

"Missionary Society."

"Oh, I had no idea . . ." Mary said.

"Don't draw back and look like you're afraid to talk to me," Elaine said brightly. "I'm not particularly religious—don't go about praying over folks who don't want it or humming hymns under my breath. Don't find myself talking to or about God much between one month and the next, in fact."

"Then why are you going clear around the world as a missionary?"

"It's the other way round. Want to see the world, you understand. Say, would you mind if we got outside and really sloshed around in the fresh air a bit? Been stuck in the city so long I'm rather thirsty for it."

"I'd love that. I'll take you down to the beach. Wear walking shoes."

They headed out a few minutes later, and as energetic as Mary was, she had to struggle to keep up with Elaine's long strides. Once outside, the guest went on to explain her "calling." "Got bored of the tea parties and such so I worked for a medical-mission home office in London last year. Just for something extra to fill my time. It was a real revelation—and not in the spiritual sense. I discovered that the people they sent out who wrote back were admirable and irritating in equal measure. You see, the churches ship off these dear, kind people whose souls are pure gold and whose minds sometimes seem to be pure mush. Concentrating on Higher Things, I suppose, instead of looking at what they're standing in the middle of. The kind who wait till they're out of some medicine before they send back for more, as often as not. Then they're without for months. One of them slipped through the filing system and wasn't sent any living expenses for a full two years before he asked what was wrong. Or maybe he just didn't notice until then.

After a bit, it just seemed to me that they needed somebody out there who understood real life and basic mathematics."

"Then you won't preach or whatever missionaries usually do?"

"My goodness, no! Can you imagine me converting the heathen? They'd run from me in droves. I'll be a central point for money and supplies and books and such for several missions all over China. A sort of glorified clerk, actually. Ought to suit me to the ground. Henry always says I'm too damned organized for my own or anybody else's good. Been learning Chinese and a bit of medicine to get ready. Just look at that view!"

They gazed out across the Channel without speaking for a few minutes. Mary was sorry that Elaine was going to go so far away and so soon. She felt that here she might have finally found a real woman friend. Elaine seemed to be as Aunt Nell might have been as a young woman. "Will your brother be going as well?"

"Henry? You'd have to truss him up like a sheep to market before he'd get involved with missionaries. He doesn't want to go anywhere, and besides, one of us has to stay in England."

"Oh?"

"Is that your boat down there? Is it seaworthy?"

Mary was curious why one of them had to remain in England, but the opportunity to ask had passed. Perhaps that was deliberate on Elaine's part. "Yes, it is. Want to go out?"

"I'd adore it. Let's go quickly before Henry gets unpacked and catches us. He might go all protective and spoil our fun."

"I don't think he'll miss us. I asked the butler to show him to the library. I thought he might like to see it."

"See it! If it's got more than two books, you'll never get him out," Elaine predicted.

She was quite right. When they came back to the house an hour later, Henry Turner didn't even hear them enter. He'd climbed the small ladder that ran along the main wall on wheels. Mary said, "I'm afraid you'll come down looking like the dustman. It's been awfully long since they've all been taken down and cleaned. Fifteen years at least, I should think."

Henry descended the ladder with reluctance. "This is a

remarkable collection. I've already run across things here I've only heard of and never actually seen. Amazing!"

"Oh? Well, a number of Beechams have been avid book collectors, including old Philippe, who built Castlemere. Mostly we are 'map mad,' however. Still, I've found some interesting things in here to read from time to time."

"How in the world do you know where to look?" Henry asked. "It's a jumble."

"Now, Henry—" Elaine warned.

"Just by puttering round until something strikes my fancy," Mary replied. She looked around as if seeing the library for the first time. Books were stuffed in wherever there was a space that would accommodate them. "It isn't very well-organized, I suppose."

Henry smiled and glanced up at heaven. " 'Not very well-organized,' " he repeated. "It's not organized at all. I've already run across a wonderful old copy of *Morte d'Arthur* stuffed back behind a set of works on African geography. If there's a connection there, I fail to see it."

"Henry, Mary and I have been fishing," Elaine said, brutally changing the subject.

"Sorry," Henry said with an understanding grin. "None of my business how you sort out your things. I've enjoyed browsing around. I hope you'll let me do a bit more while we're here, Miss Beecham."

"Your sister and I have agreed we're all to be on first names. And yes, I'd love for you to spend as much time as you'd like in here. It's a room that should be enjoyed. My father used to be at that desk most of the time, and I've spent many happy hours here with him. Shall we have our tea in here?"

"Lord, no!" Elaine exclaimed. "Henry will be wandering off and petting books the whole time. What about that terrace just outside?"

"Did you catch any fish?" Henry asked, proving that he could tear his mind away from books.

"Not one," Elaine answered, taking his arm and guiding him out the French doors. "But we're determined to try again. You must come along next time and charm them out of the water for us. Or perhaps you could read to them and they'll all bob up to the surface to listen," she said, making a face at him meant to convey a rapt fish.

Summoning Bartlet to bring tea, Mary followed brother and sister outdoors. "The butler says my brother-in-law,

Jamison, has gone into town and my sister is lying down with a headache. It will be just the three of us," Mary said.

Elaine had bent down somewhat inelegantly to examine the tufts of moss between the flagstones. "How beautiful! Just like little padded bits of green velvet."

"Alex liked it too," Henry said. "He brought a bit back to school to show me once when he'd been here. But it dried out and fell apart. We tried to plant it, but it didn't take."

"I used to sometimes pull up a bit just to stroke like a little soft animal," Mary said. "My father hated that. I had no idea Alex had ever noticed the moss. Come to think of it, this is where I first saw Alex. I was a very small child. About seven, I think. He'd just come from Singapore to start his English education and Aunt Nellanor brought him out to tea. I was hiding in that wisteria. You and Alex must have been very close when you were young, Henry."

"Like to think we still are, though there's not as much time for letters as either of us would like. He was quite remarkable as a boy. Knowing him was the only thing that made school tolerable."

"Remarkable in what way?" Mary asked.

Henry took a sandwich and cup of tea from the tray Bartlet had brought out. He sipped and chewed and considered. "Most chaps either go for the books or go for sport. Alex had a nice gift for both. Made him very popular with everyone."

"I can't imagine Alex being terribly interested in sports," Mary said. "I guess that's because he's never talked about them much."

"Oh, he wasn't awfully keen. And not good enough to be much of a threat to the chaps who lived for those things, but good enough to reliably hold up his end on rowing or cricket or whatever was going on. Same with his studies, really. Didn't put people off by showing off how brainy he was, but just quietly did awfully well. Was a big help to me several times, I can tell you. I remember a time . . ."

Henry went on to tell a long amusing story about a mathematics test he wasn't prepared for and Alex's efforts to beat the information into his head in the last hours. Mary listened with interest, not only because the story was funny and well-told but also because it was an odd sort of revelation to her that Alex had this friend and a whole area of his life she knew nothing about.

Elaine picked up the theme and told about the time a tutor of hers had quizzed her on material she had not prepared for. Her creative answers were much more entertaining than the proper ones, she explained. By the time they'd finished tea and laughed themselves quite silly at recollections of childhood antics, Jamison turned up from his trip to the village and took Henry away to show him some of the best hunting spots. Mary had the feeling Henry wasn't nearly as interested as he politely pretended.

"Hate to seem a sissy," Elaine said, swallowing a yawn, "but I could use a bit of a rest."

"It's the fresh sea air," Mary said. "Whenever I've been in London and come back here, it takes me that way too. Feel free to creep away and have a good nap. Dinner is at eight. We're disgracefully informal here; don't bother to dress for dinner."

"I love that phrase. It always conjures up a mental image of everybody sitting about the table in their knickers and vests."

Mary went to rest as well, smiling to herself and wishing these delightful people could stay forever.

They intended to visit for a long weekend; Mary managed to get them to extend it to a full week. It was the most pleasurable week she'd had for a very long time. Elaine's personality, though strong, didn't pall. Instead, Mary came to like her more every day. Henry was delightful company as well. He was bright and witty in a quiet way and seemed to have a pleasant story to tell on nearly any topic. He even managed to get along quite well with Jamison—no small acomplishment.

On their last day, they took luncheon on the cliffs. Henry carried the big picnic basket and the women carried blankets to the very edge. Their napkins kept blowing away and the gulls made nuisances of themselves, but it was a happy party. "When will you come back?" Mary asked.

"Whenever you ask," Elaine replied.

"Tomorrow, then. Just pretend you've left and come right back."

"We can't just move in on you," Elaine said with a laugh. "The Missionary Society office needs me. Besides, people will think we're some sort of poor relations if we stay forever."

"Not if there was a good reason to stay," Mary said. "I've been thinking about the library . . ."

At this, Henry nearly dropped his plate. "You have?"

"Yes, you're quite right. It's a shame to have a fine library and not even know what's in it unless you stumble over it. I wonder . . ."

"Are you actually offering to let me get my hands on it?" Henry asked.

"If you'd like. Perhaps if you'd just tell me where things ought to be put . . ."

Henry didn't quite roll his eyes in disbelief at this naive remark, but it was a near thing. "I'm afraid there's much more to it than that. It's months of work—repairing bindings, cataloging, cross-referencing, researching printing dates, not to mention the work of the actual physical rearranging. Some of the shelves are already sagging from the weight, and all the wood needs to be treated."

"Oh, I just thought you'd sort of put things with like things. Geography books on one shelf, novels on another—"

Elaine yelped with laughter. "Now you have aroused *his* missionary zeal."

"I'm so sorry. I had no idea I was suggesting such a big job. I wouldn't have dreamed of imposing—"

"You're not trying to back out, are you?" Henry asked.

"Do you mean you'd like to—?"

"I'd love it. How soon may I start?"

The summer arrangements were soon settled. Henry Turner went to London to get his reference books, cataloging materials, and clothing and returned within a week. Elaine would come down every other weekend on Friday and stay through Monday. "I shouldn't be selfishly taking you away from your family when you're going to be halfway round the world soon," Mary said to Elaine on her next visit.

"Oh, we haven't any family to speak of. Just a few cousins we're barely acquainted with. Papa passed on last year and Mother's been gone for ages."

"You have no other brothers or sisters?" Mary asked.

"We had a brother," Elaine said rather shortly. "I wouldn't mention him to Henry, if I were you. A sore subject, if you know what I mean."

Mary wasn't sure she did, but clearly wasn't invited to ask any more questions. "I used to wish I had tons of brothers and sisters," she said instead, "but every time I really thought hard about it, I realized it would have meant less attention for me from my father and Aunt Nell. Still, a houseful of children always seems a wonderful idea."

"You shall probably have dozens of your own, then."

"Me? Oh, no, I think not. I'm afraid I've passed the threshold of spinsterdom." Mary tried to make it sound like a joke, but was appalled at how sad she sounded.

"How old are you?" Elaine scoffed. "Eighteen or nineteen?"

"Twenty-three."

"You can't mean it! Still, you've got a better chance than I have. I'm nearly twenty-eight and quite decidedly beyond the pale. Of course, I'm not sure I want a husband anyway. Men can be such terrible bores. Marriage isn't the sort of thing you can try out and change your mind about if you make a bad choice. Still, wouldn't it be wonderful to have mobs of children to raise and teach and take care of?"

"It would indeed. If Alex would come back here to live, at least I'd have a niece and nephew."

"Not much chance of that, is there? Henry tried to talk him into it. Misses his chum, don't you know? But he said Alex talked as if he wouldn't be back for years and years. Said you did such a fine job with the company and Castlemere that there was no need."

No need, Mary thought. If only she were as dithery and incompetent as Hester, he probably would have returned. *That* certainly wasn't fair! She half-wished she could bring herself to play the fool just so he'd dash back to take care of her muddles.

"I don't suppose there's any reason for him to uproot his family," she said. "It's selfish of me to want them here. And I'm going to want it even more when Henry's finished the library and you've gone to China. You can't imagine what it means to me to have you both here."

"I don't leave for China for months. And Henry will spend the rest of his life in the library if you give him half a chance. He's divinely happy in there, you know."

"I didn't know. I've hardly seen him."

"You can't just wait for him to come out. Beard him in his den, don't you see? The only way."

"I just hate to disturb him. I'm afraid I'll interfere in his system."

"The more difficult the job is, the happier he'll be. If *I* really wanted to please him, I'd sneak in at night and move things about so he has to start over every day," Elaine said with a naughty grin. "Henry can brood if he's not very busy with something very difficult. It's hard for him, having no compelling reason to work. Family's always had plenty of money—not an excess, just plenty. Invested in nice safe boring things that need almost no attention at all. If he were to go around the city working as hard as he'd like at banking or whatnot, people would think he was ruined and had to. Hard for a man in his position. Would have been hard for us too, but you've got the spice company and I've got the Missionary Society to keep us busy."

"But I admire that need to do something. Men don't always have it, and it seems women seldom do. I wish my sister's husband had a little of it. I've never seen anybody quite so content to accomplish nothing."

"Do you really think he's content? Seems to me that under all that high-living, hard-drinking sportman business, he's a very unhappy person."

"Possibly he would be, under any circumstances."

"What about your sister? Never seem to see much of her. Hope I haven't offended?"

"Oh, no, it's not you at all. Hester's well on her way to becoming an invalid and I don't know how to stop the process, I'm afraid. Someone once told me there was a proverb about being very careful what you wish for because you might just get it. Hester is a perfect example. The one thing she wanted in the world was Jamison, and unfortunately, she got him."

"Pity. It could happen to any of us, though. What do you want most in the world, Mary?"

"I don't know," Mary answered quickly. As close as she'd grown to Elaine, she couldn't share her innermost feelings on that one subject. "I think what I want most is to find out what I want most."

Elaine threw back her head and laughed. "Wonderful way to put it! I'll have to remember that."

"And you?" Mary asked.

"Hmmm. Probably to find a group of people who will let me boss them around and then love me for doing so. Henry won't let me boss him on anything important. For all his lovely manners, he's quite strong-minded. Henry quite likes you, you know. He might even be smitten."

"You *can't* mean that," Mary answered, embarrassed and

more pleased than she would have expected. "He hardly speaks to me. I don't mean he's rude. Just rather quiet."

"Just so. He sometimes gets terribly quiet around people he cares about. Hmmm, maybe—"

"Don't get that look in your eye, Elaine Turner. I'm not the one whose life you're going to manage!" Mary said with a laugh.

"I suppose I would make a heavy-handed matchmaker. Still, you ought to think about it."

"Not for a minute. Let's go fishing and talk about other things," Mary replied.

But she did think about it. More than she wanted to.

Hester, suffering from the heat and Mary's attempts to "bring her out of herself," managed to convince Jamison that they should spend the rest of the summer in the north someplace. He was most uncooperative until she ran down old friends of her mother's who had a castle near Edinburgh. Mary was glad to see them go at first. Hester had turned into a silent martyr, the last sort of individual for Mary to abide with good grace. And while she and Jamison had come to an unspoken and very uneasy truce, it was a relief to have him gone as well.

She was astonished, therefore, to discover how lonely and big the house seemed without them. She spent the morning on household accounts and whatever items of business required her attention, then usually went for a long walk before luncheon. But the afternoons stretched out endlessly and the evenings were even longer. She and Henry dined together and sat about for a bit every night trying to make conversation, but for some reason it was difficult when Elaine wasn't around. They kept stumbling into unexpected pits of silence. She always sensed that his mind was on the work he'd really rather be doing. This wasn't happening as she'd hoped. She didn't care a whit whether the library was set in order; she'd invited him to sort it out for the sake of companionship, and he wasn't much of a companion.

Eventually she decided that while Henry Turner might be quite content to work alone, he was going to have help whether he liked it or not. At least it was something for her to *do*.

"I'm going to help here now," she said as she walked in one day after luncheon.

His response to her overly firm offer to pitch in was

flattering. "I'd love to have you help, and considered asking you. I just thought you had no interest and I'd be regarded as a resident pest. What would you like to do?"

"Henry, don't be silly. You know I haven't the faintest concept of what there is to *be* done. Just give me a job and if I can manage it, then you can give me another one."

That summer turned out to be the most wonderfully tranquil of her normally hectic life. And when she thought back to it, the day she insisted on helping was the real beginning. Often, in later years, she looked back on what began so nicely and ended so tragically and wondered if there hadn't been signs or omens she should have noted but missed. There were precious few, and she wouldn't have known what to make of them even if some inner voice had said, "Take note of that. Be careful."

She moved from gently dusting the least-valuable volumes to progressively more important work. Mary was pleased and very surprised at how much she came to enjoy her jobs. Henry, invited to open his mind, was delightful to spend time with. He was a natural teacher. Through him, she first began to sense that books were a great deal like individuals. They had pasts, histories, relatives. Often a book would present an intriguing mystery. The simple question of when it was printed, for instance, could become a matter of clever detection. Content, word usage, print style, binding materials, paper quality, color, and size were all clues to be weighed and considered.

"I've always loved what was in books, I just never knew how fascinating the books themselves could be," Mary said in wonder one evening over dinner. There was no longer any difficulty making conversation. Henry had become downright chatty and he could jump from subject to subject with as much enthusiasm and agility as Mary could. In fact, by the end of the day they were both frequently hoarse from talking so much.

"Books are like a disease. Once you've got it, it's incurable and lifelong," Henry said. "It's the one thing about me that Alex never understood. He's like you were—enamored of what the books say, but not much concerned by how they came about and where they've been. I've always thought that if I could get him involved as you are, he'd succumb to the lure."

"Do you hear from Alex often?" Mary asked.

"Not often, but when we do write to each other, we pour

out volumes. Curiously, it's generally impersonal topics. One or the other of us develops a new interest or falls on a new fact, and we write about that rather than our personal life. But the friendship comes through anyway. At least in his letters; I hope in mine too. You correspond with him frequently, I assume."

"Only on business, usually."

"Did he ever tell you about the time . . . ?"

Henry began a long recital of a school prank involving the removal of the hinge pins on a great number of doors and the subsequent surprise of those who attempted to open them. That led, naturally, to an entire evening of reminiscences of the old days with Alex and Henry as an unholy pair of schoolboys. Mary went to bed that night feeling almost as if she'd spent the evening with Alex himself. It was a very nice feeling.

33

Several weeks later Bartlet announced that Miss Turner was in the drawing room waiting to see Mary. "Elaine! I had no idea you were coming down today," Mary said as she hurried into the room, taking off the sleeve protectors she wore when working in the library. "Where are your things?"

"I'm not staying—"

"Is there something wrong? You look quite distracted."

"I've done something perfectly horrible. Come to confess. It can still be remedied, I assure you."

Elaine was actually wringing her her hands like the heroine of a melodrama. Mary had to repress a smile. "Confess away, my friend. I'm sure it can't be so terrible if you did it."

"It's all to do with a childhood friend of mine. Elizabeth. Her husband died a year or so ago and she has five little children and now she's ill. She had an operation and will be quite well in a month or two but she can't go home to recuperate to her parents' because they broke relations with her over the marriage, so Elizabeth's gone to stay with her sister, but she, the sister, has quite a tiny house, so I agreed to take the children in while Elizabeth is resting and taking her medicine."

"That's very nice of you, but what is so terrible?"

"Mary, you haven't seen my house in London. It's hardly larger than a closet. Rather untidy closet, at that. Fine for me, but impossible for five children and two nannies."

"For heaven's sake, Elaine, bring them here, then."

Elaine collapsed onto a chair in obvious relief. "Do you mean that?"

"Of course I do. I'd adore having the children here as long as your friend won't mind them staying with strangers."

"You can't imagine how glad I am that you said that. Didn't know what I was going to do—"

"How do we get them here?" Mary said briskly. "Where have you left them?"

Elaine was unpinning her hat. She looked up and her wide mouth stretched into a guilty smile. "They're in your drive. Packed into a carriage like wriggly little sardines. I was going to drive off with them—to God knows where!—if you didn't offer. Could see myself forever wandering the globe—nightmare!"

Mary laughed. "Let's get them inside. Poor things are probably sticking to each other in the heat."

The children were a bit sticky, but the nannies were the ones in need of restoration. Both young women were flushed and frayed and Mary saw to it that they were immediately taken away for tea and sandwiches while she and Elaine sorted the children out. Their mother had made it more difficult by her choice of names. The three boys, aged ten, eight, and seven, were Danny, David, and Donald. The five- and three-year-old girls were Diedre and Diana.

"Elizabeth is really something of a ninny," Elaine said under her breath.

"I'm afraid to ask what their surname is," Mary said.

"And well you should be. It's DeBerry."

Mary all but collapsed in laughter and the children joined in, not knowing what the joke was, but liking the happy lady with the fiery hair.

The next hour was chaotic. Bartlet, looking like there was a death in the family, was asked to hire some extra household help from the village and to assign the present maids to ready the nursery. One of the nannies went into a snit and marched off to the village to find her own way back to London, but was persuaded to return by Elaine, who made some pretty rash promises about increases in wages. After making these promises, Elaine cravenly departed for London in solitary glory.

Henry emerged from the library and was enveloped in a swirling tide of small children. "What in the world is this? Is England being invaded?" he asked cheerfully.

"Not all of England, just Castlemere," Mary said. When the children were all settled on the terrace with lemonade and cakes, she explained. "I'm afraid it will be very distracting to your work."

"Not in the least. Some of them can help with dusting the books and the shelves. Anybody can do that."

"That's why you've been letting me do it?"

Henry laughed. "I let you do some things that involve a bit more responsibility. Seriously, I think children need jobs to do. It makes them think better of themselves. They'll be happier away from their mother if they're busy."

"I think you're quite right."

"I got the theory from my father," Henry said with mock solemnity. "Only he was talking about dogs."

As it turned out, the boys showed no signs of missing their mother the entire time they stayed at Castlemere. Henry took primary responsibility for keeping them in hand and kept them occupied from morning to night. When they weren't hauling books around—an activity they had a limited tolerance for—he had them out fishing or traipsing around the grounds. He even set up a schedule of morning exercises that half-exhausted them before they could even contemplate using their energies in anything troublesome.

Mary and the girls joined them some of the time, but little Diana and Diedre needed more in the line of emotional support. Both were desperately homesick for their mama, and Mary's days consisted of being as good a substitute as she could. She filled much of the time by reading to them or telling stories. An old dollhouse of Hester's was dragged out of storage and set up on a large table in the nursery. Mary spent many hours helping them fix up the house. They scrubbed it and repainted the exterior, and the older girl, Diedre, helped Mary cut and paste new paper onto the interior walls.

Henry always interrupted his work to have supper with Mary and the children in the nursery, and later, when he and Mary dined, they talked over everything Danny, David, Donald, Diedre, and Diana had done all day. Mary went to bed every night happy and tired and buoyed by a strong sense of having spent a worthwhile day.

"You thrive on this," Elaine said on her first visit.

"It's an illusion. I plan to collapse for a month when they go. I'll buy a wheeled chair and make Bartlet push me about," Mary said, but in her heart she knew Elaine was right. She'd never felt quite so alive before, so completely useful and valuable.

Most important, perhaps, she was finding that she could and did spend entire days at a stretch when she hardly thought about Alex at all. It was with a certain degree of guilt that she realized this was like having a burden lifted. It was a burden she had borne happily, even eagerly, for so many years that she hadn't realized the weight it exerted on her soul until she was temporarily relieved of it.

Like most good things, it was eventually over. Elaine came on a Sunday to take the children back to their mother. "She's quite fit and there are even signs that the breach with her parents may be healing. They've asked to see the children."

They were sitting on the terrace outside the library. Mary had taught little Diana how to do somersaults and the child was toppling about erratically on the mossy flagstones. "You too, Mary," she said, stumbling over and taking Mary's hand.

"Not in front of other grown-ups. They'd laugh at me," Mary said.

"Only a snicker or two," Elaine assured her. "Of course, Henry would have his image of you spoiled forever if you acted the hoyden."

"Every woman should be a bit of a hoyden," Henry protested. "I don't think Mary can really do a somersault anyway."

"I most certainly can. Who do you think taught Diana so expertly?" Mary objected.

"I wouldn't believe it without seeing it," Henry said.

"Then you shall," Mary said. She went to a clear spot, tucked her skirts around her knees modestly, and did a quick, neat turn without showing so much as an inch of petticoat. She bounded up with arms outstretched for applause.

Henry scooped Diana up and they both clapped their appreciation. "Now you see what you've done, poppet? Mary is likely to think so well of herself that she runs off and joins a circus. Then what would we do? We'd have to follow her around the countryside."

"Wouldn't you like some more tea?" Mary asked, pleased and embarrassed at the attention. Diana climbed down from Henry's lap and went tumbling off.

"No, thanks," Elaine said. "I want to take the children up to the nursery and make sure the nannies are getting all their things packed up without inadvertently taking away what's not theirs. Children, come along."

"Do you think their mother is really well enough to have them back yet?" Henry asked. "A month isn't very long to recover from a serious illness."

"She's not only ready, I nearly had to tie her up to keep

her from coming down herself. Can't fool me, Henry Turner. You like them. Afraid you're going to be cursed with her eternal gratitude, Mary—something of an affliction, given her excessive modes of expression."

"I'm the one who's grateful," Mary said. "They've been a joy. Shall I come up with you to help?"

"No," Henry said decisively. "You'd just be in the way, and you know it. Come for a walk with me instead."

Mary strolled off with Henry toward the cliffs. "I'm going up to London with them, you know," she said. "I've neglected business and have to meet with my advisers."

Henry smiled. "You expect me to believe that, do you? Mary, stop looking back at the house. They're not going to steal away while you're not looking, you know."

"I feel that they might," she said. To her surprise, Henry put his arm around her waist as they walked. It was a very comforting and comfortable gesture. "I wish they could stay at least another week. There are so many things still to do, places to show them—"

"You have moss in your hair," Henry said, stopping and gazing at her. She brushed at her mop of red curls. Henry reached up and picked loose a small green tuft, and after discarding it, returned his hand to the side of her face. "You look quite nice with moss in your hair. You look quite nice in any circumstance. I don't suppose I'd mentioned that before, had I?" he asked dryly.

"I don't think so," Mary said, very much liking the warm feel of his hand on her cheek.

"There are a great many things I've neglected to say. Perhaps when you get back from London we can talk about them?"

"Yes . . . yes, perhaps we could," Mary said. Why was her heart hammering this way?

"Mary!" A shout came from the terrace. Elaine. "Are those dolls really Diedre's, as she says, or are they your sister's?"

Mary and Henry stepped apart and smiled at each other. "Go on," Henry said. "Sort it all out. This is a weighty matter, the ownership of dolls."

Mary returned the "Little D's" to their mother with a polite smile on her face and a cold, bleak lump in her heart. She'd felt so awful about parting from them that she'd actually caught herself having some perfectly horrid thoughts:

Suppose the mother wasn't well, but suddenly died and she got to adopt them all? Suppose she just stole them and went off to some obscure end of the earth with them? What if . . . ? Mary had to go back to her room at the Mincing Lane house and give herself a mental tongue-lashing. The children's visit was a pleasant interlude in her life. Nothing more.

Nothing more!

But as she tried to concentrate on the spice business the next day in Clyde's office, she kept coming back to the thought. That wonderful month was far more that a mere four weeks of diversion. That single summer month had made a profound change in her picture of herself and her life. As a temporary mother, she had found a niche she fitted into as if it were designed for her. She was quite superior at playing dollhouse and kissing away hurts and telling bedtime stories. She'd discovered how magnificent a child's hair smelled in the sunshine and the joy of helping someone catch his first fish ever.

She wanted her own family.

And she wanted it desperately as much as, maybe even more than, she wanted to cling to her romantic attachment to Alex. How and why had she developed this mad insistence on "saving herself" for him? She couldn't have him—ever. But she'd allowed the vision to obscure a far greater panorama of dreams—a great vista of happiness that *was* obtainable! She suspected that Winston had seen through her, and perhaps that, not age difference, was what had led him to break their engagement. How stupid she was to have let that happen.

Henry Turner proposed the night she returned to Castlemere. "The work on the library is almost done," he said. "I would be very sorry if that were the end of our friendship."

"Certainly not."

"I had hoped . . . hoped that it had become more than mere friendship between us. Is that a vain hope?"

"Not on my account."

"Mary . . . ?"

"Yes?"

Ask it, she thought. No more flowery phrases. We're long past that. Ask!

"I'd like to ask you to consider something. You need not answer right away. You need never answer if you choose. I'm wondering if you'd consider becoming my wife."

"Yes," she said instantly.

"You'll consider it?" he asked, surprised.

"I've already considered it. I accept."

"Oh. That's grand. I . . . God, Mary, I've practiced that first bit a hundred times, but I guess I hadn't thought out what to say next. When shall it be, then? The wedding?" Henry asked. "Is that the next thing to talk about?"

"Soon," Mary said firmly. And then, wondering if she might frighten him off with her eagerness, she added, "It should be before Elaine leaves for China, don't you think?"

"Certainly. Mary . . . are you sure?"

"Are you trying to escape the consequences of your rash words?" she said lightly.

"Never. You're what I've waited all my life for without even knowing I was waiting."

"Oh, Henry. What a fine thing to say." Mary wanted to say something equally fine in return, but couldn't find the words. "You've never even kissed me, you know. Don't you think you should?"

Henry grinned. "You are the strangest woman! Yes, I suppose I really should and, in fact, I'd like it very much. Are you ready?"

Mary started giggling. "I don't know what I'm supposed to do to get ready."

"You could stop laughing at me."

"Oh, Henry. I'm not laughing at you! I'm just happy."

"I'm glad. Making you happy makes me happier than I knew I could be. Now, hold still."

He kissed her very gently. "I'm not fragile," she murmured. "Henry, you won't change your mind, will you?"

"Never. Will you?"

"Never."

Elaine was ecstatic. "My two favorite people in the world—married. Too good to be true, really! You'll be my sister. Couldn't have found a better one." She actually cried, which moved Mary to tears. "I take full credit for this, you understand," Elaine said, sniffling into a man-sized handkerchief she'd fished out of the bosom of her dress. "Told you I was a matchmaker at heart. Not a half-bad one, it looks like."

"Do Henry and I get no credit?" Mary asked.

"None whatsoever," Elaine said firmly. "Will you live at Denby Hall right away?"

"Denby Hall?"

Elaine looked at her with a puzzled expression. "Our home in Yorkshire. Certainly Henry mentioned it?"

"No, he hasn't."

"How peculiar. No, I suppose it's not. Henry hasn't really lived there since we were children. He was away at school and then took a house in London. Of course, it's been closed up for years. Since Father died. Take a lot of airing and rug-beating."

Mary felt a chill. A dusty, almost abandoned house in Yorkshire? It wasn't the dust or abandonment that bothered her. It was the Yorkshire part. So far away from Castlemere. Dear Lord above, how could she have been so dim-witted that she never questioned where they'd live? She'd just pictured them at Castlemere. She'd never been able to imagine herself living anywhere else.

With great trepidation she raised the question to Henry that evening as they took a last stroll in the moonlight. "I guess I ought to get somebody up to Denby Hall to get it ready. Trust Elaine to point out the obvious. Glad she did."

"Do you want to live there?"

Henry stopped walking and considered. "Not particularly. I never much liked it. Everybody is supposed to have his heartstrings tied to his childhood home, but I don't. I guess that's because I didn't much like my childhood. Where would you prefer to live?"

Mary paused. "Here."

"At Castlemere, do you mean? But it's not only not *my* house, it's not even *yours*."

"I know that, but Alex wouldn't mind."

"Suppose he wouldn't, but how would that look? Like I'd married you for your money, then sponged off your cousin the way Jamison does."

"The cases are entirely different. Jamison hasn't the means or desire to provide for his wife. You have."

"You want very much to stay here, don't you?"

Mary looked up at him and saw the understanding in his eyes. "Desperately," she said. "My heartstrings are hopelessly tangled here. I can and will get over it if I must—and I know I must someday when Alex comes back to England. But I'd like to have the time to unravel myself gently."

"I wouldn't force anything on you, Mary, dear. I want you to be happy, and if being here matters so much, we'll stay—for a while."

They walked on a few paces. "I'm being very selfish," Mary said. "It's not fair to hurt your pride. We'll go to Dunhill."

"Denby Hall. And my pride is my great flaw anyway. Won't hurt a bit to knock it down to the proper level."

Mary told Hester and Jamison her news the minute they returned from their travels. Jamison didn't like it on the simple assumption that anything Mary wanted was probably not in his best interests, but could think of no genuine argument. They all knew it wouldn't have deterred Mary for a second even if he had found legitimate reasons she shouldn't proceed. Hester, however, was thrilled and flung herself into preparations. "You must wear my wedding dress, Mary. You couldn't find a lovelier one. It can be cut down at the waist and let out at the bosom without any difficulty at all."

She rose every morning with new ideas for Mary's wedding and initiated endless conversations on flowers, food, music, rings, veils, and all the side issues that had to be considered for a grand wedding. "So little time. I do wish you'd given me another six months."

"Given you?" Mary asked. "We want to be married before Elaine leaves. She's Henry's only family."

"Yes, yes. I know that. I wanted to talk to you about your going-away shoes—"

"Going-away shoes? Hester! I don't care if I have to tie rags around my feet. You're driving me quite, quite mad with all these trivial concerns."

"But it must be right, Mary. It's a day to remember the rest of your life."

"No, it isn't. I'll forget half of it in a week," Mary said snappishly. "I don't want to get married."

"What!"

"I mean, I want to *be* married. I don't care about *getting* married."

In spite of her wishes, the day approached and Hester became more annoying with each hour. The plan was that the wedding be the first Sunday in September. Mary and Henry would go to Calais for their honeymoon and meet Elaine there a week later. They would then accompany her as far as Marseilles and see her off on her long journey.

Mary had started half a dozen letters to Alex and Anjanette the day after Henry proposed, telling them of her engagement, but tore each up before it was done. She couldn't seem to just announce it without attaching some justification. Finally she gave up and asked Henry to write the letter.

Henry left a few days after his proposal was accepted, on the theory that it was only marginally proper of them to have been sharing the house before as friends, but as a betrothed couple it was clearly not done. Besides, he had family business to attend to which had been sadly neglected for the past two months, he said. He didn't elaborate on what business, nor did Mary think to question him.

The day of the wedding finally arrived. Until the last moment Mary's primary concern was to get it over with so Hester would leave her alone. She asked Winston Foxworth-Wilding to give her away, unaware of what it actually cost him to do so. She stood with him in the entryway of the big house while the wedding guests filed into the chapel.

"You're a beautiful bride, Mary," Foxworth-Wilding said as she fidgeted irritably with a wayward ruffle at her neck. "But that scowl doesn't go with the dress."

Mary took a deep breath and forced herself to smile. "Yes, I'll terrify the guests, won't I?"

"Oh, I don't think you're half as terrifying as you think. At least not to me. There's Bartlet signaling to us. Are you ready?"

He took her arm and escorted her down the front steps and across the grassy area to the chapel doors. She stepped inside and looked down the center aisle. On either side were people turning to get a glimpse of the bride. At the front of the chapel Hester stood as matron of honor, facing her, and on the other side, Henry Turner.

Mary stared at him for a long moment, then clutched Winston's arm tightly and whispered, "What am I doing!"

He put his hand over hers and spoke quietly but firmly. "You're getting married and you're going to have a lovely life."

"But—" Mary stopped as Winston urged her forward. Her sudden anxiety almost kept her from breathing.

I don't even know Henry Turner, she thought frantically. *And I'm marrying him. I want to go back, but it's too late. Too late.*

34

Agnes pulled open the heavy curtains on a dreary Monday morning. "Time to be up and about," she said curtly. "Ugly day out there."

Mary greeted this cheerful announcement by pulling the pillow over her head and mumbling, "What time is it?"

"Near to eight, you lazy thing."

"Where's Henry . . . Mr. Turner?" Mary asked, one arm outstretched into the empty space where he should have been.

"Got some more of them books," Agnes said, starting to drag the tangled bedcovers off her mistress. "Man brought them over from the morning train. Probably a present for you for Christmas, like as not. You got your shopping done?"

"You know I haven't. I'm going to London tomorrow. Christmas is still two weeks away."

"You'd best get something nice for Mr. Turner."

"I don't need you to tell me my duty," Mary said in a superior tone, but Agnes merely made a disrespectful noise through her nose. "Besides," Mary went on, "I've got a wonderful present for him. I'm going to tell him about it today. He won't get it for quite a while yet."

Agnes looked at her suspiciously. "You sayin' what I think you are?"

"I believe I am. At least Dr. Engle says so."

Agnes grinned. "I suspected as much. The laundry lady told me she ain't seen no sign of your courses."

"The laundry lady! Dear Lord, does the whole south coast of England know before Henry?"

"Likely so. The women, anyway. You want your breakfast on a tray or something?"

"Of course not! I'm not sickly," Mary said, although in fact she did feel a bit queasy, as she did most mornings these days. It wouldn't do to admit it to Agnes, however.

Mary kept her secret—such as it was—until that night. "Henry, I have something to tell you," she said as he slipped into bed. He propped his head on his elbow and looked at her. "Henry, we're going to have a child."

"What!"

"Yes. Aren't we lucky? Late June, I think."

"Are you sure?"

"Yes. Aren't you happy?" she asked, beginning to sense that his response wasn't exactly what she'd anticipated.

"Of course I am, but it's so soon. I'm just surprised."

"And pleased?"

"Naturally I'm pleased."

"I thought I'd get a few baby things when I go to London tomorrow. I know it's much too early, but it would be fun to have them anyway. I'm sure Hester will knit all sorts of beautiful clothes. She does that sort of thing so well—"

"London? You can't go to London tomorrow."

"Why not?"

"In your condition? You have to take very good care of yourself."

"A trip to London can't hurt me. I do it all the time. It's not as if I turn cartwheels all the way," she said with a laugh.

"But the baby," Henry insisted. "It could harm the baby. We don't want anything to be wrong with it. We're going to have a perfect child."

"Probably not entirely perfect, I hope. Perfect people are so boring."

"That's not amusing," Henry said, sitting up suddenly.

Mary felt tears sting at the back of her eyes. "I'm sorry. I thought it was. Henry, what's wrong?"

He seemed to get a grip on himself. "Nothing. I'm sorry too. I'm delighted about it. It's just such a heavy responsibility—being a parent at last, or about to be. I'm hardly used to being a husband yet, and now I'm going to be a father too. It's wonderful, Mary, but a little bit frightening. Don't you feel that?"

Mary slid down under the covers and looked up into the shadows. "I suppose so, but I've suspected it for a long time, though I didn't know for sure until yesterday and I've had more time to get excited about it all."

Henry put out the light. "You'd better get some sleep if you're going to travel tomorrow."

"You don't mind if I go?"

"I always mind if you're away from me, but no, I understand. Now, get your rest." He pulled up the covers and twisted into a comfortable position.

Mary lay awake for a long time. He hadn't even kissed her good night, much less made any romantic overtures. That wasn't like him—not at all.

He'd been an enthusiastic bed partner since their wedding. Very, very considerate, but enthusiastic. Mary had tried hard to develop an interest that matched his, even though she sensed that it wasn't exactly a requirement of marriage. Still, Henry seemed to really enjoy sexual relations and she felt she owed him some response in return, even though she felt nothing more than a mild sense of embarrassment about the whole thing. Wasn't it odd, she'd thought in the few weeks of her marriage, that something a man found so rewarding could be, at best, slightly silly, and at worst, downright uncomfortable for a woman?

Only occasionally did she remember that night in Penang when she had heard Anjanette's soft, loving cries. She still flushed at the memory. Anjanette had clearly been enjoying herself. Of course, the man in her arms was Alex. Once, only last week, Mary had thought of that night while Henry was making love to her, and for a few guilty moments she'd allowed herself to imagine that he was Alex. She'd hated herself for it, felt like the very worst sort of traitor. And she'd felt something else as well—a quivering, tingling sort of heat. She'd involuntarily shivered with the pleasure of it and Henry had asked if she were cold. His words brought her back to earth with a thump, and there she would remain, she'd vowed.

She told herself that the delicious feeling she'd been on the verge of experiencing was simply not something that would have a part in her life. A loss, to be sure, but not such a terrible one. She had so much else: a husband who was a bright, considerate man, and soon a child, and, she hoped, many brothers and sisters for that child. In addition, she had the rare good fortune to have a generous income for life and interesting work that could absorb as much or as little of her time as she cared to give. And someday, perhaps this child—or another if this were a boy—would marry

Alex's boy, Richard, and she and Alex could look fondly on the grandchild who would inherit Beecham's.

Mary stirred uneasily. Why wasn't that as comforting a thought as it should be?

Anjanette sent the christening robe that had been Claudius Beecham's, then George's. It had gone to Singapore when Alex was born, back to England for Hester and her sister, Charlotte, then back to Singapore for Katie, then Richard. "As far as I know, it may have been your Aunt Nell's and her half-brother William's as well. That would mean it's also been to America, unlike the rest of us. I like to think so," she said in her letter. "I wish we could be there to see your dear baby wear it. Take very special care of your health, our dearest Mary, and please kiss the sweet baby for all of us the very day it is born. Alex and the children send their best wishes. . . ."

It was a lovely garment with layers and layers of old lace ending in a wide, deeply scalloped hem. Mary tried to imagine old William as a bluff and hearty baby wearing it and failed. She ran her fingers over the lace and wondered if Aunt Nell's baby fists had ever clutched it. Or Alex's. Had Alex been a beautiful baby?

Of all the Beechams, only Mary herself hadn't worn the robe.

Being pregnant kept bringing old feelings to the fore, old questions she'd long ago forcibly put from her mind. But now she found herself wondering about her own past. Where had she been born? That terrible boardinghouse in London? Was she christened? What had her mother dressed her in? What church? What friends came? Did she have a godmother or godfather?

How could her mother have cut her off from all of that? Gwenith Grey had deprived her of her past. Never mind that the result was good—Mary still couldn't forgive her the intent. *She gave me away,* Mary thought, suddenly feeling just as she had when she was seven.

"Mary, what's the matter with you?" Hester asked one day over tea when Mary's mind had wandered off into these murky depths.

"I was just thinking about my mother," Mary said before she could think to be discreet.

"After all these years? Why?"

"I'm going to have her grandchild," Mary said, putting

her hand to her abdomen. "This baby has kindred it will never know."

"And never want to," Hester said matter-of-factly. "Kindred? They're just common Welsh people, aren't they? I think you're being most peculiar."

"Yes, I suppose I am," Mary admitted.

She soon felt even more peculiar, but it was physical. For all her great pride in her excellent health, Mary started having problems during the last months of her pregnancy. First it was a tiny bit of spotting, which drove her straight to bed in absolute terror that she would lose the baby. When the danger seemed to be over and she started getting up and about again, she was irritable and uncomfortable and woke every morning with puffy hands and feet.

The family physician advised more rest, which Mary admitted was a good idea in theory, but which drove her mad. She wasn't accustomed to inactivity and it depressed her. Reading, napping, playing cards, and doing handicraft—those things at which the upper-class Victorian woman was supposed to excel—were boring and useless activities to Mary. Moreover, she felt she was neglecting important duties. Beecham's Fine Spices had some problems; nothing serious, her advisers assured her, but worthy of some concern just the same. Several shipments of very fine goods for which they had paid premium prices had arrived in a severely mildewed condition.

She wrote endless letters to Clyde and Winston, to which Winston finally replied with a mixture of fondness and annoyance, "We're doing all that can be done, Mary. Stop fretting about not being in London. There's nothing you could do that would alter, much less save, the situation. The financial loss won't be as great as we originally feared. If it makes you feel better to write these novel-length letters, go right ahead, but get it out of your head that you must be Doing Something."

Henry was not as sympathetic as Mary would have wished. He was very worried, but in a vaguely accusatory way. "If you hadn't insisted on walking clear to the village—"

"I just strolled halfway, not a strenuous activity by anyone's standards," she snapped.

By the last month, Mary kept remembering a remark Elaine had made very early in their friendship—something about Henry tending to be moody if he wasn't very busy.

Mary had seen nothing of it before their marriage or in the
early days, but of course he had had a great deal to do then
with the library. Now he had little to do but watch over her
and wait, and he'd started slipping into what she thought of
as his "faraway" state. He would sometimes put down the
book he was reading and simply stare gloomily into space,
as if deeply engrossed in some problem.

"Henry? Henry . . . what are you thinking about?" she
would ask.

"Nothing, just some family business," he replied as often
as not. "Shouldn't you be resting?"

That was Henry's answer to most of her questions—
shouldn't she be resting? "If I rest any more, I shall start
growing green leaves out the top of my head. I feel like a
great lazy turnip as it is."

"I know you must, Mary, but you have to take very good
care of yourself for the sake of the baby. You know that."

"I'm nothing more than a container to him," she complained in a burst of irritation to Hester one afternoon in
May. "Mary Deeoham . . . I mean, Mary Turner, has ceased
to exist. I'm not me anymore. I'm just this body that sur-
rounds the baby."

"He's just being a nervous father. I think it's nice," Hester
said, thinking sadly of how little of the same sort of interest
Jamison had taken in her early pregnancy and in the few
false alarms since then.

"I'm tired of this," Mary said, lowering herself awkwardly
into a chair. "It's like the wedding. I want the result, but I
loathe the preparation and the waiting."

Hester picked up her knitting and studied it with artificial
intensity. "I would think you could enjoy it. I certainly
would, if I were as fortunate as you. There aren't many men
who are so concerned for the welfare of their wives and
children."

"Oh, Hester. I am sorry. That was beastly and insensitive
of me to complain to you."

Mary was genuinely contrite, but in the back of her mind
was one remaining complaint she didn't voice. It wasn't her
welfare, she sensed, that concerned Henry and had turned
him into such a brooding shadow of himself. It was the
baby's alone. She just couldn't figure it out. He hadn't been
happy when he learned she was pregnant, nor did he yet
talk enthusiastically about plans for the baby after its birth.
His concern was solely with its health and well-being at

birth. It was very troubling. When Mary tried to talk about possible names for the baby or redecorating the nursery or hiring nursery maids, Henry said, "There will be plenty of time for that." But if she wanted to go down to the beach to do a little fishing or take the dogcart to town to purchase new yarn for Hester, he became distressed. "There's no need to take unnecessary risks. I can't imagine why you'd want to," he'd say sharply.

I must be more tolerant, Mary told herself. She knew her emotions were at fever pitch and her judgment was clouded. To attribute vaguely sinister motives to Henry's concern was just a sign that she wasn't thinking clearly.

It's almost over, she thought one morning in the middle of June as she woke and rolled out of bed awkwardly. As usual, Henry had risen early and she woke alone. He hadn't done that early in their marriage, and while it was difficult to get used to waking with someone else in the bed, it was as difficult to get unaccustomed to it now. Henry had grown distant. It's not just my imagination, she thought. Then she caught sight of herself in the mirror. "It's no wonder!" she said out loud with a laugh as she turned sideways and got a full-length view of herself. She gathered a handful of her nightdress at the small of her back and pulled it tight. Her abdomen was enormous. She wouldn't have believed it was possible for her body to have changed so much.

She bathed, dressed, and went looking for Henry. "The master has gone down to the stables, I believe, madam," Bartlet told her, looking just over her head. He couldn't meet her eyes these days, and Mary found it amusing. It was as if he were afraid his gaze might unwittingly stray to her ungainly figure. "Shall I send someone for him?"

"No need, Bartlet. I'll just wait for him."

But waiting turned out to be very tedious. She puttered in the library for a while, then decided she'd stroll down to meet Henry. But as she started out, she decided that she'd walk, instead, down to the cliffs to look at the sea. She wouldn't climb down to the beach; even she didn't believe she was in any shape for that sort of endeavor anymore.

It was a warm day and the walk seemed longer than ever before. She half-sat, half-toppled to a grassy spot with a fine view and sat for a long time catching her breath. She'd been there only a few minutes when she heard Henry's call. He came striding across the grass, carrying a valise. "Where are you going, Henry?" she asked.

"Better to answer what you're doing here."

She tried to control the self-pity that was washing over her in waves. "Sitting and watching the seabirds," she said with counterfeit calm.

"Have you no idea how irresponsible it is of you to indulge such a foolish whim? You could have fallen or—"

"Oh, Henry! Leave me alone. Don't be such a fussy old maid! I'm not some sort of suicidal simpleton! Stop treating me like one."

"Well!" he said, clearly shocked by her shrill tone.

"Where are you going?" she repeated.

"Up to London. Family business," he said. His voice had a shrill edge too.

"Now, Henry? What sort of business would take you away when it's so close to my time?"

"That's none of your concern."

Mary was now shocked. This man who was glaring at her wasn't anybody she knew—it certainly wasn't kind, courteous Henry Turner. Once again, as during those few moments as she walked down the aisle nine months earlier, she felt suddenly suffocated in anxiety. "I don't suppose it is," she said, coldly facing back toward the sea.

"Now, Mary—"

"*Oh, shut up, Henry.*" She could feel a sob rising in her chest and couldn't bear for him to witness it. "Don't 'now, Mary' me. Go away to London on your secret family business." She waited a long time for him to say something else, an apology perhaps, so that she could offer her own in turn. But he said nothing, and when she finally looked over her shoulder, he was gone.

She stayed there for a long while, first sobbing wildly and wondering what on earth had gone so terribly wrong with her life, then finally pulling her frayed emotions together. She was cruel and half-mad to blame Henry for her own mental instability, she told herself. It was her condition. After all, if she thought Henry had changed, what must he think of her? She'd turned into a puffy, irritable fishwife of a woman—sleeping, complaining, or crying most of the time. No wonder he was cranky with her. He had every right to be.

But to go away to London now? She could understand why he might want to escape her company, but still . . .

She lumbered to her feet, determined not to slip back into the sniveling self-pity she was trying so hard to shake. She'd go to her room, have a refreshing cool bath and a nap, and it would all look better. This thought propelled her only a few feet before she was stopped dead in her tracks by a quick, sharp pain and a searing gush of liquid down the inside of her legs. She stood as if rooted, excited that this meant the baby was finally coming and terrified that it was blood she'd felt. Trembling, she bent forward and lifted her skirts to look. No, thank God, not blood.

It struck her then that she didn't know what she should do. Run back to the house quickly before anything more could happen? No, running couldn't be the right thing. Sit down and wait calmly for someone to come fetch her? No. Nobody but Henry knew where she was, and he'd probably gone off in a snit to London. She tried calling for help, but the breeze jerked her words out to sea. Lifting each foot as though it weighed a ton, she began to walk gingerly toward Castlemere.

"I'm having a baby," she whispered in awe to herself. Then, more loudly, more joyfully: "I'm having a baby!"

35

Mary's labor seemed to go on forever. Within a few hours of the onset, she was getting very weak and clearly feverish. "It shouldn't be like this, should it, Dr. Engle?" Hester asked, taking the country doctor aside.

"No, Hester, it shouldn't."

"Can't you do something?"

"I don't know what. I'm a doctor, not God," he said crustily. "Has her husband been sent for?"

"Yes. He left a London address and I've sent Bartlet to bring him back. You don't mean . . . ?"

"I don't know. Mary normally has phenomenal ability to throw things off, but this time . . . She's not been well for months, she's very small, and she probably has little reserve of strength."

He turned away and rummaged busily but uselessly in his bag, thinking of the first time he'd seen the laboring woman. She'd been a skinny, pale child, and deathly sick. He hadn't expected her to survive that time either. Pray God he was wrong again!

Mary was half-asleep when the next contraction twisted through her. It brought her wide-awake. "Don't fight this, Mary," Dr. Engle said through her haze of pain and fear.

She could hardly see him. His face kept drifting apart so that he looked like he had two identical heads on his shoulders. "I'm dying," she said.

"No, you're not. Don't say such stupid things."

He didn't understand. She wasn't complaining. In fact, death seemed a perfectly logical, almost desirable alternative to the pain. At least, if she were dead, nothing would hurt anymore. "Whatever . . . whatever happens," she gasped weakly, "save the baby. Is it a boy or a girl?"

"You're getting a bit confused, Mary. We don't know yet."

"Oh . . . yes. Not born yet."

This was a bad sign, the doctor thought. Were her mental abilities failing as well?

Bartlet returned at nearly midnight, having made the grueling trip to London and back in a single day. "Is he with you?" Hester asked, meeting the young butler in the hallway.

He shook his head. "He wasn't there, ma'am. It's a hotel, but they say he was never there."

"You mean he hadn't arrived?"

"No, ma'am. They say they've never heard of him."

Hester laced her fingers together nervously. "But Mary says it's the address he always leaves."

"How is the mistress, ma'am?"

"I'm sorry, Bartlet. I should have said. We're still waiting. She's nearly unconscious most of the time. We don't know if she's going to live through this. You should get some rest now after your long trip."

"It you don't mind, ma'am, I'd rather just take a chair here and wait."

Mary was back in the jungle of Penang. Her horse had bolted and she'd fallen from the saddle, but her booted foot had been caught in the stirrup. She was being dragged, her muscles torn and shrieking. Alex was supposed to save her. Alex was somewhere near. "Alex! Alex!" she screamed, but she heard only a pitiful whimper that couldn't possibly be her own voice. Her head struck something and a searing pain shot across her eyes. She tried to raise her hand to her face, but couldn't make it move.

The horse had run on and now the tiger was stalking her. She tried to get up and run away, but her legs wouldn't work. She writhed and twisted, but someone was holding her down. Who would do that to her? Stop them, Alex. Stop them. Alex. Alex. The tiger will kill me. The tiger hates me for loving you.

It's coming closer. It's touching my face, licking my face with its great hot tongue. I can't breathe. Now it's gone, I can't see it.

A great slash of pain ripped through her. The tiger was tearing her apart. She tried to put her knees up to her abdomen to protect herself, but she still couldn't move. The tiger slashed her again—and again—and again. She could smell the hot, coppery odor of her own blood.

Alex! Save me. Save me.

"Mary? Mary? Wake up."

Hester's voice someplace very far away.

"Where are you, Hester?" The words were nothing more than an incomprehensible whisper.

"That's it, Mary. You can do it. Turn your face this way. Let me help you. Open your eyes now. Open your eyes, Mary. Here is your baby. Look, Mary. It's a pretty little girl."

"Did Alex kill the tiger?"

"What's that? What about Alex?"

"The tiger—is it gone?"

"Mary, you're dreaming. There's no tiger. That was a dream. Please, please open your eyes. You can do it. Look at your baby."

It took every bit of strength she could summon, and all she could see was a pale blur. "Red hair," she whispered.

"That's right! She has red hair, like yours. She's going to look just like you."

"Molly."

"What?"

"She's Molly."

Hester's deep concern was suddenly overridden by class consciousness. "You can't name her Molly. It's such a common name."

Mary smiled faintly. "I'm common." She could hear Hester's low laugh. "Molly Beecham."

"Very well, but it's Molly Turner."

Mary closed her eyes. Hester must be mad. Why would she name her baby Turner? They didn't even know anybody with that name. "Molly Beecham," she muttered once more.

Agnes was sitting at the kitchen table with Bartlet. "Poor Miss Mary," she said. "Havin' such a bad time and all."

"She don't know nuffink 'bout it. You said so yerself," the boot boy said.

"Get yourself out of here," Agnes said. "I'm not talkin' to the likes of you. Keep to your own business."

"Is she better this morning?" Bartlet asked.

"Doctor says so. Says she's gonna pull through right as

anything. 'Bout time he said something good. She's been at death's door for near a week now."

"Did she get to see the baby before it . . . ?" Bartlet began.

"Miss Hester put the mite right in her arms, but I dunno if Miss Mary knew it. Maybe best if she didn't. Just make it harder for her if she has memory of it."

"Hester? Are you there?" Mary asked, trying to lift her head.

"I certainly am. How strong and well you sound today." Hester brought over a cool cloth and laid it gently on Mary's forehead.

"I don't feel well. I feel horrible. My mouth tastes like—"

"Don't say it!" Hester warned. "Let me help you sit up. I have some nice orange juice you can drink. That will make you feel better."

Mary allowed herself to be dragged into a sitting position and even managed to help a little. "What's the matter with me?"

"You had a terrible fever. We feared for your life. But you're getting better now."

Mary frowned. There was something else she had to ask, but for the life of her she couldn't remember what it was. She glanced down at her hands. They weren't puffy anymore. In fact, they looked quite oddly pale. Suddenly she realized she could see clear to her feet. She put her hands to her abdomen. "The baby! Have I had the baby?"

"You have indeed," Hester said, and quickly rose and took away the cloth from her head.

"Where is the baby? What is it?"

"All in good time," Hester said, her back to Mary as she bent over a bowl, wringing out the cloth.

"Where is the baby? Molly! I remember. A little girl."

"Mary, you must calm yourself," Hester said firmly. "Just be quiet and I'll go get Henry."

"Henry? What has Henry got to do with it? Where is Molly?"

Hester put the cool cloth back on her head and left.

In spite of herself, Mary fell back asleep. When she next woke, long afternoon sunlight was shining across the foot of the huge bed. Someone was chafing her hand. "Henry?"

"I'm here, Mary," he answered.

He looks like he's the one who's been sick, she thought.

"Henry, where's the baby? Why won't Hester let me see Molly?"

He slowly sat down beside her on the bed. "Mary, you must be very brave. The baby is gone."

"Gone? Did somebody take her?"

"God took her. She died, Mary. She wasn't quite right and God took her back."

Mary pulled her hand away from his. *"No!"*

"Yes, Mary. You must learn to accept it. I know it's terrible for you, but it's for the best. It really is. You'll realize that in time."

"No! It's not true. My Molly couldn't die. I wanted her too badly. God wouldn't do that to me. No, no, no!"

"Hester, call for Dr. Engle," Henry said.

"Hester? Are you here? Tell me it's not true."

They gave her a sleeping draft and she didn't stir until the next day. She woke feeling much stronger physically, but her heart felt as if someone had tried to wrench it from her body. She remembered enough of the conversation the day before to know that she must behave rationally or they would put her to sleep again and she'd never find out the truth.

"Hester, what was wrong with Molly?" she asked when her sister came in with a tray with a glass of juice and a small bowl of pudding.

"Eat first and then we'll talk."

The tiny invalid's meal took forever to get down, but Mary doggedly forced herself to finish it off, then repeated her question.

"I don't know what was wrong, exactly. She was perfectly formed, but very tiny . . . Mary, it doesn't matter. It won't help you to know all this."

"I must know, Hester."

"Very well. She had no . . . no spirit, I suppose. She didn't even cry or kick or anything a baby should do."

"Did she . . . did she die right away?"

"No, not for several days. Henry hired a wet nurse from the village and took her straight to London to try to get someone else to see her. Dr. Engle agreed it was a good idea. He didn't know what to do for her."

"She didn't die here, with me?"

"No, she died in London."

"I don't believe it," Mary said.

"What do you mean, Mary? You have to learn to accept this."

"It's not that I can't accept it. I just don't believe it."

"That's your illness talking. When you're better—"

"When I'm better . . ." Mary repeated, but didn't complete the sentence.

Mary wasn't well enough to start getting around on her own for more than a month. She felt ready sooner, but Hester kept a tight rein on her. Jamison, apparently feeling that all the baby-drama had eclipsed his natural importance, had taken himself off for a long visit to friends in Germany. This left Hester with a great deal of time on her hands to devote to her suffering half-sister.

"What I'm suffering most is attention," Mary claimed loudly one day in August. "I'm going for a walk."

"You're not strong enough," Hester said. "Last time you went outside, you got quite faint."

"That was two weeks ago and it was fearfully hot. It's cloudy and cool and I'll be fine. Where's Henry?"

"He's gone to London. Family business, he said."

"I wish I'd known. I wanted him to stop by the Mincing Lane house and get a shawl I left there. I suppose he's staying in the place he always does. I could send a message."

"I don't know," Hester said, looking vaguely troubled.

"What's wrong?"

"I don't know. It's just something odd I'd almost forgotten. When you started your labor, Bartlet went up to London to fetch him. I didn't think, in view of how very ill you were, that a telegraphic message was quite the thing. The odd part of it was, he wasn't there. Henry, I mean. Bartlet said they'd never even heard of him. Henry came back the next afternoon anyway, and by then . . . well, I just never asked him about it."

"Bartlet must have gone to the wrong address," Mary said, puzzled.

"Yes, I expect that was it. I'll go with you on your walk."

"You will not. Hester, I appreciate all your attention, but I simply crave some time all by myself."

She set out, walking very slowly and carefully. She wouldn't go to the cliffs today. Later, but not today. She had an almost superstitious feeling about going back there. Instead, she set out for a clearing in the woods where she and Aunt Nell had often picnicked. She was about halfway there when

Ginger caught up with her. "Oh, Ginger! You darling thing. I haven't seen you for ages and ages," she said, stooping to pick up the cat. Hester had banished him from the sickroom, maintaining that cats carried diseases.

Ginger purred loudly and butted his head into Mary's chin, condescended to have his chin chucked, then scrambled down to attack a blade of grass with great paw-slapping skill. "Oh, I know, you're still a frisky young thing," Mary said admiringly. "Come along."

The cat followed her at enough of a distance to suggest that he just happened, by sheer coincidence, to be going the same way. When Mary got to her destination, she sat down on a long hollow log and drew a satisfied breath. She was hardly tired at all. She picked up a small dead branch and rustled it among the leaves on the ground. Ginger came flying out of nowhere and leapt on it. Mary laughed so loudly she startled a chaffinch out of a nearby tree.

"He's a fierce old thing, isn't he?" a soft voice said.

Mary turned and found she had company. A young woman in homespun garments with a fat baby in a sling across her bosom. She had pale eyes and a shy demeanor. "Hello, there. I'm Mary Beecham. I mean, Mary Turner. Would you like to sit down?"

"Thank you, ma'am, I will. I'm Betsy Whiting. I'm Mrs. Renault's granddaughter. I reckon you don't remember me."

"I'm sorry . . . I've been ill and my memory isn't all it should be."

"I wet-nursed your baby the first day. How is she getting along?"

"She died, Mrs. Whiting."

The girl put her hand to her mouth. "Oh, I'm so sorry. I didn't know. Lord, I hope it wasn't anything I did."

"No, it wasn't. Mr. Turner took her to London to see a special doctor, but she had something wrong and—"

"Yes, ma'am, I know. I went along. I'd just had little Jimmy the month before, and Mr. Turner asked me to help."

"I see. But why didn't you know she died if you went to London with her?"

"When we got there, he was gone a bit, Mr. Turner was, then the next morning another woman came. He paid me handsome, then told me to go on back home."

"That's odd. Mrs. Whiting, I don't remember my baby.

You must have known her better than I. Tell me about
her."

"Oh, ma'am, I don't know that I should say aught more.
You'll just be making yourself feel worse. I know if something happened to my Jimmy—"

"Please, Mrs. Whiting. I need to know something about
her. I have nothing of my own to store up and remember."

"Well, she was a quiet little thing. Very tiny, but perfect.
I changed her nappies and all, and she had all her little
fingers and toes and everything. I counted. Just like I did
when my Jimmy was give me."

"Did she cry?"

"No, ma'am. She was good as gold. Never fussed or
fretted at all." The girl seemed troubled.

"Did she seem sick to you?"

"Well . . . she was awfully good. Too good, if you know
what I mean. I thought then it was peculiar, how good and
quiet she was."

"How long were you with her?"

"Let's see . . . you had her round four in the afternoon, I
was told. I came that evening, then the next morning first
thing we went to London, and that next morning another
woman came. Two days, I guess."

"And she never cried that whole time?"

"Never once. You're looking pale, ma'am. Do you want
me to go up to the house and get your people for you?"

"No, thank you, Mrs. Whiting. I'm fine. I'll just sit here a
little longer and then my cat and I will go back."

"I'm sorry as sorry to be the one to have to tell you all
this."

"I'm grateful. You mustn't worry that you've upset me.
I'm tough as old leather."

Betsy Whiting and her baby went along, Ginger following
to see them off. Mary sat thinking for a long time. The story
the girl had told had upset her, but it had also piqued her
curiosity. There was something very odd about it all. Why
had Henry taken her all the way to London, then replaced
her with another wet-nurse? And why was Molly such an
unusually well-behaved baby?

She asked Henry about it when he returned the next day.
"I met Betsy Whiting in the woods the other day when I
went for a walk. The girl you took to London with Molly."

"Yes?"

"Why did you send her back and hire someone else?"

"She was so talkative she was annoying me beyond measure," Henry said. "Of course, I was so distraught I suppose anyone would have."

"Betsy Whiting, talkative? She seemed very quiet to me."

"Let's don't talk about it, Mary."

"I have to, Henry. Where's Molly buried?"

"That's an odd question."

"It's a perfectly natural question. I'd like to visit her grave when I'm well enough to go to town."

"You'd just upset yourself needlessly. Mary, you have to just forget all about her. She's not buried in London anyway. I took her to the family cemetery in Yorkshire."

"When—exactly—did she die. And how?"

"Mary, I won't indulge you in this morbid curiosity. It's not good for you. It avails you nothing. I'm going to ask Dr. Engle to see you again. I'm sure when you feel better you'll be able to put this all behind you as if it never happened."

"As if it never happened? Henry, we had a daughter. A living, breathing daughter. How could you expect me to forget?"

"I don't mean you should forget. I know that's impossible. But you must stop dwelling on it."

"Henry, I can't. I must know about her death. Otherwise, it's as if she isn't really dead." As she spoke, the words cut through her like a knife. That *was* what was troubling her, and she'd never realized it until she heard herself speak the words. There should have been some private wrenching-away, some deep, instinctive knowledge that the baby was truly gone. But she'd never felt it.

"Mary," Henry said sternly, "I'm getting truly concerned for you."

"Is she dead, Henry? Really?"

"Of course she is. I don't want to hear any more of that kind of talk."

I don't believe him, she thought.

"Henry, why don't you stay in the Mincing Lane house when you go to London?"

"I've told you before," he said, easier now that the subject had changed. "I feel awkward there without you, and it's inconvenient to the people I have to see."

"What people are those?"

He gave her a long, cool look. "Bankers, lawyers, people who handle the family's affairs."

Mary was warned by his gaze, but couldn't let it go—quite. "The hotel where you stay, is it nice?"

"It's adequate. Why do you ask?"

"I just wondered if you actually go there."

Henry looked away thoughtfully for a long moment, then said, "Mary, you must learn to be more careful of what you say. You've been very ill. A brain fever. People might just think your wits are addled if you continue to say such strange things. Do you understand me, Mary?"

She met his politely threatening gaze, her mind in a turmoil. "Yes, I believe I do," she said.

36

Letter from Mary Beecham Turner to Elaine Turner, March 1879:

My Dearest Elaine,

What a comfort and entertainment your letters are. I don't know what I should have done all these years without them to look forward to. I've always intended to keep them carefully put away to present to you on your return as a sort of diary of your adventures. But I read and reread them until they are smudged and tattered. I'm afraid you'd be ashamed to get them back.

As for your question about my cousin Alex's visit—it didn't happen. He was to have arrived in mid-October, just for a short visit, as I told you, but as he was ready to depart, his son became very ill. He sent a message, but we had no way of knowing that as we rushed to Southampton to meet him. Much confusion and milling about and questions until All Was Revealed. Henry and I were naturally very disappointed. Another letter arrived shortly, saying the child had recovered, but by then press of business on the islands prevented Alex from coming. We're hoping this year. His letters refer more and more often to a permanent move.

Hester is at Castlemere this month and sends her love. She and Jamison are off on another of their trips in a few weeks. America again this time. As I believe I told you, they went to South

Africa last year and were gone for nearly eight months. It was the longest Hester and I had ever been apart and it was hard on both of us. This mad dashing about the world is most difficult for her. She doesn't like travel particularly, and Jamison can't be a good companion. His drinking has become, I believe, a serious problem, though she denies it vehemently. His fine looks are going. He's beginning to have a squashy, bloodshot look.

I've been very busy with spices. We've invested heavily in some property in Mexico and are growing progressively better capsicums—what most people call peppers—every year. We need not bid against other buyers for our own crops, of course, and that cuts down on the cost, but at the same time it increases the risk enormously and there have been heart-stopping rumors of bad weather from time to time. Unseasonable rain can rot tons of product in mere days, but so far the reports have been wrong or exaggerated, thank goodness.

But enough of that. This letter has a purpose I've been reluctant to put into words. I must first extract a promise from you, my dear friend. You must swear you will not tell Henry of this. I know I'm asking you to divide your loyalties, and if you cannot do so, I beg you to tear up the remaining pages of this epistle without reading them. Henry is your brother and I would understand entirely if you did not wish to accept my confidences.

I shall therefore proceed, in the hope that you are reading:

You asked in your last few letters when there were to be more little Turners and I have avoided answering the question. I must now tell you I don't believe there ever will be. To be quite frank, Henry and I haven't lived as husband and wife since Molly was born. Nearly three years now. At first he claimed only to be considerate of my delicate condition, and as you well know, I was disgustingly weak and ill for more than six months after the birth. But even when I was quite recovered, he continued to live in different rooms.

To be honest—and you will find I intend to be quite horribly honest in this plea—I was somewhat relieved at first. I knew I was not in good condition to have another child for a while and that was my only interest in marital activities. But when I tried to get him to come back to our bed, he—I don't know quite how to say this—he treated me as though my interest were practically "whorish." It was quite devastating and embarrassing and I quickly gave up my attempts.

Don't misunderstand, dear Elaine, your brother is not cruel or unkind to me. In fact, he is a gentle, considerate, and loving husband as always, save in that one respect—and one other, which I will address presently. No one who knows us would ever credit that there is a single flaw in our marriage—I hardly believe it myself. We are dearest of friends and intellectual companions and if it were not for my desire to have a family, I should be entirely satisfied.

Well, perhaps not entirely. There is something else that troubles me deeply and it is the real purpose of this letter. (I suppose you're wondering when I shall ever come to the point. Forgive me if I must sneak up on it and pounce as my old cat Ginger is wont to do. Yes, Ginger is still with me. He's determined to live to an enormous age and still frisks about as a kitten.)

Henry goes somewhere every month or so. You must know about it. As I recall, he was making these mysterious trips even during that first summer when he cataloged the library. I discovered shortly after Molly's death that he hadn't been going where he said he was. After that, I admit I checked on the destination he gave me and found that it, too, was false. I faced him with it and he was furious. It was the only time I have ever seen him lose his temper, and it was terrifying. He wasn't violent or ugly, merely so cold that I felt I had been buried in a glacier.

He told me it was simply none of my business and never would be. I imagined another woman;

in fact, I imagined another wife and perhaps
children. What else could be so important? I'm
still not sure but that this is the explanation, and
I'm turning to you for an answer. I confess I
have tried desperate measures to find out for
myself. As awful as it is of me, I have had him
followed, but he seems almost to sense the follower. He goes first to London, then always
manages to disappear, usually in a crowd.

I must, however, make a final confession that
is the most damning. I don't know quite how to
sneak up on this, so I shall tell you right out. I
don't believe my baby died a natural death. I
have no real reason for thinking this but a mother's instinct—and a few shreds of information.

First, I closely questioned the doctor who attended Molly and me. He said she was an extremely lethargic baby but had no obvious physical
deformities or ailments. Of course, he only attended her for the first afternoon and night of
her life. I must admit that he sees nothing strange
about her death. Second, Henry hired a local
wet nurse to bring the baby to London to see
another doctor, but for no apparent reason dismissed her the next day. Again, to be fair (and I
am trying to be fair), he said she annoyed him in
his distressed state. Quite a reasonable explanation, I suppose. Third, Henry refuses to tell me
which doctor this was and will not admit to a
specific burial place.

As to this last point, I understate it greatly to
say he refuses to tell me. It goes far beyond this:
on several occasions he has implied that further
inquiries on my part will result in dire consequences. The threats are very subtle and carefully
veiled, but the meaning is that he will put about
that I'm insane if I continue to question him.

Oh, Elaine, don't shake your head at this and
believe I am insane. I know my suspicions sound
deranged, but I'm not mad. I swear I'm not. But
the threats, frankly, terrify me. We both know
of men who have had wives put away, and the
more the poor dears protest their sanity, the
more insane they appear to be. It can be done; it

is done. Henry could do it. Legally, if not morally. I am known to be something of an eccentric, out of step with normal standards. It would take little to convince a judge that I'm abnormal. Moreover, Henry and I both know I would be hard pressed to maintain a dignified and reasonable composure, should it come to that.

Dear sister-in-law, what can I do? Where should I turn for answers but to you? I'm sorry to burden you with tales of your brother, but I must. My only other friend in this world is my sister, Hester, but I dare not admit a word of this to her because she would inevitably tell Jamison and he would love above all else to have me out of his way. If it ever crossed his mind that there was a way to get me locked up, he would exert every energy to make such a fate come to fruition. I fear, unreasonably, to even put these words to paper for terror that somehow he might see them and have the idea planted in his fertile mind.

Does Henry have another wife? Another woman? Another child? Has he written to you of the mysteries surrounding my little Molly's death? Was there an accident? Something he fears I would blame him for? (Don't misunderstand, I would not accuse Henry of being responsible for Molly's death—but he must have some reason for concealing the true circumstances.) Is he, in fact, planning to have me put away, as he hints? I shall not ask you the obvious question: am I insane? For I know the answer. I am *not*. I am confused, frightened, misled, and misinformed, but not insane.

I fear to send this, but I shall take my fate in my hands and do so. I beseech you to destroy this the moment you finish reading it. If you choose not to answer my questions, I shall not question you further, but please realize, dear friend, that I am desperate for enlightenment. And only you can provide it.

> Your loving sister-in-law,
> Mary Beecham Turner

Letter from Elaine Turner to Mary Beecham Turner, May 1879:

> My dearest friend,
> Your letter has torn my heart in two. I know nothing of your child's death but what you your-self have told me. Of the other, I have sworn to Henry that I shall not reveal what he wishes to conceal. I cannot break that promise. I can say this, however: ask him about our brother. His name is Franklin. I cannot say how much I re-gret that I cannot tell you more.
> Your eternal friend,
> Elaine Turner

Mary's impulse was to run and find Henry and shout, "Franklin? What about Franklin?" But she managed to control herself and keep quiet for several weeks. Mean-while, she searched through her memory for anything she might have heard about a brother. She had a faint memory of either Elaine or Henry saying there was a brother who had died. But Elaine had mentioned him in the present tense. Was the error in Elaine's grammar or Mary's own memory?

Mary tore Elaine's note into tiny scraps and burned them. She silently puzzled over the message for three weeks. Henry usually left on his mysterious journeys on Mondays. On the Monday when he came to breakfast in his traveling clothes, Mary felt her heart give a lurch. She managed to talk pleasantly to him and pretend to read the newspaper as he passed her pages. When he finally rose to leave the table, she took a deep breath and said, "Henry? Are you going somewhere?"

"Yes, up to London."

"To visit Franklin?"

There was a paralyzed silence. "Franklin?"

"Your brother, Franklin," Mary said matter-of-factly.

"My brother died years ago." He spoke blandly.

"No, he's living and you visit him every month," Mary said bravely. She wasn't at all sure she had it right, but she was sure that nothing but a strong bluff would work.

He sat back down heavily. "Elaine promised she'd never tell anyone."

So it was true! "She felt I had the right to know," Mary said, and thought: *Forgive me, Elaine.*

Henry got up again, looking ten years older, and paced back and forth across the room several times. Eventually he spoke. "Then you might as well know the worst of it. Get your things and come with me."

Mary had a thousand questions, but sensed that she must not ask any of them. Henry's state was as fragile as a house of cards right now. A single wrong word might bring the whole structure down—on her. She hurried to her room and packed an overnight bag and came back downstairs.

"You won't need that," Henry said listlessly. "Leave it."

But he was always gone for at least two days. Still, she didn't argue. Henry had sent the driver of their small open carriage back to the stables and took the reins himself. She sat beside him, silent, trembling with curiosity. He drove for several hours and they exchanged hardly a dozen words. At one point he stopped at an inn at a crossroads and got them tea, which they drank together as strangers. Mary hurried inside to use the facilities, afraid Henry might actually be gone when she returned. But he was there, sitting erect and remote. Finally he turned down a country lane.

Were they nearly there—wherever "there" was? If so, it was only a half-day from Castlemere. All those trips clear to London were for the purpose of evading a possible follower. Mary had been right that he feared detection. As if reading her thoughts, Henry suddenly said, "He moved here just before we married. He used to be in Scotland."

"Yes, I see," Mary answered. She didn't see at all, but was afraid to show ignorance.

They turned into a long private drive and approached a tall iron fence with spikes at the top. A man sitting high in a gatehouse climbed down and unlocked the gates. They rolled through and he relocked them behind the carriage. As they neared the building she could glimpse through the leaves, she saw two men sitting out in a sunny patch in wooden chairs. Their legs were tied to the chair legs. Mary suddenly felt a blanket of fear fall over her. This was an institution of some kind.

An asylum!

And she was now locked on the inside of it.

Had she played into Henry's hands? Had she sealed her own fate? Was that why he'd told her not to bring a bag? He'd threatened to impugn her sanity; perhaps this was the culmination of those threats. Dear God, she'd just docilely ridden along like a goat to market! She considered leaping down from the moving carriage and escaping. But escaping to where? A nimble man couldn't climb that fence; she wouldn't make it halfway. No. She had to behave sanely even though her heart was hammering at the top of her head.

"The grounds here are very attractive," she said as the first step in her campaign to appear utterly normal.

He turned and smiled slightly at her. It made her arms and legs feel numb.

They pulled up in front of the large vine-covered brick building which had once been a grand home and now had thick bars at the windows and neglected shrubbery trying to obscure the lower floor. Mary nearly fell getting out of the carriage. Henry caught her, set her on her feet, and said, "Careful."

She very nearly threw herself at him and begged to be taken away, but he didn't give her time. Taking her elbow firmly, he led her to the front door. A huge man with a nearly bald head and a black eye that was turning green and yellow opened it. " 'Afternoon, sir. Ma'am," he said.

Henry nodded to him. Mary did the same, though her neck almost cracked with the effort. They ascended a long curving staircase with fraying carpet and dust balls gathering in the corners. At the top, Henry guided her along a wide hallway lined with closed doors. Mary noticed that most of them had heavy locks. They turned into another corridor and reached another flight of stairs. At the top of these they were once again in a door-lined hallway. Oddly, the further they ascended, the darker and gloomier it became. These doors were all bolted and they had the bottom six inches or so cut off. A few battered tin trays sat in the hallway and Mary realized the doors were made so these could slide underneath.

A slovenly woman sat on a wooden chair at the end of the hall under a dust-coated window. She rose when they approached. "Been real quiet of late, yer honor," she said to Henry. "Don't know but what yer wasting yer money on them mattresses and clothes and like, though. He just tears 'em up soon as he gets 'em."

Mary realized she'd been holding her breath. They were talking about a man. Not about her. Thank God she hadn't acted the lunatic and tried to escape in the driveway.

"My duty is to provide for him. What he does with what I provide doesn't matter," Henry said. "Open the door, please. My wife wants to meet her brother-in-law."

The woman stared at Mary with a sly, mocking look. "Better her than me, yer honor."

She went back along the hall, sorting through a ring of keys. She tugged on one of the heavy wooden doors, which opened out. Inside was another door made of bars of metal. The attendant moved away and Henry gestured to Mary to look in.

She was aware of the smell before she saw him. The room reeked of urine and excrement. The odor enveloped her and she quickly put a handkerchief to her nose and tried not to gag. The room was almost bare. There was a bookshelf, but it was bare of books or ornaments. A mattress was on a single frame, but there were no sheets and the mattress itself was shredded and bits of stuffing littered the floor. Hooks on the wall showed where pictures had once hung. There were runny stains on the wall where someone had apparently thrown food or drink.

A man was huddled by the small window. He wore only rags that had once been trousers, and a single shoe. His hair was medium length, but tangled and wild. As she stared at him, he looked up. The features were Henry's, but not Henry's. The eyes were wider apart, the mouth slack. His expression, though alarmingly blank, managed also to be malignant.

"Franklin . . ." she said softly, thinking she might reach whatever mind existed in there.

The man—her brother-in-law—rose slowly, with cautious feral movements, and came toward the door. The smell grew stronger. "Franklin, my name is Mary," she said very gently. And as she spoke, she put her hand through the bars.

"Mary, no!" Henry said, but the words were hardly out of his mouth before Franklin lunged forward with the speed of a great cat and pulled her arm. He jerked it toward him. Mary was slammed forward against the bars, cracking her temple and bruising her breast.

As Henry grabbed her to pull her away, Franklin bit into the flesh at the side of her hand. She screamed and fought, and at the sound, Franklin dropped her hand and ran to the far corner of his filthy cell.

Mary fell against Henry, her hand gushing blood and her

vision blurring with the impact to her head. Henry scooped her up. She must have fainted, for when she was next aware of her surroundings, she was in the carriage, lying on her side with her head on Henry's leg. Her hand had been bound in clean white bandages. The carriage was moving very slowly.

"Henry?" she said struggling to sit up.

"Lie still," he said, patting her shoulder gently. "I should have warned you. I'll never forgive myself. It was selfish and ugly of me. I just wanted you to be shocked. I should have looked out for your safety. Just rest, Mary."

She obeyed him for a while, then, once they were outside the hateful locked gates, said quietly, "I lied to you, Henry. Elaine didn't tell me. She only mentioned his name. I pretended to know the rest."

He stroked her arm. "It doesn't matter anymore. Don't let it trouble your conscience."

They rode the rest of the way back in silence, but it was the silence of peace. When they got back to Castlemere it was dusk. Henry took Mary to the big master suite and removed the bandages from her hand. "It's not nearly as bad as it first looked," he assured her. "How is your head?"

"It only hurts a bit," she lied.

"Would you like a dinner tray up here?" he asked solicitously.

"No. If you'll just ask Bartlet to wait dinner until I bathe and change, I'd prefer to have a normal evening."

"Nothing will ever be normal again," Henry said.

"Of course it will. Everything is going to be better than ever now. I promise you."

Henry didn't seem to hear her. "I'll send Agnes up to help you."

"No, I'm fine." The moment he was out of the room, she stripped off her clothing. In spite of the long ride in the open air, she could still smell the stench of the asylum on the cloth.

They both picked at dinner, and the minute it was cleared, they went to the library. Henry sat down at the desk and Mary silently took a chair across from him. "He's four years younger than I am," he began abruptly, as if determined to get the story out as quickly and efficiently as he could. "He was born defective. From his birth on, they told my mother he would never be normal. She loved him the more for needing her love. She spoiled him, indulged him in everything he wanted. I know that's the way of mothers. She couldn't be faulted for it. But by the time he was four or five, he was uncontrollable. It made childhood a living hell for Elaine and me. He attacked her when he was only seven. A dinner knife. He stabbed her with a dinner knife—and Mother comforted him when Elaine screamed with pain."

Henry was fiddling with a letter opener as he spoke. He suddenly realized what was in his hands and put it aside. "We never told anyone about him. When company came, he was locked up in a far wing of the house, but it destroyed my mother to do that, so before long it became the rule that there simply weren't guests at Denby Hall. Ever. Alex never even knew about him, and Alex was about the closest friend I had."

"Alex wouldn't have liked you less, Henry. Neither do I."

Again Henry acted as if he hadn't heard her. He was resolved to tell the story and get it over with. "When Franklin was fourteen, mother died of pneumonia. Nobody could reach him then. He never spoke, only garbled nonsense that Mother alone understood. With her gone, nobody understood. Father hired two men to be his keepers and companions. One day when he was sixteen, he indicated to one of them that he wanted the candy the man was eating. The keeper told him no and he killed the man."

"No!"

"In a single blow. Then he attacked the other man, who'd come to the aid of his coworker. Franklin strangled him to death." He was telling the story in a curiously flat tone, as though it weren't quite real, but the dead white of his face testified to the reality and the pain it caused him to tell Mary. "Father had him put in an asylum. It was the only thing to do. They're equipped to handle such violence. We couldn't have any other deaths on our heads. Father died five years ago and I took over responsibility. I can't help him."

"You do all you can. Henry, you sound like you think this is somehow your fault. You must know it isn't."

He looked up at her. "It's odd you'd use that phrase. You see, it *is* my fault—not in the sense of being to blame, but in the sense of carrying the fault. It's inherited. My mother had an older sister who was the same way. That's why Elaine has never married. It's why I didn't intend to, but I loved you too much for my own good or yours."

"Henry, it was coincidence about your aunt and your

brother. You and Elaine are completely normal. I think you're—"

"Molly wasn't."

The words froze in Mary's mouth. "What?" she finally gasped.

"She had it too. That's why I took her away. I could tell the first time I looked in her tiny face. And I knew you would love her like my mother loved my brother. Without the mother's love and spoiling, a person like that might not become violent. She might—"

"Are you saying Molly *is* alive?"

Henry looked up at her, squinting slightly as if against a harsh light—or a great pain. "Of course. You didn't think I could let her die, did you? She's our daughter. Yours and mine."

"Where is she?" Mary was trying to control her voice, but she could hardly get her breath.

"With some nice people. They'll be good to her without being *too* good. I chose them very carefully."

"What people, Henry? Where is my baby? Where's Molly?"

He said nothing. Mary stood, leaned across the desk, and grasped his hand with her bandaged one. "Henry, you must tell me. She's my child. *You have to tell me where my baby is!*"

He looked up at her again. "Yes, I suppose I must," he said listlessly. "I'll take you to her tomorrow."

"Now, Henry. Right now."

Rubbing his temples, he said, "Tomorrow. I promise. But, Mary, go away now. I'm too tired, too sick to talk anymore."

She knew he meant it; he'd been pushed as far as he could be. She wanted to shake the rest of the truth out of him, but sensed it couldn't be done. Not tonight. "Very well, Henry. But we will leave at dawn."

There was no reply. She went slowly toward the door, and as she opened it he said, "Mary, it was all because I love you so much. And her. And Molly too."

"I know, Henry," she said, and in a strange way she knew it was true. He was a good man who had done a terrible thing because it was the only thing he knew to do. They'd go get her in the morning and she'd prove to Henry that she could raise her own child without turning her into a monster like the one she'd met earlier in the day.

She was just stepping into the master suite when she heard the gunshot.

At first she thought the sound came from outside, but in seconds she heard footsteps and shouting downstairs. A door slammed and someone screamed. She ran back down the stairs. Tripping on her skirts, she nearly tumbled, then caught herself and continued. But the fall had slowed her down. By the time she reached the library, the hall was full of servants. Bartlet was standing outside the door and a maid was sitting on the floor sobbing, "Oh, it's too awful. Too awful!"

"Bartlet, let me in that room."

"No, ma'am."

"I must go to my husband."

"It's too late, ma'am."

She flung herself at Bartlet. "Too late? Too late! No, no, no! He didn't tell me yet. He didn't tell me where Molly is. He has to tell me. Henry! Henry," she screamed, trying in vain to get past Bartlet, "tell me, Henry. Tell me! *Tell me.*"

37

"Poor Henry, almost no one of his own to mourn him," Mary said to Winston Foxworth-Wilding.

"He had only Elaine and this brother you told me about, didn't he?" Winston asked, pouring her a cup of tea.

She was sitting at the desk where, a few nights earlier, Henry Turner had put a gun in his mouth and pulled the trigger. Mary was dressed in widow's black, her hair dragged into a severe knot at the back of her neck. For the first time he could remember, she actually looked her age. A new sort of maturity had replaced the childlike innocence in her face. It was be no means unattractive, but he regretted the sorrow that had brought about the change.

"As far as I know. There was that cousin who came to the funeral and wouldn't even stay the afternoon," Mary said. "I believe he blamed me. How little he knew. And Elaine won't know for weeks yet. I posted a letter to her yesterday. I didn't quite tell her the truth; I didn't want her to feel she had any part in his death. I said someone I'd hired found out where he went before I received her letter. No reason for her to suffer any more than she is bound to. She and Henry were very close. I didn't write another word about Molly to her."

Winston realized she was talking just to fill the void. The funeral that morning had been a pathetic affair. Mary's business advisers had attended in lieu of family—Hester and Jamison were in America—and a few local people had come out of respect for Mary herself. And there was also the one Turner cousin, a sour young man. A sad little turnout for tortured Henry Turner.

Mary looked down at the desk. "I searched it inch by inch the next morning. The desk. He was here alone for a few minutes and I hoped he'd left some sort of message. It wasn't until early this morning that I realized that he'd shot himself for that very reason—so he wouldn't have to tell me where Molly is. I believe he sensed that my desperation to know would have overcome his reluctance to tell me. So he had to die to keep his secret."

She paused for a long time. "Damn him."

"What now?" Winston asked.

Mary looked up. "Now I find out. She cannot have disappeared without a trace. I've been thinking about his brother. He put him away, but did his best to provide for him. The woman at the asylum said something about all the clothes and bedding he provided going to waste and he said it was his duty to provide it anyway. I'm sure he would have done no less for his own child. You see, Winston, he did love her and want the best for her. He just felt, with his mother as the worst sort of example, that any mother would turn such a child into a monster like his brother."

"Are you sure he was wrong?"

"Winston! What a cruel thing to say!"

"Perhaps, but you must consider it nonetheless. What if Henry were right? I think you might be a terribly indulgent mother. Could you deny a child for its own good? Especially a child whose needs and disadvantages were far, far greater than most?"

"Of course I could. I'm not a fool. Will you help me?"

"I don't know. I'm not certain you're doing the right thing."

Mary leaned back and sighed. "Nor am I, Winston. But I'm certain I must find her. I must. There will be a record somewhere. I've asked his banker and attorney to bring down all the documents they can put their hands to."

"Mary, we're discussing a man who went to a great deal of trouble to make sure he wasn't followed when he went to visit his brother. Do you suppose he just wrote out monthly checks to someone 'for maintaining Molly Turner'? You know better."

She looked up at him and smiled faintly. "There's no victory in winning with a good hand. Aunt Nell taught me that. Henry can't have hidden my daughter so well that I can't find her. You see, I have hopes that . . . No, never mind. You'll just scoff at me if I say it."

"Probably so. When has that ever stopped you?"

"I hope he was wrong. About there being something

wrong with her. He was obsessed with the subject. Just before he died, he claimed he knew the first time he looked at her. I don't believe he knew; he merely feared to see some defect and imagined it was there."

"Oh, Mary! You're going miles out of your way to make yourself even unhappier than you are. Don't get such hopes up. Let me have these papers you get and I'll do your searching."

"No."

"Don't you trust me?"

"I trust you to protect me—like Henry did. I cannot bear any more protection. I must have the truth. All of it."

It took her three months.

Henry's family's business concerns were far more wide-ranging and complex than she would ever have imagined. She had to learn a great deal to even begin her search. Clue after clue came to nothing. She made a journey to France to pursue the destination of a small monthly payment, only to find it was his continuation of a bizarre little legacy his grandmother had left to a convent that supported two elderly nuns on the benefice.

Another line of inquiry led through two lawyers and a bank in Canterbury, only to end with a horse surgeon who had once been severely injured by a kick in the ribs while treating one of the Turners' animals. It seemed Henry was devious even when there was absolutely no reason. His money ran in curious channels, sometimes flowing together with Elaine's inheritance in such a way that it was nearly impossible to unravel. "Never mind sorting out which is hers," Mary told the lawyer she'd hired to help her. "I want her to have all of it."

She discovered that Henry was in the habit of transferring large sums of cash from one bank to another for no apparent reason, and Mary investigated every one of these from the date of Molly's birth onward. One extremely large draft seemed the answer, until she traced it to the asylum where Franklin was incarcerated.

"That's why there was no legacy to him in Henry's will," Mary told Winston. "He put him there before our marriage, but apparently didn't decide that was where he would stay until much later. He put a large amount into a trust. I suppose it was so that I would never know. I'm sure he's done the same for Molly, but I've hunted down nearly every penny from the very day of her birth on and there's no sign of it."

"What will you do now?"

"I'll work backward."

"What do you mean?"

"Back as far as I can go. I won't find Molly, of course, but the challenge of unraveling all this mad complexity has got a terrible hold on me. You see, it could be something he put away for another reason before her birth and simply designated a new purpose without its showing on the subsequent records."

In a way, that turned out to be the truth of it. A substantial sum, even by Henry's standards, turned up in the record six months before Molly's birth. It had been paid to a Mr. Jones and deposited in a bank in Inverness. Mary wrote and inquired of the circumstances of deposit and disposition of the money. The reply was vague. Mr. Jones had turned power of attorney for the account over to a local lawyer. They were not at liberty to say more. She wrote to the attorney they mentioned. His reply was so very circumspect that it rang an alarm bell in the back of Mary's mind. She knew it could have nothing directly to do with Molly, since the sum was transferred so long before her birth, but mentioned it to Winston as another of Henry's curiosities.

"I'm going to Inverness next Tuesday anyway," he said. "I'll see if I can find out anything about it, if you want."

Mary put the matter out of her mind until Winston returned from his trip. He called on her at Castlemere and was uncharacteristically serious. "You remember Mr. Jones?" he asked.

Mary was picking some of the last of the summer's roses. She sat down with her basket and shears on a chair next to Winston. "Mr. Jones? Oh, yes. The mysterious man in Inverness."

"I made inquiries. Rather devious ones, if not downright fraudulent, actually. I have grave doubts about telling you this . . . but Mr. Jones was Henry himself. He went there to interview people and set up a trust fund for a family he selected—for Molly to live with."

"What? Wait. This can't be right. The money was paid out months and months before she was born."

"Yes, it was," Winston said gravely.

"I don't see . . . Do you mean he made arrangements to give her to someone even before she was born!"

"Only conditionally. I'm only telling you this because I believe something you said the day of his funeral may be right. He made these arrangements because he *expected* that there would be something wrong with the child. You may be correct in hoping that he only imagined he discerned the family fault."

"Winston! Have you seen her?"

"No. I was afraid to—afraid I'd feel compelled to keep the information from you if I did. I don't think I could stand keeping such an important secret from you."

"But you know where she is?"

He handed her a slip of paper. "This is the name of the people she's with. The Stotts."

Mary leapt up, scattering roses. "I must go!"

"Calm down. I've bought your train tickets and told Agnes to pack for you. The train leaves in an hour."

"Oh, Winston! I can't believe it. I can have my baby home with me in a few days. It's too wonderful for words! How will I ever thank you, you dear, dear friend?"

"Mary, you may not want to. I don't know if I've performed a service or committed a crime." He took her by the shoulders. "Mary, I'll be at my London house. Ready to come to you if you need me."

"Don't be so glum. It's grand. My Molly. My own baby Molly. What do you suppose she looks like? Oh, dear. *I* look like a gardener. I must dress. There's so much to do . . ."

Mary was still almost breathless with excitement when she reached Inverness, though there had been a few dark intervals when she reflected on just what Henry had done. All those months while she was eagerly awaiting the birth of their child, he had already made arrangements to take it from her. She tried to understand, to sympathize with the terrible fear that had made him do such a thing, but she couldn't. All she could think of were the precious years of her baby's growing up that she'd missed.

She hired a driver to drop Agnes and the luggage off at the inn Winston had recommended, then proceeded a mile or two out of town to the home of Gerald and Elvira Stott. It turned out to be a rambling stone farmhouse with laundry strung on a line across the side yard and pretty beds of flowers around the front. A toy wagon was parked on the front step and Mary could see a rope swing tied in a big oak tree. There was a cheerful, homey sloppiness about the place. A plump woman in her late thirties came to Mary's knock on the door. She had a scarf tied around her head and held a broom. A little boy with a thatch of blond hair hung on her skirts. "Yes, ma'am? Can I help you?" the woman said with a welcoming smile.

"Mrs. Stott? I'm Mary Turner. I believe you have my daughter."

The broom fell against the doorframe and Elvira Stott put her hand on the little boy's head. "Mrs. Turner? But I thought . . . Mr. Turner said . . ."

"He said I didn't know about her, or you. Yes. But Mr. Turner died several months ago. Please, Mrs. Stott, I must see my child. I've come to take her home with me."

"Oh . . ." The expression of loss on her face was all the proof Mary needed that Henry had indeed chosen well. "She's gone down to the creek with Teddy and Margo. They ought to be back anytime. Will you have some tea while we wait?"

Mary had to content herself with a few more minutes' delay. Elvira Stott served a fine tea in a spotless parlor. "Forgive me if I've not been mannerly, Mrs. Turner. It's all such a shock. I'd honestly forgotten that Moll was someone else's child. She's so much a part of our family. I don't know how we'll get along without her. She's such a dear baby."

"She's . . . she's normal, then?"

Elvira Stott set down her teacup gently. "Normal? You mean you didn't know? Oh, Mrs. Turner—!"

At that moment the back door opened and there was the sound of children's voices. A girl of about ten came skidding into the room. "Mama, you should have seen the deer we— Oh, I'm sorry." She dropped a polite curtsy to Mary.

"Margo, this is Mrs. Turner," Mrs. Stott said.

Behind her, a lanky boy who looked to be nearly twenty came in with a tiny redheaded girl on his shoulders. "Teddy, this is Mrs. Turner," Elvira told him. "She's come to see Moll."

He reached up and grabbed the little girl at the waist. She was hanging on to his hair, but he got her to turn loose by putting his mouth against her bare leg and blowing to make a loud noise. She giggled as he set her down.

Mary was transfixed by Molly. She was very small, very delicate, and had very, very red hair and blue eyes. Mary could hardly get her breath. This is my child, she kept thinking. My pretty child. My Molly.

The boy Teddy gave Molly a little shove in the back. "Meet the nice lady, Moll."

Molly turned, instead, and hugged his legs.

Elvira went over and picked her up. "She's sometimes shy of strangers, Mrs. Turner. Here, Moll, be a good girl . . ." Molly had grabbed Elvira's blouse and was trying to hide. She was starting to whimper. "Now, now. None of that, pet," Elvira told her firmly. She sat back down in a chair across the room and made Molly turn around and face Mary. The child looked terrified.

Mary rose and went to her, but before she could get close, Molly's face twisted into a mask of terror. She let out a horrible scream and twisted around to hide in Elvira's bosom. "I can't imagine what's wrong. She's normally so cheerful. It may be your dress. Black and all. She's never seen anyone in mourning," the woman explained.

"I understand. I'm new to her. I'll just sit here quietly," Mary said. She was nearly choking on her words. She wanted to snatch Molly away and wrap her arms around her. She longed to feel that small body against hers and blot her tears as a mother should.

But Molly wouldn't be comforted. Finally Teddy took her out to the kitchen for a cookie. "It may take a bit of time, Mrs. Turner," Elvira Stott said. "Of course, you're within your rights to take her away now—"

"No, of course I wouldn't. She's frightened of me. I'll wait until she's used to me. Mrs. Stott, I need to know what arrangements my husband made with you for her care. I wouldn't want to deprive you of anything."

Elvira gave her a politely reproachful look as if to say: What more could you deprive us of? "Your husband has been very generous, more than we ever asked or expected. He gave us this farm and the house outright, and quarterly we receive a stipend for her food and clothes. We don't use it. It goes right back to the bank. You may have it back, if you like. As for her future, Teddy and the girl he's to marry come winter will care for her when Gerald and I are gone. They're both very fond of her and very patient and will be good . . . Oh, I guess I'm talking out of turn. What I mean to say is, those *were* our plans."

"Mrs. Stott, you've cared for my child with love and excellent care. I can see that very well. I don't want to hurt you, any of you. I won't hurry your family or Molly. If I seemed abrupt when I arrived, it's just that I've waited so terribly long."

"I understand that. I truly do. I'd feel the same way if she were mine. Mrs. Turner, why don't you come back for dinner and let Moll get used to seeing you here. And if you don't think it would be too disrespectful of Mr. Turner's memory, would you mind wearing something else? A nice red or yellow dress, if you have one. Molly loves bright colors."

"Of course. Thank you for telling me. I feel so empty and foolish, not knowing anything about her. I appreciate anything you can tell me."

But the red dress, hastily purchased, didn't do the trick. Molly wouldn't eat her dinner, or even willingly stay in the same room with Mary. Shaken, Mary returned to the inn and cried half the night. The next day, when she returned to the Stott farm, she didn't go inside. "She's so fearful of being in the same room, I thought perhaps the outdoors might seem safer to her," she said to Elvira.

"An excellent idea. I'll have Gerald put some chairs in the shade for us."

Molly stayed as far away as she could. Once she started to wander off. Teddy called to her to come back, and when she kept going, he caught up with her and gave her a sharp smack on the bottom. Mary started to rise and Elvira put a hand on her arm. "Best not to interfere, Mrs. Turner."

"But he struck the child. My child!"

Elvira didn't take offense. "Yes. Sometimes it's the only way to make a point with her. It didn't hurt her. He'd sooner die than harm her, but she must learn to mind him. He's her future—or he was to have been. You'll have to be very firm with her, Mrs. Turner. What it takes another child ten times to learn, it takes her a hundred times. Or more. Some things she refuses to learn—or can't. We don't know which it is."

"Does she talk yet?"

Elvira shook her head as if mildly surprised that Mary would even ask. "She talks something. It has the cadence of English, but none of the words."

"But she's more than three years old. Will she learn to speak?"

Elvira Stott shrugged in a way that indicated loving unconcern. "Perhaps."

They watched her play for a long while. Mary marveled at

how good Elvira's children were to Molly. She was clumsy and didn't seem to understand most of what they were doing and saying, but they were never unpleasant to her. When she tried to take the littlest boy's wagon away, he slapped her hands. She started to cry and he patted her softly on the head, but he kept the wagon. When she walked in front of the rope swing, Margo took a fairly bad fall to avoid colliding with her, then patiently waited until Molly went on to resume.

At one point Molly stumbled into a tree and bumped her head. She started to run to Elvira for comfort, but saw Mary sitting near her and veered away. Mary waited until Molly was engrossed in drawing in a patch of dry soil with a stick, then slowly rose and began to approach her. She'd never even seen her own child close up without Molly being in tears. She'd edged up to about ten feet away when Molly noticed her. Her eyes went very wide and she dropped the stick. Her underlip stuck out for a moment, then she burst into sobs.

Teddy came on the run. Picking her up, he said, "I'm sorry, Mrs. Turner. She just doesn't know you're her mother. Ma is the only mother she knows."

So Elvira had told the other children who she was. "Teddy, do you think if you held her, she'd let me come closer?"

"Let's see. Moll, old girl, get your face around here. The nice lady just wants to see how pretty you are."

But Molly just wailed so loudly and violently that Mary became alarmed at her crimson face. She backed away and returned to where Elvira was still sitting. "Don't take it personally. She'll probably take to you before long."

"It's so hard . . ." Mary said, looking away so that the other woman wouldn't see the tears pouring down her face.

Worse was to come. Late in the morning a man came to the house to deliver a package. Molly was playing with a doll next to the path to the front door. The man leaned down and patted her on the head. Scooting away a foot or so, Molly went back to her doll. "Does she know him?" Mary asked.

Elvira chuckled. "I hope not. I don't. He must be new to town."

She didn't realize that her words had cut a slice through Mary's heart. It wasn't strangers that frightened the child—it was Mary specifically.

Late that afternoon, Molly disappeared. One minute she

was playing in the midst of the other children, the next she was simply gone. The family seemed to have a drill ready for such a thing. Elvira and the children quickly fanned out to check the creek, the well, a steep ditch, the barn loft—all the most dangerous spots first. Within ten minutes Teddy returned with her from behind the barn, where he'd found her sitting and sucking her thumb. "She hasn't done that for months," Elvira said with disappointment.

Mary came back again the next day. And the next. And the next. "She's not getting any better—about me. Is she?" she asked Elvira finally.

"I'd like to lie to you," Elvira said. "But, no, she isn't. Her behavior is getting worse too."

"Besides the thumb-sucking?"

"General naughtiness. Nightmares. She's not eating right either."

Mary was watching Molly walk across the lawn. The child kept glancing uneasily over her shoulder at Mary. She looked more than frightened. She looked haunted. "I wanted her to love me," Mary said bleakly.

"She should. You're a good person. You'd be a good mother to her," Elvira said, knowing exactly where this was leading. "I'm sorry."

"You're the better one," Mary said. "Let me just stay the rest of today."

"You're welcome to stay as long as you want."

"No. It's selfish of me to even stay this long. My very presence harms her. Teddy and his wife will take good care of her . . . ?"

"The best care in the world. He loves her as dearly as if she were his own, and she adores him."

"You can't imagine . . ." Mary paused, trying to get a grip on herself. "You can't know how much this hurts me."

Elvira put her hand over Mary's. "It's just that we're where she started. If she'd stayed with you, it might be us she'd fear. I know that's little comfort now, but it's the truth."

"Is there anything I can do for her? Or for you?" Mary asked.

"Pray," Elvira Stott replied.

"Please pack our things. We'll leave as soon as we can get away," Mary told Agnes when she got back to the inn.

She sat down on the edge of her bed with a handkerchief balled up in her fist.

The maid looked at her mistress's tear-ravaged face. "The little girl . . . ?"

"She's staying here," Mary said. "Where she belongs. Oh, Agnes . . ."

Agnes sat down and took Mary Turner in her plump arms and rocked and soothed her just as she had the day the scrawny child had come to Castlemere.

38

April 1880

The sounds of the party insinuated themselves through the closed door. Hester Beecham Hewitt crossed her arms on the dressing table and laid her head on them for a moment, being careful not to muss her hair. She was so tired; always so tired. This was the second time this month for one of these house parties. If Jamison had his way entirely, there would always be crowds of his friends at Castlemere. His raucous, high-living, hard-drinking friends. That way he'd never have to sit across from her at the long dining table and simply make conversation with his wife.

She lifted her head and looked at the mirror. No wonder he felt that way. If only she could be a beauty; then he'd love her. Beauty and spirit were everything to Jamison. She could—and did—pretend spirit. That was what exhausted her. But she couldn't pretend beauty. If she could, she would. For him. For his love. *I'm only twenty-five*, she thought miserably. *What will I look like at forty?*

Pinching color into her sallow cheeks, she rose and went back to the party. There was a tiny unused minstrel gallery that overlooked the ballroom, and she ducked in there for a moment instead of passing. Looking down, she could see Jamison moving around through the swarms of guests. He had a drink in his hand. When *didn't* he have a drink in his hand? But it was early evening and he wasn't drunk yet. He never got really drunk until ten o'clock or so. The rest of the day, from the time he got up in the late morning, he was merely drinking. Ale, beer, wine, sherry, brandy, Scotch—whatever was closest at hand.

Mary had put the cellars under lock and key years ago, the very day after Portia's funeral. "The Castlemere cellars belong to Alex. I won't have Jamison sloshing his way through them and Alex getting only the dregs when he comes back," she'd said. But it hadn't made any difference. Jamison merely ordered crates of his own supplies.

Hester looked down at him with a potent mixture of love and hate. The drinking was starting to harm his looks. He'd probably grow fat and bleary and red-nosed when he got older. But for now, he was as handsome as ever to her. As she watched, he set his drink down with a languid gesture to dance with a girl named Mildred Devane, the daughter of some London friend of his. This was the third time Milly and her father had been on the guest list in the last few months. Hester thought Miss Devane was a trashy sort of girl—an embarrassingly generous bosom, flashing eyes, sultry manners. But Hester went along with the pretense of liking her because Jamison expected it of her. Hester tried to go along with everything Jamison wanted.

Milly Devane glanced up and spotted her in the gallery. She said something to Jamison with a sly smile and he looked up too. Hester forced herself to look bright and amused and waved gaily at them. They both looked away.

Hester left the gallery and went downstairs. She crossed paths with Mary at the foot of the steps. "There you are, Hester. I've been looking everywhere for you," her sister said briskly. Did Mary always have to be so energetic and forceful? When they had returned from America last October she'd seemed extraordinarily subdued—because of Henry's death, Hester assumed—but she had gradually come back to being just as bossy and sure of herself as always.

"Yes?" Hester asked, knowing Mary wouldn't seek her out except to complain about something. What was it this time?

"Hester, you must make your husband stop fondling that Devane girl in public. Castlemere isn't a brothel, as he seems to think. It's disgraceful the people he insists on inviting here. Her father's no better. The man is nothing but a garden-grade gambler. He never looks a woman in the face. Only her bosom. Haven't you noticed?"

"Not having much of a bosom, I haven't."

Mary looked at her sharply. "No need to be that way with me, Hester. I'm only concerned with how Jamison's behavior and choice of friends reflect on you and on Castlemere. You must not forget this is Alex's home now and Alex's reputation at stake, even if he's not here yet. But he'll be back very soon to stay. It's time to take this seriously. Now, are you going to talk to him or shall I?"

If she could only get a few good nights' sleep, she'd feel up to this sort of thing. "Yes, yes. I'll talk to him," she said wearily.

"You're not sickening, are you?" Mary asked, putting the back of her hand to Hester's forehead.

Hester backed away from her touch. "I'm fine."

But Mary pursued her relentlessly. "Won't you let me take you to a doctor in London as I've been asking, dear? You do look so tired and run-down."

"Will you stop clucking over me? It's most annoying!"

Mary looked hurt for a moment, but said, "Very well."

Hester found Miss Devane and Jamison at the buffet table. "Oh, Mrs. Hewitt, what a very lucky woman you are," Milly gushed.

"Am I?" Hester asked, taking a plate and putting two tiny cucumber sandwiches on it. She had no appetite, but Jamison had started making remarks about her being too thin and she was trying to force herself to eat more.

"To be married to the handsomest, most charming man in England."

"Yes, of course," Hester said, giving Jamison a smile she hoped he would return.

But his attention was on Milly Devane. "What a thing for an innocent girl to be saying! Your father will be trying to horsewhip me, next thing you know."

"I can handle a horsewhip too," she said with one of those sidelong glances that made Hester want to grab her by her perfect throat.

"Can you really?" Jamison drawled.

Something passed between them that made Hester feel giddy. Something raw and terrifying. "Jamison, I would like to have a word with you for just a moment." He didn't reply. "Jamison!"

"Yes, yes. Very well. You'll excuse us, Miss Devane?"

Hester led him to the hallway which was mercifully untenanted at the moment. "Mary says—"

He immediately threw his arms up in a gesture that knocked the small plate from Hester's hand and sent it spinning across the marble floor. "Mary says, Mary thinks, Mary wants. I don't give a goddamn what Mary says. Fuck Mary!"

He was much, much drunker than Hester had suspected.

"In this case, I agree with her. You're giving far too much attention to Miss Devane. People are noticing."

He grabbed her arm, propelling her into a darkened corner of the hallway. "People notice this house and the money we spend. That's all people notice, Hester. I could have the bitch in the middle of the ballroom and people would just dance around us, so long as we're rich."

Hester tried to keep her emotions under control. "Please don't talk that way. You've had too much to drink. You know you don't mean such an ugly thing."

"I say what I mean. You're getting to sound like Mary yourself. You'd better watch that, my dear."

He started to walk off, but Hester ran and caught his arm. "Please, Jemmy. Please don't leave me here. Let's talk. Just us. The rest of them won't even notice if we go on to our room. I want to talk to you."

"You want to nag me. I know the difference if you don't." He jerked his arm out of her grasp.

"No, Jemmy. You're wrong. I just want to be with you." She was hating herself for inflicting this self-humiliation, but couldn't stop. "Please come to bed now and forget about . . . everybody else."

"Oh, bed again. You don't want me. You just want my seed."

"Jemmy—"

"Don't 'Jemmy' me. I know what this is about. Well, I wish I could get you with child again. Believe me, I wish you had a dozen brats so you'd leave me alone."

He strode off, leaving her blinking back tears. She must not cry. It made her look ugly, and that would make him angrier. If only babies hadn't come into it again, she might have gotten him away from Milly Devane. But babies always came into the arguments, ever since the beginning of the marriage. It had gotten much worse since the last trip. If only they hadn't gone back to America again; it stirred up all the old memories for both of them.

It had been her fault, of course. At least partly her fault. She blinked again, trying hard not to remember that hideous day in Iowa or Ohio or one of those awful bleak American places the train went through on the first trip. But the memory was too vivid to push aside. It had become almost a constant companion.

She'd become ill in the morning and the train conductor had insisted that she and Jamison disembark in some godforsaken place, where she was taken to a hotel. A doctor who smelled of horses was called, and by teatime she'd miscarried. A tiny baby boy. He and the nurse with him thought she hadn't seen the body, but she had. It was smaller than most of the dolls she'd had as a child, and a terrible purplish-gray color with boy parts between the tiny, spindly legs. They didn't think she'd heard either, not even when the doctor complained, "If only that good-for-nothing bum of a husband would get up here instead of carousing around town like he owned the place."

She never knew specifically what Jamison was doing, but when he finally came back late, drunk, she was utterly distraught. She was in an agony of grief and pain. "Where have you been? You left me all alone here with these strangers. I can't even understand half of what they say. They're savages and you—"

"Don't get yourself into such a taking, as my old nurse would have said," he dismissed her with a slur in his voice.

"Taking? We've lost our child! Our son, Jemmy!"

"We'll have others. Isn't there anything in this place to drink? I think I'll just go downstairs and—"

"We'd better have others," Hester had said in a voice so shrill it stopped him at the door.

"What does that mean?" he asked.

"It means that's your job. To give me children. You've been bought and paid for, Jamison, with good Beecham cash. And that's the service you're so very generously paid to provide."

She hadn't meant a word of it. Not any more than she'd meant the awful things she said to Mary a few months earlier, but it came spewing out like acid vomit, against her will. She put her hand over her mouth, horrified at what she'd said.

"I see," he said coldly; then he suddenly lunged across the room and dragged her out of bed. Except for Portia's occasional impatient slaps, no one had ever touched her in anger, and she yelped with surprise and pain. But he hauled her to the battered dressing table and flung her at it. "Look at yourself. Just look!"

She was appalled. Could that really be her in the flyspecked mirror? Her hair was loose and still stuck to her face by dried sweat. Her skin was mottled red and white and there were dark circles under her colorless eyes, gummy and crusted from crying. She could smell the blood running down the inside of her leg, could smell her armpits, could smell her stale breath. She was disgusted.

"There isn't enough money," Jamison said coldly.

He left her crumpled there and didn't return for two days. He was beginning to sober up, but was uncontrite. She tried to tell herself he had been too drunk to remember what had been said, and since neither of them ever referred to it again, she never knew whether he remembered or not. He'd "done his duty" since then with dreary regularity. For five long years they'd had intercourse every Tuesday and Friday except when she was menstruating. On those occasions, those dreadful monthly reminders of everybody's failure, she merely said at dinner, "Not tonight," and he nodded bored understanding and looked faintly relieved.

But she didn't cry anymore. Not when he would know about it. She became a fanatic about her appearance, spending at least an hour a day on her hair and throwing away a fortune on clothing that looked awful on her no matter what she paid for it. And when she was around him, she was unfailingly cheerful. Pretty is as pretty does, her governess had told her. If she acted pretty, maybe Jamison would come to see her that way.

Now she had ruined all her good work by acting jealous and ugly about Milly Devane. It was all Mary's fault. She could have ignored it all—she'd had plenty of practice—if only Mary hadn't interfered and made her be a nag.

If only these fools would leave, Mary thought to herself. If only she had the right to tell them to. But it wasn't her home, it was Alex's. She was herself a guest. Soon—sometime next week—Alex would be here and then they'd see what happened to Jamison's friends and hangers-on. Alex would clear them out in no time. Pray God he'd clear Jamison out too. This was the real homecoming, and it would mean that she, too, would have to finally leave Castlemere, but it would almost be worth it to get Jamison out.

A young man was weaving his way across the room toward her. Last time that one was here he'd cornered her in the hall outside the map room and had actually planted a filthy wet kiss on the side of her mouth before she slapped him off. She wouldn't be caught again. Dodging a servant with a tray of drinks, she slipped out of the ballroom and hurried up the stairs. Once in the safety of the big master suite, she let out a breath of relief. She should have gone to

London. Knowing that before this influx of Jamison's friends, she'd stayed on anyway, feeling she had to protect the house from him. Not so much from physical harm—although his friends spilled drinks and ashes on everything—as from the pure malignancy of the man.

She sat down at the small desk near the window that faced the sea and took out her current diary. But she wrote only for a few moments before closing the small book and putting it back. She would have to get out of this room before Alex and Anjanette arrived. Where would she put the diaries then? Perhaps she could have this piece of furniture moved along with her and replace it with something else. But what? She started doing a mental inventory of what else might fit this space.

Her thoughts were interrupted by a light knock on her door. She went to it and without opening it said, "Who is it?"

"It's me. Agnes."

"Come in, Agnes. I thought you'd gone to bed. I told you I didn't need any help undressing tonight."

"I know that, miss. I may be getting older, but I'm not stupid," Agnes said with her customary frankness. "But Cook went out to dump some washwater and—you know that little spot of drive you can see from the kitchen garden? —she thought she saw carriages coming along our drive. I thought you should know."

Mary was smoothing back her hair and shaking the wrinkles out of her skirt with an air of someone going to battle. "I certainly should. If those low-life friends of Jamison's think they can just drop in here anytime of the night, they're mistaken. This isn't an inn! I'll send them packing so fast they won't know what happened."

She flew down the steps and arrived at the bottom just as Bartlet, whom she brought along when she stayed at Castlemere, opened the front door. It was cold for April, and rainy. She saw only a shadowy figure and she strode forward saying, "I'm very sorry, but it's much too late for us to receive visitors. There are accommodations in town that I'm sure you'll find satisfactory."

"I doubt it."

"Alex! Alex, is that you?"

He stepped into the light and she flung herself at him, then quickly stepped back to look at him. "I'm so sorry. I had no idea. Your letter said next week. How . . . ? Why . . . ?"

"I lied," he said with a laugh. "I didn't want the whole crowd coming to meet us."

"Come in. Come in. No, where are Anjanette and the children? You haven't left them someplace, have you?"

"No, they're in the carriage. Who *are* these people?"

A crowd of young men with one very inebriated young woman had come into the hall singing a bawdy song. They gawked at Alex, as if trying to remember if they knew him.

"These are friends of Jamison's. I don't imagine you find that hard to believe."

"Not in the least," Alex said, studying them with distaste.

"I'll never ask anything else of you the rest of my life, Alex, if only you'll let me be the one to tell them to go home. Please, Alex."

"I would consider it your favor to me," he said gallantly.

Bartlet was still standing next to Mary. She turned to him. "Get the footman and the boot boy up and have them bring in Mr. and Mrs. Beecham's things. And tell Agnes to light a fire in the nursery for the children. We don't want to freeze them on their first night in England."

The last words were spoken as she rushed past Alex and down the steps to the first of the two carriages drawn up in front of the house. "Anjanette!" she said as the door opened and a figure stepped out.

She threw her arms around the older woman and almost reeled back in shock. Perhaps it wasn't even her. This woman was skeletally thin.

"Mary, how wonderful to see you again," she replied in an exhausted voice. She sounded twenty years older than Mary remembered.

"You must have had a terribly long day," Mary said, trying to conceal her distress. "I'm so sorry, but I've got your room. I know you don't want to wait for me to get my things out tonight. You need a good long rest, but we'll put you in a warm cozy room tonight and have you properly settled tomorrow."

As she spoke, she took Anjanette's elbow and guided her up the stairs. Alex followed her and took Anjanette's other arm. "No, I would not like to cause upheaval. Just a little rest . . ."

Servants were unloading trunks and suitcases and the two youngest housemaids were carrying the sleeping children past them to the nursery. Once inside the door, Mary was even more shocked by Anjanette's appearance. Her fair skin had a milky-blue color and her lovely blond hair looked dull and thin. She smiled at Mary, an obvious effort. "You look more beautiful than ever, dear, dear Mary. I'm so glad to see you again."

Mary hugged her, taking great care for fear of crushing her. "And I'm glad to see you again, Anjanette. This time it's forever, not just a visit."

Bartlet cleared his throat. "Mr. Alex, I've put out that young man in the Prince William suite. It has a nice fire and no drafts. If that is satisfactory . . . ?"

"Quite satisfactory," Alex replied, and without another word, scooped Anjanette up in his arms and went up the stairs with her.

Mary stood rooted, watching as they disappeared around the turning of the staircase. Her heart was pounding as if she'd run a very long way, and she had a sick feeling in the pit of her stomach. Suddenly a voice at her side startled her.

"What the hell is all this?" Jamison asked, making a wide sloppy gesture at the pile of luggage that was accumulating just inside the doorway.

Mary said, "Only that Alex is back and your friends have to get out of here. That is, if any of them are sober enough to walk."

The footman edged past carrying a small humpbacked trunk. "Pardon me, Mr. Hewitt," he said. The words were innocent and courteous, but the bold, rather impatient look he gave Jamison made clear that even the servants understood the difference this made in his standing.

Jamison straightened up with an attempt at dignity. His eyes glittered with malice. "This place is the reason I put up with you and your whining sister, Miss High-and-Mighty Mary Beecham. If you think I'm giving it up, you're mistaken. Badly mistaken."

Mary smiled. "We'll see, won't we, Jamison?"

Mary spent the next morning emptying the house of Jamison's crowd. In some cases it was much more of a challenge than she had anticipated.

"But I can't leave. Jemmy said I could stay on as long as I wanted," one nightshirted young man wailed when she and Bartlet bearded him in his room. "I've given my rooms in London to another chap until June."

"I can't tell you how sorry I am," Mary replied, "but my

cousin has come home and his wife is ill and must have quiet."

"Oh, I'll be ever so quiet, Miss Beecham. You just don't know how quiet I can be when I put my mind to it."

"I'm sure you can, but it just won't do. Bartlet, would you help Mr. Desmond here with his packing?"

One by one, they drifted off, some more willingly than others. It was all Mary could do to keep from standing in the doorway rubbing her hands together each time one of them went.

Of Jamison, there was no sign. Mary had no idea if he even knew that she was exterminating his house party. Hester crept around red-eyed and quiet, not helping Mary, but not hindering her either. Nor was Anjanette up and about, but that was Mary's doing. She'd given orders that breakfast and luncheon should be sent to her in bed and that nobody was to visit her until she herself asked for company.

Alex and the children, however, were everywhere. He seemed to be trying to introduce them to all of Castlemere with the intensity of a man who fears it might be gone momentarily. Richard was a sturdy little six-year-old whom nobody would suspect of ever having been sickly. Small and compact, he had his father's glossy dark hair and clear blue eyes. But he was excruciatingly shy. Katie, who had celebrated her eighth birthday just before leaving Singapore, was the image of her mother, with straight flaxen hair. She was a rather prissy, self-important little girl who was wary of Mary from their first encounter. Katie had come downstairs carrying Ginger draped over one arm. "Oh, no, Katie, you mustn't be rough with him. He's a very, very old cat and doesn't like being picked up."

"He likes me. He asked me to carry him," Katie replied loftily.

Alex managed to half-offend both his daughter and his cousin by saying, "She reminds me of you when you were little, Mary. Bright and bossy and a bit eccentric."

Mary was anxious to talk to him about Anjanette's health, but for the whole of the morning and early afternoon, she couldn't get him away from the children for a talk. He took them to the stables first, then came back and said, "Mary, why don't you come along with us to the beach?"

That was when the full force of the situation finally struck her. Alex was going to show *her* beach to his children; but now it was *their* beach. Forever. She felt sick with jealousy and regret and loathed herself for it. "No, thank you. I have riffraff to dispose of," she said, turning away quickly before he could press his invitation.

Anjanette asked that Mary and Hester join her for afternoon tea in her room. She looked better than Mary had expected, which was a relief. Rest and warmth had brought some color back to her face, although that face was alarmingly thin. "My dears, what a rudeness of me to arrive at your door in such terrible condition," she said, holding out her arms for hugs.

"Not our door, Anjanette. Your door," Hester reminded her.

"Nothing you do could be a rudeness," Mary added.

"Sit, my dear cousins. Come. Close to me."

The two young women sat on the bed, one on each side of her, each holding one of her hands.

"There are things I must say before we talk of old times and daily matters," Anjanette said. "As your elder, I insist that you listen to me and obey." It was the firm loving tone she had used to the natives in the *kampongs* near the plantation on Penang. Mary and Hester nodded. "This is a big house. A huge house. A *Beecham* house. The papers say it belongs to Alex, but Alex and I believe that morally it belongs to all of us. All the Beechams. You and Hester have never known another home—"

"But—" Mary began.

Anjanette held up one bony hand for silence. "I know you both have other property, and if you love it and wish to live there, of course we will not stand in your way. But we wish most ardently that you will both stay here forever. If not forever, at least for a few months. As a favor to us and our children. Katie and Richard do not know their English family; they are too young to remember when you came to Singapore."

"Do you truly want Jamison and me to stay here?" Hester asked, casting a quick victorious glance at Mary.

"Most surely we do. Alex and I talked about this before we came. Many times. You know he has loved this house since he was a boy, but it is not the mortar and timbers and stones he loves, it is the family in the house. The Beechams."

Mary felt her eyes stinging. To cover her emotion she said, "I must get along and start getting my things out of the master suite."

"Why?" Anjanette asked. "Do you mean to put me out of this room? I like this very well."

"But you should have the master suite," Hester said with more force than usual. "It faces the sea and is the biggest—"

Anjanette shuddered. "I hope I make no offense, but I don't wish to face your cold English sea and the winds. This room looks out over the . . . the chalk downs? Is that the phrase? It is very beautiful."

"But you are the mistress of the house now!" Hester insisted.

Anjanette smiled at her, then at Mary. "I am not even the mistress of myself while my health is so poor. That is the other favor I wish to ask—of you, Mary. You English say to the person who pours the tea, 'Will you be mother?' This I ask of you at Castlemere. Mary, will you be mother?"

She paused, her gaze locked with Mary's. "Will you take my place?"

39

At first, Mary believed that life would miraculously get easier if only they could settle into a routine. Later she wondered why she'd thought it would make the least difference, but during those first days she held steadfastly to the belief that it wouldn't be so painful to be near Alex if only she could get accustomed to a daily domestic system. It was quickly apparent, however, that there was little prospect of establishing any kind of routine. Castlemere seemed as busy with strangers as a railway terminal. First there were the nursemaids for the children to be interviewed and hired. Due to Anjanette's illness, and Hester's incompetence (in her sister's view), the job fell to Mary. She also continued to take charge of all the domestic decisions that should have fallen to the mistress of the house. She was used to this, but had expected to shed the duties, and now they seemed overwhelming.

In addition, there was a steady stream of business acquaintances Alex invited to Castlemere. Again, because of Anjanette's frail health, he didn't wish to leave, and therefore had to ask others to come to him, which they did with varying degrees of eagerness. Those who sold spices to Beecham's were glad to visit; some of those who purchased resented the trip and made it known by their grumpiness and impatience. Clyde Gordon, though clearly delighted to have Mr. Alex returned to England, was eager to get back to the warehouse, and stayed only two days and paced about looking at his pocket watch and the train schedule the whole time.

The other important contingent of visitors was the doctors. Dr. Engle, knowing nothing of Anjanette's medical history and even less about tropical ailments, recommended several London physicians. At great expense Alex prevailed upon no fewer than five of them to examine his wife at Castlemere at various times during the first two weeks after his family's arrival.

If Mary had her secrets, Alex had deeper ones, or so she feared. To her questions about the diagnosis, he was cheerfully vague. "Oh, she's getting along as well as can be expected," or, "A bit of rest ought to do wonders for her," he would reply.

"But what did the doctor say, exactly?" she would ask.

"Just a lot of big words."

Mary didn't quite know what to make of all this. Because Katie was so attached to him, and almost always trailing him about, Mary virtually never had a private moment with Alex. And he was unrelentingly cheerful around the children. Was he not discussing Anjanette's condition because he genuinely had no cause to worry, or was it because there was something dreadfully wrong with her and he didn't want any of them to guess?

When the fourth doctor departed, Mary contrived to be approaching the house, as if returning from a brisk walk, as he was leaving. "Oh, I'm so sorry I missed meeting you earlier," she said as he came down the wide front steps. "It's Dr. Curran, isn't it? I'm Mary Beecham." (Neither she nor anyone else remembered—or acknowledged—that she was actually the widowed Mrs. Turner.) "I'm Mr. Alex Beecham's cousin. I hope you found Anjanette well?"

All of this was delivered in her most aggressively charming manner. But to no avail. Instead of answering her question, he merely said how nice it was to meet her.

"Well, then. What's the verdict?" she asked, coming to the point.

"The verdict?"

"On Anjanette's health."

"I've discussed the patient with her husband."

"I'm certain you have, and Alex will no doubt tell me all about it, but I do like getting information firsthand when possible," she said, smiling coquettishly in spite of the snub.

"And if that information were your concern, I would be glad to supply it."

"But of course it's my concern. I'm a member of the family."

"So you say."

"So I say? Whatever can you mean by that, sir? Certainly

you don't think I'm someone else pretending to be Mary Beecham."

"I mean nothing, young woman, except that you are asking me for information you have no right to, and I don't propose to be flirted into indiscretion. Now, if you don't mind, I have a long journey ahead and would like to commence it."

Mary could feel her face burning and merely stood speechless and mortified on the bottom step as he hoisted himself into his carriage and rolled away.

"It doesn't always work, does it?" a voice behind her drawled.

She turned quickly and found Jamison standing a few steps above her. She was so furious at his having witnessed the scene that she could feel herself trembling with indignation. "I can't imagine what you mean, Jamison."

"You need a set-down like that more often. To keep you humble. You could use a little humbleness." He lifted a brandy snifter in a toast. It was smudged with fingerprints, as if he'd been nursing it along for hours. Or days.

"You mean 'humility.' You're drunk and it's only the middle of the day. That's disgusting."

"Being drunk is the only way to get through the middle of a day at Castlemere. Or hadn't you noticed? No, of course not. You're too busy running around giving orders and snooping into things that are none of your business."

"My cousin's health is my business."

"Your cousin's *wife's* health you mean. Do I detect a bit of the carrion crow in your interest?"

"What do you mean?"

He grinned as if he'd discovered the pot of gold at the end of the rainbow. "You understand me perfectly well. When she dies, you think you're next in line. That's it! I'll bet you fifty pounds right now that you're wrong. He's got some little Malay sweetheart tucked away someplace already. Or one of those eager Singapore spinsters with lots of money and no bothersome brains. Do you have any idea how ghastly women with brains actually are?"

"You're despicable!"

Jamison had lowered himself to the front steps and was leaning back on his elbows, gazing at her with insolent delight. "Aha. Struck home, haven't I just?"

"You most certainly have not, and what you're suggesting is the most disgusting thing I've ever heard."

He rose with more speed and grace than she would have expected. "Disgusting, yes. But true, little Miss Mary Beecham. How could it have taken me so long to figure it out? It's so obvious. It's written all over your face. Probably all over your body—"

She slapped him so hard it made the palm of her hand go numb. He stumbled back, almost fell, but recovered his balance and grabbed her arms in a painful grip.

"Take your hands off me this instant!"

"Why? Because they're not his hands? Oh, it would be different then, wouldn't it? Where do you two do it? In your room after poor old Anjanette has had her sleeping potion and dropped off into a stupor? Or do you go for the bucolic—romantic trysts under the oaks? Or possibly just quick grabs in the hallways?"

"Jamison, I despise you. I absolutely loathe you. I've tried hard to keep from admitting it even to myself because of Hester. But you are evil and I'm going to get you out of Castlemere before you have the chance to say any of these ugly things to anyone else."

"You think so? We'll just see about that." He was starting to sway.

"We certainly will. Now, take your damned hands off me before I scream."

"What a way for a lady to talk." He spoke with a sneer, but did release her.

She climbed a few steps, then turned and looked back down at him. "I'm not a lady where you're concerned, Jamison. I'm your enemy. Do you understand that? Your worst enemy. We are at war and I'd advise you retreat now while you have the opportunity."

She could still hear his laughter after she'd gone inside and closed the heavy main door.

Once again, Mary went to visit Anjanette in her room after dinner. Alex was there and the children were just having their good-night kisses before being taken up to the nursery. "I don't want to go upstairs," Katie objected. "I want to stay here and take care of Mommy."

"I'll take care of her for you," Alex assured her. "I need you to watch over Richard for us in the nursery."

"Nurse does that," Katie persisted, emphasizing her point with a pirouette that landed her in Alex's lap.

"Then you can help her. Off you go." He picked her up,

tilted her upside down to kiss her mother good night, then handed her over to the nursery maid.

"I'd like to talk to you about a domestic problem," Mary said when Katie and Richard had gone. "Alex, would you stay and give your advice?"

"Mary, dear, what can it be?" Anjanette said, alarmed at the intensity of her voice.

"It's Jamison. Or rather, I believe, Jamison's drinking."

"What's he done?" Alex asked. He could almost feel his temperature rising at the mention of the man. So far they'd had remarkable luck in keeping out of each other's way, but Alex was never quite able to forget his presence and Anjanette's insistence that he be allowed to stay for the sake of keeping Hester happy.

"It's not so much a matter of doing as saying. I'll not repeat it, nor do I want anybody to talk to him about it. We had an argument and I'm certain he was so far beyond reason that he doesn't even remember it."

"I'll have him out of here within the hour!" Alex said, rising from his chair before the fireplace.

"No! No, Alex. Please don't. If you make him leave, Hester will go with him and none of us wants to drive Hester away—"

"You know that's true, Alex," Anjanette said. "Mary, won't you please tell us what he said? I think Alex could talk to him and—"

"No! I'm sorry, but it was horrible and ugly. He'd love to repeat it to Alex and I'd feel soiled. Please understand."

Husband and wife were both staring at her, Alex with an intensity that led her to suspect that he understood quite well. "I'm sure we don't want to make anything worse for you, Mary," Anjanette said. "But if he's intolerable and you don't want him to leave, then what is there to do?"

"Well . . ." She twisted her hands in a nervous gesture Alex had never seen her use. Whatever had gone on between them had seriously upset her. "I think we should try to cure him," Mary said, at first hesitantly, then in a rush. "You see, he's quite a greedy, unprincipled person when sober, but he's downright wicked when he's drinking. If we could keep him sober even a few days, perhaps—"

"Isn't that really Hester's place? Not ours?" Alex asked. He was still thinking that turning Jamison out altogether was the best plan.

"Of course it is, but Hester can't do it. Won't do it," Mary answered.

Anjanette backed her up. "She's entirely in his thrall, Alex. Is that the English word? She feels for him great love and fear of losing the little love he returns."

"Then who's going to stop him drinking? And how?" Alex asked.

"It can't be me. I got so angry this morning that I ranted about how I was his enemy and I'd get him. I don't know what he might do to me if I tried to get him to do anything. Besides, with the idea I have in mind, it's not my place."

As serious as the subject was, something made Alex smile. "Why am I not surprised that you have a plan? And why do I have the feeling that I'm going to figure as the villain? What am I supposed to do? Abduct him and cart him off to some institution?"

"Actually, I had in mind that Castlemere would serve as the institution. Abduction can be so tedious. This saves you the trouble."

Alex laughed. "You can make the most absurd things sound almost reasonable. What is Hester going to think of all this?"

"Hester is going to be furious with us," Mary admitted. "With me, because she's certain to realize I'm behind it. But in the end, I think she'll be grateful. I know his drinking is a terrible trial to her and she'd like him to stop, but she can't make him do anything herself."

"Very well, when do we start putting the bars on the windows?"

Hester wasn't told of the plan in advance. The first she knew of it was two days later when Jamison came into the writing room that afternoon. She looked up from her correspondence at his bellow. "What is it?"

"All the decanters have been drained out. Even the ones in our room. What right have you got—?"

"I don't know what you're talking about. Jamison, you really shouldn't go around the house in your dressing gown. Especially in the afternoon."

"Aren't you listening to me? The brandy, the port, the sherry, everything is gone." Suddenly, as if struck by a thought, he turned and left the room. Hester began to get an inkling of what was going on, which was confirmed when he returned a few moments later. His face was flushed and he looked disheveled. "The cellars have new doors and locks and Alex has the keys. You put him up to this, didn't you, you bitch!"

Alex had been prepared for Jamison's reaction. Bartlet was under orders to report as soon as Mr. Hewitt came downstairs. Having received this report, Alex now stepped into the writing room. "I don't care for your words or your tone, Jamison. And you're quite wrong. My cousin Hester knows less about this than you do."

"Why have you hidden it?" Jamison asked. His voice had a frantic edge that made Hester's skin crawl.

Alex's bearing was casual, but his eyes were hard. "My wife and I are considering a religious conversion that would involve abstinence from alcohol. This is a sort of dry run, if you will."

Even as distraught as he was, Jamison recognized this as a grim joke. "Too damn stingy, eh? Well, I'll buy my own, then. Bartlet, I need to send someone to the village—"

"I'm afraid that's not how it works, Jamison," Alex said. "You're not going to drink anything stronger than lemonade in this house. The entire staff has been informed and they've been reminded whom they work for."

"Oh, the Lord Beecham act! Is that it? Couldn't wait for old George to pop off so you could dash back and play the rich gentleman." Jamison was pacing the room, talking too fast, fidgeting his fingers nervously.

"Even as pickled as your brain must be, surely you see how untrue that is. George has been dead for years, Jamison. Try another." Alex was standing perfectly still, only his eyes following Jamison's progress. But his stance made Hester think of a tightly coiled spring, ready to explode. The electricity of the barely suppressed violence in the room was crackling around her.

"You won't get away with this. I'll go get it myself."

Alex smiled tightly. "I'm afraid you won't. I've hired on a half-dozen local boys to watch all the doors of the house. They're being generously rewarded for keeping you from leaving the grounds."

"You bastard!" Jamison dashed at Alex and swung what would have been a stunning blow if it had connected. But Alex stepped aside, caught the other man's arm, and jerked him around in a circle. "Don't try that, you fool. You've swilled yourself right past your prime. Your arm is no better than your brain."

"You can't keep me a prisoner!"

"But that's exactly what I'm doing. Try to focus on the essentials. I'm sure you'll understand it sooner or later. Believe it or not, I'm trying to help you. Not that I think you're worth it, but Hester does, and we all love Hester. So I'm going to blow away the fumes and see if there's a man left. I'm betting there isn't."

Alex stared at Jamison as he spoke, and thought: Why am I doing this? Just in the few years since he'd first met Jamison, the man's handsome face had started to sag, his eyes had gone dull, his physique was starting to run to flab instead of muscle. This was a man on a downhill course who didn't want to change, who was probably beyond recovery. And if he were saved from himself? What would they have then? Jamison had been a wretched individual even before the drink got such a hold on him.

But Alex glanced at Hester, her face chalk-white, her posture cowering, and he knew the answer to his question. For reasons beyond anyone's understanding, she loved this man, and it was his duty to her to try to rescue Jamison. Poor Hester, so young and so unhappy. Without a father or brother to look after her interests, the job fell to him.

Jamison shook himself free of Alex's grip and paced the room once more. "This is Mary's doing."

"Mary had nothing to do with my decision," Alex lied.

Jamison ignored the protest. "She said she was my enemy. I should have known she'd go to you to get at me. You and she—"

"That's enough!" Alex said sharply. "We've all had more of your opinions than we want."

"Opinions? Opinions! What I know is fact, and I'll prove it to all of you. You'll see. I'll prove it all!"

On this line he made his exit, ruining the effect by bumping into the edge of the door. He cursed and slammed it behind him.

"Hester, I'm sorry—"

She put the heels of her hands to her eyes. "I know you mean well, Alex, but it won't help and it will make him despise me all the more. It *was* Mary's idea, wasn't it? She's always hated Jamison."

"Hester, this was my decision and it wasn't based on what anybody thinks of Jamison, but what we all think of you. Would you like to go away until it's all sorted out?"

"I would. Yes. But I can't leave him."

"You can, you know. Divorce, as unsavory as it is, isn't impossible."

"Divorce? I don't notice you divorcing Anjanette just because she is ill."

"Of course not, but—"

"There's no difference. Jamison is merely ill. That's what none of you understand."

And when he was well, he was a son-of-a-bitch, Alex thought, but said, "That's why I'm trying to force a cure on him, Hester. He'll never do it himself. You know that, don't you?"

"I suppose I do. It just seems so cruel. It would be better if we just went away someplace. I have a house a little north of London . . ."

Alex took her hands and waited until she reluctantly looked up at him. "Anjanette and I don't want you to go away, Hester. We want you to stay here and be happy."

Tears filled her eyes. "Am I going to be happy? Ever? It seems like I've spent my whole life waiting for something just a week or two away that will make me happy."

"I can't promise you happiness, but I'm trying to help you find it," Alex said, kissing her on the forehead. "Now, you'd best take a few of your things into another room. I don't believe you'll want to share Jamison's for a few days."

"Yes. Very well."

She walked out, head held high, bony shoulders squared bravely. Poor little Hester, Alex thought. Am I trying to help her or merely make life a little easier for myself by drying Jamison out?

"You were very nice to her," Mary said.

Startled, he turned quickly. She was standing just inside the French doors. "You were listening?"

"Not on purpose. I heard Jamison shouting and came to protect Hester. When I heard your voice, I stayed outside."

"You really believe you *can* protect Hester?"

"I have to try. I promised Papa. I've made a muddle of it so far. I've made a muddle of quite a number of things," she added, picking up a glass paperweight and staring at it as if there were a secret contained in its glassy depths.

She looked every bit as helpless as Hester and—he could admit only to himself—much more appealing. She might make muddles, but she worked at it instead of letting life roll over her. If Hester had Mary's strength of character, she wouldn't have married Jamison in the first place, much less be in the cowering, fearful state she was in now. Of course, few men and fewer women had Mary's backbone and determination. Not even Anjanette. He felt a sudden sick jolt of guilt and squashed that thought as quickly as it bloomed.

"Mary, I think you had better stay out of sight today. At least out of Hester and Jamison's sight." He knew he sounded curt, but didn't dare sound otherwise.

She looked up from the paperweight, pain in her eyes. "You blame me too?"

"Of course not, but Jamison does, and he's not to be trifled with anytime, certainly not when he's in an ugly mood. And I think you're going to see an ugly mood like you've never seen before."

40

Mary stayed in her room all day. It turned into the longest day she'd ever lived. Used to activity, she hated her self-enforced imprisonment. The big master suite that she'd always loved had never seemed so cavernous and empty. She wrote in her current diary, but found her inner thoughts too confused to express well. She tried to read some of Portia's old novels, still in their rows in the small bookcase beneath one of the windows. But she was easily distracted; the stories were trivial and the characters vapid. She had lunch on a tray in her room and then tried to take a ladylike nap, but was too restless to relax. She killed the remainder of the afternoon on some needlepoint, an activity she despised, but underwent as a sort of self-imposed punishment.

Once she heard some shouting outside and nearly toppled out the window trying to find out exactly what was going on. She couldn't see anyone, but the sounds from around the corner of the house made clear that Jamison had tried to leave the house and one of old Tutin's great bearlike nephews had stopped him. Later there was a ruckus in the hallway—voices raised, something crashing against a wall and glass breaking—and Hester fled past, sobbing. Mary flung the door open, intending instinctively to run to her sister's aid, but Hester was gone and Alex, his face white with anger, simply gestured brusquely at her to stay in her room.

Later, when Agnes came to collect her dinner tray, Mary insisted that she stay. "We can play some cards."

"With you? You cheat," Agnes replied, hands on hips.

"I won't cheat. I promise. Besides, it's not really cheating to remember what's already been played."

"That's what your old Aunt Nell used to say, but she had

419

a funny way of 'remembering' cards that *hadn't* been played. You got the same way about you."

She let Agnes win a few hands, but neither of them had her heart in it. Finally, when it got dark, Mary got undressed and Agnes started brushing out her long hair. "It's an awful time for everybody, isn't it?" Mary said. "Poor Cousin Alex has so much to worry about already, and now he's having to put up with Jamison as well. It's all my fault really. If only I'd kept Hester from marrying him to start with—"

"You? What business was it of yours, missy? You think you're some sort of god what can make everybody do what you think is right?"

"Don't be daft!"

"Me? I'm not the daft one. You just think back—there was nothing you nor nobody else could have done to stop Miss Hester from jumping into bed with him." She gave a great jerk to the brush, yanking loose a tangle.

"Don't be so vulgar, Agnes." Mary's eyes were tearing from the pain.

"'Tis the truth, vulgar or not, and you know it. Seems to me a person has to think fearful high of herself to go taking blame or credit for things that aren't none of her affair to start with."

Mary turned around and put her arms around Agnes' waist, no mean feat these days. "Your methods are astringent, but you do have a way of making me feel better. Now, go away and let me get some sleep."

"That would suit me just fine. You be sure and lock the door after me."

"Yes, all right. Good night, Agnes."

She sat for some time staring at her reflection and engaging in a mental dialogue. Was Agnes right, that there was nothing she could have done to stop Hester? She'd tried to tell Hester the truth about Jamison's character and hadn't been believed. Perhaps she could have tried some great thumping lies. But Hester had thought the truth was false; she'd have never believed lies, no matter how creative.

Becoming aware of a cold draft, Mary rose and closed the window, then crawled into bed. She huddled, shivering, until the bed warmed up a bit; then it seemed too warm and she flung aside some of the covers. Eventually she fell into a restless sleep.

* * *

She knew it was a dream, but couldn't seem to escape it. The walls of the house were closing in on her. Like a mechanical monster, Castlemere was shrinking into itself, and as it shrank, the air became thick, the scent of rosemary grew claustrophobic. Suddenly there was a sound, a sort of gurgling laugh. She was awake on the instant and aware that she'd forgotten Agnes' advice about locking the door.

The room was dark, only a shaft of watery moonlight cutting across the foot of the bed. She lay rigid, frozen with the terrified knowledge that she wasn't alone. The rosemary scent, overwhelming in intensity, remained. It wasn't part of the dream. She could hardly breathe. It was as if all the childhood nightmares had come together in one awful waking moment. Someone—something—was in the room.

"I told you I'd prove it," a menacing voice growled.

Mary sprang bolt upright, her heart pounding violently. "Jamison, get out of here!" she croaked. She was nearly gagging, but whether from fear or the rosemary odor, she couldn't tell.

He lurched into the beam of moonlight for a second. "I saw him. Came sneaking out of his room. Thought I didn't know. But I was watching. He's here."

Mary tried to edge away. There was a lamp on the table at the other side of the huge bed. If she could get to it, she could throw it or hit him. He was obviously reeling drunk. It wouldn't take much to knock him out. She tried to get her voice under control and speak calmly. "Jamison, I'm going to call for help if you don't get out of here right this minute."

"Call? You call? No. I'm going to call. Everybody has to see. Where is he? He's hiding someplace. Coward. Dirty coward bastard Alex. You can't hide. Come out. I want everybody to know . . ."

Mary drew a deep breath to scream, but he seemed, in some animal way, to know. He lunged at her. It was as though a wild creature had sprung from the darkness. "Let go of me!" Mary said before he clamped his hand over her mouth. She tried to struggle toward the lamp so she could fight him, but he was leaning on her, his knee on her thigh. The pain was excruciating. Nearly fainting, she found a scrap of energy and used it to bite down as hard as she could on his hand.

He screamed and fell forward, clutching his wounded hand to his chest. She was trapped by the weight of his body across hers. Her leg was broken, she thought. She tried to scream for help, but all that came out was a whimper. Jamison was thrashing around now, as if he'd lost something in the huge bed. "Where is he? He's here. I know he is. I'll find him. Then everybody will know what you two do! It's not me that's evil. It's you."

Mary tried to push him off, thinking she could flee, but he was too heavy. Panic overcame her and her breath starting coming in short, uncontrollable gasps. She was racked with nausea. Frantic, her fists balled, she starting hitting him.

"Stop that!" he shouted.

She was making incoherent noises, short, rasping shrieks of fury and pain. Then, when she felt the very last of her energy start to ebb away, he shifted his weight and she managed to free her legs. Scrambling, she flung herself out of bed, landing painfully on the floor. "Help me! Help!" she managed to scream. She tried to get up, but was too faint.

As she sank back to the floor, she heard the door crash open and light washed over her. "Mary! My God! What's happened?" Alex said, bending over her.

"Jamison . . ." she whispered, gesturing toward the bed.

At that moment Hester appeared in the doorway. She was in a heavy nightdress, her lank hair streaming around her thin shoulders. "What . . . ? Jamison!" She ran to the bed, ignoring Mary, very nearly stepping on her in her rush to get to Jamison.

"Just breathe slowly. It's all right now. I'm here. I won't let anything happen to you," Alex was saying softly. "Where are you hurt?"

"My leg," Mary wept. "I think it's broken."

She was crumpled facedown on the floor. He carefully turned her over, talking to her gently the whole time. "Just relax. I'll take care of you, Mary. That's it. Easy, now."

She was so tiny and frail under his shaking hands. Dear God, don't let her be hurt. She was the color of milk.

"Alex! Alex, help me with Jamison!" Hester cried.

Alex hardly heard her. Mary was on her side now. He slowly eased her onto her back and gently straightened her legs. Her nightdress was pulled up and he could see a livid red-going-purple mark on her thigh. But the leg was straight. "Mary, I don't think it's broken," he said.

"What . . . ?" she mumbled. She was only half-conscious, but was clinging to his sleeve with one small hand.

"I'm going to carry you to the sofa. It's too cold on the

floor," he said, growing more and more alarmed at her extreme paleness. She was starting to tremble violently and her teeth were chattering. "Sit up just a little," he said, slipping his arm under her back. She transferred her frightened grip to the front of his shirt. Putting his other arm under her knees, he stood up, lifting her as though she were no heavier than a doll.

"Here now, what's all this?" Agnes said from the doorway. "I heard a crash. My God! Miss Mary! What's happened to her?"

"Her?" Hester screamed from the bed. "Doesn't anybody care about Jemmy? There's something wrong with him. I can't get him to wake up."

Alex eased Mary onto the small sofa that was set perpendicular to the fireplace. Agnes had grabbed a pillow to put behind her mistress's head and was tucking a mound of blankets around her before Alex had her fully settled. "Agnes, ring for Bartlet and have him get the doctor here as soon as possible," Alex said. "What *is* that smell?"

"Rosemary, sir," Agnes said, brushing Mary's hair back out of her face.

"I know that, but why is it so strong?"

"Alex, come here! Now!" Hester said in a voice shrill enough to be heard throughout the house.

Alex put his fingers to Mary's throat and felt the pulse there. It was strong and regular. "Agnes, after you've given Bartlet his instructions, please go to Mrs. Beecham and tell her Mary and Jamison have had a little tiff. Tell her exactly that: just a little tiff. I don't want her worried. I'm sure she's heard the commotion."

"Yes, sir. She'll be fine now. Miss Mary, I mean."

Only then did Alex turn his attention to Hester. She was kneeling in the middle of the big bed. Jamison, sprawled facedown, was making repulsive gasping noises. Alex came around the far side of the bed and tried to turn him over. As he did so, Jamison flung out an arm and liquid splashed his wife and Alex. Somehow he'd kept his grip on the neck of a bottle.

"What is that?" Alex said, reeling back from the overpowering stench.

Hester pried the bottle out of her husband's hand. "It's the rosemary oil Mary has put in the wash water. What's he doing with it?"

Alex groaned. "He's drinking it, obviously."

"Drinking oil? But why . . . ?"

"The oil is distilled in grain alcohol. Good God, if I'd known he was that desperate—"

"Grain alcohol? But he couldn't drink that. It's poison. Jemmy wouldn't drink poison. He must have thought it was something else."

"Hester, stop babbling. It is poison and it doesn't matter why he drank it. We've got to get it out of him."

Mary, in a mild state of shock, never knew how truly hideous that next hour was for the rest of them. In a stupor of pain and fear, she was unaware of the basins, the glasses of egg whites and mustard, the vomiting, the doctor's frantic attempts to control the patient. She knew nothing of the violence of Jamison's final spasms. She didn't hear the ugly, garbled accusations he made with his last breath, nor did she hear Hester's hysterics when it was over. She only half-woke when Alex summoned Tutin's nephew and another of the young men who were guarding the doors and asked them to take Jamison's body to his own room. She was only faintly aware of the doctor examining her leg and pronouncing it whole and unbroken, but terribly bruised.

Agnes stripped the bed, cleaned up all the disgusting evidence of the horror that had occurred, and wept silently when Mary cried in her sleep for her Aunt Nell—as if the old woman hadn't been dead for years on years now. Agnes wept, too, at the sight of Mr. Alex's agonized face as he bent over Mary and put his hand to her pale cheek. He looked like a man in hell—as surely he was, with a sick wife in his own room and this broken, fragile girl in here.

She watched from the corner of her eye as he leaned forward, resting his face against Mary's and whispering something he knew she couldn't hear, but which he needed to say. He's in love with her, Agnes realized with a certainty she'd rarely known. Sick in love, poor dear man. Agnes quickly left the room and mopped her eyes with her sleeve.

Mary was confined to her room until the morning of Jamison's funeral, three days later. Her leg had become swollen, but under Agnes' surprisingly solicitous care had gone back to its normal size by the second day, although a great patch had turned quite horribly black. Alex had come in early the first morning to tell her what had happened. "Do you want to be moved to another room?" he asked

when he'd finished his blunt account of Jamison's ignomini-
ous death.

Mary pleated folds of the counterpane between her fingers. "You mean because he died in this bed? I suppose I
should be sensitive and vaporish and say yes, but . . . Alex,
a lot of people have died in this bed. My grandfather and
grandmother, Portia, and who knows how many other Beechams before them. That's simply one of the things beds are
for." She glanced up, and at the sight of the corner of his
mouth twitching, she blushed. "I mean, well, I don't intend
to let Jamison rule what I do, whether he's dead or alive."

"Good for you. I should have known you'd say that. I'm
going to go now. I have to prepare some story for the
children, but I'll stop back and see how you're getting
along."

"Alex, where's Hester?"

"In her room. The doctor's given her something to make
her sleep."

"Does she blame me?"

Alex opened his mouth to deny it, but meeting her candid
blue gaze, said, "Why can't I lie to you even when I know I
should? Yes, I'm afraid she does. But it's the shock. When
some time has passed, I'm sure she'll see it wasn't your
fault."

Mary laced her fingers together and looked down. "But
will I see that?"

"Mary, if you're going to start throwing guilt around, you
had better throw it at me, not yourself. I'm the one who
locked up the bottles and posted the guards."

"But because I suggested it."

"Are you saying that I'm as spineless as Jamison? That
I'll do anything that anybody suggests? Believe me, if I'd
suspected for a second what would come of this, I'd have
ignored you."

"No, of course not. But, Alex, I feel awful. You see, I
only partly wanted him to be made to stop for his own
good."

"You also wanted to see him made miserable? So did I. I
actually enjoyed the prospect of seeing him squirm, to tell
the truth. I felt he had it coming for all the grief he'd caused
you and Hester and meant to keep on causing."

"Did you really?"

"Mary, what you have to remember is that he would have
gone on making Hester's life a daily hell. He was getting

steadily worse and he'd have never gotten better on his own. Whatever our secret, base motives, we did try to do what was right even if it was for the wrong reasons. He was killing himself, Mary. Bottle by bottle. Because I interfered, he killed himself sooner rather than later. It's just a question of time and that's for my conscience to deal with."

"Because we interfered."

He ignored this. "What we both have to remember is that Hester's free of him now. She could have spent another ten years having her heart broken over and over again. She'll never thank us for it—you couldn't stand it anyway, and neither could I—but she's young and resilient. Her spirit will heal."

Mary looked directly at him. "But, Alex, it's better to be miserable near someone you love than to lose him. I know that."

He reached forward and took her hand. After a long silence, he said, "I know it too."

"Alex—"

He shook his head. "Let's not talk about any more secrets. Not today. We might be swept right out to sea on a tide of them."

Alex didn't come back to see her alone. He accompanied the doctor twice, and he brought the minister, who was having a hard time getting any sense out of Hester about funeral arrangements. Mary made all the decisions about the plot, the flowers, the music, and even selected the mourning rings that would be given to the guests. When this was done, Alex brought Anjanette. She looked shaken, but healthier than when she arrived. Her concern, however, was all for Mary. "You shouldn't get out of bed for at least a week."

"But I have to get up for the funeral," Mary protested.

Anjanette and Alex exchanged a glance. "You don't mean you think I shouldn't go, do you? Unthinkable. People would say I was being hateful because I didn't like Jamison. Hester would hold it against me forever." It never crossed her mind that Hester might resent her attendance more than her absence. "What have people been told about his death?"

"That he had a fall. Everybody assumes he was drunk, but nobody says it," Alex replied.

"And what about me? How is my condition accounted for?"

"You are grief-stricken on your sister's account."

Alex made one more visit, this time with the children. Katie bounced around the room, poking into drawers, spritzing herself with Mary's perfume, and chattering all the while. "Do you know Uncle Jamison is dead, Cousin Mary?"

"Is he?" Mary said, wishing she could get up and tie the child to a chair. She wanted to shout, "Sit down!" as Aunt Nell had done so many times when Mary herself was a child.

"Yes, he fell down and was killed," Katie explained. "Now Cousin Hester doesn't have a husband. She's very sad. You don't have a husband—are you sad?"

"Katie, how many times have I told you not to ask people personal questions?" Alex said, taking a china ornament out of her hands and replacing it on the dressing table. Picking her up around the waist like a sack of grain, he sat down and kept her on his lap.

Richard had crawled onto the bed and had cuddled next to Mary. She rested her cheek on his soft, clean hair. It was the same glossy black as his father's. Was Alex's hair this soft? Mary wondered, staring at him.

Undeterred by her father's restraints, Katie plunged on. "Papa says he'll take me to London when Mommy is better and we'll shop for pretty things. You have pretty things. Does your papa take you to London?"

"He used to, when I was little."

"Where is your papa?"

"He's gone to heaven," Mary said.

"Like Cousin Jamison?"

"Not quite."

"I have a new dress for the funeral. It's black. Mommy says everybody wears a black dress to funerals. Except boys!" Katie went into gales of laughter at the idea. "Mommy says you're not going 'cause you're sick. Are you sick like my mommy, Cousin Mary?"

"That's not what your mother said, Katie," Alex said. "And I think you've said quite enough yourself."

"Well, she almost did. She said she didn't think Cousin Mary should go. I heard her. So did you."

"Katie, go back to the nursery."

"Papa!"

"Now. I'm sorry, Mary. I shouldn't have brought her," Alex said after she'd flounced out of the room. "Nor should anyone ever speak in front of her—about anything."

"Anjanette should have told me herself. This is her home now and I wouldn't do anything to upset her. I'll stay home with Richard and we'll find some quiet game to play." Mary forced a smile and ruffled the little boy's hair.

But the morning of the funeral was gray and dismal. Richard had a sore throat and a slight temperature and the nursery maid wouldn't let him out of bed. Mary got up and limped around her room, testing the bruised leg. After a few trips back and forth between the window and the door, she was convinced she was almost healed. Shaky and a little wobbly, but well enough. If Anjanette was worried about her health, she was worried in vain.

Mary rang for Agnes. "Have the rest of them gone to the chapel yet?" she asked.

"Just as I came up."

"Then help me dress quickly."

"You can't walk about like this."

"If you and Bartlet help me, I can. Hurry with that dress. The one I wore to Portia's services."

The stairs were worse than she had anticipated, but she made it before the service was half done. Not wanting to cause any stir, she slipped into the back pew of the small family chapel with the servants. Agnes sat on one side of her, Bartlet on the other. The rector dithered, unsure of how to deliver a eulogy to a man he'd met only once and then under trying circumstances. Jamison had been in his cups and kept calling the rector and his ilk "silly old farts in skirts."

Alex and Anjanette were in the front pew with Hester between them. She kept leaning toward Alex, as if on the verge of fainting. At the rector's signal for the final prayer, Mary slipped forward on the kneeling rail. Bowing her head, she bit back a whimper at the pain it caused her to kneel. She relished the agony as she prayed silently, "Dear God, forgive me my spite and wickedness. Please, please make Hester happy now. Punish me any way you want, but please give Hester a happy life. Hester's only mistake was loving somebody who wasn't worthy of her. She doesn't deserve to be made miserable for that all her life. And please, God, if you can see a way, don't make Hester hate me forever. . . ."

A discreet nudge from Agnes alerted her that the service was over. "Amen," she whispered, and stood up with the others. Alex and Anjanette were coming up the center aisle with Hester hanging limply on Alex's arm. Mary's eyes filled with tears at the sight of her sister, so devastated by grief. "Oh, Hester." She spoke involuntarily, and though the words were hardly more than a whisper, Hester heard her.

Stopping so suddenly that Katie stumbled into her, Hester stiffened and stared at Mary. Her mouth worked soundlessly for a moment as Alex tried to gently drag her forward; then the venom spewed forth: "Murderer!" Hester screamed.

Bartlet and Agnes moved in toward Mary, almost crushing her in their effort to protect her. "Hester, I—"

"You killed my husband! You murderer. You lost your own husband and you resented me for having Jamison. You wanted him yourself. He told me!" She was gasping, straining against Alex's encircling grip. "You killed him. You did it on purpose. You ought to be in jail! I hate you, Mary! I hate you, I hate you, I hate you."

In a single motion Alex bent over, thrust his arm behind her knees, and scooped her up like he did Katie when she misbehaved. Nearly running over the rector, he had her out of the chapel in a matter of seconds. The rest of them stood frozen in attitudes of shock. Anjanette was the first to speak. "We all know that Hester is nearly out of her mind with sorrow. She didn't mean a word she said and I think we should all forget we heard anything." She took a long, commanding look around the small chapel, gathering them in with her eyes. Then, taking Katie's hand, she walked on with dignity, just as if nothing untoward had happened.

Jamison's few friends followed her, pointedly not looking at Mary, who stood rigid in the back row. Agnes and Bartlet both had an arm around her, holding her up. A few neighbors came next; then the servants began to file out. The cook, a crusty woman who'd never been known to smile, patted Mary on the shoulder as she went. The village twins, who were upstairs maids, bobbed quick, guilty curtsies as they passed her. When the others had all left, Bartlet and Agnes let Mary down. "Thank you both," she said softly.

"I'll carry you, miss, if you like," Bartlet offered.

She smiled weakly. "Thank you, Bartlet, but I'd rather just be left alone for a while. I can walk, but I have some more praying to finish first."

*   *   *

Late that night, Mary slipped quietly to Hester's room. Opening the door, she said softly, "Hester, may I come in?"

The lights were out except for a small candle on the table beside the bed, but Hester was sitting up. She said nothing, so Mary gingerly sat on the bottom of the bed. "I know how you must feel about me, but I want to ask your forgiveness anyway. I know you won't give it. And you're probably right—"

"Did he hurt you badly?" Hester asked. Her voice was hardly audible.

"No. I'll be fine. It's just a bad bruise," Mary said, surprised.

"I'd actually thought about it myself, you know."

"About what, Hester?"

"About putting him away in a rest home to cure him. But I was too selfish. You see, I knew it would be best for him, but I knew he would never stop hating me for it and I couldn't risk his hate."

"Do you hate me?"

For the first time, Hester looked directly at her. "No, I don't hate you, Mary. But . . . but I don't love you either. Not now. You did what I didn't have the courage to do and it took him away from me. Just as I knew it would. Dear God, he's gone. Forever. I just can't accept it or understand it. How could it be, Mary? How could I love him so much and how could God take him from me? What have I done wrong to deserve such?"

"There's no answer to that, Hester."

"Certainly not from you. You have no idea what it is to love as I loved."

"Hester . . ." She almost poured out her secret about Molly, just to somehow prove that she did know to the depths of her soul what it was to love and lose someone dear. She hadn't told anyone but Agnes and Winston about Molly.

But Hester didn't give her the chance. "No, you didn't really love Henry Turner. You just wanted to be married. I could tell. You're so smart—all head and no heart. You don't understand what it is to love a man so much you'd give up your own life before you'd lose a moment with him. You'll never have your heart broken because you don't have one."

"Is that really what you think?" Mary asked, astonished

that someone so close to her could be so utterly wrong. Could that possibly be what others thought of her?

Hester leaned over and blew out the candle. After a long silence she said, "He hit me. It broke a tooth."

Mary didn't know what to say, but wished she could drag Jamison Hewitt out of his grave and repay him in kind.

"It was the day before . . . before he died. He pulled my hair and said I was ugly and hit me. He really, truly hated me, Mary. I think he would have eventually killed me." She was speaking in a flat voice, as if reading an unfamiliar passage in a book. "Did he hurt you badly? No, I already asked you that, didn't I? I'm sorry he hurt you too. But you shouldn't have made Alex take away the drink. It was the only thing Jemmy loved."

Mary was, for one of the few times in her life, completely speechless. And for once she had the sense to realize that she was wanted only for listening.

"Mary, sit beside me," Hester said, her voice breaking.

Mary did as she was bidden, crawling up the length of the bed and putting her arms around Hester. "I'm going to leave here," Hester said in a minute. "You can understand, can't you? I don't think I can ever be happy at Castlemere."

"Where will you go?"

"Oh, my house in Kent, probably. It's very pretty and peaceful and there's a nice woman who's the housekeeper. Someday I'll invite you to visit me. But don't come there until I do."

"Whatever you want, Hester. I'll do anything you want."

They sat silently for a long time and Mary could feel Hester's hot tears dropping on the bodice of her dress. Finally Hester said, "Why wasn't I the one who died? It would have been much more sensible. Jemmy would have been happy without me and I'm miserable without him. It's not fair."

"Oh, Hester . . . dear Hester, nothing is fair. Nothing."

41

─────────●─────────

When Hester left Castlemere the next day, Mary went with her. Hester was going to London to stay with friends while she had some more black dresses made before going down to her house in the country. "Why won't you stay with me?" Mary asked.

They were riding the train. After years of promises, a new spur line of the railroad had finally opened from the village, making the trip to London an easier journey. Neither of them had ridden the route before. Hester leaned forward as if the scenery were so interesting that she could think of nothing else. Mary didn't ask the question again.

Hester didn't speak for many miles, and when she did deign to talk to Mary, it was with sarcasm. "I suppose Alex made you come with me. Did the two of you think I might leap out and throw myself on the tracks if I didn't have a guard?"

This was a new strand in Hester's personality, but while Mary would normally have picked it out and held it up to ridicule or at least examination, she meekly said, "No, in fact Alex didn't want me to leave today."

"Oh? Why? Is he anticipating some other crisis that you could throw yourself into?"

Mary just shrugged. She'd vowed she wouldn't cross Hester in any way, but that didn't mean she had to cut her heart open and let her sister rummage around in the contents. Mary was leaving Castlemere as a penance. It was a quiet little bargain she'd made with God after she left Hester's room the night before. She would give up Castlemere and Alex's presence and in turn God would make Hester's life happy. At least, those were the conditions she'd offered.

She'd had no sign of His participation in the deal, but she was going through with her part anyway.

The odd thing about it was that Alex seemed to understand without her having told him a word of it. "I have to leave here," she'd told him at breakfast.

They were alone in the room at opposite ends of the table. He laid his napkin aside and looked at her as if he were reading her thoughts in her face. "When will you go?"

"Today. On this afternoon's train with Hester."

"If you must go, you must. But I wish you'd wait until your leg is fully healed."

"That doesn't matter. I'll be quite as comfortable, or uncomfortable, in London as here."

"Do you want me to take you to the village?"

"No, Bartlet and Agnes are coming along. They can take care of everything."

He looked out the long windows for so long she thought he'd forgotten her. She rose to leave the table, and as she passed him, he reached out and took hold of her wrist, saying very quietly, "I'm sorry you have to leave."

Mary stopped and put her free hand over his "So am I,"

"What do you think would happen if I kissed you once before you go?" he asked, looking up at her with a self-mocking smile.

"Thunderbolts? A plague of frogs?" she answered lightly, but her heart was thudding.

He rose and slowly put his arms around her. They gazed at each other, savoring the moment, knowing it was the last time there would be such a time. When his lips met hers, however, it was not a tender kiss, but a hungry, almost angry kiss. She returned it in kind. He held her so tightly she couldn't get her breath, and when finally she pulled away, it was with a gasp.

"Oh, Mary . . ." he said miserably.

She stepped back, still trying to regulate her breathing. "Alex, please tell Anjanette and the children good-bye for me. I . . . I can't."

She heard the door from the kitchen hall opening and fled, thinking even as she ran up the stairs that she hadn't found out if his hair was as soft as Richard's. Now she'd never know.

"What *is* the matter with you?" Hester asked, dragging her from her reverie. "Your face is red. Does the motion of the train make you ill?"

"Yes, that must be it," Mary answered.

*   *   *

For two months Mary had no direct contact with Castle-mere. She wrote once a week to Anjanette, making the same inquiries about the children and reporting tediously on the weather. She and Clyde compiled a report on the business twice a week for Alex, but she was careful that there was nothing remotely personal in it. She also wrote often to Hester, and a gradual thaw took place between them through the post.

Alex came to London three times and she contrived to be very busy each time. Once she made a visit to Portia's cousin in Southampton; her absence exactly coincided with his days in London. The next time, she extracted an invitation to stay with Hester—an international trade agreement would have been easier to negotiate. The third time Alex came, she threw herself on Winston Foxworth-Wilding's mercy. "I'm sorry, Mary, but I'm looking over the final copy of the book before it's actually printed. Any errors have to be corrected now, and it's very tedious work."

"I'm wonderful at grammar and punctuation, Winston. Let me help."

She proved herself an adept, if maddeningly meticulous, proofreader. They finished in less than half the time it would have taken Winston by himself and they used the extra time to see some of the sights in London that they were both normally too busy to bother with. They attended an opera and a play and on that Sunday afternoon went for a long leisurely carriage ride.

"I was sorry I missed Jamison's funeral," Winston said as they rolled along. "I was in Edinburgh doing some research on the Celtic book. I didn't even know until it was all over."

"Did you go to Inverness?"

"No. Have you been back?"

"No. And I won't. At least not for a long time. Elvira Stott writes to me every week about her. I'll have to be content with that. Hester appreciated the lovely letter you wrote to her about Jamison," she said, suddenly changing back to their original subject.

"What really happened to him?"

Mary told him the whole story, not neglecting her own part in it.

He listened with cool detachment until she was done. "What is all this breast-beating? He was a complete loss to society, to family, to business, to himself. He wasn't even evil on a grand scale," Winston said. "He was merely a petty tyrant who was using up your sister's precious youth at a rather alarming rate. You can grieve his loss if you want, but I certainly won't. In fact, I'd be proud in a nasty way if I could claim any part, however small, in bringing about his demise. How is Hester getting along?"

"She's living at her house in Kent. She let me visit and there's a bespectacled young rector there who is most attentive."

"Hardly Hester's class," Winston said with a smile.

"I wouldn't care if he were the cobbler's idiot son if he could make Hester happy. This young man obviously adores her. I told her she ought to marry him quickly."

"I imagine she was grateful for your advice."

"No need to be sarcastic with me, Winston. It runs off me like water off a duck. She didn't deny her fondness for him, but told me a long, confusing theory about grief coming to maturity—or something like that. I didn't understand a word of it."

Winston laughed. "No, of course you didn't."

"What does that mean? That I'm an insensitive clod-pate?"

"No, my dear Mary. Only that you're so very single-minded. You see a goal and head straight for it without pausing or looking aside. Hester, however, has a great need to have her bags packed and the itinerary mapped out and somebody to run ahead and make sure there are no potholes."

"You're forgetting that Hester's the one who made a hasty and thoroughly ill-advised marriage," Mary argued.

"Yes, and that's one of the reasons she was so unhappy. It was a very un-Hester-like action, all that raw passion. Speaking of passion—"

"Oh, look at the lake! Aren't those ducks adorable?" Mary said quickly, all but leaping out of the carriage.

Late that evening, after they'd returned to Mary's house, had a delicious cold supper and more talk, Winston announced that he had to leave. As they stood in the doorway, he said, "How long can you keep hiding from Alex, do you think?"

"Whatever can you mean?"

"Mary, you forget I'm involved in Beecham's. I'd be a fool if I didn't notice that you're avoiding him every time he comes to town."

"It's a bargain I made with God," Mary said simply. "He seems to be keeping up His part of it and so must I."

"Well, that certainly has a primitive sort of charm."

"Oh, Winston, don't be so arch."

"I'm sorry."

"So am I. I didn't mean to get ruffled. As a matter of fact, Anjanette says in her letters that she's feeling stronger every week and wants to bring the whole family up in another month or so to do some Christmas shopping. I can't and won't hide from that. It would be rude to her."

"Call on me if you need me," he said, dropping a brotherly kiss on the top of her head.

"Thank you, Winston. I probably shall, you know."

As it turned out, she needed him very shortly.

They were to come the first week in December. Two days before the anticipated arrival, Mary devoted the day to her own shopping. Although her treasure of a housekeeper, Mrs. Coomb, could be trusted to arrange for flowers, linens, meals, soaps—all the details—Mary preferred to make these decisions herself. With Agnes in tow, she set out early. By midday they were loaded down like an expedition to some foreign clime. Nearly buried in paper-wrapped parcels and bunches of hothouse tuberoses that cost the earth, they returned to the London house.

Winston met them at the door. At his serious expression, Mary's exuberance faded. "What's wrong?" she asked, nearly falling from the carriage in her dread.

"Come inside."

Once behind closed doors in the library, Mary drew a long shaky breath and asked, "It's not Alex, is it? Nothing's happened to him."

"No, not Alex."

She collapsed into a chair. "Who, then?"

"Anjanette. She's had a heart attack."

Mary put her hand to her mouth. "Oh, no! Poor Alex. Is she . . . ?"

"Not when Alex sent the wire."

"To you?"

"Yes, he didn't want you to be alone when you got the news."

"I must go to Castlemere. Will you come with me? Please, Winston."

"If you need me, of course."

"A heart attack! People recover from heart attacks, don't they?"

"They do, but Anjanette's been in ill health for years. Mary, she could be gone already. The wire came hours ago."

It had been a sunny day, and was still very warm for December when they arrived in the early evening, but Castlemere seemed as doomladen as a German castle in the winter. In the few short months she'd been there, Anjanette had become a favorite of the household staff. The maid who opened the door was weeping openly. Mary flung her hat aside and gave the maid the huge bundle of tuberoses she'd brought along. Then she ran up the stairs without even pausing to ask what the situation was. Winston followed more slowly, unsure just what his role was to be.

He climbed the long staircase and approached the open door of the Prince William suite, where Anjanette had apparently remained, even though Mary had abandoned the master suite. Two maids were huddled just outside, clinging to each other and crying quietly. Winston looked in the door.

There was a fire in the grate, making the room oppressively hot. Anjanette was propped up slightly in the bed. Her eyes were closed and her breathing so shallow as to be almost imperceptible. Alex was at one side of the bed, leaning forward, holding her hand in both of his, and looking at her as if he might bring her back by sheer strength of will. The man looked half-dead himself. Mary had knelt at the other side and there were tears running down her face in a steady stream. "Anjanette, I've come. It's me, Mary."

Anjanette turned her head slightly and opened her eyes for a moment before they fluttered shut again. "Mary . . ." she whispered. There was an ominous rattle in her breathing.

Winston became aware that another figure had joined him in the doorway. "Oh, Dr. Engle . . . ?" he said quietly.

The man shook his head sadly. "Nothing to be done," he answered in a hushed tone. But he slipped into the room and, standing next to Mary, lifted Anjanette's wrist, taking her pulse. Then he laid her hand back down as though it were porcelain and came back into the hallway. "Terrible pity," he mumbled to himself. "Especially for the children."

Mary was running her fingers lightly, lovingly along Anjanette's arm and speaking softly. "Anjanette, you must not leave us. Please get better."

The older woman gave her a ghost of a smile. "Mary . . . don't . . . cry."

Mary wiped her eyes on her sleeve. "I won't cry. I promise. But you must get well. You *must.*"

"Mary . . . will . . . you . . . pour?" Anjanette asked, then slowly turned to face Alex.

Mary put her forehead down on the counterpane. Winston stepped in and put his hands on her shoulders. She rose slowly and said, "Anjanette, I'll be back to see you. You'll be better in a little while. I know you will." She glanced at Alex, then turned and let Winston lead her away. He closed the door gently behind them, leaving Anjanette and Alex alone together.

"What did she mean?" he asked Mary as they walked slowly down the hallway.

"She was talking about tea," Mary said in a preoccupied manner. "About serving tea."

Mary and Winston waited in the map room. It had grown dark, but the curtains were open. The fragrance of the tuberoses filled the room. Winston went to the window, wondering how such an exotic scent survived in a house of mourning. He stayed there, watching the shadows become part of a greater darkness. On the horizon there were occasional flashes of lightning. He hated these winter storms. Behind him, Mary sat at the desk where George had first showed her the magic of maps. Neither of them spoke.

In less than an hour, Alex came in. Though he'd never been a soldier to Winston's knowledge, his bearing was stiffly military. "It's done. She's gone," he said flatly. "The doctors kept warning me this could happen, but I didn't believe it."

Mary had stood when he entered, but she made no further move toward him. Winston glanced at her and thought: The queen is dead. Long live the queen.

"I'm sorry, Alex," Mary said.

"Yes . . ." There was a distant rumble of thunder. "There's going to be a storm. The ground will be wet."

Winston let the silence stretch as far as he could bear before saying, "What shall we do first? Would you like us to help you write to her people? They're in Java and Holland, aren't they?"

His brisk practicality broke the spell. Alex put the heel of his hand to his forehead for a moment, then said, "Yes, yes. There is a lot to do, isn't there?"

He went to tell the children and Mary went to the Prince William suite. Dr. Engle was putting away medicines in his bag. Mary sat down and looked at Anjanette. The struggle done, her face in the repose of death was lovely. Mary hadn't been aware of the lines suffering had added until they were erased. She appeared so much younger and so very beautiful. This must have been what she looked like when Alex married her. No wonder he'd loved her.

No wonder they'd all loved her.

Mary stayed at Castlemere for another week, miserable herself but eager to be of whatever comfort she could to Alex. But he didn't seem to want or need her comfort. He turned to his children instead, and seemed obsessed with making sure they felt the loss of their mother as little as possible. He moved them into his room so that they wouldn't be lonely in the nursery. "Richard often has nightmares," he said when Mary questioned the advisability of this move. "I want to be there if he needs me."

Before long Mary was forced to admit to herself that she had no place in the small grieving family. She had become an intruder at Castlemere. With a grave sense of failure and loss, she went back to London. "You know where to find me if I can help in any way at all," she told Alex. Please need me, she thought.

"I'll come to London in a while," was all he replied.

For three months she heard nothing from him. "I want to help them, Winston," she told her old friend who had seen her through so many other sorrows. "Not just Alex. The children too."

"You can't. It's that simple. You can't," he told her bluntly. "You ought to know by now that there are griefs we must face alone. You've faced your own."

In March a letter came from Alex. "We'll be passing through on the way to Hester's Friday. I've decided to take her up on her offer to keep the children for a while. I'm told there's a two-hour stop between trains. Will you take luncheon with us?"

She had three days to wonder what it was about. Was he going somewhere that he needed to leave the children with Hester? Why hadn't he asked her to keep them? She had offered repeatedly. Never mind that it hurt her feelings—

he'd never know. She met them at the station and had a carriage waiting to whisk them to the London house for a quick meal. She was astonished at how tired Alex looked. Even the children were thin and edgy. It must have been terrible for them. Why hadn't they let her help?

After a light meal, the children went into the tiny garden and Mary sat with Alex over dessert. "You're going to Hester's, your letter said."

"I'm leaving the children there. She's been begging me to leave them with her for a while. I thought at first they should be with me, but I've decided I'm the worst person in the world for them to keep company with. It will only be for two or three months."

"And you? Where will you go? Back to Castlemere?"

"No!" he said. "I'm going to do some traveling around Great Britain. There are a great many places I've meant to see and never bothered with. This is as good a time as any. I'm not good for anything else. I thought I'd go to the Lake District and see the Highlands and Loch Ness and Warwick Castle."

"That ought to be very nice for you," Mary said.

"I hope the weather remains good," he replied.

They fell silent for a moment; then Mary said, "We're talking to each other like strangers, Alex."

He looked up and met her gaze squarely for the first time. "It's the only way I can talk to anyone right now, Mary."

"I understand. I felt that way once . . ."

"When Henry died?"

"Henry? No, it was after that. Someday I'll tell you about it."

Alex studied her for a moment. "Is that a promise?"

"Of course, if you promise to come back here as soon as you're able."

"I will. Mary, don't look so worried about me. I'm going to be all right. Just give me some time."

"I'd give you anything you want, Alex."

42

Mary had a surprise caller the first week in June of that year. "A lady to see you, ma'am," the new maid said.

"Elaine!" Mary cried as she entered the drawing room. "I was about to send a search party out to China for you. You haven't written for ages. I can't believe my eyes! Here you are in England!"

"Surely you knew I'd return as soon as I was able," Elaine said. The words weren't exactly cold, but they lacked the warmth Mary had expected. "Franklin is my responsibility now. I'm only sorry I couldn't abandon my job immediately."

"Elaine, you needn't have come. I'm paying Franklin's bills and I have my people send him special food and extra blankets and clothes and anything else the people at the asylum might not provide. You didn't think I'd abandon my duty, did you?"

"It's not your duty. It's mine." Elaine was definitely cold now, "I don't imagine you go see him."

"No. He doesn't know me," Mary said. The truth was, she couldn't bear to ever get near the hideous place again, but even if she did force herself to go see him, it would do him no good. "I don't think he'll know you either."

"That doesn't matter. Someone must visit him."

"I'm sorry, Elaine. I didn't know you'd feel that way."

"Of course you didn't."

"Elaine, please take off your hat and sit down to visit. What is the matter?"

"The matter? You ask me that?"

"I do ask."

"I want to know the truth, Mary. I suppose you thought to spare me in your letters, but it's time to tell me."

"What do you mean?"

"My brother Henry took you to see Franklin, then killed himself for it? Do you honestly expect me to believe that? I'm insulted that you'd take me for such a fool. He didn't want you to know about Franklin, but having told you, he had no reason to do something so utterly horrible. What did you say to him? What did you do?"

"What did *I* do?" Mary said, angry now.

"You must have injured him horribly. He was so intent on keeping Franklin a secret—you must have threatened him with it. I can think of nothing else that would have made him take his own life."

"Do you really think so little of me?" Mary said, appalled.

"I think nothing of you. You're beneath my consideration," Elaine said. "I simply want to know how you killed Henry."

"You can't imagine how wrong you are. And how evil it is of you to speak to me this way. Elaine, I thought we were friends."

"I thought so too. But I've learned better. You killed Henry. I curse the day I actually destroyed that insane letter you wrote to me. If I still had it, I'd have you put away like Franklin. But I'd put you in the nastiest, filthiest asylum I could find. To imply that a sweet, kind man like Henry had some part in the death of your child. Outrageous! You're both mad and wicked. And to think I actually felt sorry for you! And told you about Franklin. You didn't fool me with that story about finding out about him on your own. I hope God will forgive me for the part I had in all this."

"Elaine, I'm sorry for the burden on your conscience, but I have nothing on mine. There were matters between Henry and me that you know nothing about, nor will you—ever! Now I think it would be best for both of us if you leave."

Thank heaven she knew nothing of Molly. Who could guess what she might do if she did?

"I'll spend the rest of my life trying to forgive you, Mary, but I doubt I will accomplish it," Elaine said, striding toward the door.

Mary followed her. "You'll be wasting your energy, hating me."

"Probably, but I can think of few greater pleasures," Elaine said.

Mary was still standing at the front door, shaking with

impotent fury when a carriage pulled up. "Mary? You look a thousand miles away," a familiar voice said.

"Alex! Why didn't you tell me you were coming?"

"I did. Didn't you get my letter. Mary? What's the matter? You look like you've seen a ghost."

"In a way, I have. The ghost of a friend. My former sister-in-law."

"Henry's sister, Elaine? I'm sorry I missed her. We've never met."

"Nor are you likely to now. Please, come in. You are staying, aren't you?"

He had planned to take a hotel room, but there was a heartfelt plea in her voice he couldn't ignore. "Mary, I think you'd better tell me about all this. I've never seen you look so shaken."

They went inside, passed through the dining room and out into the tiny city garden. "It's all so secretive and ugly and distressing. I'm sure you don't want to hear it. You've problems enough of your own," Mary said as they sat down on either side of a little wrought-iron table.

"I'm sick to death of my problems. I'm a good keeper of secrets, you know."

"I'm not sure where to start," Mary said. "It's about Henry's brother and my daughter."

"Henry had a brother? Other than the one who died young?"

"No, he didn't die. Neither did my Molly. . . ."

It took her nearly an hour to get the whole story out.

"My God, Mary! I'd never have guessed," Alex said when she finally stopped. "What can I do?"

"Nothing. That's the worst of it. It's too late for anything to be changed."

"Surely not. Have you gone back to see her?"

"No, and I shan't. She's terrified of me. It would just hurt both of us. The awful irony of it is that I had to do just what I hated my own mother for doing. I had to leave my child with someone else for her own good. I suppose there's a lesson in that, but it's one I wish I'd never learned."

"Mary, it breaks my heart that I didn't know and had no way to spare you this pain."

"That's just how I felt about you when Anjanette died. Alex, I've been rattling on about myself forever. So selfish of me. You look fit and wonderful. How were your travels? How are you really?"

"I'm fine. I've seen everything I've ever wanted to see, and a lot of places I didn't. I'm sick of traveling and starved for the sight of Castlemere. I'm going down first to fetch the children back from Hester—at least that's one of my alternatives."

"What do you mean? What are the others?" Please, God, don't let him say he's going back to Malaya, she thought.

"It depends on you."

"Me? How?"

"When I left here the last time you said you'd do anything for me. There is something I'd like you to do."

"You have only to ask," Mary said, wondering what he could possibly need. Probably to come to Castlemere and help get the children settled back in.

"Then I shall. Mary, it's probably indecently soon to talk about this, but I've had a lot of time to think. There's been something between us ever since you came to Singapore so many years ago. I've tried to deny it for a long time, but it was always there—a fire that insisted on burning, no matter how I tried to put it out."

"Yes . . ." Mary said, her heart racing.

He rose and came around the little wrought-iron table. Kneeling before her, he took her hands. "I don't want a single favor from you, Mary. I want everything. I want you. I've wanted you for a very long time. Will you marry me?"

"Oh, Alex, I've waited to hear that question since I was a child."

"Does that mean yes?" he asked, standing and pulling her into his embrace.

She wrapped her arms around him and looked up. "Oh, yes, Alex. Yes, yes. Forever and ever yes."

Hester's "cottage" in Kent, as she called it, was really quite a large house, but it was mostly one story, of good solid chert and flint rock with a homely thatched roof. This old-fashioned construction and the climbing roses that nearly covered it gave a cozy intimacy that was very dear to her. The greatest part of its charm, she had finally admitted to herself, was that it was so utterly unlike Castlemere in every possible way.

There was no long, bleak, treeless vista along cliffs, no perpetual drone of the sea slapping at the land, no salt-laden air whipping at one's face and clothing and hair. Instead, there were orderly hedgerows marking off the fields and lanes, and clean, gentle inland air filled with the scent of rich earth and flowers. Instead of the cavernous rooms and halls Philippe Beecham had loved, the cottage was a haphazard rabbit warren of little rooms, all leading into each other.

Since moving here the summer before, Hester had made only one change—she had had the two rosemary bushes flanking the front door torn out and fuchsias planted in their place. She dearly hoped never to smell the scent of rosemary the rest of her life.

June in Kent must surely be as close to heaven as people are allowed to get in this life, she thought as she strolled through the tiny formal garden, cutting roses for the vases inside. Except for the warbling of a robin, it was quiet too. Almost too quiet, if truth be told. Alex's children had come to stay with her in March, three months after Anjanette's funeral, and she'd come to love the sounds of children's voices around her. But they were gone for an hour or two today, playing with Reverend Douglas Fargate's little girl, Priscilla. Motherless Pris was a shy, dainty child with her father's big brown eyes and mannerly ways. Oddly enough, she and talkative, outgoing Katie got along beautifully and they both adored playing "little mother" to Richard. Richard didn't much care for it.

Dear Douglas seemed to enjoy seeing the children together as much as she did. He swore they didn't interfere with his sermon writing, and when they'd taken down half the books in his library to build a playhouse, he praised them for their cleverness. Such a good man. And he was so very nice to Katie, who was taking her mother's death badly. He took her for walks and never seemed to become annoyed with her perpetual chatter.

Hester knew she would marry him eventually and they would have a contented life. But she was in no hurry. She had one hideous marriage to be cured of first, and it might be a long process. It had been a few days more than a year now, and she still dreamt of Jamison often and sometimes thought she heard his voice in a crowd when she visited London. Before she would be ready to think of marrying again, she had to learn to stop wondering "What would Jamison think?" when she bought a new hat or made plans. At least she had learned to put him—and herself—into perspective. He hadn't loved her at all, and while she'd been consumed by a terrible passion, she hadn't really *liked* him for a long time. It was like a slow awakening from a bad dream.

In the meanwhile, she was simply enjoying life as she had never enjoyed it before. She had grown up under Portia's thumb, then put herself willingly (oh, how horribly willingly!) under Jamison's. Now, for the first time, she was her own person. She ordered her household as she liked, planned her gardens, meals, wardrobe, and reading material to her own wants and needs. If she wanted eggs for supper and bonbons for breakfast, there was no one to nay-say her. It was heady stuff and she wasn't eager to exchange that freedom for another bondage, no matter how sweet or comfortable.

She gathered up her roses into the wide flat basket and went back to the house, sucking on her finger where a thorn had drawn blood. As she came in the kitchen door, the housekeeper met her. "I was on my way to find you, ma'am. Your sister and cousin has come to call. They're in the morning room."

Hester dropped her basket of roses and ran to greet them. "Mary! Alex! I had no idea you were coming today. What a fine surprise. You haven't come to take the children away from me, have you, Alex? I'm enjoying them so much. You told me I could keep them until Saturday next."

He hugged her and said, "No, I just wanted to see how they and you are getting along."

"They'll be delighted to see you, as am I."

"Katie . . . ?" he asked.

"Better every day. I promise. It's been terrible for her, but she's a sensible little girl in spite of her flighty talk."

"Richard?"

"As always. He asked once where his mother was and I told him that she was in heaven. Alex, I know it was hard for you to part with them, but believe me, they're happy and well here."

He sat down and leaned back in the overstuffed chair that Hester had brought from her own room at Castlemere. "Hester, I've thought often of that day of the funeral when you insisted on bringing Katie and Richard here—"

"And you refused me."

"Yes. I'm sorry you didn't just steal them. Those few

months with me were awful for them. You were quite right. I wanted them near me for my own comfort, not theirs."

"I didn't say that," Hester protested.

"No, but you'd have been right if you had. I'm glad to have such a wise and loving cousin."

"Oh, Alex . . ." Hester said, blushing with pleasure. "They've gone to play with Doug's daughter. I'm certain he wouldn't mind if you went around and brought them back."

"I think I'll do that, if you don't mind. Mary?"

"No, go on. I want to talk to Hester," Mary said, smiling.

When he'd gone, Mary, who had been pacing around the room sat down next to Hester and said, "You look heavenly, Hester. You're putting on some weight and it suits you."

"Certainly that's not what you're so eager to talk about," Hester said.

Mary looked surprised, but didn't comment on Hester's new bluntness. "No, it's not. I have the most wonderful thing to tell you. I . . . Alex and I are going to get married."

Hester's mouth dropped open in amazement. "You can't mean that."

"But I do. He asked me yesterday."

"Mary, Anjanette's only been dead a little more than a sixmonth."

"Hester, I'd never told you, but I've loved Alex forever. Since the first time I saw him when I was a child. And he . . . well, he's loved me too. Not since then, but for a long time."

Hester shook her head. "No, Mary. He loved Anjanette."

"Yes, I know he did. But he loved me as well."

"Anjanette died only half a year ago."

Mary got up quickly. "Would you stop saying that over and over. Do you think I don't know?"

"Have you gone mad?"

"Oh, Hester, I wanted you to be happy for me. I'm so happy I'm about to burst."

"I'd like to be. But this is insane. It shows a disgraceful lack of manners and common sense both."

"Manners? Do you think I care—that either of us cares—for what people think? Hester, we have a chance for happiness. Is it so awful to want to have that chance?"

"But you should wait. There's no reason to rush into this."

"Yes, there is," Mary said bleakly.

Hester raised an eyebrow. "Oh?"

Mary sat back down and said quietly, "I can't let him have second thoughts. I'm terrified that he might change his mind. Hester, I've loved Alex ever since I knew what love was. Before that even. He's the only thing I've ever wanted in my life. You *must* understand that."

Hester took her hands, which were icy. "I do understand, but, Mary, there are things you don't seem to understand, and you should. No matter what Alex feels for you, he loved his wife."

"I know that!"

"But you don't see what it means. He *loved* her. She was his companion, his history, the mother of his children, his partner—his lover."

"I don't deny any of that."

"But it can't be put aside, packed away so quickly. It takes time. Even if Alex were an insensitive man who hadn't reciprocated her devotion, it would be too soon. But she was a part of every aspect of his life. Don't you remember what I told you before about grief?"

"Hester, I'm sure all of that is true for you, but it's not true of him. He wouldn't have asked me to marry him if he didn't mean it."

"I'm sure he thinks he meant it. Just as he thought the children should stay with him when Anjanette died. He changed his mind about that after a bit."

"But that was only in the days right after her death. This is months."

"Mary, there's very little difference. They'd been married for many years. Nobody gets over love that quickly."

"I don't pretend that he has, Hester. I loved Anjanette too, and I haven't stopped just because she died. But don't you see, we can share that grief, learn to accept it together."

"No, you can't. Grief is solitary."

"Perhaps for you. But it doesn't have to be. Alex and I love each other. We will endure it together. I can help him because I loved her too. Oh, Hester, I wanted you to be happy with me and for me."

"I'd like to, but I think you're both making a terrible mistake."

"You're just thinking about what other people will say."

"Mary, I'm long past caring about society's strictures. I've defied them myself and seen that the world didn't crash down around my ears because of it. No, I wasn't thinking of that at all. If there's one thing I learned from Jemmy, it's that as long as you have a great deal of money, people will accept you. At least accept you as much as we care to be accepted. I'm thinking only of you and Alex and what's best for you."

Mary looked away. "I thought you'd be happy for me—"

"I want to be. If you'd told me this a year from now—"

"A year! Hester, I've lived for Alex's love for so many years—"

"Then waiting another shouldn't be impossible."

"But I've done my waiting already! I've waited for him since I was seven years old!"

Hester got up and walked across the room, knowing that nothing she could say would convince her sister. She must stop arguing with her, and yet it was all wrong . . .

"It's perfect, really. We'll be putting the two halves of the company back together," Mary was saying. "I think maybe that's what Papa hoped all along. And we both love Castlemere. Hester, I won't even have to change my name. Think of it. None of that tedious changing of monograms on my handkerchiefs like you had to do." She laughed a little shrilly.

Hester turned, making herself smile. "As if you would sit quietly and embroider. If you'd done that when you should, all your linens would have a T on them now."

Mary suddenly ran across the room and embraced her. Hester was surprised and touched to discover that her invincible sister was trembling like a baby rabbit. What an extraordinary reversal of their usual roles. Had Hester grown so much stronger? Or Mary more vulnerable?

"Hester, please, *please* be happy for me. With me. Wish us well."

Hester hugged her tightly "Oh, I do most heartily wish you both well. Most heartily."

Mary didn't mention any of the conversation to Alex. In fact, she made a dedicated effort of will to forget all Hester's dire warnings. Hester just didn't comprehend that this was a very special circumstance. Nor did Hester understand how desperately in love with Alex Mary had always been. All Hester said might be true of other people, but the very intensity of Mary's passion would make it all right. These were not ordinary circumstances. She didn't resent the fact that he'd loved Anjanette. She'd loved Anjanette herself so very much.

What's more, Anjanette herself would have understood. Perhaps *had* understood for a long time. She would have wanted Alex to be happy, and Mary was going to make Alex happy. It was her sole aim in life, because her own happiness would depend on his. Anjanette would approve, even applaud Mary's aims.

"Are you sure you and Hester didn't fight?" Alex asked.

They had a first-class carriage to themselves on the trip back to London. Mary had been very quiet. Now she took his hand and leaned her head on his shoulder. "No, we didn't. She just gave me a lot of matronly advice."

"Which I'm sure you took with good grace."

Mary looked up at him, smiling. "Naturally. I'm the most agreeable of brides-to-be."

Alex grinned back. "If only Nellanor could hear you say that!"

The remark, meant in the friendliest way, was like a dash of cold water in her face. Nellanor. Dear Aunt Nell. What would she have said of this precipitous marriage? She certainly wouldn't have minced her words.

It didn't bear thinking about.

43

Mary stretched and yawned luxuriously before opening her eyes. Then she rolled over and cupped Alex's hand where it lay on her naked breast. Alex's hand on her breast. How utterly extraordinary! She hadn't suspected she could be so happy. Nor had she had so much as an inkling what love could really be. To be loved entirely—all over—physical love as well as that of the heart! Why hadn't anybody ever hinted at how perfectly bodies fitted together? It was the most marvelous revelation life had to offer.

Alex nuzzled her neck. "It's not morning again, is it?" he complained, nibbling her earlobe.

"Mmmm. Do you think we ought to get up? Hester will be bringing the children this afternoon."

"But not until this afternoon."

"We didn't even leave the room yesterday and I think it's pretty outdoors."

"We'd have gotten out yesterday if you hadn't put on that lacy chemise—"

"—that you took off before I'd even found my stockings."

"But it looked so good coming off. The way your breasts showed through the lace was irresistible. Don't ever put that thing on in front of me if you actually want to go someplace."

She smiled. "Still, we ought to get dressed, just so we can have the fun of getting undressed later."

"You're sounding like an old married lady," he said.

"I am. I've been married a whole week now. A whole week! It seems like minutes and it seems like forever. Do you have any idea—any idea whatsoever—how desperately much I love you?"

Alex rolled onto his back and stretched, grinning. "Some."

"And you love me too. Say it."

"I seem to recall having said it about a million times this week."

"You must say it a million times a week from now on. It makes me all tingly. Even the soles of my feet want to touch you," she said, curling up sideways and gently running her feet up and down his leg. "To think, I'd never seen your knees before. Isn't that amazing? I loved you so much without even seeing all of you. You have gorgeous knees."

Alex laughed. "Nobody has gorgeous knees. Except you. And you're so delicious everywhere that I hadn't given much thought to your knees yet. Let's see . . :"

He sat up and, starting with her knees, slowly kissed his way all the way up her body. "Oh, Alex, stop! No, no, don't stop. Don't ever, ever stop. Ohhh—"

He laughed as he stroked the inside of her thigh. "I should have known you couldn't even make love quietly. Since the first time we met, you've talked."

A memory flashed through her mind, a memory from Penang. Anjanette didn't make love quietly either. She was sorry she remembered.

"What's wrong?" Alex asked, noticing a subtle change in her movements.

"Just a little muscle cramp in my leg," she said breathlessly.

"Hmmm, I guess I'll have to massage it out. Where's the cramp?"

"I'm not telling." She giggled. "You have to find it."

"You think I can't? Is it here? Or here? Or maybe here?"

"Oh, Alex, that tickles . . . or something."

"More likely the 'something.' "

They dressed and undressed twice before finally leaving the room. As Alex opened the door of the master suite, he looked back and said, "I like to see you in that mirror. It's like having two of you. An embarrassment of riches, I think it's called. Let's get some more mirrors so there can be dozens of you. And there's something else I want—"

"Anything, my love. Anything."

"I want to have a portrait done of you. A great, huge, gaudy portrait. I want generations of Beechams after us to know what an unbelievable treasure you are."

"Oh, Alex," she whispered, tears coming to her eyes. She'd scoffed at the concept of crying out of happiness before, but this week she had repeatedly learned the meaning of the phrase.

"I want you to wear something red. No . . . I know what

I want. Remember that garnet-colored dress you wore the night we all went to the Residency ball in Penang? Do you still have it?"

"Yes, I think so. Someplace. But it's so old."

"Then have another made just like it."

"Why that dress, Alex?"

"Because I loved you in it. I mean, I first began to realize I loved you the night you wore it."

"I loved you the first time I saw you. It was here at Castlemere. On the terrace. You were so beautiful—"

"Beautiful? Good God, I was a skinny boy with ears like the handles on a water pitcher."

"You were a god."

"And you were a pixie—hiding in the wisteria."

"You remember that?"

"Of course."

"I didn't think you even knew I was alive."

"How could I not notice a child who could throw herself into the sea just to get my attention?"

"I didn't do it on purpose. Let's walk down to the beach and maybe I'll fling myself in again."

"No need. You already have my full attention."

"I know that. Oh, I know."

They sat for a long time on the big flat stone. Mesmerized by the waves and the hot summer sunshine, Mary said lethargically, "I'm tired."

"It's a nice sort of weariness, isn't it?" Alex agreed, leaning back on his elbows and stretching his legs out.

"I hope to feel this way all my life from now on. Though a real nap by myself might be refreshing."

"And lonely."

"Alex, about the children—I'm uneasy."

"Why on earth should you be? It's not as if you don't know them, or they you."

"Well, they haven't been told. What if they don't like the idea of our being married?"

"Why shouldn't they?"

"It will be a surprise to them."

"Children love surprises. And they love you."

"Richard does."

"So does Katie. Her manners are just a bit strange."

"Do you remember the last time we were here together?"

"Of course I do. It was a moonlit night and you told me about George's will and who you really are."

"Were you surprised?"

"No, I'd suspected it. Not the marriage, of course, but that George was your real father. There was something very strong and binding between you and him that transcended mere legalities. I saw that in Penang. And since then, I've seen you so often in Katie that I would have known for certain that you were a blood Beecham. Some gabby gene that surfaces from time to time—"

"I'm not as talkative as Katie."

"Katie is your image."

"Alex! I was never as odd and outspoken as she."

"You were and are. Nobody knowing you and Janette would ever suspect Katie was her daughter and not yours."

Something about the way he spoke her name made a chill go up Mary's back. It was the intimate, familiar use of the diminutive, she supposed. It made it seem, for a moment, as if she were still alive. Or still alive in his mind.

"Do you miss her?" she asked impulsively.

"I haven't had much time to think about it lately. She'll be here in a little while."

"I meant Anjanette."

"Oh."

"Do you?"

He stood up suddenly and made something of a production of picking up a sea-gull feather a few feet away and smoothing it out. "Of course I do. What sort of callous ghoul do you take me for?"

"I'm sorry. I shouldn't have mentioned her."

"Why not? Are we to pretend she didn't exist? I'm sorry, Mary. You just took me a bit by surprise. Here, put this in your hair. . . . No, sticking up in the back, like an American Indian."

It was like a miniature squall at sea, blowing up and dying. Mary let out a long breath of relief as she tucked the feather into the hastily pinned knot of hair at the back of her head. "There! Do I look like an Indian maiden?"

"With that flaming hair? Not precisely. But you look wonderful anyway. You're getting too much sun. You'll burn. Let's go back to the house."

Why did his consideration seem like a rejection? Mary wondered as she climbed up the cliff behind him. Just her imagination, she was certain, and her nervousness about the children's return.

Apparently Hester, too, was nervous of the outcome of the announcement and had inadvertently conveyed her unease to the children. They arrived late that afternoon and were fretful. Richard clung to Hester like a barnacle and Katie glued herself to Alex's side. Mary felt rather left out, but attempted to make bright conversation on the way to Castlemere from the train station. "There are two new colts in the stable. After you've had naps, I'll take you down to see them," she promised.

"We don't take naps anymore. We're too old," Katie said.

"Nobody's too old for naps," Mary said. "I like naps."

"Only little children and sick people take naps," Katie persisted. "My mama took them because she was sick and died."

That left Mary with nothing further to say on the subject. "I have a new doll for you, Katie. Wait until you see how pretty she is. Perhaps we can make her some new clothes. I'll show you how to sew. Would you like that?"

"No."

"Katie, that's quite enough of your rudeness," Alex said in such a firm tone that she mumbled an apology and retreated into sullen and complete silence. He reached over and gave Mary's hand a reassuring squeeze, but she failed to be reassured. This was going to go badly. She was positive of it and helpless to think what to do about it.

Once in the house, the children were taken upstairs by the nanny and the nursery maid. Hester joined Mary and Alex for a late tea. "You didn't tell them, did you?" Mary asked her sister.

"Good heavens, no. That's your job, and one I have no desire whatsoever to usurp."

"No, it's my job," Alex said, setting down his cup untasted. "And I believe it's one best done immediately."

"I'll come with you," Mary said, rising.

"No, if you don't mind, I think it would be best if I talked to them alone."

"Oh, I see. Very well, if you think—"

But he was gone.

Mary made conversation with Hester for a few moments, but neither of them really had her mind on climate or horticulture, and in a while Mary said, "I have to go to them."

"No, Mary. Leave Alex to deal with it. They are a family and must sort it out among themselves."

"But I'm part of the family too. I was before, and I'm even more so now."

"You've married Alex. Not the children. It will take a while with them. They must be courted too."

"I didn't see you courting them! You just took them in and they didn't mind."

"I didn't marry their father," Hester said softly.

"Well, I did, and so it's my business."

When she got to the nursery, Alex was sitting on a little chair with Richard on his lap. Another man might have looked quite foolish in that position; Alex managed to retain his dignity in spite of the awkward posture. Katie was standing in front of him with her hands on her hips. "No, Papa! No! No! No!" she was saying.

"Yes, Katie. Even if you don't like it, you must be lady-like, and soon you will come to like the idea very much. I promise you."

Katie heard the door and whirled to face Mary. Her face was red. "You aren't my mama!"

"No, of course I'm not," Mary answered with false calm.

"I don't want a new mama and I don't like you, Cousin Mary."

"Katie, I won't allow that sort of talk," Alex said.

"Then I won't talk at all!"

Alex started to speak, but Mary forestalled him. "Alex, I think Katie and I need to have a private talk. Would you and Richard like to go see the new colts?"

"Mary, I can handle this. Katie is being rude and—"

"Please, Alex."

"Very well, but I'll be right back," he said, standing up with sleepy Richard draped over his shoulder. He reached out with his free hand and touched Mary's cheek before lightly kissing her. The sight made Katie go rigid with fury.

No sooner had the door closed behind them than Katie said, "I meant it. I don't like you."

Mary drew on a reserve of calm she didn't know she had. "I know you don't right now. But you used to like me and you'll like me again someday if you let yourself."

"No, I won't. My mama died. I don't want a new mama."

"Katie, please sit down and listen to me."

Rebellious and angry, Katie still had her manners well enough inbred to obey, albeit reluctantly. She perched on the front two inches of a nursery chair, as stiff as a block of ice. Mary sat down across from her. She'd never been in this room much; when she came to live at Castlemere, she'd had her own room and spent much of her time in Aunt Nell's company, not nursery maids'.

She drew a breath and said, "When I was a little girl about your age, I lost my mama too. She died like yours did. I came to live here, just like you have. It was strange to me and there was a woman who was married to my father and I didn't like her at all . . . Katie, are you listening to me?"

Katie gave an almost imperceptible nod.

"My Aunt Nell told me I must be nice to her and I would start to like her and eventually I would love her. And do you know what? As wise as Aunt Nell was about most things, she was wrong about that. I learned to get along with my father's wife, but I never loved her."

Katie looked at her with surprise.

"Do you know why that was? Why my Aunt Nell was wrong? Because my father's wife didn't like me. You see, if she'd been good to me, I would have loved her, just like Aunt Nell said. And that's the difference between us. Both of us lost our mothers, Katie, that's the same. But your father has married somebody who loves you very much. You and Richard. People can have only one mother. I want you to know that I understand that very well."

Still refusing to meet her eye, Katie mumbled something. When Mary asked her to repeat it, Katie said, "What did you call her?"

"Who? Oh, my father's wife—I didn't know what to call her at first, so I called her 'ma'am' and then I made myself call her 'Mama.' But later I got brave and called her by her Christian name. You don't have to worry about that, though. You've always called me Cousin Mary or Mary. I don't want you to change that."

Katie was silent for a long time, then finally turned her head slightly and looked straight at Mary. "I love Mama."

"I know you did. So did I. She was a wonderful person."

"Papa loves Mama."

"Your papa loved your Mama," Mary said, firmly emphasizing the past tense. "And he loves me now."

"No, he doesn't."

"He does, Katie. You know that. You're not a baby. We got married because we love each other. And we both love you and Richard."

"I won't be your little girl," Katie said, but it wasn't spoken as fiercely as her earlier statements. As she spoke, she picked up one of the toy teacups and turned it over, as if to look at the china mark on the bottom. The accidentally adult gesture tickled Mary.

"You don't have to be. We'll just stay cousins like always. But we will be very nice to each other because if we aren't, it would make your father very unhappy and we don't want that, do we?"

"No . . ."

"Would you like to go see the colts now?"

"I suppose so," Katie said, rising with deliberately airy unconcern.

As they started down the stairs, Katie stopped and looked at Mary. "You aren't as pretty as my mama."

Mary stifled a smile. "I know I'm not. Your mother was very beautiful. I thought so the very first time I saw her. You look very much like her."

"Do I? Oh, do I really?"

"Very like."

At the bottom of the steps Katie stopped again. "You're not exactly ugly," she admitted. "Your hair is just a funny color."

"Yes, I guess it is," Mary said, smiling.

Mary wouldn't have thought anything could mar her happiness, but it did. That night Ginger died quietly in his sleep. Mary emptied out a large walnut jewelry box and curled him up in it with his favorite blanket, then carried the coffin and a shovel to a secluded spot near the stream—a favorite spot of his for catching birds. When she had tamped the earth down on the cat's grave, she sat for a long time. She was stunned by how very bad her pet's death made her feel. The troublesome, fireplace-despoiling creature had been a part of her entire life at Castlemere. A flood of memories washed over her. George had picked Ginger out for her, and she could remember vividly the pleasure she had felt holding the little fuzzy body and hearing its rattling purr.

Twenty years. Ginger had lived to a great age for a cat. And his passing left an unexpectedly large hole in her heart.

It was as if an entire era of her life had now closed. Ginger had been her childhood. Now it was well and truly over.

Mary had a good long cry and returned to the house. She met Alex near the stables. "Where have you been and what's the shovel for?" he asked.

"I was burying Ginger."

"Oh, Mary. I'm sorry. Why didn't you tell me? I'd have gone with you."

She set the shovel back by the stable door and took his arm. "I know, but it was something I had to do by myself. Ginger and I . . ." The rest of the sentence clumped up in her throat.

"I understand," he said, patting her hand.

44

"I hate to say I told you so——"

"Mary Beecham, I don't know anybody who enjoys that phrase more," Hester said. It was the fifth afternoon of her trip to bring the children back and she was due to return to her cottage in Kent momentarily. She and Mary were waiting for her bags to be loaded on the pony trap.

"Still, you were wrong in all your gloomy predictions. There have been a few bad moments with Katie, and that one tantrum Richard threw about the milk at breakfast this morning, but it's working out quite well. The children have accepted me."

Hester paused before speaking. "So it seems. Well, nobody could be happier to be proved wrong than I am, Mary. But still, I don't think you should be too cocksure."

"There you go again!"

"Just store it up as one more thing you can tell me I was wrong about someday," Hester said easily. "I think having Richard and Katie take all their meals with you and Alex is an awfully good idea."

"Alex suggested it," Mary admitted with a noble sense of fairness. "He said he and Anjanette always had them to meals even when they were very small. He's not like most fathers, who just want them tucked away out of sight until they've grown up and learned all their manners from someone else."

"Not like our father——"

"Our father was quite a bit like Alex," Mary corrected her. "He liked having us around."

"He liked having *you* around."

"Don't be silly, Hester. Papa adored you," Mary said, uncomfortable. "Oh, here's the pony trap. Are you sure you don't want me to go to the village with you and wait for the train?"

"Quite certain. I hate farewells, especially when they're the ordinary, everyday kind." She gave Mary a quick hug. "I do wish you well, you know. Alex seems very happy and he deserves his happiness. So do you. If you should need my help, you have only to ask."

Mary saw her off, then went upstairs to dress for dinner. On the landing, she met up with one of the upstairs maids carrying a vase of roses. "How lovely they are this year," Mary said, pausing to smell the flowers.

"Yes, ma'am. My mother grows roses too, but not half so nice as these. She grows them red climbers you see on walls."

"They're beautiful in their own way."

The two women moved off in different ways, but Mary took only a few steps before pausing. "Stella, where are you putting those?"

"Why, in the Prince William suite, ma'am. Like the master said to."

"I see." Alex must have invited someone to visit and neglected to mention it. Well, it was time they got back into the world. Still, it was odd that he would forget to talk to her about it.

She asked after dinner. "Visitors?" he asked. "Not that I know of. Why?"

"I just wondered why you had flowers put in the Prince William suite today."

He looked perplexed for a moment, then said, "Oh, I told Stella that some time ago. It just makes the room seem nice, don't you think? I like having flowers around. I guess it comes from growing up in the tropics, where there are so many all the time."

"But, Alex, nobody even goes in that room. Isn't it a waste?"

He hesitated. "I suppose so. It just seemed . . . well, I was thinking I guess of how much Anjanette always enjoyed having roses near. It was her favorite scent."

"The roses are for Anjanette?"

"In a way, I suppose they are." His voice had gotten cool and remote.

"Alex—"

"If you resent the waste, you can remove them."

"It's not that. It's that . . . well, Anjanette isn't there to enjoy them and—"

"But I enjoy knowing they're there."

Mary suddenly sensed that she was on dangerous ground indeed. "Then they shall stay for as long as they're in bloom!" she said with a bright cheerfulness she was far from feeling. "It's quite nice, really. I wish I'd thought of it."

Mary tried to forget the conversation, but it kept coming back into her head. A few days later, she told the maid, "Continue to put the roses in the Prince William suite, but in the fall, when they finish blooming, you may discontinue."

"But there'll still be some nice dahlias, ma'am."

"I know, but there's no need to put them in unused rooms."

That afternoon, Mary went to the rooms in question. The roses, a yellow arrangement today, were in a tall vase in the sitting room. Mary sat down in the rocker that Alex had sent for when Anjanette first arrived. She liked rocking chairs and there had been no reason to remove it after she died. Mary sat down in it and leaned back. There was a strange grating sound and she stood back up and shifted the chair. There, under the rocker, was a key. She picked it up, studied it for a minute, and went downstairs.

Alex was in the map room, going over some shipping bills. "Isn't this the key to that box in the stables? The one you were looking for this morning?"

Alex took the key. "I'll be damned. It certainly is. I wish I'd had faith it was going to turn up. I went ahead and had the lock replaced. Where did you find it?"

"Under the rocking chair. I wonder how in the world it could have gotten there."

Alex folded the stack of papers and replaced them in their envelope. "I must have dropped it. I didn't think to look there."

"But . . . when would you have dropped it? You had it the day before yesterday."

Alex set the envelope aside with a stack of others. "I go in that room occasionally."

"Occasionally? How occasionally?"

"That sounds rather accusatory. Are there rooms in this house that are forbidden to me?"

"Of course not. It's your house."

"Our house."

"Why? Alex, why do you go in there?"

"Is there some reason I shouldn't?"

Mary put her hands out in a gesture of despair. "Yes. Yes!"

"Why?" he asked coldly.

"I don't know. But it's not right. If you need to be alone, why can't you go somewhere else? This is a huge house. There must be a dozen other rooms."

"Mary, you're talking nonsense."

"No, I'm not. I want to know why you go there. It's because of Anjanette, isn't it?"

"What if it is?"

"Alex, do you need to . . . to 'commune' with her? If there's something wrong, why don't you talk to me?"

"I do talk to you. All the time."

"Too much time—is that what you mean? Would you like a recess from me?"

"Remember what you told me about burying Ginger? That it was something you had to do by yourself. In a way, it's a little like that."

"But I was only off for an hour or so."

"And Ginger was only a cat. Anjanette was a person. It takes longer. Much longer."

"But it's been weeks!"

"Mary, you're looking for a fight and I haven't got the time to oblige you. This paperwork is stacking up faster than I can clear it away. And we've lost that shipment of ginger on the ship that sank and I've got to find some other suppliers to meet our needs this year. Could we postpone this discussion?"

"I don't think so."

"I meant that as a rhetorical question. Now, you can either help me get through these bills or you can leave me alone to do it myself. Which will it be?"

Mary turned and ran from the room.

He had dinner sent in to him on a tray. Mary ate with the children and then went for a long walk. When she got back, after dark, he was at the door. "Where in the world have you been? I was worried."

"I can imagine how worried."

He put his arm around her and led her upstairs. "Come to bed and let me tell you how sorry I am about being such a bastard this afternoon."

"Are you really?"

"More than I can say. You just took me by surprise and I acted horrible. I've told Stella to close that room off and ignore it until and unless you tell her otherwise."

Later, after they'd made love luxuriously, he kissed the top of her head and murmured, "Have you forgiven me?"

"Entirely."

"It's not as if I haunt that room. It's just that . . ."

"That what, Alex?" she asked when the silence stretched out.

He turned to face her and cradled her face in his hands. "I don't know if I can explain it. It's as if a part of Anjanette is still there. I visited her grave, but that's the place she's dead. Those rooms are where she was alive."

"Yes?" Mary's heart ached, and she wanted to cover her ears, but she sensed this was something he needed to say and she needed to hear.

"I feel, sometimes, like I've turned my back on her. By loving you so much. And I go there rather like making a duty call. No, that's not all it is. That makes it sound like I think of her as a maiden aunt."

"Do you still love her?"

He drew back, studying her face in the pale moonlight. "Of course I do. I'll never stop loving her. Did you think I would?"

"I . . . I don't know."

"It makes no difference in how I feel about you, Mary."

"Yes, it does!" The room seemed suddenly to have gotten colder.

"No, it doesn't. I love you entirely."

"But you love her too. Still. So you can't love me entirely."

His hands fell away. "Mary, you're making me feel that I have to explain something unexplainable, to excuse something that needs no excuse. Do you want me to forget I ever knew Anjanette? Ever loved her? I can't do that. I spent most of my adult life married to her. We have two children."

Mary burrowed closer to him, shivering. "No, I don't want that. I just want you to love me so much that you won't think of her. I know that's ridiculous of me, but I'm jealous."

He smoothed her hair back from her face. "There's no need to be. How can I convince you of that?"

"I don't know."

"It's only been a short while since—"

"I didn't force you to marry me. You asked."

"Of course I did! And I'm glad I did. I just meant that there are some things that can't be rushed, no matter how much we might want them to be."

This was too close an echo of what Hester had told her to comfort Mary. "I'm being childish and selfish, Alex. Please forgive me."

"I could forgive you anything, my love. And it's especially easy when you've done nothing wrong. Now, go to sleep and we'll start fresh tomorrow and forget all about today."

"Yes, you're right," Mary said, and yawned theatrically.

But she lay awake for a very long time.

He did seem to forget the conflict. Pointing out that they'd both neglected the spice company, Alex suggested that they go up to London for a few days and both work like whirlwinds to clear up details left too long unattended. The children were to be left behind. Mary was glad, for the first time she could remember, to get away from Castlemere, at least for a few days.

They spent long hours together at the warehouse and arranged to have business guests every night for dinner, thereby fulfilling a great many obligations in less than a week. Whatever differences and misunderstandings they might have had in other areas of their lives, in regard to spices they were in perfect accord. They shared a tremendous love of the product they sold, the history of it, and the pure sensory appreciation of it.

They met with Clyde Gordon, with their banker and attorney and a brash young man who promised better cartage service at a lower price. After interviewing him, they agreed to use his services on a trial basis. They purchased a piece of land the Beechams had coveted for several generations—land that adjoined their own London warehouse on Mincing Lane—and with Clyde, drew up plans for the immediate expansion of their storage facilities. One morning they gave Clyde a bonus and purchased a thousand new oak barrels and smaller casks. Another day they personally supervised the repacking and return shipment of an inferior load of cloves.

It was exhilarating and exhausting. They fell into bed every night almost too tired to make love. But in a sense, they didn't need to; they'd been making love all day. Quick kisses over a barrel of capers, hands held while sorting through bills, winks when Clyde wasn't looking. And the heady, pervasive scent of spices filling their senses and clinging to their hair and clothing.

"But we're newly wed, Mary. We must try . . ." Alex said one night as they clung to each other, trying to stay awake.

They did try, and laughed themselves to complete exhaustion with the effort. Mary woke up smiling the next morning.

It was as if they were under some sort of magic spell which, if not quite broken, was seriously dented when they returned to Castlemere. In the letters waiting for their return, there was one from an aunt of Anjanette's.

"She's going to be in England this week and expects to visit," Alex explained half-apologetically. "If we'd been here when it came, I could have written back and stopped her, but I'm afraid she's on her way now."

"Of course she should come," Mary said firmly.

"Anjanette's family is positively addicted to grave-visiting," Alex explained. "Whenever anyone in the Java branch of the family died, at least a pair of them came clear out from Holland to 'call on' the grave. I suppose that's why she's coming."

The elderly aunt, as it turned out, didn't travel alone. She brought her son, his wife, their three grown children, a spinster daughter of imposing bulk and volume, and a small army of servants. None of them spoke English. They stayed for three days, which seemed like an equivalent number of years. When Alex introduced Mary as his wife, the visitors made a valiant attempt to control their disapproval of such a precipitate marriage, but failed. It was clear from their manner and expressions that they considered this breech of propriety entirely Mary's doing, not Alex's.

At first Alex considerately attempted to translate everything they said (at least everything he wanted Mary to hear), but the effort became tedious in the extreme. Little of interest was being said, and it was being said in a half-dozen variations each time. After a while, he was translating only the high points of the conversations, then gave up entirely. It was just like visiting the *kampongs* with Anjanette in Penang.

The evening before their departure, Mary sat through a complete meal during which not a single word was addressed to or understood by her. The only sound that was familiar to her was the name Anjanette, which recurred every few minutes. The conversation apparently moved from cheerful reminiscences (Alex smiling and laughing—what about?) to discussion of the poor motherless children (Katie and Richard petted, kissed, cried over), and from there to sympathy for Alex's situation (many suspicious glances at her). Mary had come to recognize that grim, set expression of his as the one that hid genuine sorrow.

Mary grew angry, but was unable to focus the feeling on its precise source. She didn't like these Dutch visitors, but they weren't the only problem. There was something different about Alex when they were around. He became their Alex, not her Alex. They were upsetting him and making her helpless. She felt quite outcast in her own home.

On the third day, they got around to the point of the trip, the visit to the grave. Mary didn't feel well that morning and was tardy in getting ready. When she rushed downstairs, mouth full of apologies, however, she discovered that she hadn't held them up at all: they hadn't waited for her.

"Wait for you?" Alex asked when she chided him after their departure that afernoon. "I had no idea you wanted to go along."

"Do you mean I wasn't even expected to accompany you? I wasn't even invited?"

"Well—"

"Alex, an innkeeper's wife is treated with more courtesy than you and Anjanette's relatives have treated me! I'm not a deaf-mute housekeeper. I'm your wife. I understand they didn't come here to see me, but they could have at least acknowledged me. *You* could have acknowledged me."

"I haven't ignored you."

"Oh? Then tell me what I was wearing at dinner last night."

"Wearing at dinner? What a peculiar question."

"I had on the garnet dress. The one . . . ." Mary suddenly ran out of words.

"Oh, Mary, I'm so sorry. What a brute I've been to you. You did look beautiful. I did notice. Truly. It's just that they had me so undone—"

"I know that and I wanted to be of some help to you. And to the children. And I couldn't because nobody would talk to me."

"They weren't saying anything worth hearing."

"The whole dinner talk was about Anjanette. Why

shouldn't I want to hear? I knew and loved Anjanette too. In fact, I probably knew her better than any of them."

"Yes, but not as family."

Mary was stunned. "What difference does that make? And for that matter, I am family. I was *your* family before we were married and now I'm stepmother to Anjanette's children."

Alex suddenly ran out of patience. He ran his hands through his hair. "Oh, Mary. Let it go, will you? Do you have to talk everything to death? They were morbid, depressing people I had to put up with. They're gone. They won't ever come back. What difference does it really make?"

"Alex, they came between us. You *put* them between us."

"I didn't invite them."

"No, I mean you let them exclude me. You excluded me."

"Mary, we can't live in each other's pockets every minute."

She clenched her hands together and looked down so he couldn't see her face. "I thought we could," she said in a small voice. "I really thought we could."

He put his arms around her then. Laying his cheek on the top of her head, he rocked her gently back and forth. "Oh, Mary. Dear, beloved Mary. Without you my life would be desolate. If I slam doors in your face, it's just because I need to slam a few doors. Please understand. Please be patient."

That night, when Alex put out the light, he crawled into the big carved bed, gave her a long kiss, then turned over to go to sleep.

"I don't understand at all," Mary whispered into the darkness.

45

They didn't talk again about Anjanette's relatives and Mary came to peace with herself about it. No matter how much she wanted to be a part of every aspect of Alex's life, she quite simply hadn't been a part of his first marriage. It was childish of her to have expected Anjanette's family to throw themselves at her with kisses and congratulations. They'd not even known of Alex's marriage when they arrived and couldn't have suspected that Mary had grown up at Castlemere and counted it her house every bit as much as Alex's. They came for a purpose: to grieve their kinswoman. It was a legitimate purpose and Mary had no right to complain. Or so she told herself firmly and repeatedly.

Even if she were wrong, Mary was determined not to act put upon. She and Alex and his children were a new family, with rough edges to be smoothed out and accommodated. The children had lost their mother, the mainstay of their young lives. They were at loose ends and Alex was distressed on their behalf. Her first duty, for their sake as well as hers, was to keep everyone happy.

And for a while after that, she felt she was succeeding. Whenever her own feelings were hurt, she reminded herself that the little ones were but children and Alex was both a widower and a new husband—a difficult pair of roles to play at once.

Then Katie and Richard came down with measles the first week in September. Old Dr. Engle's son, who had started in practice with his father the year before, attended them. Though they didn't speak of it, both Alex and Mary kept thinking of the last child in this house who got measles, Charlotte Beecham, who had died during Alex's first visit to Castlemere. "It's a very mild case in both of them," the

469

young physician assured them. But it relieved little of their anxiety.

Within a few days, however, they saw the truth of it. Richard was virtually well and Katie, while very spotty, wasn't desperately sick, only sick enough to be very, very cranky. Feeling that the little girl's illness gave her the perfect opportunity to prove to Alex just how maternal she really was, Mary threw herself into the nursing. But two full days of it were nearly all she could take.

When Alex found Mary the third morning, in the map room, studying a proposal a new shipping company had sent to solicit their business, he said, "What are you doing down here?"

Mary looked up, keeping her finger on a list of figures she was analyzing. "Here? Where else would I be?"

"I thought you'd be upstairs with Katie."

"No, the new governess, Miss Millbridge, is reading her stories this morning."

"Oh, I see."

"Alex, what's wrong? You sound angry."

"No, I'm just surprised. Don't you think you should be with Katie instead of this strange woman?"

"Miss Millbridge is the living, breathing essence of conventionality. There's nothing the least bit strange about her," Mary said with a laugh. But seeing that Alex wasn't amused, she added, "I spent the last two days with Katie and she much prefers Miss Millbridge to me."

"That's not how it should be."

"Perhaps not, but she does. Alex, Katie and I are slowly coming to our own understanding. At least, I think we are. We don't force ourselves on one another."

"Good. Good," he said, picking up the papers she'd already looked at and glancing through them.

Mary went back to the figures where she'd left off. "I keep having a suspicious feeling about this proposal. It looks too good to be true. What do you think about these numbers?"

"What about Richard?" he asked.

"Richard who?"

"My son Richard."

"I'm sorry. I thought you were talking about business. What about Richard?"

"Don't you think he needs you? I was just up to the nursery and I thought he looked pale."

Mary bit back the impulse to say: Then why didn't you

stay with him? "Alex, the doctor saw the children not an hour ago. He says they are both doing splendidly. What is this all about? Please stop shuffling those papers about and tell me."

"I'm just concerned about the children."

"You needn't be. They're fine. Call in another doctor if you don't have faith in young Dr. Engle."

"It's not that. He seems a very bright young man. It's just that Anjanette—"

Mary stiffened at the sound of the name. It was the first time she'd been conscious of having done so when it was mentioned.

"—always stayed with them whenever they were sick."

"And so did I. But Richard is well and Katie is getting better quite quickly. They don't need me, but I thought you did. We promised these people"—she tapped the papers—"an answer this week. Clyde is holding a shipment for our decision."

"You're quite right," he said with a strained smile. "I'm making too much of nothing."

His capitulation made Mary feel guilty. After all, his wife had died only a short time before. It was natural, even admirable, of him to be overly concerned with his children's health right now.

"You look this over, Alex, and do whatever you wish about it. I'll go upstairs if it will make you happier."

The rest of the morning was uneventful. She dismissed Miss Millbridge and read stories and played games with Katie and Richard. Alex stopped in several times and grinned with approval and contentment. Mary mentally chided herself. If it was rather boring to spend a morning this way with a fretful little girl and a shy little boy, they were good children and it was a very small price to pay for everyone's happiness. Alex was obviously pleased at her sometimes inept attempts to be a good mother to his children.

If anyone was to blame for her occasional unease, it was herself. She simply hadn't thought out the fact that when she married Alex, she had automatically become a step-mother. She would get better at it, the more practice she had. Already she was beginning to appreciate the pleasure in seeing a child learn and grow and develop. Why, the smile on Richard's face when he finally mastered the rules of the card game she'd been teaching him was worth it. As time went on, he'd learn more and more about important things and she'd have that glow of satisfaction over and over.

Both children took long naps, in spite of Katie's philosophical disapproval of such childish activities. When she woke, it was as a result of a bad dream. Mary tried to comfort her, but was rebuffed. "I don't want you! I want my mother!" Katie said, thrashing free of her embrace.

Mary backed away and said softly, "Katie, you know your mother is gone."

Katie sniffled into her pillow for a few minutes, then lifted a tearstained face. "This pillow smells."

"It's the rosemary oil. I have it put in the rinse water."

"My mother put cinnamon in the sheets and things."

"I know. That's where I got the idea. When I visited your house in Singapore. You were a little girl, not even two years old yet."

"I don't like this smell."

"I'm sorry. I've always loved the rosemary smell," Mary said patiently. "Do you know why the house smells like it? I'll tell you a secret—"

"I want the cinnamon smell," Katie declared implacably.

Mary hadn't realized Alex had come in the room until she heard him reply, "I think Mary can probably change to cinnamon, sweetheart."

She turned and looked at him for a long moment, then turned back to Katie. "No, I'm afraid I can't. Katie, your mother did things in certain ways. I do them in different ways. She liked cinnamon. I like rosemary. When you are a grown woman and have your own house, you can choose whichever you prefer, or have no scent at all."

Katie gave her a long, defiant look. "You're mean to me. You aren't nice like my mother."

"Mary—" Alex began.

But she held out a hand to stop him and continued to speak to Katie. "You're quite wrong. I'm very nice, but I'm nice in different ways than your mother was."

"You didn't like my mother."

"I loved your mother. But she's gone now. As sad as that makes us all, we must get along with each other without her. Now, I'll leave you alone for a while until you think about all this. I'll come back later and we can play some more card games if you like."

"I don't want you to come back. I want you to go away."

"I won't do that. This is my home."

Mary rose with what grace she could manage in spite of her furious trembling. She walked past Alex without looking at him. She went downstairs to the map room, but hearing the sounds of two of the maids talking as they tidied the room, decided she didn't want to face anybody. She slipped outside and started walking. Without even considering it, she automatically headed toward the cliffs. Instead of climbing down the steep path to the beach, however, she sat down at the very edge, her skirts billowing around her like a pincushion.

"Oh, Aunt Nell, why aren't you here to help me? You'd have that child straightened out in an hour. I've had weeks and I'm just making it worse. She hates me. I don't deserve to be hated by her. I'm not to blame for her mother dying. My own little Molly is terrified by me, and Katie despises me! What am I doing wrong?"

She sat staring out to sea for a long while before hearing the soft scuffing of someone approaching through the sparse grass. She knew without looking that it was Alex's footsteps. "You'll get a sunburn and freckle," he said, sitting down beside her.

"I don't care. Alex, I wanted to tell her about the rosemary in the plaster—"

He reached out, took her hand, and kissed the palm gently. "Let's keep that as our secret for now. I like having secrets with you and I treasure the memory of the day you told me. Do you remember that?"

"Alex, I remember everything about you. Everything. I could tell you what you were wearing and how you had your hair combed that day."

He laughed.

"I mean it. I don't think you've ever understood how completely and utterly I love you—and loved you since I was a child. I've never loved anyone else. Not even for a minute."

"Foxworth-Wilding?"

"Not the same way. He sensed it even when I was trying so hard not to believe it myself. That's why he wouldn't marry me. He could sense it. I didn't want you to know. You were married to Anjanette."

"I hated the idea of you marrying him," Alex said. "And I felt like hell for such a selfish feeling. I knew he was a good man who would devote himself to making you happy, and I still went nearly mad when I thought of you in his arms, maybe bearing his children. It was a bad time for me, and worse, in a way, when the engagement was broken, because I felt such enormous relief and such overwhelming guilt at being relieved. Then, the next thing I knew, you were actually married to Henry Turner and you were going to have a child. My old friend Henry! I nearly ate myself up with jealousy and guilt over the jealousy."

"You never told me before."

"I couldn't admit it to myself." He put his arms around her and she moved sideways to lean back against his chest. He put his hands over her ears and tilted her head back. Kissing her forehead, he said, "Your hair smells wonderful in the sunshine."

She tilted her head sideways, and as he nuzzled her neck, she said, "Aren't you scared that somebody will see us sitting out here kissing in broad daylight?"

"Scared to death," he said languidly. "Mary, let's come back here tonight and take off all our clothes and go swimming and make love on the beach."

"On those rocks?" She laughed and shivered with delight. "We'd be bruised all over."

"On the big flat rock."

She relaxed in his arms, rubbing her cheek on his wrist. "Alex, I've been talking to Aunt Nell. Asking her what to do."

"And what has she answered?"

"She hasn't. Isn't it just like her to refuse to reply? Honestly, I don't know what to do about Katie."

"Just be patient with her. She really likes you a great deal, but she's having a bad time. I know this is made even harder on you because of your little Molly. You have a special need to be a mother to Katie. Maybe if you could do the cinnamon thing, at least in the nursery linens . . . ?"

Mary sat up straighter. "Alex, I can't do that. I don't know exactly why, but I'm certain it would be the wrong thing."

"How can it matter?"

"I can't make part of the house Anjanette's. She is gone and Katie must accept that."

"Mary, it's such a very small concession."

"But it's an important one, Alex. Can't you see that?"

"No, I'm afraid I can't."

She pulled away and turned to face him. "You're angry."

He shook his head sadly. "I simply don't understand why you're taking a stand on something so trivial. She's very young and desolated. Mary, you're forgetting that she had Anjanette as the central figure in her entire young life. Until a few months ago, Katie had literally never been away from her for more than a day or two. Now she's gone forever."

"That's the point, Alex. She *is* gone forever. And I'm here—forever. Things have changed whether Katie likes the change or not."

"Why can't you help ease that change?"

"I have tried, but not by trying to be an imitation Anjanette."

Alex looked away toward the horizon. "What a peculiar thing to say."

Mary was stunned at the ice in his tone. "I'm nothing like Anjanette and I don't want to be."

"Anjanette's qualities aren't something to be scorned," he said.

"Nor are mine, Alex."

In spite of the warmth of the sun, she started shivering when the moment stretched out and she realized he was not going to make any reply. It was like swimming in a warm sea and suddenly paddling into a frigid spot of water. Inexplicable and frightening. She sensed that she had inadvertently drifted into very dangerous territory. I don't dare say anything more, she thought.

"That breeze is chilly when the sun starts getting low," she said, standing up and brushing grass off her skirts.

"Yes, it is," he replied in a preoccupied manner and without meeting her eyes. After a moment he stood and took her arm in an alarmingly formal manner. "Let's get back to the house. I've still got to write that letter to the shipping people. Their offer is, as you say, almost too good to believe, but I think we ought to give them a try on a limited scale and see if their performance is what we'd hope for."

They walked back, talking business, and while Mary made the appropriate replies, a voice inside her head was crying: What am I to do? What is wrong?

It turned cold early that evening. The sun was swallowed by a fierce bank of rolling black clouds. The warm Indian summer, as Alex said the Americans called it, was over almost like a candle being snuffed out. A frigid wind blew in from the Channel and the servants scurried around closing windows, pulling heavy drapes, lighting fires, and searching in wardrobes and drawers for warm clothing. Mary stood at the bedroom window watching the raindrops striking the glass and thinking it should have stayed warm for one more night. If only they had been able to go down to the beach as Alex suggested! But had he meant it, even when he said it? And if so, had he changed his mind? It was probably just as well the weather had kept her from knowing.

Mary didn't sleep well that night, and woke up cold and out of sorts. She tried to remember if she'd had measles as a child and couldn't recall. When Agnes came in to bring a freshly pressed dress she asked her.

"Yes, miss. That you did, and a spottier mess I never hope to see. Miss Nellanor was right upset, she was. The old lady had planned some sort of trip to see some cousins or such and said as how you did it on purpose just so you wouldn't have to leave here."

"Oh, yes! I do remember. Well, that's not it, then."

"It's the change in the weather. You ought to stay abed for the day."

"No, I'll get up in a minute. Just leave the dress, Agnes. I can get into it by myself. How are the children this morning?"

"All over the place like fleas on a dog. That Richard is such a sweet little thing. He wanted to go outside, but I told Mr. Alex he ought not. And Miss Katie is talking about going to London with her da to shop for new clothes. She is outgrowing things, and now, with this cold, I don't know 'bout all those fancy things her mama got her when they first came."

"What did her father say about taking her to London?"

"Oh, he was a dear man. Said he'd take her next week. Just the two of them. Isn't that nice? Not many little girls have a father what would take so much trouble over them."

"No, not many," Mary said. If only she didn't have this headache, her stomach wouldn't be so queasy. "Agnes, I think I will stay in bed for a little longer."

Alex came in a few minutes later. "Agnes tells me you're ill. What's wrong?"

"No, not ill. Just tired."

He sat down on the edge of the bed and patted her leg. "You've been trying to do too much. You deserve a lazy day. Just stay here. The children are frantic to get outside. I'll have them bundled up and take them to the village for a few hours. The house will be quiet, so you can sleep."

She felt foolish tears of self-pity come to her eyes. Why couldn't he have offered to stay with her? It was considerate of him to make the offer he had, but she'd far rather have had him near. No, she'd rather have had him *want* to be with her. She knew she'd be sniveling like a child herself if he didn't leave soon and get it over with. "Would you ask Agnes to bring me a hot-water bottle?" she asked.

"Mary, you are ill!"

The genuine alarm in his voice warmed her more than the hot-water bottle could. She quickly reassured him. "I'm fine. I promise. In fact—"

She stopped herself abruptly. There was no reason yet to tell him of her suspicion. Better to wait and be quite sure. It was too soon to be certain yet. Besides, if she was right, she wanted to set the stage properly, not just blurt out something so important without thinking. "In fact, I've got a dress fitting this afternoon and I plan to be up and about long before that."

But rest didn't help as much as she'd hoped. She awoke just before noon feeling stupefied, not refreshed. Forcing herself to get up, she had some tea and a biscuit before the dressmaker arrived. She even behaved well about all the standing straight and still for the fittings. It was one of her least favorite activities in the world, but she endured it as a sort of penance for having argued with Alex.

That night at dinner, the children were full of stories about their day. "Papa took us to the beach, Cousin Mary. It's fun. There's this big flat rock where you can sit and throw rocks into the ocean. You ought to go there sometime," Katie said.

Mary knew it was unworthy of her to find the remark irritating. With a smile at Alex, she said, "I've been there a few times. I grew up here, Katie."

"My mama grew up in Java," Katie said.

"Yes. I know."

"My mama wouldn't have liked today. She didn't like cold weather."

"I *love* cold weather," Mary said. It was a lie and a stupid thing to say besides. "I can show you all sorts of nice places around here. Trees that have lots of bird nests—"

"Mama didn't like birds very much."

Why doesn't Alex stop her? Mary wondered frantically. "Didn't she?"

"I like birds," Richard said. He slid off his chair and came to crawl up onto Mary's lap. At eight, he was too old for laps, but she wouldn't have let him go for anything. She hugged him and smoothed his fine charcoal colored hair out of his eyes. "So do I. Would you like to see some birds' nests? The babies are all grown up and gone this late in the year, but you'll know where to look next spring."

Richard looked up at her with those clear blue eyes that

were so much like Alex's and said softly, "Are you our mother now, Cousin Mary?"

Mary had barely opened her mouth to answer when Katie screamed, "No! No, she's not our mama!"

Richard turned his head so quickly that he bumped Mary's chin with a sharp crack. Mary bit her tongue and could taste blood, but she said softly, "Alex . . . ?"

As if summoned from some sort of trance, he stood up and lifted Katie unceremoniously from her chair. Depositing her in front of Mary, he said, "That was a very rude outburst, young lady, and we are waiting for your apology."

"I'm sorry, *Cousin* Mary," she said mutinously through gritted teeth.

"I accept your apology, Katie. Now, go back to your place and we'll have dessert," Mary said. Dear God, she was sick to death of being patient and reasonable and trying to act impervious to Katie's antagonism. Her supply of understanding and sympathy was down to the last few drops. "Richard, do you want coconut cake?"

He was cuddled up to her, nearly asleep. It had been too busy a day for his first time out after being sick. She had the nursery maid summoned to take him up to bed. As soon as he was gone, dessert was served. Mary cut a piece of cake and smiled at Katie and Alex. He returned the smile, Katie didn't. "My mama didn't like coconut," she said.

"Oh, Katie!" Alex said wearily.

Something inside Mary snapped. "It doesn't matter whether your mother liked this dinner or not, Katie. She's not here! Do you see her at this table? She's never going to be offered coconut again, so it doesn't matter if she liked it or not."

"Now, Mary . . ." Alex said, alarmed.

"Alex, this has to be taken care of once and for all."

"Katie only meant—"

"I *know* what Katie meant. Katie meant to harass me and make me unhappy. I'm sick and tired of it." The hurt that had been building up in her for weeks suddenly rushed to the surface, washing her along in its tide. "Anjanette is dead! It's tragic but—"

"You hated my mother!" Katie screamed.

"I loved your mother. She was the closest thing I had to a mother myself. But that doesn't matter. What matters is that she's dead. It's awful, but it's true. And I can't help it. It wasn't my fault." Mary was screaming too. She suddenly heard herself and was appalled.

Katie flung herself out of her chair so violently that the chair fell over backward. She ran from the room.

Mary stared at Alex, stricken. "What have I done? What has happened to me?"

He didn't move from his place at the other end of the long table. He made an aborted gesture and looked away. "Oh, Mary . . ." he said, and gulped back whatever else he'd intended.

She put her head in her hands, forcing herself to find a tiny, shriveled reserve of sense. "I'll . . . I'll go to her. I'm sorry, Alex."

Fighting back the sobs of despair that threatened to overwhelm her, Mary went upstairs one agonizing step at a time. Katie was in bed, sniffling and hiccuping. Mary drew a long breath and said, "We both behaved very, very badly and upset your father. I'm sorry for my part of it. I've told him that and I'm telling you."

There was no reply.

"Katie, I love you and Richard and your father very much. It pains me terribly that none of you cares as much for me as you do for your mother. That's why . . . that's why I get upset. It's not a good reason, but it's the only one I have. I know it hurts you that she's gone and I know you want to hurt somebody back. I'll try to understand and remember that. But you must try to keep in mind that I have feelings too, and you shouldn't be mean to me for no reason."

"I wish you'd go away and leave us alone," Katie mumbled into the pillow. It wasn't said belligerently, but with genuine sadness.

Mary blinked furiously. "I suppose you do wish that. I . . . I'm so sorry you feel that way. Good night, Katie."

She left the room, nearly blinded by the tears that now flowed unheeded. Stumbling in the darkened hallway, she made her way to the room that had been Aunt Nell's all those years ago. The bed was stripped and dust-sheeted, and she fell on it, sobbing. "I've botched it, Aunt Nell. I finally got what I always wanted and I've ruined it and I don't even know how it happened."

She must have fallen into an exhausted sleep. She woke feeling boneless and beaten. Staggering to her feet, she went to the window, opened it, and took a deep breath of the cold air. This could be fixed, somehow. It had to be fixed. She would talk to Alex. He did love her and somehow together they would find a way to be happy together. As miserable as she was, she knew that he felt every bit as bad or worse.

The hallways were dark; she made her way to the master suite out of lifelong familiarity with the big house. Opening the door, she said, "Alex, I want you to know I'm sorry. I know I keep saying that and you probably don't believe me, but I do mean it. Just tell me what to do, what to be, and I'll do it. Anything . . ."

She waited.

And waited.

There was no reply and she suddenly sensed that she was alone. She'd made her plea to an empty room. And she suddenly knew, and hated knowing, where he was. She went down the hallway like a sleepwalker and opened the door of the Prince William suite. Alex was sitting in the rocker. A single candle flickered fitfully in the draft from around the window. He'd removed his coat and shoes; his shirt was open at the neck and rumpled.

"Alex? Why are you here? Why aren't you in *our* room?" When he didn't reply, she went on, "I've talked to Katie. I don't know if she listened, but I've done all I can."

He turned and looked at her then. His expression was ravaged. "Mary, I wish I could make you understand . . ."

"Understand what? Explain everything, anything, to me. I want to know what's wrong with me."

"It's not you. It's just time. There hasn't been enough time. I'm the one to blame. I should have realized that grief can't be turned off. It has to run its course like an illness—or a gestation."

"Are you talking about the children? About Katie?"

"Yes. And myself. It's . . . it's just too soon."

She steadied herself with a hand on a pie-crust table by the door. "Alex, she's as dead as she's ever going to get. That's a hard, ugly, cold truth. Can't any of you grasp that? And can't you see that I'm not her and that's not a failing?"

"Nobody suggested that it is."

"Suggested it? I've been pounded nearly to the ground with the reminders. Anjanette stays with the children every moment; so should I. Anjanette gave them apples for a special treat; I shouldn't, therefore, give them oranges. As if it's a moral failing. Anjanette didn't like coconut and I, low creature that I am, do like it. Anjanette liked the scent of cinnamon and I prove my utter depravity by preferring rosemary. Anjanette was an accomplished seamstress and I'm probably on the direct route to hell because I can't sew a straight seam. Anjanette didn't like birds; what is the matter with me that I do? *Suggest* that I'm inferior? You might as well take out a page in the *Times* and announce it."

"Mary—"

"I'm not finished. I've got a few things to say and I'm going to say them once—all of them. I loved your wife. Nobody could know her and not love her. She was kind and gentle and wise and serene. I admired and respected all those traits and I know I don't have any of them. Not a damned one! But for God's sake, Alex, I'm good in my own way. I'm smart and energetic—"

He stood up suddenly and grasped her by the elbows. "—and beautiful and so desirable you make me nearly insane sometimes with the need to touch you. You're funny and madly curious and there are a thousand other wonderful things about you that I love so much I can't find the words."

"Then . . . ?"

"Can't you imagine how that makes me feel? To love you for being so very different?"

"I don't see . . . ?"

"Don't you comprehend guilt at all? If you had been anything like Anjanette, in any way whatsoever, I could tell myself it wasn't so callous and unfeeling of me to love you so desperately. It's because you're different that I feel so disloyal to her. It's an insult to her memory. More than her memory. I loved you when I still had her as my wife. God forgive me for that! Like the children, I have to keep her alive. Her body is dead, but her spirit will stay alive only as long as we go on loving her. I owe that to her."

"But, Alex, can't you love her without it being at my expense?"

"Apparently not," he said miserably. "I don't know how to solve this, Mary."

"You mean you don't want to."

"I shouldn't have married you so soon. I've done something terrible to all of us."

Mary was made reckless by her despair. "That's very little help right now. Oh, I know. Don't tell me. Anjanette wouldn't have said a thing like that. Anjanette was never sarcastic. Well, you're absolutely right."

Alex balled his fist and crashed it down on the delicate table. "Don't you realize? She hadn't been dead a year when I married you. I didn't even honor her memory enough to wait a decent interval. I wanted you so much that I buried her like you would a . . . a pet. Have the backyard funeral, then go to dinner—or bed—and forget about it. She was my wife! The mother of my children. And I . . . I forgot her in your arms. And I was happy to cast her away. Then."

"So you have to go back and honor it now? No, Alex. It's too late. You must forget her."

"That's the one thing I must *not* do."

Mary suddenly felt completely drained of emotion. She had been furious and on the brink of hopeless sobbing only moments before, and now his words were like a sharp slap to stop hysteria.

"I see," she said in a voice so calm she thought for a second it must be someone else's. "Very well. You'll have to make a decision, Alex. This is your house; they are your children; Anjanette was your wife. It's all up to you. You can choose to live with a dead wife or a live one. There is no clock ticking for me. I'll wait forever if I have to."

"Mary, don't be melodramatic. I know I've said all of this badly, but I want you to understand. I love you."

"I think you do. No, I know you do. But not enough."

"Mary, don't say that. You sound jealous."

"Of course I'm jealous. I'd have to be a lunatic to be otherwise. And the worst of it is, Anjanette would hate all of this. She would hate being made into a plaster saint to be venerated to the point of making all of us dismal. She loved us too. All of us. If her ghost could speak to you now, she would plead with you to forget her and be happy. She lived her whole life for your happiness."

He looked stunned and was speechless. She knew she had gone too far. Said too many things that could never be taken back. She had burned her bridges. Turning away slowly, she said, "Good night, Alex."

She walked out of the room, waiting only a moment to see if he would follow her. But he didn't. With enormous care and a bit of the serenity she had admired in Anjanette, she went to the master suite, threw a few things in a valise, and went quietly downstairs. She let herself out the kitchen door and went across the wet grass to the stables. She interrupted a game of cards between the groom and two of the stableboys. "I need to be taken to the train."

"The train, miss? This late?" the head groom asked.

"There is an eleven-o'clock train to London, isn't there?"

"Yes'm. May I ask, where might you be going?"

"I don't know. I just don't know."

46

Alex was at the stables before seven the next morning. "Can't you get that pony trap ready faster? I've got to catch the first train!" Out of the corner of his eye, he caught sight of Katie, still in her white nightdress. "What are you doing out here? How did you escape Miss Millbridge?"

"I came to see the kittens, Papa," she said, holding out a ball of orange fur as evidence. "They're big enough now to take inside, I think. The stableboy gives them milk in a bowl."

"That doesn't explain what you're doing out here at this time of morning without being properly clothed," Alex said shortly.

"But it does, Papa. I wanted to take this orange kitten to Cousin Mary. It looks just like her cat Ginger that died. I want to surprise her. She'll like this kitten."

Alex sighed. "Mary's not here."

"Where is she?"

"I don't know. I assume she's gone to London."

Katie set the kitten down, and it scampered back to its family. "Oh, Papa. Did she go away because I was so awful to her? I didn't mean to act so ugly."

"I know you didn't. Neither did I, but we've all been unfair to her. The only thing she did wrong was to be stupid enough to love all of us."

"Yes, Papa."

"Do you understand what I mean?"

"That it's not her fault that Mama died."

"Exactly, and whether we meant to or not, we've been acting like she was to blame. You do want her to come back, don't you?"

"More than anything. I like Cousin Mary, Papa. I was

just sad about Mama. I've been bad, Papa, and I don't think Mama would like the way I've been."

"I think the only person your mama would approve of right now is Cousin Mary," Alex said.

"Mrs. Haycraft, I'm sorry to arrive at your doorstep without warning," Mary said late the next afternoon. It was an effort to even speak with conventional courtesy. Mary felt that something essential inside her soul had wilted and shriveled.

Giving her a friendly, if puzzled expression, the lady replied warmly and at length in an East Anglian accent so thick Mary had to puzzle it out bit by bit. The gist seemed to be that the house at the crocus farm was Mary's property and always kept ready for her to visit. Further, Mr. Haycraft, the croker, was too busy with the harvest to be available until later, but could be summoned if necessary.

"That's quite satisfactory. I came only for a rest, not to supervise or interfere with his work."

How long would Mrs. Beecham be staying? Mrs. Haycraft asked.

"I have no idea. Perhaps a very long time."

After a solitary dinner Mary had no appetite for, but nibbled at to be polite, she fell into bed before it was even fully dark. It had been a long, exhausting day, virtually without sleep. By the time she arrived in London the night before, she had decided she couldn't stay there; it was the first place Alex would look for her. It wasn't that she didn't want him to find her. The fact was that she didn't want to wait there and find that he *hadn't* come after her—and she was convinced he would not follow her. Or worse, if he did, would come out of a sense of duty. Dear Lord, if there was anything she couldn't stand any more of, it was duty. Anybody's.

So she'd come here, where she'd once taken a trip with her father. It had been the spring before his death. They'd talked about coming back in the fall for the harvest, but he'd died before then and she'd never returned. That had been . . . how long ago? Only seven years. It seemed like decades, so much had happened since then. She was no longer the happy girl she'd been then. Now she was a woman bone-weary with defeat.

She'd thought of the place often and with fond longing, especially in the autumns when the fragile, valuable crop of saffron had come into the London warehouse. Mary returned to the crocus farm like a wounded animal, wanting nothing more than peace and quiet. Emotional oblivion. She didn't want to think about Alex or herself or what had gone so terribly wrong between them. She didn't want to talk to anyone who might urge her to ponder the imponderable. Determined to vegetate, she slept that night through as though drugged, and didn't really waken until midmorning. Mrs. Haycraft brought her a tray with breakfast enough for five. The odor of eggs and sausage made Mary feel that her stomach was about to turn itself inside out.

Mrs. Haycraft nodded knowingly at Mary's nausea and made arrangements, as Mary asked, for transportation into Bury St. Edmunds.

The doctor there confirmed her suspicion, such a happy suspicion only a few days ago, now a fact that filled her with confusion. Pressing her palm to her abdomen, she tried to imagine the child she carried. Boy or girl, like her or like Alex. If only she'd been certain earlier—would that have held them together? Would the prospect of a child have kept Alex from dwelling on his disloyalty to Anjanette, or would it have made him feel more committed to Mary and thus guiltier?

During those first days, she tried very hard to simply not think about any of it. Thinking—feeling—was desperately painful. She took long walks along the raised paths that cut across the fens and forced herself to pretend her usual interest in business. Acre after acre of crocuses were beginning to bloom like a vast amethyst carpet. The purple shimmer was so beautiful that even she was captured by it.

Mr. Haycraft and his seasonal workers were out before dawn, and at first light, when the flowers opened, they began the delicate, tedious business of clipping out the bright orange stigmas. Each flower had three, which were laid carefully in small boxes the workers carried. A boy collected the boxes, replacing them with empty ones, and took them to the drying sheds. There Mr. Haycraft himself supervised the next stage of the process. With Mary's help (which he took in good spirit, though she was clumsy and preoccupied) he separated the stigmas and laid them out on shallow trays which fitted into a framework that took up most of the interior of the shed, which he called a cupboard.

Each tray was moved and turned twice a day until the stigmas had dried to threads. Then village girls who worked seasonally picked them over and packed the threads in small caskets to be sent to the London warehouse. The broken or deformed stigmas were dumped together to be ground up later. Since ground saffron was so easy to adulterate with other ground flower heads, it was traditionally of far less value than the whole product.

"How long have you done this work, Mr. Haycraft?" Mary asked as they worked.

The answer, which she expected to be expressed in years, was given in generations. He was the fourth in his line to work saffron for Beecham's. And his sons, he said, would serve the fields of her sons.

Her sons. . . .

Mary had written to Hester from London, swearing her to secrecy. A return letter came on the fourth day of her stay at the crocus farm.

"Alex has been here," Hester wrote. "I reluctantly honored your request and didn't tell him where you are, but I did have to tell him I'd heard from you and you were alive and well. He's frantic with worry. . . ."

Mary read this merely as Hester's interpretation.

"I have an idea of what this is all about and I urge you to get a grip on yourself and face the problem. Though you married in terrible haste, you *did* marry and can't simply turn the clock back by running away. Mary, patience has never been one of your virtues, but I beg of you . . ."

Mary folded the letter without reading the rest. Patience! It was all very well for Hester to pontificate from her sweet, happy life in Kent now that her impetuous, ridiculous infatuation with Jamison Hewitt was over. Surrounded by her roses, her quaint thatched roof, and her patient suitor, memory packed away in cotton wool, Hester saw everything in simple terms. Well, perhaps it was simple: Alex had loved and lost Anjanette and hadn't been ready to remarry. Just as Hester had warned her. As for running away, well! What else could she have done? Stayed at Castlemere, watching his love for her disintegrating hour by hour? The fight for his love was the only fight she'd ever lost.

No, she hadn't really lost the fight, she thought late the afternoon of her fifth day of exile. She had merely given up. It was probably the only time in her life that she'd given up on anything she wanted.

The harder she tried to put the thought out of her mind, the more it intruded. She had quit the field, forfeited the battle. Not a tactic Mary Beecham often employed. Not a tactic at all.

Late that afternoon, she left the drying shed where she'd been helping Mr. Haycraft and went for a long walk. A fog was rolling in from the Wash as she made her way along the path to the river Nene. She sat on the bank, heedless of the dampness that would stain her skirt.

It must have been just such an afternoon when King John's men crossed somewhere near here. Perhaps right here. She glanced at the ground, half-expecting the point of a crown to be sticking up from the soil. But of course there was no such thing. The fog grew thicker and the outline of the far bank began to blur and appeared to shift. Her perception of space grew hazy. It was no wonder those ancient men had become confused and disoriented.

And in what romantic fog had she lost her way?

She closed her eyes for a moment. She could hear the muted sound of the waves lapping at the bank and could imagine the cries of distress, the whinnying of terrified horses, their hooves mired in watery muck, the screams of men's terror as the quicksand started to swallow them down to death. The sounds must have been muffled, but horrifying.

Suppose, she thought to herself, reopening her eyes, suppose King John had stood here on this very bank. What must his thoughts have been as his small army and all he valued were sucked down? Despair, fear, horror. But courage too. Had he sat here as she was doing? Or had he waded in, trying to save his men and his treasures?

Mary suddenly shivered with a vision. It was as if her chances of happiness were sinking slowly from sight, joining the bones of men and horses, long dead and forgotten. Could she watch placidly as that one single treasure of her life disappeared forever? Had King John merely sat here on the damp bank wringing his hands pathetically and observing as all he valued sank from view? No, certainly not. He must have raged and fought and cursed the fog and the quicksand. He must have done all he had in his power to snatch back what fate was taking from him.

Mary stood up suddenly, turning her back on the fog-shrouded river Nene. No, she wouldn't give up either. She'd had to give up Molly for her own good, but not Alex. Not Alex! If there was a chance left of saving the love Alex once felt for her, she was going to fight for it, not retire from the field like a fainthearted sissy. He might not love her like he loved Anjanette. He might never love her that much, in that way. But she wasn't going to run away from her heritage because of it. Her father had left her half the company because he knew she'd take care of it. He'd have been crushed with disappointment to see her not even taking care of herself. And Aunt Nell! By God, Aunt Nell would have jerked her around by the braids for moping about and giving up. Mary Beecham a quitter? Aunt Nell would be outraged at the idea.

And as she thought of how very dear Aunt Nell was to her, Mary suddenly realized that she knew something she had to teach Alex: that love had many faces, each equally beautiful in different ways. He had the evidence, he'd just never been aware of it. Just as he loved his children and loved Anjanette in wholehearted but different ways, he could love Mary without feeling it betrayed anyone. Somehow she'd make him understand that. She wasn't sure how—or how long it might take, but he would see!

Hitching up her skirts, she started back along the path. Plunging through the fog, she sometimes actually had to bend over to see which way it turned, but she safely found her way back to the house. "Mrs. Haycraft! Mrs. Haycraft," she said, running in the door. "Oh, there you are. Please ask to have a carriage brought round for me. I'm going back to Castlemere. Then help me pack, if you would. I need to leave immediately. There's no time to lose."

Mary left the cottage at the Wash without even changing her clothes or tidying her hair. "Please drive quickly!" she urged the driver Mrs. Haycraft had summoned from his work in the fields. The cottage wasn't even out of sight when her carriage passed another careening up the road.

"Stop!" she called to the driver. In the brief second of passing, she had recognized the face in the window. Climbing down from the carriage, she looked back through the fog and saw the other vehicle also stopping. Alex leapt out and signaled for his driver to go on. "Mary!" he called.

For a moment she could hardly move; then she ran to meet him and he swept her up and swung her in a circle. Setting her down, he held her tightly for a long moment, neither of them speaking until Alex drew a long breath and said, "Dear God, I thought I was going to comb every hedgerow and closet in England to find you. Finally I remembered this place." He set her down and looked into her eyes. "Mary, I have so much to tell you."

"Alex, I shouldn't have left. I—"

"No, Mary. Just for once in your life keep quiet and let me talk. You were right. Absolutely right about everything. I realized it the night you left, but by the time I came to tell you, you were gone. And then as the days went by and I couldn't find you, I realized something far more important. I've awakened every morning thinking that I simply couldn't get through another day without you. You've become part of the fabric of my whole life. Such a short time to have meant so much."

"Alex, there's something I have to tell—"

He put a finger to her lips. "I've been an ass, Mary. Worrying like some foolish philosopher about the inherent dishonesty of loving two women so much. That night, when we talked, I suddenly saw how fortunate I am. Instead of torturing myself and you with it, I should have rejoiced in my extraordinary luck. You see, Mary, I *don't* love two women. Not anymore. I had the tenses all wrong. I love one now. You. With all my heart and soul."

She smiled, tears blurring her vision. "May I talk now?"

"Could I stop you?" he said, grinning.

"I have something important to . . . Alex, what *is* that strange sound?"

"Oh, my God, I nearly forgot him." He reached into the deep side pocket of his coat and gently pulled out a squealing orange bundle of fur. "This cat has lived on my person for nearly a week. Katie made me bring him along to you."

Mary put out her hands and took the little thing. "Alex, he looks exactly like Ginger did. Oh, what a precious gift. Did Katie really send him along?"

"She did, and if I'd known what I was letting myself in for, I wouldn't have let her. Do you know how often the greedy little creatures want milk? Not just want—demand! Try to imagine how many times I've stopped to satisfy him. I'm acquainted with every farmwife from here to Castlemere."

Mary had a sudden absurd vision of Alex stopping every few miles and begging for a cup of milk for a kitten, all the while searching for her. She suddenly started to laugh. The kitten snagged onto the front of her dress and crawled up to snuggle under her chin. "Oh, Alex, it's too . . . too funny for words."

"Perhaps I'll think so too, someday," he said dryly. "But not quite yet. You do like him?"

"I adore him and I love you a thousand times more. But, Alex, I'm afraid I'm going to have to share that love pretty soon."

"Oh? With whom?"

She gently pulled the kitten loose from her bodice and put him back in Alex's coat pocket. Ignoring its sad little meows for the moment, she looked up at her husband and put her arms around his neck. "Can't you guess? Can't you really?"

"You don't mean . . . ?"

"I do. A baby. Do you mind?"

"Mind? *Mind!* Mary, nothing could make me happier." He kissed her tenderly.

As he kissed her, the kitten struggled out of his pocket and burrowed between then. Mary took it in both hands and said, "What about a name?"

"For the cat?"

"No," she said with a laugh. "The baby. I thought perhaps Max. It's partly my name and partly yours."

"Whatever you want," he said, smiling. "Are you ready to go home now? To Castlemere?"

She looked up at him. "Just try to stop me and you'll find what sort of stuff Mary Beecham is really made of."

47

June 1927

It had grown dark and there was a wind whistling through some distant part of the house, making a faint but eerie moan. Neither Natalie nor Mary paid it any heed. Natalie put down the last diary and went to sit gingerly on the side of her grandmother's great bed. "Oh, Grandmama," she said, taking the older woman's hand. She held it to her cheek for a long moment, then said, "Is Molly still alive?"

Mary drew a long breath, as if building up strength. "Yes, alive and very happy with the Stotts. The older boy, Teddy, took her into his family when he married. She was fifty-one years old last week. My baby—fifty-one! She's a loving auntie to Teddy's children and grandchildren."

"You've seen her?"

"Dozens of times. I went to Inverness every few months as long as I was able. I write to the Stotts and they bring her to town for shopping and I get to see her from a hotel window."

"Never closer?"

"Only once. By accident. I ran into them on the street. She . . . she seemed almost to know me. And was still afraid."

Mary turned her face away.

"It wasn't your fault, Grandmama," Natalie said.

"Don't you think so?"

"Of course not."

"I . . . I used to think perhaps it was because I didn't love her enough. Because she was Henry's child. Not Alex's."

"That's nonsense and you know it!"

Mary turned back to face her and smiled. "For a second, you sounded just like Nellanor."

"I'm proud to hear that," Natalie said. "Does anyone else know about Molly?"

"Only Winston and your grandfather knew. And Agnes. Dear old Agnes. Gone ten years now. Bartlet probably knows, though I never told him. My attorney drew up the trust to support her, but he doesn't know who she is." She paused, her strength ebbing. Natalie waited patiently. "In my will, I've made you executrix of the trust. I wanted you to know why—and who she really is."

"I'll look after her, Grandmama, as you would want. That's what you wanted of me, isn't it?"

Mary took another deep breath. It was obviously painful and there was an ominous rasping sound to it. "You must . . . leave her . . . with the Stotts."

"Of course I will, but I'll visit often, as you did. But, Grandmama, let's talk more about it tomorrow. You must rest. You look very tired."

Mary closed her eyes, and her hand in Natalie's grew limp. "Yes. Now I can rest. . . ."

Natalie called young Dr. Engle, who came just before midnight and said, as Natalie had feared he would, that there was nothing to do but hope. "It's her will—and God's— now." But he stayed and sat with Natalie. At two in the morning Mary's breathing grew more labored and he gave her an injection that seemed to provide some relief. She neither woke nor responded when he spoke to her.

At dawn, Natalie rose and opened the curtains. Faint pink light flooded the room and lay in a diagonal bar across the foot of the huge bed. "Natalie . . ." Mary whispered.

She ran to her side and bent close. "Yes, Grandmama?"

Mary looked straight at her for a moment before her eyelids fluttered shut. "Remember . . ." she whispered.

"Yes, Grandmama, I'll remember. I promise."

After a long moment, Robbie Engle came around and gently laid his fingers on the inside of Mary's wrist. "It's over, Natalie," he said softly.

"Yes. Yes, I know," she replied.

Natalie took one last glance in the mirror as she adjusted the veil on her black hat. She picked up the final diary from the nightstand beside the bed and made one more visit to her grandmother's room. It was empty now. The nurse had gone and all the bottles and vials of medicine had been cleared away. The enormous bed was neatly made, with no trace of the woman who had died there two days ago. The windows were open and a summer breeze was billowing the curtains. Natalie pulled open the secret drawer and replaced the diary. Later, she would come back with a carton and take the small books with her; they were her most important legacy from her grandmother. This would be her father's room, now and someday, as his only child, hers. Then the diaries would come back.

She looked at the bed and could imagine her grandmother propped up against a bank of pillows still—ordering the world as she wished it. "Yes, Grandmama, I promise I'll see that your Molly is looked after," she said again, just as she had said three days earlier while Mary Beecham drew her last breath.

She turned away quickly and went downstairs. As she descended, she noticed a figure standing in the dim hallway. She instantly recognized the lanky stance and the sandy hair. "Oh, Albert, I'm glad you've come," she said, rushing forward into his arms. "I didn't know if my wire would reach you in time."

He paused a moment before saying, "I quite liked your grandmother, Natalie. I would have come whether you wanted me or not."

"Oh, I do want you here. She summoned me a week ago, then hung on by force of will until I'd finished a project she assigned me."

"A project? What was that?"

"To understand her secret. To read her diaries. She kept them from the time she was a little girl until . . . until a few months after she married Grandfather Alex. Then she stopped. I suppose she didn't need to confide in them anymore because she had him."

Albert was perplexed by this, but waited, his arms around her, for her to go on.

"There was one last entry, Albert. It was at the end of the last book and I didn't discover it until this morning. It was written only ten years ago when my grandfather died. I remember the funeral and how dignified she was. I was only eleven or so then and I didn't have any idea until this week how terrible it must have been for her. He was the center of her world from the time she was a child."

"It was the worst day of her life," a voice said behind her, "and one of the worst of mine."

"Papa! I didn't know you were there," Natalie said, turning, but not stepping away from Albert. "Papa, there were so many things I didn't get to ask her, but one in particular has been on my mind all morning. What happened to Richard—Grandfather Alex's son from his first marriage?"

Max Beecham, the dark-haired, blue-eyed image of his father, Alex, said, "Richard—I'd almost forgotten Richard entirely. I never knew him—not to remember. He died of a lung complaint when I was about two. Mother said once that my father would have died of grief over it if he hadn't had your Aunt Katie and me." He'd gone to open the front door as he spoke, and looked out as if searching for someone.

Natalie left Albert's side and went to take her father's arm. "It's a sad enough day, Papa. I didn't mean to make it worse by reminding you of Grandfather Alex."

He took her hand and gave it a squeeze.

"You've been talking about Father, haven't you?" Natalie's Aunt Katie said, coming in from the dining room. She was an awesome woman in her mid-fifties, with thick still-blond hair and an imposing, well-corseted figure. If any of them present had ever seen her mother, they'd have been surprised at how much physical resemblance there was and how little similarity of personality. "I can always tell by that look, Max. Oh, Albert . . . isn't it? Glad you're here."

She came and took her half-brother's other arm. "I've been thinking about Father today too. As terrible as it was for her to lose him, it would have been worse for him, I think. Their marriage was an example to us all. Sacrilege, really, a funeral on a fine day. Ought to turn cold and rain a bit. The least God could do for her. I'll bet He's quaking now at the thought of her turning up at His gates."

This made them all smile and broke the morbid spell.

"I've been thinking . . ." Natalie said. "Would anyone mind if I asked Bartlet to sit with us in the family pew?"

"I've already asked him," Max said. "He was pleased, but said he'd keep to his place with the servants. I think I'll go over to the chapel. It can't hurt to be a bit early."

"Quite right," Katie said briskly. "Take the outdoor route. Fresh air. A bit of exercise. Do us both good. Max, you spend too much time at the office. London's bad for your health, and that wretched tumbledown house in the city is a disgrace. You'll be moving down here now, won't you?"

Natalie and Albert, hand in hand, followed them, Natalie smiling that Aunt Katie was still trying to boss her "little brother" around. "Albert, when this is all over, will you go with me to Inverness? There's someone I have to meet."

"A friend of your grandmother's?"

"Someone she loved and looked after from a distance and whom I will now see to. I'll tell you all about it later. It's a long story that Grandmama entrusted to me."

The words were all said, the prayers prayed, the hymns sung, the coffin lowered into the ground. The friends and business associates had decently withdrawn, and now it was only the family standing by the grave. Natalie's father, Max, stepped forward, stooped, and took a handful of the soil and paused for a long moment before dropping it onto the lid. Then Great-Aunt Hester Fargate, a frail old lady with sparrow-brown coloring, came forward on the arm of her equally frail husband. She swayed alarmingly and Natalie thought for one awful second that she might actually topple into the hole, before Max took her arm and put a little handful of dirt into her black-gloved hand.

"Who could have thought I would outlive her? She was so . . . so terribly *alive*," the old lady said as Max led them away.

Katie, flanked by her two sons, big florid men in their mid-thirties—twin cousins Natalie had never been able to tell apart—stepped up to the very brink of the grave and looked down as if making certain the coffin was actually there.

When they moved away, Natalie motioned for Bartlet to go ahead of her. He, too, stood very near the edge, and closing his eyes for a moment, moved his lips silently. It might have looked like a prayer, but Natalie was certain he was saying one last thing to the mistress he'd served nearly all his life. Albert moved as if to assist him, but the elderly servant opened his eyes and gave him such an affronted look that Albert backed up hastily.

It was Natalie's turn. She slowly approached the grave and bent to drop, not a handful of soil, but a branch of rosemary she'd broken from one of the bushes near the house. With a soft swish, it fell onto the lid. Natalie could smell the pungent oil on her gloves.

"Yes, Grandmama, I will remember," she said.

ABOUT THE AUTHOR

Janice Young Brooks is a native of Kansas City, where she lives with her husband and two teenaged children. Her novel, *Seventrees*, received the prestigious American Association of University Women's Thorpe Menn Award for literary excellence in 1981. Her other novels, *The Circling Years* and *Crown Sable*, are also available in Signet.